AN
INSULAR
POSSESSION

AN INSULAR POSSESSION

TIMOTHY MO

Paddleless

An Insular Possession

First published in Great Britain 1986 by Chatto and Windus
This edition published in 2002 by Paddleless Press

Paddleless Press, BCM Paddleless, London WC1N 3XX
email: timothymo@eudoramail.com

British Cataloguing in Publication Data
A catalogue record for this book is available from the
British Library

ISBN 09524193 8 6

Cover and book design by Surface Impression Ltd
Printed and bound in Great Britain by Cox & Wyman

CHAPTER I

The river succours and impedes native and foreigner alike; it limits and it enables, it isolates and it joins. It is the highway of commerce and it is a danger and a nuisance. Children fall off fragile native craft; drunken sailors topple from the decks of the Company's chequered ships. Along with the rest of the city's effluvia the river sweeps the victims out to sea. Thus for centuries it has fulfilled the functions of road and, as rivers will, cloaca. Its appearance changes, if not its uses. Most often the water is a sullen grey. At its mouth it stains the clean blue sea yellow-brown, the colour of tea as drunk in London. Somewhere, at its source, the water must run pellucid from some untainted spring. Logic dictates this. Practice, as always, is another matter. Where the river rises thousands of miles inland it seems already pregnant – with silt, with life, and with the opposite of life. For here already are bodies, though not the stalwart corpses of the foreign sailors down the stream, but those of babies, victims of the prevalent cult of infanticide. Most are female. Here, in the backlands, the landscape is bleak and sterile, as of a world never properly born. The river winds a sinuous course through lazy, rumpled hills, thinly covered with scrub and here and there some crazy, crooked conifer stark against that margin where sky silhouettes hill-edge. There are no habitations especially evident, although it is the foraging human hand which has left those hills so bare of wood. Bandits make their lairs here in artful caverns or concealed depressions where their settlements lie unseen from the river. Otherwise, there are a few hardy charcoal-burners, half brigand themselves, whose lonely fires wink at night on the slopes.

Only on the river is there life and traffic of a sort, though this, too, is sparse and on the water as well predators are not unknown. But the river flows on, gathering strength and volume from a thousand tributaries, and as it swells so does its capacity to bear life and the commerce of life. The few insect craft which can be spied from the heights of the hinterland reproduce and multiply until they have become a swarm. There are tiny three-plank craft, urgent as homunculi, thrashing their single stern-oar like a tail. Awkward barges, full of salt or coal. Graceful mandarin boats which skim the river like so many dragonflies, with gaudy shields between their oars and dragon's eyes painted on the bow. Flat, comfortable house-boats. Lean, suspicious craft with their decks full of staring cut-throats. Rope-drawn ferries, glorified rafts these, noisome with livestock, which cut across the grain of the river's traffic, bank to bank, one whole mile. At this point on a misty morning, and all mornings seem to be misty here, it is possible to lose sight of the opposite shore altogether, and then one feels cut off from the world and its companionship, enisled in some forlorn spot, although the river echoes and magnifies, as water will, the lowing of the buffalo, the honking of the hogs, and the crying of the children. But then the sun lifts the mist, parts the curtain, and there you are, nearer your destination than you thought, though the fierce current has almost taken you too far downstream.

And so to Canton, old Canton, already in Chase's and Eastman's day an ancient place with a dubious and blood-stained past, though it has also been a cosmopolitan resort for all kinds and complexions of men whom curiosity or commerce, or both, have brought halfway round the world and back again. In some cases: not back again. For instance, the city has a mosque and in the mosque the tomb of an uncle, one of the many uncles, of the Prophet, whom silk and porcelain brought here more than a thousand years ago. The Muslims have their Imam, who is their headman and regulates them in the same way as the President of the Select Committee of the Supracargoes of the Honourable the East India Company regulates under the jealous eye of the Celestial Viceroy another group of barbarians, called the English.

The traditional green roof-tiles, gilded eaves, and scarlet columns of the mosque (little more than an architectural cliché) do little to distinguish it from the mass of petty, eclectic Chinese temples which are scattered throughout the city. Even its round six-storey minaret, its elevation spoiled by the detritus which has accumulated around its first two floors, is unremarkable except for the two trees which grow for no apparent reason out of the cracks sixty feet above the sustaining ground in its top storey. It is surpassed in height by all the city's pagodas. Of these, three, more or less in line, dwarf the others and to a very receptive eye (and the city's collective eye is singularly receptive in matters of this kind) can be said to resemble a ship's masts. So the city is a rather cumbersome and over-crewed junk in full sail, like those which float in the river which laves its sordid banks, advancing along the line of her destiny which is quite often to be blown off course or entangled in the archipelagoes of history. It is said that if one of the city's masts should topple, then shipwreck will befall her. Naturally, we know this is the merest superstition, but it is matter of record that the city was sacked in 1649, five years after the conquering Manchu had founded their dynasty in the northern capital, Peking. Xenophobic and stubborn, as they will prove with the European, the citizens of Canton refuse to receive the conqueror. A million Cantonese, they claim, perished in the massacre which followed the lengthy siege and even allowing for a certain licence, the river would have been glutted with the bodies of its city, the water reflecting the flames by night.

But time and the river sweep on, Manchu and Chinese accommodate, and the water's floating population starts to thin again. To Whampoa island and its anchorage where lie the ships of the British and their cousins, the Americans, is twelve miles or two hours' rowing in a well-crewed ship's gig. As one proceeds downstream, the tall masts and latticed ratlines of the merchantmen become visible several miles off, well before the river starts its majestic curve around the anchorage.

At this point the river has undergone a complete transformation of character and so has the traffic it supports; as well it might, for it is effectively two streams now, at the confluence of the west and north rivers which mingle to form the Pearl. There are other islands here. Dane's and French, with their bamboo grog-stalls for the roistering sailor, scene of many a brawl, while on the hillsides lie the graves of earlier visitors, often from previous centuries though the names are familiar enough. Williamson, Duval, Svensen, say the mossy headstones. And

Flint, Bellini, Hof, and Zamora. They sleep peacefully. On goes the river. It is open countryside now upon either bank; gone are the stilt houses of the city and their casual filth. Here and there a water-wheel spins its splashing buckets while a boy watches the blindfolded buffalo put its shoulder into its patient circle. Chocolate and veridian, the fields spread their pattern across the plain, broken in places by the tight wool balls of the trees which signal a sheltering village. On the left bank there are low ranges of hills upon the horizon but on the right the plain extends itself into the haze. Again, there are pagodas, constructed for precise geomantic purposes which remain obscure to the foreign mariner, except that he uses them as transits, for the sandbanks at Second and First Bars are hazardous, even for the native river-pilot. At least the river's bars are a predictable ambush; they become submerged and exposed with the rise and fall of a tide but they do not change position. It is the river itself which is fickle and mischievous. It is never the same for longer than a season and in ten years will cut itself new channels, flood what was land, retreat from its bed to leave bird-haunted mud flats and strange smooth stones, create peninsulas and enisle what was once part of the main. In the heart now of the delta country, it is no longer possible to speak of a single river so much as a maze of interconnected waterways which fragment the solid land until what at first sight seemed to be an unbroken, surrounding terrain is revealed as a jigsaw of curiously shaped islands, small and large, with no connection with their fellows. This can become apparent either suddenly, with elevation, as recently in modern times from an aircraft, or slowly, as it might to a hydrographer like Captain Belcher or the great Horsburgh. Who sound as they go, circumnavigating what they think of as an infinitely extendible coast, only to find it island, until one day their painstaking labours can be integrated into a larger chart which shows in an instant as the blatant truth of retrospect what was never once apparent at any single definable moment of the task.

Only at the river's mouth, its end (or, for the foreigner, its beginning) does its true nature, like the silt it bears, become soluble. Then at the *Bocca Tigris* the islands are, discernibly, islands: Tiger Island, Taicocktow, Chuenpi, with their low fortifications and embrasures, the conical islands like fangs in a tiger's mouth, a resemblance which did not fail to strike the Portuguese who were the first European navigators to float upon the estuary. The Bogue, as contracted into the English from the more evocative Portuguese, marks the end of the river proper, the Inner Waters of the Empire. The silty waters flow out, the banks of the estuary widen to twenty miles, to forty, and for a while there are no more islands visible, only sea, with waves and glitter where the dugong sport. Mermaids those early navigators thought them, and one pities the privations they endured to cause them to mistake those creatures for women. Perhaps they heard them in the first night, before they saw them, for their cries of distress are heart-rendingly human and the mothers do suckle their young, afloat upon the waters of the gulf, from breasts that are disconcertingly like the female mammary gland. They gambol across the course of craft making the twenty-mile passage down the gulf from Lin Tin island to Macao and across from Urmston Bay into Lantao Sound. Possibly, they are less buoyant than they appear at their play, for one never encounters their carcasses, or if one does, on a beach, it is invariably of an adult. Only in mid-gulf are they to be observed. Around the sheltered waters of the islands at the base of the estuary's rough isosceles, around Lantao, Hong Kong, Lamma or the Ladrones, you will not find them. There fishermen spread their nets upon the beach in a terrible stink of rotting algae, while their salted catch shrivels and curls on rocks beneath a baking heaven. Under such skies the still sea glitters until it hurts the eye of the non-navigator and he, the landlubber, must slant his eyes in an ironic imitation of the epicanthic fold of the Oriental. Once seen, the islands are bare and precipitous, though some have a thin, distempered fleece of pale-green scrub, and are made up of decomposing granite, pebble, and fringing sand, on which, in their season, the typhoons will confer a rich harvest of flotsam. Typhoons arrive in the South China Sea in the summer, the period of the south-west monsoon, towards the end of which time also arrives that other primitive force of nature, the British sailor, and then the sky darkens, the waves on the dull sea become long and regular, and the fisher villages batten down with boulders on their roofs. The winds strike, there is a lull as the eye of the hurricane, its still centre, passes – and then, the final onslaught. The estuary becomes the cockpit of the elements. Monstrous waves form, they seem as high as the bad, jagged peak of Lin Tin island itself and smash into whatever land they find. In seas like this, flimsy native craft are doomed and even the Company's chequered thousand-tonners must look to their survival.

And what of Canton and its river? Are they, too, hostage to the season? The waters forced back up the swollen channel, the banks burst, the river-boats capsized and the stilt huts blown into the raging waters?

No.

While the estuary is ravaged, in Canton the skies are blue and the air calm; at worst there is mild drizzle and a breeze which is invigorating rather than threatening. For the typhoons obey quite precise meteorological laws which dictate that those hurricanes should be seaborne forces which can only afflict the coast and islands of the province. Once inland a few miles or so, the winds are dissipated and an extraordinary calm succeeds. In the tranquillity of Canton one would never suspect the savage onslaughts the islands were suffering.

CHAPTER II

Corpulent O'Rourke shifts on his chair and the rattan creaks protest. His huge, bulbous nose, a fiery red globe in the violent vermilion his own work so frequently affects, appears around the side of the easel; withdraws again.

'Mr O'Rourke!'

O'Rourke shifts his plenilunar buttocks, vast in buckskin, and the rattan is again abused. He nibbles the splayed wood fibres at the end of his brush. The portrait is not to his satisfaction, nor, for that matter, the sitter. He prefers them pretty and nubile. His lower lip, which is wet and pendulous, pouts. He looks, and it is fortunate that Mrs Marjoribanks cannot see it, exceptionally ill-tempered.

'Mr O'Rourke!'

He relinquishes brush for knife, momentarily alarming Mrs Marjoribanks.

'Mr O'Rourke, pray did you not hear me when I addressed you a few moments ago? You have not spoken for an hour.'

'Madam,' says the old rogue, 'there are friends of O'Rourke's who would envy you the rare distinction of witnessing him wordless for quite one minute. If I am silent, it is but the tribute genius pays to art. The painter may daub to commission, but his Muse does not.'

'Mr O'Rourke, surely you are not so Thrasonical as to declare yourself a genius?'

'Madam, I am and have.'

Boaster, grand prevaricator, story-teller, wit and conversationalist of mighty reputation (his young friend Eastman thinks so, at any rate), O'Rourke retreats behind his easel. Mrs Marjoribanks, who is three-quarters profile to the artist, makes a *moue* and rearranges her skirts. She mischievously disposes of her hands, which are large and, like O'Rourke's nose, red, though for different reasons, in a new position.

'Madam!'

She takes a deep breath and holds it a while.

Grinning Ah Cheong, O'Rourke's valet, brush-cleaner, cook, general factotum, man beneath the stairs, and − I am afraid to relate − pimp, enters.

'Mastah Eastman just now come chop-chop say you plomise give him sketch-y lesson today, you no lemember bimeby?'

'The divil he does.'

O'Rourke glares round the side of the easel at Mrs Marjoribanks, although his terrifying frown is merely necessary to keep the pince-nez from slipping off that extraordinary nose. He takes another, smaller brush and fastidiously mixes a colour on the palette. It is a deep crimson, a sort of scarlet with body, which is destined for Mrs Marjoribanks's mouth, now down-turned (that is to say, her mouth in the painting).

'Give him glass but-lan-day, tell him bimeby finish?'

'Sherry, Ah Cheong, give him the sherry.'

'Me thinkee Mastah Eastman likeee but-lan-day, Flenchy one number one.'

He retires, still grinning, to serve Eastman his glass of cognac and to steal one for himself, too, from the Company's well-stocked cellars. He used to give Eastman a gruesome cherry brandy, his own favourite tipple as served by the captains of Indiamen to their native river pilots, but one day Eastman rebelled.

Eastman is a young man of twenty-four whose fair hair is thinning somewhat at the front. He has been heavily marked by smallpox and part of the bottom wing of his right nostril has been destroyed by the same disease. But his pleasantness of expression and frank blue eyes redeem his appearance, much in the same way as O'Rourke's is enlivened by the humour in the sharp brown eyes behind the pince-nez. The two friends like to make a butt of each other's ugliness. 'Until you came, sir,' O'Rourke is fond of announcing, preferably very loudly in a public place, 'I had the distinction of being the ugliest man in Macao and in Canton the second ugliest. People would point: "There goes O'Rourke," they would say, "the ugliest fellow I ever saw," and my appearance would thus excite comment. In point of eminence it was a remarkable distinction. Now Eastman has come, than whom there is no more hideous man in the East, and I am no longer distinguished to the public view.' This is one of only two things they have in common, the second being a passion for drawing, for as well as a difference in age of almost half a century (O'Rourke, who was born in 1772, will soon be sixty-two) there is another distinction between them. Eastman is an American. Fortunately, O'Rourke is not a stock Company Briton; he isn't even English at all: he's – what else – *Irish* and there is more than a faint touch of the accents of his native Mayo in an otherwise cosmopolitan address. Eastman is from Virginia and this is his second sojourn in the Orient, the first as clerk in an Anglo-Dutch firm in Malacca, and he is beginning to think he is an old hand in this part of the world.

Mrs Marjoribanks is released, rather unceremoniously, she thinks, since she knows Mr Marjoribanks's guineas will be perfectly welcome to O'Rourke. Downstairs Eastman bows to her on her majestic way out. She sniffs at him. Then Eastman comes up to the top floor, the drawing lesson is postponed (O'Rourke out of patience, of which he never has a very large store anyway), and both enjoy a restoring glass. Pretty soon, they are engaged in a discussion which in different forms has been exercising them for some months. Let us conceive of them as actors in a play, for Walter tends to histrionics on this issue.

O'ROURKE. 'My dear and noble young friend, your arguments do credit to your heart, less to your head. *(Your health!)* You talk of vast and national interests and such interests are not to be disposed of according to the dictates of mere private conscience.' EASTMAN. 'But such is precisely the foundation of my belief. There can be no distinction between the public interest and the private. The public weal is merely the aggregation of many private interests. To alter a national policy, one must first appeal to individuals and it is the appeal to conscience which will most readily effect this transformation.' O'ROURKE. 'Now you are talking like a Quaker or Radical, sir.' EASTMAN. 'Radical I am not, nor would ever wish to be one of those misguided men. Quaker, as you well know, Harry, I could not be.' O'ROURKE. 'Ha! Ha! You are a young rogue for all your sermonising and philosophising.' EASTMAN. 'I make no claims for myself, nor do I advance myself as a model of right conduct. I simply assert what is truth and has an existence independent of its advocate. The Company and the Free Traders, both, connive in the corruption of an empire's morals and the destruction of the health and vital forces of His Celestial Majesty's servants.' O'ROURKE. 'Come, sir, you surely overstate your case. The drug becomes an evil only when it's abused. Why, I have myself seen in India how our sepoys will carry about their persons a tin box of pills, of sticky morsels rather, of the finest Patna opium to recruit themselves when they have exhausted their physical capacities. I have seen those blackamoors, almost dead of tiredness or wounds, sink by the wayside and I would have wagered a month's commissions that neither musket-butts, the threats and blandishments of their officers, no, nor the very fear of death itself would have roused them as they lay. Yet I have seen those same rascals swallow half a pill, washed down with a mouthful of cold tea, and within the hour put an army of Mahrattas of ten times their number to the rout.' EASTMAN. 'Tell me also how the drug will relieve the dying agonies of the grandfather, soothe the madman's disturbed brow, sustain the paupered young mother's failing energies, and as Godfrey's Cordial give peace and restoring sleep to the ailing child.' O'ROURKE. 'Sir, you steal the very words from my mouth.' EASTMAN. 'Sir, the Company and Free Traders steal the bread from the Chinese and in return give them an unadulterated poison.' O'ROURKE. 'You debate with me, Walter. But, pray, drink the poison Ah Cheong has given you and we will fill the glass again, if you please. There. Now you will admit of the drug's powerful medicinal properties. I will confess when it is abused it is an evil, but that is properly speaking in the power of the user. The drug itself is not evil. Will you not consider the gin-shops of London, the miseries and violences the drunkard inflicts on his family, the thousand sailors' brawls of which we ourselves are the disgusted spectators daily in Hog Lane or Whampoa, and will you not then admit that it is alcohol which is the greater evil? The opium eater's tranquil somnolence is a mere reverie besides the retching and uproars of the drunkard. Taken in moderation, opium is no more harmful than tobacco.' EASTMAN. 'Now it is you who trifles. There may be no comparison between alcohol or tobacco and opium as banes. The vice fast fixes on the eater. He cannot be without it. Without it he will as surely die tomorrow as with it he will die in the space of a few years.' O'ROURKE. 'Well, then, as a man of some little experience....' EASTMAN. 'You are a man of great experiences, Harry.' O'ROURKE. 'Then I assert that it is patent to the man of experience who has knocked about this globe that the vicious propensities excited by the drug have been greatly exaggerated. Walter, besides, were the British not to supply the drug some others would surely fill their place. Nothing could be more certain than this. Already your countrymen, yes, you Americans, sell their Turkey opium here. Do you not consider that the Spaniards, the Portuguese, aye, the Portuguese of Macao surely, would not at once indulge those wants which the British neglect to supply? The trade in opium provides the Company with fully one tenth of its Indian revenues. Without this source of silver, India would become ungovernable. Without India there would be no empire, no navy, no protection from the tyranny of a Napoleon or the insults of any petty despot. Consider, 'tis opium which pays for the Company's purchase of teas. So addicted are our own turbulent populace to that herb that by law the Company must keep one year's stock of teas in its warehouses at London. What would our own dangerous classes do without their precious tea? To what use might some unscrupulous demagogue not turn this want? And, consider, Walter, the revenue on tea, small as it is, pays for fully half the annual cost of His Britannic Majesty's Royal Navy. An income to the government of three or four millions a year, raised from the population in the most trifling and painless way. Only a fool could throw away such a thing upon a whim. No opium, no tea, and without tea we should not have had Reform to face this two years past but Revolution.' EASTMAN. 'Whim it is not. We are not concerned with others. Were Britain not to abandon this noxious traffic, then it will never be extirpated. To argue as you do is to perpetuate this evil. It requires someone to make this initial act of relinquishment. Your argument could apply equally to the terrible traffic in slaves. Britain, to its eternal credit, led the way in its suppression. Your practical arguments as to the ready appearance of a supplier of proximate resort could apply to slaves, to the drug, to, to....the engines of war and destruction which also are instruments which are neither good nor bad in themselves but partake of those qualities in so far as the use to which they be put be good or its opposite.' O'ROURKE. 'Sir, you should look to His Celestial Majesty to put his own house in order. One sovereign state cannot interfere in the domestic affairs of another. If there are Chinese smugglers of opium, then it is the Emperor in Peking who must extirpate them.' EASTMAN. 'The Honourable Company, you will also tell me then, merely instructs the *ryot* to grow his crop, sees the fields of India white with poppy, sells the drug to the Free Traders and then, like Pilate, washes its hands of the consequences. Because there is no carriage of the drug in its own bottoms but in the ships of the Free Traders, it believes, you will also tell me, that it has no responsibility for this wicked trade? Humbug, sir. The Company's guilt, the guilt of Britain is transparent to the unbiased mind.' O'ROURKE. 'Ah, Walter, and you are very biased.' EASTMAN. 'Well enough, Harry. Now will you do me the inestimable favour and privilege of criticising, without the smallest mercy, these feeble productions of my pencil?' O'ROURKE. 'The Praia Grande at Macao, will it be? Yes. Ah, Walter, now with the arm of this figure you make the mistake so common to the dilettante. Thus now do I change it…and here…my dear boy, I am so much disinclined to say so that the words stick in my throat….but at your stage you might well be better advised *to copy from the work of a master, than to draw it from the life!*' EASTMAN. 'Well, then, in that case all amputees should have a preliminary dram.' O'ROURKE. 'Ha! Cheong, brandy!'

CHAPTER III

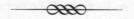

The Factories (which is where O'Rourke is staying while he executes his commissions in Canton) occupy a space of about nine hundred feet frontage and six hundred depth, with a square and a riverside esplanade. It is here our two friends 'bend their steps' – as Harry likes to say – after their warm but amiable discussions on opium and the other drug, art. In fact, there exists nowhere in Canton but the Factories for O'Rourke to stay. A jealous government has restricted the foreign traders to this minute and exceptionally frustrating enclave. From here they may not stray. No women may be brought here, no firearms; they may not initiate themselves into the mysteries of the Chinese language, ride in sedan-chairs (even if they wished to indulge in one of the few forms of land transport capable of replicating the exact symptoms of seasickness), enter the city gate, or petition the mandarins directly. Of course, the foreigners do have in their possession light sporting-arms; they even contrive, once in a while, to bring up to the Factories white women, crones like Mrs Marjoribanks, just so the Chinese know they have done so out of pure mischief. (Of native prostitutes, boat-girls, who cater to their pressing needs, they have an abundance at the Factories).

These, by the way, are Factories in the sense of trading-posts manned by Factors, not in the sense of industrial manufactory, as carried out by those mechanic classes whom both O'Rourke and Eastman are at one in regarding as so dangerous.

The English Company has been sited here since 1715 and trading to Canton for rather longer than that. There are also other nationalities: American, of course, Spanish, Swedish, Austrian, Dutch, French, each with their own Factory. In all there are thirteen Factories. Actually, no one has seen an Austrian or Swedish ship in living memory.

Architecturally all the Factories conform by necessity to the same curious plan. They are, with the grand exception of the English Factory (and the English dominate the Canton trade), fairly narrow, maybe six or seven yards across, but extend backwards several hundred feet. Their length is broken up into smaller sections, or little houses, of, say, ten yards' depth. They have three storeys. The top floors are walled off from each other, resembling a row of tiny one-room cottages or, though built before the significant conjunction of steam and iron, a line of railway carriages. Each facing its successor, they have no view worth speaking of, beyond each other's walls. These are offices and living quarters. They are numbered going backwards: No.1 French Hong, No.2 French Hong, No.13 New English Factory, etc. The ground floors, however, are flagged with large granite paving-stones and run as uninterrupted corridors, hundreds of feet long, beneath the offices and bedrooms of the top two storeys. In these long, shady arcades lounge native servants and messengers, while shroffs test silver by ringing the coins on the paving-stones. Also to be seen are a few storage magazines against the walls, and halfway along, narrowing the corridor, a secure treasury with heavy iron doors. Strategically disposed stand hand-pump fire-engines in green and red. These are wonderful and vital pieces of mechanical apparatus, for fire is an ever present and deadly hazard, not so much within the well-ordered region of brick, stone and granite which is the foreign enclave, as spreading possibly from the rambling, densely packed and often tinder-dry native city behind, which thrusts its shaky terraces hard against the noble walls of the Factories. Such conflagrations gutted all but the Honourable Company's magnificent premises on November 1st, 1822, though new and more glorious buildings soon arose, and there have been innumerable minor alarms.

The Thirteen Factories themselves are ranged closely together, separated into three blocks by the aptly named Hog Lane, New China Street, and Old China Street. Tall flagpoles dominate the river in front of the Factories and the Union Jack droops now on the failing breezes of the south-west monsoon before the English Factory, which is the headquarters of the Honourable East India Company, trading to China. Known simply as *the* Factory, a collective designation which extends to occupants as well as building, its architecture is grandiloquent and it is furnished accordingly. Palatial pillars take an open terrace eighty feet out to a Corinthian portico. Behind is a vast, airy dining-room, with tall windows flung open to the river. A crystal chandelier depends from the ceiling, reflected in the mahogany of the banqueting table. A life-size portrait of George III, brought as a gift by Lord Macartney's embassy in 1793, and spurned by His Celestial Majesty, hangs at one end of the chamber. The display of plate and candlesticks is simply prodigious. Further on, there are also a billiard-room, full of clicks and laughter, and a library, full of smoke and the smell of calf bindings, as well as various bureaux for the President and the Select Committee of Supercargoes he presides over, not to mention the empty, north-facing attic which usually serves as Harry O'Rourke's studio while in Canton.

Magnificent as the building is, time is running out for the Company in China. Their monopoly on tea exports has been successfully challenged by the Manchester and Scottish Free Traders, upon whom the Company is, in any case, dependent to carry its opium illegally into China and thus relieve it of any but indirect odium for the nefarious trade. The Company, as Eastman says, is not unlike Pilate, and public hand-washing is a tactic it has never scorned. The Company will be dissolved in China in 1834, in a few months' time, and its functions taken up by a Superintendent of Trade, appointed by the Home Government, probably some well-connected nobleman, nobody is quite sure who yet.

So, though the banqueting table glows as richly as ever, the silver sparkles, and an invitation to dine with the Select and then smoke a cheroot on the terrace is still coveted, life winds down. About the Factory there hangs an air of sadness. The clicks and laughter in the billiard-room will become ghostly echoes, the excellent library will be broken up and auctioned piecemeal, the cellar vied for. Now O'Rourke, so long resident on the coast that he can even remember the old Factories, goes to his room. Where we will leave him with his cigar, his sketch-books, and a glass (or two) of eau de vie, while Eastman proceeds to the bachelor mess of Meridian, Remington, Remington & Co. at No.7 American Hong.

The mess are mostly young bachelors, with the older married men single by necessity in Canton, while their ladies languish in Macao. They are a cheerful crew, high-spirited, well-educated, and generally fond of each other's company (the underlings if not the partners, who are sombre men), which is as well, considering that there is no escape from anyone. Eastman, punster, wit, and accomplished mimic (particularly of O'Rourke and P- a former member of the Select) is fairly popular, though at times he can offend with sarcasm and irascibility. Tonight, September 7th, 1833, he is neither sarcastic nor irascible and fits well into the prevailing mood of jollity and jubilation. Meridian (as we will call them for short), having nearly foundered four years ago on an unwise speculation in indigo, have recovered impressively over the last eighteen months. What is more, they have achieved this without soiling their hands, ships' bottoms, or consciences with drug. Some other American houses (though none of the British Houses of Agency) are also abstainers from this fabulously profitable traffic. Meridian import Canadian ginseng,

North American furs, sandalwood from nameless South Seas islands, sea-cucumbers and bird's nests from the East Indian archipelagoes, and exchange these for silk, porcelain, lacquer, curios and some tea which they export to Boston and Philadelphia via the Cape of Good Hope and the South Atlantic.

Young Gideon Chase, a New Englander seven years Eastman's junior, is a clerk with him in the running of these ventures and now greets Walter in his shy way. (He is very young at almost seventeen and Eastman is quite sure he was never so callow.)

'We had quite given you up, Walter.'

Eastman sits himself at the dining-table in the chair Gideon has pulled out.

'Harry O'Rourke detained me. I do confess when the old rascal starts prating about his precious art, not to mention his unmentionable experiences, I find myself oblivious as to the hour.'

'Ha! Down at the flower-boats, I calculate, Walter.' This is Ridley, a vulgar New Yorker. 'Dallying with Ah Soo and Ah Sam in their flowery bower,' says young Johnstone. 'Conclude to go to the good Dr Colledge for blue ointment and mercury,' interjects another spark.

'You know very well I have lost my salary to Ridley's damnable dexterity with the cue and the ball, God damn him,' says Eastman, 'and Ah Soo's charms are not for the impecunious.'

'Our dinner awaits, gentlemen,' says Jasper Corrigan, senior partner until the arrival of Remington, who is presently at St Helena. He does not like the conversation of his young gentlemen to grow too unbridled. But, 'May it cool still more,' says Ridley, who is difficult to repress. For dinner, a relatively modest affair this evening by Factories standards and one which would certainly make Harry O'Rourke grumble, is constructed around an excellent cold buffet of York ham, fowls, beef, abalone, and local crayfish, preceded by clear broth, with curried mutton and rice. There is champagne first, then a first-rate claret, fruits and pastries, washed down with some of Mr Bass's finest, and then a glass or two of port or Madeira to aid digestion. Beef tea is drunk, curry sampled, then, 'Let us discuss this modest collation,' says Corrigan, and subsequently, over the Madeira and crystallised fruits, the conversation moves from the humdrum quotidian to an elevated sort of topicality: they discuss the latest issues in Boston, London, Philadelphia, Fort William, Trincomalee, and Peking as they affect their place in the world. Ministries, their fall and their successors, the demise of the Company, the question of rupee remittances and bills on London at three hundred and sixty-five days' sight, piracies in the outer waters, the Portuguese in Macao and Timor, are bandied around over the golden wine and nuts. Although on the spot, these merchant adventurers have the sensation of being far removed from the events which will shape their lives and fortunes. To return to New York or Salem entails sailing across three oceans and could take almost a year. The British Governor-General sitting in the Council of India is at least three months away, maybe six with an opposing monsoon. For return despatches to come, even assuming an unlikely speed of deliberation in Calcutta, will take six months, by which time a crisis may well be over or a tiny cloud have become a storm. As for communications with London, well, nothing under a year could be reasonably contemplated, though steam-packets either side of Suez might cut a few months off soon.

'Who are the worst cunctators,' says Eastman, who is grotesquely proud of some scraps of classical education whipped into him by an old Loyalist at Norfolk, 'the Celestials or our Cousins? The Company, in its day, would make no decision on the gravest issues. The most vehement representations of their Select Committee at Canton registered as nothing with the Court of Directors in Leadenhall Street.'

'Walter,' young Chase whispers, 'what is a *cunctator?*'

Quick as a flash, Ridley says, 'One who has supped too well at the altar of Hymenaeus.'

Corrigan, in the role of young gentlemen's mentor, does not seem to hear. Chase, who came out three years ago at the age of thirteen as the orphaned ward of an uncle with connections, is lamentably uneducated both in the classical and the worldly sense, and the smoking-room sally is lost upon him. 'Gideon,'

25

says Eastman kindly, 'it is one culpable of excessive delay, though the consul Fabius called Cunctator was so dubbed for a correctly exercised prudentiality.'

'I guess the Cunctator knew when to exercise boldness, too,' says Ridley, 'while the Company's acts have always been characterised by vacillation and a womanly timidity. The grossest insults of the Chinese went unresented when by a timely application, nay, a timely display of force, they might have been brought to their senses. The excesses of the Chinese have gone so long unchecked that there must, I fear, be expenditure of blood and treasure before matters may be improved. Had the Company taken earlier a firm stand on its trading prerogatives and the rights of its servants, then all might have been settled bloodlessly.'

'There, Ridley,' says Eastman, who, as we know, is opposed to the traffic in opium but is otherwise as keen as the next man to open the empire to trade, 'you speak truth. The supineness of every committee here has been a reproach. Rather than imperil a single leaf of tea, the Company would require its servants, as men, to swallow the basest of insults. The pride of its servants may have been hurt but the Company's pocket never.'

'The new Superintendent – a superintendent, by the way, Gideon, is one charged…' Chase throws a walnut at the detestable Ridley, who ducks it neatly, '…with the task of overseeing affairs. Therefore,' continues Ridley smoothly, 'we should all hope that he will see what is wrong and apply his powers vigorously to prosecute matters with zeal and despatch. I, for one, am heartily tired of being pelted with bricks, mud, and worse for the horrid crime of attempting a stroll on the city walls.'

'Is it right, though, Ridley, that we should force the Chinese to trade with us when it is not their wish?' enquires Chase, the naive boy.

This draws thunder from above in the shape of Jasper Corrigan. 'Of course, it is right, Chase. Trade, important as it is, is merely the vanguard of civilisation. We are not merely the servants of Mammon but more so the agents of a great and revitalising influence. It is our duty through the instrumentality of trade, to bring China into the family of nations and, indeed, into a free and unimpeded intercourse with not only the rest of mankind but our Maker. Trade will bring civilisation to the half-civilised Chinese and, as naturally, the great truths of Christianity will follow in the wake of trade. I labour in the firmest of convictions that our efforts are hallowed work.'

'Aye', 'Indeed', 'Well spoken', 'Fine sentiments, Jasper', and palms slapped on the table indicate an overwhelming consensus among the little company, who enjoy their cheroots and another glass or two of Madeira before retiring to bedrooms above the offices.

CHAPTER IV

At six the next morning Chase and Eastman are to be found in mid-stream opposite the Factories in one of Meridian & Co.'s jaunty little two-man skiffs. They wear only their trousers and white shirts, which the breeze ruffles, but perspire as they pull up the river. This is their regular exercise. There is nowhere to ride, one soon becomes tired of walking (on the rare occasions vigorous pacing is possible on the choked quay), and this is the pleasantest way to 'shake up the liver' before breakfast. 'Put your back and thigh into it, Gideon, when you have the will. That's it, well pulled, Gid.' In response, the little craft shoots over the water. It is possible to attain a respectable velocity in the middle of the river when it is clear, as now, and soon the pair are past the sandbank at Shameen and its floating brothels, the two small forts on either bank, and are nearing the Fati flower-gardens, to which, as a special concession, they are allowed to resort three times a month.

Their shirts, which will be laundered by Meridian & Co.'s servants, now stick to their backs and they gasp with exertion. 'Gideon, I think we have done our duty,' Eastman manages, 'to both ourselves and the bodies with which our Maker endowed us.'

'You cry for quarter, then?'

The young cub steps up his rate and Eastman is obliged to follow, laughing so much that what little wind he had left is soon expended, with the result that he catches a crab and the skiff slews round. Eastman collapses over his oars which are somehow mixed up with his elbows, one forward and one astern. 'Mercy, you rascal. I shall have an apoplexy.'

'About we go.'

The current is now with them and without a great deal of effort they are quickly abreast the forts again, where they see Jasper Corrigan at the tiller of a small sailing-dinghy, threading his way through the lines of sampans and house-boats which crowd this stretch.

'There is a man of discernment, Gid. We should profit by his example.'

They put their backs into it again and actually overhaul a becalmed Corrigan who nods curtly at them. It is a moment's work to carry the skiff into the boat-house and, after a quick wash and a change of shirts, it is in to breakfast.

At eight work starts in the office. It is not by any means a demanding way of earning one's daily crust and, indeed, work is probably a misnomer. Gideon seems to do most of it. Without exception, the clerks are all from good families, gentlemen adventurers to the man, who would never have descended to such occupations at home. Would they? On the other hand, it is certainly worth noting that they are nearly all younger sons. Eastman, to be frank, is too volatile, too fitful, maybe too clever, to be good at this line of work. He sits on his tall stool, checking the entries written into the account-books in Gideon's copper-plate. Eastman himself has a beautiful hand, firm, flowing, regular, elegant without any unnecessary flourishes; it could well be a graphologist's nightmare, for so far from reflecting his character, which is naturally headstrong, irascible, tempera-mental, and unstable, it positively misleads. It is the handwriting of a bishop and, at that, one whose strong point is administra-tion. Administration is not Eastman's forte, nor does the graceful handwriting figure largely in the ledgers of Meridian & Co. Possibly Gideon could manage quite well without being supervised, though the thought has never once crossed his loyal sixteen-year-old mind. Now Eastman pulls the ledger away from Gideon's spluttering quill ('Walter, I beg you, show some care!') and runs his finger down the entries.

'To cotton (finished) 600 bales at $10 per bale $6000

'To olibanum (garbled) in chests at $100 per chest 20 chests $1000

'To tin pigs $15 per piece 500 pieces $750

'To cotton checked dress $1 per piece 500 pieces $500

'To bird's nests 700 at $10 each $7000.'

'Is it satisfactory, Walter?' Gideon enquires anxiously.

'Satisfactory, my dear Gideon? It is fine, handsome. Continue with a will,' and Eastman pats his pocket for a cheroot. 'I expect I shall conclude to go to see the silver being shroffed on account of the goods. You may pursue your labours without me for the time being,' and he trots down the stone stairs to enjoy his mid-morning smoke with great complacency. Afterwards, he does actually go to the shroffs, those expert native employees of Meridian & Co., and watches them assaying the silver which the Chinese merchants have paid into the treasury on account of Meridian's goods. Spanish and Mexican dollars, 'chopped' with the assayer's seal so many times that they have become totally defaced, 'shoes' of Chinese sycee silver which indeed do remarkably resemble footwear, and simple broken lumps of specie are strewn carelessly (at least it might seem so to a novice observer) on the stone flags. So deft are the shroffs that they can tell by touch, sometimes, when they have been passed base metal in the guise of precious or when a coin has been hollowed, the silver excavated and replaced with lead. Such forgeries, though not unknown, are nevertheless very rare, for there exists a remarkable mutual trust in financial matters between the 'Hong' merchants and the foreigners. Each of the thirteen 'Hongs', that is to say the Factories, has its own Hong or Security Merchant, from whom they nominally rent the premises and who is the guarantor of their good conduct. He is the medium through whom they transact their buying and selling in the non-clandestine trade, which is primarily teas on the export side. In fact, the Hong merchants, with the exception of the fabulously rich Howqua, are all heavily in debt to the foreigners and paying them vertiginous rates of interest on the capital they owe, such that it is exceedingly unlikely that they will ever balance their accounts again. They are not happy men: respectively 'squeezed' by venal and rapacious mandarins, dunned for interest by their foreign creditors, permanently short of capital and liquidity, life for them is a long-drawn series of frights and vexations. When they fail, as they sometimes spectacularly do, they can expect exile to Ili in the remote and freezing north-west. Many would like to quit the business, but they are forbidden to do so. Some wretches die still in harness, as it were, and it is common for their distracted heirs to be impressed into the business in the father's place. All in all, it is testimony to the resilience of the human spirit (irresponsibility, some of the harder-hearted creditors would call it) that they should appear on the surface such cheerful and large-minded men, even if they frightfully mangle the English language.

Minqua, Meridian's Hongist, is at the shroff's this morning, and Eastman greets him with a 'Well, Minqua, chin-chin you velly well, today,' to which Minqua replies: 'No.1 today, ony No.3 wifee, she too much makeum leg bad,' by which Eastman understands that Minqua himself is in rude good health but that his second concubine is still suffering from the ulcerated leg which the Honourable East India Company's young surgeon, Dr Colledge, is treating (*gratis,* of course). Eastman condoles with him. He is fond of old Minqua (grandson of the first Minqua, who founded the house in 1730, and son of Minqua II, who opened dealings with the fledgling firm of Howden, Meridian & Co., as it was then).

When Eastman first came out to Canton, Minqua invited him to his mansion on Honan island for dinner and then sent him back to the Factories in his own boat. The old fellow loves to play whist and cheats shamelessly when he gambles with Meridian's young gentlemen, which they are under instructions to allow, within reason, Jasper Corrigan making good their losses.

'Too muchee bad silver today, Minqua,' Eastman chaffs him (there was a single counterfeit dollar in with the thousands of others three years ago).

'Eiyah! All good!' Minqua says. 'But bimeby you give um back Minqua.'

The silver, as Minqua points out, is only temporarily in Meridian's coffers. In a few weeks' time, Meridian will use much of it to pay for the teas and other goods which they will export, on their constituents' accounts, to Boston and also to Europe where very likely it will evade King William's duties, much to the satisfaction of Jasper Corrigan, who not only lost a midshipman brother in the war of 1812 against the British but also knows that the English behave very much like thieves here. First of all, they do not confine themselves to clandestinely transferring opium to their hulks, those floating warehouses, in the Outer Waters at Lin Tin island but also trans-ship legal imports, like cottons, rattans, or pepper, in order to escape the ordinary Chinese customs dues. His own ships pay the tax of 'measurage'. He resents it, finds it arbitrary and extraordinary that the rate of his liability should be the length of his ship, rather than the goods it carries, but still pays. The various 'cumshaws' to the servants of the Hoppo's department, that is the Imperial Commissioner of Taxes, must also be paid to expedite handling of cargoes, and even hardened demi-smugglers like William Jardine or James Innes find it expedient to oil the wheels of bureaucracy – often, appropriately enough, with 'sing-songs', that is with pieces of Birmingham mechanism: cuckoo-clocks, fancy chronometers, musical boxes, chiming watches, clockwork pornographic tableaux, that kind of thing. In the Palace at Peking, gathering dust, in a special pavilion, repose the ingenious toys and timepieces of Midlands artificers and Swiss craftsmen.

Which show that the prevalent corruption has reached the throne itself.

Despite his avowals to the contrary, that he merely wishes to cherish tenderness for the barbarian from afar, the Emperor is now deeply implicated in the Canton trade and his household revenues are usefully boosted by it. Remote Emperor, wily mandarin, ruthless British Free Trader, hard-headed Yankee interloper, pompous Company official, swaggering secret-society smuggler, and opium-growing Bengal *ryot* are linked by a devious web of dependence and repulsion, necessary coopera-tion and mutual hostility and, curiously enough, without the tension inherent in the confrontation of opposites, the system would probably not have held together so long.

The Company always affected to despise the money-grubbers, those hard-faced men from Manchester and Edinburgh who did the Honourable Company's dirty work for it. In fact, the Country Traders (as those MacLeans, McFarlanes, and Smiths were called, together with their correspondent agents in Bombay or Calcutta) were at first expressly prohibited from a Canton residence. The city was the Company's preserve. Trespasser be gone. But the bullish simply stayed put, while the cunning bought consulships from strange powers: His Prussian Majesty, His Bohemian Majesty, and claimed immunity and the right to abode on a technical ground. But as the drug-trade burgeoned, so the money-grubbers came at first to provide a convenient alibi for the Company in the face of the Canton Viceroy's fulminations and, finally, an indispensable means of carriage for their Indian opium after they had sold it at the Calcutta auctions. By Eastman's day, the tail is pretty well wagging the dog.

At the moment he and Chase step on the stage, we must imagine them as heirs of an economic system best conceived of as two intersecting triangles, perhaps even as a Star of David, whose sides, though invested with discrete identities, when amalgamated add up to a wholly different economic formation. We have: the West India and the Atlantic Triangle. And − the East India Triangle. The former is the senior.

Both are of an extraordinary, a classic simplicity, Cartesian almost in their ruthlessness and clarity. We may even ascribe an inventor and a date to the first system, that distinction belonging to the great Elizabethan discoverer (in all senses), cut-throat, and admiral Sir John Hawkins, who in October 1562, set out from Plymouth to West Africa on the first part of a wicked geometry. There, where the continent bulges out into the Atlantic Ocean, he bought Negro slaves from the native rulers, trading manufactured metal items, such as copper nails and arrowheads for men. With his holds full of purulent humanity he is wafted by the trade winds to Hispaniola. There he exchanges slaves with the Spanish for a more fragrant cargo of spice and West India produce: a roaring trade, for the governor prevails on him to discharge a cannon or two to excuse him to King Philip. And home, then, on the final leg. He has thus a triple gain. So successful proves the second voyage, two years later, that the Company pays sixty per cent on its shares. This will seem a trifling dividend when compared to the dizzy profits to be made in the succeeding centuries, when English and Americans come to own the cotton and sugar plantations of the mainland and Caribbean islands and also the men and women who work them and produce the tobacco, the cane, the molasses, the rum. It will take three centuries to perfect the operation of this huge engine of enrichment (for the few) and enslavement and degradation (for the many).

But a brilliant idea! To make someone work for you (in a climate you and your kind would find difficult to endure) for nothing, for ever. To possess them! And the investment grows – you own the children they produce. British ships supply. Americans and Creoles own. And in the early days of the system copper-coloured men of that New World toil as slaves, too, (though less hardy than the Africans who shall replace them) hacking out silver from the earth's bowels for a small band of swarthy white men. This provides the fuel and lubricant for the entire engine – and some of that vital commodity will still be circulating two and a half centuries later when the second triangle is added to the machine. In the meantime, the black men labour on the plantations. Generations, white and black, are born and pass away. A whole ancestry extends itself which has never known freedom.

Now begins the second of the unholy trinities – whose sides pierce and intermingle with those of the first. The cotton the black men grow across the ocean goes in its raw state on ships to a damp coast on a small island in the north-west Atlantic where impoverished white men and women, and their children, also torn from their homes in the countryside, but slaves only to a pittance of a wage and technically free except in their thrall to the iron laws of political economy and supply and demand, act as spinners of this cotton, and others of their ilk as weavers. And so the cotton, in the form of cloth now, or even manufactured piece-goods, continues its journey west to east, crosses the oceans to India, where it is sold to brown men on a subcontinent who will be growing poppy for the white men – but later … much later. These blooms of *Papaver somniferum,* by the way, are white, not scarlet as we know the flower of the wheat-fields. For a couple of centuries, before the advent of the white flower, the traffic with the Occident has indeed been a lucky red for the Emperor and his subjects. They possess that which the West ardently desires: tea, silk, porcelain, and…rhubarb. *Rhubarb?* Yes, you see, the Chinese believe this is what the rude Western trader really wants; that it is the lure which has brought him over the perilous, dragon-haunted sea; that the barbarian bowels are naturally constipated and without the rhubarb to open them, they shall die. In any event, the Chinese have no desire at all to exchange their herb and silks, magical commodities, first for the barbarian's tawdry woollens and, later, his cottons.

Now this is most inconvenient. It is to throw a spanner into the very works of the machine – much as the Luddites at home.

However – as yet – the Chinese cannot be coerced by dragoons who are German mercenaries, or very well be transported to penal colonies in the Antipodes. With reluctance, with very great reluctance, the engine's operators must expend that commodity which they detest above all others expending, even blood: they must pay for their teas in hard bullion, silver. For a hundred years and more, then, the balance of trade between East and West remains firmly in favour of the Orient. The East India Company simply cannot square its books in its trade to China. In India, although its corrupt servants make fabulous personal fortunes, though it seeks not an administrative or a territorial but only a trading empire, it finds itself implicated in the monstrous expenses of maintaining and extending its rule. It teeters on the verge of bankruptcy; has to be baled out by the Home Government.

And then...opium.

The Chinese *will* take opium. Only a few chests at first, but the volume of the trade increases at an extraordinary compound rate, much in the same fashion as the merchant's daughter, when offered her reward by the despot, in all innocence asked for a single grain of rice on the first square of her chessboard, two on the second, four on the third, and...not all the granaries of the East could supply a bounty so prodigious. And thus does the trickle of opium become a torrent, such that the terms of trade are irreversibly shifted and the outflows of silver from the Empire become enormous – to the point where the currency is debased almost to the point of valuelessness and the law of Gresham, contemporary of Hawkins, begins to operate. The value of the opium imported now greatly exceeds the value of the teas exported. The British may declare the slave trade illegal in 1807 and abolish the institution of slavery in 1834 (although their cousins do not), but then who needs unwaged primary producers, who still have to be housed, clothed, cured, if necessary, and always fed, when you have a market of *consumers* in thrall to your product, to whom you have no responsibilities whatsoever?

And so, the second triangle takes shape: India the creditor of China through her opium. England in debt to China for the cost of her teas. But then: England turns out to be the creditor of India – the Company must service its ancient loan from the Home Government. Thus, at last, is the geometry of the arrangement completed to the satisfaction of its inheritors.

The tea? Goes to comfort and stimulate the poor white cotton-workers in the main, so that drug of a kind is at work at all corners of the triangle. And the wonderful thing is that the engine seems to be self-fuelling. Even the slaves reproduce themselves in an unbroken line. Everyone is working for the same small group of white men and producing something that someone else wants. What do the small group of white men want? Silver, capital. No one else seems to want it.

The silver-gainers, the accumulators of capital, would be quite astonished and angry to see such a crude and erroneous blueprint of the machine they are sure does not exist anyway.

Triangles? Bah, sir.

Walter Eastman's part in all this, on this particular day, moment of blazing, immolating truth to which the centuries have led, alas apprehended only as a diversion from numbing, humdrum routine, will be to take young Chase along to Minqua's warehouse to watch Mr Atkins, Meridian & Co.'s English tea-taster, at work.

That is, naturally, after a fine tiffin.

As a basically responsible, if sometimes erratic, employee, Eastman passes a self-denying hour at the table in mess. Gideon has some of the soda-water Meridian's last ship brought.

Then it's off to Minqua's.

Atkins is already there. He's a bald, stocky Yorkshireman with a big red face, not at all the thin, ascetic type you might expect to be undertaking this subtle and delicate work, for such it is. The wooden boxes, lead-lined to insulate the contents from salt and damp during their lengthy sea-passage, are already being prepared but Atkins has just plunged his arm into an unlined chest from Minqua's tea-broker, who resides to the north in Fukien, and is sifting the leaves betweeen his stubby fingers. He sniffs them. They are excellent: a good, fragrant leaf, with the firing in the pans perfectly done and not a trace of adulteration: that infamous colouring agent, Prussian blue; stones; or inferior additions of tea-dust, leaf-sweepings, and God knows what else. The tea-brokers, driven by necessity, are not as scrupulous as they used to be and Meridian, in Corrigan's words, had to entertain seriously the complaints of some constituents the season before last. The American and continental markets prefer 'green' teas to 'black' but Meridian deals in both and buys and exports Hyson, young Hyson, gunpowder and Congou. Two coolies are preparing the gunpowder tea in a corner of the yard. Eastman enjoys this particular spectacle and beckons Gideon over. The coolies have their hands on a wooden crossbeam above their heads and stand on balls about double the size of a man-of-war's 32-pound shot. Supporting themselves on the beam, they are walking the spheres along its length, turning them with the soles of their bare feet (which are very dirty indeed). Inside the balls, protected by a tough skin of canvas, is the powdery tea, which is being compressed and shaped by the rolling and the coolies' weight. Stripped to the waist in baggy, black trousers, their queues hanging down their meagre backs, the men tread sullenly. Gideon imagines Atkins on the beam manufacturing with his prodigious weight a satisfactory ball in no time. He is about to share the joke with Walter but Eastman says in a pedagogical sort of way: 'This form of manipulation is one of the most interesting and curious parts of the whole process of preparing the teas,' and Chase decides levity would be unbecoming a junior writer of less than eighteen months' standing with the firm, so 'Yes, indeed, Walter,' he says meekly, but a moment later: 'Ped-ipulations, surely?' – which truly feeble adolescent effort meets with the scorn it deserves.

Now Eastman enters Atkins' tea-room, that holy of holies, shrine – one supposes – of the anti-Bacchus. Its windows face north, it is totally free of dust, grease, and (still more remarkably for the heart of a major southern Chinese city) of odour.

Gideon, who has visited a mosque in Oman, feels like kicking off his shoes. In handsome wooden cabinets along the walls stand rows of glass jars and on others stacks of small tin boxes, all containing samples of teas of former years, carefully labelled for purposes of comparison. There is a thermometer for plunging into kettles of boiling water; sand-glasses for timing the infusion; cups, of course, with little lids; wooden trays; sieves. Not present are cake-stands, sugar-basins, milk, or tea-pots.

Atkins comes in, wiping his face with a red and white spotted handkerchief.

'Still sultry, Mr Eastman, sultry and close for September,' he remarks.

'I guess you should clarify the animal spirits with a cup of your own finest Congou, Atkins,' says Eastman, 'it can be a great refreshment in this climate.'

'Something stronger is indicated, sir,' the portly tea-taster says, winking at young Gideon. 'Will you take a glass of Mr Hodgson's brewing with me?'

'Why, Atkins, I allow you surprise me,' says Eastman.

'Mr Chase, will you be surprised too?'

'Thank you, not.'

Eastman holds out his foaming tankard to be refilled. 'Do you ever speculate, Atkins,' he enquires, 'as to the appearance of the neighbourhoods in which the plant is grown?'

'The Bohea Hills, you mean? I have only McKenzie's engraved sketch to go by, who was able to disguise himself in native costume. My person would be harder to conceal, I believe.'

'I guess so,' says Eastman, eyeing the speaker lugubriously.

Perhaps slung across a pole, Gideon thinks, like a hog.

'You dare to smile, sirrah?' Eastman says.

'He who can smile in this climate is a man of valour,' says Atkins. 'Take some tea, then, my boy. Its heat will make you perspire and that'll cool ye.'

Gideon accepts, though he is himself a coffee-man by patriotism and disposition, finding tea watery and insipid.

'I'll give you the 1827 Hyson, which you may find you enjoy.'

Gideon does not. However, he is relieved to see Atkins has dispensed with thermometer and sand-glass in the brewing of his little cup. He would not like to be a nuisance. As if reading his thoughts, Atkins says: 'The assaying of tea is an art and not a science. It is the man, and not his instruments, which is the most important. There can be no substitute for my experience and intuited knowledge.'

'Then why the paraphernalia at all, Atkins?' Eastman asks carelessly. 'Why the records, the samples? I know full well that the utmost reliance can be, and is, placed on the talent of your nose alone. Would affairs not be simpler if we dispensed with all this and relied on your original genius and that of your rivals in the other houses?'

Atkins now smiles. 'And my craft, gentlemen, how would that be secured and transmitted? How would it best be preserved for the posterity of those who shall be our successors here? For progress can only be made upon the discoveries of one's predecessors, where each generation would merely repeat the mistakes of the earlier and the sum of knowledge would never grow.'

'You mean as with the discoveries and experiments of the

great painters of the past? Or, better still, that it must accumulate like the capital of the speculator? I allow that is a comparison which is more ingenious than meaningful.'

Gideon, who is never personally offended by Eastman, is forever being offended on the behalf of others by his remarks and is in a perpetual light sweat of anxiety that, if not blows, at least high words are going to be exchanged because of Walter's most unfortunate manner (which Gideon knows himself is not so much tactlessness or boorishness as the straightforwardness of pure intellectual honesty). Poor Gideon. But bluff old Atkins is the last man to take umbrage where offence was not intended, and he merely snorts. He and Eastman go off to confer with the Fukien broker's agent, while Gideon stays to watch the coolies balancing precariously on their globes. A strange world, thinks Gideon.

CHAPTER V

From THE CANTON MONITOR
March 20th, 1834

Per *Harpy,* recently arrived from Calcutta

Superintendency of Trade. From our friends in Calcutta, the City of Palaces, we have it on the best authority that Lord Napier of Merchiston has been offered, or will shortly be offered, the position of Superintendent of Trade and His Britannic Majesty's *de facto* minister at Canton when the Honourable Company's monopoly shall have been dissolved in April. Such tidings will gladden the hearts not only of that portion of the foreign community here composing His Britannic Majesty's subjects but also of all others, including our transatlantic Cousins and companions in exile (and *quondam* enemies) who stand to benefit as much as the English Free Traders from the prosecution of a vigorous British policy, though of course the Americans have never been officially excluded from the trade in the consignment of teas as have their British cousins. They assuredly will not suffer from free competition and the abolition of a vexatious monopoly. Britannia's wont is to be generous and the benefits which she may extract from the jealous Celestials she will not be seeking to guard unto herself, where others might.

It is perhaps a work of supererogation (and even a source of chagrin) to recapitulate those insults meekly submitted to by the Honourable Company, insults which its servants might have resented as men but were obliged to endure in their capacity as *employés* . Let it be said directly, though, that if the Select's actions as a body might have been misguided, no personal reproach may be levelled at its constituent members as individuals. That they were, with very few exceptions, men of honour whose every deed and action in their ordinary lives partook of the qualities of candour and magnanimity, no one who has taken their station in Canton for more than a few months can ever allow himself to doubt. That their decisions in their official capacities led, however, inexorably to the present lamentable state of affairs must be equally evident to all. The surrender of the wretched gunner of the *Lady Hughes, anno* 1784, to be cruelly strangled by the Chinese authorities, after the firing of a salute had accidentally killed a boat-woman by its discharge, was an act of contemptible pusillanimity, but one full of consequences down to the present day. Those irksome restrictions which make our everyday lives less pleasant than they might be, the arbitrary, excessive, and irrational levies of the emperor's myrmidons (which taxes, one might make so bold as to add, His Celestial Majesty stands in no danger of ever seeing, his officers having very large holes in their pockets indeed), the scorn and contempt of the ignorant, long-nailed mandarins and also the brickbats and epithets of the Canton rabble which assail anyone unwise enough to step outside the strait-ened confines of the Factories, the description of 'barbarians' and worse, the confinement of trade to Canton when everyone knows we had Factories at Amoy and Chusan in the previous century – all these may be laid at the door of the Company, either sitting as the Court in Leadenhall-street or as the Select Committee of Supracargoes at Canton.

The only measures which have ever proved efficacious against the insolence of the Chinese have been those inspired by a manly and determined firmness. A post-captain of the Royal Navy, nay, the humblest midshipman, has ever had the ear of the highest authority at Canton, where the august President of the Select may only 'treat' with his humble petition through the medium of the lying, cringing Hongists. Do we not recall the occasion when the Hoppo and his rapacious underlings demanded the due of measurage from a British frigate, come to cleanse the barnacles from her hull in the Inner Waters? When Jack Hoppo enquired as to the vessel's cargo its valiant captain struck the table with such a fist the glasses jumped. 'Cargo? Cargo, sir?' quoth he, 'the only cargo, sir, a British man-of-war carries is powder and shot, shot and powder, sir, and I shall unload it against your forts, if such is your will.' And with every blow of his fist upon the table, the rascally mandarins leapt back a step in terror, their hands pumping before them, until they fell through the door and in a heap upon the companionway.

Then the gallant captain took them upon the quarter-deck. 'Did you,' enquired he, 'see His Majesty's pennant flying at the mast-head? If you did not, I desire you will take a good look at it on your way to Canton, where you may tell the Viceroy that you have seen a flag that has never been dishon-oured and – please God – while it waves over my head, it never shall!'

Thus the gallant Captain Maxwell. It may be superfluous to add that the frigate stood for the estuary without paying a single *candareen* of tax.

Lord Napier, we know, is a naval man, who saw service at Trafalgar as a midshipman, though he did not have the honour of being in Lord Nelson's ship. He is a cousin of the inventor of logarithms and we have no doubt his calculations at Canton shall prove as satisfying and profitable to the foreign community as they will constitute a source of disquiet and discomfort to the venal authorities of Canton.

Let us never again be willing witnesses to a repetition of those disgraceful scenes which marked the mob's invasion of the Factories three years previous when only good fortune limited loss to the destruction of quay and gardens. If the high road to Free Trade and riches in China may only be reached through a river of blood, then let the blood which is shed be Chinese. We would see, if we had to, whether the Corsican's whiff of grape-shot might prevail as well against the rabble of Canton as the Paris mob. Let us have a Napoleon, if we must.

CHAPTER VI

Old Harry O'Rourke is on the prowl, not (for a change) for young female flesh – that terrible, unpredictable itch which possesses him sometimes to the point of unreason but for *subjects* for the other fixation which grips his mind. They really are subjects for one reason for the vividness and strength of O'Rourke's best work is not so much his technical adroitness, knowledge of the inherited tricks, gambits, schema of the profession – product of years in the life-class and intensive scrutiny of the works of dead masters – but a gift for identifying with what he draws. Even his buildings have a character which appears rooted in three dimensions. This applies to his drawings, be it with his favourite pen and ink, or his water-colours, or even, in the fashion of the great man's youth, the 'oil sketch', fruit of a rapid afternoon in the open. By contrast, the commissioned portraits are quite dead. They *are*

objects, reified, embalmed in oil. He is never so happy, so brilliant, as when padding the streets with his box and his pad, perhaps with a small portfolio securely stringed and tucked under his arm. In the pocket of his coat, a garment which appertains to the previous century, and which the old fellow will insist on wearing in the hottest weather, is a bulge. Extra lead pencils? Pen, ink? No. A brandy flask, as cumbersome and antiquated as the coat. Thus accoutred, he sweeps the crowded square with its hucksters, sideshows, cook-stalls, jugglers and mountebanks. But these he passes by; his albums of the past three decades already burst with delightful studies of charming children whirling enormous swords, of barbers scraping the inner eyelids of their customers (which is why so many of the Chinese are blind physically as well as − in the opinion of the missionaries − morally), of squatting coolies wolfing their victuals. Instead he seats himself on the wharf at Jackass Point.

Upon her back a girl of seven carries her infant brother in a gay cloth sling. Their home is the small sampan moored to the quay and the tiny substitute mother is scrubbing the deck. Despised as are the boat-people by their fellow countrymen, forbidden, for instance, to sit literary examinations, or intermarry with landfolk; disapproved of as they are by the missionaries, who have some justification for believing them imps of the devil, since most of the prostitutes resorted to by the foreign sailors (and one foreign artist) are recruited from the ranks of the boat-girls (or boat-boys); yet still the barbarians have some regard for them. For in this stinking, ramshackle, haphazard city are they not the only natives who keep their homes in ship-shape order, clean and neat? Do they not compose a large portion of the handful of Chinese who can speak English, even if it is only the fractured Canton lingo which, let it be said, they manage a good deal more intelligibly than foolish old Ah Tom, the Hongists' linguist (so-called, Eastman says, because he speaks only one language, Chinese)?

O'Rourke works with bold, decisive strokes, different from Eastman's fussy detail. He might seem slapdash next to Eastman, though the easy fluency of line is deceptive. In the end the marks may look similar enough, though O'Rourke's have taken half the time. But where Eastman, the gifted amateur's, drawing is competent enough, it lacks the conviction of the professional. Old Harry O'Rourke has invested his work with emotion and the bare lines are instinct with life. His figures will be incomparable with Eastman's because, though, to say the least, he's an imperfect man, jealous, conceited, and bad-tempered, he possesses that magnanimity without which any creative artist's view of the world, never mind how perfected in the techniques of its time, will never go beyond an imperfect imitation of the visible. Whereas what O'Rourke offers at his very best is a perfected alternative world, which at the same time is no distortion of the real, for if he changes by leaving out all that is inessential to the illusion, at least he imparts nothing that is false. He tends to see things as they are, not as they are supposed, though, paradoxically, it is his view which seems willed. It has to be said Harry has been unlucky. He would have been better off as a Renaissance artist; born, say, in an Italian city-state or even patronised by some German princeling when his kind of inspired draughtsmanship, deceptive cool technique infused with feeling, was more fashionable. *Sprezzatura,* nonchalant ease; though, in fact, with Harry, often as not, this is purely a social pose, rather than a professional affectation. For he may go through ten painstaking drafts in the studio, ruthlessly discard the fruit of what had seemed a productive afternoon on the hill of Macao. Even so, his works do have this tendency to look better from a distance, if you take a few steps further back than usual, and to talk of the deceptively negligent manner of the late Titian or even Velasquez in this regard is to make the conceited old monster purr. (But do not, on pain of severe displeasure, talk to him of the Chinese brush-masters whose suggestions, brilliantly effective invisible cues, constitute the acme of minimalism, daring manipulation of blank space). Alas, Harry has been lamentably out of stride in his own day and place. For the classical landscapes of Claude or Poussin, so admired by his mentors, for the native English scene as rendered by his peers, he has no sympathy. In fact, though he abhors the Grand Style, as laid down in the tyrant Reynolds's *Discourses,* he greatly admires the Italian masters: the shameful secret is − he was dreadfully snubbed by the Great Man, and this turned him against his precepts. Hogarth – there's Harry's man. The Cozens – father and son, splendid. Rowlandson, capital fellow. And Morland he liked: his lack of pretension, homely scenes occasionally transfigured, his technical facility, and, of course, his penchant for drink and dissipation struck a sympathetic note with the Irishman. Lawrence's speed and ease were all that Harry admired in him; *he* hacks like that. Constable, Turner? Harry has never seen a Constable. As for the latter, although Harry is a mere three years older, it has to be said he would not have had the vision or ability to appreciate the over-Turner. He would have understood neither his light nor his colours. And as for those recently modish and well-paid fellows, the history painters, soon to be swept away themselves and consigned to the realm of what they paint, well….on this subject Harry's eyes bulge out of his head. Truth, he avers, is not to be found in those grand conjunctions of personages on the field of battle or convention-room, but on the kinds of streets he pads. Perhaps so; but success is always a fortuitous conjuncture of the man and the moment. Harry might have been *the* man, but the moment, assuredly, is not his. Poor Harry. Never mind; as he stares now, the girl's back is a soft curve.

O'Rourke does not, where Eastman would, try to capture the intricate pattern of the soft clinging cloth: there is a pause, the pencil hovers, the line is described without the smallest hesitation, and there is the very curve of the young girl's back and the line alone suggests the texture of tunic and, indeed, what it feels like next to her young skin. O'Rourke does not include the baby or his sling. He has quite a ruthless eye, which eliminates what it does not want to have. So how is it, then, that the girl's back, while unbowed, unburdened, suggests weight carried and the weight of the awesome responsibility for another life? Well, this goes beyond craft, and not even O'Rourke knows. He knows that the mosquitoes are exceptionally aggressive and biting him to death and one of the buzzing assailants has just drawn a lump on, bad luck would have it, the O'Rourke proboscis. It flies off with a complacent buzzing but unsteadily (high concentration of alcohol in the bibulous old artist's blood?) and another homes in for a meal. Harry swats his cheek, dislodges the pince-nez, and says 'Drat!' It does seem peculiar that the insects should prefer his raddled flesh to the tender forms of his unconscious sitters. But, alerted now, the subject looks up and sees the elderly red-nosed devil. He is scowling and his small devil-glasses look most precarious. Accustomed as she is to the rude barbarian, Ah Lui's eyes widen, the sampan rocks, and were she not very used to the wayward inclinations of small craft, she and Ah Dee might be in danger.

'You, Devil, don't look at me. I don't like you.'

O'Rourke, whose thirty years on the China coast have left him quite innocent of the smallest knowledge of any of the lingua francas of the empire, does get the gist.

'Now, my dear, do not be alarmed. I mean you no harm, nor your little brother.' He pats his pockets for a sugar-plum or iced almond, and encounters only his flask. He proffers it, meets with no response, and has a swig of his devil-water.

'Your very good healths, my dears.' And then has another wholehearted mouthful, wipes the cap against his britches, and pockets the flask, by which time Ah Lui is on all fours at the sampan's stern. Ah Dee is too young to share his sister's prejudices (local xenophobia which, apparently, even the water-buffalo share, with their tendency to ignore black-suited peasants and charge startled, white-garbed sportsmen on their illicit snipe-shooting excursions) and burbles some cheerful nonsense at the stranger. Even O'Rourke knows this isn't Chinese; so, imperturbable in any company, he makes a rude noise, involving expired air, tongue, and lips. Ah Dee makes one back. O'Rourke holds up the little sketch. Ah Lui is tempted, on hands and knees still, to the sampan's bow. Her eyes rounden. The figure in the drawing has no face as such but she recognises herself. Surprise turns into laughter. Harry says: 'My dear, you pay Harry O'Rourke as sincere a compliment as he has received in any salon,' and Ah Lui proceeds to display the acquisitive instinct of the collector. O'Rourke pulls back his hand. 'Ah, no. It's not mine to give. Besides, it is only the instrument for the finished work.'

'You display the initial symptom of mental derangement,

Harry.' A shadow falls across the boat and Ah Lui scampers to the stern again.

'Not at all. Self-communion is the indispensable preliminary to divine. In any case I converse with my little sitter.'

Eastman throws the butt of his cheroot into the water. He inspects O'Rourke's pad. 'Charming, most charming, and more than charming. How infinitely mortifying to think that the fine little fellow in his sling will grow in the space of fifteen years into as blood-thirsty a rascal as any cut-throat presently on the river, and his tiny minder an adornment to a flower-boat in Lob Lob Creek.'

'Well, my boy, pray it shall be the sitter you meet on the water.'

'In either case, I guess they may win my hard-earned substance. What do you draw now? Not an imitation of the original, I trust?'

'No, no, I'll make them a gift of my own phiz.'

'Harry, I would not wish to give William Jardine such a nightmare.' And, indeed, O'Rourke has not spared his own feelings. In fact, he has made himself even uglier than he appears in the flesh; the grumpy frown, the nose, the pout are all recorded with fidelity so excessive it caricatures the original.

'But no vermilion?' Eastman quizzes his master. 'Then, sir, it is no O'Rourke and can never be claimed as such.'

O'Rourke says, 'You are entirely premature, my boy, and given to underestimating the resource of the true artist,' and, so saying, taps the side of his mosquito-wounded nose with a calloused, thick forefinger, which Eastman mistakes for the preliminary showmanship he'll indulge until O'Rourke dabs the drawing and reveals the gesture in its true light as stroke of inspiration, improvisation, or whatever, conferring upon his own portrait the requested trademark vermilion lips. 'Painted, if you will allow me, sir, with the life-blood of a great artist,' Eastman comments facetiously. To which O'Rourke says, 'Sir, you and your critical kind importune me as greatly as the mosquitoes.' O'Rourke shows his work to Ah Lui, but she won't come to the bow; a pair of devils are too much for even this intrepid little water-dweller. Eastman places the cartoon on the boat's bow with a copper cash as weight and says, 'A perambulation will reveal objects more worthy of your regard, Harry,' and steers him to Thirteen Factory Street *en route* to the city wall, stopping on their way at No.7 American Hong for two stout sticks.

These they may well need. They also encounter Gideon Chase and Jonathan Ridley, whom they press into the expedition, and, well-equipped, sally out by the Consoo House. Minqua is just coming down its granite steps, having left a discussion with his fellow Hongists concerning John Company's demise and the appointment of the new superintendent, whoever he may be. He is still worried, and seeing this trio of young bucks with the Fat Fornicating Old Devil, plainly bent on mischief, does nothing to make him feel better. (These are parlous times. Why can't everything be simple like it was twenty years ago?) 'Makee too much trouble go outside Factory now. Better you no go, takee skiff on river,' he admonishes them, but it is difficult enough to restrain adventurous young bloods at the best of times and quite impossible if you happen to talk the ridiculous nonsense which is all harassed Minqua has at his disposal, and the foreigners just laugh in his face and continue their purpose. Which is, in defiance of the Emperor's regulations, to proceed through the suburbs and on to the ramparts of the ancient city. Now they have passed into Carpenter's Square with its curio-shops, selling camphor chests and lacquer cabinets to the foreign mariner. These are items of quality, so the bands of roistering, grog-inflamed, samshoo-poisoned sailors who make Hog Lane and Old China Street places to avoid are absent. Eastman waves to the purser and third mate of a Meridian-consigned ship who are bargaining with a shopman. 'Not more than three dollars,' he shouts; and then they are turning down Curved Iron Railing Street into Physic Street, which is the thoroughfare of apothecary's shops. All shops specialising in a particular commodity or service are grouped together in their own streets in Canton: thus, Coffin-Maker Street, Lacquer Street, Shoe-Mender Street. These alleys are granite-paved and only wide enough to admit four abreast. Each ward has its own gates which close across the street at night, although burglars and other unsavoury types simply resort to roof-climbing, quite safe with a fall of only a few feet.

'Come, O'Rourke,' calls Ridley, 'the laggard it is whom the wolves devour.'

Old Harry is carrying only a small sketch-pad and his blackthorn, but has stopped for a sly nip in the doorway of an apothecary's. Gideon is sent to chivvy him along and in the doorway ingenuously asks, 'What can they be, Mr O'Rourke? Dried plantains, I guess?' to which O'Rourke answers, 'The preserved and wizened member of the stag, my dear boy. I own they look hardly large enough.' Gideon wonders what kind of remedy they form and also whether O'Rourke is quizzing him. Chase has become very sensitive to teasing or the possibility of it. At this moment a bucket of water is emptied from two storeys above them, most of which goes into the gutter but some splashes Gideon's snowy trousers. They hurry to catch the others up, some faint urgency noticeable for the first time in O'Rourke's gait.

'Should we not retrace our steps, gentlemen?' Gideon enquires, and is scoffed at by Ridley and Eastman. O'Rourke is on the alert for subjects, and is ready to subordinate his gross physical cowardice (which he will freely admit to) in the pursuit of his conception of excellence. Moreover, is he not with three strapping young fellows? So, 'Courage, my boy, courage,' he murmurs as he has another nip.

Gideon becomes lost. The streets wind; they make abrupt turns; cross over canals; back again over what is surely the same water-gate. And they are so full of people, Chinese that is, it seems extraordinary they can make headway at all. Separated again from Eastman and Ridley, Gideon hopes that the two leaders are not using their sticks upon the persons of the natives. There has been no open hostility yet, apart from the bucket of dirty water, which might have been an accident. They are now some distance from the Factories, and the Chinese here are not the 'traitorous natives' who so prominently figure in the Governor's edicts as abetting the foreigner in his antisocial practices (chiefly, sodomy and stealing babies' eyes). To his relief Gideon sees one of the big city gates above the mean, green roofs of the next street. Eastman and Ridley are waiting for them and together they take the steps to the wall.

The guards, sleazy, ragamuffin fellows, look the other way, jingling what is no doubt Eastman's cumshaw in their greasy purses. They have the look of the Manchu about them rather than the Chinese, and O'Rourke, who has bribed their colleagues (or perhaps themselves) into posing before, confirms that they are indeed Bannermen:

'Of the White-Bordered Banner, Gideon. Alas, the open and manly instincts of their forebears have been dissipated in centuries of corrupting garrison duty. The bordello and alms have succeeded to the hunt and the camp-fire.' (Drink only has the effect of making this hardened imbiber portentous, rather than incoherent, as with lesser men and better livers.)

The ramparts are as broad as three streets put together and considerably cleaner. The masonry is massive but it is true that there are fissures and parasites, including one great tree suddenly sprouting twenty feet up on the wall's outer face. Ridley lobs a shard down and a great flock of birds rise, squawking in dismay. Sited at irregular intervals are cannon, belonging, like O'Rourke's coat, to the previous century, and some even to the century before. Not only are they disgracefully rusty but, fixed on iron pins cemented into the masonry, they may fire only on one line and it is impossible to train them an inch to either side. Possibly it would be safer to be fired at than to fire. A valley some three miles wide stretches before them. On the other side rises the White Cloud Mountain. An Old Resident, O'Rourke has actually (in a happier and more relaxed time) picnicked in the picturesque old monastery which is sited in a gorge a few hundred feet below the summit, making the journey in a chair mounted on bamboo poles. And, of course, came away with a charming study of the old temple, which is filed in a dusty portfolio somewhere in his studio in Macao. Intervening, between city and mountain, lie dog-infested, foreigner-hating hamlets – the Ninety-Six Villages. Suicide to go there these days. Not even Ridley, striking out in front of the little party and swinging his stick in an exaggerated way, would dream of it. They continue along the wall, which is describing a lazy curve, and after a mile find themselves near a red temple, opposite small hills, mounds really, some hundreds of yards outside the wall, which overlook the city.

'Extraordinary, is it not,' says Ridley, 'that the authorities responsible for the defence of this vast city should have been so deficient in a knowledge of the military science that they should have left those hills as they are.'

'Why so?' This is poor ingenuous Gideon again.

'Why so, sir? It needs no Vauban to understand that those heights are the keys to the city. From there a single battery might dominate the city and pound at leisure any of the public buildings its commanders chose.'

'Extraordinary indeed,' says Eastman.

The philosopher of war continues: 'It would be no difficult task, knowing as we do the patient industry and large population of this country, to level those hills and redistribute their mass across the plain. The miserable stone towers they have erected barely offer shelter against the rain, let alone the deliberate fire of the well-handled siege train. Folly and incompetence on every side.'

Gideon says eagerly, 'Jonathan, you are right to opine that the means are not wanting. We do have every evidence of the industry of the people: their irrigation-works, the cutting of the Grand Canal, the Great Wall itself, if the reports of travellers may be accepted as veracious. Could not the explanation lie rather in the want of good leadership or in the petty peculations of the mandarins? Once roused, the people themselves would constitute a most formidable foe.'

'Pshaw!' says Ridley.

O'Rourke, the old hypocrite, says: 'They are sunk in a lethargy and somnolence from which they will only awake when they accept the great Truths of Christianity. It lies not in the leadership.'

Eastman, no friend of the divines, certainly not the majority of the missionaries encountered on these shores, raises his eyebrows at Gideon. 'Opium,' he says. 'Their somnolence is the product of indulgence in that most pernicious and costly of vices.' But Gideon is unusually obstinate. 'Even that is, I believe, a question more of a result than a first cause in itself.'

Ridley trips him up with his walking-stick, saying, 'Nine and thirty years of experience combined of the Chinese argue with you on this point, Chase. Your puny experience must defer to us,' and he swipes, not so playfully, at Gideon's rump as he sprawls. A very nice boy, Gideon minds neither the abuse nor the practical jokes, but rubs his scuffed palms and laughs. 'Whatever your pleasure is. Let us not spoil our excursion with disagreeable arguments.'

But suddenly, as a jagged rock, the size of an apple, whizzes in from nowhere, something extremely disagreeable does happen. Fortunately, the missile flies into the wall with a loud crack and promptly disintegrates into tiny pieces without striking any of them. But Gideon turns as pale as his trousers. Eastman says, 'Darn it,' and drops his cheroot, Ridley whirls round with his stick raised, while O'Rourke says, 'Gad,' and has a swift restorative noggin.

At first it is not clear who has attacked them. Then a Chinese head appears from under the breech of a large brass cannon twenty yards behind them. Ridley looks furious and the air hums as he shakes his stick. 'I am going to take that darned rascal by his queue, God damn him, and give him the thrashing of his darned life,' he says between clenched teeth. Gideon puts a hand out to Ridley's arm, but draws it back. He looks at Eastman, who only raises his eyebrows in that quizzical way he has. '*Con brio,* sir,' O'Rourke says, 'go to it.'

Ridley has barely taken five steps when an immense crowd of Chinese, howling imprecations and with offensive weapons in their hands, appear over the top of a flight of steps at the edge of the wall. So fast are they running that their pigtails stick stiffly out behind them and their faces bear the unmistakable signs of a zealous intention to seize the persons of the foreigners and do them serious physical mischief.

Confronted with the mob, Ridley falters, then turns his back and runs. The others already have some yards on him, including Harry O'Rourke in the van, upon whom either adrenalin or alcohol have had a remarkable stimulatory effect. He leads them pell-mell down the next flight of steps and they splash through a morass, scattering chickens and rubbish-browsing pigs on either side. The owners appear out of the doors and unglazed windows of their hovels, waving their arms and shouting 'Barbarian devils!' and 'Kill! Kill!' The faces, Gideon has time to note, as in a dream, are both spiteful and amused. A sturdy coolie is sufficiently imprudent to make at Ridley a motion of stiff hand to throat, 'significant,' as Harry O'Rourke will afterwards relate in Meridian's mess, 'of decapitation'. He has got too far away from his companions for his own good. Clunk! goes Ridley's heavy stick on the man's head and not even his turban can save him from a cracked skull. Over he goes. On rush the foreigners. 'A shrewd blow,' O'Rourke gasps as they turn down a tiny alley. 'To the right, for God's sake,' Ridley shouts. 'We shall be safe at the Factories.' Their pace slows now and O'Rourke's entire face has assumed the colour of his nose, but is it imagination or has pursuit slackened as well? They keep moving, with O'Rourke now at the rear and Eastman supporting his elbow. He waves Gideon on. Rounding the next corner, they see armed soldiers and a mandarin in his sedan-chair. Gideon groans but O'Rourke ejaculates, 'Thank God!' and Gideon sees that Ridley is grinning. The official lictors beat bystanders aside with staves and whips and, for once, the foreigners are glad to stand to the wall with the throng and not resist the mandarin's passage. (As the more truculent English like to.)

Soon they are in Physic Street, of whose balms they thankfully need not avail themselves this time, and passing down into Thirteen Factory Street again, and pretty soon afterwards, snug on the cushions and wicker of Meridian's mess, taking cold punch and drawing on hookahs, as O'Rourke embellishes their adventure. As it is hardly a unique experience, even he has difficulty holding the attention of the young gentlemen who find a new topic in the grand dinner the Company are giving on New Year's Eve to celebrate their passing. So when Gideon enquires hesitantly, 'What became, I wonder, of the fellow Ridley struck?' no one hears him, and Eastman shrugs his shoulders.

Chapter VII

'At any rate, we shall pretty soon see matters come to a head. The Company's end will also have marked the termination of this centuries old system of trading.'

The speaker: O'Rourke; the addressed: who else but Eastman; the scene: Respondentia Walk, by the riverside, which has been strangely empty of Chinese crowds these few weeks.

EASTMAN. 'Well, so it may turn out, though the purge may prove the death of the patient.' O'ROURKE. 'Think of it rather as a boil which is to be lanced. The pain of the operation, if it can be called even that, is momentary and trifling, the inconvenience and indignity of years ending in a twinkling, the system restored to vigour and health.' EASTMAN. 'I should think you might be rather sorrier than you seem. The Company, after all, was a handsome source of commissions to you.' O'ROURKE. 'True, sir, but then we artists are notorious ungrateful fellows. We are holy madmen, possessed by our own genius, which is a fickle and unsteady condition at the best of times.' EASTMAN. 'Wholly madmen at any rate and certainly possessed by the bailiff.' O'ROURKE. 'Ha! Oh Calcutta! Calcutta! I remember you not for your palaces but your dunning suitors.' EASTMAN. 'I believe Lord Napier will be importunate as the most insistent creditor. He has two pretty frigates to reinforce his claims and their broadsides could make a terrible knocking upon the doors of Canton.' O'ROURKE. 'You forget that the door of Canton is where the river disembogues and it is wonderful how well forty miles can muffle the sound of the most ardent knocking. But, certainly, milord seems an obstinate fellow if we may judge him by his recent efforts to force a channel of communication.' EASTMAN. 'Obstinate and perhaps pedantic. What matters it whether a communication be titled a Humble Petition in the Chinese or no? I can certainly see that it should be forwarded directly to the Governor, for the Hongists would cravenly tamper with its meaning where it might displease the mandarins, but to be governed altogether by mere forms of address is idle. To fight a war over titles would be ridiculous. It was insulting to the last degree that the mandarins should have translated Napier's name by the sounds of Laboriously Vile. But this is not a cause of war.' O'ROURKE. 'Not so, Walter. Men are swayed by "mere forms of address". They become more important than the substance. They will not fight for issues but for symbols, for... Jenkins' ear, for the ransomed Helen, for the regiment's tattered colours. It is the symbolising power which will make a cause from an issue. Thus are we all artists and so art is a harlot, too.' EASTMAN. 'Now you demean your Muse and yourself.' O'ROURKE. 'Sir, she is a harlot and worse.' EASTMAN. 'Well, let Lord Napier enjoy her, then. Perhaps she will not reject the Superintendent's credentials so rudely as Governor Loo yesterday.' O'ROURKE. 'Mark my words, the affair must end in the effusion of blood, if not now, then before my old life is ended and certainly within your span of years.' EASTMAN. 'Do you wish, then, that you had never forsaken the City of Palaces?' O'ROURKE. 'Ah, no. That I did not say, my young friend. Canton besieged would be a cooler place for O'Rourke than Calcutta and its creditors. But take we passage to Macao tomorrow and perhaps the thermometer and tempers will be cooler there.'

From THE CANTON MONITOR
August 21st, 1834

Bold policies of Lord Napier. Matters in Canton have now come to such a pass where our situation must be improving or it must worsen. It cannot remain the same. In the scant four weeks since the arrival of Lord Napier, so eagerly attended by all these past six months, more has taken place than in the entire century and a half of the East India Company's history of trading to China. His Lordship has shown a zeal and dispatch which put John Company's pusillanimity to shame, and we do wonder how the former high officers of the Company upon milord's establishment may feel at this sudden reversal of the old policies. By this, of course, we do not mean to level any personal reproach at Mr George Robinson and Mr John Davis, formerly supercargoes upon the Select Committee of the Company, and now respectively Second and Third Superintendents to Lord Napier, whom we have always absolved from any unfavourable personal imputations. Their conduct, as we all know, has always been decided, magnanimous, and gentlemanly in their private dealings. This we are happy to repeat editorially.

Lord Napier upon his arrival at once signalled to the Canton authorities the difference in his standing from a mere trader, for *teas and silks* the most august members of the Select were never more than in the eyes of the haughty mandarins. Without stopping to communicate, as required by the regulations of the Emperor, through the medium of the fawning and unreliable Hongists, he despatched his private secretary, Mr Johnston, to the city gates to present the ribboned credentials proclaiming him the representative of his sovereign, William IV. Needless to say, milord's commission did not bear the offensive character *'pin', an humble petition,* but was marked by those forms which characterise the correspondence of equals. It was summarily and insolently rejected.

His Lordship had made the navigation of the river's intricate waterways from the Bogue in a small but well-crewed cutter, arriving in the small hours of July 25th. The dawning of the day saw the hoisting of the national colours at the flagstaff of the British Factory. However, it will not have escaped the notice of Governor Loo that this new *Barbarian Eye* disembarked at the Bogue from the frigate *Andromache* (32) and the guns of that stout vessel provided the pass which his Lordship disdained to request from the Chinese. Did the forts at the Bocca Tigris open a plunging fire upon Lord Napier's cutter? They did not. We are happy to learn that not only has Lord Napier prevailed upon the gallant Captain Chads, commander of the *Andromache,* to delay his anticipated departure to India and remain in the Outer Waters, but we also hear that the frigate *Imogene,* Captain Blackwood, is also lately arrived at the Bogue. As the

Chinese seem so obstinate, and as affairs but yesterday seemed so much darker, we cannot but rejoice in this most timely reinforcement. Two frigates, nay, one brig of the Royal Navy, would be more than a match for His Celestial Majesty's entire floating armament.

However, we cannot but regard with regret and concern yesterday's news of the cessation of the delivery of cargoes to British ships. Whilst not wishing to adopt the truckling habits of the defunct Company, we feel it incumbent upon ourselves, nay, we feel it our duty not only to ourselves, but to our readers as well, many of whom are personally interested in the receiving and delivery of cargoes at Canton, to deplore those consequences with which any long or very general suspension of trade in the river would be attended. Lord Napier must find a course between the Scylla of apathetic resignation to the insults and peculations of the Chinese and the Charybdis of the universal destruction of that trade which we presently enjoy.

From THE CANTON MONITOR

September 11th, 1834

Reduction of the Bogue forts. Now surely must His Celestial Majesty know that he can no longer treat the scorned foreigner with such a magnificent disregard and condescension. It will now be no secret in Canton that the frigates *Andromache* and *Imogene* passed on Sunday through the Bocca Tigris and with the trifling loss of but two men killed and six slightly wounded, mostly by splinters, pounded the Chinese forts and silenced their batteries. At one point during the engagement, if such it may be called, the wind shifted and the ships would have become becalmed but for the strong tide running into the river, which carried the frigates through. The Chinese forts were thickly built and bristled with cannon but despite the advantage of plunging fire the Chinese gunners made but poor practice. Most of the shot fell short and their aim became increasingly wild as the battle drew on. The ships made a beautiful practice, throwing their shot with a precision most creditable to their captains. The parapets and embrasures of the forts were broken and many guns dismounted. Yet in the hands of Europeans, the river forts would have been impassable. The ill-drilled, indisciplined, venal, and leaderless levies of the Emperor were as naught against the superior order and resolution of the British.

We are happy to be able to make known Lord Napier's orders to Captain Chads, dated September 3rd, which have been shown to us: 'I shall ever feel it my duty as the first representative of the King ever appointed to this place and as responsible for all the evil consequences of untimely concession to act with vigour and determination, being persuaded in my own mind from numerous examples of former occurrences that an opposite course would be attended with consequences very fatal to the general Trade, the personal respectability of the merchants, and the dignity of the British Empire.'

We applaud Lord Napier's manly stand and assure him of our best thanks and consideration. Already the Governor Loo has ordered trade to be resumed and the offensive proclamations to be taken down from the walls of the Factories. We expect hourly the sight of the two sails in Whampoa. Bravo! we cry.

From THE CANTON MONITOR

September 18th, 1834

Obduracy of the mandarins and Governor. Oh! How may the face of matters be changed within the short space of a single week! In our last we gloried in the result of Lord Napier's contest with the Chinese in momentary expectation that the unceasing efforts of the Superintendent and the victories of his frigates would be attended with a rapid and inevitable success. Yet a bare seven days later matters look at a worse pass than we have yet seen.

The white sails of the frigates were descried at Whampoa at a distance of a few miles from the Factories when some gentlemen ascended to the roof of the Honourable Company's former premises on the 12th *inst*. Relief appeared at hand to the beleaguered garrison, for the tiny official establishment of the Superintendent was both effectively besieged, with Chinese soldiers situated in the surrounding streets and environs, and a garrison with the *Andromache's* sergeant and a dozen of gallant marines. Yet how tantalising, how close was that security. For the frigates were yet too large, their draught too deep, for them safely to ascend the remaining twelve miles of the river and anchor before the Factories. Under their guns how would the mandarins have dared be insolent? Alas, it was not to be. It was the river itself, sinuous, supple, devious, deceptive, opaque, winding, shallow, and treacherous as the mandarins themselves, which was the salvation of Governor Loo and his otherwise devoted city. Emboldened by the tardy arrival of the frigates, he waxed in insolence and presumption. Cargoes were awaited in vain, the soldiery grew in defiance, and once again the proclamations appeared around the Factories, accusing the foreigners of the vilest and most unnatural practices.

The Parsee gentlemen of the Chow Chow Hong, whose letter to Lord Napier we earlier printed among our columns, have redoubled their pleas to that nobleman that he might adopt such a line of conduct with the Canton authorities that trade might be opened again. While still deprecating such addresses, which we condemned in our last as timid and selfish, we might now be disposed to entertain their fears a little more seriously.

It is with regret that we learn that Lord Napier is suffering in his personal health, illness perhaps aggravated by detention in his personal restricted circumstances (How great a trial to body and spirit it is we know only too well ourselves!) and certainly by the exertions of his present position. Stands the mercury presently at 90 degrees and more, though old Canton residents will not need telling that the oppressiveness of the weather here is peculiarly independent of the range of the thermometer. In any other circumstances Dr Colledge, under whose regime Lord Napier has been placed, might recommend a sojourn at Macao to recruit the distinguished invalid's health, but for Lord Napier to fly his present position would be tantamount to nothing less than an admission of defeat in the eyes of the Chinese. We pray and wish for better news.

From THE CANTON MONITOR
September 25th, 1834

Departure of Lord Napier for Macao. It will now be generally bruited that Lord Napier has withdrawn himself and his suite from Canton. Our last was printed too soon to allow us to print *verbatim* a report of his Lordship's speech to the British Chamber of Commerce on the 15th *inst.* in which he most gracefully acknowledged the inexpediency of persisting in a course by which British mercantile interests were hardly advanced. He recognised that the subjects in dispute between himself and Governor Loo had so far transcended the realm of commercial interests that they were altogether personal in reference to himself and his position as His British Majesty's representative *in situ* and that as this was so he might retire with the satisfaction of knowing that the merchants' interests were not thereby compromised. It had been his duty to use every effort to carry HBM's instructions into execution and having done so this far without effect, he could not feel himself authorised any longer to call upon the merchants' forbearance.

The frigates have been ordered to retire to Lin Tin island in the outer estuary, while Lord Napier departed for Macao by the Inner or Broadway Passage, which debouches behind Macao and avoids the outer or sea passage by the Bocca Tigris. Dr Colledge is in close attendance on the barge of the Superintendent, while the Second and Third Superintendents, Mr Robinson and Mr Davis, were already at Whampoa upon the frigates.

From THE CANTON MONITOR

October 2nd, 1834

Cruel harassment of Lord Napier. It is with feelings of the deepest indignation that we learn of the cruel provocations to which the attending mandarins subjected a sick and already suffering man on his journey to Macao. We refer to Lord Napier's recent and lamented departure from the Factory Wharf. During the whole of his journey down the Broadway Passage until his arrival in Macao on the 26th *ult.* he was subject to taunts, delays, and a system of nuisances and hindrances so devised that they deserve nothing less than the title of torture. All which could be done to make the sick man comfortable in the barge was performed and Dr Colledge, we know, was assiduous in his most devoted attentions. The ceaseless din, however, of drums, gongs, cymbals, firecrackers, and matchlocks being discharged, both by day and night, conspired to deprive the ailing man of both sleep and rest. His Lordship arrived in Macao a few days ago, and we most anxiously await news of his condition.

From THE CANTON MONITOR

October 16th, 1834

Death of Lord Napier. Yesterday we had intelligence of the heavy tidings of the death on the 11th *inst.* at Macao of Lord Napier. He was faithfully attended to the last by Dr Colledge and passed away in the bosom of his grieving family, who had accompanied him from England in the *Andromache* and remained in Macao while he was so dangerously, and fatally it now appears, closeted in Canton. He was not denied the last consolations of his religion, ministered to him by the Rev. Elijah C. Bridgman, and may appear before his Maker in all humility as an Englishman who sacrificed himself in the service of his country and in the cause of Civilisation and Christianity. But what a sad toll this most recent initiative has taken of the flower of its country! The death in August of the Rev. Robert Morrison, first Protestant missionary in China, translator of the New Testament into Chinese, and author of the first Chinese and English dictionary on the most approved lines, was a blow from which it might be said that the hopes of the party never recovered. They lost a most able translator and Lord Napier, besides, the services of a most wise, experienced, and trusty counsellor. The Rev. Morrison is succeeded by Mr J. R. Morrison, his son, a most able linguist and interpreter, but the younger Morrison would be the first to concur in the opinion that the son is not as the father. How well Dr Morrison knew the wiles of the Old Satan made incarnate in Chinese perversity and hard-heartedness, for after the space of five and twenty years his converts numbered but ten, and those of dubious worth, for their Christian zeal was greatest at mealtimes. He lies now in the Protestant cemetery at Macao, that repose of the earthly shell which he himself wrung from the jealous Catholic government of Macao for his first wife at a time when none but Papists might find a decent burial under Portuguese jurisdiction.

The Rev. Bridgman will preach the funeral sermon and will be Chief Mourner with Mr Jardine. Officers of that service in which Lord Napier first served his country will do him all the honour in their power and shall appear in full dress uniform. Mr James Innes and Mr James Matheson will bring up the rear of the *cortège*.

This letter reached Canton yesterday at 3 p.m. and was translated by Mr J. R. Morrison.

To Howqua and Mowqua, the senior Hong merchants
Gentlemen,

It is my painful duty to announce to you the demise of His Majesty's Chief Superintendent of British Commerce in China, the right Honourable Lord Napier, this day at 10 o'clock and 20 minutes p.m.; and to request that you will cause this sad event to be made known to His Excellency, the Governor of Canton.

I am, gentlemen, your obedient servant
(Signed) T. R. Colledge
Surgeon to H M Superintendents
Macao (Saturday) October 11th, 1834

We are happy to make it known that the Chinese authorities were persuaded through the medium of Howqua and Mowqua to allow Lord Napier to depart for Macao. The request was conveyed by Mr T. R. Colledge to the Hongists (who have yet to deign to receive officially Mr Colledge's letter of the 11th inst.) at the house in Canton of Mr Jardine. We hear with pleasure that Mr Jardine, himself formerly a surgeon on a ship of the East India Company before beginning to trade on his own account, was able to impart valuable, though in the end unavailing, advice to his fellow medical man, Dr Colledge. Mr John Francis Davis, Second Superintendent, has taken up the deceased's duties and functions. Sir George Robinson becomes Second Superintendent. Captain Charles Elliot, formerly Master Attendant, is promoted Third Superintendent.

Mr Davis, in past years an *employé* of the Honourable East India Company and member of its Select Committee of Supercargoes since1827, will, we trust, continue the vigorous policies of his distinguished and lamented predecessor, rather than revive the supine addresses of his old employer.

It will not have escaped our readers' notice that our journal appears edged with a black border, which token of respect needs no form of explanation.

Lady Napier will take ship to England on the *Orwell*, accompanied, we have it on best authority, by Mr James Matheson, who will press Lord Palmerston for redress and reinforcement.

Chapter VIII

ow different are Canton and Macao (to which our story and heroes now pass). The traveller who went from Naples to Stockholm would not have felt a greater difference. For the distinctions which do exist are accentuated by the short physical distance between the two water-borne cities, barely eighty miles. The sensation is not so much of crossing a delta, mighty obstacle though that was and is, as of a continent of the mind; of performing an interior journey as well as one demarcated in space. One feels, simply, different in Macao. The skin which crawled and prickled with the dank heat of the southern Chinese metropolis tingles here, rejoices in the cooling, balmy breezes which play along the Portuguese settlement's leafy esplanades and vivid gardens. The spirit lifts, the eye is refreshed.

Pastel villas, pink, green, and blue, or just dazzlingly whitewashed, face the sea. This is presently being whipped into spume horses by the first gentle breezes of the new north-east monsoon (which is starting to supplant the dying south-west monsoon). Along the Praia Grande, the noble, tree-lined carriageway which curves around the perfect crescent bay of the Outer Harbour, can dock shallow-draught vessels, mostly fishing junks and lorchas. On the other side of the peninsula is the Inner Harbour. At the fashionable hour of 6 p.m. smart carriages, bearing the society of Macao, will trot up and down the Praia and bloods on horseback will ogle the occupants and, if favoured, retrieve a dropped handkerchief or two.

The settlement, already almost three hundred years old, is situated on a narrow-necked promontory jutting out of a large island which forms much of the left bank of the Canton estuary. A wall, 'the Barrier', is built across the narrowest part of the isthmus. Held by a debauched and lousy band of professional gamblers, bullies, and opium-addicts who masquerade as soldiers, it separates this little piece of Portugal, of the transplanted civilisation of the Atlantic, from the Celestial Empire.

In shape Macao resembles a dog's tongue, with a few carbuncles on it, representative of its low hills, on one of which crouches a flat, Jesuit-engineered fort built for defence against the Dutch in the seventeenth century: a potent work in its day but become nothing more than a monument and public urinal. The grotto of Camoes has been spared this last defilement and indignity (smelling floral rather than ammoniac) mainly because it is, through accident of entail and sale, positioned in the garden of the last head of establishment of the British Factory in Macao. Yes, the Honourable Company had premises here, too, for the off-season of the summer when (officially) they were meant to be out of Canton and privately also preferred to be in this balmier sea-zone. They were grand premises. Nothing grand about Luis Camoes, a scribbler merely, who wrote his epic *Os Lusiadas (c. 1557)* in the said Grotto (a lean-to of insignificant granitic rocks) and returned to Lisbon to die a debtor in 1580, like several of those early navigators whose exploits he celebrated. In 1802, the year Harry O'Rourke is said to have arrived from Calcutta, there was already a sense of a backwater about the settlement, a sense of a passing, not merely of a port (measurable in smaller manifests and declining tonnage, and harbour lists of smaller numbers of vessels frequenting) but also less quantifiably of an empire, a mission. And so Camoes is perhaps as representative a figure as any for the place, the Portuguese, and their empire; that is, if the artist can be said to be emblematic of anything but his own piffling neuroses. Which he transmutes, of course, into the universally and perpetually current coin of particular creation.

Alice Barclay Remington to Charles Remington

Rua da Conceciao, 39
Macao
November the 18th 1834

My dear Charlie (to whom I write as proxy for all my sweetest and dearest family),

Oh, my dear brothers and sisters! You must not think your youngest sis a good-for-nothing who has not written to her family for almost a month, for every moment almost of our days has been taken up since our arrival in Macao Roads on the *Swallow* three weeks ago and there has not been a ship departing Boston-bound to whom I might with a free mind consign my mails since four days after we landed. Uncle was in a fret to land as soon as we had the harbour in sight but he had to wait with the rest of us, for you must know that the harbour (rather, both of them, for there are two, the Inner and the Outer) is quite silted up from the earth washed down by the river, so large ships (and apparently even the little *Swallow* is a large vessel by this reckoning) have to lie a mile or so to sea and wait for boats to take them off, both passengers and cargo. You would have laughed, dear brother, to see Uncle stamping up and down the deck while his hands wrestled with each other behind his back and all the time he struggled to keep his feelings from showing on his face! The river is quite, quite yellow here from all the silt – as yellow as the China Men's faces, Aunt said, though, of course, she had yet to see any of them, the river-pilot not yet having come on board to take the *Swallow* up the river to Canton – or rather Whampoa Anchorage. Canton, they say, is quiet now and that wicked man Governor Loo (who, it is said, as good as murdered poor Lord Napier) is allowing the foreigners to do their trading freely (except, of course, the traffic in drug). Uncle says even at the height of the dispute (which was really a little war) the Americans were allowed to come and go quite freely, while the British were hindered from doing so because of their own obduracy and *bellicosity* (Uncle's word). Well, we all pray and hope that there will be a peaceful resolution of all this strife without effusion of blood, even China Men's, for did not the one Maker create us all, of whatever colour our skins, and should not we know better than the poor heathen Chinese the value of our Redeemer's own blood? Tell, Mother, dearest Charlie, that she need not worry on Uncle's account. Canton is *quite* safe now and we Americans are not hated by the Chinese. Have I said that before? Oh, I am sure I am repeating myself (as Aunt Browning always used to exclaim in front of us children).

But our house is *beautiful,* Charlie! Such a sweet, snug, dear little house you never saw. Dearer even than our own little summer-house when we were small. Of course, our Macao house is not small but really quite grand. Let me tell you the colour first, which is pure white, unlike the houses of some of the Portuguese merchants which are brightly painted. (Port-you-gooses, I heard some crusty old English gentleman calling them only yesterday.) The *Dezembargador* (who is *very* grand and the chief judge – I had thought he was a mere *employé* in charge of the unloading of the ships!) has his house painted red and the windows white. Our shutters are dark green, which complements most handsomely the whitewash. We are housed on three floors, with a grand reception-room on the ground, occupying the entire floor of the building, which is not small. Here (Aunt and I have decided but Uncle doesn't know yet – poor man!) we can hold our parties and balls, there is room for more than two hundred people, which is the entire *Societé de* Macau. Let me now take you to the second floor where is found a private withdrawing-room for ourselves which I shall furnish just so and according to my taste (which, as you know, Aunt and Mother have always complimented me upon). I shall make it as elegant and snug withal as lies in my powers of discernment and Uncle's pocket. There is also a dining-room, a library, a billiard-room, and a study for Uncle. Our bedrooms are on the third and topmost floors, and there is room for more besides (if you ever decide to accept Uncle's offer of a place as a writer in Meridian & Co.). I almost forgot to say, which is the most charming of all, and shall be my bower and constant solace, there is a beautiful garden or rather gardens, for it is on four levels and laid out most prettily in ascending terraces, with steps, and curious rocks, and grottoes, and a little Chinese pavilion (or pagoda as they term it) in which I shall sit under a spreading tree and think fond thoughts of you all at home and maybe cry a little tear or two and under which, dear brother, I sit now and listen to the feathered songsters perched overhead as I write this foolish letter to you all from,

Your loving sister,
Alice

Rua da Conceicao, 39
Macao
December the 18th, 1834

My dear Charlie (and to you all again, my dears),

Although only four weeks separates this from my last (but Oh! how great a variety of experiences may be crammed into such a month that a whole year in Boston could hardly compare for observation of men and manners and experiences learned) you will not in all probability receive what I have under my hand until three months after my first has arrived, such is the timing of the mails. Never mind, you must all make allowances and I, for my part, will strive to write to you as freshly as when the incidents I describe were first imprinted upon my mind and senses. I have adopted the resolution to which I am determined to adhere, that from the first day of January, 1835, I shall keep a journal, and the pages from this I shall send to you all every three months or sooner, so that you shall know all that happens to me and in this little place of ours and as freshly as it occurs. Also, such a procedure will stop me repeating myself in my letters until I drive you all to distraction – or to slumber.

Uncle is come back from Canton, which is all the news I meant to impart to you. He has brought with him such a collection of bachelors, young and old, from Canton as ever spinster could desire (be she young maid or old and I, Charlie, am fast in danger of becoming a chaperone myself than Aunt's ward). The young gentlemen of Meridian & Co. are a fine set of young bucks, and shocking rakes they seem to think themselves. In fact, they are a most amusing and eligible set of young gentlemen, though it is true that the families of some are not wealthy. Still, their appointments in Canton, by all accounts, are most comfortable and they do not lack for every luxury. When Uncle told me of their cheroots and their port and their hookahs (or water-pipes, which is the Indian word), their claret and their servants (two

68

for every gentleman, Charlie!), and their easy chairs and their verandahs, and the crystal and the plate – I could scarcely forbear from wondering why they go to the bother of coming down the river to Macao at all! Of course, there are no ladies allowed in Canton (European or American, I mean), although two years ago Mrs Marjoribanks, wife of the then President of the East India Company, caused a scandal when she went up the river to reside a few days at the Factories. Perhaps it is the want of the fair sex and the softer and politer intercourse their society always encourages which drives these gay bachelors to Macao when they tire of the amusements of their own fellowship. But then, Charlie, one notorious old curmudgeon (whose residence is Macao, although he visits Canton from time to time for lengthy periods for reasons I shall disclose later) said to me:

'Madam, I am an old bear of a bachelor and our species threatens to share the fate of Bruin! What a sanctuary and preserve China is for us! I regard the Governor Loo as a game-keeper for old fellows such as myself, and you as a poacher. You must transport yourself hence!' And then, Charlie, he rolled his eyes in the drollest way imaginable and said: 'Trespasser, be gone!' I hardly knew whether to be offended or not but, really, his address was so eccentric (his nose a huge, red, broken-veined thing and his coat, Charlie, must have been as old as he was) that I laughed, for his face, though ugly, was kind and his eyes humorous behind his silly spectacles, which, by the by, were in constant danger of dropping off. I am told he is a painter of considerable accomplishments; indeed, the only artist of stature ever to come to this coast. He earned, they say, many *lakhs* of rupees in Calcutta in commissions but squandered this fortune and eventually had to flee his creditors and come to Macao, where he has resided since the beginning of the present century. Had I the wherewithal, I might prevail upon him to execute a small portrait of my good self and force it upon my loving relations.

Now, Charlie, you must be sure to write me of all your doings and treat your sis (who is far away) as you would your closest confidante. You may rely upon me to be discreet (for you know that I do not love gossip, or at least to recount it!) and, in particular, dear Charlie, do not omit to inform me of your rides to the interesting Miss Richardson.

Your loving sister,
Alice

'But my dear impetuous Gideon, you talk of the most formidable task, of years spent closely closeted with texts as rebarbative in style as they are barren in instruction. The fruit, I will make so bold as to observe, will not be worth the awful labour of the gathering. Know you that your teacher, if such can be found, risks his head to verse you in the mysteries of his language?'

Eastman sprawls his long limbs over the rattan couch. He is in shirt and white trousers. Gideon sits forward on a small, three-legged stool, his back hunched, one palm over clenched fist. He wears a dark coat. In a corner, Harry O'Rourke's pen flies over the rough for a drawing which will be completed, after being put aside and half-forgotten, in four years' time and will be entitled *On Meridian's Verandah, Macao*. In the background will figure in order from left to right: one of Horsburgh's charts of the Malacca Straits, a globe, a telescope, hookah, fez (yes, a fez), a dog called MacQuitty, a fowling-piece, a plate of sugared almonds, a raised stand-dish of Turkish delight, a pomelo, and three decanters which contain respectively port, sherry, and Madeira.

Gideon replies to Eastman in a low and earnest voice: 'I am serious as I have ever been. My scant months in this superb and secretive country teach me already that no enduring or equal relations may be entertained between ourselves and its inhabitants, should I say their rulers, until a perfected correspondence is established between us. Only when we have learned to communicate properly with them, in terms acceptable to them as to ourselves, will we become acceptable as equals. Do you think Sir George would not laugh at Minqua's or Howqua's ridiculous speech? The weightiest matters become things laughable in their mouths. And so it is with us to them.'

'But there have been notable scholars of Chinese, my dear fellow. The Reverend Dr Morrison, the able M. Rémusat, to name but two. Their accomplishments, and remarkable they were, did not prove sufficient to break down the jealous disdain of the mandarins.'

'Scholars they were assuredly, but in the first place they were divines. As missionaries their interest naturally lay in the souls of the Chinese, not their minds, nor, dare I say it, their hearts. They loved them not as men, as their fellow creatures, but as converts, which is to say they were but, but…as accessories to their pride. To those divines they were merely objects, objects of their own desire, which was to possess those men's immortal souls. For the civilisation of the Chinese –' Gideon sees Eastman's eyebrows rise and amends himself, '– the semi-civilisation, then, they evinced nothing but the deepest contempt, and men contemned are men lost to the contemner – and in this case lost also to the Creator of all men. What matters it if a man has acquired the tongue to perfection when he puts it to such a purpose? His dislike becomes but the more apparent and the dividing gulf but the wider, aye, and deeper. The scholar is lost to all but himself, estranged from those who should be his flock, and his glistering accomplishment (for you are right to point to the mighty difficulties, Walter) but the mirror to his own desires and vanity. His acquisition is quite worthless.'

'Bravo, sir, bravo,' Eastman cries, applauding with the cheroot still in his fingers, 'you have me almost believing. What think you of our friend's impassioned eloquence, Harry?'

O'Rourke does not look up from what he is roughing (at that moment, the line of Gideon's back; he's good at making backs articulate, this master) but after a while muses: *'To possess an effective command but at the same time to be impotent to move the emotions…'*

'Yes, Mr O'Rourke,' says Gideon eagerly, while Eastman tosses a pink and white cube of Turkish delight to MacQuitty, who sniffs suspiciously at it, growls, and, amazingly, eats it. Gideon waits in vain for reinforcement from O'Rourke's quarter but the only sound is the faint squeak of his nib. Eastman

71

has got on the Turkey rug and is wrinkling his nose at MacQuitty, who barks back. Gideon sighs. He pours himself a glass of Madeira (this is what bad company will do) and starts flicking through an old issue of the *Gentleman's Magazine*. It will soon be dinner anyway and he really must stop being so self-assertive. No gentleman should quite so obviously insist on being the centre of interest.

'Oh, he's a darling. Mmm. I could kiss his dear little nose. What a sweet pet you are.'

'He's an intelligent lad, Miss Remington. A little spoiled and wayward and he likes to have his own way, or he'll pass into a sulky decline, but a gallant companion in the marsh for a day's sport, I'll assure you.'

Gideon shifts uneasily in his chair. MacQuitty, though, is curled complacently in Alice's lap and, were he a cat, could be said to be basking. He does emit what sounds uncannily like a purr.

'What a cold, black, damp little nose it is!' and with this Alice actually does apply her mouth to MacQuitty's dented promontory, who darts out his long pink tongue wetly at her cheek. Gideon lets out an inarticulate little cry and quickly crosses his legs. He blushes, but no one seems to have heard him, and Walter, anyway, is much too preoccupied with sparkling in the present circumstances, which is to keep the company of Alice Remington on the second lawn of her uncle's mansion in the Rua da Conceicao at afternoon tea.

'Do take a second cup, Mr Eastman.'

'Why, thank you, I shall, Miss Remington.'

'It is a delight to be in the home of tea. At least as near as the jealousy of the Chinese permits. I have always adored the herb. Coffee to me appears crude and cloying by comparison. Perhaps I am unpatriotic. Am I unpatriotic, Mr Eastman?'

'Let us all be hanged for traitors.'

'A most refreshing cup,' Gideon lies. 'So much more cooling than coffee. This, I surmise, is the 1832 Congou. What is your opinion, Walter?'

Up go Eastman's eyebrows.

'Of course, I should not be babbling in front of you gentlemen whose daily business it is to traffic in teas and who know everything there is to know about it.'

'Far from it, Miss Remington,' says Eastman, 'far from it. Some of us are as green as the teas we ship on our constituents' accounts.'

Alice sees Gideon's cheeks redden and, being kind and the hostess, steers talk away to another topic, such as: 'That brilliant bird, Mr Eastman! Do look behind you – how heavy it seems. It can barely fly.'

Eastman rotates, but is too late.

'It barely cleared the garden wall. The plumage was extraordinary.'

'Then it was undoubtedly an escaped bird from Mr Veale's aviary. He has many such – rare and exotic birds from all the countries you could think of within the Tropics. Have you visited his gardens yet?'

Alice has not.

'Then we must form a party. The grounds and aviary are one of the sights of Macao. Veale, too, a *rara avis* in his own right; foremost among the many eccentrics of our little society.'

'I am sure you travesty the good Mr Veale and do an injustice to the community I have just had the honour of joining. Do I look so eccentric, Mr Chase?'

'You look, you look...ordinary, quite ordinary, I'll assure you, Miss Remington,' stammers smitten Gideon. 'Quite ordinary, really.'

'Why, Mr Chase, you are cruel and most ungallant,' Alice says to the poor young fellow, whose tea has been one long delightful torment.

'And you, Miss, are a little vixen and tease,' says Aunt Remington, whose elongated shadow in the five o'clock sun falls across our little party on the lawn.

Eastman is on his feet and Gideon follows. 'A seat, ma'am, pray take mine,' and Eastman slides it deftly beneath Aunt Remington. This is a quick-thinking cavalier, for it means Eastman can now seat himself, arms containing his knees, on the

73

red rug at Alice's feet. Gideon looks out of the side of his eye at irregular intervals to see whether Eastman's elbows are touching Alice's knees. They aren't, but you'd need sharp eyes to know it. Aunt Remington is evidently in need of treatment at Dr Colledge's gratuitous ophthalmic hospital for natives. Once, Alice catches Gideon's measuring eye and smiles, whereupon his face burns and he prays she has no conception of what passes through his mind. He fancies he is already in love with her, and yet he is also jealous of her – jealous of her effect on Walter. Walter is his hero. His model, his exemplar. But ... how she is ravishing, saintly, an extraordinary and superior creature; only a few years his senior but, oh, how immeasurably his older in terms of experience and easy sophistication. Yet she is pure, too, pure as the...Gideon looks for an unusual and forceful simile and fancies he finds one ... the *driven snow*. In fact, latest news, rather amazing in its way, is that snow *has* fallen on Canton, an occurrence rare enough to happen only once a century. Of course, here, by the temperate, mediating sea, which warms in winter and cools in summer, there is a slight refreshing nip in the air and the lawn is briefly white in the early morning but not a flake has there been, nor ever will. Only Alice's cheeks have kept their roses longer than was the case with other arriving belles and now she is grateful (over-grateful, perhaps, Gideon thinks) for the shawl which attendant Eastman drapes around her shoulders.

'Thank you, Mr Eastman. It is kind of you to consult my comfort.'

Eastman is now assiduous in engaging Aunt Remington in conversation; a chance to ingratiate, which Gideon has missed.

'And from Mexico, ma'am, the latest news? We are starved for reports in our little world. We feed too much upon ourselves, our petty cliques and rivalries.'

The Reform Act in England, the gallant Poles, crushed by the Russians four years ago, the French monarchy are brought forward and discussed. Eastman is notoriously well informed and has an opinion on everything, anywhere ('Regale us, Eastman,' they cry in the mess and then pelt him), but he is quiet and attentive now as he listens to Aunt Remington with a steady gaze which does not leave her face. Aunt Remington is not fooled. Though she and Remington are, speaking relatively, a young uncle and aunt, she has fifteen years' more experience of young men and their wiles than Alice, and that's enough. Nevertheless, this is not to say that her head can't be turned slightly by a long-legged, listening young man whose chin is on his knees and apparently undivided attention hers. So she plays the cosmopolitan to Eastman's news-starved provincial, while Gideon has the opportunity at last to engage Alice single-handedly in light conversation, and can think of simply *nothing* to say. (Can Eastman really have been so artful as to engineer all this?) until Alice enquires, 'Your parents, Mr Chase, they must miss their son sorely?'

Gideon hesitates. 'Both my parents are dead.'

This is rather curt but, even for Alice, Gideon does not feel like expanding on the subject.

'Oh, how terrible, Mr Chase, at your tender years.'

This is not how Gideon would like Alice to look at him. But the kind-hearted young thing's eyes have filled with tears and it is, after all, attention of a kind. 'So have you been alone many years, you poor boy?'

'I have an uncle, Miss Remington, my mother's elder brother. He is a partner in a mercantile house in Boston and he was kind enough to care for me as a child and also to find me a place with our great house here, your uncle's house, for which I presently have the honour of working.'

'And how old were you when your uncle sent you away?'

'I had attained my thirteenth summer, ma'am, when I first left for these shores,' says Gideon a little stiffly.

'Oh, Mr Chase,' sighs Alice and dissolves Gideon's protective reserve utterly.

'But,' he continues in a different and lower voice, Eastman and Aunt Remington discussing the state of affairs in post-Napoleonic France, 'when I had arrived here, there was found to be no suitable position for me, and I sailed home on the same ship, which was the *Aurora* of seven hundred tons.'

'Without setting foot on land,' Alice breathes, rather than enquires.

'I was able to walk a few hours by the bankshalls of Whampoa,' Gideon says. He continues now, without being prompted, 'Subsequently, another place was found for me and having acquired some small experience with my uncle's house I was able to secure my position with Meridian. This was some eighteen months after my first arrival on these shores. Since when, I trust, I have conducted that portion of the house's affairs entrusted to me to its advantage and my credit.' He smiles. This is to give his last words the sort of tone he has learned from Eastman, the tinge of irony rather than conceit.

'The wicked man,' Alice thinks, not, of course, with reference to Gideon but his uncle.

'Oh, Gideon is seventeen men,' Eastman interrupts (Louis Philippe has been relegated), 'a Solomon for each of his years.'

'D-n you, Eastman,' thinks Gideon savagely, but with sufficient mental restraint actually to envisage that strong word in truncated form.

Aunt Remington barely shivers, but Eastman picks up the polite and almost imperceptible command (which Gideon would certainly have missed) and cries: 'But we shall all have pneumonias if the *mala arias* of the summer do not take us off first. Let us go in, and then I greatly fear we have overstayed our time.' He shepherds Aunt Remington down the mossy steps of the terraced lawns.

Alice, of course, does not require such assistance from Gideon.

CHAPTER IX

'Would you have signed?'

'Sir, I would not.'

'But, my dear Walter, the petitioners seek to do all you have been desiring. How many times have I heard you declaiming the virtues of Free Trade and unrestricted opportunity? How many times have we not descanted against, nay, felt the arrogance and prejudice of the Canton mob and not wished for redress for insult and injury?'

'Sir, I am no friend to the Chinese, but well know that the British merchants do not seek to open a wider trade or facilitate a legitimate traffic but merely to prise open a broader channel down which they may pour their poison. They are devious, sir, and deceitful. Their overweening craftiness fully matches that of the Chinese.'

'And you, Gideon?'

'I should rather have been drowned in the river with the unwanted daughters than been signatory to an address so disgraceful.'

'Well, you have both the excuse at least of being Americans. As for me, it concerns me not. I am no trader but a dirty-handed dauber.'

'Your hand, Harry, is not so soiled when caked with all your paints as those of the drug-hawking petitioners.'

O'Rourke, at his most benevolent after a dainty breakfast of paw-paw, kedgeree, cold fowl, ham, curry, eggs, rice, biscuit, guava preserve, plantains, and figs, washed down with a bottle of claret and four cups of coffee, rustles the foolscap pages of the *Canton Monitor* which Ah Cheong has resourcefully ironed crisp against the humidity. He adjusts his pince-nez. *'A petition addressed to His Majesty in Council from the merchants resident in Canton dated December 9th, 1834,'* he reads in his rich brogue. 'Well, now, is that not formal enough for you?'

Eastman snorts savagely. He snaps a biscuit in half, as if it might be the neck of Matheson, head of the British Chamber of Commerce. Gideon merely looks sombre.

'Let's see now,' O'Rourke goes on remorselessly. 'They want a Plenipotentiary, then, do they…sufficient force to exact reparation…most unsafe of all courses to adopt when treating with the Chinese government, or any of its functionaries, is that of quiet submission to insult …blah, blah …may compromise the honour or bring into question the power of our country …etcetera, etcetera …' O'Rourke seems to have become a little dry; taxing work, reading out aloud; more claret is the obvious remedy. He gulps the glass Ah Cheong has filled (not a mind-reader, just a cynical old retainer). 'Pompous, pompous, but no more than to be expected of that old Scotch windbag. A damned restless, loquacious sitter. One would not mind so much but that one word in ten is intelligible to the Sassenach. Still, his guineas are good as anyone else's.' The pince-nez are slipping and O'Rourke scowls ferociously to keep them on. 'They start talking sense now: you and I know, Walter, 'twas the river which defeated poor Napier. Here they ask for steam-boats which may negotiate the shallows with their small draught. *Fit them with a pair of 10-inch howitzers which may fire grape, canister, or shell…as it would be a novel arm of warfare so…it would create astonishment and terror…a steam-boat and a frigate to stand off the mouth of the Peiho River and threaten Peking…demand with the mouths of their cannon reparation!* (I like that, "mouths of their cannon".) Well, how think you of these warlike councils?'

'The councils are good, the means effective; the end it is which is so deplorable. But if this vast empire is to be prised open, it shall have been by the instrumentality of a most monstrous vice – perhaps it is inevitably so. Perhaps it may only thus be opened to a legitimate trade. Perhaps the awakening of the minds of the many and the generations as yet unborn can only be accomplished at the price of the stupefaction of the intellects and wasting of the bodies of a few millions of depraved addicts.'

Gideon bursts out hotly: 'How can you talk like that, Walter? I know you do not feel or calculate in such a cold and wicked way. You are a good man. You sounded then like some perverse and estranged philosopher.'

'A Teuton,' O'Rourke says drily. 'And you, young man, you are a good deal too enthusiastic. Drown your enthusiasm, sir. We shall have more claret brought. Cheong, claret.'

Rua da Conceicao, 39
Macao
February the 25th, 1835

My dear Melissa,

- and thus do I begin my 'secret correspondence' with my dearest sis. I do not wish to conceal matters from Charlie but there will always be news to impart which I could only do freely to you; besides I would bore poor Charlie. Well, we have had here the most wonderful season. It has been one long jollification from beginning to end. Such a succession of balls and dinners you would never imagine, more of them in two months than you would have in an entire year – two years! – in Salem or Boston. First of all, on Christmas Eve, we were all invited to the British Superintendent's for a dinner. Lord Napier had occupied a house belonging to Mr Jardine on the Ridge of Macau, but Mr Davis, who succeeded on Lord Napier's death, was on famously bad terms with all the Free Traders and particularly Mr Jardine and the two Mr Mathesons, owing to his connection with the Honourable Company, for whom he had worked since before the battle of Waterloo! He entertained us at the old English Factory, and, as you may well imagine, it was something like the destruction of the Imperial Guards at this dinner. Oh, the long faces and the gloomy looks! I felt quite overcast. The Parsee gentlemen, of whom there are a great number at Canton, many living outside the Factories in the native city, which they are not supposed to, had also been invited and came at the end of the meal to pay their respects, which they did most humbly. These worshippers of the sun are British subjects, mostly from Bombay, though the British do not really accept them as so, with names like Cowasjee, Mukherjee, Framjee, Everythingjee. Their acknowledged head is a Mr Jamsetjee Jeejeebhoy, who they say is as rich as Croesus and a close crony of Mr Jardine's. They think it likely that he will end as Sir Jamsetjee, rather than plain Mr Jeejeebhoy, which was already fancy enough for anyone.

The day after was a good deal livelier, and from this time on our little season may be said to have commenced. We went, Uncle, Aunt, and myself, to a midday concert given by the band of the Portuguese garrison in the open air in the grounds of the Monte Fort. In the evening we attended an opera at the Playhouse, which I had not seen before, *The Barber of Seville,* which I much enjoyed, given by a touring company of Italians, who received an *encore* and much applause. Following this, a light supper at the Macao premises of Russell & Co., our largest American firm (who, I regret to say, traffic in drug). The floor was later cleared of the trestle tables and we were able to dance. Dance we certainly did, for I did not miss a single turn. Ladies, did you not know, are scarce in supply in Macao, especially young, single ladies, and it may justly be termed a Paradise for spinsters. Even Aunt had to dance several dances with the gentlemen and Uncle was very merry at her expense over her swains, young and old (and, my dear, some of the gentlemen were *very* old and very breathless, and one quite feared for them). Your sister, too, was panting from her exertions − for ladies can pant as well as horses − the music and dancing going on until well after midnight, when we finally returned home at the desperate hour of four *ante meridiem.*

New Year's Eve, too, we celebrated in fine style, this time at Dent & Co.'s Macao premises. Fifty of us sat down to dinner in the open, a little cramped, I fear, but all was gaiety and joviality. When they brought out the huge plum pudding, they were unable to get the brandy in the ladle to burn, try as they would, and when it did take finally, a small air blew it out again. Mr O'Rourke, the celebrated artist, was in charge of these incendiary operations, and everyone was laughing at the poor man's fumblings. When the draught extinguished the ladle for the second time, he said, 'Hang it!' (only, Melissa, dear, it was a *much* ruder word) and he said there was insufficient vapour and promptly drank half the brimming ladle to the guffaws of the young gentlemen who were shouting at him all this while. This time it took cheerfully and the flames, blue and yellow (only Mr

O'Rourke told me afterwards they were purple and turquoise and I had seen them wrongly), were so beautiful as they seemed to wash the air almost. Am I so silly? Then Mr O'Rourke held the ladle under his chin and pulled the most frightful face. It was quite ghastly as the shadows and the fire flickered over his big red phizz (which is extraordinary enough in the ordinary light and circumstances of the day) and, I have to confess, I gave a little scream. Following which, of course, each of the young gentlemen present *had* to have the ladle to hold under his own nose to make the lady of *his* choice scream – by which time the brandy in the ladle was exhausted, whereupon Mr O'Rourke had to begin his work of an incendiarist all over again. Then there was the new year of the Chinese – quite perverse in all things, they wear white for a funeral where we clothe ourselves in black, read their books from back page to first (so a young gentleman from Boston told me, who plans to study the language), they also have to begin their year a month or so after ours, only the date of that changes every year! How strange and various are the ways of mankind, which our one Maker has ordained! There were gongs gonging and firecrackers cracking in the streets until I thought I would go deaf. This was some days ago.

Uncle is back up to Canton on Monday and there is a great deal more activity resumed on the river now than before Christmas. I must take my leave of you now. Be sure to write often as you may to,

Your loving sister,
Alice

PS In rendering my account of all my doings, I almost omit to mention the great event which took place here on 26th *ultimo,* which was the great fire at the Cathedral of the Catholics, St Paul's. It raged so fiercely it was quite impossible to get near it, leave alone extinguish it. Soldiers, even animals (Can the Papists be so *blasé?)* were regularly quartered in it, and it is believed some straw started the blaze which eventually quite gutted the building, leaving only the front standing at the top of the wide flight of steps from the Chinese town. It was built for the Portuguese by Japanese converts, who were skilled masons, in the century before the last, and was (I have to confess) in its way a noble edifice. Now only the façade remains. Mr Arden, the chaplain to the Superintendent's mission and formerly on the Hon. Co.'s establishment, says it is fittingly so, for it is a religion which depends on hollow forms and empty ceremonies without the substance of true worship, which is the true and unimpeded relationship of our spirit to God. I have to agree it is so, but shame it is that the *building* should have been destroyed.

CHAPTER X

Things have indeed picked up, as Alice says. In Canton the young gentlemen of Meridian have actually to work sixty minutes of every hour in order to wipe out the backlog of the past few months. Ships have been laid up, idle and unfilled, at Whampoa, though at Lin Tin island in the Outer Waters of the gulf the clandestine trade of the hulks has been continuing, mainly because the demi-piratical 'scrambling crabs' and 'fast dragons' were always able to maintain a sporadic service of opium collections. Because of this, the British have not materially suffered. The Americans were not included in the Viceroy's proscriptions, yet ironically it is those in the legitimate (that is, non-drug) trade who have seen their business worst interrupted. Chests of teas lie in the godowns; furs, pepper, rattans, betel, still fester in the ships' holds. Gideon's quill scratches and sputters, along with everyone else's except, naturally, Eastman's. Without a word, Gideon will take a sheaf of papers from Walter's desktop and add it to his own diminishing pile. The boy's efficiency has not gone unremarked by Jasper

Corrigan; Chase is clearly too good for this mechanical clerking (though he'll have to undergo a few more years for the good of his young soul). 'Too callow yet, I calculate – we'll knock the darned tomfoolery out of him,' Corrigan thinks, as he tours the office with hands behind his martinet's back. The clerks' backs are almost parallel to their desktops during the partner's brief visit. As Corrigan goes down the stone stairs an inaudible collective sigh rises, perceptible almost as a lowering of pressure in the air. But it would not be over-imaginative to believe Gideon a little less whole-hearted than usual. And once, when no one was looking, did he not look up and sigh, quite heavily?

In the billiard-room, where his shooting has always been mediocre, his game becomes perfectly atrocious. In fact, he and Eastman are soon banned from play and relegated to sliding the score-pegs on the wall, Eastman for burning a hole in the green cushion with a particularly negligently placed cheroot, Gideon for miscuing and ripping a four-inch-long slit in the baize sufficient to expose the slate. At night, he is restless in his iron cot, though the nights are cool and a blanket comforts. In the mornings he doesn't spring from bed with his accustomed alacrity after the servant has placed the jug of hot water by the wash-basin. (The lad has been shaving, with pride, since his fourteenth birthday.)

Eastman thinks his young friend might be declining. Ague, bubonic plague, cholera, consumption, dysentery, fever, pneumonia, and typhoid, in alphabetical precedence though not necessarily in order of deadliness, have a habit of carrying off colleagues in Canton. They can be personages of distinction, like Lord Napier, or humbler men who go to obscure graves on an island in the river, lamented only by a handful of acquaintances, who will soon forget them. When Gideon fails to make his usual hearty tiffin and dinner (breakfast being another matter entirely where anyone's appetite, except the mighty O'Rourke's, can occasionally become jaded), Eastman grows concerned. He sees himself, failing anyone else, as somehow *in loco parentis*. 'Gideon,' he accuses him, 'you are moping and out of sorts.' Gideon denies this indignantly. 'In fact, you have not been yourself since we left Macao. I have not heard your laugh since Harry O'Rourke scorched his nose on the brandy ladle.' Gideon looks evasive. 'The weather, Walter, it is an oppressive clime,' he mutters. Eastman seems to have abandoned his languid pose as he continues mercilessly to interrogate Gideon. 'Oppressive? Nonsense. The air is delicious. There is a frost on the roofs in the morning. If you find it oppressive, then you are indeed sickening.'

Jonathan Ridley must add his ten cents' worth. 'Tonic. Dr Colledge will prescribe admirably for you.'

Gideon, if he was not Gideon, could be said to glower.

'When did you last have a motion?' Eastman enquires. 'Was there anything unusual about the stool?'

This is too much even for Gideon. 'For God's sake, Eastman,' he roars and strides off for a walk around the square.

'Water on the brain,' says Ridley loudly. 'It can be relied on.'

'What young Gid needs is his liver shaken up,' says Johnstone, talking down the line of his cue. 'I calculate there is a lump in the baize which has misdirected my ball.'

'A lump in your eye, you mean,' Ridley says, potting red. 'The boy thinks too much, which is unhealthy at any age, particularly his. White in off the red, which was a masterly stroke, if I say so myself. Vigorous activity is the remedy best applied to Master Chase. Damn it, there is a lump. Three, if you will, Walter.'

Eastman, who is sitting on the refreshments sideboard with his long legs up and chin on his knees, puts a cue behind his head to slide the score-peg. 'If there's anything wrong with Chase's liver, I'm damned,' he says. 'You pair of bucks go to row with him at dawn. He could become stroke oar and chief desperado on a scrambling crab if it was his will tomorrow.'

'Then,' says Ridley, leading the general laughter, 'he needs apply for a position with Messrs Jardine and Matheson. But you, Walter, are his mentor and you will agree he needs distraction. You will recall how young Hayes moped before blowing his brains out. A darnation poor affair that was. I am not saying that Chase is not made of sterner material.'

'You have brushed the ball with your sleeve, Ridley, are penalised a point, and surrender play to Johnstone.' Eastman is already jumping off the sideboard as Ridley's cue, launched like a javelin, thuds into the wall, knocking away mouldering plaster and sending five geckos scurrying for cover.

A chance to eliminate several contemporary birds with one stone comes a few days later. One of the Meridian-consigned ships, kept late by the trouble with the Chinese, has to leave only half-full, or fight the full force of the new monsoon on her way home. She needs her chop from the mandarins and other final details of lading, according to Ridley, must be supervised before she can drop down the river. He and his cronies, then, plan an excursion which shall combine business with a day of sport: take a pair of guns each; an easy row with the stream down to Whampoa; sort the formalities out; a day in the salt marshes; dinner on the *Saxon* and… a hard row back against the flow. But this last is put to the back of the collective mind. They have all been working much too hard, are bored, rather frustrated, and, of course, it will be good for Gideon. Good for Gideon begins to have the comfortable ring of a motto. Unfortunately, Jasper Corrigan has to be informed. This is not an impulsive, if illegal, perambulation of the city walls for which no other notice than the rising of one's own spirits and pulse has to be proffered, but a consequential matter. It is the loss of company time, rather than the breach of the laws of the empire, which is germane. Still, Corrigan hesitates. His young gentlemen have worked loyally. After all, this is a cyclically trying time. For five, seven, maybe ten years one flouts regulations with impunity. Then comes a period of reaction, triggered by the arrival of a new viceroy, sporadic imperial wrath, a hint from the mandarins that the price for turning a blind eye is now subject to review and increase. The last few months do not fit this predictable pattern; they seemed different. Nevertheless, there exists a lull. Both sides seem anxious to pick up the threads; life, quotidian life, as the individual knows it, goes on and young men are always a volatile quantity. If they are not to an extent (always to an extent, Corrigan thinks judiciously) indulged, then the ensuing mischief will be even worse. So, after humming and hawing as only he knows how, Jasper gives his permission.

'Do not, though, gentlemen, while afloat on the river under

any circumstances relax your vigilance. And should insult be offered in any hamlet you might stumble across, you are to withdraw instantly without resenting it. Of course,' he continues, 'should your lives and property appear to be endangered, you may resist. Such is your right under natural law, we talk not of the extraordinary laws of the empire.'

'Oh, with eight barrels between us, we shall be safe enough,' Ridley says cheerfully, not at all reassuring Corrigan.

So, a starry pre-dawn finds Ridley and MacQuitty (for he is Ridley's dog), Johnstone, Eastman, and Chase at Jackass Point in their boat-cloaks, with a leather gun case apiece which Ridley sees safely stowed, and then it's a matter of grappling with the boat-hook past the lines of junks and sampans and into the middle of the stream.

The break of day finds them by Whampoa island and buoyant in the river's noble, pagoda-girt anchorage. Asleep under his voluminous cloak, Gideon has failed to notice the misty, distant banks sliding past, while Eastman touches the tiller now and again and the other two dip an oar. Softly, softly, they glide. Bump goes the boat. And bang again, as it knocks the merchantman's side. Gideon jerks to; under the cloak, he is now uncomfortably hot. Gun cases go up; hoisted are a box of pickles and a case of books, presents for the master and mate. Then Gideon gets a hand up. The boat tilts, air and sea are alarmingly below, and then, the hard hand relinquishes his own and he is on a deck holystoned white as any man-of-war's. The bosun looks very suspiciously indeed at MacQuitty but the gun-cases are already neatly stacked and, in fact, as the remaining three come over the side with as great a panache as if they'd been doing it all their lives, their little group is the only assemblage on the deck that is ungeometric.

It's a far bigger ship than Gideon's *Aurora* on which he originally arrived on these shores, and considerably better run. In fact, as the cunning Ridley knew all along, the only work they have to do is hand the ornate chop over to Captain Gale. (Yes, this Connecticut master's life was made miserable until he came to command.) A hearty breakfast is served in the saloon, not quite as damaging as the way in which the Factories start the day. Gideon pushes some victuals, as the pancakes and bacon seem to be known afloat, around his plate and then concedes the unequal struggle in a cup of black coffee.

The first and third mates want to come as well.

Ridley can see why a tramp with the guns might be an attractive prospect before the awful tedium of nine months at sea. 'I trust you nautical fellows,' he says, 'can point a fowling-piece as well as your long Tom, but do you make the distinction between a duck and an albatross?' There is more in this vein, such as Eastman's: 'For God's sake, sir, have a care of us in your aim, but you could put Chase out of his present misery.' (Eastman is beginning to think he has an inkling, and is merciless: in love and war etc.)

It now shapes up to be a splendid day: good company and, hopefully, good sport.

They push off with the boat-hook and the mates rig a little jury-sail which sends them skipping along the grey surface, over the jolly wavelets. The river is very wide here, pale hills in the distance, tiny pagodas, mulberry trees along the banks, paddy, canals, vegetable-beds. They will not proceed along the main branch, but choose to go down a tributary which soon sprouts arms of its own; they pick the largest of these. A gust skims them down. The water is mirror-smooth. They steer down a tempting mouth. Treetops meet from opposite banks. Under the canopy there is a silence, a dead enclosure, sensed as deafness rather than the absence of sound. Chase swallows. They turn again into a still smaller waterway. The sails clap; wind rustles through the sedge.

The mates head straight at the bank. What's happening? Ripples now – of alarm – among the sportsmen. Gideon braces himself for an impact, has visions of bodies knocked flying into the stern-sheets, guns discharged, men overboard. And – nothing. A hiss and scratching as they knock the reeds aside. Then suddenly they burst through into a lake which stretches its mournful immensity for further than the eye can see. Somewhere wildfowl call lugubriously. The mates, who seem to have a wonderful ability for sorting dry land, the real thing, out from the less than firm, steer for a grove of bamboo. Out they jump, and fail to sink to their knees in mud. MacQuitty follows, barking. He cocks a leg, thinks better of it, and turns to watch his owner disembarking. (He's a bulldog, by the way, no particular connotations of anglophilism intended by Ridley.) On shore Gideon and Eastman receive the guns from Johnstone in the boat – they were, of course, empty all the time, although Ridley had a charged pistol in his belt.

'Very well, gentlemen,' he says, 'I invite you to load.' From his horn flask he taps black powder down the barrel. Oakum, lead shot, more oakum follow. Johnstone's rammer rattles as he follows suit and Eastman is only a little less handy. Gideon observes these manoeuvres. He succeeds in locating his ramrod under the barrel (he has a single-barrelled weapon of Ridley's, the others' are double-barrelled, Eastman's weapon an under-and-over).

'Ah, Gideon, place the butt on the ground while loading,' Ridley says. He exchanges glances with Johnstone, who is just seeing to his priming. 'Allow me, Gideon,' Ridley says with unusual kindness – he's a keen shot and like all real experts is indulgent with beginners. 'You will be able to prevail on that to go off,' he says. 'Do not cock the hammers and keep it pointed at the ground.' He shows Gideon how to carry the gun in his crooked arm.

The sailors return from their reconnoitring expedition. There are no signs of habitation in this dreary spot. Should they leave the boat unattended? To have it stolen or damaged would be an intolerable nuisance and perhaps dangerous. On the other hand, guarding it entails someone missing the best of the day's sport. They decide to hide it, upturned, in the bamboos with leaves piled over the keel. MacQuitty feels impelled to establish some claim on their means of return. He stakes it in the only way he knows how. He cocks his leg and sprays away for dear life. 'No manners, like his master,' Eastman says, 'a spaniel for a retriever, certainly, but MacQuitty? Whoever heard of a bulldog as hunter's companion?'

'I'll not hear a word against him,' Ridley says. 'We'll divide into three parties. Eastman, do you and Chase go together, our friends of the *Saxon* will prefer each other's company, and Johnstone, MacQuitty, and I are used to each other's ways on these excursions. We'll meet here in two hours, take refreshment, and set off in opposite directions again.'

He and Johnstone stroll off along the lake shore, followed by the mariners, while Eastman takes Gideon inland. 'You will not, Gid, my dear fellow,' he says, 'be offended if I request you to walk beside me rather than behind me.'

'By all means. Why should I take offence? Oh, I see.' Gideon touches the hammer of his fowling-piece nervously with his free hand. After a while, however, he begins to feel more comfortable; this is a dashing as well as the safest way to carry a gun. He feels he cuts a figure and wishes Alice were there to see.

Up till now they have been walking across a ridge on hard ground, but they start to descend and arrive on wild grass. They cross a small stream.

'Observe that it must flow into the lake, Gideon. Therefore, we should bear to our right. Were there trees, one could cut notches in them (had we the forethought to provide ourselves with knives, that is).'

Gideon starts to worry. He has a copy of the *Canton Monitor* in his coat. Surreptitiously, he tears a corner off, rolls it into a ball in his pocket, and then drops the screw of paper on the ground. He repeats this manoeuvre every fifty yards, hoping that no wind will spring up. They now traverse broken ground, with mud, large stones, and water-channels so regular they must be the work of man. Still no wildfowl. 'What an extraordinary country this is, Walter, to support such a vast population and yet to have large areas such as this, quite desert. We could be the only rational beings for miles around. And yet we foreigners have touched only on the fringes of this vast empire.'

Eastman grunts. He, Eastman, master, as he sees it, of the penetrating and epigrammatic, hopes young Chase is not going to get prolix on what threatens to become a hobby-horse.

'What energies, what talent, must there be in that teeming mass of humanity which is now so wastefully, so wilfully misdirected!'

'What markets!' Eastman retorts. 'What fortunes to be made! So much bibulous paper, I tell you, to absorb the surplus production of Europe.'

'Ah, Walter, I am sure if you knew the Chinese, you would not hate them so. Yet you cannot really hate them, else you would not be so warm on the subject of...'

'...the accursed drug. It is not that I love the Chinese, but that I despise the peddlers of the poison, the smug, arrant humbugs of the Dents, the Jardines, the Inneses.'

'Well, I don't hate them. I do not hate anybody. And if I did hate them, I would conclude to study to understand them and when I did comprehend them, then I could hate them no more.'

'Surely to understand an enemy clearly is but to have better reason for hating him?'

'No, for then you could place yourself in his position and imagine what it was like to be him. And if you could become him, then you could no longer hate him.'

'Aha, my young friend, but what if he hated himself? What if he was full of loathing and contempt for his own wretched hide and despicable actions? What then?'

'Well, I do not think Mr Jardine hates himself.'

Eastman has the grace to laugh, but counter-attacks with, 'Am I to presume, are we all to understand, that you condone the actions of the rascals who stoned us on the walls, or the cut-throats who kidnapped Catchpoole of the Company, that, indeed, you have assumed their character? Then we would be excused wearing swords when you came to dine.'

Gideon's turn to smile. 'But imagine me as the Viceroy or the Provincial Judge. That is what I really meant, an initiate in the mysteries of their writing and their books, the acknowledged monarch of those pedantic *literati*.'

Eastman is quiet for a while. 'Then,' he says slowly, 'you talk of something quite other. You talk, I believe, of losing your immortal soul. No, no.' He waves Gideon silent. 'I do not mean it in the sense the missionaries would use it, not in any theological sense, but I mean that you would lose all that had gone towards the fashioning of you, the influence of your dear friends, your education, the good in you, and, yes, what bad there may be in you, all those acquisitions, moral or material, which have made you what you are. You would stand naked, shivering, lost, and, my boy, quite alone and removed. Enisled in, in, the sea of life! Ha! I sound like some damned poet. But it is true, you talk of as deep an isolation as man can know – and among his fellows all the while, there's the tragedy. Madness lies there, Gideon.'

'Think you so when I would have the whole tribe of man for my family?'

'Aye, every man a brother and none a friend. No, your ideas are too fantastical, too thorough-going and perfected for your own good.'

'I had thought I heard Harry O'Rourke say the same to you,' Gideon observes drily.

'Shoosh, man, look!' Eastman's pointing finger indicates the skew-whiff V of birds straining in the sky. Gideon brings his gun to his shoulder. 'For God's sake, Gid. Grape from a thirty-two-pounder would not harm them at this range!'

Gideon brings the weapon down.

'You would be better off at the present time to imagine yourself as one of the great shots of the day, or even a competent one, rather than as Confucius.' But Eastman's tone is affectionate. They trudge on. The land becomes marsh. Water glints. Suddenly, four birds rise to their left. Eastman wheels and fires, one barrel after the other. Startled, Gideon also turns, describing a ridiculously dangerous arc, most of which seems to be filled with Eastman. Fortunately, he doesn't succeed in pulling the trigger and, fortunately, too, Eastman doesn't seem to have noticed. Unscathed, the duck fly on.

'Damn,' says Eastman, sounding just like he does when he has failed to pot a billiard-ball. He is about as good a shot as he is a billiards player, thinks Gideon. He waits for Walter to reload. From an indeterminate direction come two heavy reports, a pause, and two more in quick succession.

'Hmm,' says Eastman.

They walk on, rather more alertly than before, and come, at length, to the origin of the ducks – which is not the huge lake they originally sailed into but a sheet of water of finite proportions which are more immediately apparent. Quite a decent pond, though, reminding Gideon of one near his uncle's in New England.

Four shots, so close together they sound like one, echo from, perhaps, the other side of a distant clump of trees.

In some reeds Gideon spots a flash of green and brown and discharges his one barrel – *boom!* – straight into the vegetation. A spray of water erupts. 'Chase!' Eastman cries in outrage. Gideon has fired with the butt an inch from his shoulder, enough to get a painful kick right on the collar bone. He's deafened, there was a flash from the hammer, and the powder stinks. Two startled ducks whizz out of the reeds.

'God damn it,' says Eastman, with a heavy emphasis on each of the words.

Gideon's head rings, his shoulder hurts like the devil, and, yes, he confirms with evidence on his fingers the suspicion that his nose is bleeding. But he feels a curious elation.

'Well, you know, I almost bagged them,' he says in a far-away sounding voice.

'Bagged them?' Eastman says incredulously. *'Bagged them?* Since when have sportsmen opened fire on sitting duck? This is sport, Gideon, not avian massacre.'

Obviously not as taken aback as Eastman feels he ought to be, Gideon says, 'Well, at all events I missed them,' looking, however, into the reeds to see if there's a floating carcass or two. Ripples still disturb the surface. Eastman turns away, saying something that sounds very like 'Bah'.

Gideon reloads his piece, rather more dextrously than at his first attempt, he feels. They proceed. All this time shots have been echoing around them; the others seem to be blazing away. Whether this has scared away all the birds in their vicinity they cannot say; certainly from now on there is a notable absence of wildlife. After half an hour's dispiriting tramp, Eastman consults his watch and announces they should be returning. He bears towards the direction of the last shot they heard some ten minutes ago.

'But, Walter, where can you be going?'

'To rejoin our companions, naturally.'

'Then the best means of achieving that goal would be to retrace our steps to the rendez-vous we have mutually agreed upon.'

'I am indebted to you for your unsolicited advice,' Eastman says testily.

Gideon recognises this as part of a formulaic, rude Eastman business letter. 'And wipe that grin off your face,' Eastman adds. They march off, Walter with a confidence soon to be undermined. Now, of course, there are no shots to be heard at any price anywhere. Most disobliging of the others really. After a while Eastman halts by a group of boulders. 'Do you know,' he says in a puzzled voice, 'I am sure I have...'

'Quite,' Chase says grimly. 'I recollect them distinctly as well.'

'It is easy enough to be critical. What constructive plan do you have?'

'As a matter of pure fact, I have been laying a paper trail,' the callow youth says primly.

'You have been what, sir?' the other roars. 'That is, that is ...' The word which springs to Walter's mind is 'cheating', which is ridiculous.

'I guess we shall, to a certain extent, have to retrace our steps, Walter.'

To a certain extent, Walter would like to wring Gideon's neck or, better still, pepper his insufferable backside with No.3 birdshot. However, necessity compelling, he follows. After a little backtracking, hesitation, and circuitousness, Gideon finds the last (or first, depending on which way you look at it) of the paper scraps. 'All we have to do is to follow the long chain of its fellows back to our starting point,' he says reasonably enough.

'Kindly refrain from stating the obvious, Gideon,' Eastman replies coldly.

'Were we Chinese, of course,' Gideon says cheerfully, 'we should be picking up these fragments and reverentially bearing them in a vase to the river to make a ceremonial disposal of them. Such is their reverence for the written or printed word.'

'Printed? Did you say printed?'

'Of course, did the Chinese not invent printing before the German, Gutenberg?'

'That is not what I meant.' Eastman examines a scrap. He peers at it, trying to identify the source from the few legible words of text. The inferior paper has soaked up dew from the grass. A suspicion forms. 'Can this be…'

'The *Canton Monitor*,' says Gideon.

Eastman flings the scrap of paper away. 'Am I indebted for finding my way home to this, this…rag, reeking of the evil poison its sponsors purvey, its scandalous opinions broadcast in the execrable prose of the illiterate Irishman who calls himself its editor?'

'Yes, Walter.'

A brisk walk of twenty minutes sees them back to their starting-point. The others cheer ironically. MacQuitty barks a welcome. He brings a soft, drooping mass of feathers and bill to them in his mouth and drops it at their feet. This is merely one of a brace; all told, the others have accounted for eight brace.

'A darnation fine morning's sport,' one of the mates tells Eastman.

They have arranged their bag over the leaves on the upturned boat's keel, the beautiful plumage set off to advantage against the brilliant green when glimpsed through the latticed frame of the bamboos. A pair of guns lie crossed against the boat, completing the tastefully contrived tableau. Eastman's fingers itch for what they manage best, neither gun nor cue but…. a pen or brush. Still life is actually what he realises most successfully and, in this kind of accomplishment, does not suffer by comparison with O'Rourke, who regards it as a form of necrophilia, the objectionable object, nadir of artistic endeavour. (And has told Walter Eastman so.)

'You are doleful failures at either form of the "pot",' says the odious Ridley.

'At least they have not administered each other the *coup de grâce*,' chips in Johnstone. Our two heroes smile manfully.

'Rum, young fellow,' the first mate says.

Gideon wonders what's so strange about failing to hit those charmed ducks, then sees the sailor is proffering his hip-flask. He shakes his head.

'I calculate it can only improve your aim, young fellow.' Gideon laughs and has a nip. Pretty soon the sailors have their pipes going, Eastman soothes his feelings, ruffled more than the dead ducks' feathers, with a good cheroot, while MacQuitty stretches himself over Ridley's boots. After a quarter of an hour's recuperation, Ridley jumps to his feet and with intimidating zest cries: 'A further few hours' sport, gentlemen, before we return to the *Saxon*.' The appalling prospect quite numbs Gideon, extinguishing the warm glow which the good-natured sailor's tot had instilled in him, while the tip of Eastman's cheroot brightens to an angry scarlet.

However, the others are apparently all genuine eagerness to go, though is Ridley's grin somewhat more maliciously amused than usual?

'Come, sir,' the detestable fellow says to recumbent Eastman, kicking the sole of the latter's boot. 'You may find more fowl in the quarter we beat. We will take yours. Give them a sporting chance, hey, Johnstone?'

'Certainly, certainly,' says the latter, straight-faced.

'Will you not take MacQuitty with you?' suggests Ridley helpfully. 'He'll flush the birds for you.'

'Mind you don't shoot him,' Johnstone adds.

'A kind thought,' Eastman replies with commendable suaveness, 'but we'll not torment the poor brute with pining after his master.'

'Oh, he's a damned carefree, disloyal sort of a dog,' Ridley says airily. 'Shoot him, if you have the will,' and he sets off with Johnstone and the sailors through the bamboos. MacQuitty trots after them in his barrel-chested way (not unlike the first mate's nautical gait), but Ridley says curtly, 'Sit,' and MacQuitty obeys, only his twitching ears and drooping tail (the most emotional parts of him), registering his disappointment and chagrin. Chagrined, too, are Chase and Eastman; however, a challenge is a challenge: of MacQuitty's mettle as a dog and theirs as sportsmen. The trio wander disconsolately along the lake shore for a mile. It is not so wild as their previous walk. Gideon notices some fishing-stakes protruding out of the mud and nets farther out. There is a boat in the distance. No duck, though.

'Do you suppose Ridley imitates the call of the wildfowl?' Gideon suggests.

'I have always thought,' Eastman says, 'his own conversational voice peculiarly resembled the cry of the mating mallard. Must his bag all be female?'

This seems to restore him to his old self. Accordingly, when MacQuitty, trotting ahead in his heavy-bodied way, suddenly flushes a duck from reeds, he is far too benignly disposed to murder it effectively. His barrels swing too slowly; even as he fires, he knows the bird is safely past the blast of pellets, the successive recoils of the shots coming as twin kicks of a disappointment already deadened by its anticipation. He blames not the lapse of time nor his own sluggish reflexes but the gun's design. 'Side-by-side is an infinitely better contrivance,' he mutters. MacQuitty has gone up to his chest in the water; now he turns and looks at Eastman, then returns to shore to shake his coat dry in disgust. They continue their walk. After a while they come to a little rise and, on reaching the top, see an inlet of the lake below which is full of water-grass and, more to the point, duck. MacQuitty is about to bound down among the floating fowl and scatter the prey to the guns but Eastman kicks him smartly in the ribs, making him jump sideways and growl. He puts his finger to his lips to impress stealth on Gideon, taking him as far down the slope as possible without alerting the duck.

'When I fire, do you press your trigger as well.'

'But, Walter ...'

'Quiet.'

They raise their guns. An instant later Eastman discharges his topmost barrel. Gideon fires, then a split second later Eastman's under-barrel goes off. This time Gideon has kept the butt pressed tightly against himself, with the result that there's the same bang and flash, but against his shoulder only a soft and almost voluptuous push. Down the barrel, he sees an explosion of feathers, marking where a duck had floated. His nostrils fill with the stink of powder, his ears sing, but he feels a thrill. Eastman, too, has hit a bird, with the contents of his second barrel, firing immediately after the recoil of the first and sending a climbing duck cartwheeling back into the water it strained to leave. Before the reports have died away, MacQuitty's down the slope, splashing through the water to come back with the trophies.

'Wonderful, wonderful shooting, Walter.'

Eastman, who ought to know better, beams, hurrying to

reload, which Gideon does as well, with fingers that shake. Next moment a flight of birds passes overhead. The hunters swing their weapons to the shoulder, firing directly up. Three closely placed reports crack and echo, one after the other. A classic moment. But this time Gideon's blinded by the sun coming through the clouds, and an instant later finds himself lying on his back with a painful shoulder. Through his watering eyes he sees a long, black streak whistling skywards through the flight of birds, and then it rotates slowly about its own axis and starts to fall, descending with increasing speed, like some angry bolt of heavenly vengeance, straight down on their heads.

'Oh, my God, Walter,' Gideon wails, quite paralysed. He's sure the awful missile is going to impale him straight in his manly portions, yet he cannot for the life of him move his parted legs. He shuts his eyes, reopens them, and is just in time to see his ramrod lance into marshland, as if the soil were the consistency of the quivering bean-curd the Chinese love to fry. It is engulfed and promptly vanishes from sight for ever.

'Well,' says Eastman, his genuine astonishment inspiring him to understatement and language less strong than usual. 'Good gracious me!'

He helps the abashed Gideon to his feet, then brushes him down. 'In your haste, Gideon, you must have omitted to remove it from the barrel after you had recharged the piece, and then fired it out along with the shot. Really, you are fortunate that the gun did not burst.'

'Ah,' says Gideon. 'Ah.'

They resume their walk, Gideon not quite *hors de combat* as Eastman has obliged for the reload with his own tool. They skirt some of the greenest, most treacherous grass Gideon has ever seen; jump a ditch, push aside bamboo – and stumble into a clearing. And there, Gideon receives the nastiest shock of the day: seven of the rascalliest, dirtiest, most heavily armed and sinewy Chinese ruffians he's ever seen. Squatting on their heels, they sharpen three thin stilettos and a broad-bladed dagger on a glistening grey whetstone which heavy service has reduced to the same wafer-thinness as the knife-blades themselves. All carry muskets or light fowling-pieces and on a tripod is a gingal, a heavy two-man gun, six feet long, decorated with red tassels, capable of throwing a one-pound iron ball (lead's expensive) half a mile. MacQuitty growls; his hackles rise. Does he know what these fellows like to do to dogs? Gideon swallows, no saliva left at all. The men stay still; they don't scowl, glare, or even look directly at the intruders but without exception they have the maddest, emptiest, most dangerous eyes Gideon has ever seen; eyes which recognise no laws, limits, rules, or philosophies; they carry no baggage in the head. The question is, Gideon asks himself, will they simply cut our throats or will they *mutilate* us first as well?

Eastman strides into the midst of this sub-lodge meeting of the Grand Society of Rovers of Rivers and Lakes (or, in a word, pirates, for that is what they are).

He picks up a brace of duck.

'How much-ee this two piece give-um buy?' he briskly enquires. Eliciting no immediate response apparent in those fourteen vacant, frightening eyes, he holds up two fingers. 'I give-um two copper cash,' he says.

No one looks at him.

Are we invisible? Gideon wonders deliriously. And also, more to the point, has Walter taken leave of his senses? Eastman, with culpable disregard for the safety of others, Gideon thinks, throws down his under-and-over – which also leaves him defenceless. He indicates three brace: 'All right-ee, make-um better price buy one duck. Him belong all together one me give-um quarter silver dollar.'

For the first time traces of interest begin to show on the impassive, brutalised faces. Suddenly, one of them, obviously the captain of the gingal, holds up a forefinger and with the knife-edge of the other palm makes a hacking gesture at the finger's joint.

Gideon's knees weaken; he feels like fainting. Not *that;* anything, *anything* but that.

Eastman laughs scornfully. 'Half-um?' he says witheringly 'half-um? Me tink-ee makee half-um silver dollar can buy all market hab got Canton-side.'

The leader of what Gideon now thinks of as 'this motley

band' repeats his earlier eloquent gesture which Gideon now understands to be indicative of the vulgar fraction, rather than exclusively minatory.

Eastman sighs. 'All right-ee. Gib, er, ten duck,' he holds up his fingers, 'then makee half silver dollar price, good pidgeon gib you.'

The man nods.

Eastman finds a Carolus dollar in his jacket pocket, places it on a stone; the fattest man in the group picks up the chopper. He hits Eastman's dollar precisely down the middle, picks up the two halves, lays them on top of each other for comparison, rubs the edges together, and presents one to Eastman. They clasp hands on the deal.

'Very well, Gideon,' calls Eastman cheerfully, 'do you take two brace and I may manage the others.'

Heavily burdened, they leave the convocation to crash through the bamboo thickets back to the lake, then along its shores in due course to rejoin their fellow-hunters.

'I fail to understand,' Gideon says in puzzlement. 'Those rascals, for such they appeared, might with trifling loss have overpowered and killed us for all our dollars, not to mention our watches and fine weapons, which they surely coveted. Yet instead they chose to bargain with us over comestibles.'

Eastman laughs. 'My dear Gid, I thought you, as our philosopher, intended to conceive yourself as in the shoes of anyone you chose. Know you not that a Chinaman will not rob you by offering violence when he may rob you legitimately in the way of trade? Half a silver dollar indeed! He might derive more glee from swindling us than performing us the service of cutting our throats from ear to ear. In fact, if I was not mistaken, those were Jardine rogues – though that would not necessarily have stood in the way of any throat-cutting, had they been so inclined. Also, my dear Philosopher and Comprehender of the curious ways of all Mankind, trifling loss – as you so familiarly put it – may mean that our three barrels might account for the life of only one man, but I conclude to assure you that that man would not account it trifling to lose his dearest possession.'

'Oh.'

Walter claps Gideon on the back, causing him to stagger dangerously with gun and birds. 'My dear head-in-the-clouds young friend, you are too much in the way of general theorising. You must temper it with your acquisition as to the particular and circumstantial. Listen to that old rogue O'Rourke.'

Whistles, cat-calls, unoriginal jeering greet them at the boat, which turn to astonishment at their haul. On this occasion the others have been less fortunate, with only three birds between them. Eastman is modestly dismissive but gives MacQuitty a pat – though MacQuitty won't even sniff the birds, let alone pick one up in his velvet mouth to drop at Ridley's feet.

They launch, and enjoy the sail back.

Dinner is (what else?) roast duck with turnips. 'Fair winds and an unfair price at the end of it, Captain Gale,' says Johnstone. 'Fine claret, this.'

'Will we be able to come up next season, Mr Eastman?' enquires Captain Gale.

'We can bank on nothing,' says Walter gloomily. 'Sooner or later, let it be later, our Celestial friends will need their notions of themselves readjusted forcibly. Let the British do it.'

'Well, I am quite safe aboard ship at all events. I fear for you gentlemen in the Factories, Americans or not.'

Gideon keeps quiet. Through pursed lips, he expels four lead shot which rattle discreetly on his plate. He has a delicious sense of physical tiredness combined with mental alertness. The waters lap below. It is dark outside and the saloon is cleverly lit. What brilliant company. How fortunate to come to the other side of the world, yet to be able to share one's exile with such friends as these. 'My dear Eastman...'

'Aaagh!'

Captain Gale has turned violently away from the table. He makes a strange gargling, his face creased with pain. He spits out something which tumbles with a clunk on to the china; then fumbles in his mouth with thumb and forefinger, whence he produces an appalling sliver. Now he spits blood. 'Some claret, sir,' says Ridley, pouring from the decanter. 'Swill it around the mouth.' He and Johnstone are solicitous. A circle of concerned heads forms about Captain Gale but the tough old salt dismisses the accident. 'A broken tooth is of no consequence. I guess the surgeon shall lance it with heated wire. Shall you not, Mr Vaughan?'

'I will, Captain. But you had better abandon claret for brandy, and plenty of it.'

'With a right good will, Mr Vaughan.'

Ridley picks up the offending object from Captain Gale's plate as the Goan steward clears the table. He wipes it on a napkin. It is a rusty-looking sphere of about the size of one of the cob-nuts in the dessert dish which Captain Gale will so unfortunately be precluded from sampling. 'Iron?' says Ridley. 'I thought only the lowest natives were so poor they could not afford lead. You should have requested me for some.' He hefts the ball thoughtfully before wrapping it in his handkerchief. In the boat, on the way back, a journey for which Captain Gale has lent them two Lascars, nothing – not even threatening to duck him – can stop Ridley grinning from ear to ear. He even delivers an otiose little lecture on the way to shoot: 'Which, by the by, my good Gid, is to aim where the target bird *will* be when the shot arrives, not where it is in the moment of taking aim. That's pure history, my boy, an event long in the past, and you will miss. You must anticipate what its present situation is going to be and take a lead. Of course – splash away, Eastman, you wet yourself, too, as we are in the same boat, so to speak – a pair of darnation cunning shots like yourselves need not heed my advice.'

In fact, the only event which might make an impression on Ridley's immense and odious egregiousness, loss of the ivory-tipped ramrod from his single-barrel fowling-piece, he will only discover the next afternoon. On instructions, Gideon will disclaim any knowledge. The boy's learning, Eastman thinks.

Chapter XI

From THE CANTON MONITOR
July 9th, 1835

The present juncture, only a little more than twelve months after the cessation of the Honourable Company's functions and monopoly in China may present a point of vantage both appropriate and convenient from which to review the events of the past year, and the manner in which our expectations, fond or otherwise, have been disappointed. Let us avow at once, frankly and firmly, that our hopes been most cruelly dashed. The anticipations generally entertained regarding the monopoly's demise and the advent of Free Trade have not been fulfilled. In a purely financial point of view, some speculations might be said to have flourished better during the time of the Company. Tea is now at a glut on the London market, owing to the circumstance of the throwing open that trade to all comers. The great number of vessels which resorted to this port to take on cargoes of tea at the ridiculously inflated prices the brokers were demanding merely combined to drive down each other's profits at the London auctions. Now those same shippers cannot prevail upon the wholesalers to take their teas at any price. Stocks of teas are on hand, it is estimated, which will supply all conceivable wants of our domestic population for three years. To think that the law required the Company in its time to keep a year's stock in their warehouses lest the froward and turbulent urban populations of our island might even temporarily be deprived of what has become to them increasingly a staple of existence. *O tempora! O mores!* Yet if change and reform have not been wholly as desired (and would that it might serve for an example to some of our fire-eating Radicals at home), in one respect has our little revolution at Canton been insufficiently thorough. One baneful nuisance remains, one impediment to the proper workings of a new and cleansed system, one mote in the eye, one tiny abuse, which may yet become the source of huge and endless mischiefs, one engine which, we will not say may work the overthrow of all the Free Traders have striven for because they cannot be resisted – such is not in the nature of things – but which may spoil or delay the perfection of the new system of trade. What is this sprig of Lucifer? We refer, of course, to the Finance Committee at Canton of the Honourable East India Company, which has inexplicably been allowed to continue in its functions, and promises to wreak chaos out of all proportion to its few members and puny premises. It is as if the Pretender had been allowed board and lodging in White-hall and permission to keep on his tatterdemalion court at the accession of Hanover. (The many distinguished Lowland gentlemen resident here, none more distinguished than Mr J.-, would vehemently repudiate the first suggestion of sympathy with the House of Stuart.) However, we digress. In what sense may the operations of the Honourable Company's Finance Committee jeopardise the present prospects, for bright prospects there are, despite the present depression? By, we say, throwing open participation in the Canton trade to any *parvenu* or adventurer who happened to have the desire to chance his hand. In the past the traffic was the resort of a body of most respectable and established capitalists, men who would have been the adornment of any profession (we do not say trade) in any of the great and fashionable cities of the world. They ventured their own funds, substantial fortunes which had been thriftily accumulated over a long period in a traffic in which they were well versed. Do we not well recall Mr J.-, not the least of these men, with justice declare the traffic in drug 'one of the most gentlemanly speculations he knew'? Are their works of charity, their munificence as patrons of the arts not well known? Indeed, are the evidences not all around us? Yet now, by presenting funds on demand in Canton, virtually to whoever asks for them, the Company through its indiscriminate financial advances encourages a class of speculators the least likely to promote the stable and orderly expansion of the sibling trades in drug and tea. This is not a beneficent and natural competition within the open market; the operations of these interlopers present a spectacle of unbridled anarchy.

Our language is strong; so, too, are our feelings on this most important subject and its gravity must be our excuse. For some months now His Majesty's several representatives in this spot cannot have been ignorant of what went on before them. It passed unremarked before the bland and imperturbable eye earlier this year of Mr John F. Davis, in succession to Lord Napier HBM's Chief Superintendent of Trade in China, self-esteemed scholar and quondam *employé* of the East India Company. Mr Davis's views and dispositions are well known to us of old. However, even with our long experience of the quirks of the supracargo, we must confess our surprise at the warmth and indiscretion of the Superintendent's remarks to the effect that the British merchants' important petition to His Majesty in Council of December 9th, 1834, was both 'crude and ill-digested'. It was, indeed, our little community which found Mr Davis himself somewhat hard on the digestion, with the result that we were all rather less dyspeptic when he made his unlamented departure from the estuary January past. His successor, Sir George Robinson, came to his appointment with all the advantages inherent in his situation: *viz.* that he was Mr John Davis's successor, beside whom any man might appear as a disciple of reason and paragon of popularity. Alas, Sir George's incumbency, while so far free from the abrasive and personal discourtesies which marked the short-lived reign of his predecessor, has been characterised by an excessive leniency, even partiality, towards the Chinese, whom one might be forgiven for describing as the assassins of Lord Napier, and a certain distance from the British community. We refer, of course, to the *established* houses.

Nevertheless, lest our reprobations appear too ungrateful, it affords us the most lively and unalloyed pleasure to repeat in our columns our approbation of the determined and assidious attention to his duties demonstrated by Captain

Elliot, formerly Master Attendant, when making his representations at the Gate of Canton for the release of the shipwrecked sailors of the *Argyle,* and his more than assiduity, his courageous and manly bearing when knocked smartly over the head and rudely bundled from the city, he and his. Can the gorgeous uniform, gilt buttons, epaulettes, braid, cocked hat, and all, of a post-captain in His Majesty's Navy ever have suffered such indignity so meekly? The time is coming upon us when sterner measures must be the order of the day. There can be neither safety nor dignity while we sit here unprotected at Canton, with the rabble at our backs, rather encouraged in their opprobrious conduct than restrained by the mandarins, and the river before us. Let us recall the eighth of those Resolutions Sir George Staunton proposed before the House of Commons on the 16th of April 1833, Resolutions which sent a thrill through the hearts of all of us connected with the China Trade in whatever capacity. Sir George, it will be recalled, recommended that in the event of an embassy proving unsuccessful (and how well he might have presaged the fate which awaited Lord Napier when Sir George himself as a ten-year-old pageboy accompanied the fruitless embassy of Lord Macartney to Peking in 1793) that: '…it proving impracticable to replace the influence of the East India Company's authorities by a system of national protection emanating from the crown, it will then be expedient (tho' only in the last resort) to withdraw the British commerce altogether from the control of the Chinese authorities, and to establish it in some Insular Position on the Chinese Coast where it may be satisfactorily carried on, beyond the reach of acts of molestation or oppression, to which an unresisting submission would be equally prejudicial to the national honour and the national interests of this country'.

To which one may perhaps be permitted to append a heartfelt 'Aye!' and the 'Hear! Hear!' with which the honourable members undoubtedly received Sir George's most pertinent recommendation. As an editorial codicil, may we not suggest one of the commodious and picturesque harbours in the vicinity of Lantao and Lamma islands? There the mariner would find deep water and shelter beneath the massy peaks of either island, the trader frontage for his godowns on their spotless strands, and water in the torrents which cascade in pearly sheets from their unscaled heights. *Lantao!* There may be a name which will be written on a glorious and immortal page of Britannia's destiny! The Gibraltar of the East. Lantao! (We say it again.) Lantao!

From THE CANTON MONITOR
July 16th, 1835

A letter to the editor from two unnamed gentlemen

Sir,

We have observed your personal opinions as expressed through the medium of the news-sheet it is your honour to conduct weekly, which has inspired our hopes, as regularly dashed, that you might hold your opinions more weakly. In fact, sir, we doubt whether they may be opinions which you hold yourself, rather you may be an adherent to the parties which are interested in those beliefs. We would at least admire the *consistency* with which you have advocated your opinions in your organ, or at any rate your masters', for if your beliefs have changed, it is but by hardening. The *consistency* of your masters' beliefs is soft, treacly, viscous, inspissated, of a darkish hue, and tending to harden when the balls are removed from the mango-wood chest and exposed to air. Those vital organs of theirs, which according to the ancients was the seat of the emotions, might appear hardened and dark when removed from their own chests. Is our meaning clear enough? We deplore the truck in poison on which your masters' fortunes and your own journal are established exclusively. The substance and happiness of a few selfish individuals are founded on the stupefaction of the intellects, the wasting of the bodies, and the misery of the unoffending families of a mass of wretched addicts. Are we to assume that the sole and cogent reason for your failure to advocate the utter extirpation by root and branch of the unhappy inhabitants of this empire, for you seem perfectly willing to bring fire and the sword to them, is that were you to slay all of them, your masters would no longer possess the market for their noxious ware? We fail to understand why in our dealings with the Chinese we cannot find a happy medium between a cringing and meek submissiveness (which with both mandarins and rabble is but an invitation and incitement to further excess) and the extreme bloodthirstiness you are pleased to advocate. Think you that the jealous mandarins will part with a grain of sand from the estuary's meanest rock without the effusion of a river of blood? You speak of the numerous works of private charity and the public patronage of men of arts and letters (do you, sir, include yourself and your two pages of foolscap in this latter august company?) of which your masters have proved the willing sponsors. Humbug. Are the murdered man and his wronged family to be grateful to the assassins for defraying the cost of his funeral? The source of these riches taints all the good uses to which they may be put. Not all the perfumes of Araby will cleanse those hands of their foul crime in purveying the means of self-destruction to their fellow beings. We doubt we shall see our missive inserted among your columns, which seem to espouse but a single point of view, but it is our intention to Chase and Chasten you, and from our darts you will find no Shield.

VENATORES

In printing the effusion above (hot-blooded enough for any Spaniard and prolix enough to require a river of ink at any event) we make no apology, nor were we goaded into so doing by the most unjustified taunt with which it concludes. The Company, in its day, and in its territory (and, as is still the case in its Indian Possessions where a hapless editor may find himself put on the next ship home for treading in print too closely on the heels of the malversations of the Collector of Dagallee Wallah or Smoakamee Hookah, or wherever) the Company, we say, operated a virtual censorship on the legitimate expression of Free Opinion. Then, even the Canton Monitor was obliged force majeure to trim, to come up on the indirect tack, to abandon the manly assertion for the clever insinuation, when, speaking in a general sense, John Bull found the rapier more handy to his task than the cudgel. We, the Free Traders, stand not only for Freedom of Trade within the limitations of the preconditions of probity and security (which the newcomers manifestly lack) but also for a Free Press (though, again, a Free Press is not a licentious Press, which we should never stand). Our correspondents' letter (if not the work of one fanatic) is licentious enough for anyone. Do we have a mangy Tom Paine in our little number, some thin-shanked, addle-pated Robespierre who loves the Celestials? Is it some foolish missionary (but we are well acquainted with all those gentlemen who would never abuse the numerous kindnesses shown them by the Free Traders)? We should say, from the letter's heat, and the flowing ornate hand, that it is the work of some jealous Portuguese of the mouldering, decaying settlement of Macao. It has been carried thence, we note, by passage boat on the 7th inst. and it arrived on the 8th in time for insertion in our present. Since Lin Tin island became established as the resort of the opium-hulks, the Portuguese settlement's fortunes have sensibly declined. Happy would they be to deal in the drug which this jealous José or Pedro affects to despise. Yet they cannot for fear of the hawk-eyed mandarins who hover on the other side of the Barrier. Were we in need of further argument to support our contention, here we would find it. If the Emperor will not concede some eligible situation, some suitable island possession, then let us take it. Would our correspondents find that occupation more odious than our present one of journalist?

'Oh, no, it does nothing like justice to the original. A very feeble representation. Is that your opinion, Gid?'

Gideon looks nervously at the formidable Harry O'Rourke, then at the canvas on its easel. 'Well,' he equivocates, 'of course it is but half-completed and until the finishing touches are put to it, I guess we cannot judge. It certainly does not flatter, but then Mr O'Rourke is no society portraitist. 'Warts and ...'

'Pshaw!' says O'Rourke in disgust, surprising Gideon, since Eastman's far ruder comments never evoked such a contemptuous response. In fact, Harry took it in his stride, beaming behind his lenses. Gideon imagined him as having had a very good tiffin. Now he scowls at young Chase, his eyes darkening. 'Speak your mind, spit it out, sir.'

Gideon stutters, Eastman smiling wickedly in the background.

'Do you,' says the irate old painter, 'feel it lowers a man in your estimation that he should have to earn a living in the world? The very greatest artists have painted to order. To do hack's work is not to vitiate the entire body of his work, it is merely to do hack's work *ex tempore*. The muse is not pure, you young fool, she's a harlot and you'll accommodate yourself to life the better when you find that the objects of your adoration, if you have the one, are not to be worshipped as goddesses. Further…'

'But, Mr O'Rourke, you are putting words in my mouth,' says mortified Gideon, 'I intended no reflection on your stature as an artist…'

'The statements were to be discovered implicit in what you said,' O'Rourke continues remorselessly, 'and I detected views of the most lamentably Philistine kind of which I shall do you the service of disabusing you and do me the honour of realising this: no criticism can offend a workman of ability and integrity. 'Tis the assumption that he *will* be which offends, for it implies he is inferior.'

Gideon feels, rather reasonably, that O'Rourke's own display of testiness would seem to condemn him out of hand on his own terms. He opens his mouth, then thinks better. 'Besides,' says O'Rourke, wiping a brush, 'this is not commissioned work.'

'Aha,' says Eastman, eyes glinting, 'now we come to a truer story. Do you paint for love of your art, sir? Or for love of your sitter?'

'Sir, I love neither. The one is an addiction, the other a …'

'Dalliance?'

'A diversion for an old man. My remaining hours drag.'

'Harry, we weep for you, you old humbug.'

O'Rourke grunts unamiably. He pads around the commodious studio, which is, of course, north-facing, on the top of an old house near the Monte, access won by dangerous, juddering stairs, some lacking a plank or two, so that the general impression is of mounting rungs. 'Jacob's ladder,' Eastman calls it. There are fine windows and in the new tiled roof O'Rourke had put on (new, that is, twenty years ago) a skylight. Generally, it is an imposing and elevating sort of place, worth its initial outlay many times over in the extra guineas it puts on commissions, as Harry realises. Shortly, Gideon will catch the outrageous old pontificator out in another inconsistency, for when Eastman says, 'Say! Harry, your visitors are damnably dry,' and O'Rourke insists on seclusion and total concentration as his inalienable right, Chase says: 'But surely the muse cannot object, Mr O'Rourke, for if a public woman as you assert, then we may assist, if one believes Casanova, in the capacity of spectators.' Then he wonders if he's been too gross. But Eastman slaps his thigh, says 'Bravo!' and makes himself at home. He is about to pull the bell for Ah Cheong when that factotum pops up, grinning, always grinning, with only his head visible above the level of the floorboards. 'Missy Lemington,' he lisps in the Canton lingo Gideon has grown to hate, 'waiting downstair go bimeby,' and all is made transparent as O'Rourke shies a clammy rag at his retainer's head.

Enter Alice moments later.

The gentlemen have rearranged themselves: Eastman languid on the window-box, hand on cane, Gideon staring sternly out of a window, arms behind his back, O'Rourke chivalrously at the trap-door to receive his pretty sitter.

'Oh, Mr O'Rourke, you dear man, what an agreeable surprise,' says Alice as she places her little hand in his crude paw (which is damp and still smells of the horrible cloth). 'I had not seen Mr Eastman or Mr Chase (who I am sure is cutting me at the window) for *so* long that I thought they had quite made up their minds to abandon me in this dreary place.'

O'Rourke's face contorts into a sort of baffled rictus as he seeks to bring the emotions of gratification (at pleasing Alice) and annoyance (at being bested by the crafty young bucks) under voluntary muscular control, with the result that as he alternately blinks, scowls, and grinds the stumps of his ancient brown teeth, his pince-nez fall to the end of their red thread. 'Your slave, my dear,' he says, 'your very willing slave,' bowing her in and then wiping the spectacles on the cloth, which conclusively films them.

'Mr Chase, sir, you have shamefully neglected me.' Alice bears down on the blushing, routed young man and extends her arm, fingers out, which Gideon takes, hideously uncertain what to do with it. He finds himself bowing and kissing the hand in question, not at all what he was expecting, but which seems to have been the right thing to do, for Alice moves on to Eastman to deliver a charming rebuke to him as well.

'You are unjust,' Eastman defends himself with mock indignation, 'we arrived here only on the evening of the seventh and had merely time to dash off a note or two to our friends (and not so amiable acquaintances) in Canton. Then we needs must unpack and settle ourselves in before dealing with the several pressing affairs of our employers. Oh, how you are cruel and unfair.'

'Harumph,' says Harry.

'Shall I place myself again in the chair at the window, Mr O'Rourke,' Alice enquires. 'I dare not steal a look at the canvas, howsoever I may be tempted, though I see Mr Chase and Mr Eastman conferring behind the easel.'

And indeed the young men are in turn ostentatiously inspecting O'Rourke's work, then scrutinising the original and whispering while shaking their heads gravely.

'Why, you are quizzing me!' she exclaims, laughing. 'How odious the pair of you are to behave so!'

O'Rourke is thoroughly out of sorts by now. Brusquely, he throws a sheet over the canvas, then shoos his young friends away, catching Eastman a smart, back-handed blow on the arm. 'Away with you, I say. I will not be a butt. My work will not be mocked. Nor will I be judged by a pair of young jackanapes with an excess of time on their hands. To the devil with you, and take your tomfoolery elsewhere.'

The pair retreat to the trap-door, O'Rourke advancing on them with an oily brush, and tumble after each other down the steps.

'The old bear has claws, Miss Remington, teeth, too, though rather short-sighted,' Eastman calls up. 'We shall raid his honey store.'Which they proceed to do, spurning the cherry brandy Ah Cheong and his master (though for different reasons) would like to foist on them in favour of an ambrosial malt (presented Harry by a pleased Scots factor), during the trial of which Eastman puffs enough smoke from O'Rourke's cigars to daunt a swarm of bees. 'First-rate *seegars* these, Harry,' says Eastman complacently when the artist and his sitter descend more than an hour later, light dying, which has been more than enough time for substantially lowering the level of the bottle. 'May we continue the enjoyment of our tobacco, Miss Remington?'

'Damn your coolness,' says O'Rourke, who cannot be angry with anyone for long, least of all Walter. 'Will you be employing the leaves of my album to light them?'

'Oil more combustible, Harry.' Eastman grins at Alice. She does her best to keep a straight face. These pair of young wags do seem to be particularly carefree and feckless youths, though Gideon Chase is apparently more sober-minded. Perhaps the strain of being in Canton the last few trying months? They must look forward to. ...whatever it is they like to do in Macao. Uncle has remarked on young Chase's application, marking him out over his (Uncle's) whisky and cigar as a brave young fellow who *puff, puff* might with seasoning arrive at a partnership in the fullness of time. All in all, Alice is glad of the men's arrival and, after Uncle and the missionaries between them, a little levity is refreshing rather than to be wholly reprehended.

Nevertheless, she is a little scandalised by the cavalier way they seem to treat Mr O'Rourke, almost as a buffoon, when it is universally acknowledged that he is not merely an individual of surpassing talents but a man of genius, 'the finest painter ever to set foot in the ultra-Gangetic East' *(Straits Courier and Singapore Free Press,* read by Alice in Mrs Marjoribanks's house two years out of date). 'Of course,' she thinks, watching Eastman polish O'Rourke's pince-nez for him on his own spotless shirt, 'he is a terrible old quiz in his way, but his drollness is deliberately assumed and you do not, at least, I do not yet, I hope, judge a man by the cut of his coat. Rather by the opinions he dresses himself in, whether they be good or ill, his own or purloined second-hand from other men, and the companions he keeps, whether they, too, be wholesome or the reverse.'

Can these rowdy boys best be described as wholesome, with their flushed faces, tousled hair, and the fumes they have made? But Alice has always adored the manly smell of a cigar, or rather coming into her father's study when the perfume of tobacco has been redolent rather than immediate, perhaps historically impregnated into the leather. The actuality of the practice of cigar-smoking, as opposed to its fragrant, fainter aftermath, is more acrid, harsher, maler, making the eyes sting and water, and the soft throat rasp. ('Ooh, papa, it's so big, and brown, and wrinkled!') Alice doesn't know whether it's repellent or exciting or a bit of both. But *why* can't they be a bit more like Father?

This, of course, would be rather to defeat the point. However, there is obviously no real harm in these youths, she decides. For their part, the young men, whose behaviour is admittedly different from their comportment at the tea-party on the lawn, when chaperoned by Aunt Remington, are intoxicated in ascending order of degrees proof, by Macao, by the Hebridean nectar, and by Alice.

Somehow, with a sleight of hand well worthy of himself, O'Rourke has made the malt disappear. Tea comes, courtesy Ah Cheong, who is genially abused by his master. 'Bring spoons, you heathen devil. Some preserves for the bread and butter, and cut the seed-cake before you bring it.' He pours the tea himself. 'Due precedence should be paid the sex, madam,' he says, parading his notorious misogyny, 'but forgive an old bachelor exercising his rights in his own lair. Milk, my dear?'

'Of course, one of the Chinese fashions by which an inferior expresses his subordination to an elder or a superior is to pour tea for them. They set some store by the practice. A curious inversion, is it not, Mr O'Rourke, sir?' This (who else?) is Gideon.

'Invert yourself around the bread, my boy. As a storehouse of useless informations you are second only to Ribeiro. Excellent bread. The Portuguese are capital bakers. Poor soldiers but capital bakers.'

O'Rourke's antipathy to the sex may be entirely apocryphal; his reputation as a trencherman is founded on solid fact, and he proceeds to demolish bread and cake, as minor postscripts to tiffin and a teasing preface to dinner. At the conclusion of this insignificant little repast, the young men escort Alice home through the crowded, cobbled alleyways of the ancient settlement and vie with their clearing sticks and what they imagine is wit.

Dear, gallant boys, Alice thinks.

'I shall send it by the next ship to my doting family. It is fortunate that he was able to accomplish the greater part of it before you arrived. Whether 'tis a likeness of their dear *departed* sister and daughter they may best be judges for themselves.'

'Oh, my dear Miss Remington, it most faithfully captures your habitual expression and not only that, which any of the native charlatans might have imitated in their worthless way as, indeed, for a trifling consideration, they will with their perfect facility for any of our visiting sea-captains or ship's surgeons, but it also most wonderfully shows you as you are... within yourself.'

'Oh, but are my lips so *very* red, Mr Eastman? And should I wear such a vacant look about my eyes?'

'Miss Remington, O'Rourke will give us all the rubiest lips. He does love his vermilion. But this is a most amiable eccentricity of his. And life will, as he avers, always imitate art. Why, have you not heard him assert that after he had 'pickled 'em in oils', Howqua's wife and her children were to be seen about their courtyards many months afterwards with the itinerant mountebank's crimson grease-paint on their lips? The noodles had decided they must live up to Harry's gifted eye. I am the sallowest of mortals as you may observe, but have lips like corals where Harry has taken me on his canvas.'

'My nose, is that so very *short?*'

'Now I do believe that you are fishing for compliments – and shall have them. It is a most charming nose and O'Rourke has rendered it perfectly. But, again, it is not a question of the individual features in themselves or a mere imitation of them.

That I could endeavour myself, but Harry captures, I guess, something like the soul.'

'Oh, yes! You do endeavour yourself. Mr O'Rourke himself had remarked on your talent during one of our sittings.'

'Well, Harry is a rare being. What he says behind the back is altogether kinder than his strictures to the face. He is the most merciless critic.'

'The best kind, Mr Eastman, if truly disinterested.'

'Ah, have you suffered usefully, Miss Remington? Perhaps the pangs of rejected authorship, which are amongst the sharpest stabs felt by the heart of man.'

'Oh, my daubings are not for the public viewing, nor my scribblings. I am no novelist or poet. I am earth-bound in the jottings of my daily avocations, which are of no interest beyond the moment and the writer. I lack the soaring gift. I should, however, like to enjoy the advantages of Mr O'Rourke's instruction and advice. I should like ... in my small way... to *draw*. He, however, became so gruff, I was quite frightened!'

'The old curmudgeon! I shall horsewhip him!'

'No, no. I crave you – do not mention it to him. My temerity deserved such a reception. To treat him as a drawing-master! It was odious, presumptuous.'

'Then you misjudge him. Harry O'Rourke is beyond pride – not that he is modest but because his belief in himself is unshakable.'

'Oh, those are admirable qualities in a man, Mr Eastman. Do you possess them?'

'I should certainly have the forwardness to offer myself as your drawing-master, were it not altogether too sour a prospect for you.'

'Oh, but how wonderful! I should derive the greatest profit and enjoyment from it. But how selfish I am – I should merely be taking advantage of your great good nature and depriving you of the opportunity to profitably employ the time in your own practice.'

'My dear Miss Remington, I expect that you are mistaken. In the first instance, my own scrawlings are beneath consideration. In the second and more important – and I have this from the fount of all painterly wisdom, our friend Harry himself – to teach has the effect of clarifying one's own impulses bringing him to a discovery of his own habit of working, which had been a thing buried and mysterious till then. In fact, our rubicund friend waxed so bold, he observed that the less skilled the disciple, the apter a foil he might be to his master.'

'Oh, Mr Eastman, I scarcely know what to say. You are too droll for me.'

'I should exhort you, in that case, to endeavour to be unworthy my instruction. But your aunt has shown the rest of the party the glories of your garden and we must give young Chase his tea. Not a word to Gideon of our arrangement.'

Gideon has been most unlike Gideon. As Walter Eastman is preoccupied himself, he has not had time, or more to the point, inclination, to notice aberrant behaviour. For instance, it is half past five in the summer morning. Young Chase's narrow bachelor bed has evidently been slept in, for it is rumpled in that barely disturbed way which can never be counterfeited. His jug's empty and there's grey water in the basin, cleanly boy. The window is open, admitting the salubrious sea-breeze. He doesn't smoke anyway. What an innocent room it is. Halfway down the Ridge to the bazaar is our innocent. Going up the hill, antlike in groups of three or four, are a procession of hopeful hawkers, as well as official suppliers of milk, fruit, and meat, gardeners, other menials, and domestics for whom there is either no room or no trust in the households they serve. Going down hill is ... just Gideon. The Chinese stare or, more pointedly, ignore him. They refuse to acknowledge his nod, even the man with the pomelos and bananas, who is the wife's cousin of the *compradore* of Meridian and builds into his prices the ten per cent *ad valorem* which the venial agent of that great house routinely takes as his perquisite. Of course, if he didn't, the fruit-seller would inflate his price and Meridian would still be worse off. A rational and equitable arrangement this, and indeed a quite open one, but which does unfortunately have the effect of inspiring contempt all round in the involved parties: the foreigner for the cheating, petty Chinese; the Chinese for the stupid, careless foreigner. It is an accumulation of such small, silly, mutually diminishing contacts, pinpricks like this, which do not even deserve the title of collisions, which has brought about the chronically recurrent major condition where the other party have ceased to be seen as people, but as simple objects of dislike and ridicule, and where the behaviour of the best must be degraded to that of the worst. It is a law which is as iron as any of those of science, grammar, or perspective, as Gideon will know. At the moment, he proceeds downhill, literally and metaphorically, trotting increasingly fast down the greasy cobbles, for to slow will be to skid and whoops-a-daisy. Sweating, even at this cooler hour, he arrives on the flat and has to execute a shuffle, a hop, skip, and a jump; followed by a rapid side-step to miss the mess (that is, what are specifically designated 'loathsome nuisances') at the top of the Rua dos Lojos. To the right at the bottom past a native barber, across a line of noodle-stalls where coolies are already breakfasting, down five flights of stairs, up two, and along a railed terrace, where a venerable banyan's bunioned roots break through the restraining plaster and its boughs shield a dozer. But this could be Portugal; certainly, if it were an oak. Now he clatters down a cobbled slope; three left turns downhill, and it is unmistakably China: low, squalid habitations; meals cooked over charcoal in the open on braziers that look like inverted flower-pots; a heap of blackened rags that turns out to be a beggar whose ghastly mutilations and sores are self-inflicted; naked children with a string around the waist and orange streaks in their hair. Gideon picks his way between the stinking puddles; the cobblestones are no more. At the side of a house more substantial than its neighbours (walled around, five storeys) he halts. Before he can knock, a small door opens and after taking a furtive look down the street, he steps inside the courtyard.

'Naturally,' Eastman says, 'beyond a certain point it is impossible to teach. That is, as Harry says, one helps the child to discover his balance and walk, but after that he may choose the direction in which he proceeds.'

'Well, I am sure that you will find that I am yet at the crawling stage.'

'I believe you are altogether too modest. It is a pretty talent, and that is a fact.'

Aunt Remington is pretending to read under a parasol in the bright sunshine of the lawn's centre; actually, she is watching the bees buzz around the flower-bed and enjoying the fragrance of the exotic blooms. Very few are familiar to her and the tiny, old Chinese gardener has no English at all, not even the names of his gorgeous charges. *'Lairng,'* he says grinning and pointing at the flowers, then, under Aunt's insistent interrogation, *'Lairng fa,'* he exclaims again, of quite a different species. He really is an aggravating old fellow, Aunt thinks crossly. They inherited him, of course. He and his beautiful growths were there long before they ever came and will be long after they have departed. To the old gardener, the present occupiers are of less significance than the blooms of a single season, which may fade and die, but then return the following year, which is more than the tenants of the house ever do. He sees himself, with some justification, as the garden's real owner.

Alice wants to draw some orchids the old man has been tending with particular devotion. 'See how perfect they are, Mr Eastman! The thick flower, the curving, delicate tendrils.'

Eastman thinks their cultivator would make the better subject.

'Indeed,' he agrees politely, 'they could form a useful exercise, though I expect a little difficult for a beginner.'

'Oh, dear,' says Alice, disappointed.

'A firm foundation, Miss Remington,' Eastman lectures her, 'one must commence with that or the rest is lost. Sketch rather…the little pavilion.'

Alice stares hard at it, looks at the paper (beautiful paper Walter has provided), then at the pavilion again, as if she might transfer the image from her eye to the blank surface before her. 'Should I…should I…imagine it as on the paper already and then proceed to trace its outline?'

'Ah, yes,' says Walter, surprised, 'that is one method of proceeding. Yes, indeed, that is precisely the method employed with the camera obscura.'

'The what, pray, Mr Eastman?'

'The camera obscura, my dear Miss Remington, is an ingenious device whereby an image of an object viewed may be thrown on to the surface one wishes. It is quite simple. One constructs a room the inside of which will be dark. In the front wall he pierces a hole. When the conditions are suitable, that is, if the light is sufficiently brilliant, an image of the object viewed will be cast through the hole on to the opposite side of the room. Indeed, one may construct a box as an item of portable apparatus and obtain an image on the panel opposite to the hole. One merely draws around the outline of what one views. When mirrors, lenses, and levers are employed the whole forms a handy and conveniently operated machine.'

'But how clever! And is this a new discovery?'

'Indeed not. The principle was known to the ancients. An interesting and perverse aspect of the phenomenon is that the image obtained is cast upside down on the wall of the chamber, or panel of the box, as it may be. It is also the case that the smaller the aperture may be made, so much the better defined is the representation of the external world. It will, however, be a dimmer image and would require a day – such as this – of the brightest light. The fitting of a lens of a convex nature would also be of a help.'

'Mr Eastman, I had simply no idea of this, though I have observed a silhouettist at work in Philadelphia.'

'A quite separate process,' Eastman says, 'which operates upon principles which are decidedly different.'

'And does Mr O'Rourke avail himself of such an aid?'

'My dear Miss Remington,' says Walter laughing, 'Harry would, I guess, as soon avail himself of a gallows. If you wish to avoid his ire abstain from all mention of 'the fiend's own contraption'. Canaletto was notorious for resorting to that device, and Harry despises him beyond all others. Now I can see you are made bashful with my talk of Canalettos and O'Rourkes. Do you remain seated here while I remove my awful and inhibiting presence to the right side to sketch the pavilion from that angle. Draw freely, for this should not be an ordeal for you and your mistakes will but point you the way to the right quarter.'

Alice compresses her lips; she puts her pencil on the paper, making a small dot; then removes the pressure. So far, so good. She has made her mark without committing herself to anything: that is, the dot could become a straight line, upwards, downwards, or, indeed, in any direction; a curve; a circle; etc. She finds it a frightening sort of liberty, which impels her towards extending her first hesitant line up and then down, which she hopes will represent a wall of the pavilion. She continues with the roof, which is somewhat less obliging as it is rounded. Meanwhile, Eastman is shading in, crosshatching, fussing away after having got down the outlines with a commendable despatch which nearly, but not quite, matches his irascible old mentor's. Now, if he only knew, he's spoiling it. This is probably a question of temperament rather than pure technical ability as gained and painstakingly refined, the acquisition of a vocabulary of forms. Or, indeed, talent, that unfair and inexplicable ability Harry was born with. The old buffoon is both more venomous than Eastman (hear his jealous remarks about his rivals!) and also more generous. The smooth Eastman's vocation should be critic, commentator. And he proves it now with the excellent advice he gives Alice. She, at first, won't show him what she's done. Quickly, she flips the block over. 'Oh, no, Mr Eastman. You must not see. No, no. It is too bad.' A playful struggle ensues for possession of the pad, Alice rather more earnest than Eastman, and if during the tussle their fingers should meet, it is only a delightful coincidence which Alice's continued resistance will merely prolong. Aunt Remington has dozed off under her awning, or is perhaps pretending she has, since (though Alice would find this hard to believe) a difference in age of fifteen years is not so great that Aunt has forgotten what it is like to be Alice. So, her eyes are shut at least while she reclines on her rattan chaise-longue in her blot of shade on the lawn's dry, green parchment, while she hears the bees drone, gardener's water patter from his watering-can over the brittle leaves and − more distantly − Alice's laughter which tinkles over the rill of the Chinese water-garden.

'I must surrender, Mr Eastman, you are too persistent and too cruel and my arms are *so* weary,' and, with that, she lets go.

'But this is fine,' Eastman lies valiantly. 'Creditable when one bears in mind that it is your first attempt. Of course, a little guidance is necessary.'

'But you are the most patient and lenient of guides, Mr Eastman.'

'For instance, allow me to explain to you the laws of perspective. Now, one of the differences, the main difference, between a painting by a native and one by a foreign hand, is that the one completed by the former will appear to be flat and unnatural. It may be of persons or of the craggy landscapes they are so fond of putting upon their scrolls and fans.'

'Do you mean that the one appears to go backwards and both the personages and objects are *solid?*'

'Then I allow you grasp the principle perfectly.'

'Oh, I am not quite so foolish as you must expect, Mr Eastman. We have heard of perspective in a painting in our town and I daresay there are those to whom your camera might not be so obscure.'

'Miss Remington, I do most humbly beg your pardon. I expect I have offended you.'

'If you have, Mr Eastman, you are most freely pardoned. Perhaps you may explain to me in further detail the mysteries of depths in a picture.'

'It is, Miss Remington, a question of lines apparently parallel but parallel lines which in fact *do* meet, although, of course, strictly speaking, parallel lines may never meet, though extended to infinity.'

'Poor lines!'

'Allow me to demonstrate. Now there is a vanishing point. Regard, if you will, *my* pavilion.'

'But how wonderful!'

'I take no credit for it. It is a mere party trick for us of the nineteenth century – for the men of four, five hundred years ago, to employ it was the discovery of genius: but that does not make us their superiors. Harry convinced me so. He says that the means a painter may employ he must take from his predecessors, such as a child learning a language, which he did not invent. At first he lisps childish things, then his syntax, his lexicon of words,

121

become those of an adult, and he may speak naturally his own sentences and ideas without a thought for grammar and construction. Thus he grows out of a manner and paints according to his own lights.'

'Oh, dear, I shall never be thus, but babble the nonsense of childhood for ever.'

'You shall not. Now, come, draw me a pair of lines.'

What's Gideon been up to? Well, his course will certainly never cross Eastman's, although they might be said to follow parallel vocations. Let us follow him through the door in that nondescript mud-brick wall. (He has penetrated it several times by now.) Once into the flagged courtyard, all changes. There's an ancient Pomerac tree, gravid at this season with its long crimson fruit, a tiny pond, which is the haunt of a green porcelain toad, while the visitor's foot crunches on sapless leaves which have lain there since last autumn, when Napier died, for the tenant of the house is rather absent-minded. When Gideon first came, he entered (we remember) stealthily, like a thief, which was no more than what he was in the eyes of the native authorities, although with the essential distinction that he is a thief who steals with the connivance of the household. Up the stairs he goes, which are as venerable as O'Rourke's but considerably firmer. They still squeak: in descending order from treble to bass in a scale which seems to Gideon to replicate the eight tones of the Mandarin dialect. He never fails to smile to himself at the private joke and Father Joaquin Ribeiro, SJ, who is the occupant of the house, is always glad that his young friend is in such a good humour and so obviously pleased to step through the door to his chaotic study. 'Good day, my son,' he greets him in his heavy accent, 'how eager you must be to commence your arduous studies,' running the words together, slurring his vowels, and gobbling the consonants in the way typical of his countrymen. The words themselves are almost perfect, as befits the polyglot missionary who is master of eight languages (two dead, three rebarbatively complicated, one which has more exceptions to its rules than rules, and the seventh plainly the work of the fiend).

'Would that my abilities matched my inclinations,' says Gideon, seating himself at Father Ribeiro's huge teak table, which could place all the officers of a regimental mess down to the lowest ensign or cornet but is simply not up to the task of bearing all the reverend father's manuscripts. More folios and volumes line the walls or are piled like rock-formations on the floor. There are an ancient bronze globe, a brass telescope, and a collection of the primitive instruments of navigation which Father Ribeiro's countrymen employed to guide them on their first voyages to the East. 'Throw down those papers, my son,' he exhorts Gideon, 'they are not important.'

With care, Gideon transfers the Father's forty-year-old dissertation on the nomenclature question – Father Ribeiro is numbered among those who would employ the term *Shang Ti* to describe God in the Chinese language – to one of the floor's stacks, where it reposes uneasily on the Father's translation of a wildly pornographic eighteenth-century Chinese novel into an elegant and wholly worldly French. 'And have you been able to pursue some studies without my supervision?' Father Ribeiro enquires gently. Gideon nods. 'Withdrawn in your own room from the general sight, my son?' Gideon nods in the affirmative again; he wonders what penance could be imposed for an unfavourable answer. Perhaps one hundred copies of an unusually complex ideogram, based on obscure radicals, to be depicted with a bald brush.

'Good, my son,' says Father Ribeiro, concluding his usual catechism. 'Do not let it slip your mind that your instruction is a work attended with some danger for your teachers. Any knowledge you may acquire of the Chinese language is, where the mandarins are concerned, a thing purloined. However, I am happy to tell you that following argument – he will always argue – I have been able to secure the services of a native teacher for you.'

Gideon looks pleased at first, then, as it occurs to him that he may lose the companionship of Father Ribeiro, says hesitantly, 'Father, of course, I'm sure that I am delighted that my studies may be advanced. I calculate that my obligations to you are already heavy, but I shall be sorry, most cast down in a personal point of view, that I shall no longer…'

Father Ribeiro's swarthy face breaks into a smile of infinite benevolence. 'My dear …Gideon …you labour under obligations which, how do I say in English, are entirely of your own devising. It is always a pleasure with me….no, I should say, it is my pleasure to serve my old friend Harry O'Rourke. I reciprocate the many small services he has performed on my account these last thirty years and more. To find you, yourself, the young friend of his recommendation, a youth of such application, such distinguished talents, may I say, such personal charm and goodness, is additional happiness which was entirely unexpected. Of course, I do not say I would make such efforts so cheerfully were you to apply any knowledge you may obtain towards proselytising in the interests of your belief.'

Gideon smiles: 'Of course, Father, I guess the endeavour of saving souls is much like any other business: one hardly recruits competitors.' He knows he can make these Walter-like remarks to the good Father, a man of latitude in all respects, and Father Ribeiro does indeed take the pleasantry in the spirit in which it was offered, laughing as he says: 'Would Mr Jardine lend Mr Dent a ship? I think not. Charter, certainly. But then one cannot lease the command of a language, unless it were one learned in infancy and forgotten by the adult. On the question of the missionaries despatched by the, you will forgive me, heretic churches, only one has acquired more than the rudiments. I refer, of course, to my friend and late great adversary, Dr Morrison. An excellent scholar – but one whose converts, after labours lasting a quarter of a century, numbered less than the fingers of his hands. Well, *de mortuis*…'

Gideon feels he ought to set the balance straight, though he is no bigot. 'The medical missionaries sent in recent years by the Universal Reformed …'

Father Ribeiro holds up his hand. 'My son, we talk of the cure of souls, not the repair of bodies. An ophthalmic hospital offering gratuitous treatment? My son, we are concerned with opening the eyes of men to their Maker.'

Gideon decides to abandon a subject potentially so contentious even where a man as broad-minded as Father

Ribeiro is concerned. He says, 'Father, I trust that this will not mean the termination of our interviews?'

'Gideon, my son, my dear young friend, this would be to distress me unutterably, and further,' he adds slyly, 'how should I set about reclaiming your immortal soul, in such dire jeopardy at the present straits? You shall not remain the pagan you are.'

'Heretic, Father, heretic,' says Gideon.

'Well, my dear young heretic, your tutor in any case cannot come to visit you in your quarters without exciting suspicion and you yourself most certainly could not penetrate to his and leave with your person intact and your clothes unsullied. No, my son. Therefore, you must receive both him and the lessons he has to inculcate where else but here?'

'Father,' says Gideon anxiously, 'this is to expose yourself to danger, at least inconvenience, on my ...'

'Tush!' says Father Ribeiro, whose knowledge of the language with more exceptions to its rules than rules extends to its idiom and expletives, many garnered during an interesting association of more than three decades with his Irish friend Harry O'Rourke, who has lapsed so many times his immortal soul ought to be black and blue. Not once in those twenty years has Harry been to confession. (What an interesting catalogue that will eventually be, thinks Ribeiro grimly.) Harry *has* been spotted in attendance at a service or two. Father Ribeiro is ungenerous enough to believe that Harry was present for purposes which were strictly professional, reconnoitring the House of God the better to commit its internal proportions and furniture to memory rather than his own soul to its Habitant. Harry's expert eye certainly wandered.

'My Chinese teacher,' Gideon interrupts Father Ribeiro's own wanderings, 'I may take it he does have some knowledge of English? One of the European languages would be useful, though my own knowledge is but scanty.'

'Not one word of the English language does he possess,' says Father Ribeiro cheerfully. 'Better so, than he should have any acquaintance with the corrupt species of Canton English.'

'That fractured lingo,' says Gideon, quoting their mutual friend.

'Indeed. To speak a depraved language will result in the eventual degradation of the speaker's own mind. No, Ow knows only Chinese and the Latin I have taught him. That is, he is master of two written languages and speaks many more.'

'How can that be?'

'There is but one written form of Chinese, the one to which you address yourself. The different spoken dialects, the court dialect, for example, and the dialect of Canton, which may be as different as French from Spanish, share the same written form. The ideographs are merely pronounced differently.'

Gideon is relieved. 'The one form is bad enough.'

'Ow is a native of this region and therefore his "baby" tongue, as I like to call it, was the *patois* of Canton. However, as a man of letters and ambitious functionary, he was obliged to learn the court or Peking dialect in addition.'

'That being the language of the mandarins and the adjudicators of the literary competitions?'

'Indeed. Ow was himself once a mandarin, that is he was a licentiate of the examinations in expectation of office but those anticipations were thwarted. It is a long story, but he has no reason to love the mandarins. I will myself continue to oversee your studies and mediate between you and Ow for some time. Patience, I regret, is not his strongest suit. Ah ... I should not use that expression. Ow would be wasted as an instructor in the elementary principles, but when you have progressed beyond your first stumbling steps in the language he will prove a most excellent interlocutor and guide. In the meantime, my son, apply yourself, always apply with the greatest diligence.'

'I calculate on so doing, Father.'

'You poor Mr Eastman. Are you not too fatigued?'

'Not in the least. No exercise can be too strenuous, nor too arduous after the stupor of Canton. Our limbs cry out to be stretched.'

'Do, I entreat you, allow me at least to instruct the bearers to wait a while, so that you may rest and recruit yourself a little.'

'What these wretched, half-starved men can endeavour, I may.'

Up the hill of Taipa island, then, they continue to climb, Alice in her palanquin, Eastman talking to her through the open window. At the rear, one of the Remingtons' houseboys bears Walter's easel. Today, he'll essay a water-colour. No Aunt Remington. Alice will sketch.

Walter removes his jacket, light beige linen which is already darkening under the arms and between the shoulders. Alice sprinkles some eau de Cologne on her handkerchief, passing it to Eastman, who accepts the comfort. The cologne starts to do its work, evaporating and drawing the heat from his face. A very slight breeze ruffles his thinning hair. There is, thank God, only half a mile left. The cooling effect of draught and evaporation now makes him sneeze; his skin crawls. 'Ah, darnation,' he says to himself.

'Bless you, Mr Eastman.'

At the top they find the view they've sought. Macao lies below, across about a mile of water: Praia Grande, Monte, boats, villas. The Remingtons' house is hidden. Eastman directs the setting up of his apparatus, oversees the placing of Alice's stool. He suggests she begins with the curve of the bay, building up from there, then begins himself to paint with pleasure, commencing with a framing branch in the top right quarter. It is a strange sort of day, now overcast with clouds scudding overhead, now brilliant, the fast shadows moving over the yellow water again. Quite an interesting problem for an aspirant with water-colours. The grasses hiss and flutter. Sparrows cheep. Over the harbour the kites and buzzards circle endlessly, the latter recognisable by their square tails, the kites forked. Eastman has become oblivious to sounds now. He mixes his colours with urgency, as his conception seizes him. The water he sees as primrose where it is in the sun and chocolate under shade (not so bizarre to any who have tried to capture that part of the estuary under those conditions), then the clouds, the horizon, where all three seem to meet, he fuses in a play of light and the hawks, as inverted black Ws or figure 3's, squiggled with a movement of the brush, are the clasps which hold the planes of sky and sea together. He thins the sky with a film of water, darkens a patch of cloud. Stands back and feels excited. He has worked fast, for him.

'May I spy?' It is Alice, whom he has been neglecting in his absorption.

'But, Mr Eastman, there is no tree here.'

'No tree?'

'Yes, the branch which runs along the top of your picture, it does not exist.'

Eastman stares at her.

'Is there something wrong, Mr Eastman? Pray, do not look so.'

Eastman pulls himself together. 'I beg your pardon, Miss Remington. Most humbly I do. No, it is but a device, not exactly a convention, perhaps an accepted fiction, by which I may draw your eye in, make the scene complete and… somehow more outstanding.'

Alice seems to accept this. She proffers her drawing, which is certainly an improvement on her first efforts in the garden, with the perspective basically correct. Eastman appears in it at his easel. 'Ah, yes, you see, what I do through artifice you, Miss Remington, have accomplished through instinct. You see how my small figure will give an approximation of the scale of your landscape. If you will forgive my churlishness and insufferable egotism, my head as depicted by yourself defies the law of proportions.'

Alice laughs. 'I recall our lesson. The child's head, was it not five times to the body? I forget.'

'I calculate from the largeness of my head here, Miss Remington, that you must suppose me either very immature for my years or else monumentally vain.'

Alice's laughter tinkles again. Then she scrutinises Eastman's work with closer attention. 'How, how…*stormy* it is in your painting, Mr Eastman. So tranquil, yet so full of a force impending.'

This is better, Eastman thinks, adjusting his view of Alice again. 'No, no, it is quite calm, though I do take your point. I have tried to capture the true essence of the day. The effect of *chiaroscuro* I was explaining to you when we were drawing at the Monte Fort the previous week – I have tried in my way to accomplish it. It is hard for a mere *dilettante*. Harry, in remarking Mr Gainsborough's ability to…'

Plop! goes a large raindrop on the back of Walter's hand, then another. 'Gracious heavens!' They look up from Walter's work, which has so absorbed them, to a contemplation of the real sky. This has darkened very considerably and the clouds are black and many. A gust hits their faces and then heavy rain falls in its train. They run for the palanquin, Eastman taking the opportunity to help Alice under her arm. Unfortunately, there is room inside for only one: so Eastman, not to mention the bearers, are wet through by the time they descend to the boat, which will take them back to the Praia. The painting? Washed out by the rain, unfortunately, so it will never hang with the O'Rourke on Eastman's wall. Still, Walter is not unmindful of the other irony it contained. He is uncertain whether to be cast up or down by it, really: that his eye surpassed his ability to interpret what it recorded, that his metaphor of a transient moment should have contained, unconsciously, the seeds of an actual development. A cheroot consoles.

Venerable Ow shoots his prodigious cuffs, a foot wide without exaggeration, and bends his hands back at the wrists in a mantis-like way. What a queer old fellow he is, thinks Gideon for the tenth time. He simply cannot make Ow out. At first he thought it was because of 'the dark intricacies of the mandarin mind'. (Ribeiro just smiled). Now he has started to see Ow as a true personal eccentric, one whose repertoire of quirks, moods, and old-maidish fancies he has just begun to plumb. What whimsical airs the old fellow likes to give himself! A young girl couldn't be vainer! or an old dowager more crotchety. Gideon has just learned to interpret his huffs as huffs, his spasmodic irritability and sly jokes for what they are. Considering the mental anguish involved in learning Chinese, Ow is a good name for an instructor. The language, says Father Ribeiro, half-jokingly, has been specially designed by the devil to insulate the Chinese from the glad tidings of Redemption contained in the Gospel. The onomatopoeiac teacher himself is small, fragile, quite bald (which relieves him of the degrading necessity of wearing his hair in the queue imposed by the Manchu conqueror) and the possessor of the longest fingernails Gideon has ever seen. They are quite six inches long, covered in sort of scabbards which protect their brittle length. They click as Ow takes up his brush or when he touches the little thimble-cup of tea Gideon ceremoniously pours for him at the beginning of their lesson. Father Ribeiro has versed his young friend in Chinese etiquette, explaining that what he must inculcate in himself is an attitude of mind as well as the discipline and powers of retention so necessary to build up a store of recognisable characters. 'What is asked of you, my son,' says the reverend Father, 'is to *accept*, to become a blank sheet on which will be inscribed the accumu-lated literary wisdom of a passage of whole centuries. The spirit of the lands from which we came is, alas, to enquire, to tear down, to scrutinise. To learn the language of the Chinese is perforce for you to become something of a Chinese yourself or at least to adopt for a while their habits of thought.'

'Then, Father, was there not a danger of you losing your Faith while you were acquiring the rudiments of the language?'

'No, *au contraire, mon cher,* faith is precisely the endowment of the Chinese mind; that, and a certain fortitude which is not ignoble. But that their faith is misplaced, it shames many of your compatriots and mine. They are as sturdy vessels full of a loathsome liquid, but empty those same vessels and fill them instead with the wholesome doctrines of enlightenment and a brimming Christian charity, and they shall be as the glorious acquisitions of God.'

'Hmm.'

'Regard this obstinate old fellow here,' says Ribeiro, indicating Ow, 'a man good so far as man may be good, though not free, you will observe, from his little vanities. What a convert for the Church he would be, with his mental powers and constancy. He is the stuff of martyrs. But no, he is lost in his wicked wiles and perversity.'

Gideon looks nervously at Ow but reassures himself. The teacher knows no English after all. However, all but the Anglo-Saxon component of the tongue seems permeable to the old fellow's understanding and he certainly knows he is the subject of the conversation, for he chuckles mischievously and says, *'Obstino invictusque,'* and sips his tea with great complacency.

'Invincibly ignorant, you old Machiavel,' Father Ribeiro says, with the liberty of a friendship so old and so intimate it is no longer possible to tell whether it is love or contempt which unites.

'Ha-hum, harumph,' says Gideon, artificially clearing his throat. Ow gives vent to a burst of the birdy sounds of the northern dialect, the 'r's and 's's guttural and far back in his throat in the typical Peking style.

Father Ribeiro retorts in the same tongue with similar energy, some congenital Iberian volatility in an address otherwise as nearly perfect as his English. Gideon wonders if he is a witness to a major falling out among dear friends. It transpires they are discussing the best method by which to teach him. Ow, stickler and classicist, wishes Ribeiro to teach Gideon in the way native children progress: that is, he will learn a character and its sound, but not its meaning. Soon, he will have a sentence by rote, later a verse or 'paragraph', eventually a page, finally (and hopefully) a book or 'volume' which he will be able to recite faultlessly *without understanding a single word of its meaning!* Then, and only then, will he be taught the significance of the characters. Father Ribeiro feels that the grown man will have more incentive if he is simultaneously taught the meaning of the shapes he is learning to recognise and reproduce. Ow sticks to his guns. Ribeiro surrenders. Gideon is set, once more, to the Trimetrical Classic. While Ow enjoys his tea, cracking the occasional melon-seed between his teeth and looking extremely like a rodent now, rather than an insect, Ribeiro points to the characters and Gideon drones their sounds. Now and then Father Ribeiro corrects Gideon's pitch or pronounciation. Ow nods, beating his dainty cloth boot in time. Once, he corrects Ribeiro correcting Gideon.

CHAPTER XII

Alice Barclay Remington's journal

August 25th, 1835. And thus do I begin a new era in my
diary, committing myself all trustingly to the care of my
Maker. If this small record of my daily doings and my inmost
thoughts will serve on perusal to chasten or to humble me
in the sight of my Creator, then it will have answered some
useful purpose. Tomorrow a week in the Mercy of Jesus
Christ our Saviour and Lord, I shall celebrate my twenty-first
birthday. Oh! how solemn and momentous an occasion that
should be! On that day I shall become an adult, a woman in
name if not in fact, and should put away all girlish things
behind me. Were I a man I would come into man's estate and
Oh! were I a man, I should be the man whom no man could
master. As it is, I shall inherit the money left in trust for me
by Grandfather and have the income of course, only applying
it in accordance with Father's instructions, as Grandfather
would have wished. I shall have the grandest of dinners to
celebrate! Uncle has promised!

August 26th. Mr Eastman called in the afternoon to criticise
my progress with the drawing. He is so stern when he does
so, but I am no longer frightened of him. When I was, I
rather rose to his well-founded comments and was tart with
him, merely to conceal my inward confusion. But now I can
accept and learn with truest submission, like a real disciple.
He seems so clever and knowledgeable and besides is a most
amiable and high-minded youth! Would that all could be like
him. He came in company with Mr Chase, his friend, such a
handsome, quiet sort of boy, as I have always found him, a
fine young person, with a mind and a will of his own, though
much under his elder's influence. Mr Chase appeared
abstracted often, though always polite and attentive as is his

wont. For some unaccountable reason, his voice seems to have changed, it is more lilting, has more *range,* is more flexible and alive …and I run out of epithets for Mr Chase's voice! It is most odd – I mean Mr Chase's voice. I had some chance of speaking to this young gentleman and found that though he does not speak much, what he says is pithy, to the point, and, in short, well worth listening to. He has a sort of morbid shyness about talking about himself, not entirely unbecoming, think I, but I was able to draw him on the lives they generally lead in the Factories. Also, he spoke warmly and at length of Mr O'Rourke – who he says is a second father or perhaps uncle to Mr Eastman, and a tempering, sobering check on his wilder enthusiasms. I cannot imagine words less suitable to apply to Mr O'Rourke, for all his many good qualities (and he is a *dear),* than the foregoing, viz. temperate, sobering, etc. Mr Chase, though, smiled (not at all in an odious or superior way) and said I little knew the truth. He said Mr O'Rourke was a man of years and experience as well as genius, that – if I recollect him correctly – he would know the correct paths to follow, even if he might choose not to follow them himself. Mr Eastman, he said, is a man of great contradictions, subject to fits and starts, and unpredictable moods; his enthusiasms, while noble, and pursued obstinately to their conclusion once espoused, are Quixotic. He said it would be impossible to tell whether he would come *pro* or *contra* in any issue, that Walter would not know himself according to any rational system of calculations, and it would depend very much on the temper and frame of mind in which it found him, but once his mind was made up, he would not swerve. And who should steal quietly behind us at this moment but our topic of conversation himself who very coolly said: 'Digestion and a good cigar, and I'm yours, Gideon,' and he added a quite vulgar 'hey' – permissible, of course, in the circumstances, which were very *familiar.* He spoke with a blocked nose which rendered his words more lugubrious than they were. Mr Chase looked a little confused, but they are certainly good friends and I should imagine he would never say anything behind his friend's back that he would hesitate to speak out in a plain and manly way to his face. So he laughed, and Mr Eastman clapped him on the back. Both will be at the dinner Uncle is giving.

August 27th. Wrote to my dear family, pouring out my thoughts and feelings. A thick packet to go on the ship. A present of curious fruits to Uncle arrived from Minqua, the Hong merchant, accompanied by his red card. Such spiky, dry, brown-looking things; they seemed mere husks but were fragrant and full of juice. Uncle said they are from the far south, in Yunnan, Land of the Clouds, which apparently is almost not China at all. Also some preserved Chinese fruits, I did not like these.

August 28th. Rode on the Praia in the cool of the evening with Mr Arden, Third Chaplain to the British Superintendent of Trade. One would never think he was a man of the cloth! Later, he galloped on the beach, waving his hat. He rides to hounds in his native Northumberland.

August 29th. Rained hard all day. I feared it might be a presage of one of the mighty hurricanes, called typhoons, such as the one which struck after Mr Eastman and I returned from Taipa island. Houseboy said, 'No, Missy Lissee, just rain, rain, no wind.' The rain falls in white columns, it is so heavy, turning slowly in what slight wind there is. I hear the water running, its *guggling* (there is a word I could only use, or invent, for my private diary) and the splashing and echo it makes in the drains and gutters of the garden. I watch through the streaky window and feel content and happy with my mortal lot. Rain *will* have this effect on me. Mother used to tell us children that Father proposed to her on such a day in Grandmother's drawing room in Salem, that he put a hand on the rocking-chair while kneeling and fell forwards on his face! Aunt Remington hid his umbrella, she says, so that he was forced to stay in the house and make his plea!

August 30th. Bright sun, but still too damp to sit in the garden. Mr Chase, Mr O'Rourke, Mr Arden, Mr Veale (keeper of the fine aviary), and sundry British gentlemen (both traders and officials) to tea on the verandah.

August 31st. Mr Eastman sent a charming cartoon of himself. His trousers rolled around his calves (which in life, of course, are not the lean shanks he caricatures), feet thrust into a mustard-bath, grog steaming by his hand, and sneezing into a handkerchief. *'Dauber seized by consumption',* runs the legend below. Poor man! He really should have brought an umbrella that day. I grow fond of this youth. He will come tomorrow; he has promised. Aunt and I busy all day with preparations, commanding servants, hanging lanterns. Oh! I hope most earnestly that it does not rain. Tomorrow Aunt and I will put each other's hair up. We do not trust our native servants. The dress I had made from the patterns brought Aunt on the *Audacieuse,* I shall wear for the first time.

The water magnifies a strange sound, a new sound. It carries over the brown flood which is now streaming into the sea; it bounces off the amphitheatre of tall hills and steep islands which encircles the Bocca Tigris; echoes and re-echoes around the heights and back over the water. The river knows the mewing of the gulls, the harsh call of the white sea-eagle, the chant of the boatmen, the cry of the dugong, the creak of ropes and boards, and the varied music of its own waters. But this is like nothing else. It is a giant's panting, the wheezing of some ailing sea-monster, but regular, monotonous, unfailing. And as it nears, and one hears the sound itself, rather than its reproduction off the cliffs, it has an explosive quality to it, and behind that, a steady, deep thump. It starts to sound now like...a *sneeze!* Helpless, although regular and in series. At-choo, huff-puff, *at-you, at-you.* Dirty smoke appears, blown round the small headland of Chuenpi. Now there's also a splashing underlying the throbbing and the wheezing and the sneezing. And here it is: the devil-ship to end all devil-ships. To the thunderstruck fishermen, spreading last night's nets and catch on the rocks, to the scurrying soldiers on the parapets of the fort, to the bewildered, gesticulating mandarins, who believe they see the work of a sorcerer, the demon craft is plainly on fire. Flames, as well as smoke, belch out of the long metal pipe in its centre. Wheels, like the irrigation wheels of the paddy, thrash the water. It moves, slowly, admittedly, but it moves, against wind and against the river's mighty will. Not a sail is spread. On the other side of the narrows, a sampan whirls past, carried at speed by what until now has been an irresistible conjunction of natural forces. They steer quickly away from the panting, glowing devil-boat, narrowly missing a reef of jagged rocks. In the bowels of the devil-boat a bell rings. The sneezing fits increase in incidence, the thumping deepens. The foam about the wheels, froth before, thickens and to the natives assumes the appearance of buffalo-curd. The strength of the opposing current in the narrows is prodigious. Flotsam spins past at a rate of several knots. But, if anything, the devil-ship is making greater headway. It butts the current, rising to the swell, cutting the waters with its knife-edged bow. Now it passes under the forts, their antique cannon and intimidated soldiery. Gongs beat, flags are brandished, tiger-masks flaunted. In vain: the fire-boat is so much more impressive. It is smaller by far than the devils' sailing-ships, which would tower over it; yet they are helpless against an opposing wind and an adverse tide, where this conquers both. Elements, that is. For the craft appears to be unarmed, except for the lightest of brass signalling guns at the stern, unlike the unwieldy floating batteries which have forced ingress in the past and then been thwarted by the river's wiles. Wisely, the new devil-ship has not asked for a pass, for it is doubtful if one would have been vouchsafed. In due course, the reports of the Bocca magistrate and commandant will reach Canton, although by then the floating inhabitants of Whampoa will have been able to see the new arrival for themselves.

'Oh, I shall sorely miss the two of you. How dull will be my days, as I occupy myself with the circumscribed round of the spinster in Macao.' Alice is half-joking and half-serious.

Gideon smiles wanly. He is not sure whether he is pleased or relieved. On the one hand, he will certainly miss Alice; though he will be glad to be undisturbed. On the other, it means he will have Walter to himself. Strange how he does not resent Alice's interest in Walter, but is made uneasy by Walter's neglect of him for Alice. A queer world, and that's a fact.

'My dear Miss Remington,' says Eastman, like Alice not entirely without an edge of real meaning behind the persiflage, 'your admirers are legion. How will the departure of a brace of the conquered be noticed?'

'By the principal, naturally, Mr Eastman, and you are very cruel and flippant. I do not have a legion of admirers. I certainly do not encourage them, if I do.'

How the misogynist O'Rourke would relish that last conjunction of contradictory statements! thinks Gideon, who feels himself getting older and wiser by the day. Sometimes he feels *very* cynical. He is thinking of taking up smoking, maybe a pipe, but is afraid Walter will laugh at him.

'Then it is you who are cruel not to give them a crumb of consolation,' says Eastman, 'the poor fellows. You break hearts, Miss Remington, truly you do. Was that not a killing little gown, Gideon? Did not His Excellency the Dezembargador appear peculiarly smitten? And Mr Arden the chaplain, did his thoughts not become rather slaughterous than priestly when his hopes of the last dance were dashed?'

'Who was it but you who so rudely dashed poor Mr Arden's hopes of the concluding whirl,' says Alice, laughing despite herself, 'You are very wicked and must not blame the consequences of your own wrongdoings on others, who may be entirely innocent.'

'What is this unseemly uproar?' asks Aunt Remington, coming up the garden. 'I do calculate you young people must be laughing at me.'

Our two young heroes are on their feet at once, vying to surrender their chairs to Aunt.

'Thank you, Mr Chase,' she says, 'I know you at least would not mock my grey hairs.'

'Your one grey *hair*, Aunt,' says Alice, 'which was not being

137

remarked on. It is, alas, I who am the butt of these ungallant gentlemen.'

As we know, Alice and her aunt get on well. Uncle can be a bit of a frump, although fortunately the visits to Macao of seniors and juniors in the house of Meridian do not exactly overlap (as at present). On the whole, the partners leave the Factories later and return to them sooner than the clerks. Besides, apart from the close season of the south-west monsoon, which is now ending, the young men even during the busy season can get short leave of a few days in Macao. With an earnestness, therefore, which she is unable entirely to conceal, Alice alludes to such possibilities: 'I do trust that I shall not be entirely bereft of your guidance during the winter, Mr Eastman. I had felt myself improving greatly, or as much as lay within my powers.'

'Oh, your work is really most accomplished now. There is little to be desired, and to be sure, if there is any credit, it is entirely due to yourself for your own perseverance. But certainly, I shall be happy to continue to view what you have drawn and pass on what advice I may, whenever I have the occasion and opportunity to be down from Canton.'

Aunt Remington seems to smile to herself, but whatever thoughts she has are inscrutable to the young people.

'You may contrive to send up your sketches on the passage-boat, and Walter append his criticisms,' says Gideon helpfully. 'Might he not even set you some exercises in ascending order of difficulty for you to complete and post to him for his remarks?'

'You seem to have a regular system of things already set up, sirrah,' says Eastman. 'The fertility of your invention never ceases to astound me. How is it that you are so very quick in solving other people's perplexities when they themselves have barely addressed their minds to them?'

'Ah,' says poor Gideon, who kicks himself for his indiscretion. *No one must have the smallest suspicion.* But Aunt Remington has had her interest aroused.

'Indeed,' she says, 'Mr Remington believes the river-traffic will be utterly transformed. The *Jardine* steamer from Aberdeen, I hear, made her passage through the Bogue to Whampoa with the most miraculous swiftness.'

'Swiftly,' Eastman says, 'and with a sublime disregard of the river's will. She moves quite independently. Communication between here and Canton must soon become a matter of hours, under any circumstances, rather than days and nights. The same wholly altered the character of the log-trade from Natchez to New Orleans.'

'Of course,' says Gideon, 'we should not think of making use of the bark of Morpheus to convey the productions of Apollo.' He had been going to say Venus, but remembered himself. Really, he appalls himself sometimes.

'Oh, one should not be too particular in affairs of this kind,' says Alice. 'Surely the sooner is the better in all cases. It is but the conveyance after all. Do you not think so, Mr Eastman?'

Gideon looks keenly at Walter and is a little disappointed when he says, 'We shall have to take our opportunities as we find them, Miss Remington.'

Opportunism is precisely what he does not associate with Walter.

Chapter XIII

From THE CANTON MONITOR

November 19th, 1835

Tranquillity reigns on the river. In the Outer Estuary and on the Inner Waters calm prevails. Trade, this season, has gone on, as it opened, in circumstances of the most perfect normality. Such is the state of affairs which applies to both the 'open' trade and the sales of drug as carried on around the anchorage of the opium-hulks at Lin Tin island. The 'fast crabs' and 'scrambling dragons' continue to ply, unmolested, in full sight of the government's revenue cruisers, who seem content with their squeezes as presently exacted.

Silver paid into the treasuries on account of opium deliveries continues, as it has done for the past more than two score years, to exceed considerably the amount of specie used to pay the Chinese for their teas. Yet tea remains a drug on the London market and the ready supplies continue to overhang and depress the prices at the auctions. We blame the influx of petty new speculators who have invaded Canton to take what pickings they may but our readers are familiar with our views on that contentious topic, and the respectable agree already with us on this point. Our preaching will hardly convert those directly interested in the opposite camp.

The Factories now present a scene of bustle and animation, such as can only gladden the hearts of all the foreign residents, of whatever persuasion, denomination, or 'house'. How different from a twelve month previous! We welcome back all those gentlemen from Macao, who rejoined our number recently, including our 'hunting' friends who favoured us with their thoughts at the end of the last season. We hope that they have been suitably 'chastened' and enjoyed their stay among the Portuguese. If they have wives, now must they be chaste again in Canton and if they are so very unwise as to 'pot' at us again, then we must chase them from the field.

HBM's Chief Superintendent of Trade, we learn, has also removed from Macao. Henceforth, his station shall be a floating one. He has taken his establishment aboard that pretty craft, the *Louisa,* which will remain off Lin Tin island. We believe Sir George Robinson has removed from Macao, doubting that place to be sufficiently secure from the jealousy of the Chinese. Certainly the small Portuguese garrison, even were they to be instructed to defend Sir George and his staff, could not long prevail against the Chinese, pressing, as they would, from behind the Barrier, in superior numbers. We do not mean by this to sully the honour, disparage the determination, nor belittle the military genius of our Oldest Ally, merely to point out that a peninsula, such as Macao finds itself situated upon, is not a position which is either readily or easily defensible. (We shall not remind our hosts of the time when the British took the place, necessity compelling...) Nor, perhaps, will our Allies need reminding as to the problems of general strategy which arise in defending a peninsula. At any rate, Sir George's ark may in the meantime answer very well as a floating island, impregnable as it is uncomfortable. It will do for the winter, but the open anchorage around Lin Tin will not serve to protect against the typhoons of the summer. We would urge the Home Authorities through Sir George to consider well yet again the taking of some Insular Position along the southern coast of China.

Eastman wrinkles his mutilated nose in disgust, looking – Gideon thinks – like a frog in his high-collared, bottle-green coat. With theatrical disdain, he ceremoniously tears the *Canton Monitor* December 3rd, 1835, in two, then into quarters, and yet again takes three strides to the south window of Gideon's room, 13 American Hong. 'Now, Walter,' Gideon says, 'recollect kindly you fling those mutilated pages from my verandah. I fear not the wrath of the editor of the *Canton Monitor,* who may or may not be passing by, but I should tremble to arouse the indignation of our own compradore. Besides, the only persons inconvenienced, I calculate, are certainly not the *Monitor* but the coolies who must dispose of the waste paper.'

Always an advocate of the primacy of the rational voice, Eastman arrests his arm in mid-throw. 'True, Gid, true,' he mutters.

'And, after all,' Gideon points out, again very reasonably, 'by destroying one copy of his journal we actually benefit the editor, for whoever might have been able to peruse your copy *gratis* will now have to purchase one himself, thereby augmenting the sales of the *Canton Monitor* and also, therefore, the income of its proprietors.'

'Gideon, you are a most insufferably egregious young prig.' Eastman throws the crumpled pieces on to the fire, which has been a comfort on this unusually cold evening. 'You are fast taking on a very base mercantile character.'

'But we are merchants.'

'There are merchants, I guess, and there are merchants. We are not the likes of Jardine at any rate.'

'That is a fact. Still, we ought never to despise those who provide us with our livelihoods, and Mr Corrigan and Mr Remington are on terms of the most perfect amity with Messrs Jardine and Matheson, not to say Dent and Innes. You are surely not saying the partners of our house are grasping and small-minded men?'

'My dear Gideon, there is nothing small-minded about the way Jardine has grasped his fortune. It amounts to an overweening rapacity.'

'Well, whoever is the patron of the *Monitor* is the richer by your fifty cents. In fact, though you profess to despise it so and never fail to roast the editor, you must, I calculate, be one of its most regular readers. Why not, therefore,' Gideon adds in all innocence, 'take out a subscription and save yourself money?'

'Gideon!' roars Eastman. 'I warn you, sir.'

'Of what, sir?' asks Chase, retreating round the table.

'Of the toe of my boot, darn your insolence.'

142

Gideon flees, with Eastman in pursuit. Over go the chairs, Eastman ably jumping them as they lie on their sides; then a jug and basin; finally a pot of ink and a quill and...'I am so sorry, Gideon, I have scattered your papers. Forgive me. Let me fix...but what is this?'

Spilled on the floor lie three black bricklets and five or six tufted bamboo sticks. Eastman recognises the latter as the brush-pencils employed in Chinese calligraphy. He picks up the small tablets, which have a Chinese character stamped on them. A faint fragrance rises and, yes, on sniffing the objects, which are in fact perfumed cakes of the finest native ink, he confirms the scent emanates from them. 'What are these?'

Gideon quickly takes the inks from Eastman and gathers the pencils together. 'They are, er, *Celestial soap.*'

'I should think they rather blacken the countenance than clean it. Which might, I allow, explain the condition of some of the faces of the filthier denizens of this city.'

'Well, I expect if they wear white to a funeral, they are certainly capable of fixing their toilets with black soap.'

'Ha! We have a wit here. Is it not true they also begin their books from the back?'

'Is that a fact?' Gideon enquires. 'That is a "rum notion", as old Harry says.'

It will be noted that this reply, though disingenuous, is not actually a falsehood, as was the prevaricating answer to Eastman's earlier question about the 'soap', which was distinctly slippery of our young hero. This is what comes from mixing with Jesuits.

Eastman, though, has picked up a stray fragment of the *Canton Monitor* which has missed the fire and is shrivelling and curling up in the heat like a salted fish on rocks. By the way he holds it, face creased, nostrils twitching, it might as well be a rotten fish. 'Bah!' he says, scrutinising the broken sentences on the scrap, and throwing it into the flames. It starts to scorch and then go brown; then, before it is properly consumed, rises up on the hot air and is wafted up the chimney. 'The pen mightier than the stake and pyre?' he observes gloomily.

Gideon pats him on the back. 'Do you calm yourself. I declare that you are obsessed with the miserable rag.'

'I am.'

'Well, but consider this, if you will allow me to observe – the *Monitor* is merely an organ of opinion, not a creator of it, still less a mould in which any in our little community would choose to shape his thoughts. Will it influence anyone who can see the true face of selfishness and brutality in its sentiments into adopting a mode of behaviour which they know to be dishonourable? Of course not. Nor does it really confirm its adherents in their thought or practice, for they already are the most shallow and selfish of men, concerned only with their own precious skins and futures. It but reflects an attitude of mind with which we are already familiar. How can it achieve anything which is important? Would you seize all the mirrors in the Factories, for that is all it is? Walter, you must see this.'

'Yes, yes,' Eastman bursts out, 'but it is a most outrageous provocation to me. I despise the rag, its patrons, its opinions, and the humbug who edits it. I do detest all it stands for.' Eastman actually clenches his fist, and places it over his heart.

'Drink some water and calm yourself. Here.' Really, Walter is so volatile Gideon expects steam to vent through his ears, like the experiment he saw conducted in Boston with potassium and sea-water, surely no more volatile a combination than Eastman and opium. Eastman rights a chair, jabs a cheroot into the feeble coals the compradore provides (far less ardent than himself), puts his long legs over the fender, and commences puffing.

'Perhaps we may compose another letter,' Gideon suggests, thinking it might do Walter rather than the *Monitor's* readership good. Eastman sucks away, blows two leisurely smoke-rings, rubs one boot against another, and, long after Gideon has decided Walter was too abstracted to have heard him, drawls: 'By your own argument, that would be, I expect, a most superfluous and profitless exercise. It would, I imagine, be the greatest self-indulgence, for what good would it do except to relieve our own feelings? I should say *my* own feelings, for I know you do not fully share them.'

Stung, Gideon says: 'You don't do me justice. How often do you fail to do so. It is true I am not so vehement against the purveyors of the drug as you, but I recognise the drug itself as a bane, none the less. You hate a, a....an ideal thing in a philosophical point of view. But I fear its real effects upon the people I see around me, a people who might be our equals in every respect, if not our superiors, were it not for the crushing hand of the ignorant and venal government which holds them in thrall. I don't know why you hate the Free Traders so, but I believe it is hate which moves you and not a softer feeling and more kindly for the Chinese.'

'Oh!' – and it is no very understanding Oh! but an extremely sarcastic interjection.

An uncomfortable silence follows. Gideon's face is hot and flushed. Eastman continues puffing, staring into the red coals. Gideon picks up a copy of *The Gentleman's Magazine*. He feels terrible. It is he who has attacked Walter but he who feels hurt. At length Eastman throws his cigar-butt into the greying embers, pulls up his slack trousers, yawns, and stretches to his full six feet. Gideon looks timidly over the top of his periodical. 'I, er, Walter, I wish ...that is, I trust...'

'Good night, Gideon.'

'Walter...'

From the stairs. 'Yes?'

'No, I forget my words.'

'I will see you at the boat-house at six o'clock in the morning.'

'Oh, *fine,* Walter, capital.'

'Bring small-swords and a second.'

Alice Barclay Remington's journal

February 12th, 1836. A terrible fit of the 'blue devils' today. I moped about the house all day, a thoroughly disagreeable sight for Aunt, and vented my ill-humour and spleen upon the servants. Oh! the spinster's lot is a humdrum one anywhere. How much the more so in this little out-of-the-way portion of the globe, where I languish for want of the society of my dear family and friends at home. Matilda Bunyard, who was rather the friend of Harriet Hardwicke than mine, wrote to me from home. She is engaged and her betrothed is an attorney-at-law from Boston, a Mr Johnson. I do not know him. Soon I shall be an old maid. Perhaps my present thoughts, so gloomy, are but the natural reaction after the festivities and celebrations of the end of the last year. This is an unnatural life which we lead here. Either we are full of the most unnatural dash and gaiety, with scarcely time to think, or the next moment plunged into despond and a terrible species of inanition. It is a melancholy condition for a young girl and conducive hardly to a good balance and salutary cheerfulness. I am too melancholy to write more today.

February 20th, 1836. On the Praia Grande today, walking with Mr Arden, we encountered Mr O'Rourke, the painter, and a companion. Mr Arden espied them first. Mr O'Rourke was under one of the spreading banyan trees, seated on a whitewashed stone which had, I suppose, been dressed by a China Man. Another such stone served as table between himself and his acquaintance. I say acquaintance because I may, I trust, hardly describe such a person as a fit companion for a gentleman like Mr O'Rourke (which, it is generally conceded, Mr O'Rourke is in the last resort, although a little eccentric and loose in his appearance – matters forgivable in an artist). But his companion was a low, ruffianly-looking, greasy man in a shabby and dusty habit. His face was swarthy, his fingernails as he moved his chessmen (for that is what they were amusing themselves at) rank, and his teeth when he laughed – which he did rather too much in a high-pitched way – brown and broken. And, Oh! lest I forget (as if it were possible to forget), his mirth emitted a most powerful aroma, the reverse of wholesome, of that potent bulb, the garlic, which seems equally beloved of the Latin and the China Man. For he was a Portuguese. Even though his habit, his cassock I should say, was black and of the priestly cut, I would not have taken him for a man of religion. (His hat – and I forget the word of the sect for it – he had placed on a stone beside their flagon! and wore on his head a red and white spotted kerchief, which I recognised as both ancient and Mr O'Rourke's. Mr Arden greeted Mr O'Rourke politely, though of the opposite religion, and would have fain got away without acknowledging Mr O'Rourke's opponent (and his own, of course!) but that in the most hail-fellow-well-met way (and with, by the by, a great blast of garlic) he bade Mr Arden a 'Good day!' which Mr Arden acknowledged coldly, although (as one would expect of a gentleman such as he is) with the most perfect correctness. He is, Mr Arden informed me, a priest of the Romish sect and in fact a member of that conniving and subtle order, the Jesuits. He is a missionary and has illegally resided in Macao. He is reputed an excellent linguist; although, as Mr Arden says (who rightly scorns to learn an inferior tongue), one can admire the accomplishment, while reprehending the purpose to which it is put.

Mr O'Rourke has been recently to the Factories to execute a number of commissions (I *do* trust a portion of his remunerations found their way back to Calcutta, where dwell his deserted wife and three children). He said the great scare of the month previous when the fire in Carpenter's Square had threatened to spread to the Factories themselves had caused great consternation, not least among the Hong merchants, who feared the obstructions and squeezes of the mandarins had it come to rebuilding those establishments in these uneasier times. Mr Chase, he told me, and Mr Eastman, my good friend, were both well, though without a great deal to occupy them. (Why, then, should they not correspond more often? Out of sight is, I expect, out of mind where these young gentlemen are concerned once they are installed again in their splendour with their servants and their hookahs and their claret.) I should not complain. Short as these young gentlemen's time was in Macao at the last festive season, Mr Eastman was again unstinting in the attention and time he gave to my drawing. Might I be too vain to imagine he found my company not altogether a thing monotonous? But, alas, their stay was all too short.

Whilst Mr O'Rourke spoke to me, Mr Arden looked this

way and that, and it was quite comical to watch him strike his boots with his cane, scuff the dust, and harrumph and huff, always avoiding the eye of the chess-players. At length the Portuguese priest made a move which quite drove Mr O'Rourke into a corner and it seemed there would be no escape for him (Oh, this is a very devious and cunning Order!) and Mr O'Rourke was forced to turn his attention from myself to the game in hand. Mr Arden was not sorry to go.

In the evening brushed Aunt's beautiful head of hair one hundred strokes. She seemed a little oppressed.

CHAPTER XIV

The senior partners sit on the balcony: boot-heels over the railings. Wicker creaks; there is the musical gurgle of the river. Fainter than that, the various brouhahas and domestic rituals of a mysterious but also, nevertheless, obviously homely way of life carry from the stews and mazes of the native city, the sounds punctuated in the abrupt and jagged way characteristic of the arrhythms of quotidian life. Aggregated, they may form the regular beat of history. From the billiard-room: clicks and laughter. But the senior partners are older, less humorous men, not given to recreation. Money constitutes sufficient amusement for them, the swelling figures, encroaching across the squares of their accounting-books and carried over on the succeeding columns of the ledger, a diversion enough.

Remington says: 'Yes, but our duty to ourselves coincides with our obligation to our constituents. If we go under, that is, should we be unable to meet our obligations, then those for whom we act as agents are also ruined.'

Corrigan, who never likes to commit himself to anything and can be a sombre dog, says nothing but purses his lips and shoots out a brown stream. Remington remembers him mostly as a *young* dog in the great house of Meridian & Co. in the early years of the century when both were 'writers' in Canton and Manila. This was more than thirty years ago, a very long time to have known someone or, more precisely, to have been aware of his existence. There have been great gaps in their acquaintance. The Anglo-American War of 1812 was one, when Corrigan remained in Canton with the tricky task of coexisting with the enemy on a practical, day-to-day basis in the tiny community. It was rather hard to think of fellow-exiles one had known for years as enemies overnight, hallucination made harder to accept as reality by the fact that their respective nations had been at war six months before they heard of it, while they had been carrying on their daily lives quite unaware they were drinking and playing with mortal foes. Equally, it did not escape anyone, peace might well have broken out six months before they got wind of it and were treating each other as hostiles when, in fact, they were all good friends again. Peace 'breaking out' was an aptly ironic term coined by some anonymous wit (O'Rourke subsequently claimed the accolade) since an end to fighting was as violent a shock to the carefully rewoven fabric of their everyday association as its initial eruption. During the war, Americans did not attend the British Factory's social functions and vice versa. On the other hand, taking the air on Respondentia Walk, a curt nod was permissible to employees of the Honourable Company and to the country traders (the Free Traders of the later period). A brisk 'Good day to you, sir' at the unavoidable encounters replaced the previous 'How d'you do, Dent?' or Beale, or Magniac, as the case might be. And on the river when the young men's skiffs crossed, the usual good-natured hurly-burly was replaced by a great punctiliousness, giving the other due precedence. As they had all been trading rivals, anyway, in a state of competition for goods, markets, and prices, it was in a sense quite easy to shift the game on to a higher level – the jostling between nations.

Remington was in New York, Corrigan around the delta and Macao, always anxious about British men-of-war or privateers which might be lurking a few miles out in the gulf, waiting to pounce on a Meridian ship. Arrival of British men-of-war at Whampoa caused consternation at one point, but the British commanders stayed in port, while the American vessels slipped in and out, with more discretion than usual. Corrigan, who, unlike Remington, had to work his way up through the house without the advantage of blood-ties, patronage, and a gentleman's manner, had the more taxing work – and, indeed, it was his adeptness at Canton in the war which secured him his partnership five years later. Remington renewed his association with Corrigan after the war, when he went to reform their office in Manila and made a couple of trips to Macao, where he stayed with his old associate and had the chance to smoke a cigar and drain a dram or two.

Then, eight years later, Corrigan had a short spell of two years in the Boston headquarters of the house. Their last meeting was five years ago when Remington's outward ship, consigned for Manila, by a grand fluke crossed at Rio with Corrigan's inward ship to Boston. They had time for another smoke and a glass in Corrigan's cabin.

Neither man ever had much capacity for change in him, and the middle-aged man is remarkably similar to the young. They were never callow and they will never be wise, either. Popping in and out of each other's lives has left them better friends and more familiar than an unbroken association would have done. What they see again in the other confirms them in their opinion of themselves, and the increasing greyness of the hair and the furrowing of the brow, hardly noticeable to their families, merely confirm the workings of an ineluctable process. Weight, though, in the sense of avoirdupois, is not part of this scheme, for both are lean men whom the years seem to have desiccated, brittle as the bird's nests they import.

Now Remington, oblique but persistent, returns to the theme Jasper Corrigan will not be drawn on. Remington, of course, is quite familiar with the wiles of Corrigan. 'I admit,' says Alice's uncle, 'that our founders did not participate in the trade, but then, I guess, it was hardly opened at the time and was a mere trickle compared to the torrent we see now.'

'A seventeen-fold increase since the beginning of the

century, I calculate,' says Corrigan, who has an inclination for figures and doesn't at all mind committing himself to a statement of fact.

'Now is that a fact?' Remington's surprise is assumed. Corrigan doesn't pick up whatever cue Remington intended but his jaws work grimly on the quid of tobacco their house grows in the Philippine islands, cuts, cures, and, as cigars, rolls as well, before carrying it in their leased ships.

'What we must ask ourselves, old friend,' Remington says, 'is this. Would our founders have refused to participate in the trade had it then presented the opportunities which offer themselves at the present day? It is my very considered belief that they would not have spurned them.'

On the river a mandarin boat skims past, lanterns burning at the bow and mast. From their vantage point, the partners can see the dark shapes of the crew, huddled around a brazier on their haunches at their evening meal.

Remington persists. 'As I have said, Jasper, our responsibility is not merely to ourselves, but also our constituents. There are difficult and uncertain times to come. Until the present, we have managed on the legitimate trade. True, our profits have not been so large as they might have been, had we not fine consciences. But these are dark and dangerous days. Soon, the *only* trade possible will be the clandestine traffic, simply because the mandarins have not the means to suppress it. Our cottons and fancy piece-goods may easily be impounded on the quay here, where a small chest of opium-balls, the value of a barge full of cloth, may go up the channels of the river by devious paths.'

'You are eloquent, Frederick,' Corrigan says, and after thirty years Remington is uncertain whether he is being ironic. Jasper, Remington thinks, is one of the few men of his acquaintance in Canton unsubtle enough to make such a remark without the slightest nuance other than its strict meaning. So he just says, 'Well, when the arguments are intrinsically so powerful, any speaker must appear a cogent advocate. It is not the wrapping which is well fixed but the matter.'

Corrigan says – not too quickly, and we can see how he managed at Canton during the Anglo-American hostilities –

'Speaking of fine wrapping and a small substance, I hear a young gentleman of our mutual acquaintance has been paying close and marked attentions to your niece.'

'It would be surprising if I were not cognisant of the situation, while you were.'

'I guess I didn't mean to imply that you were ignorant, old friend.'

'On the other hand it is certainly convenient to feign ignorance of some things.'

'Then I calculate you ape His Excellency, the Governor of Canton.'

'Allow me to observe that nothing would be more likely to be productive of mischief than ill-judged attempts to interfere in matters of this kind.'

'Surely so, surely. Nothing, I recall, inclines more to a course of action than to be prohibited it by one's seniors and betters. There are no two ways about that.'

A silence ensues. Remington, who knows his man, is content to have broached matters and will let Corrigan make up his own mind. He can raise the question again in the coming months. More likely, he muses, Jasper will.

While the partners manoeuvre, the young gentlemen will roister. Their usual scene of operations, Meridian's billiard-room, is tonight rowdy beyond all previous nights, and it has been a Bedlam in the past. The excuse for mass drunkenness is that it was Ridley's birthday three days ago. Since he was stuck down at Whampoa for two nights, the celebration is belated but all the more enthusiastic for that. Ridley himself is a bit under the weather and rather less than his usual boisterous self on such occasions, owing to the vast quantities of French wine and ship's rum he took while at Whampoa for the two nights. Captain Borg insisted, once he heard it was the young agent's birthday, and the old salt drank him under the table. This, as any at the Factories will testify, was a feat. However, Ridley is starting to feel better now, whether it's a question of the hair of the dog, or having been unwell out of the window before that. They'd got to the twenty-second of his twenty-six years, each heave of the boat-shed tarpaulin, customarily resorted to on these occasions, sending him nearer the ceiling, when an appalling liquid belch, and Ridley's face starting to match the green baize, alerted Johnstone to the possibility of a disaster for the table and the certain poisoning of the room's already none too sweet atmosphere. Accordingly, they hung Ridley out of the window by the heels, while he puked in a throttled way; then, the merciless young hounds tossed him four more times, while the faithful MacQuitty barked under the bulging canvas and snapped at their clattering heels. This piece of hooliganism accomplished, they leave Ridley laughing on the billiard-table and blowing his nose.

Gideon, his face flushed, has been jerking the tarpaulin as energetically as anyone, and were Jasper Corrigan here, rather than on the balcony with Remington, the partner might have second thoughts about the steadiness of this young fellow whom he has been marking for advancement in due course. In fact, Gideon is paying Ridley back for the tossing he received on his own seventeenth birthday, when Ridley was ringleader of japes which got somewhat out of hand, culminating in the house's youngest employee being knocked senseless against the ceiling. However, revenge Corrigan would understand.

'Would bathing profit Ridley?' Gideon asks Johnstone meaningfully, who says, 'I think I get your drift.'

Ridley springs off the table and picks up a cue. 'You will float with me, you rascals,' he warns.

'Oho!' says Gideon. 'The peasants resist, my lord.'

'Hither, men-at-arms,' calls Johnstone.

Is it evident enough that young MacLean has recently received a packet of the novels of Walter Scott, despatched by his Edinburgh uncle, and donated to the Meridian mess library?

'Surround this upstart cur,' says Eastman, placing a wicker basket on Johnstone's head. 'Arm from the rack,' calls MacLean, and the cues rattle. MacQuitty gets under the table, behind his master's legs, his hackles rising, and he starts to growl. 'Avaunt, Grimalkin,' says Gideon, rather inaccurately since MacQuitty is a red-blooded dog who loathes cats. 'At you, sirrah,' shouts Ridley and 'Crack!' go the cues as Johnstone parries *quinte*.

Ridley is no mean hand at quarter-sticks; his eye is keen, timing uncanny, and co-ordination superb. The blows clatter round poor Johnstone's head and, really, it's a good thing he's wearing the wicker basket. Finally, Ridley gets him where he wants him, and a smart rap on the knuckles sends Johnstone's cue flying out of his hands. 'Quarter!' cry the others in unison as Johnstone drops to his knees and MacQuitty chases the cue as it rolls along the floor. 'Varlet, you are spared,' says Ridley magnanimously, while the others cheer anachronistically and 'Bumpers!' Eastman bellows, prompting Gideon to pull the sash for the native servant. This latter, a patient and good-humoured soul, almost a family retainer in the manner of Scott, is inured to decades of youthful excess. He enters with half a dozen bottles and the chit-book, which Ridley generously signs. With the extra alcohol, things begin seriously to degenerate: there is talk, for heaven's sake, of hoisting a dead cat from the flagpole of the British Factory, where the Union Jack has not flown for eighteen months. As their predecessors had never dared perpetrate such an enormity at the height of hostilities between the two nations, it is as well that Ridley himself scotches the idea. A raid on the flower-boats, those floating palaces of perverse pleasures? A rampage down Hog Lane and into Carpenter's Square?

They settle for laying a gunpowder trail to the door of the Chinese customs house. As the fiery snake fizzes away, Ridley lobs an apple against the door. Oh, the Chinamen's faces!

Fr Joaquim Ribeiro, SJ to Gideon Chase, Esq.

> Rua Joao Evangelista
> Macao
> April 8th, 1836

My Son (and dear young friend),

I had the satisfaction and pleasure to receive the latest exhibitions of your growing accomplishment by the six o'clock passage boat this morning, when also I wended my way to the market for the buying-in of the fish, for today is Friday. (A heretic may not know this, my son.) Like the fish, your most recent compositions show the eye bright, the scales shining and firm (being the linear integuments of the characters you now so very competently are drawing) and altogether a great delight to behold. I am glad to hear you set your time aside with an hour in the morning and an hour at night, for discipline is as essential as genius and an innate ability for the language. We will build on solid foundation and, therefore, your progress must be slow at first. Do not be impatient, my son. If the first principles are secure, your later progress will be all the faster. That is, you must now master the radicals of the characters, from which you will develop the range of the scholar with many different varying ideograms. Especially, do not weaken your health by long burning of the lamp at night. I would rather you did your hard studies in the morning. Leave evening for some leisurely practice of the characters you have already acquired.

Ow cast his cloudy eye over your latest missives, and I convey and interpret his small grunt as favourable to yourself. This is most gratifying. He is in many ways a difficult man (in himself, I do believe, and not as a specimen of a Chinese scholar) and will doubtless prove a hard and exacting taskmaster to yourself in due course, but I believe he has taken an interest in what you may do, and this is most important. To proceed to details: you have confused the third character with the sixth in your first exercise. You must also strive for a more flowing touch. I do not refer to the 'grass' script, or running hand, which is a shortened and peculiarly difficult form of characters you may later master, as used in communication between cultivated *literati,* but I mean that at present your work is excessively square and childish. But we are all children at one time, my son, and must walk before we can run. And the most accomplished scholar is but as a child when compared to the wisdom of God, which passes the understanding of man. Your renderings from the Chinese into the English are excellent (that is, so far as it is permitted of me to judge, the difficulty here lying not in my understanding of the Chinese but a less than perfect ascertaining of the English language which lacks all rules itself, whereas its speakers are subject to all manner of insufferable restrictions.) The difficulty, as with any tongue, will be the translation from the English into a correct and idiomatic Chinese. It would have been a boon had you even an acquaintance with Latin in your dealings with Ow. However, let us be grateful for your extreme youth, your diligence, the quickness and keenness of your understanding, and the retentiveness of a powerful memory. I talk to myself now, my son, which is the sign of madness. Soon the summer will be here again and we may have the opportunity of renewing our personal meetings. I present you with the assurance of my most distinguished esteem and salutations. May the blessing and guidance of God always be with you.

J. Ribeiro.

Gideon Chase to Fr Joaquim Ribeiro, SJ

> No.13 American Hong
> Canton
> May 5th, 1836

My dear Father Ribeiro,

I have the honour to acknowledge your most recent communication in which you very kindly assured me of your continuing regard and interest, as well as most patiently giving me once more the benefit of your constructive criticisms. I am most sensible of the obligation your kindness puts me under. You commend my industry. Really, there is no merit where the work presents itself as of such absorbing interest to the student. I am endeavouring to alter the style of my calligraphy in the direction you suggest. I am only too aware of my manifest inadequacies in this respect but perhaps conscientiousness and application will remedy the want of natural ability in this regard.

In respect of my midnight lucubrations, I fear we are a very dissipated crew here and, all too often, the hours which should be profitably and rewardingly employed in the pursuance of my studies are wasted on the worst and emptiest revelry. However, I contrive to make an hour for myself even after such entertainment and am, I can still say, abstemious relatively in the matter of intoxicating liquors.

I regret to say I have learned that Mr Eastman and myself have been delegated to remain at the Factories during the slack season and that it is most unlikely that I shall be able to snatch more than a week in Macao in the next four months. I may console myself by reflecting that the enforced stay affords me the opportunity to perfect my grasp undistracted and that, in my case, it would have been too soon to have enjoyed the full advantage of the attention of Ow *seen-sang*. It is a source of keen regret to me to have to defer the renewal of our acquaintanceship and the instruction and benefit I may derive from your personal example. I understand that Mr O'Rourke intends making a professional visit to the Factories in the near future and perhaps it may be convenient for you to entrust to him supplies of ink and brushes as well as copies of more difficult books for me. It is too dangerous to purchase them at Canton. In the meantime I take this opportunity of enclosing my latest exercises and assuring you that I remain,

Your most obedient dutiful student,
Gideon Chase

Alice Barclay Remington to Walter Eastman, Esq.

> Rua da Conceicao 39
> Macao
> June the 1st, 1836

...Oh, but how provoking it is! How cruel, how unfair! More than for any selfish reason, I am anxious for the effects

157

upon your health of such a long and enforced stay over the hot summer months. I have often heard Uncle remark on the 'deleterious consequences' (he is a grim old Uncle!) of a Canton residence in the wet months. Doubtless, he intends to show you no favouritism. You intimated to me that it was not only the balmy zephyrs which would draw you to Macao this season, but rest assured that you should not be the only one to mourn your absence. Let it not, though, however irksome, be a consideration which will add to your burden of fretfulness in such a lonely and unhealthy place. I could not bear the thought of that. As you specifically anticipated my desire to intercede on your behalf (a most powerful, direct, and natural response on my part), I will honour your confidence in me. Knowing Uncle as I do, I doubt but that my tearful pleas would have had more than the effect of soft rain on the granite of Camoes' grotto. Oh, you too suffer the fate of exile! Yet how noble of Mr Chase to offer himself up voluntarily to share your plight! More than ever do I think him a fine and generous youth. It must have been hard for him to abandon of his own volition the prospect of balls and regattas and all the convivial diversions (such as they are) of our little society here. But then one would expect no less from a friend of yours and, of course, he has the benefit of *your* society. As to Mr O'Rourke …

CHAPTER XV

R ain distresses the river's grey surface, making it seethe like an oil painting attacked by a strong reagent. It is quite a light rain – 'hair-fine' rain, *mo mo yew,* in the local patois which Gideon has yet to acquire – and from the shelter of the balcony seems like a rolling mist. But appearances are deceptive, for when our budding linguist sticks his hand out, he feels the tiny drops prickle his skin. The far bank, more than half a mile off, is invisible where drizzle, stream, and steely mud merge in the low landscape. The drooping flag which drips in front of the American Factory pretty well sums up Eastman's spirits, for he, too, feels like a wet rag. It has been raining hard for the past week, fiercely and irregularly, relenting for an hour or so, while the roofs and vegetation steam in bright sunlight; then darkening again as the heaven's coffers open and pelt raindrops the size of the Carolus dollars the shroffs strike on the pavement. The sound on the tiles above his head is not unpleasant to Gideon. The rushing and gurgling in the gutters and storm-drains, the pattering of the drops, have provided a soothing lullaby to help him concentrate and sustain him in his lonely efforts. By lamplight he has looked through blurry windows, walked by himself through the Factory's echoing arcades in the early mornings, while the droplets swell and fall from the arches.

But this fine drizzle is irritating in the extreme, where the monsoon torrents exhilarated. As a result of the week's chronic downpours, the river is high, inconveniently, if not dangerously, so. The Factories Square and quayside walks are flooded to the depth of a foot. To go anywhere at all you have to step into a boat. Even to visit a fellow-maroon in the Factory along the way. So they are now doubly prisoners, hostages of both the elements and the Chinese. As ever, despite the state of the river, they are forbidden to ascend the terraces to the drier native quarter. However, the particular cloud of the foreigners proves silver-lined to the boat-people, who can earn a copper cash or two by plying their homes for hire. The vagueness of the river's margins brings about a corresponding unsureness in the status of the water-dwellers, who are condemned to float without putting much more than a foot on land: be born on the stream and, river-borne, die. And because uncertainty is a kind of freedom in this rigid society, they find an emancipation of the spirit. They chatter, shout at the foreigner, and Gideon would like to think their excitement and cheerfulness are not solely brought about by the prospect of gain.

Unfortunately for the boat-people, Eastman and he have

rigged up what looks very much like a coracle in which they steer erratically round the square. There are a few younger men in the other Factories; mostly, though, it is the old who have remained.

And so ... it is four o'clock. Our two friends sit on the Meridian balcony, regarding the swollen, grey waters. Gideon returns from sticking his hand out to lie back on the wicker chaise-longue next to Walter and put his feet on the balcony's edge in imitation of his senior. Eastman is glum. *'Que je m'ennuie,'* he says. As we know, Walter can be intolerably affected, but this still seems enviable sophistication to Gideon.

'Ah, Walter, when you are tired of Canton, you are tired of life.'

A great sigh indicates that this may be precisely what Walter is, tired of life.

'What is your book?'

'Tiresome at any rate.' And Eastman throws it from him. Reading the spine as it lies upright on its calf covers, Gideon sees it is Washington Irving's *Sketchbook of Geoffrey Crayon, Gent.,* which deserves a much better fate. Rip Van Winkle is pretty much who they will both feel like whenever they get to see Macao again. Eastman picks up a volume by Ridley's favourite, James Fenimore Cooper, but to divert Walter, Gideon says, 'Quaint to reflect, is it not, that we come halfway round the globe as adventurers here, when the unknown lies just beyond our own doorsteps at home.' Eastman grunts, but he fiddles for a cheroot, which is always a good sign. 'In fact,' continues Gideon, 'we commence our affairs here among a people already demi-civilised, while in America or Canada we stand on the edge merely of a vast and unknown continent, peopled in parts with the rudest savages, painted, naked, and slaughterous.'

Eastman puffs away, bringing instant relief from the mosquitoes. 'Not to mention the bison, would you say, or the mountain-lion, or the grizzly bear?'

'Yes, sir, that's so,' Gideon says eagerly.

'Hmm.' Puff-whiff-puff. It is a more comfortable and reflective silence now. 'Y-e-e-e-s,' drawls Eastman. 'But I find it stranger still that to reach the western shores of our country

160

entails a sea-voyage to the very bottom of the world, as it were, and then back up again, traversing the entire coast of the *South* American continent.'

'I guess it may take as long as a voyage to China?' Gideon prompts him, knowing the answer very well.

'Under normal circumstances the voyage is of the same duration, more or less. But should the storms in the extreme south prove unnaturally violent, and if the vessel is driven back around the Cape, it may well prove longer.'

'Gracious.'

'That is so.'

Gideon, who knows his Eastman, lets Walter have another puff or two and proceed in his own time. Which he does, saying ruminatively in a cloud of smoke, 'Johnstone, among his other deeds, has doubled Cape Horn.'

'Is that a fact?'

'Yes, floated in what he says is the most beautiful and commodious harbour he has ever viewed.'

'In the South or North Americas?'

'The beautiful, green, and desert coast of California. They saw no man.'

'Well, the steamer will result in a greater traffic on that coast, wild though it be now. Our country is on the verge of a great opening of its horizons, physical and mental.'

'Hmm. Steam, I venture to agree, will be the medium, but I rather figure it will be the railroad which is the agency of exploitation.'

'But what will make men resort to that coast in sufficient numbers to justify the prodigious labour of laying an iron track across the wastes? What body of men will accomplish that, in despite of the elements and the savages? Easier almost to cut a vast canal across the fever-swamps of the isthmus.'

'As to your first question, the answer is perfectly simple – lucre. What else? Is it not that which has brought our employers and ourselves to this dreary spot? Regarding your second question, your last comparison would, I think, have suggested the answer to you, of all people.' Eastman raises his eyebrows mischievously.

161

Gideon doesn't mind being made the butt of Walter's wit if this is to cheer him up from his present despondency. 'I am not sure what you mean.'

'No? Canals? Prodigious, ant-like industry? Our Celestial friends, of course. Ship twenty vessels full of the rascals across the Pacific or round the Cape, and there you have your mechanic force, perfectly adapted to the task. With, of course, allowance made for the proportion who will perish on the voyage.'

Gideon is horrified. 'That is a cruel suggestion and most unworthy of you, Walter.'

'I expect unworthiness has nothing to do with it, Gid. Wickedness? What is wickedness? What is its value per picul? There is only loss or profit, efficiency or procrastination. Will wickedness detract from the product's value, taint its flavour? Is it some form of imperfect packing? Did the sugar on the raspberry tarts you ate in your youth taste the worse for being sweetened with the tear of slavery – for it should have tasted salt, but it did not. Did you think of the nigger who cut the cane? You did not. Merely to exist is to be involved in the system others have created to tend your daily needs.'

'Monstrous, Walter, monstrous.'

'There is a Cape Horn of the mind, too, which is as difficult to double as the real. Monstrous? Yes, I allow that its waves are monstrous.'

'But, to pursue your analogy, you seem almost to glory in the shipwreck.'

'Myself? No. You misunderstand me. I would rather rely on my own arithmetic and experience than the treacherous fires you would light at the cliff-top to drive me upon the rocks.'

Now, as Gideon starts to look extremely perturbed, Eastman laughs in what is for that young man quite a kindly way. 'Ah, heaven help me, what a villainous wretch am I to torment your poor understanding so.'

'I guess I understand you perfectly well,' says Gideon coldly.

'Oh! Oh! What have we here? We have taken umbrage.'

'You are most impossible, Walter, cruel and impossible.' Gideon resorts to a dog-eared *Blackwood's* exchanged with the English Factory.

'Even the Chinese do not read their books upside down, Gideon.'

Chase starts to laugh. 'Well, if my opinions are so topsy-turvy, needs must I shall read differently from the rest of mankind.'

'And the rest of mankind has long since fled this gloomy spot.' His own last words remind Eastman that Gideon has loyally stood by him, and he feels guilty. He sets out to be as charming as possible now. 'Well, let it be an Eden. What d'you say?'

'I say it is time for refreshment.'

Without having to move more than his arm, Eastman pulls the sash on the wall, causing a bell to ring out of earshot in the further nether regions of the Factory, which is a fair illustration of causes and remote effects, knowledge of the repercussions of a distant event which is certain even without the immediate proof of the senses – all of which is germane to the preceding discussion. 'Coffee chop-chop,' says Eastman to the aged mess-boy. 'Sweet biscuits and syrup.'

'And some plantains,' Gideon adds.

They sit companionably in the rich aroma of coffee and cigars. How food will blunt man's natural instincts of aggression! thinks Gideon. We are not as rational as we would like to think ourselves. Walter's pale face in repose, his eyes shut as he lies back against the wicker, has marmoreal qualities. The prematurely receding hair on his forehead gives him the appearance of a Roman emperor, though doubtless the smallpox pits would not have appeared. 'Has Harry O'Rourke ever taken your likeness?'

'No.'

'Strange.'

'He sees me, I guess, as a free spirit. He only paints Free Traders.'

'But I recollect his sketching a group of us on the verandah. Where can that have been?'

'It was probably MacQuitty which interested him. But I do begin to recollect. I expect you crave immortality through Harry's brush yourself?'

'I do not.'

'I doubt he took the conception further. For every picture or drawing he finishes, he will abandon ten.'

'Spendthrift with money and profligate with his talent.'

'Admirable generosity of soul. Does the rain abate?'

Gideon goes hopefully to the edge of the balcony. At the moment he is filled with a great love for Walter. 'A trick of light merely. The clouds are closing in.'

'Are you so sure?'

'Yes, the river's surface is speckled and so are the waters over the square.'

'We could have alleviated the monotony with a cruise in our little craft.'

'Really, we should go half-naked in it, I guess, and paint ourselves blue.'

'Dangerous. The English Factory would have resented the insult by peppering our ancient vessel with birdshot and sinking us.'

'If Corrigan's tarpaulin can sustain our weight or even Ridley's, it is surely sufficient armour against No.3 birdshot discharged at the range of seventy yards.'

'In that case our Cousins would undoubtedly resort to a heavier load. There's nothing so unsporting as your true sporting gentleman.'

'Let me try your cheroot,' Gideon says suddenly.

'My dear fellow, allow me to present you with one of your very own.' Walter offers Gideon his case, and waits smugly for manifestations of unease: choking, wheezing, and, hopefully, green-faced Gideon dashing for the balcony to vomit on the face of the waters. No such fun. 'You cub, you've done this before, I'll wager.'

'Never, I'll assure you.'

Gideon blows out smoke with great composure, just catching a cough on the way out of his dry throat. His eyes water slightly; however, he bears up coolly under Walter's keen regard. 'Hmm, we shall have to get you down to the flowerboats before long.'

'No, thank you, Walter.' Gideon hopes he does not sound priggish. Eastman goes to the balcony, standing between two red pots of camellias, the houseboy's pride and joy. 'It is somewhat abating, I should say. I believe a brisk pull to the Dutch Folly and back will be entirely beneficial to our systems. We'll take the coracle to the boathouse and transfer there to the skiff.'

As this gives him the chance to get rid of the cigar, Gideon is glad to acquiesce.

Pandemonium. Distant shouts. Bare feet slap on the stone arcades. Volleys of shrill Chinese expletives. Gideon jerks to in bed. He rears up, hands on the mattress. What can this be? Is there another fire? Thieves? A groan escapes from Gideon's lips. He puts his feet on the floor, which is pleasantly cool, despite the awful damp heat of the southern Chinese summer. He has not slept well, has a headache, and a tongue which is doubtless yellow and slimy. Bright daylight breaks through the curtains as he parts them; so it's not likely to be thieves and, in any case, fires happen in the dry season. Coolies and Factories servants are splashing through the puddles in the square from which the river receded six weeks ago. By this hour Gideon has usually long been up, applying himself profitably, but the weather has oppressed even him. He pulls on his trousers, doesn't trouble to tuck in yesterday's shirt, and thrusts his feet into leather slippers. Chinese in considerable numbers are crossing the square, but he is the only European out. There is a jostling throng outside the French Hong, which parts to admit him. Perhaps they fear blows, though he bears no stick. The bodies close in behind him. Men stand on tiptoe, peer sideways, crane their necks. At the front, they whisper. A man lies on the floor. Gideon recognises him as a coolie attached to the French Hong; a gardener, he would say, from his straw hat which lies beside him. His face is a dreadful grey-blue, the eyelids fluttering and the orbs rolled back into the head so that the whites show as thin slits. His chest rises and falls rapidly but he only makes shallow gasps. No one helps him. He lies quite alone in a little circle formed by the staring faces. Gideon drops to his knees beside the man. His black trousers, as is usual in his class, are rolled up to the knees. One calf is heavily swollen and an angry purple. The other leg is normal: that is, wizened, malnourished and veiny. Gideon does not wish to touch the leg. He feels sickened. A huge bead of sweat runs off the sick man's forehead. Nothing would induce

Gideon to mop it with his own handkerchief. The very thought makes him queasy. He thinks of the professional beggars around Hog Lane and Carpenter's Square, their loathsome deformities, festering sores, and self-inflicted mutilations. Perhaps this coolie, decent-looking employee of the Factories though he seems, has contracted the bubonic plague? Gideon draws back. The coolie's breathing has altered for the worse: an awful rattling as the expired air leaves his throat, an arching struggle as he sucks in to renew his life. The swelling seems to be travelling up the man's thigh to just beyond the knee, while the purple darkness is also encroaching on the unsullied flesh. Should he loosen the man's trousers?

Thwack!

'Get back, ye damned rascals!'

Swoosh, thwack. The air hums under successive blows of Dr MacGillivray's stout walking-stick.

'Eiyah!' (Exclamation comprehensible even to one as lamentably ignorant of the area's dialect as, say, Harry O'Rourke or even Dr MacGillivray himself.) MacGillivray's florid, moustached face appears at the front of the crowd. A thin-faced coolie winces, clutching his cracked elbow; he stares balefully at Gideon, who is not at all responsible for inflicting the pain on him. Another fellow jumps and then steps smartly aside as the doctor jabs him in the kidneys with the point of his formidable weapon. Gideon looks up from the prone coolie, as much to let the doctor see he is a fellow-foreigner as for relief and proper instructions. He does not relish a lusty whack across the shoulders with that stick. MacGillivray, a notoriously crusty old fellow who is surgeon to one of the richest British opium Hongs, doesn't recollect the name of the humblest member of an American house but, so small is the community, he knows perfectly well who Gideon is. 'D'ye pray for the soul o' the departed, laddie?'

'I ...'

'Well, ye may be premature if ye do, but not if ye go on like that.'

Dressed in a heavy coat, despite the heat, MacGillivray bends forward and transfers his black valise from hand to hand as

166

Gideon pulls him free of each constricting sleeve in turn. 'Now then,' he says, sinking down slowly and at the great risk of his trousers. 'Y-e-e-e-s,' he says, picking up the coolie's by now ballooning calf and turning it in his large hands with the sandy hair on the knuckles. He lifts the straightened leg high in the air, Gideon seeing the sole quite black, with scabs of dirt flaking off.

'Aha.'

Gideon looks at MacGillivray with anxious interest.

'Come here, laddie. It won't bite, not the leg anyhow.' Dr MacGillivray rotates the calf and on the back Gideon sees two small holes, set close together. 'Puncture marks, laddie. What's your diagnosis?'

Light breaks in on Gideon. 'The unfortunate man has been stung by a snake.'

'Ye're a sharp boy,' says MacGillivray sarcastically. 'Smart, as ye'd say. What kind o' snake?'

'A…er….poisonous serpent?' Gideon hazards.

'A *poisonous* serpent,' MacGillivray repeats, reaching for his bag and bringing out a sharp knife. 'A poisonous one, eh? Yes, I believe we may safely assume that from the condition of the fellow's lower extremities, not to mention his laboured respiration. In short, the fellow is half-dead.'

Gideon turns away as the doctor cuts two horizontal slits, one above and one below the punctures. When he looks around, MacGillivray is pressing beside the incisions. His blunt fingers squeeze out a small amount of blood and clear fluid. He grunts. He cuts a thick strip of cloth from the coolie's pantaloons. With this and the two flat halves of a seasoned bamboo, which obviously belong to the coolie and which lie beside him, MacGillivray improvises the tightest tourniquet he can around the victim's thigh. Gideon looks hopefully at him, wondering if it would be presumptuous to offer assistance which he now finds he is prepared to offer within reasonable limits (*where's the snake?*). He is beginning to feel rather ashamed of his earlier repugnance and timidity. Dr MacGillivray, however, shakes his head. 'The horse has bolted,' he comments, rather too elliptically for Gideon. 'See the size o' those holes, laddie? And consider, if ye will, the space intervening between them. Only a

167

hamadryad's fangs could have inflicted such a wound.'

'A hamadryad?'

'A king cobra to the vulgar, laddie. I would estimate its length as at least twelve feet, very possibly more. The head would be the size o' a wee dog's and the fangs an inch and a half, or more, in length.'

'Gracious!' Gideon shifts nervously.

Dr MacGillivray ties the final knot in his tourniquet. 'I fear we are too late with this poor fellow. The venom already circulates in his system.'

The coolie's breathing has become laboured and shallow to the point where he can hardly be said to be respiring at all. The discoloration has spread up the thigh, under what is left of his pantaloons, and into the loins, and is now visible again seeping past the waist-band and up his bare torso. 'Paralysis,' says Dr MacGillivray, elongating the second 'a' with what seems like ghoul's relish but is only broad Scots. 'Convulsions will shortly ensue, followed by death.'

A few moments later the coolie jerks spasmodically and then again more violently, his spine arching as his body comes off the stone floor. Gideon puts his hands over his face.

'Aye, it's no a pretty sight.'

The coolie's arm twitches and the flapping hand strikes Gideon on the knee. He shudders and draws back. The convulsions are becoming less violent. Before long, they cease altogether, to be succeeded by complete immobility. The man's chest is still but his eyes are open. MacGillivray snaps his case shut. After a while, Gideon realises that the man's staring eyes are sightless. He is dead. Gideon remains on his knees. He tries to swallow, but finds he has insufficient saliva. The coolie's eyes stare fixedly at the ceiling. Gideon wonders whether to close them. He is still reluctant to touch the corpse.

'There's nae more we can do for him. Ye canna even pray for his heathen soul.' MacGillivray puts a big hand on Gideon's neck, which makes the young man's flesh creep. 'Ye're as white as a ghost.' The doctor puts a hand under Gideon's arm and lifts him up. 'I'm putting ye under my regime, laddie, and my instructions as a medical man, d'ye no hear, are that ye should follow me directly to my quarters, this moment, mind, for a medicinal dram.'

MacGillivray brandishes his stick to clear a path through the fascinated crowd and Gideon allows himself to be guided out into the square. The bright sunlight makes him blink. For a moment he feels giddy, but MacGillivray supports him. 'I've had a queer turn or two in my time as well but there are worse sights for ye to get accustomed to.'

Gideon nods. 'I guess I should apologise for my weakness.'

'Och, ye didna exactly swoon like a young lassie.'

'Will the snake still be a danger to all in the vicinity?'

'I'm a doctor, laddie, not a diviner, but I would hazard the opinion that it is long gone. It is the water they enjoy, being cold-blooded creatures. The coolness is grateful to them. As an old Indian reptile myself, I have often to resist a powerful inclination to jump in the nearest tank. It's the floods which attract them, d'ye see. Every year is the same.'

In MacGillivray's chambers Gideon is compelled to knock back a generous glass of whisky, which burns and makes him gasp. Then he's gruffly sent about his business.

Walter breakfasts in his shirt-sleeves. 'Halloa, the laggard!' he greets Gideon, saluting with his second cup of coffee.

'Something terrible has happened.'

'Yes,' says Eastman, sniffing, 'you've taken to drink, which in our climate is a terrible thing at this hour and at your age. Every bottle a nail in your coffin, Gid.'

'No, Walter. It is no joking matter. A man has been stung by a snake in the French Hong and has just died of its venom.'

'May I be pardoned for hoping that his initials are W. J.? Or even A. M. or J. I.?'

'It is some poor, nameless coolie. Oh, it was a dreadful spectacle.'

'Ah,' says Walter carelessly. 'I thought you said it was a man. But now it has become a coolie.'

'I know your callousness is merely assumed, though it would doubtless offend many others.'

'It would not surprise me to see you walk on the face of the waters the next time the square floods.' After this there is a silence. Gideon helps himself to eggs and grits from the chafing-dish and a portion of curried fowl. Eastman pours him a cup of coffee.

'Thank you, Walter. Say, where d'you go?'

But Eastman is out of the door and clattering down the stone arcade to vault the flight of steps to his room, whence he returns with ...his sketch-book and lead pencil.

'Where are you heading?'

Eastman chooses a pear from the splendid wooden fruit-bowl, sinks his teeth into it, and lobs a rosy apple at Gideon. 'This will prevent your bowels from becoming bound, at any rate.'

'Walter?'

Inarticulate sounds from a mouth full of juice, as Walter's back goes through the door. Gideon mops up yellow yolk with absurdly pink ham, nursery colours these, and regards a syrupy biscuit unfavourably. Then he drops his knife and fork with a clatter, gulps his coffee, and follows Walter through the door, polishing the apple on his trousers as he goes. Eastman is on the other side of the square. By the time he himself has crossed it, Gideon has lost sight of him, but he follows the faint whiff of cigar, until it leads him to ...French Hong. Eastman perches on a shroff's stool at what he obviously believes to be the most effective angle to the corpse. He is surrounded by whispering Chinese but the pencil flies unusually freely and, indicative of absorption, the cheroot clenched between his teeth has gone out. Occasionally, he waves irritably to clear spectators from his line of vision. Squinting, he sights down the line of his extended pencil at the feet of the corpse, for technical reasons which are no doubt perfectly valid but which remain not only obscure but macabre to Gideon. 'What in heaven's name do you do, Walter?'

Eastman's pencil-top moves erratically. When he regards the corpse intently again, Gideon realises he will not get an answer. 'This is a ghoul's work,' he protests. Eastman continues to ignore him. He seems genuinely absorbed. 'Really, Walter ...' Gideon continues feebly, then trails away. The circle of Chinese specta-tors has, if anything, grown since Dr MacGillivray's unsuccessful attempts to save the victim. The Chinamen whisper quietly among themselves, spitting or chewing betel. The coolie's eyes stare fixedly but purposelessly at the ceiling; they could be artificial orbs of porcelain. Gideon understands the meaning of the hackneyed description 'glassy'. The coolie's leg, he sees, has swollen in the short space he has been away to almost twice its normal size. The flesh near the bite has gone black. Surely mortification cannot have set in so quickly, even in the heat? Perhaps it is the effect of the venom. Certainly, there is as yet no smell, other than that of the press of curious humanity behind him; even that is inoffensive, in the way the labouring class of Chinese merely seem to smell stale at worst, as opposed to the meatier reek which the sailors in Hog Lane trail behind them. In fact, the crowd seem more interested in Eastman and his drawing than in the corpse. Gideon is finding it hard to adjust settled notions. Certainly, those in the forefront of the crowd are now becoming a nuisance. Walter speaks to Gideon for the first time: 'Do be a good fellow and drive these Chinamen back.' He speaks so reasonably and so pleasantly, and a moment later is engrossed in his work again. Gideon looks uncertainly at the crowd. He has no stick, nor would he use one if he had. He thinks of Moses, who threw down his staff and conjured it into a snake. And then... *'Yauh daih she...'* he remarks conversationally to the crowd. There is no discernible reaction. *'Gobihn,'* he expands. '*Very* big, over there.'

The front row of onlookers stare at him, as if he were mad or a corpse himself. Or, indeed, as if he possessed the mesmerising power of the hamadryad he assures them is in the room. He gestures, but realises his arm-span fails to do justice to the fabled dimensions of the creature. There is little reaction from his audience. The massed coolies continue to regard him with appalled fascination, a situation which, it seems to a dismayed Gideon, may be indefinitely extendible. But then there is a hubbub at the back, curses, the all too familiar sound of blows given and received with a stick, and the faces and raised arms of Smethwick, butler of the French Hong, and his Chinese underlings, appear as the coolies melt and slink away. 'Avast,' bellows the portly Smethwick, who likes to give the impression he was a bosun when he was merely steward of the saloon in his seafaring days. 'Good morning, sir. Remove that body,' he bellows in the same breath, simultaneously touching his straw hat with his left hand to Gideon and brandishing the stick in his right at his gang.

'You will oblige me by leaving the man where he is,' Eastman says quietly without looking up.

'Beg pardon, sir, he'll start to stink. Disease from dead bodies, sir. He'll be high by noon, or I'm a Frenchman.'

'That is enough of that, Smethwick,' says Eastman sharply. 'You will withdraw until I summon you.'

'Orders from Dr MacGillivray, sir.'

'Thank you, Smethwick,' Eastman says coldly. 'My orders are for you to retire until I require you to enter.'

'Very good, sir,' says Smethwick dubiously. 'Belay that,' he roars, driving his grinning men before him like black-clad sheep.

Eastman is now into shorter strokes. Gideon comes over quietly and peers over his shoulder. It is quite a remarkable drawing in its way. Eastman has played a trick with the perspective, so that the coolie's feet, of which one black, upturned sole is visible, the other drawn up under the raised knee, appear disproportionately large. The angle of the neck, the lolling, foreshortened head with the rolling eyes, and the abandoned sprawl of both arms and one leg suggest hideously the casual untidiness of death. In fact, though Eastman is at the moment accurately portraying the dimensions of the swelling on the bitten calf, its discoloration and the suppuration, the whites of the coolie's eyes do not show, nor have the arms quite the twist he delineates. Gideon checks the model to confirm his belief and is correct. A darker line, rapidly executed, indicates the shadow of a fold in the coolie's breeches and, by extension, suffices to suggest the entire scanty outfit.

'The spectators, Walter, where are they?'

'I omit them.'

'Why?'

'Because I choose so to do.'

'But they are a part of the story, perhaps the largest part.'

'I do not tell a story.'

'But every picture should tell one.'

'Is that a fact?'

'Surely so,' says Gideon with more confidence than he feels. 'At least,' he says with emboldened conviction, 'in this case, where ... where the significance of the man's death resides in the attitude of his fellows, their lack of sympathy, their failure to be involved in his tragedy.'

'Next,' says Walter, 'you will be quoting the lines of the Dean of St Paul's.'

'Of whom?'

'And I, at least, am done,' says Eastman, springing up. 'Or am I?' He walks slowly around the body, inspecting it closely. 'Hmm.' He holds up his pad.

Gideon can hear shouts and scuffling outside.

Smethwick rushes in. 'For God's sake, sir, allow me to remove the body. They believe you wish to use the eyes for magical purposes. I cannot hold them much longer with my small numbers.'

'Very shortly, my good fellow,' Eastman says. 'Directly I am through.' Smethwick is sweating and his hat has been knocked off. There is more shouting outside and he rushes back.

Eastman continues his perusal of the corpse.

'Walter, I implore you, cease this grisly and prurient inspection. You have accomplished the task of representing this unfortunate accident as even more revolting than it is in actuality. Must you gloat so longingly on it now? There is no need to dwell on this dismal scene.'

Eastman smiles thinly. 'Is speed the criterion of tastefulness, then? Were there some means in existence of capturing this whole scene, so distressing, so very distressing to your finer feelings, in an instant and recording it for the wider audience commanded by art, would it then become less distasteful to you? I have the right, and I will assert it against anyone, to exercise my craft on any subject that takes my fancy.'

'For God's sake, Walter,' cries Gideon frantically. 'Pack up your possessions if they have not altogether possessed *your* mind to the point of unreason, and let us in heaven's name go.' He grabs Walter's arm and pushes him through the door. On the way they meet Smethwick, mopping his brow with his spotted kerchief, who has come back to seize the corpse, by force if necessary. A

173

howl of execration greets them outside but Eastman simply smiles disdainfully in the manner of an aristo before the sans-culottes and walks unscathed through the gauntlet, with Gideon at his heels. Behind rise cries of jubilation, followed by a murmur as Smethwick's coolies emerge with the corpse. Gideon finds his shirt quite transparent and adhering to him, but Eastman's springy step indicates his self-satisfaction.

All this before eight a.m., Gideon thinks.

At a re-set breakfast table, where the inner man is restored, mostly the inner man's nerves, with coffee, Eastman is wholly unrepentant. 'Johnny cake?' he enquires brightly, holding the plate out to Gideon.

'Thank you, no.'

'Then put down that apple. It is a perfectly good piece of fruit, which another may enjoy if you do not altogether sully it with your paws.'

'Walter,' Gideon bursts out. 'You anathematise the opium-smugglers and the Free Traders but MacGillivray at least endeavoured to save the poor man's life, where you callously used the awful circumstance of his demise as material for your hobby. His tragedy was merely an accessory to your dilettantism, fodder for a, a ...grotesque and offensive egotism.'

'Allow me to observe, Gideon, that you have a fragment of toast on your upper lip. Pocket Savonarolas should have clean mouths before they commence preaching. But do you flay away, and I shall endeavour to repent, most truly I will.'

'How can you claim to be superior to those whose blind cupidity and turpitude you so rightly scorn when....'

'I am in the right now, am I? This is capital intelligence.'

'...when they demonstrate that humanity and sense of brotherhood which links all men – and you simply scoff at it, or worse.'

'Bah!' Eastman's lip curls. 'Think you that one man's life is as aught when the destruction of thousands, hundreds of thousands by this accursed drug comes into the balance? MacGillivray – whoever it might have been – Jardine himself, it matters not. They might draw the venom from one coolie's system but they pour a poison as noxious as any snake's into the bodies of a myriad and give it circulation in this benighted empire.'

'But one man's plight may stand for that of the many. Have I not heard you say that to Harry O'Rourke so many times? That one moves the individual first, necessarily, in order to work even the vastest transformations of conscience.'

'That, Gideon,' says Walter grandly, 'appertains to entirely a different argument. Are you going to eat that or no? Well, for God's sake, put it back where it belongs. No, in this case,' he adds totally inaptly, 'you may count me as among the disciples of Malthus.'

As Gideon's acquaintance with that philosopher is non-existent, Walter (whose knowledge is only tenuous) has the advantage of him, and he drops the matter. The seven years between nineteen and twenty-six are, it may be seen, long ones.

Walter Eastman to Alice Barclay Remington

> No. 12 American Hong
> Canton
> August 7th, 1836

…well, and in short we do very well for ourselves here. I am become quite a Philosopher of the Verandah; instead of a barrel I live under a muslin net. Our colleagues and compatriots must soon be returning here from their all too brief sojourn by the sea and, everything regarded, perhaps it was a boon in disguise that we were never permitted such a liberty. At least I have no fond memories to sigh over, because there were none in the first place.

Gideon is excellent company. He is in many ways a most remarkable youth and his intellectual powers seem to be augmented in strength with almost every day that passes. As you know, he did not enjoy the advantages conferred by the foundation of a good and uninterrupted education, but more than makes it up now by a course of the most unremitting study and application, though precisely what he studies, I know not. He was seated yesterday on the balcony, while I regarded the river – which (thought I) flowed towards you, and I was struck by the contemplation of how you must some days hence feed your eyes upon those same waters I so mournfully gazed on, except what I saw as grey would be bright yellow when it reached you. 'What do you read?' asked I. 'Oh,' said this most egregious cub, 'a little light reading, Hegel's *Philosophy of Right*.' He has the fanaticism and, perhaps I am cruel to say, the lack of discrimination of the true autodidact.

I send you (you will not fail to have noticed!) a representation of the gigantic cobra which slew a coolie of the French Hong some weeks back. You will note its beautiful markings, the bulging sinews which ripple along its body, the fire of its eyes, and its quick, darting tongue. I have taken the liberty of having drawn it half-erect and ready to strike with its dripping fangs the unwary passer-by. Could the lady with her hands in the air be yourself? Certainly she is armed with a book and pencil. Actually, all is the greatest licence on the artist's part, as I have never seen a cobra in my life and certainly not the beast which struck the Chinaman. But it most certainly existed, and Gid will vouchsafe the punctures he saw on the dead man's leg.

I may end, I hope, by touching on a matter near to my heart. It is customary in this house for those who have remained at Canton over the dead season, as have we, to be released a few weeks earlier than the others for Christmas in Macao. However, it is not beyond hope that I shall be able to take a few days in the autumn, busy though that time customarily is for us. My dear Alice, if you will allow me ...

Fr Joaquim Ribeiro, SJ, to Gideon Chase

> Rua Joao Evangelista
> Macao
> August 8th, 1836

Excellent, my son! Truly excellent! Your progress is faster almost than my own at a comparable stage. You do not possess the facile affinity for language of the polyglot, whose comprehension will always be quicker in the early stages but whose understanding and penetration will likewise always be doomed to shallowness. Rather, my son, yours is the progress, the mighty advance, I might say, of the true scholar, slow in its early growth but waxing stronger and ever faster till like a mighty tree it o'erspreads and o'ershades, providing the shelter below its massy boughs where lesser men may refresh and rest. And yet you also, I will affirm, have a peculiar affinity for the language which – as I have often remarked – might have been devised by the Foul One to defy the attempts of Christ's emissaries to bring Truth to the benighted Heathen.

Of our own dear, benighted, and always prejudiced heathen, I have to report that Ow is still impervious to the great Truths of our Lord and resists my arguments with the greatest composure, quaffing the while a sweet liqueur of my native country, for he has no objection to ardent spirits, while contemning the comforts and consolation of acceptance of the glad tidings of the Holy Spirit. And yet, like Plato or perhaps even his beloved Mencius, he is a good man. Yesterday, one of his prodigiously long fingernails broke in its ivory scabbard, a source of great chagrin to him. *O vanitas!* But what a thing to concern one, the length of one's nails. I believe this was of greater concern to him than the entire Sermon on the Mount, which I had been arguing with him.

O'Rourke delivers this to you by his own hand, together with a packet I have had made up for you of the most fine perfumed ink-blocks. Ow sends you his own Red Ink Stone, an antique piece (of some high intrinsic value) on which you may mix the bricks of pigment with water – but not, I beg you, unrefined river water! I am afraid the gift has reference to one of the profane novels (one of the multitude of licentious works in the language) of which he is so fond. Too hard as yet an exercise for you but in the course of time…

'The heat has a most disagreeable stimulatory effect on me,' grumbles Harry O'Rourke. Who is a very welcome addition to the band of maroons in American Hong, presently smoking on the verandah.

'How can that be disagreeable, Mr O'Rourke?' asks Gideon, who has been rather excluded from the general conversation. 'I guess you should be grateful for any access of strength or nervousness in this clime. The heat sends me into quite a torpor.'

The others exchange significant glances amongst themselves. Eastman looks wryly amused, while old Harry himself chuckles, not unkindly. Gideon wonders whether O'Rourke refers to the irritating symptoms of prickly heat or even *dhobi* itch, that unwholesome affliction of the area most politely termed the upper thighs, which might have a goading effect on the unwilling body. 'Is it…is it…a *tickling* sort of feeling which afflicts you, Mr O'Rourke, sir?' Gideon enquires politely, and might as well have operated with a feather on sensitive portions of the anatomy himself – the soles of Eastman's bare feet, Ridley's armpits, for they roll and guffaw, while Eastman actually drums his heels in glee.

'Ignore these young rogues' unseemly mirth, Chase,' O'Rourke says. 'My grey hairs will not be mocked in vain and your youthful candour does you credit. As for these rakes, they were but yesterday weaned from mother's milk.'

'Ah,' says Ridley, who has kept Harry company on the passage-boat, his eyes lighting up, 'they do say Old Kingqua imbibes the cupped milk of a wet-nurse in order to… ah …'

'…. restore and retain his failing virile powers,' Eastman finishes his sentence for him. 'I believe the horn of the African rhinoceros has to be ground into the beverage.'

'Which must give it the consistency of plaster.'

'But surely the desired effect when it shall have set?'

'One assumes the privy member has not been destroyed in its entirety by the effects of disease.'

'It is extraordinary, is it not, gentlemen,' contributes Gideon, 'how the race is obsessed with the physical manifestations of manhood. One might say the principle is verily enshrined in their vernacular culture.'

Amazement. Open mouths. The pronouncement falls like a bucket of river-water on this jolly, unbuttoned conversation of men. Eastman is too surprised even to hurl a cushion at the head of the upstart prodigy. 'Ah, yes,' says Ridley. Harry beams at young Chase. Gideon himself is a trifle disappointed by the reception of his little *aperçu*. (*Aperçu* is, you have already guessed, a word of Walter Eastman's.) He sinks back into the wicker-work, a puzzled half-smile playing around his lips, the beginnings of that air of baffled pedantry, scholarly imperviousness to the vulgar rebuff, which his expression will, on and off, assume from now, until by late middle age it is very nearly habitual, cracked always (since it's Gid) by occasional flashes of shrewdness and humour. (But all that's another story.)

With decision, O'Rourke says, 'I shall take your likeness tomorrow, Gideon.'

Now Eastman does shy his cushion. 'Elected to the pantheon, darn you,' he says. 'How shall I vent my spleen and envy?'

'Vent it at the flower-boats,' rumbles Harry. 'You blades shall be my bodyguard or at least my fellow-revellers.'

'Fellow-debauchees, I calculate,' says Ridley.

'If you desire, my boy,' says the old lecher imperturbably, 'if you wish, and if you have the capacity.'

'Do you accede, Gid, to this revolting proposal?'

'By all means. It should prove a most interesting and instructive excursion.'

'You amaze me. Do you feel quite well in the head lately?'

Nine p.m. A great many claret bottles roll under Meridian's mess-table; in fact, the young gentlemen will have their work cut out to explain the quantities to Jasper Corrigan when he sees them itemised on the steward's accounts. The port decanter has been refilled twice, brandy savoured. With inflamed faces the foreigners lurch across the square to the boat-sheds, a curious, straggling line to the watching Chinese, the notorious young stick-hitter swaggering to the fore, that strange, barrel-chested dog at his heels; the smallpox fop following him with the too great steadiness of one inured to drink, fighting its effects; the Fat Fornicating Old Devil staggering on his cane, one arm supported by the sober dangerous Stripling Who Knows Talk.

They take Jasper's cutter. Gideon steers. Without incident, he brings it alongside the bedecked barge in the side creek, some three-quarters of a mile below the Factories.

Bump. Lap and gurgle of the river. Not a sound from the interior of the big house-boat. Gideon can already smell the heady aromas of the blooms in their pots on the roof. Ridley raps on the gay shutters with his stick. 'No, you young fool,' hisses O'Rourke urgently.

'I could swear I saw light a hundred yards off,' Eastman says.

'Push off, push off. Go round again. Smartly at the tiller, Chase.' Gideon obeys Harry. They circle the flower-boat slowly, no sound except the faint ripples at their bow.

'Hulloa, what was that?'

'Your young ears are sharper than mine.'

'The squeak of the rowlock, I think,' Eastman suggests.

'No,' Gideon is emphatic, 'an animate sound.'

MacQuitty, who has been resting his paws and snout on Jasper's water-breaker, puts his front legs on the gunwale. His ears prick up.

'It was not unlike a squeak, though, Walter.'

Then again it drifts over the water, unmistakable this time: a giggle, repressed female laughter. 'Aha!' Ridley exclaims. 'So its fair occupants *are* aboard. Let us lay alongside and mount, in a manner of speaking.'

'Slowly, slowly.' Harry has been restoring himself at the flask. 'The passengers may be adorned with petals, but the crew carry poignards.'

'I calculate the crew are defined as the body of persons who do the work.'

But the boat has bumped again. As Ridley, despite O'Rourke's strictures, is about to grasp the sides of the boarding-steps, a door opens. A man steps out, followed closely by two more. As might be expected they are, in Eastman's muttered imprecation, 'perfect specimens of ruffians', not dissimilar to the pirates and smugglers they encountered on their shooting expedition in the marshes of Whampoa. True, these are not so heavily armed, bearing only cudgels and short swords, but

180

their aspect is every bit as villainous; hardly surprising since there is a vigorous mutual recruitment and interchange between the two similar vocations of floating-brothel bodyguard and river pirate, both being members of the same secret society, the Brotherhood of Rovers of Rivers and Lakes. A bald, burly fellow, clad in baggy breeches to the knee and a shiny black cloth waistcoat which exposes his swelling pectorals, deltoids, and biceps, puts a glinting hand on the railings and with the edge of the other hacks at his throat in that eloquent local gesture so familiar to foreigners.

'I calculate he wishes us to go, Walter.'

'How sharp of you. I also allow that is so. We must retain you as our interpreter.'

Ridley looks to O'Rourke for guidance. 'Stand we our ground. On no account provoke them, Ridley.'

Gideon holds the tiller tightly. He wonders whether to address the men in their own language; his grasp of the dialect is improving. The necessity of revealing his knowledge to the others is obviated by the arrival of a fourth man on the flower-boat's deck. In a loose silk gown, fat, pasty, with long-nailed fingers that are revealed by the light of the swinging lantern he carries to be covered in jade rings, this individual receives deference from his hired desperadoes. Recognition, too, from O'Rourke, who calls out to him: 'Woo Sang!' The fat one comes to the railings but the glow of his lamp is too feeble to illuminate the boat. 'A lucifer at once!' Eastman strikes a match, which sputters evilly under Harry's face.

'*Ah,*' chorus the armed ruffians in unison. '*The Fat Fornicating Red-Yanged Devil.*'

Gideon grins in the darkness.

'What do they say, Harry?'

'They greet one of my years and dignity with a respect you puppies would do well to emulate. Throw the painter to them.'

'Certainly not, Mr O'Rourke.'

'The *rope*, Gid, the rope,' Eastman says kindly.

The Chinese lash the cutter alongside and the foreigners climb agilely, or not, as the case may be, on to the flower-boat. MacQuitty, never welcomed on boats, follows, wagging his tail,

181

oblivious of the baleful looks the bodyguards cast on him. Fortunately, there are no chow or lapdogs with whom he might become embroiled in territorial disputes.

In a very commodious room, richly furnished (mother-of-pearl inlaid black cabinets, chairs, tables, scrolls, paintings, vases, lacquerware), in the Chinese taste, is...no one. How disappointing! 'Bring on the bevy of lily-footed beauties,' says Ridley, flinging himself into one of the chairs. It proves a hard and extremely uncomfortable home for his athletic young buttocks. 'Darnation, are the beds softer, Harry?'

'Behave yourself, whelp, or you will have your throat cut and float in the river. Had you the benefit of my wide experience, you would also understand that a hard divan is aptest for purposing pleasure.'

Gideon draws out a round stool, which looks like a perforated bucket. He picks up a volume from the table, opening it, of course, at what a foreigner would consider the back. The vocabulary is somewhat idiomatic for our aspirant but, interestingly, it appears couched imperatively and in a hortatory tone not dissimilar to the precepts and analects of the sages which are his staple exercises. O'Rourke observes with a mischievous look on his face. As Gideon idly turns the pages, he comes upon a crude cartoon or, better, diagram, the meaning of which is wholly and immediately explicit. 'Aaah, ah ...' says our bashful hero, colouring and turning over to yet more graphic art on the next page. O'Rourke leans over. 'Inferior to some fine Japanese prints I have seen,' he comments evenly. 'The native artist's ignorance of the laws of perspective is particularly ludicrous here, is it not?'

'Well, yes ... I calculate so ...that is ...' Gideon is actually rather fascinated by the depiction, its very primitiveness lending it force.

'The man's member grossly exaggerated, of course.'

'You'll be pleased to hear,' Ridley chips in, leaning over, too. He whistles. 'One is irresistibly reminded of the battering-ram in *Ivanhoe*, or is it *Quentin Durward?*'

'Was it the crossbow slots they battered?' enquires Eastman. Further tediousness is cut short by the arrival of fat Woo

Sang, plainly the proprietor of this palace of floating pleasures. He pumps his depraved-looking hands together, bowing in his oily way. O'Rourke executes a *roué's* bow of the previous century (which was indeed when he learned it). From whom? An *emigré* dancing-master, *ci-devant* marquis, sheltering – if that's the correct expression – in icy Dublin. Harry's spine is a little stiff but, then, some stretching will be a beneficial preliminary for the old fellow this evening.

'Orh, orh,' says Woo Sang, making the deferential glottal sounds.

'Enchanted, enchanted,' Harry replies. 'You old villain.' (Under his breath). Then, removing his weight from his thrombotic old legs, transfers his bulk to an ebony throne. An ancient female retainer enters with tea-pot and thimble cups, followed by an equally wasted male servant with what looks like … a tray of opium pipes! Fat Woo gestures angrily. Gideon glances at Walter. Fortunately, he seems not to have noticed. Woo sidles over. With a beam which reveals fearful black teeth, he displays a bottle of cherry brandy with the air of an auctioneer unveiling the afternoon's prize lot. His expectations are dreadfully disappointed as the foreigners indicate their disapproval in the varying degrees of their ages and temperaments, and his unctuous air is replaced by one of a lugubrious dismay. How hurt he seems! 'Woo,' observes O'Rourke, 'is one of the most unmitigated humbugs of my acquaintance. Without speaking a word of his language, that is quite apparent. Brandy, you old rascal.'

'But-lan-day?' Woo echoes him. He shakes his head. 'No hab got.'

'Hab,' O'Rourke contradicts him.

Woo shakes his head.

'You mean you won't give us any.'

'Perhaps, Harry, he doubts your ability to engage subsequently,' Ridley suggests. O'Rourke ignores this. MacQuitty, who has been beside Ridley's chair, growls and pads over to the curtain through which the ancient retainers have disappeared. His head and heavy chest part the cloth, hindquarters still visible, and his tail starts to thump. Giggling behind the arras. 'Ah,' says his master, 'he has flushed the birds from cover. Are our guns loaded?'

Enter Woo again, with a flunkey who presents O'Rourke with a glass of what must be brandy. Harry swills the amber around the balloon, then proceeds to enjoy it ostentatiously. Woo snaps his fingers, and there hobble out from behind the curtain six simpering courtesans with white faces, flowers plaited into their head-dresses, tiny hooves, and fluttering fans. Ridley is very taken aback. O'Rourke smacks his lips. Another sip sees the end of his brandy. Woo, beaming again, gestures at his blooms; rare exotic orchids is the plain implication. Too exotic, alas, for Ridley, who would much prefer the large-footed, tanned, and unaffected Tanka boat-girls *au naturel* – the customary resort of this bad young man. However, in for a penny, as Harry says … And: 'Which do you desire?' asks O'Rourke, the only member of the party now showing any zest for the enterprise. 'Which do I dislike the least?' Ridley asks himself.

'Gideon and I will act the parts of the crowd,' Eastman says swiftly. 'Will we not, Gid?'

'Oh, yes, certainly, Walter, I never had any other intention.'

'What is this?' Ridley enquires anxiously. 'Do you abandon me?'

'We do,' says Eastman cheerfully.

'Come now, make your choice, my boy, or I'll make it for you.'

The courtesans giggle. One of them expectorates into a spittoon. 'Be swift. That one? She has American manners, I'll warrant.'

'Not unless I conclude to contract her consumption.'

'The one with the blue head-dress, then. I shall have her companion on the right.'

O'Rourke indicates to Fat Woo. Woo makes a gross gesture, of unimaginable lewdness and yet great obscurity, fluttering his fingers at waist-level, the other hand two feet away by his ear. 'No, no,' O'Rourke says, waving his hand dismissively. 'We shall dispense with that.'

Ridley looks greatly relieved.

'There can be nothing more discordant and depressive of the

184

amorous faculty than to be serenaded on the Chinese lute. Nor will we eat his disgusting confections of the unmentionable parts of various animals.'

O'Rourke having indicated the foreigners' choices, Fat Woo sends the courtesans away. They stagger on their three-inch feet, agitating their fans like giant humming-birds, it might seem, in order to lighten the burden on those deformed extremities. Woo smirks at O'Rourke, withdrawing backwards, fawning and pumping his hands. 'What a thorough reprobate the man looks,' Eastman comments with disfavour. 'Do you not worry on account of the very likely circumstance that he has sampled his own wares?'

Harry slaps his huge thigh scornfully. 'My dear fellow, even were the inclination there (which I seriously misdoubt, having observed the catamites and low actors with whom he consorts), the ability would be wanting.'

'Say again?'

'He is a eunuch.'

'Well, damnation bells.'

Harry lets this information sink in. The others regard Woo with renewed speculative interest as he disappears up the companionway, quivering jowls wreathed in false smiles.

'That would, I guess, explain his pasty complexion, reedy voice, and,' says Ridley, looking slyly sideways at Harry, 'vast girth.'

Gideon, logical as ever, but still sometimes wildly uninformed, is puzzled. 'From his general bearing I am correct, I calculate, in surmising that he is the proprietor of this establishment, if not of several others? Then why submit himself to such a dreadful mutilation? Could he not purchase, as is the custom with these unhappy women, some orphaned male child at birth and have the operation performed upon him by proxy, as it were? Such is the practice of the Turks with their harems.'

'You misunderstand. He has actively *sought* this condition. Able but poor youths who lack the advantage of patronage will have the operation performed as their means of advancement. They join the self-perpetuating body of eunuchs at the imperial court, that evil which has afflicted all dynasties in their decline.

Ribeiro will tell you of the history better than I can.'

'Who will?'

O'Rourke ignores this, smartly turning the tables. 'Your too obvious repugnance is misplaced, Walter. After all, is not the artist the man who is capable as progenitor, while the critic is …'

'…as the eunuch. Or perhaps a procurer. You are too cruel, Harry.'

At this moment a flowered head appears from behind the curtain.

'We are commanded. Follow me, sir, and acquit yourself manfully.'

Ridley grimaces, but rises. 'Stay, MacQuitty.'

Walter and Gideon are left to cool their heels. What does Walter do? Has a smoke. Gideon inspects the scroll paintings. They are not works of any great distinction. Through the window, which is made of translucent shell, the lights of the Factories glow like constellations in a misty sky. Woo Sang returns, wearing, for no very apparent reason, a black cap with long side-flaps like the drooping ears of a despondent dog. Gideon is sure it's an official's hat, perhaps a district magistrate's; he surmises it is a harmless vanity of the *castratus,* who like the rest of his ilk is forbidden office, he now dimly remembers Ow saying, though they command an influence equal to, or even greater than, the highest mandarin's. 'What a fascinating history this man's might be,' he says aloud, as much to himself as to Walter.

Woo's face wears an entirely different expression, mischievous, genuine humour in the smile. He beckons Gideon over, finger to lips; then tiptoes with exaggerated stealth past the curtain. Gideon looks at Walter, who shrugs. They follow the eunuch.

Behind the curtain is a passageway, disappointingly like that of any ship, with doors on both sides, presumably leading off to cabins. Fat Woo beckons from an open door. Again he presses his fingers to his lips. He removes a brush-painting from the wall – a very salacious one – revealing behind it a small brass disc the size of a one-mace coin. Sliding the cover of the peep-hole away, he peers through. His shoulders start to shake. Tearing

186

himself away with obviously very great reluctance, he beckons the young foreigners over. Eastman stubs out his cheroot on his heel, and claps his eye to the hole.

'What is it, Walter?'

No reply.

'Walter?'

'Don't be such a damned simpleton.' But there is a chuckle behind this shortness. 'God damn this for a spectacle!'

'Walter, I have to insist you tell me.'

'Now we know.'

'Know what?'

'We know there exists a portion of the great man's anatomy more rubicund still than his nose.' Eastman steps aside. 'See for yourself.'

Gideon applies himself to the aperture, a little awkwardly, as he is neither as tall as Eastman nor Woo Sang, whose height indicates origins in north China or, alternatively, as a simple consequence of his condition, growth untrammelled by the need to develop the appendages of procreation. Gideon is also frightened of spiking his eye at the hole. Or having it poked out by someone on the other side. Who would, he thinks, be entirely within their rights.

The scene swims into focus, at least parts of it do. He turns away hurriedly. 'No, no, Walter. This is too gross an invasion of our friend's privacy.'

'I seem to recall a passage of Boswell as regards Dr Johnson, but never mind… our little trespass is not so heinous or unprecedented as you seem to feel Gid.'

'Precedented in literature perhaps, but still to be reprehended in the reality.'

'Nonsense. Ah, do I carry my pencil and sketch-book in my pocket?'

'Walter, even you could not contemplate…'

'I can,' says Eastman cheerfully, 'I could, I would, but, alas, the means are deficient.'

They leave Woo Sang at his spy-hole. In the main saloon again, Gideon says, pompously even in his own ears, 'I shall have to inform Mr O'Rourke.'

'Why not? It may add to the old reprobate's pleasure. In fact, he probably already knows, I should guess.'

Gideon is taken aback. How odd. However, Walter certainly seems to have spiked his guns. 'Well, whether Mr O'Rourke is good enough to overlook the impertinence, it is still ...' His voice trails away under Walter's mocking grin.

'You are almost too good to be true, Gideon. What would my solace be without you?' and he claps him on the back.

Under an ebony chair, MacQuitty gazes mournfully at them but refrains from whining. His ears prick up. Ridley returns. He picks himself off the floor and trots over to lick his master's hand. For that bumptious young man Ridley looks strangely crestfallen. Gideon regards him with a mild horror; his nose does not actually seem to have fallen off. Gideon knows he is being unfair, for he has always been aware of the covert traffic in boat-girls, brought in and out of the Factories on behalf of the foreigners by the likes of O'Rourke's valet, Ah Cheong, for an hour's discreet pleasuring. Yet those tawny, bare-footed daughters of the river do not inspire the same uneasiness in him as these professional native courtesans, whose skin is as good as cold and scaly to Gideon. His year's toil has changed only his intellect, not his feelings, he thinks regretfully.

'The difference,' Ridley says, 'between fresh meat and hung game,' and he grimaces.

'What can you mean by that, sir?'

'I mean that the experience is not to be repeated. Those hooves!' Ridley gags. 'The odour of the golden lotus anything but fragrant, I'll assure you. And the cost! Thrice almost an hour of Ah Soo or her sorority.'

'And did you,' Eastman asks, 'did you, my bold lad, accomplish?'

The reason for Ridley's hangdog air now becomes apparent, as he looks evasive. 'Not entirely, to speak truth, I....er .'

Eastman laughs pleasantly. 'Then you still have your health, after all. And who is to gainsay you play the straightest cue of us all.'

'Ha! Ha!' laughs Gideon, surprising himself as his own mirth rings flatly in his ears. His seniors turn their heads in amazement, and then regard him with devastating scorn.

Eastman's eyebrows rise once more. 'Puppy', he says crushingly. Poor Gideon reddens. He sinks into a chair; arms splayed, trying to get his hands as deep into the pockets of his tight trousers as he can, kicking out his legs. Even MacQuitty decides to bark at him.

'The prerogative of years is that age knows to extend the prolongation of its pleasures, while youth, though more ardent and capable of returning successively to the fray, will be over-impulsive. You boiled over fast, my boy.'

'He failed even to simmer, Harry, and that's a fact.'

'Gad! Call at once for one of Woo's disgusting philtres. How pale you look, my boy.'

'With reason.'

While the others are in conversation, Gideon is able to regard Harry with something like equanimity. Perhaps, he reflects, he can be more dispassionate about O'Rourke because he is older. Of course, Gideon has also seen, if fleetingly, the activities which engaged Harry, and there is less mystery.

'What about me do you regard so fixedly, young Chase?'

'Oh, nothing at all, I'll warrant you. I daydream.'

'The palace of nocturnal pleasures is a curious place to do it,' Eastman observes drily. 'Shall we not tarry, then?'

'Away, away.'

MacQuitty is first into the cutter, leaping over a thwart, then securing his favourite position on the water-barrel.

Ridley and Eastman allow Gideon, as the fruit of his temerity, the lion's share of the hard pulling back to the Factories quay. Next day his hands will be blistered.

CHAPTER XVI

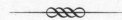

'What a capital notion to come by the back passage. I congratulate you on your acumen.'

'The *Inner* Passage, Gid. It is known as the Broadway or Inner Passage. Back passage has quite another and more opprobrious connotation.'

'Of course.' Gideon colours. Then laughs at himself. The banks glide by at the rail of their boat. It is a glorious, sunny December day, with the thermometer at sixty-five degrees. To come by this inland branch of the mighty delta is to have another experience altogether from the sea-passage of the estuary through the Bocca Tigris. This is tranquil, picturesque, to gaze on a landscape made by man, where the Outside Passage is the reverse of calm, can be tempestuous through archipelagoes and under cliffs whose grandeur has nothing to do with the enhancing handiwork of man. Peach and orange groves, rustling, unkempt fields of sugar-cane, pagodas, a country mansion or two of some wealthy merchant or scholar-official, the occasional puff-ball of a village's sheltering arborage; in fact, the entire motley components of the Chinese landscape pass under the casual examination of the two young foreigners.

'How strange,' Gideon muses, 'that this beautiful scenery should be so delightful to us, who would willingly dawdle our way to Macao, and yet the same was a vexation of the spirit and, indeed, a mortal nuisance to Lord Napier.'

'Speak for yourself. So far as it concerns me, the time cannot pass by too quickly which intervenes between us and our destination.'

Gideon is hurt. He enjoys every moment of the journey in Walter's company. Well, almost every moment of it. As if reading his thoughts, Eastman says, 'Not that I will disallow there are compensations: one's companion, for instance.'

Gideon feels a warm glow. How he loves Walter. More so, rather than less, for the way he treats him. 'We shall be in Macao for dinner, I guess.'

'Straight after, I expect. It will be a cold meat supper for us, and we shall have to kick the steward to get it. But let us be diverted by our voyage while we may.'

A light wind ruffles what is left of Eastman's thinning blond hair. Gideon feels it fill his own shirt and pull at its capacious sleeves, chilling him deliciously as his fine perspiration evaporates. Evaporation, as when water cools through the sides of the large, porous earthenware pots at the Factories, is a scientific principle familiar to Gideon.

This branch of the river is relatively narrow, varying from two hundred yards at its broadest to barely fifty in places. There are a great number of fishing-stakes, generally in the middle of the stream, which effectively halves its width. For their shallow-draught junk, this hardly presents a difficulty. The entrance to the Inner Passage, though, opening off the main river a mile upstream from the Factories, is deceivingly large.

'Who in the name of God are those?'

Gideon follows Walter's finger. In mid-stream, near a line of stakes, is moored a small sampan. At the stern-oar stands the usual boatman, but three shrouded black figures, rather round-shouldered, sit on the gunwales. If it is possible to say anything in this tranquil, sun-bathed setting appears sinister, it is those sombre, crouching silhouettes, who bear all the menace of the Inquisition.

'Friars from Macao?'

'If so, they have rowed a good thirty miles. I don't expect the good brothers are noted for their prowess in this regard. In any event, the risk would be too great. Some French missionaries were executed, decapitated, when apprehended under similar circumstances a few years before your time.'

'And yet the purveyors of poison travel without molestation.'

'On that score you are becoming as single-minded as myself. Have I warped your brains, too?'

'We are influenced by different motivations and reasoning, but our conclusions are the same,' replies Gideon, squinting against the afternoon sunlight, which shimmers on the water. 'Now, just who or what may those figures be?'

'God damn it – one of them has fallen in!'

'I saw!'

If it were not for the evidence of his own eyes, corroborated by Walter, Gideon would think he was imagining things. For a start, there was hardly a splash at the time. The boat's other occupants continue to sit imperturbably on the side, not even glancing behind to ascertain the fate of their companion, still less rescue him.

'I may be crazy, Gid, but that fellow concluded to topple in quite designedly.'

'Not mistaken. I thought so as well. Yet he was fully dressed in his black cowl.'

The dazzle on the waters is quite painful to regard now. As they sail smoothly along, the strange sampan falls behind; pretty soon it is lost in the sparkle of refracted light.

'How may sailors see under such conditions?'

'They must squint, as we do now. No wonder then that the figure-heads sometimes look like gargoyles. Of course, the Chinese mariner's eyes are already perfectly adapted by nature to his task of look-out.'

On this, as on previous occasions, Gideon regrets Eastman's tendency to flippancy. 'I am sure some device involving smoked or stained glass would be as practical as a compass.'

'Franklin, I'll say, should have been a Bostonian, not a son of Philadelphia. You continue to amaze me. How suitable such an apparatus would be for the sea which burned "like a witch's oils".'

'Had I a crossbow, I would loose it at… I don't know what. No albatross follows.'

'How about those black-garbed, black-hearted villains who let their friend drown?'

'Fine target. A good butt for wit or bolt, methinks.'

'Now you confuse the language of good Sir Walter with that of true poesy.'

'Of true inspirational genius, is Mr Coleridge's inspiration not directly attributable to, in great part, the vice you most abhor? That is, the sickly dreams and vivid fancies induced by drug?'

'*Was,* Gideon, was. That is your answer and my retort. What I would say is that opium may have provided the stimulus to his fancy, but at what fearful cost? The poet died but two years ago. What might he not have been spared to attain in a ripe old age?'

'Say!' says Gideon, 'the year after I came out!'

'So,' parrots Walter, 'the year you came out. Anno Gideon. How fortunate for Mr Coleridge to have secured immortality by this happy coincidence. Lord Napier as well, why not? I am sure they would repose the happier for this gratifying intelligence.'

Gideon laughs. 'How egotistical I am! You are right to chide me.'

Eastman offers his young friend a cheroot, which he declines.

'Not at all. You are the very principle of selflessness personified, as I guess I should well know. In any case, how does one measure the world and its great men except through your own eyes and your own experiences?'

'Ah, you are so much older and so much wiser than I am!' Gideon's artlessness is so obvious, his admiration so unaffected that Eastman is completely disarmed. At the Factories, before the others, he would have been embarrassed. Here, alone (that is, except for the crew of Chinese and Portuguese half-castes), just the two of them on the river, he may show his feelings as openly as he can. Of course, it does not lie in his power to be as ingenuous as Gideon but he discards for a while the cloak of irony with which he conceals...an empty spirit?

'You will not think so when we are both ten years older. Perhaps you will grow to despise me then, if we are all spared to see those far-off days. One's point of view is, after all, a matter of perspective. I don't talk of painting, mark you. A decade may make as much difference as a century, or as little as a month. How speedily does a child grow, how rapidly do its faculties develop. The first four years of life are momentous, the last four sluggish by comparison. Perhaps the ten years from forty to fifty years of age are as two years from one's twenties. Certainly, the passing of a year of childhood would seem as long as ten years of old age. No, you will grow away from your old friends and learn to despise them.'

'Oh, no, Walter, I shall always study to admire you. You do not despise Mr O'Rourke, do you? You must see more that is great and worthy in him with every day that passes. And yet you first were privileged to make his acquaintance more than five years ago.'

'I'll allow so, but then I am not Harry and you are not me.'

'You are mistaken. I shall always love and esteem you.'

193

Sometimes, even for those who know him well, Gideon's earnestness can prove a little overpowering. Such is the case now, as Eastman laughs lightly to break the spell of his young friend's seriousness. 'Well, see how highly you may regard me after our residence in Macao.' He adds slyly: 'I fancy you are rather in love with the fair Miss Remington.'

Gideon's face turns as red as the sail of their junk. 'Ah, no…that is she could never…you are my…'

Eastman says, 'What did I not remark? The three or four years between you now are as an unbridgeable gulf. In ten years they will be meaningless, but long before then I have no doubt we shall all be suited. Yes, no doubt.'

The wind sighs through the rushes, perfectly summarising Gideon's mood. Eastman prefers him wistful to gushing. 'Come,' he says, let us go to the bow and see the linesman sounding. The navigation becomes intricate twenty miles above Macao.'

'I guess I shall lie in the saloon for a while. I am still tired from our unseasonable start of yesterday.'

'Very well. If you hear me shout *"Ladrones!"* and there is the clash of steel on steel, you will know we are under attack by pirates.'

'I will know you are mercilessly quizzing me. Call me to see the view if I am asleep nearing Macao.'

Eastman is left to the enjoyment of his cigar and a contemplation of the river. Although he has never travelled by this particular route before, he has seen an album of Harry O'Rourke's containing some excellent views composed in the happier days when the Company made the annual passage by the Broadway in considerable comfort and some splendour, taking with them a milch-cow to provide en route for tea, as they liked to drink it. Harry has a drawing of her on her barge, regarding a pair of water-buffalo with a great lack of curiosity.

The sun is starting to sink, but the river still shimmers in the dusk. From a village on the right bank, larger than any they have passed so far, rises the blue smoke of the rice-straw fires on which evening meals are being cooked for the peasants now driving their beasts home.

Eastman can hear the strange whistles the young boys use to

control the lumbering buffalo, whose horns and bony heads have the massive quality of a tiled Chinese roof. He fancies he can smell the rankness of the animals. A boy sees his foreign face over the side of the boat and shouts *Faan Gwai!* He lobs a stone which, as Eastman is fifty yards away, falls woefully short. Walter retaliates by pretending to level a musket at the boy, to the extent of pulling the trigger with his forefinger. But the boat glides on, leaving Eastman and the boy staring at each other, as they both diminish into the distance, representatives of baffled, inimical cultures. In the 'saloon', which is not the comfortable, brass-and-mahogany-appointed sphere of recuperation found on a Meridian vessel, Gideon nevertheless sleeps the deep sleep of a young and energetic person. One who is used to rising very early and dulling his brain by taxing it with repetitive, monotonous, and exasperating exercises. He dreams…maybe of Alice Barclay Remington, maybe of Father Ribeiro and Old Ow, or maybe even of entertaining this strange trio at some vastly improbable and wholly eccentric function, where he has to play host and reconcile everyone's idiosyncrasies to the others', a task as labyrinthine, exigent, and fraught with unexpected hazards as the descent of the river's final miles, which the half-caste river-pilot has now to negotiate, grounding once or twice (fluvial equivalent of an awkward halt in conversation, aftermath of some *faux pas* by one or other of the guests in Gideon's dream) but getting off again with the tide by dint of shifting cargo and crew to port or starboard (in much the same way Gideon would have to trim and steer the talk to some safer, less contentious topic); so that as sleeping Gideon by turns frowns and cringes, oblivious of the cares and tensions of those who labour on his behalf, he does, in fact, experience the very same range of emotions as the master of the craft on which he and his dream are borne. It is a most exhausting reverie. Bump goes the lorcha, and 'Ah!' gasps Gideon as he comes back to the world and ease at the same moment as the boat's master can shed his reponsibilities to his craft and passengers.

Eastman, no dreamer and no good friend …is already on the quay.

* * *

'OH, SHERIDAN'S WIT is incomparable. The neatest turner of the phrase apposite who ever lifted pen.'

'I am so glad you should think so, for then we agree. Not about Mr Sheridan (for I do not possess the knowledge to compare him so confidently with other playwrights) but that we should choose his play in preference to Mr Congreve's.'

'Oh, I guess Mr Congreve will not feel jealous. After all, he is dead these hundred and more years. But in point of view of light, satiric comedy, Sheridan has no peer and certainly Congreve is no rival.'

'It is *The Rivals* which Mr O'Rourke wishes to stage.'

'What a splendid choice! In the first instance Harry's or yours?'

'Do you know, Mr Eastman...'

'Not Mr Eastman, I crave you. Do you write your charming letters to me as Mr Eastman? Must I be to you as the departed Mr Congreve?'

'Walter, then. And you must have the freedom to call me Alice.'

'Even when your uncle is present?'

'Even when that awful ogre should hear. But to answer you, I don't quite remember. It seemed we found ourselves in agreement from the very beginning, while ranged against us was Mr Arden.'

'Let him ever be opposed to you.'

'*Mr* Eastman! You are impossible and very hard on Mr Arden.'

'I am contrite but unrepentant.'

'I am not sure you can be both. Well, I still do not know if Mr O'Rourke very cunningly bent me unawares to his opinion, for I do not seem to recollect ever being an admirer of Sheridan to an immoderate degree. We did attend at a performance of *The Critic* in Boston some years ago now...'

'*The Critic* is a most excellent play. Sagacious, pithy, full of the most amusing observation, most cunningly crafted.'

'Oh, dear! I knew I should not have confessed my want of taste.'

'But, I was on the point of saying, in a sense a difficult play fully to appreciate. It is perhaps a play for a coterie. One would relish it the more for having trod the boards himself, or for having suffered on his own behalf the pangs of rejected authorship. No stab, not even the thrust of the assassin's knife, may be so keenly felt, I'll allow.'

'How often have we heard you say so!'

'I guess Harry and I are the most perfect egregious bores and our stock in trade in danger of becoming very worn.'

'There now! I did not mean to insult you.'

'Oh, I am proof against the world's barbs. You will not find me as Sheridan's playwright who writhes in an ecstacy of simulated mirth and real mortification as his assumed "friends" read aloud to him, as if the merriest jest in the world, the wounding notices which his little *jeu d'esprit* has won for him.'

'Oh, yes! Oh, that was comic, truly it was! How vainly did he strive to jest, how spiteful were his friends.'

'And how execrable the work they later stage – with the ambitious tyro's guineas, of course.'

'I begin to appreciate the play more with every minute.'

'Still, its full flavour is for the Thespian.'

'Mr Eastman?'

'Walter.'

'Walter, again! Surely you are too young to have had successive careers in the theatre, letters, arts, and commerce? I know we Americans are noted for versatility in our employments, but you seem a veritable prodigy.'

'Ah, no. I have been only a dabbler. What profession comes to mind which demands as the desirable ingredients for its success the writer's ear for a telling phrase, the eye and instinct for shape and line of the artist, the acumen of the man of trade, and the actor's flamboyance and his ready ability to step into another man's shoes? I cannot think of the calling. Did it exist then I might be a dilettante no longer. I speak so familiarly of the stage, my dear Miss Remington…'

'Alice.'

'You are right to rebuke me. But the theatre, the boards, and grease-paint are quite familiar to me as my parents were themselves *devotees of the buskin and the sock*. Yes, they were actors.'

'Oh, but how interesting.'

'They were travelling actors, strolling players, but that was in the years before I made my first appearance on the stage of life, as it were. My father was a tragedian.'

'One would not have it guessed it from you.'

'From my demeanour, you mean?'

'Yes, you seem so gay, so …'

'I accept the compliment. As to the general fact that my progenitors were mountebanks, well, perhaps I may be pardoned for not advertising it.'

'For what conceivable reason?'

'Because, as you well know, dear Alice, there are those less kind than yourself, who would regard it as a low vocation. Perhaps they are right.'

'Then they are ignorant, low people themselves who should slight the profession of a Forrest or a Kean.'

'And your uncle? Will he allow you to appear? What does that make *him?*'

'Oh.'

'Forgive me.'

'No, no, you shame me, and you are right.'

'I am sorry. I guess I did not mean to embarrass you. It would certainly be unsuitable for unmarried young ladies such as yourself to take a role, even before the restricted audience of our little society.'

'I am sure Uncle could have no objection to amateur theatricals in themselves. After all, we often used to perform our little mummings before our parents when we were little.'

'The garrison of Macao, though, is not the bosom of one's family. He is right to be jealous of exposing his charge to the vulgar gaze. It would be a dereliction of his duty as guardian. I guess I am sounding very uncle-ish.'

'Indeed. What an ogre you are, to be sure.'

'Ah, I espy the work in question. Not a very handsome edition, I am *bound* to believe.'

'Mr O'Rourke had fifty copies composed and printed on Mr Matheson's handpress, and stitched and glued, so he informed me, by the Chinese handyman called Nankin Jack.'

'Ah, Jack. More of a huckster, I would observe. Which is the contemporary and equal of the obliging Mr Matheson.'

'*Mr* Eastman! You forget yourself. Do you not apologise for your rude words?'

'For appearing unseemly to a dear friend, yes. For traducing a black-hearted villain, no.'

'Really, I hardly know what to say.'

'Will you require me to withdraw? I should be disconsolate.'

'No, no, I beg you, do sit down. But you are cruel to speak so of Uncle's friend.'

'Friend?'

'One who is received and entertained is a friend; the more so here in our little society.'

'I had no idea. In fact, you amaze me.'

'Oh, dear. Have I been indiscreet? It is Uncle's affair.'

'Your indiscretion, or may I call it, your confidence is safe with me. Would I show your drawings to anyone without your expressed permission?'

'Oh, I am sure you and Mr Chase laugh unkindly at me when you are by yourselves.'

'I assure you not. In any case, has anyone ever seen our young Mr Sobersides laugh? He is immune to mirth, Gideon.'

'Shall we have the pleasure of his company this afternoon?'

'I fear not. He is much given to disappearing, whither I know not, and re-appearing without so much as a word of explanation.'

'Then we shall wake Aunt and have our tea.'

Chaotic as ever, Father Ribeiro's study is bathed in the gold of the late afternoon sun. Beyond a certain point, it seems, further dust will not accumulate on his grey manuscripts. Sunbeams shafting through the open balcony-window pick out the fluffy debris in the air, also turning the fine down on the back of Gideon's wrist into copper wires. How subtle of the Chinese language to have different words for hair, he reflects: one for the shock which curls atop his young head, one for the sleeker growths of the body.

Head bald and spotted like a bird's egg, Master Ow beams at

his foreign disciple. Apart from matching the time of day (there is, the old gentleman believes, a favourable conjunction for every action, moods synchronising with the hours of his necromantic calendar), Ow's mellowness is also the product of the glass of cherry brandy Father Ribeiro keeps handy for his old friend. And administers when Ow gets too much for him altogether. He can be very haughty; on a hair-trigger for a huff. Gideon smiles back. Now Ow looks distant. Really, the old fellow is too flighty by half, as temperamental as a young girl courted. Father Ribeiro decides it is time to top him up. Ow shakes his head but Ribeiro keeps pouring. 'Drink, drink,' he exhorts him, in the local patois.

In the court or mandarin dialect, perhaps the tiniest of snubs to Ribeiro, Ow says to Gideon: *'Within the Four Seas all Men are Brothers'*

Gideon echoes the classical sentiment with: *'Why then do all Strive and Contend?'*

He is unsure whether the old gentleman is testing him, or telling him in a kindly way that it is not his fault he is a barbarian. However, Ow appears delighted, and the beam reappears. What excellent teeth he has, Gideon thinks irrelevantly. Ow uses them to split open a salted melon-seed, of which Father Ribeiro has stock. The good Father himself has difficulty concealing his gratification at the way things are going. Theoretically, formally, the situation as presented to Ow is that he assists at, lends his persona to, a tutorial conducted by Ribeiro. The old *littérateur* considers himself far too grand to act as a mere instructor, particularly to a foreigner. With all the diplomacy, finesse, and worldliness for which his order is celebrated, Ribeiro weaves the strands of a context which may prove acceptable to Ow. In fact, Ow's own cast of mind is naturally inclined to the pedagogic, rather than the personally creative, a preference reinforced by the native tradition of scholarship which is traditional and exegetical rather than innovative or experimental. Prestige accrues to the master who has himself once been the disciple. Ribeiro, with elaborate casualness, picks up one of the streaky folios of which he is himself the author, turning his back to leaf idly through the pages. He has been leading Gideon through his drills, hoping Ow might interject some fancied pearl or other into the exchanges, but, though emanating an aura of general benevolence, Ow has been silent. It has occurred to Father Ribeiro that he might have overdone things with the cherry brandy but now Ow takes the bait. Ribeiro waits; his success will be to preside over his own redundancy. He will skilfully phase himself out. Father Ribeiro looks significantly at Gideon, who takes the hint and pours a tiny quantity of tea into Ow's cup. This is of symbolic rather than practical consequence since Ow is clearly sticking, in all senses, to Ribeiro's ghastly liqueur. But the old gentleman accepts the homage in the spirit, so to speak, in which it's offered, graciously inclining his head. Ribeiro waits. He sneaks a look into the ancient flecked mirror over his mantelpiece. Ow nods away, but he's not actually saying anything. Gideon, the exasperating boy, is not pressing his opportunity. Father Ribeiro sighs heavily, releasing the appetising aroma of the garlic bulbs in which his tiffin-time *cozido à Portuguesa* was stewed.

'Some character practice, my son,' he exhorts the pupil who is outgrowing him. 'Take up your brush...'

'..and walk,' says Gideon impertinently.

Father Ribeiro takes blasphemy in his stride. 'Our Lord helps those who help themselves,' he says rather Calvinistically. 'In the first place the inspiration must be your own.'

Gideon applies himself to the very complex characters he is now learning. He will never, actually, be more than averagely competent as a calligrapher. Someone who, in fact, will never know what talent he might have possessed, what celebrity attained, had life been otherwise, is ...Walter Eastman, of course. Whose hand does just what his eye commands, whose understanding of space and pattern is innate, and whose memory is at once quick and retentive but also in many ways quite superficial and facile. The very qualities required. To be the complete classical intellectual in the native tradition is also to be a mediocre artist; that is one bereft of all originality. Slow but powerful, quite dull (for the keenest blades are the first to have their edges notched), Gideon proceeds with brush and ink. No question of Eastman matching him for real solidity of mental accomplishment. Beyond a point, a relatively advanced point, it is true, Walter will never improve at anything he sets his hand to; whereas Gideon's growth is less spectacular but on the other hand it's unlimited. Ow is familiar with the fables which were among the first secular works of the West to be translated into his tongue, the simple plots, pithy sententiousness, and wholly self-advancing nature of the worldly advice enshrined in the maxims proving so much more compatible with the nature of his culture than the perverse, self-sublimating doctrines of the man who died with the thieves; death on the kind of cross on which the lowest native parricides suffer the slow and lingering death of a thousand cuts. In fact, the missionary press had a small commercial success on its hands with the printing of successive editions of *Aesop's Fables*. Ow looks fondly at the foreign youth, whom he thinks of, rather unfairly since Ribeiro has found his early progress swift enough, as his Tortoise. Today, Gideon wears a bottle-green coat with shiny but cracked brown boots, and as he cranes his neck for relief in its terrible stiff collar, Old Ow is tickled by his resemblance to one of the slow-moving, crusty reptiles.

'*Cur risus?*' enquires Ribeiro in the dog-Latin in which they have taken to addressing each other in confidence, since Gideon can now more or less understand what they say in the native dialects. (Naturally, this gives him incentive to pick up some Latin as well.) Ow explains. Father Ribeiro rolls his big brown eyes in despair. Is he to regard his companion of more decades than he would like to count as a venerable ascetic and monumental scholar, or as a naughty, overgrown schoolboy? He seems to be both with equal conviction and naturalness.

Impish Ow beckons Gideon over. Who obeys, squeaking a little in Eastman's discarded old boots. He shakes his head over Gideon's square, competent characters before rewriting the sentence in his own flowing, sophisticated cursive script. Gideon looks rueful, but Ow kindly repeats the little Mencian quotation he has inscribed – as it turns out – on one Joaquim Ribeiro's dissertation on the proper appellation of God. The long-dead controversy over the Chinese Rites has an unhealthy hold over

Father Ribeiro's mind, for the antique polemics between the Catholic Orders long ago ended in a reversal for the Jesuits and the end of their supple accommodation with forebear-worship and Confucius, which, quite against the overwhelming evidence of their own eyes, as they joined their converts in sacrificing and praying to the ancestral tablets, *they regarded as no worship at all!* However, Ow's action cuts Father Ribeiro to the quick, and, horrified, for there are limits to a Jesuit's tolerance, the good Father snatches his life's work from the saintly pagan. Ribeiro seizes a brush himself, grinding the deepest ink possible, the consistency of syrup, in a tiny pool of water on his ink-stone, before painting over the no less black pantheistic five-character sentiment of the departed sage and disciple of Confucius, a man, Ribeiro will admit, under serious interrogation, as good as any of the humane sages born before the Advent of the Redeemer. Are they all doomed to perdition, Ow is given to enquiring with a straight face and a glimmer in the eye, consigned to torment and flames as the reward of their goodness, simply because of their misfortune to have been born too early to have enjoyed the opportunity, at least, of accepting the glad tidings? Ribeiro generally gives his Order's stock reply, but is troubled. Pressed, he will admit he himself is uncomfortable reconciling the Mercy of God, which quite often appears identical with cold indifference, cosmic practical japes, or at best sublime annihilation, with what he understands as compassion on a humanly comprehendible scale. However, he is ruthless as he submerges Ow's beautiful, if borrowed, sentiment under an inquisitorial wave of ink.

Gideon produces for Master Ow a sheet of the excellent Chinese writing-paper he has contrived to obtain in Writing-Implements Street, Canton, through the medium of Harry O'Rourke's resourceful valet, Ah Cheong. Ow feels it appreciatively between long-nailed thumb and forefinger, and Gideon makes a mental note to present him with a quire; which, he is sure, will prove more gratifying than the traditional present of fruit already offered. Ow hesitates, then writes on the right hand of the page in a column seven characters. Gideon frowns; his lips move silently. *'My face is smooth and lustrous as the last beauty of*

Shang's,' translates Father Ribeiro, having placed his own youthful exposition high on a wardrobe. 'Master Ow invites you to indite verse, my son.'

'Say!'

'A traditional and innocuous form of recreation among *literati*. You must match his line with one of your own, and thus the verse is formed of couplets. Of course, the composition is not quite so simple as it might appear, greater or lesser merit accruing as you balance your opponent's line with artificial antitheses or rhyme, or merely the striking reference.'

'I follow, I guess.'

'Too difficult for you at present, my son, but I shall take up the gage on your...'

'No, Father. Let me see...*But with royal vermilion or pencil's mascara I may be adorned.*'

Father Ribeiro applauds, banging his great, gnarled fisherman's hands together, while Ow nods approvingly at the sense of the young foreigner's characters, if not their execution. 'Beautifully turned, my son. It would have been enough in itself to have seen that the old rascal referred to the paper upon which he composed but then to pursue the conceit as well....Vermilion, I may take it, is the red ink with which the Emperor marginally annotates his minister's scripts?'

Gideon nods with what he hopes is unassuming modesty. He is not used to being praised, or to thinking he has done well. However, even he can see he has distinguished his young self on this happy and auspicious occasion.

Under the players' feet the bare boards of the old company's warehouse creak and squeak, the odd ancient joist going off, as pressure is released, with all the loudness of a pistol-shot, the report echoing among the lofty rafters and startling the pigeons who have taken to roosting on the beams. This may be construed as the strollers' revenge, for the birds' droppings have spattered the dusky planks white and black and the players rehearse at some peril to their persons and garments, steering increasingly erratic courses around the props of their makeshift stage, which resembles a very rickety raft on a timber sea. The gentlemen, of course, have the advantage of *perruques* in the fashion of over fifty years ago, the grey powdered wigs providing both helmet's protection and camouflage to a hit. Less lucky are the ladies, who for mere rehearsals have not troubled to dress their hair in the old style. (If one of the odious birds by some glorious mischance had managed to direct its deposits on to one of those ornate and towering masses – how aggravating it would have been for the ladies, how diverting for the gentlemen!) The gorgeous full skirts of not a few of the former – turquoise, peach, magenta, and lavender – are already streaked with the liquid waste of the dirty birds. Mischievously, in fact, some of the gentlemen have so managed their movements as to have succeeded in manoeuvring the younger and prettier of the ladies directly under the perching birds where, naturally, it is only a matter of time.

Plainly, it is an amateur production – in the best sense: the players are enjoying themselves too much to be professionals. It is true that the half-completed backdrops shiver rather, that, despite a universal disposition to overact madly, the untrained voices of most of the cast tend to get lost in the godown's rafters, that people speak much too fast, stutter, and fluff their lines (despite the leaves of script they all carry), stay on far, far longer than their parts allot (Oh, stagestruck! Reluctant exits!), and that many of the gentlemen – but not, on the whole, the ladies – *will* persist in turning their backs to the audience. As it is presently an audience of one, which sticks its long legs out, teetering on the back two legs of its chair, it is of no great consequence. The audience wears a look of great long-suffering on its face which it does not trouble to conceal, has an extinguished cheroot in its hand, and a copy of Sheridan's masterpiece in its lap somewhat less the worse for wear than those of the players. In short, the audience is not enjoying the theatricals as much as the cast.

'No, no, please, Mrs Harrington, kindly do not persist in loitering in the wings. Your part, for the moment, is over. Sir Lucius O'Trigger and Acres have the stage to themselves during this scene, and you shall plainly be visible to the audience in that station, I do assure you, as well as being placed in momentary expectation of a pistol-ball in your body from one of the duellists. We do not, do we, I expect, wish to stir our friends in the audience to unintended mirth?'

'Well, Mr Eastman,' says Mrs Harrington coldly, 'I am sure I don't know.'

'And you, Sir Lucius,' continues Walter, now not the most disgruntled person in the godown, 'when you say, *"If you please, sir, that will be very pretty small-sword light, though it won't do for a long shot,"* it is a line which is knowingly comic. That is, its humour is apparent to our friends in the audience, although not the utterer. I should recommend you, therefore, to invest it with a good deal more drollery, though to be consistent with Sir Lucius's character, a perfectly straight face. D'you follow me? You, as the actor, may point the entire absurdity of the statement without stepping outside the limits of the character you personate. It is a fine balance you must strike.'

'Too darned fine,' growls the country booby, Acres, who is played in this production by our friend, Jonathan Ridley. 'You are a mountebank's mountebank, Walter. If our trifling imperfections are not apparent to ourselves, will they not be invisible to the spectators as well?'

'Aha!' says Eastman glibly, 'there you do speak in character, old friend. That is precisely the kind of opinion, I allow, which might be held by a bumpkin such as you actually play.'

'Gentlemen! Gentlemen!' exclaims Mrs Harrington, who makes, let it be said, a most charming Lydia Languish, and knows it. 'You will be at the business of discharging pistol-balls at each other next. Pray, don't use such hard words to the other.'

'Billiard-balls, madam, billiard-balls only. But I shall declare an adjournment for refreshment and reflection.'

'Shall we play to the comedy's conclusion afterwards?'

'Indeed not. We shall return to Mrs Malaprop and Sir Anthony Absolute, the second scene of Act the First.'

'But, Mr Eastman, that is to return almost to the commencement! And you had pronounced yourself most satisfied with the rendition of those exchanges!'

'My dear Mrs Harrington, it is a fact that we labour under no particular obligation to pursue our practice in sequential order. An undue reverence for the whole, I should say, merely impedes an understanding of how the parts may work and operate together. As to the circumstance that our Sir Anthony and Mrs Malaprop do handle well their parts, it is indeed so. But my advice is this: perfect your best talent. Why trouble to improve what will never be more than mediocre?'

Mrs Harrington turns very slightly pink. 'Do you choose to call *me* mediocre, Mr Eastman? I find your manner most insulting.'

Eastman, who will quip for nothing less than victory, opens his mouth to say something he would possibly regret later, but fortunately someone more diplomatic forestalls him. 'You are ravishing in your part, Mrs Harrington. How any of our gentlemen will watch you with equanimity, I do not know,' and taking the offended prima donna by the arm, Alice Remington, an interested observer of dramatic proceedings, escorts her to the trestle-table where fruit-cup in bowls and plates of cucumber sandwiches await – not without casting a frown of rebuke back at the tactless director. Who mutters to himself something about mutton dressed up as lamb before he climbs on stage to impart his advice to other members of his company. These are: *Sir Anthony Absolute,* the very figure of that gouty, testy old gentleman; *Captain Jack Absolute,* his dashing scapegrace son, played by the handsomest of young fellows in Macao (too long a part for Johnstone to get up in time, so it went to this blade from the English firm of Dent & Co., leaving Johnstone himself with the minor part of the cunning servant, *Fag,* a role he clearly relishes). Let us not forget *Mrs Malaprop,* that wonderfully grotesque creation, and what an extraordinary creature she is in this production, like nothing else on earth, rouged to the eyeballs where her face is not a deadly white, black pimple-patches, dyed (it *must* be) hair, greasy red lips in a caricature of a cupid's bow, glasses at least half an inch thick atop a strawberry of a nose, and feet of a drayhorse, making the sides of vast black pumps bulge like the hull of a man-o'-war. She isn't unlike a seventy-four under full sail, played by no other than ...But Eastman has already vaulted the stage and throwing an arm familiarly around Fag's neck (who wears a three-cornered hat to help him feel more like a coachman), starts to harangue his amateur cast on the errors of their particular ways with R.B.S.'s immortal lines. They take it in better part than Mrs Harrington, who is being mollified at the refreshments-table, but then, apart from being bigger souls than Mrs Harrington, they also have the advantage of knowing their Eastman. Walter moves confidently around stage, a gesture here, a turn there, an inclination of the head after this particular line. Bring the audience into the play, he exhorts. For this, a slightly different angle of the body suffices, a broader movement of the arm. Let there be a longer pause here. And, most important, *speak up.* Those addressed listen, impressed. Really, there is no end to Walter's accomplishments, you would have thought he'd been treading the boards since infancy. Alice Remington, who can be trusted with a confidence, smiles discreetly to herself.

'Now,' says Walter briskly, 'shall we endeavour to do justice to Sheridan's glorious wit, more even than you contrived so ably a while ago.'

'Which particular glorious instances had you in mind for us to commence with? Line sixty of wit? Or shall we take it from the start of the scene?'

'My dear Mrs Malaprop,' says Eastman with a courtly bow, 'I would not consume so on your patience. We confer to your sex, your outrageous appearance, and posterior genius.'

'Harrumph,' says Mrs Malaprop, prodding her glasses back on to her nose with a thick forefinger and then pulling a silver flask out of her petticoats for a nip (the creature's breath already perfumed with the heady fragrance of the Hibernian still).

'Line one hundred and eighty-four, Sir Anthony?'

'Your servant, madam.'

Eastman retires, the players collect themselves – mainly Mrs Malaprop gartering her flask – and with commendable gusto begin at:

MRS MAL. *There's a little intricate hussy for you!* (Ever on Eastman's side, Mrs Malaprop has chosen the line after Lydia Languish has, appropriately enough, made a flouncing exit.)

SIR ANTH. *It is not to be wondered at, ma'am. All this is the natural consequence of teaching girls to read. – Had I a thousand daughters, by Heaven! I'd as soon have them taught the black arts as their alphabet!*

MRS MAL. *Nay, nay, Sir Anthony, you are an absolute misanthropy.*

SIR ANTH. *In my way hither, Mrs Malaprop, I observed your niece's maid coming forth from a circulating library! – She had a book in each hand – they were half-bound volumes with marble covers. From that moment I guessed how full of duty I should find her mistress!*

MRS MAL. *Those are vile places indeed!*

SIR ANTH. *Madam, a circulating library in a town is as an evergreen tree of diabolical knowledge! It blossoms through the year! And, depend on it, Mrs Malaprop, those who are so fond of handling the leaves will long for the fruit at last.*

'Mr Eastman! You have determined to exclude me from the production!'

'Shh!'

'Shh!'

'They rehearse splendidly. Do not, I beg you, interrupt them, Mrs Harrington.'

'I do not require you to give me lessons in etiquette, Miss Remington. We have different ways in which gentlemen conduct themselves before ladies in England. Mr Eastman, you must answer me.'

Walter's concentration is on the stage; it becomes apparent that he has not chosen to ignore Mrs Harrington, he simply does not hear her.

…but, Sir Anthony, (in a cracking falsetto which veers uncontrollably between a squeak and a rasp) *I would send her at nine years old to a boarding school in order to learn a little ingenuity and artifice. Then, sir, she should have a supercilious knowledge in accounts, and as she grew up, I would have her instructed in geometry, that she might know something of the contagious countries. But above all, Sir Anthony…*

'Mr Eastman!'

The beatific half-smile leaves Walter's face to be replaced by a frown of irritation.

'Sir, you treat me shamefully.'

'Mrs Harrington, you amaze me.'

'Not content with passing slighting remarks on my address, you appear bent on eradicating me from playing any part at all.'

'Then you credit me with genius I do not possess, for I am

at a loss to see how the play might proceed without you.'

Mrs Harrington stamps her foot, actually stamps it (a very dainty foot). 'Do not trifle with me, Mr Eastman. I wish you would apologise to me.'

So far the players have been carried along by their own momentum and gusto but now the distractions on the periphery break in on their charmed circle. The intoxicating certainty of lines and responses is not proof against such intrusion; convention and illusion fail together. Sir Anthony and Mrs Malaprop turn in annoyance to the source of the disturbance somewhere in the shadows and, once again, the warmly imagined Bath drawing-room of half a century ago becomes a dingy godown on the fringes of civilisation as the cast know it.

'What the deuce is happening down there? Some damned vixen raising her voice, is it?' – and, no, this is not Sir Anthony who calls angrily down, but the authentic voice of Mrs Malaprop.

Half-weeping, Lydia, that is Mrs Harrington, says, 'You use me very hardly.' She addresses the ungallant Eastman, of course.

Mrs Malaprop glares into the gloom (and naturally *she* is exempt from considerations of chivalry), prodding her pince-nez back on her flaming nose with a calloused, turpentine-roughened forefinger. 'Damn it, Eastman, do we have the stage and the benefit of your undivided attention, or do we not?'

'One moment, pray, and your indulgence. Perhaps you may glance over the preceding lines while I am otherwise occupied.' Unruffled, Walter addresses himself to the slighted heroine, his urbanity proof, he would like to think, against any of the slings and arrows Macao has to offer. Mrs Harrington is not, in fact, in everyday life a particularly difficult person; however, as Eastman reflects, the boards and a dab of grease-paint seem to inspire everyone concerned with a fit of airs and graces.

'My boy,' booms one of Macao's most formidable personalities from the stage. 'I propose a solution. Do you take the part of niece to my aunt and we should all be spared the vapourings of the sex.'

Collapse of Mrs Harrington.

Eastman, with a mind now to the quality of mercy, says quite kindly, 'My dear Mrs Harrington, restore yourself with yet another glass of fruit-cup, which will preserve your voice, and we shall take the scene from its inception.' Mrs Harrington dabs eyes and nose with lace handkerchief, sips at the glass which a quietly sympathetic Alice Remington hands her, and restrains the tiniest of discreet hiccups. Really, anybody would have been upset. Then she mounts the stage, not without casting a venomous look at Mrs Malaprop, to commence that wonderful scene with her maid, Lucy, in which they are frantically casting under toilet and sofa the risqué novels borrowed by the young mistress and deploying instead the improving sermons recommended by her aunt. Mrs Malaprop glowers back at the indulged actress as she passes, but any tension there might be between them is wholly productive, for it invests their exchanges, which culminate in Lydia's banishment to her room, with a real edge of suppressed animosity, such as professionals might be unable to simulate.

Walter is delighted. Now how to extort such performances from the principals on the night?

'But how tiresome for you, my dear Walter.'

Eastman is not sure he likes the young whelp's tone. Gideon's voice physically broke some time ago, of course, so that the present ups and downs, as it were, only represent the veering between an assertiveness Eastman for one believes to be entirely premature and the diffidence which would be seemly for one of his unadvanced years. 'Tiresome is a word which is barely strong enough to describe the travails of the theatrical manager, but I'll allow you convey the general sensation.'

'It was noble in you to assume the burden. Do the company not appreciate this?'

'Nobility in others is something one always resents. But I look not for thanks or laurels after the event. It is in the knowledge of a task well done that my satisfaction must reside.'

'There speaks the Walter we all love and admire. Whatever the job, to do it well – once you have set your hand at it.'

'Yes, yes, Gideon,' Eastman says testily, already tired by the day's amateur theatricals. Gideon makes allowances for this. *He* endures no such tribulations. 'I expect you will be ready by New Year's Day,' he enquires with tact.

'Ready or not, the performance must be given.'

'Well, I calculate you may count on the indulgence of the audience.'

Eastman explodes. 'That is what I do not wish on any account to have. You have succeeded in grossly contradicting yourself. Did you not claim on my behalf the distinction of a workman's proper pride in all I undertook?'

'Ah.'

Silence.

Gideon says after a while, 'Does your responsibility extend, Walter, to the provision and purchase of scenery as well as the direction of the play itself?'

'It does, even to the printing of the handbills.'

'Tickets and programmes, too?'

'As we are not a professional company, admission will be by invitation. It shall be by general invitation. Programme, I had not considered that – but now you bring it to my mind, I believe it would confer a finished touch upon the production. Yes. The handbills and invitations would need to be printed in any eventuality.'

'Perhaps I might be able to be of assistance to you there in the setting out the bills and the dealings with the printer.'

'Had you a printer in mind?'

'Harry had mentioned the possibility of an illicit run on the ecclesiastical press. I believe the Portuguese authorities might turn a blind eye for the occasion. But, yes, I most gratefully accept your kindest of offers – I will write you a play of your own entitled *The Printer's Devil*.'

'But my dear Eastman, how flattering to be immortalised by your talented pen – if not to be traduced in the portrayal by the buffoon you will undoubtedly choose to represent me.'

'Oh, I believe the casting of Mrs Malaprop to be proof enough of my percipience in that regard. Fear not.'

'I'll say so. A choice of genius on your part to fix it so. I hear that the Thespian also understudies in the role of artisan and decorator.'

'Is as useful in either. No, more so where scenery and representation are concerned, and is a veritable *deus ex machina* in one person.'

'Is that a fact?'

'Gid, you would imagine yourself transported into the streets of Bath, the cunning is so extraordinary. Every cobble perfectly represented, on the walls of the houses windows one could wish to open. I swear I can smell the flowers in their beds and hear the trees rustle.'

'Gracious!'

'I really do not know what I should have been able to accomplish without such assistance.'

'I would guess a considerable amount.'

'A great deal less.'

'In any event, I, as your assistant in the humdrum matter of administration, will ensure that recognition is awarded where due and that, in this particular instance, the name of our good friend appears both among the principals and as master of properties.'

'Mistress. But for that, I should be surprised if our good friend and senior should thank us. But as you will.'

'Oh, no! You do mistake our friend – a craftsman if ever there was one, with the craftsman's proper pride in all he undertakes, certainly, but also the labourer's proper humility.'

'*Touché!*, Gid, but I should warn you the toe of my boot itches.'

'Exit, pursued by fiend, I mean friend.'

Alice Barclay Remington to Harriet Remington

> Rua da Conceicao 39
> Macao
> December the 15th, 1836

...but then we must make allowances for our neighbour's weakness, if we would hope our own trespasses to be

213

forgiven. May I ever bear this in mind and recollect that but for the Grace of God I, too, would be as those miserable sinning women and refrain from vainglorious comparisons. I strive to be cheerful, a good niece, and content with my lot which in a material or social point of view must be considered a most enviable one – with agreeable company, the healthiest of climates, and to occupy me a round of entertainments both wholesome and stimulating. Yet is there a dissatisfaction which gnaws.

You will remember, dearest Harriet, that I had confided to Melissa that I had one particular friend here, the most amiable and talented of youths, or so I had thought. No! I still think so! But:

> Great wits are sure to madness near allied
> and thin partitions do their bounds divide.

When I spake thus to him, then retorted he:

> Else why should he with wealth and honours blest
> Refuse his age the needful hours of rest?

Verily he turned my own or rather the poet's words against me, for he must have referred in his couplet to Uncle himself! Oh, what an ingenious and erudite youth is this!

Then again. wit is not always the consort of wisdom. That he has faults and these manifold I must freely own in my private moments, and I account my communing thus with you as a private solace, tho' many is the time I have rushed to the defence of my admired one against his spiteful detractors. (None of whom would dare to utter their base sallies to his face, for so to do would be to invite the flight of pricks and barbs far sharper than the coarse product of their dull wits.

And yet he is his own worst enemy.

He is so proud and headstrong, so self-willed. I believe his noble and sensitive nature feels slights and injuries, not only on his own but on behalf of others he has befriended, more keenly than might a cruder soul. Even so, wrongs which on

214

his own account he might endure, he will not tolerate where they concern those close to him. And yet, still more, this noble youth will suffer in his spirit for injuries done those whom he has never seen, nor ever will, for those whom he had no special love. We cannot judge him by our own petty standards. Would that others might see him as I do! For he possesses, it must he said, a cruel and cynical wit which loves to mock (tho' never the innocent) and may wound and mortally offend. He has made enemies. Besides, his sense of what may be deemed risible or ludicrous is, for my taste and I am not alone, too developed and keen. For an American, he lacks seriousness, of purpose and manner. His humours may be altogether grotesque. With this, he is prone to fits of melancholy which, he says, are as fully part of his character as his promptness to laughter on other occasions.

That he has no expectations or endowment in the worldly sense is not, I need hardly tell you, dearest sis, a disadvantage in my eyes, tho' I would he a *naïve* indeed to pretend that this did not present obstacles even if they were not of my own devising. Ah, me! The path I tread is between a heaven and a hell, ecstasy and misery – and this must be what they call … but never mind, we shall draw a veil over our private feelings. I know I may trust you, dearest Harriet, with my confidence – for there is no one here to whom I may impart my secretest thoughts and feelings and hopes, or upon whose bosom I may be relieved of my deepest fears and disappointments.

Now, you must know, Aunt has procured me some bales of finest silk and will ship them to you on her private account as a present – I can already see you in the fine gowns they will make – except that you must not tell her I told you, for they are intended as a great surprise! Uncle has been withdrawn and stern but has many onerous concerns to bring the clouds to his dear brow, and I would not wish to be the source of additional chagrins to him. I do believe he sorely misses Father at this present pass, though, as we know, they did not always agree with each other. Do tell Melissa that…

Eastman holds the card at arm's length. Gideon awaits his appraisal. Walter grunts.

'It is suitably plain – but wherefore the large interval between the name of the printer and the bottom of the card?'

'I had considered bearing the arms of the Kingdom of Portugal there but then thought better of it.' Gideon looks anxiously from the sample of the printer's work to Eastman's face and back again.

'Your second thought was the better of the two, I guess,' drawls Eastman. 'Naturally, we are grateful for the protection and hospitality of our friends while we are in Macao, but such a course may be taken too far. The new republic does not need to defer to the old world's ancient monarchy. The self-esteem of John Bull, moreover, is too notorious to admit of such a flagrant display of the flag of even his Oldest Ally. After all, we conclude to play to those who speak English and Their Excellencies the Governor and Dezembargador attend out of duty, rather than pleasure. Let the sashes and decorations they will assuredly flaunt on their own persons suffice. Which still leaves a rather extravagant border to fill on your card.'

'I'll confess I have blundered most miserably.'

'The situation is not beyond fixing.'

'What can you mean?'

Walter takes up his pen. He is already smiling to himself. Wood-shavings, such as litter the carpenter's yard outside the godown where they presently stand, appear, causing Gideon to frown in puzzlement until at length it becomes clear to him that he is looking at…a mop of thick curls. Follow: snub nose, two scowl-lines between bushy eyebrows, and even before the rouged cheeks and patches appear, Gideon recognises the character. Eastman touches in a few cheeky wisps of hair poking out under the neck and around the bosom; giggles unsophisticatedly: then at the side and slightly behind, in profile, he draws the chiselled, handsome features of dashing Captain Absolute, or is it Ensign Beverley? Gideon finds something caustic in the sharpness of the features and the perfect proportions of the nose – can Walter really have succumbed to anything so petty as personal jealousy over another's looks? But he's laughing again as he executes a lovely Lydia Languish, her oval chin up as she tosses her head in a characteristic gesture. More heads and shoulders come on to the paper, thick and fast. 'Ridley!' shouts Gideon. 'No, Acres,' Eastman corrects him, as he starts on the three-cornered hat under which Johnstone becomes Fag, the coachman.

Soon, the entire cast are assembled on the card, a most pleasing collection of miniatures. Even Walter's surprised. 'I do believe fortune guided my hand.'

To his surprise, Gideon says sagely: 'Usually, you try too hard. You are fraught and altogether too conscious of your self. Dashing this off, in a moment of abandon, you have…stood outside yourself. It was in a sense not you but your talent which drew the likenesses.'

'Pshaw!' says Eastman contemptuously. 'You puppy! I was not aware you were a member of the fraternity, sir.'

Gideon refuses to be abashed. 'This is a principle, Walter,' he says with odious assurance, 'which may apply as well to any branch of artistic or even scholastic endeavour. I do not possess your very enviable talent. On the other hand, in my own small experience of penmanship, I have found just such an observation to be true, and that's a fact.'

'Your copper-plate is an adornment to the ledger but hardly partakes of the nature of art.'

'I don't refer to that,' says Gideon quickly, and then changes tack. 'Now, Walter, in shooting at a mark, or a bird, for that matter, is it not a mistake to pause to take too deliberate and lengthy an aim? Does the eye not mist, the hand shake?'

'True,' says Walter without a great deal of conviction.

Gideon goes on, 'Is Jonathan not a dashing, careless sort of fellow with the cue and has the beating of us all? Tossing a scrap of paper at the fire or into the basket, how often have you found that throwing thoughtlessly rather than to...'

'Yes, yes, Gideon, for God's sake!' exclaims Walter, laughing. 'You pile on your proofs like a missionary or natural scientist.'

'To convince another,' pontificates Gideon, 'it is necessary first to convince oneself.'

Eastman ceremoniously turns his friend round, gently plants the sole of his boot on the philosopher's trousers and pushes. 'You are rewarded with a certain Order,' he says, 'which you wear to be presented to His Excellency the Dezembargador. The Order of the Bootsole, sirrah.'

'I am disappointed in you, Walter. But must overcome my natural chagrin for the general good, and shall take your handiwork to the master of woodcuts who lives in the bazaar.'

Eastman is left baffled, then. Is Gideon still the same pompous young prig he always was? Or has a new and subtler invocation of the absurdity and uncertainty of all things, irony, compounded the simple rhythms of his Yankee speech? Gid is getting out of hand; truly he is.

The godown is transformed. Every corner dusted by an army of native sweepers, red carpet on the ancient planks, crimson as the blood on the pigeons' breasts who – I am sorry to relate – have been massacred by the steady hand and cool eye of Jonathan Ridley, utilising a half-charge and birdshot the size of caviare. The rafters are still pitted, causing Lancelot Dent, the proprietor, to squint hard, as if he might be viewing the ravages of woodworm. Dent can see into that lofty recess, thanks to the battery of lamps and lanterns of every shape and description which Eastman has commandeered from all over Macao. Only the lighthouse's mighty reflector knew impunity. Before the velvet of the curtain, full of interesting lumps which move and giggle, a nose and eye occasionally appearing where the two drapes meet, stand precisely one hunded and seventy-three chairs. In the front centre, hemmed around by red cord, are twelve seats for His Excellency the Portuguese Governor and staff, with their eager ladies. Wives would not be an accurate expression, though tactful, for these exiled sons of Lusitania have in many cases found local consolation, laying their curly heads on the breast, so to speak, of China; forming unions which Mother Church might frown on sanctifying, but which State not only benignly regards but actively encourages. For the Portuguese, cunning colonisers, have always reasoned that it is better to mix blood than to shed it. So bigamous, or unhallowed, Dezembargador's buxom concubine or aide-de-camp's lissom mistress, the unofficial part of His Excellency's entourage, with their black hair and sloe eyes, fan themselves gracefully and look demurely to the ground when they meet a barbarian stare. Some, of course, are actually bona fide wives and their strange, liquid-eyed offspring legitimate. Why are the ladies *eager?* Because they are starved of distraction in this godforsaken peninsula. Social life revolves around the guests of their outpost province. Isolated splendidly, Senhora Silveira da Costa Pinto, the Governor's *wife* (no possible doubt on that score), all flashing white teeth, beak of the Iberian aristocrat, with an olive complexion which actually withstands the onslaught of the Orient better than the peaches and cream of the English and American ladies (which degenerate after a while into a sickly alabaster), holds high her tawny head, half-smile playing round her full mouth as she regards everyone and looks at nobody. It was the same at the foreign residents' summer regatta. The cream and peaches/alabaster ladies congregate in a band of their own. Once in a while one of them will glance at Sonia Silveira da Costa Pinto, then laugh too loudly as her eyes return to whoever is speaking in her own company. As the Governor's handsome lieutenant of an aide-de-camp sweeps up to kiss His Excellency's lady's gloved hand a ripple of dismay spreads through the gathering, uniting both sections of the Cis- and Trans-Atlantic communities. Disapproval of flamboyant Latin ways is not entirely untinged with envy. The stolid factors, John Bull, Lowland Scots, or Philadelphia Brother, spread sturdy legs and clutch their lapels for moral support. Frederick Remington engages the Scot, Jardine, in a conversation which has little to do with the performance to ensue. Grim enough, those faces are. They would daunt any theatrical manager on his first night, let alone at a premiere which will also be a penultimate perform- ance. *(By insistence of the public, another showing,* says the poster, printed up well before any demand might be measured.) Our two grim-faced merchant princes talk, perhaps, of satisfying the demands of a market they know to be insatiable: a million addicts in the two provinces through which the river runs. But Eastman's run is two nights. He is pitiably nervous, though he has the style not to show it, beyond smoking cheroots one after the other as he languishes studiedly against the wall, close by the buffet-table. A display of bad manners which does not escape Frederick Remington, who himself dies for the whiff of a cigar, but feels he cannot, though no such niceties afflict the quid- chewing Corrigan. *'Damn his impudence.'* Doubly so, for now Alice detaches herself from the vixens criticising Senhora Silveira da Costa Pinto's expanse of revealed bosom and over- abundance of jewellery. She comes to lend support to Walter. Up go his eyebrows as she approaches. 'Dear Walter, so pale you look – and full of forebodings. Do not fear. I know your cast will not let you down.'

'Fearful? I fearful?' Walter laughs healthily, showing teeth which cigars have browned badly at twenty-seven. 'The question is: has Harry worked upon his stage-fright so very enthusiastically that he will be unable to stand? And Mrs Harrington. Mrs Harrington! The vapourings, the tears!'

'Her paleness may only enhance the whiteness of her neck and shoulders. She will be a most excellent Lydia.'

'Ha! In that case, pray excuse my attendance, for I must wait on my players where my duty is. Why does your uncle look so black?' And, indeed, Remington scowls most fearfully. 'I reckon it is my good self he regards under so very unfavourable a light. What can I have done? I believe Gideon balanced the ledger for me satisfactorily!'

Remington makes a small movement of his head to his niece, the precise significance of which it is difficult to interpret. The wilful girl chooses to misunderstand it, though she is one of two persons in the warehouse (i.e. Remington the other) to whom the thoughts of Remington at that moment are permeable. 'I shall accompany you to exhort your players,' says Alice. 'I am afraid you should utterly upset Mrs Harrington, should I not act as your chaperone.'

'Shall I give you my arm, or shall you, then, give me yours, chaperone?'

Under the eyes of Remington and Jardine, in much the same fashion as the Scot's eponymous steamer ran under the guns of the forts at the river's narrows, our pair leave the ordered protocols of the audience for the chaos of backstage. Where Mrs Malaprop's nose is very red indeed, Lydia Languish ready to swoon in any arms convenient, Fag thumping his coachman's whip into his palm … and: 'Where is Jonathan?'

'He… ahem….' Mrs Malaprop beckons Eastman closer '…is paying an act of homage to nature.'

'Even he afflicted? Your stocking has slipped, sir.'

'Address me as madam, sir. I am aware from the gratefully cool sensation around my calf that such has been its fate. However, I believe our friends in the audience will have more sympathy with its present situation than with it in a more eligible position.'

Ridley appears from behind a screen of terraced house-fronts, his own regular façade of cool pluck rather shaky at the present moment.

'Have you had the effrontery to commit a nuisance, sir, on one of my properties, the painstaking labour, besides, of an artist and a gentleman?'

'There was a bucket placed opportunely, Walter, behind the scenes – and I assure you, I'd as soon make my cast over O'Rourke's portrait of the head of our own house as defile those gracious houses which tremble behind us.'

'Sir, I'd *rather* you watered the dry and wizened features of the former. Indeed I'd join you.'

'Ha!'

'Oh! Mr Eastman. My lines have slipped from my memory. I have quite forgot them!'

'And could you not get *The Reward of Constancy*?'

'I *beg* your pardon, Mr Eastman? Surely even you …'

'Your first line, madam. I see that you do not exaggerate the extent of your predicament. Well, I shall be in the wings to prompt. I am told that once the curtain rises, so do your spirits, and you worry no more.'

'Sounds very much like hanging,' growls Mrs Malaprop. 'Concentrates the mind wonderfully.'

'Come, come. *Coraggio*. You have performed admirably at our rehearsals, all of you. I have every confidence we shall do justice to the genius of our playwright. Do put down your text, I crave you, Mrs Harrington. The lines of the others, as they speak, will stir your memory.'

'Walter, I believe the audience grows restive. Mr Jardine and Uncle are consulting their watches.'

'Time is money, and an appointment a debt. The wretch! He has no chair in his office lest a visitor shall prolong his stay, the old Scotch skinflint!'

'It is past half past eight o'clock, Walter, and the handbills promised the curtain would rise on the hour.'

'This is not Philadelphia or New York, Jonathan, but the borrowed soil of Portugal. Do they even garrotte their felons punctually?'

'It shall be ourselves for execution if we do not shortly commence the entertainment and, as Harry says, it will be a mercy. Let the curtain rise.'

'It shall be even as you desire, O, King!'

'Encore!'
'Bravo!'
'Splendid!'

Applause spatters through the godown. A bouquet thumps on to the stage. A single camellia follows, and another, projected by the enthusiastic one-man claque of Gideon Chase. For the Latin temperament of Governor da Silveira Pinto's aide-de-camp, the sight of drifting petals is too much. Snapping the stem of a rose in Her Excellency's nosegay, and incidentally badly pricking his thumb, he leaps to his feet, spurs clinking, and runs to the edge of the stage to present the floral tribute to Mrs Harrington. Who stoops to retrieve it, amidst renewed applause for this spontaneous piece of theatre, mostly from the Anglo-Saxon matrons, her eyes flashing and her round little bubs threatening to break the constraints of her tight bodice as she drinks in her triumph.

Quick as you like, Gideon Chase (his brain – one could say – permanently unhinged by the close study of other minds long dead and obsessed with the stylistic devices of parallelism and antithesis) vaults the stage. He bears a single bloom and the deadly weapon of romance's complementary mode, comedy. Who else does he seek…but Mrs Malaprop, bows low, and extends the token of his fealty, which the sweating red-nosed creature curtsies to accept with an awful, yellow-toothed grin as her wig falls off and she boots it into the audience. Collapse of audience. Mrs Harrington looks daggers at Gideon – whom Eastman draws to him, embraces, and says, 'No gallant, but a wit.'

Ironic cheers, whistles, and jovial catcalls intersperse the hand-clapping. The curtain sweeps across the stage once more. 'Encore,' shout perfectly genuine members of the audience, for Eastman disdains stooges. Gideon feels his is a usurper's role, stealing the limelight which is the prerogative of Walter and his cast, and makes to go while the drape obscures him. But Walter has him securely by the arm and, as the curtain parts again, brings him colliding against his shoulder as if he were on a spring. *Force majeure*, Gideon takes his bow. Sheepishly, he grins.

He is in between Walter and the amazing Mrs Malaprop. Walter releases his hand. On the wings, Ridley and Johnstone step forward and bow deprecatingly to minor acclaim. Next, the maid, Sir Anthony, Captain Absolute, Falkland, Julia, Sir Lucius O'Trigger, volume of applause increasing all this time. A pause. La Languish is clearly reluctant to accept inferior billing. The smiles on everyone's faces become a little fixed, particularly Mrs Harrington's.

'Your due, madam,' Eastman hisses, 'take it.'

The applause is becoming ragged.

Mrs Harrington's teeth are bared in a ghastly rictus, aging her ten years. Gideon smiles foolishly. Through the side of his eye he sees a muscle twitch in Eastman's cheek. Mrs Malaprop leans behind them, and a violent shove in the back propels Mrs Harrington forwards. She has to take three half-running steps to keep her balance, by which time it's too late to go back, and she drops into a curtsy, simultaneously turning her head to bestow a glance of fury on her unknown assailant. (She has three major suspects.) Applause swells. Eastman looks significantly at the formidable but wigless personage, pepper-and-salt bristle and scalp gleaming with perspiration. As she waits magisterially – yes, magisterially – and will not on any account be rushed, then, with Napoleonic timing, takes one deliberate step forwards, applause rises to crescendo. *'Bravissimo!', 'Trionfo!',* 'Harry, you rascal!'

Imperturbably, she curtsies with a massive dignity, which is proof alike against praise or the vulgar levity of her friends. She turns – credit where credit's due – and extends her blunt-fingered, wide-palmed hand to the contriver of her triumph. Walter takes the hand, kisses it, raises it, and they both bow low as the curtain sweeps across the stage for the last time. Before it does, Gideon spots Jardine and Remington sitting with sombre faces. In front of them, His Excellency the Governor looks amused. He is explaining a point to his lady, who bursts into laughter, leaving in Gideon's mind as the night's abiding image the gleam of her white teeth against the red velvet of the curtain.

★ ★ ★

EASTMAN LAUGHS CARELESSLY. His hands betray him. The knuckles whiten around the edges of the journal. The newspaper shakes. 'Oh, it is as the water off a duck's back,' he says. 'The mountebank's monstrous conceit must be his coat of proof.'

'Indeed, Walter. But this critic's darts are tipped with poison.'

'Yes, damn his impudence.'

Eastman reads from the *Canton Monitor*: *'Within a community which discovers itself in a position as remote and enclosed as ours, where amusement and diversion must commonly proceed from our own devices, that indulgence which is habitually extended to the dilettante (be he manipulator of keys and strings or wielder of pen) must be fortified by a lively sense of gratitude among those to whom his fledgling attempts are addressed. Therefore, in just such magnanimous and complaisant temper, we attended some weeks* past... – Ha! Ten days to be precise. The blockhead has sufficiency of fingers to arrive at that tally surely?'

'I beg you, Walter, do not allow yourself to be provoked. No one of any discernment would allow himself to be influenced by these calumnies.'

'*...the production of our regretted and distinguished fellow countryman's own first comedy, the elder in that family of effusions which so noted a critic as Hazlitt...*- Hazlitt, by God! I call Hazlitt an American, if he calls Sheridan Irish.'

'Walter, Walter.'

'*...praised as the finest of their kind ever to grace the stage of London. Now it is not merely an augmented and justifiable pride in our fellow Hibernian's achievements – for we are not at all ashamed to admit that we, like Sheridan, were Dublin-born (though the speech and mannerisms of the Sir Lucius O'Trigger of this production partook, we believe we do not deceive ourselves, more of the whoops and wild ululations of the "Redskin" than the Irish man, even the stage Irish man- which is a different creature altogether). No, as we say, provincialism is not at issue, but a simple desire that justice be done the work of genius, for we believe that the great Richard Brindsley must surely have been turning in mortification as he slumbered among the Poets in the Abbey. The play was staged in the godown of the former Portuguese opium-brokers of Messrs Dent & Co. (on whom we intend no reflection), and surely the production was itself no less soporific in its effects*

upon the human constitution than the wares once housed in the building
in which it was presented... – Ha! The fellow's grammar is
damnable, never mind the sentiments it clothes, but that last was
good, God damn it, indeed it was.'

'Enough, Walter, if it wounds and angers me, it must enrage
you. You will give yourself an apoplexy.'

Walter is remorseless. 'What else does our Hibernian have to
say? The costumes the sport and sustenance of the moths this
twenty years, the buckles pinchbeck, which they were, the wigs
had seen better days, which they had, the whole only partially
redeemed by Lydia Languish, as portrayed by the captivating
Mrs H. and the drolleries of Mr O'R–, although he would regret
the latter's intemperate and sometimes offensive interpolations
about leading members of our own little community which
betrayed a want of judgement and discrimination. Such remarks,
he says, are the hallmarks of – Halloa, my boys – intemperate-
ness of callow youth and their source may be discerned in the
realisation that the asides were perhaps not altogether unmedi-
tated. *We misdoubt also whether anyone but a Briton may fully
comprehend a genius so peculiarly national as that of Sheridan and
fittingly have the overseeing of such a work, but if the execution proved
wanting, the intention was laudable.*'

Gideon is finally able to relieve Eastman of the newspaper.
He uses the tongs to place it on the fire.

'That was to sneer under the impression of praising, that last,'
Walter says.

'Surely, what else?'

They watch the *Monitor* flare and disintegrate, charred
fragments borne up the chimney. 'Hot air rises,' quips Walter,
'and was that not the veriest specimen of hot air?'

'And not the savouriest. This, Walter, is the moment,
according to the native custom, when we should swear an oath
of brotherhood and revenge as we burn yellow incense-paper
before ourselves.'

'Yellow it certainly is, and that's a fact. Very well, let us have
a glass, too. My spirits could do with recruiting: Perdition to the
Monitor.'

'Confusion to its editor.'

226

Oh! What a momentous step! Today may I truly be said to have put childish things behind me! The gravity of my action should oppress me with care and worries, yet how light in heart do I feel! Even thus do we come to the choice which may make or mar our happiness for the rest of our mortal days, for as the Bard says:

> *'There is a time and tide…'*

So do I venture to put out in the frail bark of my earthly felicity on to the troubled and oft stormy sea of life, confident in the worth and loyalty of my companion. For, yes! the amiable youth whose noble qualities had so recommended themselves to me, whose flaws (for I am not blind to them) I now see to be merely the other aspect of his essential nobility of spirit, I have fixed upon to be my chosen through good or ill. I shall not write his name – I will not, I dare not. Yet, I fear my face will give me away, for must I not wear the look of a radiant happiness? O, traitor felicity! We are secretly engaged. Such was our mutual wish. It was almost unspoken, such was our understanding of the other. He it was who voiced it, as he it was who thrilled me to my very quick when he made the proposal I so joyfully accepted. Oh! How unlike him it was! His face so pale, so noble and withal so ardent, as he pressed his suit. How serious he was! Gone the assumed manner of the fop, the affected languor, the witty sallies, which I do believe he assumes to shield his inner soul from a brute and uncomprehending world – as he spoke with earnestness and simplicity which I, alone of all at Canton, or Macao, had ever heard. I am so vainglorious as to believe that not even Mr Chase, his dear friend and mine, too – much more than ever now, for does his percipience not flatter mine? – has seen my beloved (*dare* I write so?) so pure, so naked – of what the world would call sophistication and I, artifice. If it were not blasphemous, so might he appear before the Tribunal of his Maker.

He said there would be difficulties and, perhaps, sadness before us; that there would be those who would go out of their way, even delight in placing obstacles and difficulties before us *(such* is the heart of man). From this category, he was at pains to exclude Uncle, by which he pleased me greatly. Uncle, he said, only consulted my future happiness and material welfare (care I aught for that?). He did not think that he would be initially favourable to his suit — at which I expect I turned deadly pale and certainly knew I clasped his hand — but that in time he knew he would look more kindly on him and his prospects. He was but a penniless adventurer, my beloved said, but then I placed my finger on his lips and would hear no more. We looked out, then, from my little pavilion and at that moment the birds on the tree overhead, unseen to us, broke into their sweet chorus. We said not a word, nor needed to — and from henceforth I shall look upon the hour of that interview as the happiest of my life. I know that he is not what the world would call handsome. He is scarred and looks older and gaunter than his years should have left him, but he is tall, his carriage manly, and oh, his blue eyes are kind when they regard me. He has enemies, this I know well, but to me it is mysterious that the whole world does not love him, so good a man is he. Well, but now I must hide the treasure of my heart from all suspicion and prying eyes. How hard this will be! Yet for both our sakes must I endeavour to do so. Would that I had some dear friend to whom I might entrust some portion of my cares and responsibilities, but I am all alone.

Chapter XVII

A nd after Macao, Canton closes round like some giant cage. Does it matter that the architecture of the enclosure is grandiloquent, that the bars resemble Corinthian pillars, or that the key to the city's giant, rusty lock is, uniquely, carried by the foreign inmate? (The tumblers may not drop so sweetly when the key is turned from the inside.) At this time, to leave the Factories for the city or its ramparts is to depart from the dungeon as a gladiator bound for the arena and the amphitheatre's jeering crowd. Death attends the daring or unwary on that wall.

Instead of a cloud of stones or mud, this time the stranger would be met with the stabs of deadly weapons. Not even Ridley dares. Increasingly, the abusive shouts of *Faan Gwai!* become *Kill!* and *Decapitate!* How strange are men, reflects Gideon, who does dare to phrase his thoughts in a grand and simple way from which more sophisticated intellects might shrink and, accordingly, comes up every now and then with answers the profundity and originality of which he is entirely unequipped to appreciate. Well, he says to himself, nothing has happened in the last six months to alter fundamentally the relationship between native and foreigner. There have been no outrages committed on the persons of lone Westerners, the flow of opium up the river has not increased, but nor has it stopped. True, poor Sir George Robinson was recalled before Christmas, as later was his counterpart, the outgoing Governor-General of the Two Kwang Provinces, so that Captain Elliot and Viceroy Tang have one thing in common: both are new brooms. With the difference that Tang wants to sweep the alien detritus out, while Elliot has orders to brush the foreign mud up the river. Yet Elliot, a man of conscience and honour (except he intrigued infamously to get Sir George ousted), loathes the monstrous traffic and detests and despises its purveyors. As an aristocrat and a Minto to boot, he finds the Free Traders vulgar and greedy.

Why, then, has the situation become so much less forgiving, both commanders forced to work to tolerances which would have been quite beyond the capabilities of the canny engineers of Aberdeen who made such a fine job of the *Jardine* steamer? And why have matters deteriorated faster in the last six months than in the preceding six years – when, heaven knows, there were far more provocations in any given year? Steam, of course, makes things go faster by land or by sea, but technical innovation is not really the issue here, though an analogy could be drawn: affairs have been building up a head of vapour over a lengthy period, pressure rising which cannot be released since the safety-valve clogged years ago. Pretty soon, like the boiler of an early river-steamer, there will be a collapse and explosion. Can it be, young Gid ponders, that change is not slow, gradual, to be defined as a process but is in fact rapid, sudden, an event? That, once beyond a certain point, action follows action with bewildering rapidity? That men will not be rational at all, will endure outrageous wrongs (on both sides) before, dramatically, a lesser wrong sparks them to deeds?

The Emperor in Peking, for instance, is becoming very tired of cherishing the barbarian from afar and bestowing the gift of trade on him, when he takes it as nothing more or less than the opportunity to poison the bodies and morals of a substantial portion of the population of the southern provinces of the empire, drawn with impartiality from all classes and sectors, from lowest to highest. To an extent, the household revenues of the Emperor have themselves usefully benefited from the contraband trade but, by personal inclination a xenophobe who may with justice be described as rabid, the Emperor is only just beginning to get a true picture of the cost in real terms, distorted as earlier reports have been by flattery, the blatant prevarications of his venal servants in Canton whose personal fortunes are derived from the bribes of the foreign smugglers, and not least by the need of both reporter and imperial recipient of data to couch any description of the unprecedented in the lexicon of the familiar. Inheritors and products of a culture which is literary rather than numerate, Emperor and advisers still understand in metaphorical terms what may be the consequences of an

230

unfavourable balance of trade: to them the massive outflows of silver from the Celestial empire into the coffers of the seaborne Empire (which has as its flagship the triangular bark of India) may best be comprehended as a flux of life-sustaining fluids from the bowel. And Canton? Resembles nothing so much as the sphincter of the empire.

Secret Palace memorials circulate; the Emperor annotates in scarlet ink. High-minded censors, busybodies, ambitious time-servers sensing the imperial inclination, Confucian saints of a rectitude which is uncompromising to the point of mania, cranks, gentlemen essayists of leisure on their family estates – all have their pronouncements, panaceas ranging from the draconian if undeniably effective (execute all addicts) to the intelligent but unstomachable (buy all the drug and burn it). Very soon the Emperor is as sick of this torrent of paper as he is of the foreigners and their torrent of muck.

Does this itself contribute to the rapidity with which the situation deteriorates?

One memorialist of distinction stands out from among the others. Lin is his name. Presently, this mandarin is engaged on the Yellow River conservancy scheme. For the moment, even Gideon is unaware of the mental flood-waters coming to a head in the north.

Corrigan and Remington have done it. The step has been taken. From Zion to Try On, as Johnstone puts it. The young gentlemen were summoned without warning to an extraordi-nary convocation in the mess at ten in the morning – the best time to break important news, in Corrigan's view. He sounds not unlike a native horloger: the body concentrating on digesting breakfast, thus preventing a rush of blood to the brain; a good motion having hopefully already given potential trouble-makers a sense of achievement which undermines the desire to manufacture issues of contention. Also, the hour is as far removed as is reasonably possible from evening, time of potations and smoke-room conspiracies; by then things will have settled a bit. 'Gentlemen,' he begins, and waits for late-comers (among them young Oswald, the new clerk, Gideon no longer most junior). More clattering of heels in the stone arcades, then those last to leave their desks (by no means the lowest in Corrigan's estimation) find space to swing their legs on the grand old table. Having, naturally, been one of the first to abandon the ledgers, Walter Eastman finds himself in a chair at the front. Corrigan will be confronted with the disagreeable sight of his pale eyebrows and quizzical sarcastic face for the duration of Remington's address. Legs astride a back-to-front chair in the middle of the room sits the dashing, straight-backed Ridley. Gideon has worked his way down from the back but has been unable to reach Walter; he stands next to Johnstone, who has a hand on Ridley's shoulder. Corrigan smiles thinly at Oswald as he slips in. He means to indicate indulgence – an emotion without a history in that hatchet-face – and signally fails. Remington raps for silence.

'As you well know, gentlemen,' he addresses them, 'the remarkable and peculiar characteristic of this house has ever been the openness with which it has transacted its affairs: junior has always been privy to the consultations of senior, so far as that magnanimous and candid policy could have been conducted with good sense and despatch. Such has been the hallmark of our house, that and its abstention, entirely of our own volition, from the securest and most lucrative traffic open on this coast to the speculator of means. I refer, of course, gentlemen, to the trade in drug. *Gentlemen, in promulgating and perpetuating the first tradition of the house, I announce the demise of its second!*'

Three seconds of purest silence.

The young gentlemen absorb and unravel Remington's statement. There is an excited buzz, but this fades into murmurs, and finally dies away altogether without any need for the partners to restore order with a peremptory knocking: the audience is agog to hear more. Gideon sees Remington with his chain and seals, thumb hooked into the fob-pocket of his fancy waistcoat. He can only see the back of Eastman's head, thinnest part of a thinning pate. It is wholly inscrutable. Do his ears twitch, Gideon fancies? The tips – are they redder than usual, indicative of an angry flush suffusing the face? Gideon fears an outburst. Behind Remington, Corrigan sits with his legs crossed.

He spurts brown tobacco juice on the floor, jaws working only slightly more energetically than usual. He is unlikely to feel perturbed before a group of employees, mostly young enough to be his sons. He wears an enigmatic, in fact rather Eastman-like smile. Gideon's worries about his own friend are foundationless. Actually, Walter has assumed an expression of the most perfect neutrality, hardly an expression at all, which is just the attitude he wishes to convey. In its way it is a piece of acting which puts his late cast to shame. He and Remington avoid the other's eye.

'You will hardly need my assurance,' continues Remington, 'that such a step was not lightly undertaken. Depend on it, gentlemen, it was not. Nor that merely base or self-interested motives of profit influenced our councils in a decision of such moment. We did not conclude to go our new course in any such frame. Perish that thought, gentlemen!' Remington looks round his audience with more excitement than anyone can remember him betraying in years. He seems almost to dare anyone to bring such an insinuation against him; would call out such a scoundrel. Corrigan spits again. 'We act on behalf of our constituents, without thought for our own commission. As a house of agency, merely, and not dealing in our own goods as directly involved in trade...well, gentlemen, I guess I need hardly tell *you*... Ha! But we consult the welfare and interest of those who have entrusted us with their capital, their savings, the material fortunes and happiness of *their* families... Paramount in our calculations was not the return on a venture as it might be expressed per centum – so much as the security of our constituents. Gentlemen, I need not impress upon you who would risk your lives in venturing beyond this small ground that these are perilous times in which we find ourselves. At any moment the open trade might be stopped, the goods, the bales of cotton, the tea impounded. What then of our constituents, with their capital tied up and fruitless? A ruin to many, gentlemen. How could your consciences tolerate this heavy weight? How could the *partners* in our great house endure the vaster burden of *their* obligations? We should be the destroyers of so many families, the creators of so many pauper children and orphans. No, gentlemen, the lesser evil is to take up that which no one else has ever scorned. And, so, gentlemen, having renounced a policy, we should implement its opposite with a right good will, putting the past behind us as if it had never existed. We should not regret the history of our house's transactions previous to this moment. Let us look forwards, not backwards, to the future, not what has gone before – and, gentlemen, dare I say it, a smoother as well as more prosperous course for us all. I thank you.'

While Remington has been speaking, Gideon has vainly been trying to catch it might even be the corner of Walter's eye, but Eastman's face is obstinately set to the front, only the acutest, most annoying angle of cheek presented to Gideon. He wills Walter to be aware of him, stares intently at Eastman's neck rising from the high collar of his coat. Useless. Walter ignores the mental arrows, bristling in his back by now.

Corrigan gets to his feet. 'Gentlemen, I trust you will forgive us for discommoding you thus early in your day but calculate that you will agree that the cause was important enough to warrant such an intrusion into the ordered frame of our lives.'

Damned rascally old humbug, thinks Gideon with unusual warmth.

Corrigan spurts tobacco juice on to the floor.

'We do not, I calculate, require to presume on your time any further. Frederick? No, indeed. Then we will not at present burden you with the details of how the new dealings shall be fixed. Our best thanks, gentlemen.'

Chairs scrape across the floor. Talk breaks out and, as the partners leave the Factory for a stroll along Respondentia Walk, rises into a great hubbub, as if, thinks Gideon, bitterly, it were a stocks or joint venture market in which they all had something of their own to lose or gain, instead of being a congregation of the mere employees they are. He seeks out Walter, who leans against a wall in his familiar lackadaisical pose. This turns out to be not a pose. Walter is surprisingly unvehement.

'A most disgraceful episode in a history otherwise unsullied till the present,' says Gideon with all the pomposity of twenty. He tests the water. He expresses not so much his own indignation as he hopes by an exaggerated show of his own wrath to tone down Walter's – in much the same way desperate men might endeavour to check the progress of a brush-fire by lighting another in its path which will consume and extinguish it.

'D'you say so?' enquires Eastman quite languidly.

'Surely I do, Walter. It is a shameful betrayal of the policy of our founders.'

'Is that a fact?'

'I shall tender my resignation with yours, should you wish,' Gideon adds hastily, wondering if he is committing himself too deeply. It would not do to put ideas into Eastman's head that were not there before. However, the counter-fire ploy seems to have worked, for 'Whoa! Have a care, sir!' says Walter, looking quickly around them. Fortunately, everyone else is much too busy talking over each other at the same time to have noticed in the general babel. 'Those are strong words, my buck.'

Someone older might say something rather lame, but Gideon says at once, warmly, 'Oh, how glad I am to hear you say so, Walter.' Despite himself, Eastman smiles. Now Jonathan Ridley joins them. 'Poisoners to the man,' he says cheerfully. 'How will you relish that role, Walter? Not too well, I guess.'

'I'll allow that I would very much like to drop arsenic into *your* coffee.'

'Have a cigar instead. How did you find our partner's little speech, Giddy?'

'Confused, paradoxical, and hypocritical, the veriest specimen of artifice and cunning.'

'Say!'

'He presents us with a decision already taken, and has the impudence to boast of our little democracy. He deprecates gain, yet concludes by wishing for a more prosperous course. He prates in his oily way about our responsibility towards those who have commissioned us to be their agents. Do you believe he has any more care for them than he has for the wretched Chinamen whose vicious propensities he is glad to satisfy? I do expect that when he said we should not regret the house's previous history, he meant not that we should refrain from mourning its proud and unblemished record − but that we should not torment ourselves by calculating the vast fortunes we have lost ourselves by foolishly abstaining from the lucrative traffic in previous years!'

'Shush, man!' Eastman says loudly. 'You forget yourself – you orate in the market-place. Do you wish to be packed off on the next ship home? I have no desire to be your companion on a nine-month passage.'

'Well, we'll not inform on our firebrand. Hey, Gid?' Ridley gives him a great buffet on the back, which knocks the breath he might have for any reply right out of him.

'To the tyranny of counting-house and stool. Have you a cigar for a friend?'

'My dear fellow.'

Remington's butt fizzes in the black mud. The river flows weakly and there is insufficient water to extinguish it near the bank. It glows an angry red among the various unsavoury objects which are revealed at low tide, including dead cats, live rats, and, thirty yards out, what may be the black, upturned bottom of Corrigan's lost skiff, but is probably just a human corpse. The aromas, even on a winter morning, are anything but fragrant. However, the partners are highly satisfied with their morning's work, of which they believe it could be said, the briefer the better. Corrigan congratulates Remington on his address.

'Succinct, sir, always to the point, I should say, but with, ah, the requisite degree of...how shall we say? Pertinent circumlocution, direct sinuosity.'

'You call me a serpent, sir?'

'Sir, that was the garden's wisest creature, no varmint.'

'Ha!'

'No, but our young friends in general received their new instruction well. Of course, it may be said they have very little choice in the event.'

'They may always quit a labour which has become repugnant to them.'

'Well, you don't address them now.'

'Ah, just so, sir.'

Our two coevals in ... business, is it? continue their passage along the esplanade, Remington angrily pointing at the vast mound of refuse piled up in the square by its vagabond native population. He swipes at rinds with his stick, making the flies buzz. 'It should be cleared before the heat begins. We shall be visited with remittent fevers.'

They pass the British Factory, the flag drooping on its staff – put up a few weeks ago for the first time in thirty months since the Napier disaster. 'I should not like to lose any of our young gentlemen.'

Corrigan is uncertain whether Remington's abrupt statement is an addendum to his last remark – about the effects of a lack of hygiene on mortality, in which case it is a conventionally pious and unexceptionable ejaculation. Or whether it refers to his own earlier animadversions on the unwelcome contingency of any of the young gentlemen entertaining strong opinions of their own. In which case departure from the scenes of their indiscretion, if not this life, would be unlamented. It is not like Remington to utter a platitude – without a purpose – and Corrigan is confirmed in the correctness of his opinion when his partner says, 'But how gratifying it should be if *a* young gentleman felt unable under the circumstances in which he newly finds himself *etcetera* …'

They smile.

'Out of the way, darn you.'

They are nearing the boat-sheds where Factories servants under the direction of a young Englishman are varnishing the hulls of some racing-skiffs. The young Englishman, a strapping lad called Dallard with a bull-neck and no brains worth mentioning, grins at them.

'Lacquer up,' calls Corrigan, 'I calculate you may require every advantage.'

Dallard scratches his head and can think of no reply but his grin broadens.

Sotto voce says Corrigan to Remington, 'There is John Bull. Is it a mystery his countrymen are the most detested of all the foreigners?'

'Detestable or not, it is a prize-winning specimen. What do we muster against those brawny arms?'

'Ridley and young Chase.'

'Then we have lost! Chase! The deuce! My subscription is lost.'

Corrigan laughs. 'Worse than that, I have arranged a side-stake on your behalf.'

'Do you mean to ruin me, sir?'

'The English will underestimate our boys. Do you not fall into the same error.'

'This is not Bunker Hill or Lexington, Jasper, but a regatta on the Canton River.'

'They will drop like flies, but from exertion, not our balls.'

'Mere patriotism, I calculate, confounds your better judgement, Jasper.'

'It does not cloud my appetite. I expect we shall have beefsteak and onions.'

'You have, at all events. I tiffin more frugally, with Jardine. So, I guess, had better you. Let our young fops *stew* a little by themselves, if you take my purpose.'

'Right well, partner. I shall conclude to accompany – though a meal with Jardine is but a dismal prospect.'

'Meagre – but the other pickings are munificent, I'll assure you.'

'Very well, but I am fixed in my intention to avoid the haggis under all contingencies.'

From THE CANTON MONITOR
April 27th, 1837

...and what a gay and gallant sight it was that unfolded itself before us: the colourful bunting, the streamers, the flags of all the nations (the emblem of our own Union not the least prominent, though we noted with amusement the flag of St Andrew flaunted before the premises of Mr J-) and, as the dusk gathered in, there glimmered the sparkling lights both on the esplanade and afloat on the river. Calm, then, and inky black, refulgent of the twinkling candles and the greater candles in the firmament- yet what a furious lashing it had received but a few hours previous.

The watery battle did commence at two o'clock promptly. The contestants, the flower of our foreign youth, stretched their limbs and loosened their sinews on the bank or lay in postures of graceful repose, while their *cliques* exhorted and encouraged them the while, chafed their muscles, or offered a refreshment to bring the blood tingling and coursing to the surface, while the 'generals' paced about and about the glistering sharp-prowed craft, attentive to the minutest repair or adjustment which might give their champions the necessary advantage of even inches gained.

Then we launched. Oh! how tender, how solicitous! No mother bathing her infant could have surpassed the care, the gentleness with which our boats were placed upon the bosom of the waters. Our course, ye Macao-ites, was from Dutch Folly to the Fati Gardens, a goodly mile or more. The thronging boats of the Tanka people had been cleared to both sides of the stream's centre, leaving a broad thorough-fare down which the boats might freely pass, even three at a single passage. Entered were the boats of eighteen houses, thus conforming to what was not only equitable but calculated to instil the spirit of competition, for lots were drawn for six races. The victors of each course were afterwards placed 'in the hat' for a further three races of but two boats, the winners of each of these to compete for the palm against the others in a final course of three boats. Some gentlemen expressed their opposition to such a system, considering that it would have been fairer to have recorded by means of a chronometer, and noted, the interval between start and completion of the course by each boat. In such a case, it was opined, it would be possible to make a juster and nicer distinction between the merits of the rivals, for it would then be possible to discriminate between which were the faster crews in their separate races. Alas for this stratagem (for we, the editor of the *Canton Monitor,* was among this party of gentlemen, mostly British gentlemen, with a single American, Mr C- included in this number), a majority among the contestants themselves was for a choice of the victors of the several races. Winner takes the spoils! Let fortune smile on those who might enjoy the advantage of being pitted against the weaker adversaries, for does Dame Fortune not influence the issues of Love and War alike? Thus martially did the discharge of the signal-cannon give the release to the eager boats, its report echoing over the city's roofs and carrying, we have it on the best authority, even to the ears of His new Excellency the tidings of the barbarian's audacity. For are we not forbidden, our puny fowling-pieces apart, the import of the implements of war and self-defence? Nothing could be more express than the seventh of His Celestial Majesty's interdictions regarding the conduct of us, the foreigners. Mr M.- will not take umbrage when we describe his brass signalling-gun, usually employed for nothing more warlike than the firing of a salute, as a pop-gun – for we would add (and we are not altogether ignorant of the military science and usages) that the aforementioned toy in the hands of a competent gunner would be a weapon infinitely more serviceable than the rusting monsters mounted on the embrasures of the river-forts.

But we stray from our subject, which is a lighter topic – howsoever the dash and manly vigour of our gentlemen boat-crews may have impressed His Excellency when compared with the effeminate and lousy soldiery which are all that lie within his disposal.

Conquerors in the first six races were champions of the houses of Russell & Co., Meridian & Co., Dent, Innes, Jardine & Matheson, and Bevan & Co. – the first two mentioned being, of course, American houses and bestowing, as it were, a spice of amicable rivalry upon the occasion. Alas, Poor Jonathan! For the boat of Messrs Russell was soundly trounced by the brawny sons of Bevan, and Messrs Meridian vanquishing the house of Innes in securing their place among the *crème de la crème* met a most extraordinary and self-inflicted reversal.

The day's ultimate race commenced at 5 p.m., the crack of the gun signalling the hour as well as the start of the race. To the fore, and in the middle, were Messrs Dent, away to the brisk and nervous start which had ever characterised their stalwarts. A length behind with two furlongs completed, on level terms with not an inch between the bows, followed the straining crews of Meridian and Bevan.

Where the river bends and broadens, with one thousand yards completed, the gallant Meridians started, at first by well-nigh infinitesimal stages, to gain. It had been remarkable throughout the competition of the afternoon that our Trans-Atlantic valiants were thorough game cubs, a pair of bantams, tenacious of the course, and brimming with a resolve which did them and their house credit. In their previous rowings, it had been seen that they did not warm to their work until well past the half of the course and would invariably 'come on from behind' to win. Now, it was early apparent to the spectators that a similar history might unfold itself, as our young friends pulled away from their rivals until with an 'Ah!' from the banks we saw clear space between the bow of Bevan and the stern of Meridian. Now our lads began to 'give way' with a will, bending their backs into their work. Down the waters they flew. Inch by inch, they closed on the leader. Yet did our bonny boys resist our American friends. Dent gained! And, nay, it was Meridian who got their nose ahead again. But three hundred yards remain. The two camps cheer their partisans to the echo. Our cousins dance on the bank for all the world like savage redskins and, indeed, our two braves in the boat must possess the iron cords and sinews of the savage who is inured to paddling his canoe against the rapids from his childhood, for they gain, they gain! Advantage of inches becomes a space of feet, half a length. Onwards they go, they cannot, they will not, brook impediment! Victory is theirs assuredly, with a furlong to go, and we are in momentary expectation of an American victory. And then! – Our failing friends and countrymen gasp for breath – their very lungs are afire. How bitter is the cup of defeat and, in their despair, they falter, they stumble, they *catch a crab.* Slews the craft, they catch the oar of their rival and: an accident. The boat capsized. A gasp and a thrill of horror run through the crowded bank. Do we not know this treacherous river of old? Our American friends have suffered a mere glance, their impetus takes them on. But what is this? One rows on and his companion ceases! He turns and the other points to the bobbing heads. He remonstrates but, no, his companion will row no more. Backwards they pull to the aid of their late adversaries. Now comes Bevan – their stroke redoubles...Down they fly and, to the huzzas of their supporters, cross the winning line. O! fickle victory! How the chestnut will be pulled from the ashes of defeat! As the victors glide towards the bank where wait sparkling wines (and the bubbling spirits of their friends), the late favourites take their rivals on their gunwales and pull, so slowly they pull, for that shore where wait their gloomy friends.

Handsome was the conqueror's trophy, worthy of our community's munificence, lavish the repast which recruited not only the strengths of the gladiators – otiose to recapitulate the viands we viewed in such profusion, the bottles of claret, drawn up like so many ample, rubicund gentlemen, the frothy sherberts simpering in their gowns of glass. Alas! there were no ladies present, so hateful is the Emperor's frown, but, we believe, our young valiants will soon make their way and seasonal resort to Macao where they may refresh their spirits in the soothing and polite company of that which is rightly termed the gentler sex. We must remain at Canton. We are very envious and shall vent our spleen in an acerbic column.

Postscriptum. As we were preparing our pages for the press we heard reports, mischievous and entirely false, we trust, that the young American gentleman who stopped to support the occupants of Dent's boat was being made the subject of ridicule among his fellows. We would say we wholly reprobate such a course, if true, and do entirely commend his action. We are a Briton, of course, with a Briton's notion of what constitutes fair play and what foul.

CHAPTER XVIII

'No, no, but this is not coincidence.' Gideon's voice cracks in outrage. He sits at the end of Walter's bed in his dressing-gown. Walter leans across from his easy chair. Removing the red slipper from the end of Gideon's foot, he raps the heel smartly against the wall, crushing a spider which stays glued by its own juices, the eight legs still moving. 'It is confoundedly damp in those walls,' Eastman observes. 'They shall crumble within twenty years.'

'It is an act of a particular malice, for which a victim has been singled out – yourself.'

'Mind you, we, too, shall be crumbling and afflicted with ague.'

'Walter.'

'Well, sir?'

'You talk of others' rights – guard your own.'

'The only right we possess is the liberty to contract remittent fever when it may strike us. Thereafter, the bailiwick we shall have will be six feet of Chinese earth on Dane's island – and that on a quit rent.'

'Cynic that you are, you must still feel vexed at this treatment. Walter, it is to add insult to injury. Bad enough to suffer an enforced residence in the Factories during the hot season – and this will be your second such stay, when others should take their turn...'

'Allow me to observe that I scarcely need reminding.'

'...but then to charge you with the duty of initiating our liaisons with the brokers, a task they should fully realise must be abhorrent to all your feelings...'

'I expect your boots should be stretched for you.'

'Hey?'

'You have a prodigious blister by the side of the great toe. Perhaps you are getting too big for them.' Walter drops Gideon's slipper over his foot and pats it affectionately.

'And our friends,' continues Gideon in his gloomy vein, not to be diverted, 'the doors of Macao and its fellowship opened to them while we...Why, Miss Remington must...'

'I am weary, Gideon. Kindly allow me to find my way to bed. I shall see you in the morning, when I hope to find you better company.'

'Ah, Walter.'

'Good night to you,' says Eastman firmly, closing the door.

What of Walter's thoughts, as he sleeps, or maybe lies awake and stares at the ceiling's scurrying geckos, or perhaps as he breaks a sensible house rule and sucks on a cheroot, sitting up against his pillow? Quite likely he will come to at three in the morning and then open his favourite Voltaire, or perhaps a translation of Goethe, before putting it down, spine up, on his coverlet. It becomes clear that Walter's moral complexion is not to be depicted in black and white, that the world and its choices are blurred for him. For Gideon it is otherwise. Choices *are* stark for Gideon: either–or, good–bad, can–cannot, have–relinquish. Edges are yet to be knocked off him, although a certain moral angularity will characterise him throughout his long life. But the sharp certainties are in a sense founded on narrowness and ignorance – the ruthless simplicities of the inquisitor or the martyr, one who sees no other paths. In Gideon there is a lack of generosity, a priggishness: it is always easy to resist what fails to tempt oneself. To despise those who succumb is rather less sympathetic than to fall oneself (which argues a certain reckless warmth of spirit). It is, after all, very common to want to have one's cake and eat it, too. Is it so despicable to wish to compromise? To fudge a principle, thinks Walter, is not to abandon it in one's heart. And, after all, in practical terms what effect does an individual action have? Just a moment...all events are the sum of individual actions. Doesn't he say so himself?

But a principle, this is the trouble, has no shape, no face, no dear, remembered features; no warmth; is not soft or *fragrant;* might be described as seductive in an intellectual sense, but is certainly a very poor bedfellow. It tends to keep you awake, like poor Walter now. The emotions guarding this issue of principle are not necessarily very creditable either. Pride, of course, is the principal motive – as manifested in the admiration of others or in one's own lovingly nurtured image of the ideal self. Whereas an abnegation of what one espouses... is that not the ultimate in unselfishness? In this instance, the cloudy Teuton, Goethe, makes better bedside reading than that desiccated old rationalist, Voltaire.

Such are the arguments Walter rehearses in a dreadful atmosphere of cigar-smoke and moral funk. Asphyxiate himself? Almost. Convince? No.

Walter Eastman to Alice Barclay Remington

> No.12 American Hong
> Canton
> 3 o'clock (a.m.)
> April 29th, 1837

My dearest,

We are sent trials that they may make us strong. Rather than surrender to those impulses which are the first recourse of the bruised and wounded heart, we should glory in the opportunity to put our fortitude and constancy to the test which alone will prove it worthy. I mean the test of time, the trial by absence. Do not, my dearest, think me cruel and heartless for saying so. I speak only to show courage which may aspire to be equal and worthy of your own. How heavy a burden you must carry, and yet I know you are both able and willing to tolerate it. We must show the cunning and the boldness of the desperate conspirator. I know it is a role you do not relish; you are right to disdain mean subterfuge and to feel uneasiness for concealing your thoughts and inmost desires from your aunt and uncle. But it is requisite. For our future happiness we must be prepared to pay such a price of our finer feelings. The present for sundry reasons – some of which you are already cognisant of, others which I shall take pains to explain to you when next we meet – is not a propitious time for the consummation of such a decision as ours – or even its communication to the world at large. In the working out of the scheme of things we are, to a large extent, responsible for the course our lives shall take, whether an outcome shall be happy or otherwise, and it is my belief that it is the *timing* of an action which mostly determines its success. I am presumptuous enough to disagree with the Bard on the question of the degree of precipitateness required, believing, as I do, that the flood and tide will always return, whereas he who leaps in too hastily is liable to become enmired and even engulfed in the maw of the quicksands which await. Nevertheless, once the resolution is formed, let its execution be characterised by zeal and despatch. Do I sound like a scheming Buonaparte? Let me only be the commander of your affections.

I have denied in no uncertain terms to Gideon Chase the opportunity to share my exile again this wet season. That remarkable and amiable youth naturally made his preparations for the siege without a word exchanged on either of our sides. I shall be a selfish brute to inflict *my* misery on him. Besides (breathe it not in Gath) there is a very great odour of sanctity upon our Gid and, I must own, the prospect of him silently mortifying his flesh over the summer while the flame of his spirit burns all the purer – and all on my account! – is not one best calculated to amuse over these tedious months. He should not, in any event, be the most available of companions, for it appears that the reason for his long hours in the closet is the course of studies he is undertaking in the Chinese language. We discovered him at these labours when we stole into his chamber to place a dead snake in his bed. I understand he already has a great fluency. No, I shall be the happier left to my own devices and the *ennuis* of my own companionship – at least, I shall be able to cut myself without giving rise to offence. Strange to relate, when solitude is imposed on a man, he may even acquire a taste for it. My position, however, will be somewhat more tolerable than in the season previous, as I have much to occupy me – which was not the case in the desultory summer of 1836, not to mention the *longueurs* of '34 and '35.

It is in my nature, once I have set my hand at something, whatsoever it be, howso'er dark, to do it *well* – to prosecute a matter with all my energies and all the ability I may muster. I confess a certain irresolution to attend the weighing-up of the face of matters – this over, one should show address. I expect your uncle may understand such a person, and in that understanding might also find the seeds of an accommodation. In this sense, I do allow he may possess a spirit more kindred to mine than Gideon's – or, to put it another way, that the gap which opens between his years and experience and my own does not yawn so unbridgeably wide or so deep as the chasm between Chase and myself which opens at the present. But I must talk in riddles to you! I shall explain myself more clearly when next we may meet. Until then, and pending my next, I am (in the 'lingo' of old John Company),

your loving friend,

W.

Gideon Chase to Walter Eastman

Meridian's House
The Ridge
Macao
June 20th, 1837

My dear Walter,

So have you been stung yet by a deadly water-serpent? If you have it not in your power to *draw* the poison, then draw your own dying agony. (We assume you have not been bit on the right arm.) Do have your executors parcel the cartoon with your effects and despatch everything to Macao in the passage-boat as we can always do with diversion. The attractions of this place as the resort of the jaundiced foreigner, it becomes increasingly apparent to your servant with each visit, are exaggerated grossly. I do not speak with any particular malice. Our colleagues and counterparts, if not Mr Corrigan, who, I have it on the best authority, lost a prodigious wager, appear to have forgiven my aberration on the waters. (The role of scapegrace, Walter, which is yours, is easier to bear than that of scapegoat, I'll assure you.) The liquid element seems to bring out what is fickle and unstable in my character – but I should be as the Petrine rock when compared to your own good self, who is known to be possessed by the unsteady condition of genius. No, you will not wreck on me. Restrain yourself, I implore you, my good sir, from leaping overboard when you finally do embark on the craft to take you to Macao – the state of affairs is not so bad as to drive you to such final conclusions. I'll add that the promises of princes, partners, and ... women should be written, as the Dean says, on running water. Enough.

I contrive to fill my days. I would rather be arduously employed than idle and leave my mind fallow It is the trivial round which stultifies. Amusement! Mercy, I would rather be at the day-book. I parcel my days out between Harry O'Rourke and another companion, about the same in years as he. They try to teach me the rudiments of chess – abominable game! The rest is passed in reading and study. I gad about the Praia and the bazaar, collecting snippets and intelligences – you would be quite surprised to hear what goes on, I do assure you! This is only of intrinsic interest to the student and would not be considered useful knowledge, certainly not in any commercial sense, amounting as it does to no more, I fear, than tittle-tattle: a Newgate calendar gleaned from the gutter of Macao. As this town, often enough, attracts the veriest human sweepings of Canton, it is a depravity double-distilled. Useless, useless, and it shall profit me not. Scribblings in a notebook – of what use is such an album of nonsense? I blush to think that Harry made me the gift of such, odious and presumptuous youth that I am! Do I recount tittle-tattle from up the hill – a more elevated form of news, but still gossip? Perhaps they should duck me if they find me out, as should be the fate of all tale-bearers. We met in Miss Remington's garden – I there on sufferance of the pain of her severe displeasure – but such occasions greatly wearisome to your servant – also present Mr Arden, the

248

chaplain, sundry British and American gentlemen, MacQuitty (who has quite put out of countenance all the native dogs and is become the Cock and Bully of them all), MacQuitty's owner (I will not say master), Dr MacGillivray, as well as gentlemen from Russell & Co. and our contemporaries from Messrs J- and M-, these last present, I expect, by express invitation of our partners, rather aloof from us of Meridian. Do I forget the delightful hostess who, nevertheless, seemed a trifle downcast ...but I am in danger of becoming a loose-tongued Goody Chase and had better keep my observations to myself.

The cigars have arrived from Manilla, and will reach you by the next passage-boat.

Your affec. friend,
Gideon.

Walter Eastman to Gideon Chase

No.12 American Hong
Canton
July 1st, 1837

My dear and very exasperating Gideon,

Cheroots have come. Now I have both consolation and defence against the mosquitoes – conceive of me puffing fit to rival the *Jardine* steamer. Crusoe was in a better plight – he at least could grow his own leaves. How you have put me into a fidget, sir. I shall need to smoke to soothe my anxieties and thwarted expectations. On the one hand you appeal to the noblest and basest instinct in man, to wit his curiosity about his fellows, and then on the other, in the next moment, you most cavalierly refuse to satisfy the appetites you have aroused. What sort of friendly act is this? Be a tale-bearer (and I shall think none the worse of you, for Hermes was not the least of gods) or, sir, be altogether silent. No, don't be silent: shall I rather fee you as my correspondent from Macao at the handsome remuneration of a cent per line.

Your information could not be so disgraceful as the placards the Chinese soldiery have again taken to fixing upon the walls of the Factories. I will not soil this good paper by repeating the accusations of unnatural vice and the like revilements heaped upon us. John Slade favoured us with his 'true translations' – I find it difficult to conceive how this man should have troubled to learn the language when he has nothing but dislike for its speakers – we are aware the divines hate the Chinese *and* know the mystery of their tongue but they have an ulterior purpose after all. My own sentiments are notorious to you, but then I comprehend but little.

Over these last several months, I have sensed a change in the policy and sentiments of the Canton authorities towards the foreigner and his trade, more especially the clandestine trade of the British. Opium and Albion seem to be the Viceroy's twin banes. It is my very considered belief that this hardening of hearts and stiffening of resolve is not local in inspiration but emanates directly from the Emperor in his court in Peking. The provincial administration is altogether too corrupt and venal to be capable of reforming itself. Besides, the Hoppo and the Governor (apart from the great *fact* of their official lives, which is that they must recoup from the bribes of the foreigners in the short space of three years the vast outlay they have already made to purchase their offices) know only too well that the task of extirpating the trade is beyond their puny means. This is *even* if they wished to do so against their own interest. They know only too well the strength, skill, and daring of the foreigners, the stoutness of their ships, the destructive power and accuracy of their cannon. This is the courage of ignorance, a determination which is entirely phantastical, and has in my view the mark of the harem and the eunuch large upon it – that is, a correct policy inappropriately adopted and in which the Emperor has been encouraged by false and fawning flatterers, rather than having his extravagant desires bridled by subtle and worldly advisers. No politician would set his name to such a course.

As far as our own part in this sorry business is concerned,

I suppose we enter the stage on cue for the principal scene, not to say *denouement,* in which we shall play but an accessory role to the principal – Third Murderer, shall we say, to the major party's Macbeth (who was a Scot, after all) – but we shall nevertheless be in time to take our bow with the participants of the earlier acts and enjoy the sweets of a great *coup de théâtre.* How think you? On the question of arranging our various liaisons and deliveries of the new season, I may say I never had the pleasure of mixing with so thorough-going a set of rascals and cut-throats as the gentlemen of the river. Good God! I counted the fingers of my hand to check they still tallied five pursuivant to the ruffian aiding me into his boat. In exchange for our quills, ledgers, ink-stands, and stools we shall need to be furnished with at least five carronades, a few stand of Brown Bess or, better still, if our partners can endure the expense, a case of rifles, and a score of boarding-pikes, not to mention cutlasses. I do not altogether jest. Rumours abound of a receiving-ship, moored in the anchorage of Namoa some hundred miles up the coast, surprised, her valuable cargo seized and captain and crew butchered in cold blood. There was but one survivor – he climbed into the rigging and watched in horror as his ship-mates were cut down to the man. So, as you may see, it is not merely the demi-brigands of the scrambling crabs who must go armed to the teeth, but the foreign crews of the stationary depot ships who must also be able and ready to repel attacks. Certainly, they have nothing to fear from His Celestial Majesty's revenue cruisers, with their paltry pop-guns – but the pirates constitute altogether a more formidable foe – and the rapscallions esteem the distinction between *meum et tuum* as lightly as they value their own lives. We shall see. Convey my profound salutations to the old villain, O'Rourke. Who may be your other opponent at chess? On private account I have half a dozen cases of Lafite destined for me on the wings of the monsoon, one of which (you may inform Harry) shall be *tuum* and the remainder *meum.*

In hopes of your next.

Walter

39 Rua da Conceicao,
Macao
June the 28th, 1837

My dearest,

Oh! how my poor heart fluttered when I saw the familiar hand. The brilliant songsters in our tree could not beat their wings more rapidly. The sight of your personal seal was sufficient to send the blood coursing to my cheeks, red as the wax itself. Were my helpless feelings traitor to me? I could no more subdue them than I might stem the mighty flood which rolls its earthy waters and discharges around our almost island of Macao. Did you not say, long ago it seems, but how short in verity, that it was a source of comfort to you to reflect that the waters you presently gazed on so mournfully would be viewed a week hence by your friends (and those who love you?). So now, as I write, do I look out upon the face of the waters from my room.

Yet I think your plight is not so hard as mine. My dear, you are right to say I carry the burden of a heavy heart, perplexities and griefs which I may not share, for I have no friend here to whom I might entrust a confidence. Might my pent-up anguish, swollen and augmenting, burst finally as the mass of flood-waters will finally breach the stoutest dam? But I must endure.

You talk of your resolution, of how you will set yourself at any obstacle, howsoever high, once your wish is formed. Yes! I know that such is your nature! As well tell the bull in the field that he must not charge the trespasser upon his territory. But it is an obstinacy which touches on the perverse – how often have I remarked this! It is a determination which seems most arbitrarily formed and coldly held. So have I remarked your views on the world and its affairs. Do you love me for myself – or as an object upon which you may exercise and display your resolve, your manly firmness? Oh, I am unfair, I know. You must not take any notice of me – I talk to myself, wanting any other to whom I may pour out my heart – you must be both my betrothed and my dearest confidant.

Mr Chase has been most agreeable and shown great kindness to me, though, of course, it is not appropriate for me to trust my intimate thoughts to him. He has a most pleasing and gentlemanly bearing and has almost wholly lost those small awkwardnesses of manner which marred his behaviour in society even a year ago. Of course, he has a model the most suave and accomplished to form himself upon! Because he is a little younger than his contemporaries and perhaps a little more serious still than he should be, he seems lonely. I, therefore, requested – no, demanded – his attendance at a small gathering in my beloved garden. He appeared at first a trifle ill at ease but this reserve was bit by bit dissipated and I did my utmost to 'bring him out of himself'. You can be sure I was at my most gay and vivacious as I engaged him on the topics which might be of interest to him (though my knowledge of sporting matters cannot be said to be extensive). He it was who explained the derivation and meaning of *paene insula,* but I had not realised that in addition to his other accomplishments, he was a classical scholar. Mr Ridley and Mr Johnstone, among others, were present and made many jokes at poor Mr Chase's expense. He and Dr MacGillivray appeared to be 'auld acquaintance' – Dr MacGillivray, who is so very gruff his manner verges on the boorish, though it is said he has a kind heart. The two of them went to our little pond and amused themselves by poking the grasses with a stick – what they might expect to find, I surely do not know. For such a very young man, he seems to prefer the company of men years his senior than those more nearly his contemporaries. Perhaps it is a case of 'an old head on young shoulders'. I, too, must emulate this prodigy – though, I am afraid, the strain of it will bestow a sprinkling of grey hairs upon me before my time. I fear I am no comfort to you! and the despondent tone of my letters can only serve to make it *more* difficult for you to preserve the brave and cheerful face you present to the world. Forgive me, for I am weak and alone and foolish and young – and a woman.

But always your kind and loving friend,
Alice

Chapter XIX

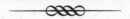

'You have betrayed your trust, sir. I never thought to see such underhand behaviour in one of the young gentlemen of Mr Corrigan's choosing.'

'Sir, if you will very generously allow me to explain my actions and the thoughts behind them, you will, I am confident...'

'You amaze me, sir. Your audacity is a thing to marvel at. I, sir, listen to the narrative of your most infamous duplicity? You are cool, sir, very cool.'

'I regret the unavoidable necessity of keeping our plans ...'

'Our?'

'...my plans, naturally, privy only for the time being, that is, until an opportune moment presented itself for their announcement. No deception was intended. Upon that I give you my word as a gentleman.'

'Gentleman? You, sir, are nothing more than a penniless adventurer...'

Eastman flushes. He bites his lip; his knuckles whiten around the bills of lading he had been carrying when summoned to Remington's private office. Until now his voice has been firm. It shakes a little as he says, 'I trust, sir, that you will acquit me of harbouring any mercenary motives or discreditable designs upon your niece. For while I perfectly understand, indeed it would be remiss of you not to wish...'

'You dare to teach me my duties to my ward? Remiss? If I have been remiss it has been in not earlier recognising you as a candidate for a sound horse-whipping.'

'Your position, sir, does not mitigate the very extraordinary tone you have chosen to adopt towards me.'

'Damn you, I will address you in any way which pleases me.' Remington holds his clenched fist six inches above his desk. Eastman waits for him to strike it. But Remington lowers his hand gently, still in a fist, and rests it on the desk. Throughout, his expression and gestures have been totally at odds with the violence of his language.

Eastman says, 'My feelings and intentions towards your niece may, I believe, speak for themselves. They are of the purest. That I am not wealthy would be impossible for me to deny. I am not altogether without resource or expectations. There is a small income, perhaps some hundreds of dollars, which will pass to me on the death of my father's sister. It is not sufficient to make me independent but may supplement whatever I should earn through my own efforts – and it would supply the difference between an adequacy and a degree of comfort.'

'Pshaw! You talk to me of hundreds. There are families in Boston or Salem with thousands, hundreds of thousands a year, that my brother would not consider for his daughter. You are an *employé* of this house, sir, and no more. One with no prospects. My niece is not to be bestowed on the likes of you. If you think by marrying advantageously to secure yourself a partnership and emoluments, then you delude yourself most seriously.'

'Well, damn you…sir, do me the justice at least of believing my desires honourable! Spurn my suit – on practical grounds – that I could not resent – it might blight my prospects of worldly happiness – but I beg you not to insult me as a gentleman, as a *man*, sir.'

Remington smiles thinly. He taps the side of his nose. The vulgarity of the gesture makes Eastman grind his teeth. With creditable self-control he steadies his voice again: breathlessness is the problem. 'Sir, you may entertain certain prejudices about me which, justified or otherwise, I ask you to place out of your mind. Examine, if you will, my proposal on its own merits. I have no worldly endowments to confer upon your niece. Nor have I the endowment of nature – I am no handsome or gallant. What I may bestow upon the object of my affections is… the treasure of a loving heart. I do not wax boastful on my own account so much as hers, when I say it is my firm belief that no man could be more devoted to her or her felicity – or might make her happier as her companion in life. Surely, sir, these are not worthless things? Are the wishes of the parties the most immediately involved to be considered as nothing at all? Your niece must have spoken to you, sir. Will you give her hand where her heart is elsewhere?'

A pretty handsome speech, my buck, thinks Remington, and says aloud: 'She has said nothing, sir, for the very simple reason that she knows nothing of this interview.'

'She…what?' Eastman turns paler even than nature made him. 'My assumption, sir…Then, then…how in heaven's name are you aware of the standing of matters as between ourselves? I had supposed the poor creature made distraught by her heavy responsibility, who turned then to you, her guardian, for that support and guidance she might justifiably expect.'

Remington's lip curls. The young man's fingers work against his palms. 'By the simple expedient, sir, of reading your disgraceful correspondence with my ward and the record of your deceit and wiles made apparent in the girl's journal.'

'You dared to open my personal mails, hers? You presumed to spy, to act the part of the ferret among my private letters and papers in her hands?' His voice is thick; it shakes. He is maddened. Remington says briskly, 'There is no privacy in matters of this nature. You intrude upon the privacy and the personal and legal affairs of my brother's family and mine. These are the weightiest of matters – which go far beyond your ambitions and the ignorance and irresponsibility of a young girl. Your letters ceased to be your property once they were despatched. I have no qualms about perusing them, I would scrutinise them as I would the ledgers and accounts drawn up by the clerks of my own firm. In fact –' Remington permits himself a thin and humourless smile – 'it was your very distinctive and rare hand, as it appears sparsely in the books, which attracted my curiosity in the first instance.'

The bills are crumpled in Eastman's fist. He is hot despite the cooler October weather, and sweat is beginning to gather in droplets at his high hair-line. He thinks hard. 'You had no right to open my correspondence,' he says dully; he is still recovering from shock; not surprisingly his powers of argument have deserted him for the moment; he seizes on the last point, the easiest for him to grasp in his present state, however minor or irrelevant, as a floundering debater might grasp at a point of procedure. 'This was not the act of a gentleman; it is, it is…little short of infamous,' Eastman gobbles pompously. But it is *I* who is outraged, who appeals to convention, he is still able to reflect with surprise through his anger and humiliation. Remington looks quite debonair now, seems to have usurped the Eastman role of lazy wit. 'Scandal and infamy, sir,' he drawls, 'were precisely what I wished to spare my brother, I calculate – you could be the master at that school, I expect – the French drawing-master. Ha!'

Eastman's lip curls. Remington's crudeness helps him regain his self-possession. 'I fear you have already made your mind up,' he says, 'to scorn me, yet will I court further indignity, if not for my own sake, then for another's. I had no wish to injure your family in reputation or substance. On this score believe me. Even now I cherish no ill-will towards your name. I heartily apologise for what innocent subterfuge I may have practised; there was no malice in it. I merely left you ignorant of my affection for your niece.'

'Ignorant? Affection? You planned to elope, you plotted to steal my charge, sir. Yes, sir. Do not deny it – I have in evidence your thoughts written down in your own hand.'

'We… ah…' Eastman grits his teeth, 'we had an understanding between ourselves, a private agreement that we should announce our intention to the world when…'

'You were secretly engaged,' says Remington drily. 'You do not deny that? Scarcely. Then it is but a short and inevitable step from the secret formulation of such a desire to its illicit accomplishment.'

'But where in the name of all that is good would I go, sir?' Eastman shouts in desperation. 'There is nowhere – you know that surely as well as I. The Factories? Impossible by reason of the jealousy of the Chinese, if nothing else. Macao? Where might I fly on that pin-head? Could I take up my station on some boat off this hostile coast? Am I a chest of drug or a bale of cotton? It is impossible, sir.'

'Do not ask me, sir,' Remington says coldly. 'I am not here to give you the directions to Gretna. You will not from this moment see my niece nor are you to attempt to open any communication with her, open or clandestine. I absolutely forbid it. Yes, sir. There is no question of a betrothal broken – there was none to begin with. Nevertheless, sir, if you truly conclude to consult her welfare, as opposed to the pursuit of a course of a folly both selfish and futile – you will appreciate the desirability of…discretion and confidentiality. You talk of one gentleman's rights as against another: there are also the duties of a gentleman. I have nothing more to say to you. No, nothing. Hold your peace, sir. You may withdraw to your work.'

CHAPTER XX

They hang motionless in the river. In the lee of the fort at Dutch Folly it is slack water. The oars sprawl idly in the rowlocks but not more untidily than Walter, who leans back against a cushion, dead cigar in teeth, with a rectangular pad against his lap and thighs. Framed in the V of Walter's knees, at the bow, looking towards the distant Factories, is the blob of Gideon's head – front sight to the rear-sight notch of Walter's legs. Gideon tugs one-handed at the line he has tossed into the stream as speculatively as the consignment of South Seas sandalwood and North American ginseng he was entrusted with importing the previous week – yes, promotion looms at twenty. The fish are wary as the Hong merchants faced with two hundred tons of goods they cannot sell, but as the fish are not already vertiginously in debt to the foreigner there is no pressure which can be usefully applied to force them to accept the worm. Perhaps Gideon should stun the fish with pellets of opium instead of the stale bread he is sowing broadcast on the water; it is the only commodity welcome to the Chinese security-merchants who, to the man, rejoice at Meridian's decision to enter the illegal traffic in drug. They will no longer have to help sell cottons and exotic produce, of which there is already a glut, to exchange for their teas if Meridian pay for the leaf with the silver of their opium profits. Wonderful! thinks Minqua – double the gain and half the work.

'Move your head, Gid, it obscures the Swedish Hong.'

'How amazing that it can, when I think of it. It is not so big! I can never understand the rules of perspective and foreshortening when you or Harry take the trouble to explain.'

'Fault in the teacher,' says Eastman briefly, instead of correcting Gideon's misunderstanding, who is not keen to remember drawing-lessons given.

'Oh, no, Walter! Not when you are the instructor,' says loyal, slow Gideon.

'Move, sir,' says Walter. 'It is a prodigious swollen head, which can mask a whole building from here.'

Gideon lies prone on his stomach, pulling hopefully at the line every now and again. The edges of the unpadded thwarts cut uncomfortably into him after a while; so, tying the fishing-line to the rowlock, he turns to Walter, taking care to sit slightly to his side. 'Am I now in your way still?'

Walter grunts, which Gideon takes as a negative.

'This is a fine day. A golden mean: neither too warm nor too cold. Cheerful but not oppressive. Light wind…'

'…which blows mercifully from us to the square's rubbish mound, rather than vice versa.'

'Ah, quite so, Walter.'

'*Go tell the court it glows and shines like rotten wood.*'

'What?'

'Sour sentiments from a namesake, brother smoker, fellow-exile, and Virginian, if you stretch a point.'

'It sounds, I calculate, not unlike Li Po, the drunken poet.'

'Unlike the earlier Walter, of course, I am neither dungeon'd nor in danger, yet, I'll allow, of the headsman's axe. Inebriated? We shall see tonight. A more congenial way of losing one's head, I guess.'

'I beg you not to do anything so foolish – you will only occasion your friends worry and confirm your enemies in their opinions of you. Who will have the trouble of putting you to your bed but me?'

'Ah, Gid, dear Gideon. I shall miss you sorely.'

'Miss me? What do you talk of?' Gideon looks anxiously at Eastman, who concentrates on some shading. He sucks the end of his lead pencil, holds the pad up appraisingly, then (which ruins the carefully careless pose), takes the cheroot out of his mouth and draws with it. 'Darnation!'

Gideon starts to laugh and Eastman joins in. 'Would I not like to perform the office of incendiary on the real Factories. Gid, it is a scene I must quit. You must confess so. How may I remain?'

'Yours is a proud spirit, Walter. But is it not possible for you to make some small accommodation? I speak in a purely selfish point of view. How sadly I should miss you. Who might be my friend? Amusing companions though they are, I may hardly hold the conversation with Ridley and Johnstone which I enjoy with you.'

'Even were I to swallow my pride and respect for myself as a man, how do you think I could retain my position? My dear fellow, I called Remington a scoundrel to his face, snapped my fingers under his nose and told him I was damned if I'd bandy words with him.'

Gideon turns on his stomach again to observe his line, disappearing into the grey murk. Some bubbles rise by it. Nothing happens when he tugs pessimistically. When he speaks again, he faces away from Walter to the Factories. 'And you would not find ready employment in any of the other houses of agency, with your known antipathy to the traders of opium.'

'The trade, Gid, the trade, not the traders,' Eastman corrects him, 'but you are right. Incompetence, a morose or a surly nature, vice, addiction to the bottle, have proved no bar to those transferring their flag from one Hong to another in the past but your servant, no. Nor should I desire such occupation. I shall take ship for Boston or New York in April. Until then... well, I shall soon tender my resignation, and shall be a gentleman of leisure at Macao, if one of limited means. Perhaps I may subsist no longer as a dilettante but by a professional pencil, as Harry. But will he call me out if I offer competition in his small market?'

'Oh, I guess he is secure in his own opinions and in the

reputation he enjoys among others. If you will forgive my plainness and allow me to observe so, you, my dear friend, constitute no threat to him. Your true abilities lie elsewhere.'

'Were my cigar yet smouldering, I should grind it out upon your impertinent rump, which is so conveniently presented.'

'It is true it is vulnerable.'

'So, Jack of all trades, master at none? Is that what you think?'

'Words, Walter, words, are your forte.'

'Mm, can you think of an employment which demands as the requisite qualities for success in its practitioners some small modicum of literary ability, a little artistic sense, a degree of boldness, a gallant address (if I flatter myself), principles existent but flexible, and the readiness to sow mischief and consternation amongst his enemies?'

'I cannot – you appear to confound the characters of the highwayman and the controversial theologian.'

'Ha!'

'But we spoke of competition here on our own small stage. The conundrum is: does the restricted setting bring out the best in an otherwise mediocre performer and enlarge his stature? Or does the smallness of his world crib the talent of he who would otherwise be greater? I have frequently pondered this with regard to two into whose acquaintance I have been privileged to be admitted.'

My good self and Harry, thinks Eastman, who can be very vain. 'I allow,' he says, 'that competition and the healthy stimulation afforded by the friendly rivalry of his peers would have concentrated Harry's mind a good deal better. Even in Calcutta he worked to better advantage. Monopoly is no good thing.'

'Indeed,' says Gideon, 'left to its own devices mankind would be complacent. There must have been not only the spur of necessity felt, but also the goad of a salutary and wholesome rivalry between prominent members of the tribe which enabled our rude forebears to ascend from their primitive state, when all was in common and degraded, to our present condition today.'

'When all is in particular and degraded. Gid, at one moment you appear to be talking about art and the next it is the steam-engine. You have a confusing, disobliging sort of way of running.'

'But precisely. Are they not closely related in their development?'

'I have,' says Walter firmly, 'sufficiently enjoyed this conversation. Desist. Look to your line. My Swedish Hong awaits its roof.'

Reluctantly, Gideon readopts the supine position; however, in addition to a deep personal shyness, he also possesses the thick hide of the true pedant, for he mutters to himself something about '...the handmaiden of...long known to them before us ...marriage of the mechanic and the clerk...' which Walter hears in snatches above the slap and suck of water as a war-junk passes deliberately near.

'...revolution in sentiment... bastion of ignorance. .. and powder would not work.'

'Quiet in the fo'c'sle.'

'Well, by God!'

The boat rocks violently as Gideon turns and gets halfway to his feet. Eastman holds up his pad for shield. 'Have you taken leave of your senses? If you are offended ...'

'Why have we not thought of this long ago?'

'Thought of what, sir? Restraining jackets?'

'*He* has only survived, and his puny organ, for want of any alternative source of intelligence! *That* is a monopoly, baneful in its effects, yet it is not one which is enforced by law or even custom. Oh, how blind!'

'Seat yourself squarely and do control yourself.'

Gideon's eyes are bright. He slaps his knees, tucks his hands under his armpits and hugs himself. 'Oh, oh, their faces! It can be done, it *can* be done. The enemy is but feeble.'

'Do permit others to share in your jubilation.'

'The *Monitor* – we shall supplant it utterly, rout its partisans. We shall found our own newspaper!'

Now Eastman *knows* he shares his boat with a madman. 'Indeed.'

'We shall sweep them off the field. That's a fact, and no two ways.' Gideon laughs happily.

'I am glad you are so confident, sir. Did I, by the by, hear you say *"we"?*'

'Yes, Walter.'

'The editorial "we" in anticipation, I guess? Rather than the pronoun of the first person in its plural form?'

'You and I, Walter,' says Gideon, slightly uneasily.

'Ah, I see, We, us. Fine. Capital. Every private soldier in the *Grande Armée* carried the baton of a Marshal of France in his knapsack, so I expect I have my font of type somewhere in my trunk, ready to assume the editorial function at the drop of a hat.'

'Oh, yours is the most able pen in the Factories, I calculate, by a very long stretch.'

'You flatter me, or, rather, recollecting your earlier animad-versions, regarding the dwarf appearing a giant among a race of pygmies, you do not at all. My dear Gid, this is not a question of writing a letter – the longest letter – of one's doings and circulating it among the largest circle of his acquaintances. It is of another order entirely.'

'Not at all. The first newspapers were composed in precisely such a spirit – they were nothing more nor less than newsletters despatched from the metropolis to the provinces – and read the more avidly, I guess, for their very informal nature. They would speak intimately to their audience in a manner our later journals could never emulate. Such is my surmise. As to the circum-stances in which you and I, *we,* presently find ourselves situate, I calculate they could not be more propitious for such an enterprise. The *Monitor* has whetted but hardly satisfied the appetite of its small public. It is pompous, ill-informed, partial, unenlivened by wit or fancy ...'

'But it has a press, Gideon. It is printed – it exists. If we allow that we had a modest capital, where might we find a press, operatives? To my knowledge, there have been three, four, maybe five brought to this coast, including the one of the Company on which Morrison's dictionary was formed – these are heavy and cumbersome items of machinery which lie like ballast in a ship's hold. Allow we laid our hands upon one such, where should we house it. And...'

Gideon holds up his hand. He smiles. 'The hard part of *my*

work is done,' he says, 'and it proved easy. The rest are but details, details merely – such as the remainder of your sketch, including, doubtless, the boat in which we sit, which may as well be accomplished over a glass and in comfort as here.' And as he hauls up his twine and gut and bare hook, he looks very pleased with himself, considering he has caught no actual *fish*.

Walter sprinkles sand over his final words. Rather more satisfying than using bibulous paper, he feels, which would not convey the idea of grit in the partners' eyes, the perfect nuisance he intends to make of himself, as well as (to pursue the conceit in an Eastman-like way) the similarity to the alchemist casting his magic dust, the allusion to the running out of the sands of…

'Time, soon, Walter,' says Gideon, spying at the window. 'They will shortly be at their constitutional. You must leave the letter while they are out, then take the passage-boat. It would never do to pass a night under their roof.'

'In heaven's name, why not?'

'It would be as a guest, no longer as an *employé* and the obligations of hospitality are reciprocal. You would be in their debt.'

'Bah! I am afflicted with no such nice notions.' Walter blows the wet sand off his note of resignation. It is in his most flamboyant hand and is, he fancies, a little masterpiece of formal insolence. '*Your most humble, obedient servant* – I do suppose that is one of the most outrageous and frequently perpetrated falsehoods in the English language.' He feels quite the journalist himself already, professional thrower of vitriol.

'Indeed. In the opposite extreme of discourtesy, I am more and more inclined to believe that the mandarins' epithets of "Devil", "Barbarian", not to mention the "Cringe and utterly obey!" with which the Third George was favoured, are merely to be read as "My dear sir, I shall be in your debt if you would bestow upon the matter your most obliging attention." No more than that.'

'D'you say? I shall still resent the Celestial insult, though, and when a gentleman asks me to do him the honour of expediting his affairs – why, I shall know what he means and will knock him down.'

'Wafer and wax. There. It is done. The die is cast.'

'Our boats burned.'

'Look forwards only, if you would avoid the fate of Lot's wife.'

'Etcetera, etcetera.'

Eastman regards the object sceptically. A wild-goose chase, after all. His footprints in the soft dust of the ancient godown tell the story: long, eager strides near the light of the door, shortening in the gloom to the pessimist's disillusioned shuffle. Parallel with his own runs the broader, shambling spoor of Father Ribeiro, whose own even length of stride, nevertheless, tells the story of greater self-possession. 'Darn it,' thinks Eastman. Dust of aeons, it seems, has laid its ghostly benediction on the contents of this forgotten warehouse. Father Ribeiro blows, stirring a small storm, invisible without sunbeams but potent enough to set Walter sneezing helplessly. This, of course, disturbs further irritant dust, making Walter sneeze yet more vastly and... on goes the cycle. Years of addiction to a fearsome proprietary blend of snuff render Father Ribeiro immune. Through watering eyes Walter begs him to desist.

'Dear boy, my son, I try only to aid you.'

As Walter removes his handkerchief from his nose and, as the prickling subsides, he fancies he can detect the aroma of garlic on the obliging Jesuit's breath. 'Ah, Father, I am grateful to you – and for bringing me to this place. Forgive me for wasting your time in this fruitless search.'

'Fruitless, my son? But this is what you require, if I am not mistaken. *Seek and ye shall find.*' He rumbles with laughter, putting his paw heavily on the object and causing Walter to recoil. He is able to apply the handkerchief in time. 'Whatever it is, Father, and it is unlike anything I have seen before, it is plainly seized up with rust and dust.'

'Despair, my son – the most awful of sins in your canon of heretics, I understand.'

Walter's eyes are now becoming used to the gloom of the warehouse. That is, in a process which will shortly acquire great interest and significance for him, his pupils, which were contracted to admit a small amount of bright sunshine outside, are now dilated to permit more of the godown's dimmer light to pass through a maximum aperture. The image cast on the retina is still, of course, upside down, though automatically adjusted by the brain, which has its stock of conventions, too. Upside down the machine might as well be left, for all that Walter knows or cares; he can now perceive that it actually is a machine of some kind. To his morbid eye it somewhat resembles the guillotine. 'Have a care, Father. Should you have the misfortune to cut yourself, the filth may poison the blood.'

'Tush!' says Ribeiro. 'Fiddlesticks!' imitating his good friend, Harry O'Rourke. 'You are a young man who uses the weed tobacco?'

'Why sure, Father,' says Walter in surprise, 'permit me to…'

'No, no,' says the Jesuit impatiently, 'the… no, my vernacular is not…you carry on your person the means of combustion?'

'Oh, a lucifer.'

'Is that what it is called?' says Father Ribeiro with some amazement. 'Extraordinary. *Lucus a non lucendo.* The unpredictable forms of the colloquial. Well, my son, strike.'

Eastman flicks the top of his boot. The chemicals undergo their dangerous reaction. Fizz, pop, splutter. A smell of brimstone succeeds that of dust and garlic. In the guttering green and yellow flame, Walter sees the contraption is half-covered by a sheet: a rectangle about eight feet long by two, with the tarpaulin thrown over the vertical frame which juts up three feet high, three-quarters of the way down its length. More than ever, this conveys macabre associations: the covered blade of the revolutionaries' device; a shrouded memorial stone, perhaps some specimen of the Gothic fantasy popular in Europe two decades and more ago and having a revival in America – this utterly repugnant to Walter's temperament. (Fashion's pendulum – the grandchildren of those who share Walter's predilections will revive something similar in a reaction against a sensibility *they* consider outmoded.)

'Retire to a safe distance, my son,' and with a neat flick of the wrist, the dexterity of the gesture probably related, Walter thinks, to familiar performance of some externally similar but arcane and priest-monopolised rite of the Church, Ribeiro uncovers the modern tabernacle. *'Fiat lux,'* he commands, 'more.'

Walter approaches with a match in each hand. The apparatus, its outlines no longer hooded, begins in the waving shadows to assume the form of Gutenberg, Caxton, and Wynkyn's mighty engine. At least as folk-memory prompts Walter, who has never seen a printing-press before. He can now observe that where the blade would be on the guillotine there is a large winged screw with a lever set through it at right angles, which holds a flat plate. The press, perhaps? The part whose function gives its name to the whole. Father Ribeiro leans over into the recesses of the contraption. He gestures for illumination. Walter passes him a match which he strikes on the wood frame. His heavy Iberian features are emphasised in the interplay of shadow and light, eyes gleaming as he investigates; so that when he turns the screw, making it shriek in its rusty thread, the kindly old Jesuit looks uncannily like an Inquisitor eliciting a confession on the rack. 'Oil, which is all that is requisite to turn.'

'To *burn,* Father?' asks Eastman, thinking of *autos-da-fé* and slow matches between the toes.

'Turn, turn,' says Ribeiro. 'To free the iron. *Pingo de oleo.* Any sorts of oils, indeed: olive oil, Chinese sesame oil, lamp-oil. My son, even holy oil I may give to consecrate your veritable crusade.' His shoulders shake. 'The fonts of letters are not here. But it is my well-considered belief that the cases of...*type?* Yes, the cases must lie elsewhere in the godown. We will return with a cart and helpers. I may answer for my converts' stalwart bodies, if not for their immortal souls.'

'Father, you truly are a tower of strength. Your knowledge is that of the encyclopaedia.'

'If my great predecessors in the distinguished Society of which I am the most unworthy and obscure member had it in their power to cast ordnance and predict the solar eclipse for the Emperor in Peking, then, assuredly, I, Joaquim Ribeiro, may recognise this tool of the devil when I see it. Luther's Iron Handmaiden. Bah! Its deadly spikes pierced Mother Church nigh mortally. As to *les encyclopédistes* – atheists, my son. Atheists and schismatics.'

'Ah, quite so, Father, quite so.'

> 12 Rua da Nossa Senhora da Nazare
> Macao
> November 3rd, 1837

My dear Gid,

Capitally, gallantly, swimmingly is how we 'come on' here. You never told me what a splendid character our good Father was. I shall burn candles; nay, I'll apostasise. Scarlet Woman? I embrace her, if O'Rourke and Ribeiro are accounted among her worshippers. To come to the point, in short, my dear friend, we possess a deadly weapon and I warrant we shall menace a few throats with its points. Can you doubt me? Could I have doubted you that afternoon as we floated idly on the sluggish stream? Brave boy! Who was undaunted and knew no perplexities.

Ribeiro, in the most capacious bag of his memory, carried knowledge − rumour, rather, though long dead − of a press secreted in some ancient godown of the settlement. It was one of the few secular presses licensed by the jealous and despotic (I was going to add priest-ridden but am in honour bound to refrain) government. Ah, Pombal! Your works did not endure. The enlightened measures of the reforming Marquis could not save his beloved Portugal! Indeed, of the statesmen of that 'Age of Reason', who is remembered but as a marmoreal lump, sport of the birds in some peeling square, while the works of the immortal Voltaire live yet in the hearts of men? Indestructible treasure! I did very nearly make a most unfortunate blunder when I mentioned the Marquis, ignorant of the circumstance that he had cast the good Father's Order out of Portugal. I understand his own excellent Italian is the fruit of a prolonged stay in Rome, where he was accepted into that mighty sodality and, all in all, his liking for this conspiracy and his coolness towards the government of Macao and − I expect − his willingness to abet ourselves must be the product of the persecutions. But I digress. (Gid, this self-indulgence, this whimsical tendency must be curbed when we enter into our editorial capacity. I rely on you.) Hidden in haste, doubtless against a future day of victory (and the visitation of black, because inky, retributions) the machinery was stilled. Yet did its operators cast over it a protective coverlet, as a blanket for a babe, alike to shield it from damp and the prowling bands of the modern Herod. It lay undisclosed, undiscovered. Ribeiro believed its demise the work of faction, inevitable concomitant of some revolution, minor or major, some upset in the bowels of government in Lisbon or Goa, which duly must in course of time subvert the government of the colony (province, rather) of Macao to be supplanted by another clique. Do we not know it in our own time? Some poisoned prawn consumed the other day in Lisbon wrenching the guts of Macao the next. It is my belief the Bishop had a falling out with the Governor and his Senate or the Dezembargador, which is how our good Father knew. How else was it kept a secret, unless the custodians of the confessional, long versed in the keeping of confidences, alone possessed the knowledge of the whereabouts? Ribeiro disclaimed all – with a twinkle in his eye. Well, when we exhumed this grave of letters, we came upon an inscription, a 'relique', not of a lapidary but a leaden eloquence, and dead men spoke to the living, their heirs. Gideon, a tear came to my eye which I disdained to brush aside. A frame of type, still standing, we found, which when we blacked and 'pulled' we discovered to be the first page of the last issue of what I shall ever think of as Our Illustrious Predecessor. Its title?

O Aurora Macaensis!

They hanged its editor, the black-hearted villains. Broke his heart first, then his neck on their garrotte.

But where is their victory now? Does he live that tyrant, with his 'wrinkled lip and sneer of cold command'? Cold, aye, in his narrow home, friend and enemy alike, persecutor and persecuted. But we shall remake our predecessor's glorious dawn! This I vow to his lingering shade, present, I make so bold as to believe, when we broke open the seals, of a kind, upon his monument and entered, the first men to touch it for half a century. Oh, it shall be the best kind of monument – one that works. *Circumspice.*

For myself, when I walk these greasy cobbles, those insidious, crooked lanes to the bay, I keep my eyes down. It is easier thus. Enjoying the air of the Praia one balmy evening, not long ago, the breeze sportive and delightful (such as will gladden your heart, lighten your step, and you will never pine for the Factories' chartered and noisome square), wavelets laughing as they lapped the shore, I crossed the path of a carriage familiar to you as to me. The horses had almost run me down, so deep in thought was I. Mostly I thought melancholy thoughts: how the strifes of our predecessors had died with them, how short was the appointed time of even the longest-lived of them, how soon we, also, would be forgotten, flown away, never known to those who should come after us, and then they, too, would have their day to be succeeded by…an everlasting night? (Not a word to the good Father!) And of that number who came after us, there would be those who would be as our mortal enemies, doubtless; those, too, who would have stood our bosom friends. Yet, never – never, Gid! – to meet or even to know of the existence of the other. How fickle, random, and arbitrary are our lives! We bump together, or not, as the balls upon the billiard-table. Born a hundred years hence (1937, what would that far-off year see?), you would never have been admitted into the dubious advantage of my acquaintance and love. And as I wandered bereft of my wits, it was merest chance I was spared to continue my poor life and pursue the history of our amity. The horse's shoulder glanced me, I swear. The brush, light as it was, spun me round by my heels, like the dervish. This, by the by, no mean comparison for I remained invisible to the occupants during our little encounter. In a moment they were past – though that second was an eternity during which I had opportunity to review the many decisions of my life, now irrevocable, which had led to that juncture – and then: they were past, leaving your servant flattened against the wall, with the echoing clatter of iron against stone ringing in his ears. She seemed gay. She wore a smile. Her face, that perfect oval, slightly lifted and inclined to the side, mouth a little open, not unlike Harry's portrait. Beside her, in hawkish profile (the bridge of that nose cuts the air), vastly pleased with the reception, doubtless, of some feeble clerical sally, some pearly specimen of the wit of the pulpit, that damned, satisfied, oily, sanctimonious, humbugging, round-collared *sky-pilot*. But for the cloth which un-mans him would I not like to have seized the whip from the coachman and horse-whipped the hypocrite. For her sake, I forbore. In my mind I yet retain, frozen, fixed, set, the tableau, framed in the window in that instant as they passed and in the next were gone with but a gust of wind to mark their passage. Would that I had been able to capture that fleeting moment, its particular impress. I cannot. The small cartoon, which I enclose, may serve to amuse in an idle hour but neither affords me a catharsis nor does justice to the scene. Destroy it when it palls.

We have much to consider. However, you should take the passage-boat, rather than travelling directly by whatever small craft you may hire. Better to arrive late and entire, than not at all, or with the loss of an ear. In any event, who would discharge your ransom? Our late employers would pay to be quit of you. I shall be at the quay to greet you, recognisable as the young man of intent looks, wild to a degree, and the lean and hungry aspect of your true Caesarian conspirator.

Always yours,

Walter

Gideon Chase to Walter Eastman

No.13 American Hong
Canton
November 6th, 1837

Say! But we are blue! Well, I come to be Friday on your island, so I may count on you greeting me on the 12th *inst*. I tendered a rather more respectful demission than yours. They concluded to make me stay – raised me to the partners' balcony on high – showed me view of the waters of the world and their riches, prospect of partnership – able and valued young man – anyone can get into bad company – fresh start. *'Vade rethro, Sathanas'* replied I. Promptly insisted I should jump if I really was the Son of God.

Mem. A horse will run you down – it will also do anything if it may avoid stepping on you. Depend on it. But better walk with your head up.

Recognise me as the young fellow of uncertain gait and green complexion at the quay.

Your affec. friend,

G. C.

PS Men live on through their works – you will never know posterity, but they will remember you. As to your contemporaries, your art is a craft (ha!) which voyages between their separate enislements and in our own small way I hope we shall build the causeways as well as burn boats.

PPS If history repeats itself, so must its cast have the same parts, only in different dress. Four centuries ago Ridley would have been a *condottiere*. Today he is a clerk-adventurer. I prefer the clerk, but it is the same man.

Alice Barclay Remington's journal

October 27th, 1837. Ah me! And all seems so futile. I did my best to occupy myself during the day, for idleness weighs heavy on me. Walked to the top of the Monte Hill with two of the houseboys and enjoyed the view of the town spread below. I did not have the heart to draw it, although it would have made a perfect sketch – a perfect subject, that is, in the hands of a competent practitioner. Descending, I bought flowers of an old flower-woman with cataracts. At least she had a milky eye. That their eyes could be opened to the great Truths of our Lord and their wilful blindness overcome! I think they were irises of some native variety. At home I put them into vases at once. Soon they will droop and die. Aunt took pains to arrange the cut stems to display their beauties to best advantage, calling me to give my opinion – but more, I think, to make me admire her handiwork and gain some compliments. Naturally, I flattered her in my best way. We dined by ourselves, Uncle being in Canton and hardly feeling like entertaining in his absence. We drank coffee on the verandah, Aunt calling for her shawl after a while, and watched the fireflies. How bright they glowed! How short their span! Brushed Aunt's hair one hundred strokes and one in her room. Then to my own lonely room. ... and some lonely tears.

November 3rd, 1837. My recent cheerfulness undermined by want of activity and matters of interest to occupy me. Assailed by the blue devils again. Oh! how hard it is to overcome my selfish desires! Uncle, I know, has not only my family's best interests at heart but my own as well. I know and believe him when he says so. Yet still is it difficult for me to reconcile myself to what in the fulness of time will be seen as the proper, the only decision. Although I already recognise his authority, I must strive to bend myself to his will with a gentle and yielding heart, for it is a rebel heart which will not surrender willingly to the promptings of reason and duty. That I might learn and profit from the example of Our Lord's meekness and His Sacrifice! But can *all* be lost? No, no. I must suppress this hope, this vain, evanescent thing, which mocks and deludes, as the lost traveller is tormented by the illusion of the water he fancies he can see shimmering on the horizon. But *was* it a mere matter of timing, a want of judiciousness of choice (which *he* always warned against – I have his letter still) in the selection of the moment to risk our little all? Can he have been so rash, impulsive? Yet how may I blame him? Ardent he is by temperament, doubly so where his heart and affections are engaged (may I not thus flatter myself now, when all such vanity is bitter and empty?). He was unable to contain and master the mounting flood of his emotion. Moved, he sought the fatal interview with Uncle. Oh, those two proud, unyielding men! I can see them now, the one pale, eloquent, impassioned, yet *dignified* and withal deferential to his senior's years and wisdom, the other calm, master of himself and the moment, sagacious, firm – yet kindly and dispassionate. For I know that Uncle's bluff exterior, so daunting to his rivals, conceals a good and tender heart. How he must have done his utmost (consonant with the dignity and superiority of his position and years) to assuage the younger man's bruised feelings when he left, still labouring under a bitter disappointment. Kind Uncle! – no one could have spoken to me more gently. At more than a month's remove, the memory of his goodness is still vivid to me. There was no rebuke, no trace of reproach in his loving accents. I could have borne it more easily! Like a babe, I broke down and wept. Harsh words, which was all my duplicity deserved, would not have moved me so much. And Uncle lifted my face, wet with tears as it was, and my eyes blinded in mist, and brushed away the fat, hot drops with his own dear hand and called me his own dear little one and the like endearments as if he were the one who courted me and was not my father's brother. Oh, dear, *good* one! Oh, unbearable moment – such aching, sweet tenderness, so hard to support, my feelings so confused, I did not know whether to cry or be happy! And I began to gasp and choke! My breath quite failed me! My handkerchief, which I had been pulling between my hands – poor innocent lace to be so abused!– dropped from my nerveless fingers. No longer would my knees support me! I swooned and fell backwards (where was my bed) but that Uncle caught me by the waist in his two strong arms and laid me gently on my bed. I felt his breath hot on my pale cheek and then he loosened the constriction around my throat (yet was it not that which had so palsied me). I opened my eyes and saw his own solicitous, anxious orbs gazing into mine. Then was I racked by a veritable storm of tears and, amazing to say, in the midst of this little tempest my entire body was suffused by the most extraordinary sensations of warmth and lightness, heat which spread from the very centre of my body in waves of feeling which ran down my limbs and set my extremities a-tingling. Oh! Again and again! I was lifted, light as an air, it seemed, in commingled pain (and yet was it not pain) and ecstasy of wonderment. Such may have been the sensations of the saints when gazing on the Glory which was Divine! Involuntarily, I gave utterance to a sigh – but it came out as a gasp – and I was racked, then, by a whole series of such, clinging the while to Uncle's arm, as I moaned and cried. Oh, poor child! He soothed me and then, pushing my damp locks from my brow, called to Aunt, who came and ministered to me and made me take a mouthful of water from her glass. I coughed and gasped. Oh, my poor heart beat so! Then Aunt spoke to Uncle in a low whisper. He left the room and returned with a small bottle. I heard the sound of the glass, its crystal tinkle on the neck of the bottle and as I opened my eyes – Aunt's wet kerchief so soothing, so cooling on my wet forehead – saw the three drops fall and colour the water purple, then their clouds thin and dissipate, and there was the cool, clear water only again. Aunt made me drink the entire contents of the tumbler, and I fell back, languishing but calm. And soon the laudanum had done its work and I slept a deep sleep, from which I awoke calm and refreshed.

My heart flutters as I remember. It does me good to remember. How infinitely wearisome do the succeeding weeks seem.

November 5th, 1837. To the sea-shore to hear Mr Arden preach in the open, his text 2 Corinthians 4 ii. The day is of great significance to the English. Addressing his congregation (which he was) on Portuguese soil (at least, only the Chinese, if not the English, would dispute it) he had to be more circumspect than he would have cause to be in addressing an assembly of sailors and marines with their officers on board the *Louisa.* Yet was he sufficiently pointed in his references to the religion of the Papists. On not a few occasions Captain Elliot, HBM's Superintendent, looked uneasy. He is short in stature but despite his own disposition towards the Chinese, which is naturally conciliatory, has the reputation of a very brave man. His hair stood up in the breeze off the sea as he stood bare-headed with his great cocked hat under his little arm. He has no whiskers. Mr Arden's gown flapped. He is unrecognisable as the retiring and quiet companion he is with me – though he fancies himself as quite the buck when the other young men are with him! That his private moments might be enlivened by a spark of the wit, force, sincerity, and animation which he reveals in the pulpit. My nostrils were a-twitch as I suppressed my yawns in the carriage of a few evenings since. I do believe the horses brushed against some native as we flew past in the darkness. But that Mr Arden is a good man no one could dispute.

CHAPTER XXI

Our young two gentlemen are *déshabillés*. Shoes off in Gideon's case, one stockinged foot on the table, the sole no longer so miraculously white, as, deprived of the Factory retainers, he has these days to launder them himself.

Trick of the trade known to the washerwoman: she flogs the hose on a stone.

On the other hand, Gideon is going to discover that his stockings, mysteriously, last longer.

Eastman has another glass of Father Ribeiro's vintage port. Fruit on a silver stand and cracked nuts stand by the decanter. He has removed his cravat but his mind is rather more concentrated than Gideon's. He brushes his cheek with his quill. Four sheets of paper lie before him. Only the first is partially covered with his distinctive handwriting, paragraphs enumerated 1, 2, 3, 4 and so on (he has got to 7). 'Ha! Gid,' he says, 'do rouse yourself.'

'My mind's empty. In due course something will come. The best is always unlooked for, you may depend upon it.'

'You are in a trance and nothing will come to you in that state. You are my "pard'ner", as the backwoodman would say, and you must undergo your share of torment and travail – mental, I mean.'

'You cannot trap an idea, Walter – though I guess mine would certainly be wild and woolly if caught at this juncture.'

'Collect yourself, sir. You work now for me. Remove your unsavoury feet from the table.'

'Say! You said you were my partner, not a plantation overseer.'

Eastman takes the feather part of his pen to the sole of Gideon's foot, clamping a hand round his ankle and tickling mercilessly. 'Ah, aagh! Quit! Desist! No, stop, you devil! Anything! Mercy!'

'See, I lay on like the overseer and you beg as the darky field-hand.'

'Damnation! Will you stop?'

Gideon's foot bangs terrifically as he drums and convulses, making the decanter jump up and down on the spot, its stopper jiggling in its neck. An orange rolls off the stand, trundling to the edge of the table before thudding to the floor.

'Ribeiro's port!' Gideon shrieks desperately, about to wet himself, and indeed it is about to fall. Walter looks round and Gideon wrenches his foot away, dealing his tormentor an accidental but highly gratifying kick in the pit of the stomach.

'Oof!' Walter doubles up. He gasps on the floor, gripping the orange.

'Well, the most damnably deadly comic pen in China is yours,' says Gideon, wiping the tears from his eyes. 'It slays by laughter.'

As he has no breath in his body, Eastman is for once unable to retort.

Enter Harry O'Rourke from Ribeiro's room above, alerted by thuds of fruit and bodies. 'What, no band of robbers?' he exclaims. 'I thought to find you dead or dying.'

'I am half-dead,' wheezes Eastman, picking himself up, 'but in hopes shortly of stealing some fecund ideas of yours. Gid has presently no contribution to make.'

'The hack scribbler's is a demeaning trade,' says O'Rourke, 'and I'm glad to see you adopt a kind of behaviour consonant with your new station. Brawling and drinking will do very well for new apprentices. You can progress to the more opprobrious vices.'

'We have no name for our organ,' says Eastman, 'and we must make a beginning with that.'

'Unfortunately, you must,' says Harry, '*Untitled News-sheet* would not do for you.'

'We already have a *Monitor* (perdition to it), a *Chinese Repository*, the missionary sheet. In Singapore the *Recorder* and the *Register*…'

'There is the *Philadelphia Star*,' volunteers Gideon, fishing for his shoes under the table, 'could we not have a *Canton Star?*'

'No, sir,' says Eastman, 'we may not.'

'Quite right,' says O'Rourke, 'a feeble, petty light always liable to be obscured by cloud. You would not wish to twinkle.'

'There are two points, will you not allow, gentlemen,' Walter says. 'One half of the title will be dictated by the place in which our organ finds itself *in situ* – or, at least, where lies its spiritual home. In the second instance, the remaining portion of its name should afford some indication as to the broad range of its sympathies. I speak in no party or political sense.' He lights up, sucking gratefully a few times, still unable to manage maximum inhalation. 'Therefore, let us apply ourselves to part the first of this conundrum.'

'Well,' offers Gideon, undeterred by the cool reception for his earlier suggestion, 'Canton this or Canton that will not do, I guess. We shall not find a welcome there. It is certainly not the source of any desirable influence.'

'Mmm,' says Eastman, 'but we must be contemporary. For good or ill, Canton is the place. We cannot pretend otherwise.'

'Good God, sir! It is your constituency. You may ignore your public at your peril. Depend upon it, sir. Where will you find your readers? You will find them in Canton. Yes, a portion in Macao (they will always need something new to occupy themselves in Macao) – but the greater part in the Factories.'

'But quite so,' murmurs Eastman, 'the point had not escaped me. And I do not think we shall find ourselves quite bereft of aid or sympathy there, tho' the helping hand may be extended under the cover of darkness. No, let us not reject that city so summarily.'

'In that case,' says Gideon, wielding not so much the philosopher's razor as a claymore, 'Macao is not to be considered at all. There will be no *Macao Chronicle* or *Macao Contemporary*.'

'Still-born,' Walter agrees, 'never to see the light of day. Call it the Macao Anything and it will not go one copy in Canton.'

'So now we are the *Canton Something*.'

'Not inevitably, by any means,' says Harry slowly. 'Be not in such a dashing haste yourself, young fellow. You rush up the stream as if Macao and the City of Rams were contiguous, with no points intervening. Such, I need hardly remind you after your journey of ninety miles, is not the case.'

'Ah!' shouts Eastman, 'will not Whampoa do? Neither of one nor the other — yet vital. Does not trade revolve around the shipping in that anchorage?'

'Not quite,' Gideon observes drily, 'I had thought Lin Tin island with its opium-hulks a deal more important.'

'Let us not forget the Bocca Tigris,' Harry says, 'where abound some splendid natural prospects.'

'Well, Walter, do you like the ring of the *Bocca Bulletin?*'

'Hmm.'

'Bulletin?' says Harry vaguely, 'now what does that put me in mind of? Civil War, surely not?' He tweaks the hairs in his nostrils thoughtfully, his mutters lost to the others.

'On reflection, it puts *me* in mind of useful knowledge and has an over-worthy ring.'

'Not at all, Gid. You do your own suggestion an injustice. It could be a means of attaching subscribers to ourselves. We have to flout a cardinal principle: the editor of a newspaper generally represents an interest. He caters to the vulgar prejudices of his readers. We shall not — we, on the contrary, will attack their interest at every moment, hold up a mirror of their true countenance. Yet must they still read our organ, even as it infuriates. There is some paradoxical desire to feel the goad — did we not take the *Monitor?* Yet how much the more advantageous if we were to supply practical informations in addition to a more elevated content — a full list of ships resorting, the date of their anticipated departures, or the length of a delay…the passengers would thank us, not the company!'

'Prices obtaining, the tides — yes, how often has one felt the want of a fuller and more accurate almanac than the most unreliable service provided by the *Monitor* — so intermittent and misleading as to be worse than useless.'

'Well, at least we possess an advantage in respect of this: we have ourselves been members of the community whose wants we would aspire to supply. Still, *Bulletin* does not afford the nicest shade of meaning apposite to our real purpose. Something on the lines of *Enquirer, Clarion...*'

'*Intelligencer*? That, I flatter myself, conveys intimations of the compendium and the spy.'

'Mmm. *Lin Tin Intelligencer.* Would do at a pinch. Could be improved on still, I allow.'

Harry speaks, audibly again. 'Meaning, or precise and subtle shades of it, is not the first requisite in this matter. The title of a newspaper must trip off the tongue, it is the rhythm, the lilt. It should echo in the ear, insinuate itself in the mind long before any meaning is registered by the intellectual faculty. In any event, long familiarity with a name robs it of its original signification – it is but a sound, with all the meaning of a bell tolling. Let it, therefore, be musical. I like the *Lin Tin Bulletin* – and there's all the menace in *Bulletin* that you could ever desire.'

'Well, I'll be darned.'

'Seconded.'

'Gideon and I are both darned and you, Harry, are an extraordinary alliterative old rapscallion.'

'But the copper-bottom rhyme is too bald alone; it might appear frivolous in the eyes of some. Besides, we need to expand the description of what is on offer.'

Silence follows, broken only by the crunching of peanutshells, until Eastman says, 'The stream which unites, aye, and divides – which is the line of our communication and severs as well, should not that receive tribute from the newest of communicators, the latest flotation of paid-up capital and shares?'

'Then it should be *The Lin Tin Bulletin and River Messenger.*'

'Ah, that I like. That is dignified and a gossip to boot.'

'Too much duchess, my boy, and not enough strumpet. *Bulletin* is dry and businesslike enough for anyone. Come out of the counting-house: *River Letter* will do capitally.'

'Mmm. How does *River Bee* sound upon the ear? Collects

clover and can sting.'

'Which, then, does need commercial buttressing, depend upon it. I know my Factories.'

Eastman writes quickly on his piece of paper '...*Bulletin and River Bee and Prices Current*. No, by God, that is a mouthful.'

Harry looks over his shoulder. His dirty, thick forefinger jabs at the legend. 'It is not the words in themselves but the manner in which you choose to exhibit them. The presentation to the eye is the thing. If you must have your tariffs, then place them on the line inferior and in a smaller style. Precedence, dear boy.'

Gideon has to add his two cents' worth: 'The conjunction "and" used twice in so short a space must needs appear inelegant, as well as imparting a certain looseness of thought. In its terseness, in its grammatical *sinew*, the most classical Chinese exquisitely avoids such a weak ligature.'

'Do you want a good kicking?'

'I would, therefore, recommend the substitution of the preposition "with" for the conjunction "and". The device of parentheses would also ...'

'Did he not richly deserve that, Harry?'

'He did, but we'll not scorn it. We'll amend accordingly. Some illustration in woodcut below is also requisite – and a motto. Some worthy and apposite quotation from the treasury of literature and rhetoric, a pearl of the statesman's wisdom, some gem of the Bard's...'

'Upon my word, this port of Ribeiro's must be heady stuff. Well, what will you fix for us? The press in the firmament, casting its rays over the globe below, dispelling the clouds of ignorance and prejudice? Moses receiving the tablet not in stone but in foolscap form?'

'I'll do nothing, you young dog, unless you adopt a more respectful tone and pass the decanter. Your obligated servant, sir. What I shall do will suit the particular circumstances of your organ and its concerns. Leave the aged Israelite out of the consideration – he never entered the Promised Land. It was left to a younger general to annexe it, hey, Gid?'

'An amusing coincidence. Let us now – I believe I can sit again upon my bruised hams – each ransack our memories for the motto the most fitting and striking under which we may mount our crusade, for it is no less. No, no ... let us commit our thought to paper in privacy. Then we may compare and adjudicate on their merits or otherwise. Your pen, Walter, unless you are already warmed to the task. My own mind is made up.'

'And mine, too,' rumbles O'Rourke, red face positively crimson now with port and self-satisfaction. Eastman puffs thoughtfully at his cigar, while the quill scratches and sputters – inspiration inclining the writer to dip over-sanguinely into the well, sterility a mere snail's trail compared to the speckled path of the fecund. O'Rourke receives the pen from Gideon, draining his glass in the same moment, and then he, too, is away. He takes a little longer than Gideon, for his quotation appears a line or two the more extensive and he is at pains to get it word-perfect, striking out a misremembered phrase or two on the way. At length he is satisfied. The pen passes to Walter, who dashes off two or three words, cigar clenched between his molars.

'What a fine parlour-game this would be over a festive season,' Walter comments. 'We could have prizes for those who culled the most appropriately disgraceful epithets for our enemies.' He takes the folded papers from the other two, pretending to shuffle and deal. 'Now let's have umpiring.'

GIDEON CHASE'S: *This America, this scene of happiness under a free government, is the beam in the eye, the thorn in the side, the worm in the vitals of every despot upon the face of the earth. A man has a voice because he is a man and not because he is the possessor of money.*- COBBETT.

WALTER EASTMAN'S: *écrasez l'infâme.* – VOLTAIRE.

HARRY O'ROURKE'S: *(Which is from a yet earlier and still more embattled century)*.

The three collaborators peruse each other's submissions. Finally, Walter sighs. 'Mine's the least, it behoves me to confess, in all regards. Harry's best, I reckon.'

'As to that I guess I'm in accord.'

'Well, don't mortify your young selves unnecessarily. As Americans, you should frankly state the difference between your organ and all others east of Calcutta. It is a great distinction. Old Will Cobbett can serve you well as to that, and the final sentiment is most pertinent. The great François Marie Arouet is perhaps too epigrammatic and too much to the point (he was a Frenchman, after all) – but then without that most noble wrath which was his inspiration and which impels you there would be no newspaper of yours in the first instance for us to seek to adorn.'

Walter flushes, Gideon can't think why. 'I believe your choice to be the best, Harry, tho' Gid's is not without merit.'

'Then use both.'

'We could place mine below Harry's,' says Gideon eagerly.

'Cobbett's below Marvell's,' Eastman corrects him.

'I think a swirling line, some piece of arabesque decoration, would mark their boundaries clearly enough, even if the differences in style were not sufficiently abundant.'

'Swelled rule,' says Eastman, chameleon and magpie, 'to bestow upon it its proper nomenclature.'

'Now is that a fact?'

'Well, Harry, you seem to have been midwife to this fledgling enterprise of mine, and quite saved the babe…'

'Godfather, my boy, this was the christening. The babe was river-born, in a basket of rushes. Let us hope it will develop a healthy pair of lungs.'

'Then, godfather, thank you for the gift of silver to the infant, for you are a founding father, too.'

'Ah, now having regard to that…'

'Discretion, Harry, is the order of the day. You may rest easy on that score. Any aid you, or our other friends, shall kindly give us will remain a confidential secret. Why should you lose your sitters and your guineas?'

'Thank'ee, my boy. The nabobs and merchant-princes are capricious and jealous patrons. That is the port talking bravely.'

'How frequently shall our newspaper appear, Walter? If the *Monitor* prints four times a month under its single editor, should not we be jointly capable of publishing twice a week? That would be to disadvantage our rivals, for their intelligence would be cold and stale after ours.'

Walter ponders, sweeping the nut-shells off the table-edge into his palm. 'Y-e-e-e-s,' he drawls, 'I reckon this to be a thornier issue than it appears. Under circumstances the most ideal, we should assuredly attempt just such an invasion of their ground – how easy to mount such an invasion when the enemy is not there to defend his works and property. But we labour under the peculiar disadvantages of our situation.' The shells blaze fiercely, lighting Eastman's pale face, and one heat-reddened ear, before it is cast into shadows. 'I have decided our sheet shall be of the same physical proportions as our competitor's – there is little choice – we are confined by the limitations of our machines, of which further presently. There will be two foolscap sheets, folded together, giving eight pages. We shall be able to place three columns of print across the breadth of our page. Four such would present a more contemporary and appealing aspect – our press will not admit of this.

'One page will be devoted to absolutely commercial and navigational informations. We still have seven to fill. I doubt not but that our pens could. Yet 'tis I who must act as the compositor, I must myself fix the formes, the work on the stone – all this to be performed personally. I flatter myself I am an apt pupil, but even the Portuguese operative who instructs me would find himself pressed – if you forgive the unintended play – to produce single-handedly those eight pages by the week. I cannot do it. But then why should we aim to match him? We must be unlike him in every sense. That shall constitute our appeal. We should be the more eagerly read if we appeared *less* often – say, we printed at an interval of *two* weeks. Then we could enjoy the leisure to improve what we wrote. And if we published our journal two days or a day previous to his – why, we'd dish him. Our viands would be fresh, his stale. In course of time, people should forget the precise week of our appearance, they should expect us and not buy our enemy's. That is, if we should truly publish the superior journal.'

'Bravo!' says Harry.

'If we are to take fullest advantage of an early appearance, we must ensure the newspaper...'

'*The Lin Tin Bulletin and River Bee!*'

'I say it proudly! *The Lin Tin Bulletin and River Bee* is got up to the Factories on publication and exposed for sale with the minimum of delay. Expedition! And not once, but always, inevitable!'

'Then we budget for squeezes and cumshaws and must have a passage-boat captain of our own in our employ.'

'I shall itemise it as a necessary expenditure.'

'Ah!' exclaims O'Rourke. 'Aha!'

Eastman's eyebrows rise.

'This, sir, is the question. The very nub, sir, the veriest. Yes, how often is art assailed by its duns. £ s.d. – you have your heads in the clouds and the feet beset by mire. Make sure your appearances are only in the black, gentlemen, do not be among the red inks.'

Eastman says, a little coldly, 'If you are giving yourself concerns for your investment, then I can assure you your anxiety is groundless. Both Gideon and I are habituated to the prudent conduct of a business and the avoidance of unnecessary...'

'By God, sir! You do travesty me. Investment, sir? I make no investment but a gift to friends. Sir...'

Gideon interrupts the spluttering and indignant old artist whose boiler-walls seem about to explode. 'Surely, surely,' he smooths the misunderstanding over, 'Walter merely meant to indicate that we intended to do both ourselves and our friends justice and that our venture was not purely Quixotic, isn't that a fact?'

Eastman, however, just goes to stand with his back to the fire and, parting his coat-tails, toasts his buttocks.

'Now, Mr O'Rourke, you may see we have given the matter some thought. Our calculations are based upon a circulation of some five hundred copies, most moderately estimated: a little more than three hundred at Canton, some two hundred in Macao, and we have discounted the negligible but still encouraging numbers we shall expect to sell in due course to subscribers in the Straits Settlements, Manilla, the Company's Indian Possessions and mayhap even further abroad to institutions, the learned, and agents of government in America and England, as our name is bruited abroad. Of course we shall print sufficient to retain a store of previous issues. Kindly peruse this, Mr O'Rourke.'

Debit			Contra Credit		
	Dolls	Cts		Dolls	Cts
To Paper, second quality, 3 reams	20	00	250 Subscriptions at $11 p.a.	105	75
To Lamp-black and oil (ink)	3	00	250 Single copies at 40¢	100	00
To Rental of Premises	30	00	Advertisements at 50¢ per line	50	00
To Wage of Portuguese Operative	15	00	Hire of Press		
To Ditto Sweeper	2	00	(as for labels, invitations, etc.)	30	00
To Passage-Boat	40	00			
To Postage to Bombay Post Office	8	00		285-	75
To Pens	0	50			
To Miscellaneous (as rags, oils, nails)	5	00			
To Cumshaws	40	00			
To Editor's Salary	25	00			
To Ass. Editor's Salary	25	00			
To Repayment of Loan	40	00			
To Dividend to shareholder	5	00			
	258-	50			
Profit	27-	25		27-	25

O'Rourke grunts. 'A pair of capital, calculating humbugs. This, thanks to God, is as Egyptian to me, but it seems the veriest moonshine. All you may know for certain are your expenses – the rest is speculation.'

'Hope,' says Eastman from the fireplace, possessor by now, one imagines, of rosy hams.

O'Rourke scowls at Gideon's accounts; he adjusts his pince-nez with his other hand. 'Am I Repayment of Loan, sir, or am I Dividend to Shareholder?'

'You, sir, are Dividend. This puts you in the standing of our Pensioner, which Mother Church could not endure. Besides, she forbids usury. Of course, the good Father could take a tithe of fifty copies of our journal, if he so desired.'

'Hmm. Then I am in more advantageous circumstances than Mother Church, for her loan is discharged without interest at a rate of slightly in excess of eight per centum, while my stock yields me a dizzy fifty per centum of income and my Principal is subject to growth while I still retain it.'

'Well, despite your protestations, I allow you seem to display your customary acuity, Harry. I expect we have twice the risk of foundering insolvent as the most secure Hong-ist; therefore, the moneys you have out with us receives double the rate currently obtaining for funds at a year's sight with Mowqua. Were you, of course, to speculate in drug, you might hope for four times the return without courting more risk.'

'Harrumph,' says Harry. 'I shall prefer to stupefy your subscribers than to corrupt the Celestial. I expect never to see the moneys again in any event,' he adds gloomily.

'Come, come. It is not like you to be so faint a heart. We must go the whole hog, or not at all. Be that not so, pard'ner Chase?'

'Downright so.'

CHAPTER XXII

THE LIN TIN BULLETIN AND RIVER BEE
(WITH PRICES CURRENT)

Wednesday, January 3, 1838
Vol.1 No.1

Oh printing! What troubles hast thou brought mankind! That lead when moulded into bullets is not so mortal as when founded into letters. – MARVELL

This America, this scene of happiness under a free government, is the beam in the eye, the thorn in the side, the worm in the vitals of every despot upon the face of the earth. A man has a voice because he is a man, and not because he is the possessor of money. – COBBETT

Extracts from pp 1, 2, 3, 4, 5, 6, 7

When a community of considerably under some thousand souls is already served by, and has competing for its undistracted attention, two established instruments of the printed word, not to count irregular or short-lived effusions of amateur or parochial talents, our little public may be forgiven for heaving a sigh of impatience on hearing the strident cries of the newcomer to the family of paper pressing its claims upon their quiet hour. Realising that to the many disinterested parties whose forebodings and strictures we would recognise as altogether innocent of malice our fledgling enterprise will appear as a work of supererogation and even vanity, we commence in the full consciousness of our temerity. Yet we dare to boast that our labours shall be in the interest of the public, even the interests of that portion of it whom we shall undoubtedly affront, and we feel no embarrassment in thus plucking at the coatsleeves of our friends and fellow exiles. For those organs for the dissemination of informations and views which have already appeared on this coast are justly dubbed *instruments*. Not one of them, to greater or lesser extent, has been free of sectional influence, tending to promote partisan views and to regard all through the specious and distorting eyeglass of interest, to the point where their conductors might not unkindly be said to have become less the tools than the accessories of their patrons and masters. We abstain from animadverting on names and titles, for we believe our meaning is sufficiently clear to all our readers.

The present affords, we trust we do not delude ourselves, a propitious and useful juncture at which to engage our public. A newly burgeoning commerce fills the estuary and, rather less openly, swells the traffic in the Inner Waters or River proper. Fast rowing-boats, seemingly with as many oars a side as there are to be found teeth in a comb, heavily armed and crewed by native desperadoes, flock around the hulks which lie off Lin Tin, vying to take off their deathly cargoes. They churn the sullen waters of the gulf as by devious means they enter the delta through its system of byways and tributaries, a watery trail of winding and looping and doubling back, which no man knows better than these rascals, until they debouch from some hidden mouth into the main channel. Abused river! You bear upon your face wares as deadly and soporiferous as the very waters of Styx or Lethe.

The Company, during the dying months of the year previous, has poured a veritable torrent of opium from its Indian Presidencies up the river and into Canton and its Province. This spite of the unavailing remonstrances of the native government and the setting into effect of a system of preventive measures which do for the first time appear more than empty words. No longer do the ruffians of the *fast dragons* and *scrambling crabs* dare to swagger in broad daylight up the main river, for the Government's cruising junks would not hesitate to give them a broadside for their pains. No longer will a cumshaw ensure that the captains of the revenue cruisers turn the blind eye of Lord Nelson to the nefarious trade. 'Twould be more than their lives were worth! That barometer, the Union Jack, which has been hoisted and summarily hauled down again as many times in the last four years that the flag-staff seems a very gallows and no wonder Jack has a phiz which is red and blue, came down again from the British Factory on the 2nd *ult.*, having flown barely nine months. With both parties determined, bent on such courses of extremity, all moderation cast aside, we believe we are not deluded when we say our newspaper enters upon this scene in a year of portentous moment.

News also reached our little communities of Canton and Macao but a few weeks since of a new era in England. How fortuitous that its inception should so closely coincide with that of our organ. Let both be new brooms, sweeping aside the dust of the old and instituting a new, freer, and better order of things. We mean, of course, the death of King William and the accession of the new, young Queen. Child-Queen we might without disrespect call her. We have it on best authority that the old King passed away and the new Queen acceded on the 20th June last. Victoria she is, let us, subjects and the free alike, hope she is not inaptly named. We doubt not but that the cannon of the puniest sloop or brig in her navy might prevail against the entire armament of the breastworks of the Bocca's narrows, yet would it be a hollow victory for Victoria if, instead of an untrammelled trade in wholesome and useful commodities, free of the onerous and venal impositions of the native officers, her triumphant arms merely opened the way for a yet greater cascade of poison. Let our small, clear voice of reason be heard in London.

We trust that we shall enjoy the forbearance and good will of our readers, especially in our early and most trying weeks. As well as endeavouring to steer a course independent of faction and sordid interest, we shall also strive to present in our few pages informations, both in a commercial and general sense, more detailed, precise, and up to the moment (and therefore more useful) than has hitherto been available publicly on this coast, save for the largest houses with their fleet boats and network of informants (we do not utter the word *spies*). Besides, we flatter ourselves that we shall insert into our columns matter of a lighter and more amusing nature to our readers than has hitherto been their fare (do we not know it of old ourselves?), for we are believers that a dish properly and skilfully seasoned will be no less nourishing, whilst a greater delight to the palate and – you have our assurance – a good deal easier on the digestion. Our declared intention and concealed order, of the great Voltaire, *écrasez l'infâme,* will prove peppery to some but our readers may still relish the aroma of our dish even as it boils in our cauldron.

We make no secret of the difficulties under which we labour, in both a mechanical aspect and otherwise. Our type is small and antique, our paper yellow, and we doubt not but that the gremlins of the press will exact a reluctant tribute from us in the sprinkling of baptismal errors from which we fear our first pages will not be free. Yet the mighty oak springs from the puny acorn, and we know our readers and friends will not be the men to judge a noble mansion by the paint which is here and there peeling.

The letters, views, and (should they wish and aspire) contributions of our readers will ever be welcome to us at our Macao office, which is to be found in 12 Rua da Nossa Senhora da Nazare. *In absentia* – and we intend not to be an editor who is bound as to perambulations and imagination by the four walls of his office (and the opinions of his proprietor) – manuscripts may with confidence be handed to the servant of the house, a son of Lusitania who speaks no English but is as discreet and trusty as those confidential retainers of those despots of the East of old (and mayhap the present) who literally wanted a tongue. And whilst not wishing to deter those of our most valued readers, and potential informants, who might find themselves acquainted with valuable and striking intelligences at a comparatively late stage from imparting their informations to us, nor to make ourselves or our gentle readers slaves of time, trussed to the dial's point, we should humbly inform all and sundry that the latest that manuscripts, or visitors calling on us in our editorial capacities, shall be considered and entertained, under normal circumstances, shall be the stroke of midnight, Mondays.

Advertisements, at reasonable rates, to be advised on application, may be submitted for insertion at our discretion until 10 anti-Meridian each and every Friday of what we are in fervent hopes shall be our long and, to our little community, most serviceable history. Your pardon — *ante meridiem*.

LATEST FROM EUROPE per *Stella*.

England. News of the death of the late King on June 20th, 1837, was brought to India in October, coming over the Straits, we have it on the best authority, from Trincomalee in a small fishing-vessel and thence overland by the system of military semaphores to Calcutta and Bombay, whence it shortly spread over the land like a fire on a prairie in a variety of means, both official and unofficial, the informal transmission of news by private gentlemen not the least speedy or effective, we have solid grounds for imagining.

For Jack Tarpaulin the national grief and great public deprivation held an end of hornpiping and skylarks aboard and the cessation of the appropriate pursuits of Mars and Venus ashore — fisty-cuffs and the consolations of the fair — for Jack was made a dull boy and had to paint all the hulls black. We doubt not he found words pithy, exotic, and incomprehensible the while to the laity as he applied his paint with his great brush as the Archbishop of Canterbury intoned the while he broke his vial of unguent over the Royal Head.

King William IV, the Uncle of the new Queen, reigned 1830-37 in succession to his brother George IV (1820-30), earlier Prince Regent. She is, therefore, the granddaughter of poor, mad George III (1760-1820), who lost in turn the Colonies and his reason. We are not yet cognisant of the late monarch's last words, whether they related as those of his recent ancestors to meat-pie or Bognor, but shall hasten to inform our readers when we know.

Russia. Sad news of the unhappy and untimely death of the poet and celebrated man of letters, Puchkin, slain in a duel in the capital of St Petersburg in the early part of the winter previous. Such was the fame and influence of the author of *Eugene Onegin* and *Le Chevalier en bronze* that a jealous government seized on his personal papers and manuscripts directly following his expiring of a mortal wound when they became the property of the Czar Nicholas.

Puchkin was far from a Radical in the social and political beliefs he held, and was a peculiarly devoted subject of the Autocrat. Yet was he stricken with grief subsequent to the executions of his friends and fellow-poets for their part in the radicals' uprising of 1825. He held the Republican Institutions of the New World low in his esteem and was an enemy to the gallant Poles from whom his countrymen stole their nationhood in 1830. He was as old as the century and the most affecting sentiments he expressed concerned the loneliness of Man amidst a sublime and unfeeling Nature. *'Vis-à-vis du bonheur, je suis athée. Je ne crois pas en son existence.' Mais, c'est bien dit.*

United States. Per USS Yorktown. At Richmond, Virginia, is projected a new asylum for the insane on the most approved and enlightened modern principles, apt for that fine and healthy township. Gentleness, moderation, and a course of conciliation should prove far more efficacious in the control and mayhap even the restoration to their senses of those unhappy patients than the brutal, degraded, and barbarous treatment meted out to the wretched inmates of the Bedlams of less than a century ago. We applaud this public-spirited work which, we understand, will be underwritten by private

293

subscription of the philanthropic citizenry. We remark, with a degree of pride and complacency permissible in an exile, that the proposal is no less than to be expected of the citizens of the handsome city of which` we are a son. We would subjoin to our pious hopes, however, the tempering reflection that this is not the first time such a course has been mooted.

Texas. An uneasy peace reigns in this territory, after the defeat and capture of Santa Anna and the rout of his army at San Jacinto in April, 1836. In the almost two years passed since the proclamation of their Republic, the Texans have not succeeded – we are not so partisan as to state – in converting the wilderness into a garden (such would be to defy and overcome nature in the arid parts in which they find their homesteads) but by the unceasing application of a system of skill and unremitting toil they have succeeded in rendering their lands unrecognisable from the ill-kempt and poorly managed areas in which are to be found the Mexicans, with their squalid clay habitations and straggling, ill-fed, and worse-used families. As fighting between the settlers antedated the outbreak of formal hostilities by some few years, resentments between the rival camps are bitter and hatreds run deep. Even now the Texans may not enjoy with easy hearts the fruits of their successes with the ploughshare or the sword, for neighbours (if they exist) will hear the neigh of horses distant in the night, mayhap the squeak of leather, or a rattle of metal – and will be roused by a distant glow which is not the dawn. The citizens of an earlier Republic, too, slept with their spears by their beds. Liberty is only for the brave, nor do we believe in the illusory concept of the intrinsic equality of man. We hope, as a consummation devoutly to be wished, that the fledgling Republic will in course of time be added to the Union.

In addition to the purely commercial digest of informations

on our eighth page, and the most detailed and informed intelligence we may collate as to happenings and the likely turn of future events in our own part of the world, the foreign news (alas, less reliable, older, and often at third- or even fourth-hand, with the inevitable loss of savour), and such lighter reading as we may find space to insert between our weightier paragraphs, we shall from time to time enliven our organ with specimens of anecdotes or definitions, both curious and we trust instructive, as they relate to our customers, suppliers, retainers, entertainers, baiters, occasional murderers and pillagers, but always reluctant hosts – the Chinese.

Did an inn-keeper possessed of an hostel the most commodious and naturally beautiful ever crowd all his guests into the smallest, dampest, crookedest, dirtiest hole of a cellar he could find and, proving alike immune to blandishment, bribe, or threat, refuse categorically to allocate to them the comfortable accommodation they well knew he had to spare?

And did such an inn-keeper, if such a paradoxical brute existed, ever survive the riot which ensued of his cabin'd, cribbed, confined, and outraged customers? He deserved to depend from his own eaves and swing gently with the breeze.

By all of which, we mean no more than to introduce, below appended, the first in what we trust will be a most amusing and, in a serious point of view, profitable series of contributions from the talented pen and well-stocked mind of our own particular and esteemed correspondent and aide.

What were those sinister forms? Voyagers on the rolling river which engirdles us, whether we be dwellers upon its bank or lodgers upon the peninsula which is all but circumscribed by the silty waters in its gulf, or travellers around the beautiful *constellations* of islands flung like stars around its estuary, will need no reminding that fishing provides alike a major source of subsistence and income for the pelagic or coastal natives who reside upon the shores of this province of *Kwangtung* and its northern neighbour, *Fukien*. How often may one descry, without remarking *(such is the effect of long familiarity upon the eye that it may render an object invisible -ed.)* the bowed figures in their sampan *(lit. – three-plank craft)*, who cast their nets with barely a splash on the placid waters, or drop their lines over the side on a speculation. Rather less apparent in their purpose are the wooden posts or stakes which constitute such a hazard to and, indeed, may altogether obstruct navigation in the narrower parts of the Broadway or Inner Passage. These, we would tell such of our readers as yet unaware *(a small minority – ed.)* are deadly entrapments for the finned tribe. Both methods of fishing require little explanation *(though long experience for the practitioner to become adept – ed.)*. Neither are peculiar to the Chinese. One method, however, which would appear so extraordinary as to be frankly incredible had it not been personally witnessed in company with another gentleman, and later corroborated and explained in a chance conversation with an intelligent and communicative native, would appear peculiar to the inhabitants of this Empire. We understand the practice is more prevalent in the north and, especially, towards the mouth of the Yangtse River *(Yangtse Kiang River? – ed.)* although far from unknown in our southern delta, and, especially, in the Broadway Passage. This, Reader, we do not abuse your credulity *(superfluous assurance -ed.)*, is the practice of employing trained birds to seize and then surrender fish! Cormorants are the birds thus engaged and the activity is carried out from boats. The birds perch on the gunwales, taking a grip with the claws of their powerful feet, their baleful and glassy eye upon the fisherman. Upon a signal, which may be an inarticulate sound, generally a glottal *(What? – ed.)* or a gesture – and sometimes both – the birds topple backwards into the water and soon are engaged upon their underwater *chase*. Their efforts are pretty generally rewarded with a rapid success and they return to the boat, often as not, with not merely one but two, three, or even more fish. These prey they allow their masters to take *(without so much as a 'pray or a by your leave' – ed.)*. Lest his hunters should so far forget themselves as to take the opportunity of regaling their appetites while submerged, the fisherman takes the precaution of fastening a brass ring around their throats which prohibits the cormorants from swallowing any but the smallest fish. These birds, for all their savage appearance, with a plumage black as night, cruel eye, razor beak, resembling nothing so much as a convocation of executioners or monkish torturers in their appearance as they perch on the gunwales, are marvellously tame in respect of their ready compliance with the commands of their handler. Of course, we must add, at the conclusion of the day's labours, the master removes the constricting ring from his feathered servants' necks, when he makes no attempt to repossess himself of the last or biggest fish, which the cormorant promptly devours, having acquired a powerful appetite through his exertions.

PURSUER

We advise our readers that they may find a list of prices current at Whampoa and Lin Tin on our eighth page, where we shall usually publish them. Every care has been taken in their collection and compilation. They were obtained first-hand by our agent – he has yet the palms blistered by the oars – and we pride ourselves they are the most reliable and recent which may be extant, a species of commercial Horsburgh.

☞ Terms of the *Lin Tin Bulletin and River Bee*. Subscriptions – $11 per annum. Single copies to be had of Rua da Nossa Senhora da Nazare, 12, Pe do Monte, Macau, at centavos 40 in business hours.

From THE LIN TIN BULLETIN AND RIVER BEE

Wednesday, January 17, 1838

Vol. 1 No.2

We had resolved at all events not to be disappointed by the reception of our first issue, well knowing that it is the greatest tree which takes longest in putting out the tiniest shoot. We expected nothing from our prospective audience but immediate indifference, though we were in hopes, nay, entertained confident expectations, that a cool reception would be by degrees converted into a hot fever of anticipation as the succeeding issues came off our press. How warming and heartening, then, to be received with such a degree of interest and show of support. We say again we had not presumed to hope for success so directly and are highly gratified. Naturally, we shall not be complacent but shall still endeavour to improve our publication and extend its circulation. As we enjoy no patronage, rather wishing to be altogether independent, the only contribution we may solicit is that of our Readers, not only in a pecuniary regard but in point of their indulgence and sympathy. Already we have received numerous letters, in the overwhelming majority favourable, and we look forward to printing a miscellany in some future issue. We append below a selection of edited correspondence, together with our replies.

One gentleman, induced perhaps by an imperfect grasp of the language of France, accuses us of being Unbelievers. That we are not. We most vehemently repudiate such an accusation. Was our own uncle not a Philadelphian, O Brother and Friend? Not a Quaker, in fact, though having imbibed at that same spring, or a similar source, from which issue the clear waters of life. This leads us by a natural course to what we have a particular desire to animadvert upon in our editorial capacity this week. We mean the distinction which is to be drawn between the man and the cloth, the promoter and the cause. We would recognise the most distressing circumstance that it is perfectly feasible for good men to engage in an immoral traffic: upon such premise is predicated our entire argument, *raison d'être,* and justification of our journal. Did we not apprehend this rationally by process of observation, reflection, deduction, we should know it intuitively from the whole tendency of our life, which has been passed among those colleagues, and still friends, whom we now believe to be deluded, albeit sincerely and with the best of intentions, regarding the moral standing of the vicious trade it is their livelihood to conduct.

By the same token, it should be admissible that *bad* men may enlist themselves under the banner of a noble cause. Where, on this coast, is that principle more perfectly and openly illustrated than among the ranks – with the best will, we cannot say they are serried ranks – of the missionaries and clergymen? Riven by internal feuds as well as denomina- tional division, concerned more with denying their rivals converts than saving souls, they collect over the span of decades their miserable handful of 'Rice Christians', beggars who find in the bowl a more potent argument and symbol than the Cross. Who could blame the Chinese for being confused when all parties proclaim the same Lord and yet traduce the other? The differences which exist must appear tiny to them besides their own indifference and scepticism. Ridicule must be the response, and entirely forgivably, of the educated native. That amongst the Divines there are men of estimable character and no little talents, we do not deny – but their merit serves merely to contrast with the shortcom- ings of their colleagues. We cannot even call the majority of them bad men but mediocrities, time-servers, wretched, canting hypocrites, who disgrace their cloth and the name of Him who endured hardness, stripes, and ignominious death, while they enjoy their stipends in security and indulge themselves in the best comforts that may be provided on this shore. We have it on the best authority that many have not the least inclination to service, that their 'call' was to an assured livelihood and a removal from the indigence, or even disgrace, which attended them at home. Who has not heard tales of the travelling preachers in our own home country who insinuate themselves into the confidence of godly and gullible households and proceed to despoil the house of its worldly goods and, infinitely more precious, the honour of its daughter? Such relations pale into insignificance when compared with the amazing actions of the missionaries peculiar to this coast. Perhaps long familiarity with their practices diminishes the astonishment which even Old Residents ought to feel. Let us phrase it in language the most simple and direct. *They go up the coast in opium-clippers and distribute Bibles with the drug!* What a cruise of humbugs is this! The wares of death dealt impartially with the Word of Life! We have seen the box of tracts brought up on deck and broken open immediately upon the unveiling of the chest of drug. No, we have seen those very tracts used to wrap an inferior and leaking ball of Malwa! Mr G-.... but forgive our presumption and ignorance, of course *Herr Doktor* G-, was first up the coast north in company with Mr H. H. Lindsay of the Honourable Company in the *Sylph* in 1832, if our memory does not fail us. Since then, numerous divines have offered their services as interpreters on board these nefarious craft – though we are informed their services are in many cases voided owing to the circumstance of their ignorance of the local dialects, which may be incomprehensible between one hamlet and the next, twenty miles away.

To their great credit, the Catholic clergy have never lent themselves to such purposes. While their reformed (reformed!) brethren and bitter enemies avail themselves of the amusements and consolations which we may find in our little society, never straying a few miles beyond safety into the hinterland, the emissaries of Rome have penetrated the very bowels of the Empire, in disguise, and at great risk to themselves, and not infrequently paying for their devotion and their temerity with their lives. Those martyrs, their sacrifice no less glorious for being in a mistaken cause, have met lonely and excruciating ends. Others, of the Society of Jesus, have risen in centuries long past to the very pinnacle of worldly power and influence at the Emperor's court – by any standard the names of Ricci and Verbiest are great names.

Would that some of our contemporaries of the Reformed Churches possessed an iota of the zeal and fortitude which characterised the every thought and action of those courtiers of the Scarlet Woman, we do not say their ability! That would not be fair — talents are not distributed equally and men cannot be blamed for their want of those qualities we admire in others. Pondering this, and other kindred matters, we relinquish our editorial pulpit.

FROM OUR READERS

Mr Editor,

I was much diverted by the form of your baptismal issue and alike instructed by its matter. It appeared to combine in a way marvellous for two simple folded sheets of foolscap, judiciously proportioned, amusement, edification, and instrumentality. As to the eighth page, I do not myself engage in commerce, so may not judge as to its accuracy and useful-ness. In conclusion, may I beg to state that I was struck, too, as to the modesty of your demand upon the reader's pocket, if not upon his higher faculties. I anticipate obtaining your second issue, on its appearance, without suffering the smallest delay.

I have, Sir, the honour to be your most truly obedient servant,
SENEX

We experienced no little difficulty in deciphering the crabbed and shaky hand of our aged patron, but find his sentiments clear, vigorous and manly. Experience is a great instructor and we find this principle exemplified in his discrimination. We would merely add that should he direct his tottering steps to our office, we should be happy not only to supply him with our most recent issue but also to relieve him of the necessity of further indisposing himself over the greasy cobbles and noisome alleys of Macao in search of his favourite reading. For $10 per annum he may take our newspaper on subscription and *have it delivered by our care and, as he admits he is not habituated to the calculations of commerce, we would do him the additional service of informing him that this simple measure of convenience will also leave him cents 40 to his advantage. As to the saving in shoe-leather, we shall permit him to perform his own solitary calculations.*

Mr Editor,

Your first cries were not those of a discordant mewling and bawling, as you seemed to fear, but those of a healthy and bonny bairn, which will rather attract attention and solicitude than jar on the ear. I trust, however, that the sentiments you take the liberty of expressing in a foreign language, even the tongue of my countrymen's oldest ally, do not indicate a leaning towards atheism and Jacobinism. Being of a serious and calculating disposition, I feel bound to observe that the lighter paragraphs of your journal, though never frivolous, may in future hold my attention for no very long period. However, it is the last, but not least, of your pages to which I shall turn at once in succeeding issues (and I hope they do succeed) as it is the best formed to aid me in my enterprises. I was fortunate to secure one of the last copies available in the Factories, but as I am in the habit of rising early, like the bird which caught the worm, I shall be among the first to procure your next and, perhaps, *corner* the market in it to deprive my competitors of a valuable aid. The price of cents 40 is not low, I will have the great presumption to observe, but then it is a commonplace that the best product will dictate its own price in the marketplace. I recommend you do not raise it.

I have, sir, etc.

HIBERNIUS

Oh, sober and frugal son of the Manse and glen! Your origins breathe from your every line and in all your sentiments. But, my dear sir, pray do not occasion yourself the least anxiety as to our beliefs in a political view. We would assure you we are no democrat, rather the reverse, and pity the poor Radical for his deluded opinions. As to atheism, we have expatiated sufficiently sup. and passim. We shall

endeavour to supply the wants of all our readers at the Factories,
although we should rather exhort our patrons to their own benefit
and, we freely own, ours, to take out subscriptions. Lest our
arguments fall on the deaf ears of our parsimonious correspondent,
we advise that for a limited period only subscriptions to our organ
may be purchased at the especially discounted rate of $9.

Land feuds among the Chinese. It may surprise our readers to
hear that the province in the metropolis of which we take
our station has been settled by the Chinese in no very
ancient times. Both Kwangtung and Kwangsi provinces
(Broad South and Broad West), which for administrative
purposes are 'paired' *(being so broad, they may endure 'paring' –
ed.)* under one Governor-General or Viceroy, though each
possess their own appointed Governor residing in respectively Canton and Kwei Lum cities, were until recent times
– speaking in an historical, rather than an individual's span –
almost wholly inhabited by aborigine tribes, as dwarfish in
their physical stature as they were backward in their habit of
life. These copper-skinned sons of Adam organised
themselves in tribes under the sway of elders. In the river and
swampy half-lands of the delta, they fished and snared, much
as their remotest forebears, when they cultivated only the
scantiest crops of yams, taro, cabbage, and red beans on
principles so crude that it might fairly be said they possessed
no grasp of the agricultural science whatsoever. At such
period the true Chinese or Han resided to the north in the
fertile areas between the two great rivers of Central China.
During such years of peace and orderly government as they
enjoyed, and they were not inconsiderable, the population
prospered and were augmented as to numbers. Pressure upon
the land and the means of subsistence inevitably grew in
proportion. The surplus populations, that is to say those as yet
unpossessed of land, were forced by ineluctable necessity ever
south. Coming over the mountain passes, or navigating down
the rivers, at last they arrived in the modern provinces of

Kwangtung and Kwangsi. Here they lost no time in driving off the aboriginal populations from the fertile lands they had failed to use to their fullest and into the remotest areas. To this day the tribes reside in the mountains and fastnesses of the south and west, distinctive alike in their physical features and colourful costume. For the Chinese they have conceived a deadly hatred and woe betide a son of Han who falls into their clutches. To this day Chinese dare not walk alone or unarmed in those areas for fear of being disembowelled or buried and suffocated alive, if captured.

No less sanguinary has been the intercourse between those first Chinese settlers and the later comers, though equally of Han stock. Of course, it hardly requires observing, the pioneers had already taken up the most accessible and fertile territories, leaving only hilly and sandy or barren lands for the new emigrants. In the majority of instances they were able to retain and consolidate their grasp upon their acquisitions and inheritances of lands, although this necessitated ever greater vigilance and a well-ordered system of defence. For this reason, more than as a protection against roving bandits or river-pirates, the villages of these provinces present a heavily fortified appearance, with walls, moats, heavy gates, and with their loop-holes and barricades slotted for musketry and crossbow resemble more military outposts than long-settled hamlets. The older situated inhabitants are known as Boon Day (Neighbourhood Folk), the interlopers as Hack Car (Guest People) and possess distinct languages and different customs – though perhaps to most foreign eyes they are to all intents and purposes of common stock. Many are the wars which have been fought between the two factions. A frequent source of discord arises over water and riverine rights, for if the Hack Cars are unable to take up their positions on the best land, they tend to be on the less desirable heights which give them, however, prior access to the streams and by damming and diverting (*Kindly recollect yourself, sir. – ed.*), they secure the most advantageous irrigation for themselves, not infrequently causing that of the Boon Days to dry up altogether. Retaliatory raids are a

304

frequent occurrence, involving the deployment of artillery and wholesale conflagration of villages, to the point where it is less germane to speak of the vendetta or feud as conducted in Sicily or Kentucky than of a system of open warfare being waged. To this end, the rival bands form militias and night-watches to prohibit the work of incendiaries and arsonists, but, despite all the precautions resorted to on both sides, successful forays are not unknown. Conflict between Hack Car and Boon Day is particularly prevalent in Kwangsi. The turbulence of these southern populations has been, not without foundation, a cause of worry and perplexity to the mandarins and the Emperor. They may yet prove the train which shall ignite a larger explosion.

PURSUER

☛ Terms of the *Lin Tin Bulletin and River Bee*. Subscriptions $9 per annum. Single copies to be had of the editorial offices which are situate at Rua da Nossa Senhora da Nazare 12, Macao. A few copies of our first are still available at centavos 40. We would advise that our press can fulfil all private needs at excellent rates where elegance and accuracy are the requirements. Terms on application.

CHAPTER XXIII

The apparition groans and regards its broken fingernails. These are ragged and quite black under what is left of them, level with the flesh. Its face is streaked and filthy, notably the high forehead where inky fingers have been run distractedly through what is left of a most tenuous hair-line.

Face is gaunt, hollows in cheeks accentuated as if by cunning application of make-up, shadows under eyes darker even than ink – which is ferocious stuff: sticky, viscous, and irritating and formed basically of lamp-black and oil. Shirt is now fit for nothing more than rags, speckled and streaked as it is, with one unfortunate sleeve torn such that it resembles the slashed and frilled fashion of a century past. Although the ink seems to want to stick to any surface it can find, however unpropitious the material, it has its own mind as to its compatibility with the alchemical elements of paper and lead, with which it is supposed to mate. It runs off the typefaces as it were mercury. These have to be rubbed with their special impregnated inking-balls as often as they please. The paper – oh, vile, wretched stuff – would be perfectly adapted to any purpose you cared to name: trail for hares-and-hounds, wadding to a charge of gunpowder, varnished for a native umbrella, concertinaed for a fan, but it has a distaste for being newspaper so strong it amounts to an overwhelming aversion. It will be thirsty in one quire, haughty in the next, like blotting-paper on one occasion and an oil-cloth the next; absorb regularly, it disdains to. The ink by itself is an itchy commodity – heaven knows what cancers it is capable of inducing, but in combination with the paper it produces a reaction akin to St Anthony's fire. The knuckles and cuticles of the compositor are worst affected; they prickle and burn as if he's been stung. Poor compositor, poor Walter. He chews them for relief.

Laboriously assembled, bit by bit, in the composing-sticks, the lead types lie in their formes. Walter has fixed a mirror into the wall above these boxes (each corresponding to two pages) to aid the task of composition and deciphering, for, of course, the lead types in their reversed form are as understandable as hieroglyphics to the neophyte. (Which, after all, is what Eastman is). The pages are dampened with water, printed, and once dry receive the impress of a second forme on their other side. Thus pages one and eight are successively printed on the same side of a single sheet. (They cannot be simultaneously pressed in one operation, for the frame and nails of the wooden hand-press would collapse under the pressure requisite to print them both at once.) When these dry, the platen kisses pages two and seven one after the other. Subsequently, it is the turn of four and then five, and on their back three followed by six. The inner and outer tympans at this moment are swung open on their hinges, joined together much like a half-crooked arm is rotated at the elbow – the inner tympan being the biceps and the outer the forearm. There is no paper on the outer tympan, so that its latticed squares look much like a window without glass or – as Walter imagines – a toy known in childhood for blowing soap-bubbles. The machine, entirely operated by hand, in a series of nine separate physical movements which do not admit of any chance to sit but only to stand or at best to lean, is still the same ancient wooden contraption Father Ribeiro discovered, given the benefit of a little penetrating oil and a few replacement nails. The *Monitor's* is a modern Stanhope press of cast iron. Although not capable of the phenomenally rapid output of the latest steam or roller presses, it does have the advantage – thanks to its sturdier construction – of a capacity to print two pages simultaneously. It is also true the rival editor has the benefit of more waged hands but then…Walter's pages dry far more quickly on their line in balmy, breezy Macao than the *Monitor's* do in sultry Canton. And by that issue known as Vol. 1 No.15, or in other words Wednesday, July 18 1838, Walter will have learned to attach a counter-weight to the platen – that is, the actual square press at the end of the oaken screw – which makes it automatically rise after it has given the paper in the closed and folded tympans its impress. This simple attachment very nearly doubles the speed at which Walter can work, and more than ever gives the platen's lever the look of a tiller and its operator the appearance of a helmsman. Production: about 250 pages in the hour, assuming you actually have the incentive to work so hard in this climate. (But Walter times his shift with an hour-glass and a candle by night.) In fact, the capacity of the press well outstrips the puny circulation of the organ it serves.

Around Walter tall stacks of old newspaper lie piled; over a thousand copies, actually. What's this? How can this be? Hasn't he said, more or less, that he sold most of the issues out?

Mem. Never believe what you read in newspapers, even a

crusading one.

Distribution was the problem. Walter's sure the demand is there. He should know. Not only is he compositor, printer, editor, composer of leading articles, chief correspondent, not to mention solicitor of advertising – he's the vendor, too. Cap on head, leathern satchel dependent from a shoulder, he's traipsed to Praia and Ridge. In fact, he was quite successful; sold two satchels full. Gideon disposed of his petty consignment at Lin Tin. Bored to death, month in and month out, on the hulks, the officers and agents will welcome anything. But at Whampoa, Canton, nothing. Subscriptions are the nub. Chase had some copies for sale at Respondentia Walk – they have no room or office, now, in American Hong, or even a welcome. No one bought. Did their old friends, Ridley, Johnstone, and the others, see him from a balcony and keep to the square's far side? Gideon is unsure. It was lonely, embarrassing; a mortification. Eastman relishes the role of romantic outsider; Gideon doesn't. A few of the Parsee traders bought some copies (to be precise, two newspapers between six of them and they bargained down to 30 cents per copy). Gideon plastered two copies against the Factory walls in Hog Lane, alongside the mandarins' abusive placards, in such a way that the eight pages could be successively read, then decamped.

Back in Macao: 'It is hopeless, Walter. I cannot tell you adequately. My spirits fail me.'

'But this is nothing, sir! Do you expect an immediate success? The pleasure is in the struggle, the vanquishing. This was but our rehearsal – and many an empty house has been succeeded by one packed to its rafters, echoing with acclaim. You cannot expect to conquer ten years of indifference at a single blow.'

'This, I have a notion, then, was why you waxed so lyrical as to our prospects in our last.'

'Oh, an old showman's trick. By public demand. Absolutely last night. Only a few tickets remaining. Positively to close.'

'Standing-room only.'

'Then you grasp the general principle admirably. You must fix the actual state of affairs to your own advantage.'

'Ah, indeed. Now, sir, I must request you to stop fixing my

articles. It is emphatically *not* to their advantage.'

'What can you mean?'

'You must quit inserting your italic – *ed*. Those facetious and inaccurate interpolations quite spoil my essays.'

'Come, come. A little wit never went amiss. I like to add a little leaven to your very worthy but perhaps doughy…'

'Wit be hanged! Damnation! You might as well preach a sermon or deliver a lecture amidst the breaking wind, flatulence, and hiccuping of an audience of unreformed drunkards!'

'Well, really! I could take offence.'

'You cannot, sir. What is *Yangtse Kiang?*'

'Now, don't trifle, Gid.'

'What, sir, is *Yangtse Kiang?*'

'A river. Have you not told me it means Son of the Ocean?'

'Just so. River. Yangtse its proper name. Kiang meaning river. When you wrote Yangtse Kiang river, you perpetrated the solecism of referring to it as Yangtse River river.'

'Ah.'

'Quite so. Now be contented with your consumptive poets and fabricating the readers' letters.'

'My dear Gideon! Do you mean to suggest that I impose upon our esteemed patrons?'

'I do – and you cannot fool me.'

'Then allow me to give you some freshly fixed mint julep in amends, as only we Virginians know how to fix it. Pursuer will have his soliloquies to himself entirely, the chorus banished.'

'Handsome fellow. Is our third "set up" yet?'

'Ah, Gid, the print will be one of your vermilion rescripts, red with my own blood. Regard these poor hands.'

'Then have a care for my palms – see there? All to record tariffs no one will ever see.'

'Well, matters, I allow, may only look up, we are so low, and that's a fact.'

From THE LIN TIN BULLETIN AND RIVER BEE

Wednesday, January 31, 1838

Vol.1 No.3

Let us consider the number 3. Or III, iii,; three, trois, tres, as it may appear under just a few of its divers significations. Is it not, gentle reader, a figure, a quantity, an amount of an import which is mightily symbolical, necromantic almost in its power? That this is no mere whimsical fancy on our part, induced by taxing hours at the 'stone' and a too liberal imbibing while secluded in our editorial *sanctum sanctorum* of a certain green and tinkling refreshment known in our home parts, we may attest merely by citing the authority of biblical precept (which would also serve to clear us of the charges of impiety and atheistical wickedness levelled afresh at us after our last). For do Father, Son, and Holy Ghost not constitute a Trinity? (Would our critics prefer the definite article to the indefinite, as indicative of rather more respect? Alas, we must be miserly with the contents of our type-cases.) What are the component elements of any army but CAVALRY, ARTILLERY, and INFANTRY? When the ancient Egyptians chose to construct their eternal homes and earthly monuments (being devilish cunning engineers, though but indifferent theologians), did they not choose the form of the PYRAMID? And what is a pyramid but a collection of TRI-ANGLES? As to congruent, equilateral, and isosceles, we shall spare both our readers and ourselves. Instances of modern triangles might be depicted thus:

ENGLAND

INDIA   CHINA

which is a specimen of political geometry where the *angles* and *inclinations* on all sides are not equal, some being rather more *acute* than others. Such a system may not persist (such is our *devout* wish). A more enduring concatenation may be expressed thus:

the which ill-starred triad may justly be dubbed perpetual, for it is beyond reformation or the free will of the interested parties.

It is, however, pretty nigh universally reckoned that three is a most auspicious number (although our informant on such matters says the natives rather consider five in that light). Certainly we would regard our present issue under such a favourable view, saying which we thank our subscribers for their indulgence and attention.

The PEOPLE fear the mandarins; the MANDARINS fear the foreigners; the FOREIGNERS fear the PEOPLE. – *Old native saying.*

Secret societies. These are of great influence and power among the natives, especially in the southern provinces, notably Kwangtung and Fukien. They draw their members from all ranks of society, including (although rarely) the functionary or mandarin class. However, most members are drawn from the lower orders, especially among travelling porters, boatmen, fruit-sellers, and the *lictor* class –that is the runners, clerks, and policemen who comprise the staff of the *yahmoon* or magistrate's residence. Even the highest official dare not too openly cross them. The Viceroy of a northern province, an eminent scholar and a stern official, secure as he thought alike in reputation and rank and in the enjoyment of his worldly possessions, was struck down in his palanquin by agents of the societies. These malefactors do not confine themselves to mere robbery and arson, but dare raise the flag of wholesale insurrection. In 1825 members of the Society of the White Lotus breached the very portals of the Imperial Palace and, streaming across an inner courtyard, would have performed the Son of Heaven the service of cutting his throat from ear to ear but that his Seventh Son seized a matchlock and, applying the fusee to the pan, sent a ball clean through the head of the ringleader when he fell dead upon the spot. This sharp-shooting scion of generations of hunters of the Tartar plains, keen of hand and eye, now rules as the Emperor Taou Kwang and, so it is related, owed his elevation above his older siblings to this deed of cool pluck.

The southern societies are known as the Triad or Heaven and Earth and Man Association. Even now, they have emissaries in the city and could project some desperate deed, even the capture of the town.

Apparent inhumanity of the Chinese. Man everywhere is the same man. How else may he be reclaimed for his Maker? Under the different veneers of varying laws, institutions, and civilisations (or, indeed, the complete or partial want of them) which may give an air of different characters, the Old Adam is the same. His nature contains the same admixture of bad and good, hopelessly commingled (for the present writer is not an adherent to that denomination of belief which views him as wholly depraved – such would be a condition infinitely less distressing), whether this *Maelstrom* of warring elements be subsumed under an integument which is yellow, black, red, white, coffee, or any combination of known fleshly tints. The laws of China, both in their ideal form and in their practical application, may strike us as ridiculous and absurd, were they not so cruel and sanguinary. What! Exile to the freezing wastes at the Emperor's caprice? His entire family, down to the babes and children, to perish to expiate a crime, as well as the malefactor who was its sole author? Yet does the black-haired race submit without a murmur.

All who have resided or voyaged upon the great river which drains three provinces, peopled by more than the population of Europe, and rolls its mighty flood down to the universal sea, know that should they fall into its metal desolation, they may expect no help from a native. Grandfather, mother, father, tender children will watch from the sanctuary of their craft impassively his drowning struggles; see his convulsive and frantic splashings weaken, desperation turn to resignation, his head bob under the surface – which is not more indifferent or neutral than they – rise, sink, and then rise no more. Yet may all this take place within ten feet of their floating sanctuary, without their so much as tossing a piece of wood to the wretched victim. Nay, should his grip arrive on their gunwales, they will beat his fingers off with any implement to hand. Nor is this an instance of a callousness peculiarly visited upon the foreigner. They will mete out such quarter impartially to any member of their race who is not of their own family. Here is the nub. The penal code of the empire states that he who discovers the corpse of a person who has met with an unnatural death shall be charged with the responsibility of ascertaining how the deceased met his end – and that until such investigation be satisfactorily concluded, the hapless finder, who may even have risked his own life in an attempt to preserve that of the victim, shall be held guilty of his death or be at the very least charged with the expenses of his funeral. Oh! What a capital black joke is this, what inversion of treasure trove! It may be imagined only too well what extortions, exactions, and blackmail might be practised on the would-be rescuer by the corrupt agents of the mandarins. They would not scruple to execute an innocent man who refused to submit to their impositions. When I recited the tale of the Good Samaritan to an intelligent and kindly native, he wiped tears from his eyes – of mirth and disbelief.

Thus a man's bond may only be that with his family, who, it may be said with justice, are in a figurative as well as a literal sense in the same boat as he. In such a way are friendship and any sense of commonwealth and sodality subverted, the naturally generous instincts of man (who would risk his life to rescue another) cramped and deformed by pernicious laws. Yet see these same folks' affecting gratitude when in similar plight, their craft capsized, they are saved by the foreigner! Truly, life is strange and holds out some perverted instances.

PURSUER

Aphorism. It is the proud and noble soul which feels a rebuff the keenest. Base and ignoble spirits, actuated by mean and mercenary motives, accept contumely and rejection without a qualm for such, they have always known, are their just deserts. It is true nobility which is killed by scorn. Like a bird it flies on high in an azure and peerless sky. Then it is struck by the pellets, a clumsy blast, an uncouth charge, of derision and spurning. It falls to the ground where it lies in the mud, a broken but still living thing.

Physician heal thyself. In Paris, toward the middle of the century previous, lived a gentleman, one La Rocque, celebrated for his wit and powers of *repartie,* which gave him entry to the most celebrated salons of that city, distinguished alike for their beauty and their learning. His attendance at dinners and banquets was jealously sought by the most elegant and accomplished hostesses of the day when his droll and fantastical conceits were accustomed to set a whole table in a roar of laughter and applause. One day presented himself to a notable physician of that *beau monde* a gentleman shrouded in a cloak of the deepest dye and his gloomy features overcast by the brim of a plumed and most funereal hat. This gentleman confided to the doctor that he dare not trust himself alone with a razor or a cord, so overcome by gloom and melancholy was he. 'Sir,' says the physician, 'I recommend you abstain from all solitary pursuits and, in especial, reading, and seek out company the most gay and vivacious, in particular that of the celebrated La Rocque, whose sallies would bring a smile to the face of Ophelia.' – 'Alas, sir,' quoth the gentleman, 'that La Rocque stands before you.'

☛ Terms of the *Lin Tin Bulletin and River Bee.* Subscriptions -$8 per annum. Single copies to be had of the editorial offices situate at Rua da Nossa Senhora da Nazare 12, Macao, at 40 cents. Limited supplies of the first two issues available on application at discount of centavos 20 per copy. The newspaper can display advertisements, announcements, and communications at advantageous rates. Its press is available for all private needs, when printing is required to be executed with accuracy and elegancy. Terms to be apprised.

From THE CANTON MONITOR

Thursday, February 15th, 1838

The lion in general disdains to notice the jackal. This cur will slink away from the kill made by the King of Beasts. In the particular circumstances of our own situation, how eligible the comparison may be can be seen from the circumstance that the cur feasts off old news which it has not brought down for itself but culled from other newspapers and that it makes its appearance some four and twenty hours previous to its senior's, after which it is promptly sent about its business. The British Lion, to alter the terms of our metaphor, would not notice a mere insect, except it might be a nuisance to others of his Pride and that he would not wish to be thought asleep or remiss. Therefore, a flick of the tail merely will suffice (we would not wish to mention our puny rival in our leading article and so shake our *colophon* at him). Aptly named BEE! How he does DRONE! But, really, he should learn to sift truth from rumour – he has to do the work of the whole hive, but still should not suck from the growths on a dung-heap (above the which we perused his gatherings, daubed on to the wall, for certainly there was not any other issue at Canton). What! Was this honey not rancid? The Queen at her Coronation already (we don't mean the Queen Bee) and the King, her Uncle, scarcely cold? This great event will not, we have it on the best of authorities, be until the summer of this year. As to the last words of the King, they were worthy of him and shame the mean-minded mocker. In his final sufferings his thoughts were for his Country. He spoke his last on the 18th of June. 'I will not die,' this Royal Patriot said, 'without seeing the sun set on the day of Waterloo,' and, hearing this, the Duke of Wellington caused the captured Tricoleur to be brought to the expiring Monarch, who gasped and whispered, 'Unfurl it, let me feel it … Glorious.' Glorious indeed.

Then all is clear when one considers the traducer was an enemy, his countrymen the Allies of the Corsican; the Hero of Trafalgar (whom he equally slights, though not in any direct and manly way) a source of terror to the *impressed* seamen of his own country. Poor colonial! We did not know that *prairies* existed in the Company's Indian Possessions, but are grateful for enlightenment on this point, although we very much doubt whether the circumstances of the breaking of the late King's death corresponded as closely to the ride of Paul Revere as the Bee would have us believe. What a farrago of nuisances fill his columns (or should we say, *cells?*) A Requiem for a half-mad Muscovite of whom no one has ever heard! A tour of the Virginia Lunatic Asylum – has he personal experience of the quality of accommodation offered by that Institution? As to those black and sinister forms, we doubt not but that they were the conductor of the Bee and his assistant glimpsed at their mischievous cabals. However, we have our consolation – *this pest may sting but once, and so doing, expires!*

'Now damnation have him for a hired old rogue, it is not even his own interests he serves!'

'Well, is it not the game-keeper who is most zealous after the poacher? When did old squire Larkins last sit up over the moonlit man-trap?'

'That I don't rightly know, as a beaver-hatted son of the land of the free.'

'You Yankees cultivate those as the height of fashion? I'll

allow the world holds no further surprises in store.'

'Oh, Walter, I am heartily sorry, truly I am.'

'Why so?'

'To overcome your natural inclination to quit the scene of ignominy and contention. You should have made your exit, as you pleased, and made a new start at home. Anywhere.'

'Now the devil take you, sir. I would rather the ship had disappeared without trace in the vast reaches of the Pacific, truly I would. How can you be so lily-livered a faintheart? Darnation take it – you could have swung for treason in the days of our grandfathers.'

'Walter, dear Walter, we have sold sixty copies of our last.'

'Fifty-eight, according to my record.'

'Even worse, then. And yet you are categorical as to the necessity of printing more than five hundred of each number…'

'We might as well.'

'How much longer can we continue to do so?'

'As long as there is breath in my body.'

'Well, sir, I do not talk of us quitting the struggle. No, though, I admit to my discouragement, even if you do not. It is the losses – how much longer can we continue to endure them? Our small capital must soon be eroded. We lose hundreds with every issue.'

'Eighty dollars the last, seventy its predecessor.'

'And we do not even draw our remunerations. No! Remove that sneer from your face, sir, you know very well, sir, that it is a matter of the most perfect indifference to me. I expect I shall not care if I never see a cent of it.'

'Can that be good grammar? Let me think. *Give* me my rollers back, you pup – we shall never see this issue. Thank you – I was fixing Pursuer's latest effusion – he is a most knowledge-able fellow: and the staunchest of friends. But I allow even his wits would be improved by a draught of sea-air. Let us catch Harry and the good Father at their game.'

From THE LIN TIN BULLETIN AND RIVER BEE

Wednesday, February 28, 1838

Vol. 1 No.5

☞ Terms of the *Lin Tin Bulletin and River Bee*. Subscriptions $8 per annum. Single copies to be had of the editorial offices situate at Rua da Nossa Senhora da Nazare 12, Macau, at cents 30. Small numbers of the three first issues remain at $10 the copy. The newspaper is willing to accept advertisements post-paid following insertion.

Gideon Chase to Walter Eastman

Lorcha *Maria* Whampoa

March 3rd, 1838

My dear Walter,

Extraordinary! Rum do's, Harry would say. Well, can you conceive, I am clean out of 200 issues. A portion of the frequenting vessels had already dropped down the river to take advantage of the early monsoon and to clear the Bogue, while matters remained so uncertain with the Canton authorities. Therefore, I was able to have taken off my hands by the ships' officers only three and twenty copies against the almost forty of my last visit. However, up at the Factories, what a different tale! Landing at Jackass Point, I resolved to 'make my pitch' squarely in the Factory Gardens and, in fact, under the British flagpole, rather than hiding my talents under the bushel of the esplanade railings as per previous occasion. Provocative, you'll say? Well, Jack no longer flies there, and I cheerfully courted the risk of the young British gentlemen stringing me up unceremoniously by the heels in tit-for-tat for the gallant Major André. I shared my station with, respectively, to the left, Nankin Jack, that peripatetic huckster of curios, with his sturdy rogue assistant, contorting himself in ecstasies the while his partner produced each trashy gew-gaw; to the right, a peep-show, very likely obscene to the last degree, doing great trade among the lower natives; in the centre before me, a swallower of swords and fire. None of these could have been a greater object of curiosity to the Square's riff-raff than your servant. A recently acquired knowledge, I will not say command, of pithy and imperative forms of the colloquial (and I dare not translate these into plain English!) when exercised caused the spectators to fall back, doubtless under the conviction that I was a warlock retailing written spells, for my understanding of the tones of speaking is as yet imperfect. A little later there fell on my ears the *hum* and *whoosh* of sticks distressing the air and the occasional dull *thwack* as a cane found the mark. Then whose heads should appear but Ridley's, Johnstone's, and the good Dr MacGillivray's, followed by sundry other foreign gentlemen, including Scotch and English. Some of these countenances bore no very friendly aspect, and I feared for the integrity (physical) of our organ of opinion, all 200 numbers I had baled with me. Good Jonathan, tho', stood by my side and in the shadow of his valorous reputation, your servant found security. Within the short space of half an hour, I was the possessor of $60 and no newspapers. Now to what cause can you ascribe this?

I shall remain at the anchorage, collecting informations for the Prices Current during the remainder of this week. You had best despatch, not more, I think, than 100 copies the which,

Your dutiful correspondent,

Gideon Chase,

– will endeavour to vend to the best of his abilities.

Walter Eastman to Gideon Chase

Rua da Nossa Senhora da Nazare 12

Macau

March 5th, 1838

My dear Gid,

Lordy! as the darky said when he shook hands with the mirror.

Remedios, who is the villainous, low-browed half-caste, both master and owner (he assures me) of the *Sonia* lorcha,

319

has this note and 200 numbers of the present, together with 50 each of the previous issues, to deliver to your care. He swears he can recognise the *Maria's* slovenly rigging when she's hull-down over the horizon ('So why you use? She too slow. No good boat. *Sonia* got two more gun each side and still make knot and a half faster,' beating his brawny breast the while) – so he will pick you out at Whampoa. Present the back numbers *gratis* to purchasers of the current. Those of the issue of February 28, No.5, which you are unable to get taken off your hands, merely leave in the arcade of the English Hong, hard by the fire-engine.

Walter.

PS Fine lad!

PPS My opinion? The old fool hoist himself on his own petard, and that's a fact.

Gideon Chase to Walter Eastman

Lorcha *Sonia*
French Folly
Canton River
March 16th, 1838

One thousand salaams, my dear sir,

Take this as good receipt for the safe delivery of 400 copies of our No. 6 through the proper or, maybe, improper offices of Remedios. I am uncertain as to the circumstance of him also taking opium up the river and discharging it before Whampoa. Certainly there is a sweet and sickly smell aboard the boat. I warrant the addict might smoke the very caulking of his disreputable craft. However, that's another matter. You were only by a small degree too optimistic as to the prospects of the last, that is No. 5. Those surplus (a mere 15 of the 200) I placed, as per constituent's instructions, by the fire-engine. May they start such a blaze as man has never beheld here!

I trust our No. 5 in the Chinese system of numerology shall prove more successful than our lucky third by the Western calculation. Pray insert the latest enclosed effusion of Pursuer, without alterations or emendations other than improvements in its grammar or the expunging of infelicities of style, for which the author and your always friend,

Gideon Chase,

thanks you.

Gideon Chase to Walter Eastman

Lorcha *Sonia*
Whampoa
Friday, April 13th (!), 1838

My dear Walter,

The success of our issue No.7 exceeds even that of No.5. As the No.7, according to the prejudice of the Chinese, is the number of death and other disasters too manifold to relate, and as I write to you on a day vulgarly held to be inauspicious, I think we may safely suppose that is what these superstitions are, namely superstitions. Yet as No.6 was less successful than No.5 (and I cannot, try as I will, descry the smallest difference between the principles on which we conducted Nos 5, 6,7 or indeed their predecessors), I may only assume there is a strong element of fortuitousness and luck attendant.

–Giddy (with puzzlement and life afloat).

Walter Eastman to Gideon Chase

Rua da Nossa Senhora da Nazare 12
Macao
April 18th, 1838

My dear Gideon,

Too much midnight study has turned your brain. You have now adopted the way of thought of a mandarin. You regard, in an enclosed and blinkered sort of way, the issue in itself, as if it could be pondered and understood in isolation. It is an inward-looking philosophising. I, however, am the heir of Descartes and I begin from myself certainly, *but* then I commence to look outwards. If the explanation lies not in the issues (I mean our issues viz. 1,2,3,4,5,6,7,8 – which is most safely in the press, by the by), then look for the causes (or cause) of their varying success outside them. Do I talk in riddles?

Now you are certainly right to complain about shipboard life (do I wonder now at the fortitude and forbearance of the British officials, tossed by the waves on board their floating citadel of a *Louisa?*). You are to come down by the *Sonia* or *Maria*, whichever the sooner, and recruit your health under the devoted ministrations of your grateful friend and partner, Walter

PS This is an editorial instruction. As the trading season and monsoon have both ended there is no need for your continual presence and the undermining your constitution in Canton. Our audience will be here in Macao again.

'Oh, no,' says Walter, lounging against Ribeiro's fountain, 'not at all. My life has been every piece as isolated as yours, more so in many ways. The hardship and the danger have been yours, I allow, but not entirely the lonesomeness.'

Gideon lobs a stone at the frog, who hides under a lotus leaf. 'Well, Remedios is not equal to a discussion on Hegel, I'll assure you, and that's a fact.'

'Nor was Hegel, and that's a fact, too. The difference, Gid, in our lots was that you were a hermit of nature, while I was a man-made exile. Damnation, I might have been a ghost for all the recognisance extended me. Have you ever walked the Praia of a balmy spring evening and not one soul, not one kindly person, fingered his brim or bade you so much as a good e'en? Well, sir, you will. We are ghosts so far as this community is concerned. No, you don't, or can't, cut a ghost. I should be surprised if we could find Christian burial in the Protestant cemetery.'

'As bad as that?'

'Not even MacQuitty will lick your hand.'

'Then we *are* pariahs.'

'No, my son,' says a cheerful voice from the balcony, 'Mother

322

Church does not disdain to embrace you, should your eyes be opened to the Truth. Why lie in the cemetery of heretics? Now, refrain from tormenting my poor frog. He is a wonderful exterminator of insects in the summer.'

'Father,' says Eastman, 'forgive us, for we knew not what we did.'

'Blasphemy,' says Harry O'Rourke, joining Father Ribeiro on the balcony, 'will not make you new friends. Why aren't you working for your stockholders?'

'The Lord fashions his instruments from the most curious materials,' says the good Father. 'These pagan lads have struck mighty blows for God's True Church. Have you read their strictures on the heretic envoys?'

'I have, and a good deal of what seems Freethinking, too.'

'As to that,' says the supple priest, 'we shall leave a Higher Tribunal to adjudicate. Gideon, you have a friend here who awaits you.'

As he ascends the creaking stairs, Gideon can smell incense and leather from Father Ribeiro's study, replacing the aroma of flowers and Walter's cigar.

'Master,' he says, entering the book-lined lair.

Ow looks both benign and mischievous. Below in the reception-room, Harry's hearty barbarian laughter rumbles. Gideon reflects on his own relative uncouthness but Ow radiates benevolence today. The old scholar is not like other people: he seems reluctant to permit them to impinge on his moods. He will not allow them to influence the course of his own emotions. If *he's* going to be bad-tempered that particular day, then he'll be crotchety, no matter what. Bring him good news, cajole, charm, flatter the perverse old monster, but he'll have his sulk. Today, he is bent on exercising kindness and a tender solicitude for his inferiors, from which course nothing, but nothing, short possibly, of an attempt on his own life by said inferiors, is going to deflect him.

'Be seated,' he exhorts his pupil, who nurtures no such murderous designs within his respectful breast. 'Amuse your teacher.'

Gideon is far too wise to consider doing this, but makes an

adjustment to the tea-pot.

'Some literary gentlemen of my acquaintance,' Ow lies, 'were struck by the facility of your Regulated Heptasyllables. When I informed them of their author's youth, they were surprised; apprised of his origins, thunderstruck.'

Gideon imagines the Literary Gentlemen in their scholar's robes, thunderstruck, overlooking a water-garden, perhaps on a miniature bridge, passing his effusions among themselves in consternation; he smiles. Ow smiles, too; he can see the Literary Gentlemen are going to be a wonderful device; glimpses immense possibilities for them. A splendid on-going joke with manifold uses, to be relished all the more as his foreign pupil is 1. sophisticated enough to be sceptical as to their existence in any but an ideal sense and 2. too respectful openly to deny their reality. (Ow, by the way, years ago adopted Arabic numerals from Joaquim Ribeiro as more rational. He's not a *bigot,* after all.) The whole farce is fairly similar to Eastman's attitude, respectively, to God and Ribeiro. 'Indeed,' persists Ow with his capital conceit, 'some of the said Literary Gentlemen hinted that your poor teacher was nothing more than a prevaricator and had composed the verses himself. Can you believe that?'

Gideon murmurs, expressing polite disbelief that anyone could imagine his teacher a teller of tall stories.

'I assure you, my dear pupil,' says Ow, fixing Gideon with his wicked eye and barely able to keep a straight face, 'such was the case. They will not admit it is within a foreigner's power to indite verse of such a standard and quite *refuse* to believe in your existence. Now is that not strange?'

Gideon chokes on his tea, some of which vents as fine spray through his nose. Ow kindly passes him from his capacious sleeve a handkerchief, convenient item of apparel he has again not disdained to imitate from Ribeiro (and which had its uses once as prop in an insulting refutation of biblical legend – Zechariah v 1-3, the flying roll of length 20 cubits and the breadth thereof 10 cubits).

'My dear pupil, I can see you are touchingly affected by this slight upon your poor instructor but beg you to compose yourself. He cares not for his reputation, save as it is made illustrious through the reflected glory of your own distinguished achievements.'

Gideon buries his face in the beautifully laundered cloth, which puts to shame Father Ribeiro, who is as notoriously careless about his linen as the lowest of his countrymen. Gideon's shoulders heave; one heel drums.

'Control your emotions, I beseech you. Your teacher does not care. Why should *you* then be distressed on his behalf?' Ow waves a taloned hand to indicate his pupil should keep the (soiled) handkerchief. Gideon wipes the tears from his eyes. On catching sight of the bland expression Ow has assumed, he has to bite his lip hard enough to draw blood.

Meanwhile, downstairs, on the lower level as it were, Harry is arguing fiercely with Eastman. Eastman desires perfection. Eastman stipulates accuracy; he is all in favour of correct detail. Harry scoffs. He believes the conception, if strong and beautiful enough, can vanquish a whole litany of petty infelicities. 'Titian's limbs,' he says, inclining Walter at first to imagine this is a new oath, until he continues, 'see how poorly accomplished these may be. Far more frequently than you would think. Look how they project from the body at angles which defy anatomy. His hands. Altogether wrong – many times. Yet how miraculous those arms and legs! They glow, they are luxurious! They are more apparent, more fleshly than this – regard! Damme, your pardon, Joaquim, they are an incitement to anthropophagi – Crusoe was fortunate not to swim to his island grasping one of his frames as flotsam!'

Walter bursts out laughing. 'Well, I'll allow you have the advantage of me. As I have never had the advantage of seeing the originals, I take your word as an Old Worlder. But it seems strange to me that one should be ready to forgive in the master the lapses one should castigate in the tyro.'

'No, sir, one does not forgive them, nor will he who committed them, but they don't detract from the realisation of their conception; they are blemishes merely.'

'I am not sure I follow your line of reasoning, but…'

'They are, then, as the typographical or literal errors in your journal. Incidental is the word I require, I think. They are nuisances but they cannot affect the meaning or detract from the nobility of an excellent essay or piece of reasoning.'

'In sufficient quantities they could destroy its sense – but I take your meaning. It would then, I calculate, be only a low and small-minded person who would be moved to hilarity by the unfortunate transposition of an 's' or an 'f' in the word …'

'Quite so, m'boy,' says Harry hastily. Joaquim, the etymologist, looks briefly interested.

'Then,' says Eastman, '*per contra,* a hack may enjoy a command of the most perfect technique, possess the most surpassing competence, and yet never be able to rise above his own pettiness?'

'But exactly,' says O'Rourke, delighted. 'Now how many times is it I have said so, or expressed the same in other words, and only now is it you take me up, you young ignoramus?' he adds, pinching Eastman's cheek affectionately.

The latter looks rueful. 'Then, I have a notion, I've been wasting my time.'

'Now how so?'

'My efforts, my practice, good gracious, my *improvement* – and there was – all so much futility. No, Harry, don't lie to me. There are no two ways about it.'

'If you become maudlin, my boy, you shall have to be sconced in a beaker of Portugal wine. What d'ye say, Joaquim?'

'Sconce?' Father Ribeiro spreads his huge hands in puzzlement. This is neither of the vivid, ever changing language of the people, nor does it sound technical. Not a Latin root? But not Anglo-Saxon…

'Later, later, Joaquim.'

'*Pois, pois,*' says the good Father, with a Latin moue and rise of his thick, black eyebrows, (being a totally meaningless but highly adaptable and expressive sound found in his own native language). 'I shall attend to our young friend, my own special young friend, if I may express a certain favouritism without insulting our dear Mr Eastman, upstairs. Will you take a glass, Harry? No? Then the world still holds surprises for this jaded mind. In this case do you take the chessmen in your pockets and we will join you, in due course, on the Praia.'

We allow ourselves the freedom of inserting below the subjoined dialogue, which, while very different from the matter we are accustomed to print in our own columns, is not, we assure ourselves, so disconsonant that it shall appear wholly inadmissible. It is clearly the work of a talented pen, we believe an English, at least British, pen, though we would not dismiss the possibility of its author being an Irishman of the educated classes, such as ourselves, perhaps some Trinity wit. However, other evidences, such as its familiarity with the Trans-Atlantic idiom and the other amusing – and less than amusing – quirks of Cousin Jonathan, incline us to suppose that our playwright (for he has had the sprightly notion, original to the last degree, of couching his unsolicited but welcome contribution in the form of dramatic exchanges) may be some returned countryman of ours. Now who should visit the desolate territories and uncouth society – the settlers more repellent than the redskins they have displaced – of the United States, but someone who *had* to? As the education of our own correspondent clearly places him above the station of that miserable class of emigrants of the 'steerage' who have been forced to depart, with many a tear, from their ancient homes, and even their dear ones, by the veriest want and destitution, and mayhap even the rude knock of the bailiff, to find, alas, often enough, after the perils, travails, yea, even bereavements (not to mention the awful affliction of *mal de mer* on which we ourselves may speak feelingly) of their voyage that there is no livelihood for them but in the lowest, most exhausting, and dangerous labours – we believe our playwright is a former protagonist of the American Wars. He may be some veteran who bears the honourable scars sustained before New Orleans, or earlier at Bunker Hill, though he would be a grey-head indeed who served his King in the Loyalist War under Cornwallis. His hand is most elegant – clear yet ornamental, delicate yet without the least effeminacy, regular without being rotund. We envy it. There is a science which claims to deduce traits of character from a man's handwriting, as well as the shape of his head. We imagine our correspondent a man of the first education, scion of some noble house – his commission first purchased, or obtained through influence, then deserved by capacity. The regularity of his hand might incline us to a suspicion that he is a nautical man, used to 'shooting the sun' and performing other nice calculations upon paper, but upon the whole we believe he is unlikely to be one of the heroes of Britannia's wooden walls, who maintained the blockade in the war of 1812, for this would have spared him the close intercourse with Jonathan to which he has had to submit and, all in all, we are inclined to suppose he is some quondam officer of the army who has relinquished his commission and taken a place in one of our British houses of agency. However, if he comes forward and identifies himself to us, we undertake to respect his confidence and should perhaps not be loth to augment his pay, should he prove to be one of the Superintendent's official establishment or, indeed, his half-pay if he has retired from the Company's sepoy service to Macao. We print in full his communication to us, dated from Macao.

SCENE – *The dark cellar or bunker of the craziest, crookedest little house of the lowest quarter of Macao. A dirty little table, one of the legs of which, very much shorter than the author's, is shored up by … a most Holy Book! On the table a guttering, smoky, and altogether extravagantly foul column of tallow provides the only illumination. Enter two cloaked figures, habited in the manner of Portugal. There are the sounds of rodents scuffling in the outer blackness, but rats are not disturbed by other rats, no matter of what size.*

FIRST CLOAKED FIGURE *(throwing aside his concealing garment and revealing himself as* SAMUEL, *a lanky and morose youth of disappointed mien and little hair):* Darn my mother, but I barked my shin bad on that thar stoop. It bides fair to break the skin and bleed. What d'ye say, Jonathan?

SECOND CLOAKED FIGURE *(flinging his cloak over a chair to reveal himself as* JONATHAN *and impaling the table with his Bowie knife or poignard. He is a sturdy lad with arms corded and sinewy from much rowing and altogether wasted in his present avocation as assassin of characters.):* Waal *(drawling)* I guess ye'll have to grin and bear it, Sam. It makes a most efficient baar-trap, and no two ways about it. We'll sit in hopes of ketching a spy or two in it by and by.

SAMUEL: Aye, that's true, I allow. *(Shifts his chaw or quid of tobacco to one cheek, the better to spit. Outraged rodent squeaks protest.)* Pry-vacy is what we be wantin', I guess.

JONATHAN: Aye, and no two ways about it, and that's a fact. Don't want none o' them Johnny Cakes or Britishers listenin' in. *(Shifts his own plug but being a younger assassin and less accomplished a spitter contrives to swallow the brown juice. Turns distinctly green in the blackness.)* Cain't be more'n two or three at a pinch, at these Cay-bals o' plotters. Say! Ain't it so dark you could hide a whole army of negurs down hereaways and no one the wiser.

SAMUEL: We should git some in for a Black Hole o' Canton. Haw!

JONATHAN *(gulping):* No negurs this part o' th' world to th' best o' my acquaintance with it *(which has been brief enough in all conscience).* Only them yellow negurs what we've been pretendin' to love for our own purposin'.

SAMUEL: Waal, when the Frenchies concluded to give *fire-water* to th' Injuns it didn't matter a d-n to the Redskins whether it be French or American firewater they was a-drinkin', so long as they got their fire-water, but who *gave* th' fire-water fixed things so as to get them Injuns' lands — so it mattered to them, durn it.

JONATHAN: So we be contemplatin' gettin' a manna-poley on that smokin' fire-water to them yellow negurs.

SAMUEL: That's a fact, and we can fix it so. Nothin' more cunning than a Yankee, less it'll be a wounded baar. Haw!

JONATHAN: Waal, dang me, if that ain't a right American trick. Don't say we ain't the equal o' any French cardinal for smartness in this You-nighted States o' ourn.

SAMUEL: They may be Disunited States, and this ain't a time for half-measures. We got ourselves in a deuced unhandsome fix here, lettin' them Britishers grab that whole yellow-negur market here. Why, we cain't fix to hold our own negurs much longer, they let any more o' those Free States into th' Union. *(Spurt, squeak)*. And that's a fact.

JONATHAN: Say, you ever thought o' startin' a circulatin' noosepaper?

SAMUEL: Waal, I could jest conclude to do such a thing. One o' our cousins negurs could read 'n write, tho' durn it, *his* master couldn't write his own name.

JONATHAN: Is that a fact now? *(Clutches table and looks significantly at his companion's hat for receptacle at a pinch).*

SAMUEL: Waal, don't sound too bad an idea o' yourn. You fix up somethin', tho' cain't say I knows anyone too strong in th' readin' line, still...

JONATHAN: *(Making his exit, left, in haste.)* Fine, fine. *(Crash and curses. Sounds of conspirator being unwell.)*

SAMUEL: Waal, durn my mother.

TROJANUS

'Outrageous! *Outrageous!*' Gideon's voice rises to a squeak, not unlike a rat splashed by tobacco juice. 'How does he dare? Does he wish to start another war? No, not even during the mutual hostilities did either party stoop to the production of such low lampoons. It is vile, unjust, vulgar.'

'Steady. You will pretty soon exhaust your font of letters, and then where will you be?'

'Walter! Do you seriously tell me you will not resent this insult – alike offensive to us as individuals, as men, and as Americans?'

'Can one resent oneself?'

'Gracious Heavens! I would almost desire *satisfaction!*'

'Well, it would give me no satisfaction at all to lodge a ball in my own brain-pan, and that's a fact.'

Gideon decides he had better cool down. He's the Bostonian, after all. How strange that the volatile Walter should be setting him such an example of steadiness and restraint. 'You are right, I guess, Walter. Whipping his lungs with a yard of steel would

330

only serve doubly to prove his point, if he believes we are such a set of lawless savages. Bowie knives, indeed!'

'Yes, I was rather proud, I'll own, of that detail.'

'Proud? Oh, I see. You study to admire the rude virtues of Leather-stocking? You do surprise me.'

Eastman sighs. 'On occasion, Gid, though one may not call you a blockhead, bearing in mind your amazing accomplishments, you are still a very obtuse lad.'

Gideon tends to be puzzled, rather than offended, by most of Walter's strictures. 'Yes?'

Walter puts his hand upon his heart. 'You look, my dear sir, upon the author of the *Monitor's* little squib.'

'Well, I'll be ...'

'Precisely. And your expletive, I allow, very much in the vernacular of Jonathan.'

'I confess myself altogether baffled as to your motives. I know you consider yourself, with much justification, I own, superior to the general run of our countrymen in the breadth of your culture and intellectual understandings. Yet I am unable to see how you think it right to cock a public sneer at them and simultaneously to augment the scanty fare in our rival's pages. And, furthermore ...'

'My dear homespun fellow! I should not have dressed you in the conspirator's cloak.'

'Hey?'

'Hey, indeed. But your reaction, of all people, inclines me to entertain the highest hopes of my little mine. It will blow sky-high. Mark my words.'

From THE CANTON MONITOR
Thursday, June 21st, 1838

So how tender a skin may be concealed 'neath the shaggiest and horridest of furs! As the bear will run to mud to assuage the pangs of his tender snout after he has so injudiciously thrust it in the bole, so we recommend to our wounded Cousins an application of plasters formed from the pap of the

Bee and the muck it contains. What a chorus of mortification! How dismal and long the faces of woe and chagrin! We have received letters (too numerous and, not infrequently, too ill-expressed to print) from the American portion of our small community, rebuking us for our temerity in giving circulation to our correspondent's little squib at the expense of our Trans-Atlantic contemporaries. Those gentlemen accuse us of poking fun not only at our professional rivals but at their glorious young Republic. They find our sketch 'offensive', 'monstrous', 'a slander'. We would merely say by way of explanation, rather than extenuation (which is not at all required), that the article in question partakes of simple truth – which shall be its justification and privilege. We do not say that all American gentlemen of our acquaintance are the uncouth specimens portrayed by our warrior TROJANUS or to be found on the pages of Mrs Trollope or Miss Martineau, but it is not at all open to argument that the manners of the New World, outside the most select circles of the finest cities (where we grant there are but little, if any, differences in breeding and language between the leading American ladies and gentlemen and their counterparts of London) are rudimentary to the point of non-existence. There is no need to descant further on the disgusting and universally practised habit of spitting (that is, the excess saliva promoted by the mastication of tobacco-quids) which, if we are to believe an unprejudiced English lady (and we do, wholeheartedly), the very senators did not refrain from indulging on the carpet of state. The fireplaces of the river-steamers (those un-boatlike craft!), the floor on which they have to spread their bedding, the hems of ladies' skirts – nowhere is there sanctuary. As to the *Monitor's* poor faith, in one gentleman's words, we do not need the writings of the intrepid female traveller to inform us that the newspapers of America – the whole disgraceful band of them – so widely disseminated in the New World – enjoy the bad distinction of being the most scandalous, inaccurate, licentious, and indecent to be found anywhere in the world, where no libel is too malicious or outrageous to be perpetrated on innocent heads – for do we not have an example, eminent even among that ruffian company for its cool audacity, circulating its poison in our little community even now? In taking our leave of this unsavoury subject, we would recommend to our readers' attentions the reflections of a past statesman of the Disunited States and quondam printer (for is it not the land of the free (negurs apart) where the lowest beggar considers himself the equal of the finest gentleman – abominable freedom!). Franklin says, 'If by the liberty of the press, we understand merely the liberty of discussing the propriety of public measures and political opinions, let us have as much of it as you please; but if it means the liberty of affronting, calumniating, and defaming one another, I, for my part, own myself willing to part with my share of it, whenever my legislators shall be pleased to alter the law; and shall cheerfully consent to exchange my liberty of abusing others for the privilege of not being abused myself.' Spoken unlike an American, but well.

From THE LIN TIN BULLETIN AND RIVER BEE

Wednesday, June 20, 1838

Vol .1 No.13

NOTICE – For Manilla and Boston via Cape of Good Hope to sail positively on the 28th *prox*. the fine American-built vessel *Adventurer,* burden 650 tons, commander W. N. Billingsworth, lying at Whampoa. Has very capacious accommodations for freight or passengers, a regular poop, and carries a surgeon. Sails remarkable fast and can make against the monsoon. One large and two small cabins still disengaged. For freight or passage apply to Messrs Russell & Co, American Hong, Canton, or Macao.

MESSRS Marklake Goodison beg to advise the public that the finest cheeses, soda-waters, crackers, eau de vie, TOBACCO-QUIDS, hams, molasses, flour, sugar, coffee, and sundry other comestible requisites are available at the most advantageous tariff at their warehouses at Rua Infante Enrico, Macao. WE ALSO BAKE JOHNNY CAKES.

AN entire yacht's fittings – *viz.* sails, ropes, instruments, charts (including Horsburgh's Directory), gig, and one brass nine-pounder Long Tom for sale by auction, Saturday, 30th *inst.* at the Macao premises of John Hollingsworth, chandler. Prior sale, preferably in entirety, also possible by private treaty, respecting which apply to the above. WE ARE PROUD TO BE AMERICAN.

To the editor of the Lin Tin Bulletin and River Bee

STRICTLY NOT FOR INSERTION

Sir,

Have the goodness to print in your most handsome face – somewhat larger than the type in which your own journal is dressed – the following matter:

Mr and Mrs Alexander R. Shillingford at Home, New Niagara, The Ridge, Macao, from nine o'clock p.m. on the Fourth of July for Independence Celebrations.

Request pleasure of, RSVP, etc.

I rely on you to set out the card to its best advantage – in a quantity of exactly 106. Further oblige me by printing ladies' dance-cards, of which for your guidance I enclose a specimen. It need not be so large and I calculate that two score will suffice. Ditto a card of fare (on which matter the compradore of Russell & Co. will communicate with you shortly).

I need not inform you that the elegant and proper ordering of the invitations etc. and etiquette is a matter of the first importance and I request you give it your most earnest attention and the favour of the best style.

Have the kindness, my dear sir, to attend yourself with your colleague (I expect there is no need for you to provide invitations to yourselves from the order of 106), and have the goodness to submit your bill 'at reasonable rates' to your bumble, obligated servant,

Alexander R. Shillingford

Plangent, buoyant: the music drifts out over the lawns and shrubbery and the rising perfume of the flower-beds seems to be the fragrance of the wlnd-borne melody itself. The grass, black now, runs out from the mansion, seeming to disappear abruptly where it drops into a sharp slope which becomes three terraces connected by steps. The fall from the last, fenced, is sheer. Below twinkle the lamps and braziers of Macao. Dots glow in clumps around the lawn – cigar-ends. Their odour mixes with the aroma of the blooms of Shillingford's garden. As the last bars of a waltz die, laughter and conversation break out in the big room. Its huge French windows are flung wide to the verandah for coolness. Walter Eastman and Gideon Chase have helped themselves to champagne-cup from the long table which runs the length of the verandah. They are now installed in a hammock-seat which swings from the bough of a great banyan, just outside the halo of light from the grand reception-hall currently serving as a ball-room. Dancers and suppers are visible; Gideon and Walter are invisible, which suits them. At their feet sprawl an assortment of former colleagues from Meridian: Johnstone in a commandeered rocking-chair; young Oswald on the sward with arms cradling his knees, not unlike the young Raleigh of a later painting (how O'Rourke would have despised that!); Ridley perched on a branch of the banyan, which has ambitions towards becoming a root; others where they can find a place.

'Well, take out subscriptions, my lads,' says Walter, sending his butt spinning end over end into the blackness beyond the banyan. 'That would be the most solid help. What d'ye say, Cousin Jonathan?'

'Yes, sir, Sam,' Gideon intones solemnly. 'A mighty great help, and that's a fact.'

Ridley guffaws and imitates a man spitting. 'Ding!' goes Johnstone, the other half of the act, imitating the ring of the cuspidor. 'Waal, missed, darnation,' Ridley drawls exaggeratedly.

'No, a hit, a palpable hit,' says Johnstone, ding-ing again for all he's worth.

'Shall we not help you in a more elevated way?' Ridley enquires.

'And what can be more elevated than the almighty dollar?' asks Eastman.

'I have a notion I'll buy a paper the more readily if my own effusions appear in print among its columns.'

'But, my dear Jonathan, nothing could please the editor more, assuming your standard of composition was sufficiently high. We cannot continue writing the whole newspaper single-handed.'

'Apart,' Gideon interpolates slyly, 'from the unsolicited correspondence of our readers.'

There is no reaction from the others, but Gideon grins in the darkness.

'What d'ye have in mind, Jonathan?'

'Oh, nothing which should aspire to any profundity. A Joe Miller or two, as our cousins say. Something from the cracker-barrel, d'you know, old friend.'

Eastman says in a serious voice, and with a perfect magnanimity, blended with just enough caution, which fools all and sundry, apart from the assisting editor, 'I guess we could consider the products of our friends' pens with a somewhat more indulgent eye – but reserving always the right to alter and amend, in short, to edit. It is Gid's house and mine, after all, and the incompetent carpenter, sparing your feelings, Jonathan, does not have to live in its ruins.'

'Well, anyhow, this carpenter seeks no remuneration for his furniture. Use it or burn it, as you please.'

'Thank you, sir,' Eastman says with dignity. 'Cigar, Jon?' Walter offers Ridley his case and then sticks his own face forwards, so that his friend can light his cigar off his own orange tip, the chain-reaction taking place as Ridley sucks vigorously. As Jonathan hollows his cheeks, and in the glow of the bright ends, his shadowed face resembles a skull. One spark drops to the black grass.

'Your servant, sir.'

The Portuguese band having enjoyed the opportunity to refresh themselves with a little white wine mixed with soda-water, the sweat-doused wretches strike up another jig, as the wealthy parsimonist and vulgarian Shillingford insists on referring to the waltz.

'Hmm,' says Johnstone, 'I guess it behoves us to dance attendance on the fair, what d'ye say?'

'God damn it, no,' says Ridley. 'Each harridan, as it is, has her card double-booked, I'll calculate. Let the withered dance with the dry. No, think better on it – send the boy. He'll do – didn't you get on famously with your grandmother, while your father cut you off without a cent?'

Young Oswald shifts on his damp hams, and grins sheepishly. Gideon glances sympathetically at him.

'Will you play the part of the dancing-master, sir?'

But Walter is oddly quiet, Ridley's facetiousness striking no answering chord; he merely laughs uneasily. Of course, thinks Gideon, no wonder the poor fellow is in a lather, and I don't blame him.

'Well, I've had my belly full of skulking in the dark,' says Johnstone, 'and am going to show my face like an honest man, God damn it.'

A ragged chorus of agreement follows.

'You're outvoted, Jonathan. Come, or we'll press-gang you.'

Cursing cheerfully, Ridley is dragged to his feet. Cigar clenched in teeth, he faces Eastman, with an acolyte on each arm. 'Don't think you shall effect your escape, Eastman.'

'Ah, no, dear Jon, this is altogether too great a ... you must ... aaagh!' – and, no, this is not Walter calling out in an excess of despair but he and Gideon hitting the surprisingly unsoft lawn after Johnstone has deftly slipped the hammock-cords. In a trice they are pinioned, arms locked, and crossing the lawn. 'Knock 'em over the head if they offer resistance,' commands Johnstone. 'This is the way we do things in these parts.'

'In this company,' says Eastman wryly, just loud enough for

only Gideon to hear. As they pass the bounteous buffet-table (which Shillingford has not stinted, far from it), the young men grab at the dainties on display. Into Johnstone's mouth, with his free hand, go two jellied eggs, entire, while his other clamps Eastman's elbow. Ridley grabs a drumstick as he's marched by the collar, strips one side neatly, and belabours his captors with what's left. As for young Oswald, his urchin hands dart among the sugared almonds, cramming his pockets with every sweetmeat he can purloin. They pass their host, smiling away to himself, indulging the young fellows. He's a plain soul, blunt and brusque, 'that damn'd expectorating boor' as one irritated officer of John Company once referred to him (for he shares Corrigan's liking for a quid without being so sour a character). 'Boys, d'you have a fine time?' he enquires. 'Yes, sir,' is the chorus. 'Yes, sir,' he repeats, hooking his thumbs in his brocade waistcoat above the thick, yellow links of his watch-chain, belly out, the shiny pumps on his feet telling the time at ten minutes before two. As Eastman and Ridley are frog-marched into the ball-room, a French naval lieutenant raises his eyebrows slightly at a countryman and brother officer, who returns a significant, very Gallic pursing of the lips. Those manners! That spitting! – for Shillingford has worked up a good mouthful which he spurts out on to the dark lawn. However, the countrymen and successors of Lafayette have their obligations on this day, and, besides, the champagne flows, veritably it does, and the buffet was sumptuous for they had shrewdly helped themselves to what they could carry well before the Americans ravaged the trestle.

On the dance-floor, a waltz is concluding. The heat is formidable. The men sweat like race-horses. Red faces, purple veins, damp jackets (the shirts were ruined after the first dance), and pumps which will have to be peeled off the feet in strips – all attest the inappropriateness of attire as well as of this particular activity in these climes. Suitable for young cavalry officers disporting themselves by the Danube, the waltz is utterly ridiculous for gentlemen of advanced years who find themselves taking their amusement on the banks of the Pearl River. Harry O'Rourke wheezes, his bunions killing him, but his lascivious old eyes are fixed on the *snowy* (really, remarkably white) *bosom* of his young partner, which heaves perilously at its restraining corsage. 'Gracious, Mr O'Rourke,' she trills, 'I do declare myself quite wore out. Is it not oppressive?'

'Upon my soul, my dear,' says the ancient lecher, 'I believe I can see your points.'

Mrs M– looks puzzled, but Harry has already pulled out his little ivory box, gift of a nabob patron from his Calcutta days, and restores himself with a generous pinch. 'Snuff, my dear.'

'Really, Mr O'Rourke,' she giggles, 'what a terrible Tartar you are.'

'Well, it was in the saddle that the Tartars took their amusements...'

'Surely not *all* their amusements, Mr O'Rourke?'

'All of them, my dear,' he says firmly, 'and we shall find ourselves chairs.' Offering his arm, he limps for the side, though it is a moot point who assists whom.

Some older American ladies fan themselves in a little group at the side; they are old indeed who do not have to dance in this male–dominated community. 'Mr O'Rourke, you poor man, you have been excessively gallant and have overtaxed yourself,' says one, an elegant lady with a pretty pair of shoulders still, shown to advantage in a crimson taffeta gown. With the liberty of a hostess (Shillingford was proud to marry above himself) and the conferred distinction of her mature years, she can add with the smallest hint of the coquette she was, 'I shall fan you.'

'Ah, how delicious the grateful breeze. And, pray, perform the same ministration upon the other side, Mrs Hollis. Mmm,' and he rolls his eyes, to the great amusement and pretended consternation of the dowagers.

'Some ice–punch, my dear,' says Mrs Shillingford to Harry's partner, 'or some mint julep.'

'Pray, apply some of this to your temples,' says another kindly American lady. 'Dear me, some of our menfolk will be victims of heatstrokes, and no two ways about it.'

'A privilege to die for you ladies,' says the old misogynist naughtily.

Mrs Shillingford stares at him over the top of her fan, a stern rebuke, but there is an answering glint at the back of her eye.

Harry thinks he'd rather like to paint this old 'un, or would have done a quarter of a century ago. Now there are some very lovely and sensitive sketches in one of his folios, dated 1806, of a young woman slightly lifting a chemise to show perfect breasts. *Perfect.* Ah.

'Well, darn me, Harry, but you look like a hired jade, flogged to the next post and left foaming at the bit.'

'Thank you, gentlemen,' says Mrs Shillingford, with her usual quiet charm but iron in her accents, 'that will be quite enough. Do not forget there are ladies present.'

Johnstone knows when he has met his match. He makes a mock half-bow, but *does* remove the smouldering stump of his cheroot from his mouth as he does so. Accomplished sycophant and oiler that he is, as well as proto-entrepreneur of the moment and budding public figure in the community, Eastman makes his presence felt with a smile of powerful charm. As he still has his arm twisted behind his back in a demi-Lord Nelson, he does not cut quite the figure he imagines. 'Ladies,' he says ingratiatingly, 'to what do we owe this convocation of grace and beauty? In this forlorn ...'

'To my husband, Mr Shillingford's, patriotism and hospitality, I guess,' returns their hostess very coolly.

'Sensible of the obligation, ma'am,' says Ridley. 'Patriots all, I calculate.'

Eastman smiles fixedly. The evening has every indication of turning out not to be his. However, in a sickly way, he bares his discoloured teeth, trying to recover by saying: 'I trust, then, his public feeling and munificence should not go unrecorded.'

'I expect,' says Mrs Shillingford, quite civilly, 'that it is a matter of the most perfect indifference to him.'

Eastman bows stiffly. He takes a step backwards. Mrs Shillingford fans herself; she smiles serenely.

'Smoke your confounded cigars elsewhere,' Harry growls to Ridley. 'I was out of breath before you came and am asphyxiated now.'

'Yes, gentlemen,' says Mrs Shillingford, 'do feel free to extinguish your cigars, even on the plates of broken victuals.' But Harry snaps his fingers to Ah Cheong, one noteworthy feature of these Macao entertainments being that guests bring their own servants. Off he goes with the butts, doubtless to dismember, shred, and sell them. Looking very much like a puce old walrus, settled on a rock among females of the species, O'Rourke sits heavily on a sofa where two obliging ladies, unhappily for him no longer in the first flush of youth, make just enough space for his encroaching buttocks.

'What is your opinion of our musicians, Mr O'Rourke? Pray, answer freely, without any constraint.'

'My dear Mrs Shillingford, they cope splendidly.'

'Spoken like an ambassador,' says Eastman quietly, without moving his lips. 'No, a Jesuit,' whispers Gideon.

'Then, of course,' continues Harry, 'I was led, like a dancing bear, by the most captivating creature. My feet padded where she willed. The Portuguese have a natural musical sense, much like the Manilla-man, and are apt at picking up a melody. That is, they are adept performers – lacking the innate ability to compose, to create, which is the peculiar gift of the *Slav* or *Teuton*. But your Latin can be a most facile imitator. In painting, of course, it is another story.'

Gideon's eyes light up; he has no small talk at all. 'Ah, Mr O'Rourke...'

'Gentlemen, gentlemen.' Mrs Shillingford raps her fan closed on the sideboard, then spreads it against Harry's chest in elegant prohibition. 'Really, you are too bad. Should they not be amusing and diverting us, ladies? It is our feet they should be making whirl and not our heads, with all this talk of slaves and rhapsodies.'

An indignant chorus backs up the hostess.

'Never heard anything like it in all my born days,' says an aristocratic-looking Virginian lady. '*Slaves* and *Two-Tones* indeed. Men were men when I had my *beaux* and I *had* them. There was courting for you. We had none of this nonsense talked, and that's a fact.'

'Shame on you, gentlemen,' says another of the formidable matrons. Now here's Eastman's chance. The unctuous youth insinuates himself among the furniture and its occupants with a tray of marinated pineapples and sherbets, which he has seized from Ah Cheong. This retainer was not at all pleased, hanging on to the heavy silver tray at the peril of its freight, an ugly tussle of will and sinews developing between himself and Eastman, until finally Walter broke his grip and nerve. Cheong now gives Eastman's ministering back dark looks, muttering pithy and unusual curses to himself, such as would fascinate Gideon Chase. The reason? Cumshaws, tips. Eastman has done him out of his perquisites from his master's friends. *He* gets nothing from it, Ah Cheong reflects bleakly, so why rob me? He decides Walter is demeaning himself out of pure spite.

Eastman fawns. 'Will you partake of a little refreshment, madam?', 'Can I send you some fruit, Mrs Shillingford?', 'Allow me to give you sherbet, my dear madam.'

Of these manoeuvres Ah Cheong is not the only disgusted spectator. O'Rourke scowls; Ridley and Johnstone raise eyebrows. As for young Oswald, he wipes his nose on the back of his sleeve, then pops an almond into his mouth, crunch-crunch, eyes darting from side to side. Walter's actually on his knees now, shuffling to serve the last of the dowagers. He is quite shameless, thinks Gideon, but it has worked. The matrons coo. Delightful boy! Oh, amiable manners! How unusual for an American (they think secretly). And it is because Walter kneels, screened by standing friends, much like some human sacrifice ringed by totems, that Jasper Corrigan, Aunt Remington, and her niece are able to stumble, almost literally, across him without the slightest warning afforded either side.

Walter is as a man stricken. He freezes in his ridiculous posture, tray extended. On his knees, he has every appearance of the traditional suitor. His pale face turns paler. Corrigan, who is an emotionless man, does preserve the facial composure of a red Indian, only shifting his chaw from right cheek to left. Aunt Remington and Alice, implicated respectively to greater or lesser degrees in Walter's predicament, command less self-control. Aunt Remington's smile glazes over, dropping several degrees of social warmth. Alice's face falls. She turns red. No ordinary blush, this. One which inflames the face, then spreads down neck and creeps across the shoulders, and tinges the bared chest and bosom (which fashion says may be revealed to a daring extent) before, doubtless, expanding imperially into zones invisible. Eyes meet. Walter has a sense of physical emptiness; fortunate and strange, because it also feels as if a midget in his stomach, armed with a plunger, is attempting to blow its contents back up his gullet. His heart is going like one of the mechanical sing-songs Jack Hoppo loves for a bribe.

'My dear Mrs Remington,' says Mrs Shillingford sweetly, 'how agreeable to have your company. Mr Corrigan, I can read your face as well as Mr Shillingford's. You must endeavour to stop thinking about business already in hand — for tonight, at least.'

Corrigan's grim features contort into an awful smile. 'Calculate I can't rightly do that,' he says. 'Otherwise Shillingford'd steal the march on me. Ain't that so, Shillingford?'

'That,' says Shillingford, with heavy jocosity, 'old friend, is a fact.' He has come in from the terrace with the French naval officers. 'Allow me, my dear, to present to you lieutenants Menetrey and Bouttier of the frigate *Colbert.*'

'Enchanté,' say the dashing officers to Madame, drawing themselves up, making stiff bows, and clutching their beautiful dress-swords. The young Americans look contemptuously at them, scorn which is fully but silently reciprocated (one would have thought these were mortal foes rather than the traditional allies they are but then one republic has become a monarchy of sorts again).

'Soyez les bienvenus, Messieurs,' says Mrs Shillingford, not very well but to the mighty admiration of her friends, *'nous sommes tres honorées de vos presences, mais il faut* ...Alexander, I do crave you, instruct our gallant friends to dance. *Oui, messieurs, la dance.* Here is poor Mrs Remington without a partner and all the gentlemen in the world merely seated and idle.' The adept hostess fans herself complacently; Shillingford did well to marry her. She manages admirably (she thinks).

Lieutenant Bouttier gives Alice his debonair appraisal. He smiles brilliantly, offers a crooked elbow, and escorts her to the floor, where the perspiring Portuguese are about to strike up again. Harry O'Rourke, slightly less purple now, is fond of the boy Eastman and not at all fond, as he would put it, of the wiles of the sex. Walter remains on his knees, having forgotten to shut his mouth, while his former colleagues scowl at the remaining Lieutenant Menetrey, who smooths the edge of a thin moustache with one finger, the other fist gripping the pommel of his sword and dangling a white glove.

'Walter,' growls Harry, gruffness belying his essential kindliness, 'do you get off your knees unless you expect to rise Sir Walter from Queen Bess's sword, and employ yourself by leading Mrs ... Mrs M–... (he cannot for the life of him remember her name) 'who languishes for the want of a cavalier.'

Mrs M– laughs prettily, showing the little translucent, grey, rather than white, teeth, which are the most attractive part of her, after the milky bosom Harry peered down. 'Oh, dear me, Mr O'Rourke,' she flutters, 'you have chosen to *persecute* me for reasons of your own.'

'Fiddlesticks! Walter, I expect you to perform the duties of a gentleman, American though you are. Damme, Shillingford, will you shoot me for that remark?'

'It can be fixed, I calculate, but not before you have represented the likeness of my wife and myself.'

'Likenesses, eh? Well, off with you, you young scoundrel.'

On the floor, Walter smiles down at the top of his petite partner's head; she comes up to his chest. His strong sense of the absurd asserts itself. The smile broadens, encompassing the encounter with Aunt and Alice.

'What do you smile at, Mr Eastman? I expect it is me.'

'Not at all, Mrs Millicent, I do assure you. No, I laugh at myself and my own follies. They are plentiful enough, and no two ways.'

'I am sure you do yourself injustice.'

To the side Walter glimpses a flash of gold epaulettes and Alice's curls. Is it accident, or does Mrs Millicent bring him away by design? Despite himself his breath shortens. That darned Frenchman. But where's the sky-pilot? Too patriotic to attend? He's steered in the centre of the room again, as if it were the most natural thing in the world, not a hint of pressure or guidance. Mrs Millicent regards his shirt-front demurely.

'Are you an atheist, Mr Eastman?'

'What an extraordinary question!'

'Do I offend you?'

'No, no. Certainly not. You are… very kind. No, it is a strange place and moment to choose to interrogate me as to my religious opinions.'

'Or want of them. I had rather thought it went with being a newspaper editor, atheism and cigars. Were you in that business in Richmond?'

'In that city and in Philadelphia, I was a Believer and had yet to indulge in the noxious weed. Does that answer your question satisfactorily?'

'Indeed.'

Eastman starts to enjoy himself. They whirl around the room with the others. All too soon the music stops. Mrs Millicent says, 'I expect I should be restored to our friends and my seat.'

'You will not dance again?'

'Alas, my card is already full, and I mean to sit out this next waltz, if I am to be able to complete my engagements.'

'My loss, then, and another's gain.'

How ridiculous it is to feel a prick of jealousy.

Walter hands Mrs Millicent to her place, orders refreshment from … whom? He and Gideon had no servant to bring in attendance. Ah Cheong turns his back. Fortunately, Mrs Millicent's 'boy' appears. Walter waits until Mrs Millicent's next partner claims her, no less a personage than the head of Russell & Co. Then he joins the young gentlemen of Meridian on the terrace, passing Harry O'Rourke, who converses with the Portuguese Governor and his beautiful wife. 'A damned thoroughbred, God damn it,' mutters Shillingford in his ear. Later she will create a sensation of admiration when she takes the floor with His Excellency's aide-de-camp.

Pyrotechnics of another kind are anticipated in the garden. Shillingford has a fireworks display arranged for the stroke of midnight. A small crowd has already gathered on the terrace. The compradore has warned his master's guests not to step on the lawn. 'Mined,' states Johnstone. Too far beyond the lights of the house to be seen, dressed in dark blue and black the underlings of the Chinese Director of Ceremonies and Worshipful Master

Pyrotechnician pass to and fro, glimpsed occasionally as shadows on the grass. Their voices rise, twittering and braying, characteristic of the local dialect, some from the lower level of the mansion's grounds. 'Are we safe?' asks a Meridian voice in the darkness, half jocularly. 'Maybe they'll take their chance to blow us to the four corners.'

'I guess not,' says someone else – it sounds like MacLean, the admirer of Walter Scott – 'not by design anyhow, for to conclude towards such a purpose they would have to meet their Maker themselves.'

'Then,' replies the first speaker, 'it would afford no consolation to have been blown sky-high by mischance. I don't trust these Goddamned heathens' power to fix the simplest contrivances. Let us hope they are not half-pay Manchus of the garrison.'

'Have no fear.' And who else could this be? 'The Chinese are remarkably skilful at arranging these displays. Did they not invent gunpowder? Why, the Emperor was already jaundiced with such when the Hudson was the preserve of the painted savage.'

Eastman smiles to himself.

'Is that that damned newspaper writer?' enquires an uncouth voice in the darkness. 'Darned if he don't love John Chinaman better than his own kith and kin.'

Eastman can see Gideon's face tauten. He squeezes his arm. Poor Gid.

'Is it safe to smoke in the magazine, gentlemen?' Walter asks. 'I expect I don't care. Blow me to pieces if you will, but I must have my smoke.'

A whole row of orange tips appear as lucifers flare. Hammering drifts up from the inferior levels of the grounds. In the ball-room the music stops again. Those at the front of the terraces are pushed on to the lawn as pressure of numbers from the dancers mounts at the back. 'Whoa!' shouts Ridley. 'We are atop the powder-barrel!'

Shillingford pushes his way through his guests. 'Beg pardon, ma'am. Jump, young fellow!' Out comes his time-piece, the size of a small orange and considerably heavier. He stands on the lawn and faces the assembly. 'Ladies and gentlemen, we must presume a little longer on your patience. It wants two minutes to midnight.' He continues to regard his watch, without looking up. Gradually the chattering dies out; now a total silence prevails. Giggling is the natural consequence. 'Hush!' – 'Shoosh!' – More laughter – silence. Shillingford has not ceased to consult his watch. Why doesn't he just turn round and wait, like all the others? What crazed pedantry is this? As the hands meet, he slowly turns to face the same direction as everybody else and, on cue, with magical precision and punctuality the first of sixty-two rockets (one for each year since *1776*) soars from the lower flower gardens to burst in a shower of red and blue balls, each one of which in turn detonates to become its opposite, blue red, and red blue. Even before the first rocket has reached its apogee and exploded, more are on their way. ('One and sixty, sixty, nine and fifty, eight and fifty...' intones Shillingford under his breath as his guests 'Ooh!' and 'Ah!') In ever renewing profusion the fireworks burst and scatter their glowing seed. Deeper detonations follow from higher up the grounds as mortars, sunk in the soil, throw up huge charges always higher. The ensuing bangs are prodigious, simply prodigious. The windows rattle.

'God preserve us,' exclaims Johnstone, 'I hope those fuses are properly timed!'

Shillingford grins in the dark.

Next moment a mortar belches, and the guests begin to count: 'One, two, three, four, five ...' and, oh, dismay! The charge fails to explode! An eerie whistling fills the air. Panic sets in. Mrs Shillingford looks questioningly, but calmly, at her phlegmatic spouse. And...*puff!* Twenty feet above their heads, there is a gentle disintegration, and a corona of tiny, multicoloured sparks. Hardly have the exclamations of amusement and wonder died away when a fizz and clattering in the centre of the lawn alert their attention to non-celestial happenings. There seem to be fireworks tied to a frame, almost certainly bamboo. Synchronisation here is less perfect than was the case with the aerial devices; nevertheless, though the pattern does not unfold quite as designed, some of the horizontal flares igniting in the wrong order, eventually there is universally discerned...the Stars and Stripes! True, the stars splutter rather than twinkle, have a habit of going out and then catching again – 'There goes Maine, God damn it!' shouts Shillingford – which makes it difficult to ascertain the state of the Union at any single moment, but the guests appreciate the conception. Applause breaks out.

'Handsomely contrived, friend Shillingford,' says King, a Philadelphian merchant, who is drinking fruit-cup and is a well-known abstainer from the opium trade. Shillingford rolls his chaw to the other cheek, spreads his legs sturdily, and spits on to the lawn. He acknowledges the approbation of his guests with becoming soberness. The last fireworks splutter out, the paper of one on fire, but finally this, too, dies out and the night is dark again. Under the acridness of the gunpowder can still be sensed the fragrance of the flowers; on humming ears falls the melody of the musicians in the ball-room.

'Dance!' cries Mrs Shillingford. 'No waltz, but good American square-dancing. Ladies, with me,' and so saying she leads her laughing, delighted guests indoors again. But then the music stops abruptly. Feet shuffle amid a general clearing of throats. Indistinctly through the now closed windows comes a raised voice. It rises and falls, drones on, halts for effect, pauses, is interrupted by applause and cheers, continues the peroration. Walter Eastman has remained on the terrace. Alone, as he thinks, he stares sombrely into the night. The reaction sets in. Even a good cigar would fail to comfort him. For the moment, tobacco is repugnant. Why does the whiff of black powder have this effect? Trappers and soldiers become inured. He feels another elbow by his. Gideon's, and it is a sympathetic pressure.

'This will not endure, Gid.'

'I do not understand.'

Indistinct forms in the garden move quickly and efficiently. There is the sound of splintering and a rattle as poles are thrown together.

'It cannot, must not.'

Gideon holds his peace. After a while, he says, 'Would you care to join our friends? I will gladly accompany you…'

'No. But do you go, Gid. I shall repair to our office. Work attends.'

'None, of which I am cognisant.'

'Off with you. I may look after myself.'

'That I shall not. We will go together.'

'I trust you will allow that I am not about to lodge a ball in my head or leap over the cliff.'

'I should enjoy the walk with you. That is all.'

'Then…fine.'

Walter springs over the stone railing, Gideon taking a few paces to go down the flight of steps. He joins Walter on the grass.

'There's a goat-trail across the side of the hill. We'll follow that.'

'But…'

'Follow.'

Walter leads the way down the terraced lawns. At the end is a tall fence. 'Now these were the bane of my boyhood, but if I rightly recall…ah, yes, here we find you.' Walter kicks a plank with the toe of his boot and leaps smartly back as it swings down where his head was. 'And its partner. Aha. Capital. Can you squeeze through after your recent indulgences? Brawny boy that you are. Fine, fine. And I merely step through in all my slenderness. Has it struck you, Gid, that Portuguese and Chinese urchins are pretty well the same specimen as that mighty pest, the boy of America?'

'You are not beyond reclamation, then.'

'What?'

They strike now across the rough grass of the hillside, with a sheer drop on the left. Fortunately, the moon has started to pop out every now and then from behind the thick veil of clouds which has obscured it for most of the evening. Hundreds of feet below extends the glorious curve of the bay of Macao, matching the crescent moon. A few lights glitter in the houses and on the Praia, but nothing on the face of the bay itself, where Whampoa anchorage on the river would sparkle with ship's lanterns. This is easily explainable: the sediment deposited by the Pearl River over the course of millennia has lifted the bay's bottom and rendered it too shallow for all but the smallest of fishing-smacks. Ocean-going ships, foreign ships, must anchor in Macao Roads, two miles north-east and the fishing-craft are all out, miles to sea, fishing by lamplight. Cloud shadows skim across those placid waters, yellow by day, but inky now.

'Oh, how it is beautiful.'

A dog barks in the distance, but too far away to have been aroused by them and, in any case, the wind is wrong. Gideon stumbles in his thin dancing-pumps, the smooth soles sliding all ways on the grass. In boots, his headstrong companion strides ahead. Stunted trees, typical of the south China hillside, cast peculiar shadows, but now they are on grit – Gideon can tell through his thin soles – and then on a familiar road, passing houses and their sleeping families. A few heaps of rags, which are the beggars, lie motionless by the roadside; even in summer, some will fail to move, come the new dawn, which is only a few hours away.

'Will you truly proceed to our office?'

'I guess I shall. Not to edit or compose, I'll assure you, and certainly not to tamper with Pursuer's lucubrations, but the press requires the tribute of oil and there's a loose screw on the platen. Don't concern yourself, but have your restoring sleep.'

'Very well, if you are indeed at peace with the world.'

'I? 'Tis the world which is at war with itself. I do not come into it.'

From THE LIN TIN BULLETIN AND RIVER BEE

Wednesday, July 4, 1838

Vol.1 No.14

☛ Terms of the *Lin Tin Bulletin and River Bee*. Subscriptions $13 per annum. Single copies to be had of the editorial offices at Rua da Nossa Senhora da Nazare 12, Macau, at 50 cents. The Bee may only accept advertisements on the basis of prior settlement. Printing in general is executed with elegance and accuracy, rates on application.

CHAPTER XXIV

Little of the world outside may impinge on the sphere of the press which purports to reproduce it. It is an environment of its own. In a small room, the large globe diminished to the space defined by four walls, even the bang and clatter of a hand-press enthusiastically but amateurishly worked, may drown the audible accidents of life, 'real' life as experienced and apprehended by the physical senses. When an annoying squeak despite fierce efforts has yet to be located and the operative insists on providing gusto-laden arias from the *Barber of Seville,* matters are only compounded. Therefore, it is not the boom but the concussion which is initial, not the ears but the feet which apprehend. Again, the foundations shudder; very slightly; the walls appear to vibrate.

'I should not work the machine so vigorously, were I you.'

'What?'

'Not so hard.'

'Hey?'

Gideon gestures vigorously with his forefinger: 'Easy, sir.'

'God damn it. The building shook then.'

Walter takes his hand off the press; cocks his fair head to one side: shouting in the street, the slap of bare feet on ancient cobbles, excited dogs, and then a horseman clatters by. 'Do we face the threat of a fire? Or an earthquake even?'

Then, boom, from the hill over their heads, and the windows clatter. The battery is firing. A goodly while later, the gunners discharge another piece.

'Well, I allow we are not being invaded. Even Portuguese artillerymen would serve their guns with greater urgency.' Wiping his hands on a rag, and still clad in the leather apron he does not disdain to wear, Eastman goes to the door. Assorted crones hobble past; every self-respecting street arab in Macao is already halfway to the Monte fort.

'I expect we should join them.'

'I see no reason,' answers Gideon stoically. He is writing at a small desk, scowling, his unconscious habit when composing, but which is not always necessarily a reflection of his mood.

'No reason, you booby? This is a newspaper which is our livelihood. What is news is our proper concern and we collate intelligences for it. Put your hat on, sir.'

Through the door they go, the budding pedant somewhat unwillingly, but it is he who reminds Walter, 'You forget to lock the premises.'

'I hardly fear we shall find the press removed in our absence, but thank you none the less.'

They join the crowds swarming up the Monte steps. The Portuguese guard have been turned out before the gate, with their bayonets fixed, but the crowd can mill in the open space in front. Gideon arrives some flights quicker than Walter. Portuguese boys in the boughs of a banyan chatter excitedly and point to sea. Being both a foreigner and a strapping lad, Gideon can see over the Chinese heads. From behind and above carries the flat report of one of the fort's cannon. Gideon feels the change in pressure in his ears. Gulls scatter, squawking their consternation. While his ears are still humming, from seaward comes an answering, distant boom, like a growl of summer thunder. An interval – and another. Is it a trick of distance, or are the ship's guns heavier than the forts? Walter would know.

'What did I tell you? We have barely time to set up the type and insert it in our next.'

'These salutes?'

'No, dolt.' Walter cuffs the side of Gideon's head playfully; only now does he take off his hot and constricting apron. 'The arrival of the British ships.'

'How do you know they are British?'

'My dear Gid, you do live in a world of your own. While you are gleaning the latest gossip from the bazaar, you omit to listen to the rumours everyone else hears.'

'I shall have to remedy this by subscribing to the *Lin Tin Bulletin and River Bee*.'

'Indeed you will.'

As he is even taller than Gideon, Eastman can see with ease

over the mob. Now he spies a gap in the crowd's ranks and in that clearing. ... a familiar straw hat. The two friends shoulder their way through the press, mostly Chinese, with a handful of Portuguese civilians.

On his little fold-up stool before an easel, just removing the battered hat and wiping his head with a red handkerchief, is Harry O'Rourke. 'A damned travail and obstruction,' he is muttering to himself. Out comes the hip-flask.

'Why are you always talking to yourself, you old madman?'

'In a world of his own, too, I guess.'

'Do you have nothing better to occupy you than to congregate idly with the vulgar and noisome populace?' Harry asks rudely. 'My only desires are a view and some solitude. Is this too much to ask?'

'And some spirituous liquor,' says Eastman with a good deal of presumption. O'Rourke swipes at him with a sticky brush, but Eastman stops it with his folded apron. 'Upon my word, a sketch in oils,' he remarks with genuine surprise, 'well, you can paint in some white sails, I expect, and it'll be a Serres.'

This is really too much for O'Rourke to support. 'Damn Serres,' he bellows 'and to the devil with you! Take yourselves away. Remove your person, sir.'

Eastman leaves unrepentantly. 'Did you see anything, Gid? Your eyes are a long way sharper than mine.'

'Not even a glimmer of canvas. The vessels stood too far out – they must, or ground.'

'Well, to work. Harry's right as to one matter – we have little time to lose.'

From THE LIN TIN BULLETIN AND RIVER BEE

Wednesday, July 18, 1838

Vol.1 No.15

An elegant and convivial celebration. The American portion of our little community 'saw in' the greatest day of their national calendar in a fittingly splendid style and circumstances today a fortnight previous. As our issue of that very date proceeded to the press some days earlier, not possessing mastery of Old Father Time and his scythe, we were unavoidably prevented from commenting on those happy rites. Glad day! – not only for our patriotic countrymen, but for our organ as well, which, by happy chance, celebrated its half year's anniversary upon that day of redoubled jubilation. Lucky thirteen! We ourselves, in our joint capacity as editor and as American, were favoured with an invitation to those festivities at the Macao residence of Mr S–. This gentleman, we are well aware, neither expected nor desired the smallest recognition of his munificence and public-spiritedness, rather the reverse, for we believe we court his displeasure in even alluding to him personally in connection with his hospitality, yet would we be failing in our duties both as guest and the conductor of the *Lin Tin Bulletin and River Bee* were we to omit to notice his disinterestedness and munificence as our host upon that most agreeable evening. May he tax us with our indiscretion, if so the pleasure moves him. The punch and julep flowed freely, as did the finest wines and brandies of France – old friend of the young Republic, representative of whom we were pleased to welcome to the company two gallant ambassadors from the *Colbert*, which left against the monsoon for Batavia some days previous. Dancing in the European style, conversation the most sparkling and agreeable, and the pleasant and unaffected manners which mark the intercourse of old friends were the ingredients of a most happy evening. The night (rather, morning!) was concluded with a wonderful spectacle of fireworks, most ingeniously contrived, and an address by Mr K– of Philadelphia, which a kind friend has forwarded for insertion below.

Speech of Mr K–

Mr K– tendered on behalf of his fellow guests and countrymen the best thanks of the company to their host. It was a remarkably convivial evening. *(Hear! Hear!)* A fine evening. Wherever Americans gathered together on this day they had a right to be gay, yet was there a serious aspect to their assembly for they celebrated their delivery from despotism. This had not been an iniquitous so much as a galling tyranny, but then the gnat's bite was more irritating than that of the dog, which was not repeated *ad infinitum*. The institutions which his countrymen and his forefathers had created represented the furthest point to which freedom and democracy had progressed. Nay, could advance. No man was unfairly taxed. There were no red-coated soldiers to flog and brand the lovers of liberty; no corrupt borough-mongers to prevent the free expression of the people's will; no discrimination by fat prelates. In this regard an unfettered press was one of the surest guardians of the people's rights. He accepted that there were excesses perpetrated, but these were the product of a partisan enthusiasm rather than a merely mischievous desire to slander. Such was the price of Liberty, and a very cheap one, he believed. He did not scruple to draw to his countrymen's attention in this connection, and he misdoubted if they were not already cognisant of it, the existence near at hand of such an instrument of Free Speech – a most patriotic defender of the good name of his countrymen. He warmly recommended its patronage and support to his fellow Americans as an object deserving of the most immediate consideration and a very worthy demonstration of their liberality (Yankees or no – *laughter*). He concluded with a wish to the effect that the present difficulties in the China trade might be soon and peacefully resolved and without recourse to bangs and fusees, louder, uglier, and more injurious than the handsome spectacle they had just witnessed, but that it would not be *their* government which would be first to shed innocent blood.

The festivities concluded with a hearty breakfast at which beefsteaks and onions consorted democratically with champagne wine.

Arrival of Admiral Maitland. Passed through Macao Roads, Thursday previous, and cast anchor in Urmston harbour, or Tongku, the *Wellesley* (74) flagship of Sir Thomas Maitland,

and her tender, the *Algerine* brig (10). Solicitous of their health and comfort, Sir Thomas wasted no time but had his family landed at Macao directly. May he be so jealous of the health of the natives!

Speculation will inevitably attend the Admiral's visit. The appearance, even in the Outer Waters, of a ship of the line, must perturb the Canton authorities. A frigate, no, a 10-gun man o' war brig such as the *Algerine,* would be sufficient to send to the bottom any squadron of his Celestial Majesty's, so the feelings of the mandarins may well be imagined as they stare down the yawning mouths of the third-rate's four and seventy cannon. Fearful sight though the *Wellesley's* cliff-like sides may be (and we ourselves descried her majestic, billowing sails from the Monte), we do not believe that an assault on Canton and her superb governors is imminent. An adequate armament would needs comprise more than such a floating battery but would necessitate also the provision of transports, store-ships, and as auxiliaries whose attachment might secure the successful outcome of the expedition, armed steamers of shallow-draught which could attempt the navigation of the river's ultimate twelve miles from Whampoa to the Factories. We believe this visit to be a display of force designed to preclude its exercise. Whether it serves to aggravate the standing of matters rather than has the effect of cowing the Chinese remains to be seen. Certainly it is difficult to imagine that matters could be at a sorrier pass. With the addition of every day, incidents and armed encounters multiply, not infrequently culminating in an exchange of fire. We are sorry to say vessels flying the American flag as well as the Union Jack have acted the part of protagonist in these fights. To be sure, there is some element of provocation in the conduct of the mandarin junks. There is little to distinguish these cruisers in the way of external insignia from the piratical craft which infest these regions (other than that the pirate-junks are more heavily armed and better handled) and, indeed, we know a colleague who asserts, with some justification, one may own, that he has discerned on the decks of the government's revenue-cutters faces previously glimpsed at the side of more disreputable craft. Whether he bear opium and contraband or a licit freight, no captain still in command of his common sense as well as his ship would permit the venal and disreputable agents of the Chinese Government to step on to his vessel. That the morality of the issue is far from clear, we must freely own. Still, to the overbearing and brutal behaviour of the British Free Traders, as opposed to the mildness of the defunct Company, must be ascribed much of the blame.

A gentleman has forwarded the following communication from Canton. While sensible of his disinterested zeal and kindness in despatching the latest occurrences to us, we feel obliged to remark that the sentiments expressed therein are peculiarly his own and are not to be construed as in any way reflecting the personal opinions of the editor or his assistant, still less the considered policy of the Lin Tin Bulletin and River Bee. *– ed.*

FROM A GENTLEMAN RESIDENT IN CANTON

The recent spate of persecutions continues apace. That the councils of government have swung decidedly behind such a course, which is not a mere aberration or the temporary agitation caused by the arrival of a new and unusually zealous officer, may be discerned from its simple duration rather than the vigour of its promulgation. Arrests of the eaters of opium and their suppliers occur daily and are so commonplace as to fail to excite comment any longer. Torture, branding, and even the executions of apprehended smugglers are rumoured to be occurring in the prison and on the execution-ground of Canton. As the legitimate trade in tea is so inextricably bound up with the clandestine traffic in drug, it may be anticipated that any dislocations felt now in the import of opium will be reflected some months hence in constrictions and insolvencies in the tea-trade, especially as regards the exports of our British cousins.

But a day or two previous, R– and myself, happily bearing stout sticks at the time, observed the aged retainer of our

357

house of agency, who from time immemorial has served us in our mess and buttery, being roughly handled and borne off by a set of rascals. Closer scrutiny revealed these to be lictors and runners of a mandarin's suite, rather than the honest cut-purses we had supposed them to be. Dashing in, we did not neglect to deal the rogues some smart knocks, sending a pair to the ground directly. However, we were greatly outnumbered and, as my proficiency with the sabre or quarter-staff is small, soon a rap on the knuckles (as fortune would have it, with the flat of a sword) sent my clumsy weapon rattling to the cobbles. Matters might have come to a very sad pass – 'We are,' thought I to myself, 'in a deuced unhandsome fix.' But I, and they, had reckoned without the skill and valour of my redoubtable companion who, dealing blows with a miraculous swiftness, dexterity, and accuracy, soon disarmed two and cracking another's crown rendered him senseless before they took to their heels, and gave up our poor, shaking, and grateful retainer to us again.

I cannot regard the Government and its servants who would seize and torment an inoffensive and insignificant old man in any light other than as cowardly, bloodthirsty, and underhand villains.

JOHN STONE

A reflection. How we may wonder at our earlier self. It is as if we regard the actions of some blundering stranger. The heart grows cold and hard, where once it was tender and warm. What was admired is no longer even despised, which was the first stage in the combustion of our inflamed feelings, but becomes an object of the most perfect indifference. Time heals all; it also anneals all. Thus do we try to fix together the shards of our broken lives.

We are pleased to advise our readers that the *Lin Tin Bulletin*

and River Bee has secured to itself premises in Canton at No.16 Chow Chow Hong, where correspondence may be addressed, personal applications made, subscriptions taken out, and single copies purchased. Our office in Macau continues to be open on the same arrangement as previously obtained.

From THE CANTON MONITOR

Thursday, August 16th, 1838

An outrage upon the River. All those Britons with the smallest spark of pride in the National Dignity will have experienced the most lively feelings of indignation on hearing of the latest and unprecedentedly bare-faced insult to the flag. This occurred when a small vessel, the *Bombay,* flying British colours, was forcibly boarded inside the river on the wholly mistaken presumption that she smuggled opium. No resistance was offered – had she proved a true smuggler, her decks full of men and bearing treble the weight of metal in her broadside of any Chinese revenue-cruiser, it would have gone hard for those who tried to board her and, owing solely to this circumstance, there were no lives lost. It is difficult to credit that the Chinese can have been unaware of the true standing of the vessel. Rumour has it that the Chinese, misled by spies, believed either Captain Elliot or Admiral Maitland to be secretly on the *Bombay.* In this case the Chinese may well find the good Admiral returning, as a courtesy, their call, though he should take passage on the *Wellesley* rather than the *Bombay.* Aptly named flagship, and as iron as the Duke! We believe her visiting cards are spherical. She sailed for Chuenpi on the 4th *inst.* where, we have it on best authority, her appearance had a most instant effect on the manners of the mandarins, whose apologies were direct and abject.

Captain Elliot was unable to prevail on the Governor of Canton to receive his credentials as an equal and without the intercession of the Hong merchants a fortnight previous when he was rudely rebuffed at the Gate of Canton. Perhaps he will now succeed. At any event, the flag flies again at the Factories.

The *Bee* drones on. In his most recent he brags of the new meadows he has found to buzz in. We are expected to believe he has a circulation of over 1000 and prints 1200 copies of every issue. We would merely remark that this statement as to his own business is as deserving of credence as the lies (a thousand pardons, *lines)* the insect devotes to the affairs of others. In the event, his compositor – that is, we are given to understand, his own fingers, which are the truthful portion of him – betrays his employer: 'We would draw to our Reader's *(sic!)* attention that we now profess *(sic!)* a circulation of over one thousand copies with every number.'

Oh, happy and unique Reader. Oh! Infinitely gullible *one!* What happened, ponder we, to the surplus 999?

Gideon Chase to Walter Eastman

No. 16 Chow Chow Hong
Canton
August 8th, 1838

My dear Walter,

Quarters are cramped but perfectly adequate in respect of the task of housing a respectable quantity of newspapers and your obedient. Shillingford's liquor cellar behind in No. 17 and his marine magazine to the fore in No. 15. Therefore, cigar-smokers may enter at their peril.

Since the cigar-smoker's assistant was last here, the whole face of matters has been altered, radically for the worse. The rude and insolent soldiery much in evidence; that is not the ragged provincial levy of Canton, the Green Standard, but reinforcement to the Manchu garrison in the New City (the Northern suburb, that is, of Canton). Their brutal manner, indeed the way they fondle their weapons as they follow the foreigner with their eyes, is indicative of their true desires to separate his head from his body. The Factories servants cowed and fearful, the lowest ruffians of the gambling-dens and brothels more than usually insolent, and even the urchins presuming to put stones in the mud-pies they were wont to hurl. Only the Tanka or boat-people continue to smile on us, and it is moot which their Government despises more – us or them. On reflection, they are the greater pariahs, poor, laughing water-people.

As I came up the river in the *Sonia,* Remedios dropped anchor at the Bogue to wait for the tide. At my reiterated request, he put me over the side into the tiny tender we tow and I made short-work of pulling over to the *Wellesley.* As well as the *Algerine,* the *Louisa* cutter danced attendance on the flagship. The gun-ports of the 74 were open and the muzzles directed at the Chuenpi forts. Much as one tends to deprecate such truculent courses (at least I should), it seemed to have been productive of the effect desired. The mandarins appeared markedly conciliatory, and the Chinese soldiers deferred to my passage. I rowed thrice around the *Wellesley* – her massive cables are as thick as my body – before an 'ahoy!' advised me that my presence had been remarked. I think the opium-hulks maintain watches more vigilant! Taking this as an invitation rather than an intimation that I should be about my business, I tied up and was on their deck in no time. I expect this resembled a plain of snow rather than any plank of a craft I ever saw. My reception was hardly hospitable, the sergeant of marines' face set like flint and his cheek as red as his tunic. However, as he could hardly knock me over the head and fling me overboard or press-gang me, he was in somewhat of a quandary. It would go hard with you, ye masticators of tobacco! Who soiled those decks might taste the cat on his back, citizen of the New Republic or no!

In this instant there presented itself from a nearby companionway a most strange and extraordinary object. I say this, though as to the article in question there is nothing intrinsically eccentric, nor perhaps would it have struck any other of our countrymen as so passing strange in these circumstances as it did your servant. Round, black, not unlike a blood-pudding, save for the crimson spot at its centre, this rose as if by its own agency from the bowels of the ship. Presently, it appeared at the level of the deck, then beneath it a face – quite a remarkable countenance by any standards, of which more later, but not a foreign face. It was the face of a Chinese. In a twinkling, characteristic of the rapid and energetic manner in which his headgear had been rising, he had swung himself on to the deck and revealed himself as a powerful, manly and well-knit fellow, with shoulders broad under his unpadded gown as any of those of the sturdy British naval officers with all their golden epaulettes included. His feet were clad in soft cloth boots, the soles as white and unsoiled as the holystoned decks of the man of war. Although his every agile and sprightly movement belonged to that of a man many years his junior, the grey hairs which showed below his cap, the wisdom and nobility of his expression, and the lines which experience had carved into his frank and unflinching features, proclaimed him somewhere beyond his fiftieth year. The seamen paused about their duties, whether on the decks or in the rigging, while, according to their several stations, the bosun, carpenter, gun-captains, master, and officers of the watch touched their forelocks, or doffed hats and put a leg forward. There was nothing of mockery in this, as I am ashamed to say I have witnessed (as you) on similar occasions, nor was the courtesy begrudged or merely commanded, but altogether the tribute of natural respect to the man's air of in-born authority. He smiled, without the smallest appearance of ingratiating himself, and proceeded to adjust the cap, which was the only article of a plain dress (other than its cleanliness and neatness) which proclaimed him to the knowledgeable eye as a military commander of the empire of the highest conceivable rank. Shortly, there followed him on deck a little, spry fellow, I should have said, but for his gorgeous uniform and the circumstance that he, too, in despite of his lack of inches, bore himself with the unmistak-able carriage of one accustomed to command as well as their bodies the deference of his inferiors and the respect of his peers. A whole procession of cocked hats and gilt rose up the stairs subsequent to this, followed by the caps of the lesser Chinese officers, distinguishable by the colour of their button, until Admiral Kwan and Sir Thomas, for it was they, were surrounded by their respective suites. To my inexpressible alarm, they began to walk in my direction, the two Admirals together at the front and their staffs behind. 'Damme,' I distinctly heard Admiral Maitland say to a post-captain by his elbow, 'a bottle and a half, and he walks as sober as a judge.' It was impossible, quite impossible, and this I later verified as you shall see, that Admiral Kwan should have understood the words of Maitland. Yet, I swear, a great grin suffused his face and he swung his shoulders a pace or two as he walked. By this time they were so close I might have touched them. Now, to my horror, the English Admiral bore straight up and proceeded to address me thus: 'You are late, sir, and I cannot abide unpunctuality. I will not tolerate it. Ashore or afloat, I abhor it.' Now was this not the stuff of nightmares? As if in a dream, I opened my mouth, but from slack jaws no words would issue.

'Come, sir. You must explain yourself.'

My frightened eyes darted from face to face, from severe post-captain to grinning midshipman. 'I...I...sir, I am not who you think I am,' stammered I, and at this a great guffaw went up. 'Do I think you are the Bey of Algiers, sir, or Buonaparte? Tell me that, sir, as you are a mind-reader.'

At this point in our interview when, I think, I should have been happy to have been fired from one of the *Wellesley's* 32-pounders, Kwan – as if veritably reading minds – remarked in an unutterably kindly fashion, *'The tides around the Tiger's Mouth* (meaning of course the Bocca) *are unpredictable and not to be harnessed to man's convenience.'*

Said I: *'This is so indeed, although I am not a river-pilot nor an interpreter.'*

Now how was this? I was readier in an acquired tongue than my own.

'If you are not our translator, sir, then who the devil are

you?' Now the terrible little Admiral had fixed me again with his awful eye.

'Sir,' quoth I, 'I have come aboard your ship uninvited, but it is true I have a command of the Chinese language.'

'Then, sir, I command you to interpret.'

'I guess I shall do so with pleasure, Admiral Maitland. I have come from Macao, where I understand Mr Morrison is indisposed – if it is he whom you expected.'

'He's a Yankee,' I heard one middy whisper. The Admiral waved me on, without a word, and I followed on their high excellencies' heels. Now Kwan turned to me and said, *'This is truly a mighty ship, but she could not float in less than the height of five men. Has the distinguished Admiral ever grounded her in a river?'*

I translated. This was the essence of Maitland's reply – 'I do not personally sail her. That is the task of her captain and, more particularly, her sailing-master. If she grounds we may shift her by dint of moving the cannon from one side to the other.'

'And by waiting for the tide. This would be a difficulty in time of war. Can such a ship turn in the narrows between islands?'

'I own she cannot, unless the wind is on the right quarter.'

'Are all the sailors furnished with swords and trained in their use, or do they merely handle the ropes and rigging?'

'Each sailor has a cutlass and pistol and is proficient in their use. They are practised in boarding and repelling incursions. Additionally, the marines are trained as sharp-shooters with their muskets. Would Admiral Kwan care to see a demonstration of swordplay and musketry?'

'Thank you. That would not be necessary.'

Now Kwan caught sight of a midshipman, a young lad. *'At what age do you send boys to sea?'*

'At the earliest, eleven or twelve. The powder-monkeys might be younger.'

'Is it punishment for delinquent youths?'

'This lad to whom you refer is … *fourteen, sir*… and his father is a dear friend of mine.'

'Might I see his dirk? Sharp enough to kill a man.'

'Yes.'

We were now nearing another companionway. 'Tell the Admiral we are taking him down to the gun-deck.'

This was dark, the roof low. Ropes secured the monster cannon.

'These can shoot more than one mile, so accurate are they, and so skilled the gunners, that they may cut a man in half with a round shot at six hundred yards – have done it.'

'*These are well-made guns.*'

'Bring up a shell.'

Kwan peered through the hinged gun-port. 'So this is what the forts look like. But the slots are in wood. Like any boat they would splinter. Those are terrible wounds.'

'What does he say? Yes, those are the worst. The Admiral has seen some warm service then?'

'*At Rabbit Hole Bay I took five ships in against fifteen pirates. I got in between the chief junk and his consort and we battered each other for six hours. Many died. After this, I withdrew, unable to capture him. Later, he sank in a storm.*'

'A brave man, upon my word, and a truthful one. No, don't translate.' At this point the midshipman returned with a small wooden box, which he bore with some difficulty. He placed it upon the deck with great care. Sir Thomas bent to open it himself when from it he removed a metal ball, the size of a pomelo, similar to a shot in all respects, save for the small metal pipe or chimney projecting from it.

'The Admiral may not be aware, but some of our guns may throw eight-inch shell, that is…' But as the translator already knew what a shell was, though never having laid his eyes on one in actuality until that moment, he took the liberty of interrupting the Admiral. 'Thank you, Sir Thomas. *This sphere is not an ordinary cannon-ball but is hollow. The cavity is packed with compressed powder which explodes with an extraordinary degree of force.*'

'*How can you prevail upon it to go off?*'

'*A fuse is introduced into the pipe and lit.*'

'*This could reach the gunpowder prematurely or become extinguished. It would also be perilous in the extreme to load.*'

'What does he say?'

'He is curious and sceptical as to the efficacy of the fuse and the wisdom of introducing it, burning, into the barrel.'

'My dear sir, it is not. The explosion of the charge which propels the shell is the means by which its fuse is ignited.'

'Ah, I was wrong, it is like this ...'

'That is ingenious – and you admit your mistakes, unlike my own linguists. Tell the esteemed Admiral that he has a potent weapon – but it is a sword with two edges, on which he may cut himself'.'

'Deuce! This is a clever fellow. Forrester, you recollect how the *L'Orient* went up at the Battle of the Nile? Tell him the shells are stored in a magazine in the bowels of the ship – and only brought up in boxes, as needed.'

'Still, with plunging fire and red-hot shot from hilltop forts...'

'First, you have to hit the ship.'

'Alas, the Manchu gunners could not hit a cow at six feet.'

'Gad, I like him more and more!'

'Why did the two ships, smaller than this but bigger than your present consort of ten guns, not use shell four years ago? Do only big ships carry them?'

'The old rogue has sharp eyes if he has been counting the *Algerine's* pop-guns. Tell him the *Imogene* and *Andromache* were provided with shells but wished to spare life and only knock the guns off their mountings.'

'How considerate.'

'Ha! Tell him we'll finish the other bottle now.'

'Gladly.'

And thus did your colleague and fellow-countryman find himself seated between two Admirals in the stateroom of a British man-of-war, toasting for the pair of them, which meant I had to drink double the quantities.

You will be pleased to hear Admiral Maitland had me rowed back to Remedios and the *Sonia* in time to catch the tide – else I would have fallen in and drowned, so inebriated was I. Since when the Chow Chow Hong has seemed a rabbit's hutch after the cabin of the *Wellesley* to,

Your always friend,

Gideon Chase

From THE LIN TIN BULLETIN AND RIVER BEE

Wednesday, August 29, 1838

Vol. 1 No. 18

ERRATA

Some absurd errors have crept into the final column of our last. p.8, 3rd column, line 70. For *Reader's* read *Readers'*. p.8. 3rd column, line 71. For *profess* read *possess*.

Such trifling misprints are, of course, still inexcusable but, we trust, nevertheless forgivable where we may depend on the indulgence of our readers.

The paragraph in question was, we assure our friends, true in substance and we make no false claims as to our circulation. The misrendering in line 71 arose as the paragraph was inserted at the last moment and not presented in written form to the compositor but dictated aloud when he misheard it.

Small minds and mean in the magnanimous may only their own pettiness see.

From THE LIN TIN BULLETIN AND RIVER BEE

Wednesday, September 12, 1838

Vol 1. No.19

A sanguinary combat. Wednesday previous, together with a party of other gentlemen from the English, French, and American Factories, in number about thirty, I had the good fortune to be present at a notable display of the science and art of *fistiana*. Rare, and indeed to the best of my recollection, unprecedented event in these parts (for the ignoble *scrappings* of the brawling sailors are not to be spoken of in the same breath as the noble art) the encounter owed its arrangement to the presence by chance in the estuary at the same time of Henshaw, a gunner in the English squadron, and Job, a man of colour of the Philadelphia vessel, the *Allegro*. Henshaw, a native of the county of Leicestershire, had attained some celebrity in the milling circles of England and among the Fancy, when his patron had been Major Frobisher. However, his material circumstances, owing largely to his own carelessness, altered when he had to run away to sea to avoid the sheriff. Aboard ship, his feats of strength in lifting cannon, felling adversaries *etc.* soon won him the esteem and admiration of his shipmates. Job had formerly been the fighting buck of Colonel Connolly of Carolina and, though pandered to in respect of his taste for beefsteaks, fine raiment, and nigger women, had fled to the northern states. Discovering freedom to be a somewhat less luxurious condition than that of the kept gladiator, he had eventually taken to the sea where, like Henshaw, in despite of his colour, he had soon become cock of his ship.

The common sailors had heavily backed their respective champions of the forecastle, a match being made for $100 a side. Further, report of the fight being bruited in Canton, a subscription purse of 50 guineas was got up to be presented to the winner, mostly by the gentlemen of the English Factory, being notable amateurs of the sport.

We made a quick passage, dropping down to Lin Tin in the quickest time I can remember when we found a large crowd already gathered. The contest was to take place on some level, sandy ground, with a few blades of grass binding it sufficiently, some yards above the beach itself – where, indeed, the mass of spectators had to stand. We were provided with stools and shooting-sticks, while the boatswains and their mates, armed with whips, kept the press at a decent distance from the ring.

Henshaw was first to peel. Fine arms, well-ribbed, and a heavy chest. He seemed in good spirits, was cheerful, and possessed a calm and steady eye. Life at sea had plainly not disagreed with him and, as he stretched his supple limbs, it was evident that the exercises with the cannon had lent to his movements uncommon strength and deliberation.

Job came up next in the midst of a crowd of well-wishers, laughing and singing, grinning broadly the while and showing a set of fine white teeth. The first mate of the *Allegro* was his chief second, Mr Donovan the ship's agent acted as his bottle-holder, and he and the Captain as his umpire. Henshaw was attended by the captain of his gun, the sergeant of marines of the *Wellesley,* and Mr Innes of the house of agency of that name stood as his umpire. On stripping, the man of colour drew gasps from the spectators. Truly, he was a model of anatomical perfection, the bust powerful and beautifully moulded, such as the sculptor might be pressed to imitate, the arms sinewy but still plastic, waist slender as a girl's, and stomach taut. Only his calves, as often with men of his species, somewhat under-formed. He was six feet tall, weighing about 190 pounds, while Henshaw stood six feet wanting an inch or so and tipped the balance in the region of 195 pounds, bearing a greater proportion of his weight in his mighty loins and hams than the coon. As they met to hear Mr Innes and Captain Hunter agree to the rules, Job looked his man full in the face, while Henshaw sturdily regarded the ground.

First round. Job, full of spirit, darts round the Gunner, not intending to plant any decisive hit but to confuse his man and spoil his guard. Gets in a few insignificant facers which Henshaw almost scorns to block. Meeting at last, they wrestle, showing not inconsiderable skill, and fall to the ground together.

Second. Job was faster on his pins than the Englishman. He now commenced to put more weight behind his blows. Two lefts in rapid succession knocked Henshaw's head back on his shoulders. Having found his measure, a most desperate right from Job split open Henshaw's cheek and sent him backwards to the ground. The nigger thus the first to tap the claret.

Third. Henshaw took more punishment but showed thorough game. Knocked to the ground by a most fearsome facer, when he rose gaily.

Fourth. Job circled his rival in a manner the most objectionable, laughing and talking to him, but not omitting to put in the most severe hits. The head was plainly his chosen mark. A good left knocked Henshaw sideways to the ground.

Fifth. Henshaw managed to parry a left of Job's and with great care planted a fine stomacher from which the spectators heard the air leave Sambo's mouth. Closed and fell to the ground together. Job complained that Henshaw had contrived to put sand in his eyes.

Sixth. Job rushed in at his adversary, dealing blows like drum-beats. Blood flowed from the Englishman's mouth and nose. A blow under the ear levelled Henshaw, who showed himself a glutton in this round.

Ninth. Henshaw's face so beaten and swollen as not to bear any resemblance to a human being. Spectators are full of admiration and wonder for his limitless bottom.

Eleventh. Henshaw secured Job's wrist as he withdrew from a blow, having lost his distance and missed. Seized him by the waist and threw him violently to the ground.

Twelfth. Henshaw parried a right from Job, returned a blow to the nigger's throat, seized him, and gave him a cross-buttock, landing heavily on him. Nigger heard to groan.

Fifteenth. Henshaw struck Job with great niceness under the heart, dropping him to his knees.

Nineteenth. The coon slow in coming to the mark and only just beat time. On the first occasion in this fight, Henshaw hit him with a facer, drawing the cork from his nose and making the claret issue copiously. A hit on the ear, placed with great thoughtfulness as the nigger staggered and dropped his hands, placed Job on the sand. He was unwilling to come out but his captain ordered him.

Twenty-first. The coon having fallen without a blow being struck in the preceding, Henshaw measured him when a right on the eye caused that organ to swell fearfully. A hit on the temple made the nigger topple on his hands where he vomited copiously.

Twenty-eighth. A mighty blow to the jaw felled Sambo, when he lay senseless and was only revived after some minutes. Henshaw received the plaudits in equal measure of English and Americans, and a case of brandy together with the compliments of the captain of the *Allegro*.

Our passage back to the Factories was made without incident, where we landed at Jackass Point at about three in the morning.

QUENTIN DURWARD

From THE LIN TIN BULLETIN AND RIVER BEE

Wednesday, October 10, 1838

Vol.1. No.21

Departure of Admiral Maitland. Sailed from Urmston Sound Friday previous, October 5th, the *Wellesley* (74) and *Algerine* (10), bound for Calcutta. Admiral Maitland had been waiting on the favourable monsoon. The *Larne* (16) only remains. During the two months previous relations between the Chinese fleet and the English squadron had been remarkable for their closeness and cordiality. Indeed, the two Admirals had become fast friends, the exchange of compliments turning into a bestowal of presents. We do believe that on both sides this exceeded the formal manifestations of good will usually required of ambassadors and that their feelings of mutual esteem were both personal and sincere. On hearing report of the death of Sir Thomas's niece, Kwan wrote the Admiral the most affecting note of condolence it is possible to imagine and exhibiting the most unimpeachable sentiments to which a Christian need not have been ashamed to own. For his part, Maitland was ready with invitations to dine aboard the *Wellesley* and, we understand, the Chinese commander actually fired one of the flagship's mighty pieces of ordnance. Prior to his departure, Sir Thomas had a case of claret rowed across to his friend and counterpart, while Kwan returned the compliment in consignments of citrous fruits, scrolls, and curios.

Yet, unhappy to relate, we doubt that the visit of the *Wellesley* will have accomplished aught but a temporary improvement in the standing of affairs in the river. To a large extent, both services are merely instruments to be set in use as and when events dictate. With the departure of the

Wellesley, the Chinese will increase in boldness and pretty soon matters will arrive where they were previously – at a pretty pass.

The circumstances remain unaltered. *Tout court,* here are the horns of the dilemma:

1. The Chinese Government wishes to extirpate a vicious trade which ruins the health of its subjects and drains its treasury of precious specie.

2. The English Government admits the immorality of the trade but cannot afford to lose its vast profits.

By putting the onus for its suppression on the Chinese Government, saying piously that one sovereign power may not interfere in the internal affairs of another, Britannia has the best of all worlds: she gets the lucre, yet washes her hands of all moral responsibility.

We do not think this can continue.

Dramatis personae. To the foreigner, inhabiting the liquid margins of this vast and populous empire, native life must remain a mystery. Not only is the book closed, but it is written in an incomprehensible hieroglyphic. True, the patient and scrupulous application of scholars and officials of the past (meaning foreigners!), including the often unjustly reviled officers of the Honourable Company, has year by year and piece by piece added to the Treasury of our Knowledge, yet this is intelligence which is confined to the higher or airy regions of China. We know in intimate detail the brickwork of the pyramid of government: the hierarchy of officers, the organisation of the Provinces, the workings of the Examination system. But what of subterranean life, if we may phrase it so, the life of the people, the vernacular life? The history of the huckster who plies his trade in the Square, his seasonal peregrinations, the network of servants and, it must be admitted, criminals, who supply our wants? Nothing, nothing at all.

In the supposition that true knowledge begins with

individuals and not principles, for out of the former may be deduced the latter but never the former from the latter, we here supply our faithful readers with some *sketches* of those about them *whom they have regarded but never seen* – which we should be pleased if they amuse and doubly so, if they perchance inform.

Verminous Tse. This scarcely human form customarily occupies a position hard by the entrance to Hog Lane, soiling the walls of the Hong with its filthy rags. Strollers may be forgiven for mistaking the recumbent heap for a pile of rubbish. Yet, O contemners! this is a ruler who has at his utter disposal the bodies of more men than you ever shall and commands an influence and credit with the shop-keepers of Canton which you shall never enjoy in New York, or Boston, or Edinburgh, or whichever is the city wherein you make your home. For this is the King of Beggars, who with his lousy and odorous army will infest the premises of any trader who has neglected to pay him and his their monthly squeeze. Rather than lose his fastidious customers, the proprietor willingly pays the King a few cash every month to secure immunity from nuisance, which the Ruler then distributes to his men. Thus, by this system, public begging in the commercial quarter of the bazaar is eliminated. Any mendicants who should dare force their attentions on shoppers receive a severe beating from the King's officers.

Woman Woo, About fifty years of age. A stout, grey-haired harridan, who affects a costume of dark blue tunic and trousers. Wears a jade bracelet. She controls the entire road of gaming booths, wherein customers wager on fighting crickets, directly without the Factories. Boxes well and disposes of a band of bullies who enforce her will. She was sold into a flower-boat at the age of seven, but insinuated herself into the affections of a rich merchant. She is a native of Amoy.

Sour Li. He is the pickle-vendor who hawks the carrots, onions, pears, and quinces in their jars of vinegar. His barrow is in the middle of the Square. This is an eminent and enviable position from which to trade. He is on this station only three days out of the seven, yet the spot remains vacant in his absence. Have you speculated, if you have remarked it at all, that this space is not seized? This, it is reputed, is the powerful functionary of a secret society.

PURSUER

Chapter XXV

W
alter can feel the change. It is almost physical. The reduction in political temperature can be sensed on the exposed skin, in prickling, not shivering. It makes the foreigner on the square wish to cover up with more protective clothing, though it is a warm January day. 'I don't care for the air of this,' he mutters more to himself than his companion.

'You would be the possessor of a thick hide, did you not remark it,' replies Gideon. 'But tell me, to be so kind, what to be exact are the signals which advise this alteration to you?'

'Now you have me in a quandary to explain. I don't know, and that's a fact. But...' Walter steps out of the way of a coolie laden with pannier-baskets, '...let me see. It is not so much the armed boats on the river, which deprive us of our exercise. No, nor that leering villain there who saws at his throat – have no fear, I shall not provoke him. Nor the arrests and executions. There could be a thousand such...'

'...have been,' says Gideon drily.

'Is that a fact? No – I reckon that it is not by large or obvious events or gestures that effects may be produced on the feelings, rather by the accumulation of little – matters not worth the mentioning, which may even escape one's own remark. The circumstance that our mess-boy no longer smiles, that the Factories servants leave the gates in bands of six or seven, rather than the one or two which was their wont, that Minqua sends his Third Son to us, instead of coming himself. Oh, and Remedios kept a slow-match burning by the guns.'

'And this is really what has combined to operate upon your sensibilities?'

'Over time and when compounded, yes. To witness a thundering broadside would be some relief.'

They have now reached the limits of the Factories precincts. Manchu soldiers lounge against the other side of the iron railings. Another group smokes long pipes on the river-wall. They wear caps, cloth boots, and baggy trousers. Around their waists they carry bandoliers of powder-charges for their matchlocks. The two nearest the railings look up from their game of dice. Blank, brutal, broad-boned faces. Most foreigners could not tell them from a Chinese. It is ironic, Gideon reflects, that his familiarity with the Chinese and their culture, new though it is, should have the effect of making these Tartar clansmen of the Emperor appear as barbaric and alien to him as they do to the Chinese – whereas to the most chauvinist of the British Free Traders they would appear as nothing stranger than another native.

The dicing soldiers call to their comrades in a language full of consonants and gutturals, which is rather more Arabic in sound than Chinese.

'What do they say?'

'I have as much idea as you. Manchu is to Chinese as Greek to Spanish.'

'Darnation, man, you are a veritable walking dictionary.'

'We endeavour to serve. Now what's this?'

Two Manchus have jumped on to the river-wall with a brightly coloured contraption of paper and rattan which would be immediately recognisable as a kite if Walter and Gideon were not prejudiced against seeing it as such. Eventually, as a string is attached to its tail, their disbelief must surrender to the evidence of their eyes.

'Well, God damn it.'

'Walter, I guess my own astonishment is equal to your own, though I would find other means of expressing it.'

The soldiers show great expertise with the launch. A tug or

two on shortened string, slack, tauten, repeat: and soon the contraption is high over the centre of the stream, flaunting its tail. The matchlockmen who had been at dice advance, insert their smouldering wicks into the wheels of their pieces, present the heavy weapons at an angle of about 45 degrees, aim quickly, and fire. *Puff! Puff!* go the reports, the priming flashing at the breech as the lengths of match in the wheels touch off the powder in the pan. The kite shivers twice. Another pair of marksmen discharge a volley over the river, with the same result.

'Do you know, I imagine I can see the balls travelling to their target.'

'Very possibly. The bore is large and their powder very weak and, besides, the bullets must climb.'

'Is that a fact? Their powder, I mean? I should amend my dictionary. I thought the reports different from our duck-shooting exploits.'

'Ha! You remember that day?'

The kite has been reeled in. The Manchus gather round it, pushing their fingers through the holes their bullets have pierced. They are careful not to obstruct the view the foreigners have of it. One of them glues paper patches over the bullet-holes. 'I am strongly inclined to believe that this display was contrived for our benefit.'

'Without the smallest doubt. We now know they can shoot straight, if nothing else.'

'They are reputed, among the Chinese, still better archers, possessing the ability to hit a mark on the gallop. Still, I cannot say I would be happy to be residing on the southern bank presently, with matchlock-balls dropping about my ears.'

The pair stroll back, trying to make the short walk last as long as possible. Others have had the same idea. Near the customs-shed, they find Ridley, Johnstone, and young Oswald.

'Good cheer! 'Tis the whey-faced scribbling poltroons!'

'Isaak Drug, I will have none of your slumbering draughts,' replies Eastman in the idiom of Walter Scott.

'Why, my good sir,' says Johnstone, 'we are embarrassed with such a superabundance, we are selling at half price.'

'Then the circumstances of the day are bad for you and worse for the natives.'

'Not for me, for my master's pocket.'

'It will mean less claret on the table for you.'

'That,' says Johnstone, with sudden gloom, 'has the distinct ring of cause and consequence.'

'Ridley,' says Eastman suddenly, 'what in the devil's name have you got under your arm?'

Jonathan Ridley, who has been hovering behind the others with uncharacteristic diffidence, tightens his grip on the parcel under his arm and circles away. His companions grin broadly.

'Oh, this fellow, you mean – the new addition to the scribbling band?'

Eastman snatches the brown paper packet from Ridley, which comprises one, two, three, four...*ten* copies of the latest *Lin Tin Bulletin and River Bee.*

'God damn it, explain yourself, sir. Do you mean to corner the market in this item? I expect we shall be enabled to raise *our* prices in consequence.'

'Struck by the lustre of authorship, we are given to understand,' says Johnstone. 'Not too bad a production, either, for the greenhorn. What d'ye say, Mr Assistant Editor?'

'I did not care for it,' says Gideon primly. 'It read more like the sentiments of a backwoodman than those of a civilised New Yorker, and generally pandered to a brutal taste.'

'No, sir – the form not the substance. Ridley is a pioneer in a new species of literary composition. Isn't that a fact, Jon?'

'See here!' says Ridley, 'this is enough, God damn it, more than enough for any fellow to have to endure. Fix your own affairs before you meddle in those of another. Walter has seen fit to approve my contribution, which I expect is good enough for anyone as he's pretty generally acknowledged to be the expert in the point of writing.'

'They are,' says the tribunal in question, 'only jealous, my dear fellow. And were I you, I should lodge copies of your lucubrations with all your friends, lest, unhappily, your own should be consumed by fire or moth. They may also read it, of course.'

'In that case,' says Johnstone, producing from his breast-pocket a scroll bound with red ribbon. Walter recoils in mock horror. 'Good God, sir, do you think I am Harry O'Rourke that you should act the part of the dun? You need not trouble to serve me with a notice to pay my debts. You shall have your fifty cents before sundown.'

'My contribution to the esteemed is naturally *gratis*,' Johnstone says. 'Peruse and do you as you will.'

'Gratefully received, sir. I should merely add that I hope that it is written with the same gusto which characterised Jonathan's. Warmth is all, where this is concerned. Believe the peruser.'

'Please, Mr Ridley, sir,' pipes up young Oswald, 'Mr Eastman…'

'Now what the devil are you about? Don't tell me *you* have perpetrated some verses for me to set up as well.'

'It's a smart lad,' says Johnstone.

'Please, sir,' Oswald says, 'this 'ere crowd's getting right ugly.'

'*Vox populi authentica,*' says Eastman, 'in all senses.' He regards the milling Chinese in the square with great disfavour, but enviable composure. 'But I do doubt if I may accept your rhymes, my lad, if they are couched in the vernacular of your spoken word – charming, apt, and nervous though it be.'

'What is he talking about, Jon – Mr Ridley, I mean?'

'I calculate, Oswald, that he is creditably not exhibiting the symptoms of panic.'

Young Oswald ponders this as it pertains to himself. The crowd, composed of elements not usually in the square – Gideon, for instance, cannot recognise any of them – have their backs to the Americans for the moment. They see the tops of the pair of ornamental iron gates, which seclude the Factories from the square, swing to. In the crowd sticks are waved.

'Act one, scene one,' intones Ridley, who is becoming a veteran at these disturbances. A little later, the first brickbat flies. 'Scene two.' Soon the air is full of missiles, clattering against the gate, flying miraculously through its tracery or sailing high over the top. Now the gate starts to shudder as the weight of bodies presses against it. 'Scene three. I trust Innes can be restrained from discharging his gun at the crowd. He had got so far as loading it previously.'

Johnstone says quietly, 'I guess we had better retire directly, but as discreetly as we can contrive. There is a boat a few yards down and I calculate the Tanka would contrive to paddle us the few yards until we are ourselves behind the gate.'

But it is too late. A boy at the back of the mob has seen. He points and shouts.

'That,' says Eastman, 'is a wretched, tale-bearing boy, who is doubtless the butt of his fellows.' But he has turned pale.

Ridley steps to the front. 'Do you all wade out to the boat, the while I shall cover your retreats.'

'Rather let me.' This is Gideon. But he sees that Ridley's square jaw juts. 'At least, I shall remain with you. Fall back, the others.' However, the Tanka boat has now pushed off.

(Johnstone's earlier trust was not entirely misplaced, but secret assistance can no longer be rendered.)

'Darnation. Can they see the fix we are in from the Factories?'

'No one's on the balcony.'

Surprisingly slowly, the mob advance. Ridley's grip on his stick tightens, while Gideon swallows, finding his mouth suddenly dry. The others have their backs against the wharf. The first rock comes not from the front ranks but from somewhere in the middle of the crowd.

'Darned lily-livered cowards,' exclaims Ridley, 'can't even come on and close like men, and there are hundreds.'

Now the stones commence flying with a vengeance. Ridley, furious, breaks his cane on one in mid-air. Gideon turns, with arms protecting his head. A violent blow on the thigh sends him sprawling. He can straighten the leg, but it is numb. The missile lies beside him: a lump of coal. Now where in Mercy's name has that come from? What a question to ponder in one's final moments! Ridley has raised his doubled fists. None of the mob appear particularly anxious to engage him, empty-handed though he is. But doubtless his minutes, too, are numbered.

'Jonathan, I...'

'Act three, scene three, and *finis,*' says Ridley grimly, without taking his eyes off a man who is a few yards in front of his fellows. He sidles nearer, obviously plucking up the courage to attack Ridley.

Gideon struggles to rise, but cannot. 'I guess he is willing to wound but afraid to strike,' he quotes, and giggles madly. Suddenly, he feels very gay. But Ridley is in deadly earnest. When the man still seems at a safe distance, Ridley shoots out his left fist and leg and then hits him with a right which is as straight as a ramrod. Over goes the Chinese. The crowd move back but in the same moment a well-aimed rock takes Ridley in the chest with a heavy thump and knocks him sprawling. As a man, the mob move in. Sticks appear; kicks, blows rain on Ridley.

Gideon shouts in the local dialect and then ... through the membrane of faintness which envelops him and which has replaced his light-headedness of a moment ago, he sees disciplined forms advance against the crowd. And these are short, spry, bandy-legged forms; native forms; forms which would be easier in the saddle. The Manchu matchlockmen.

With quick, deft raps in turn from the butts and barrels of their guns, similar to the action of paddling a canoe, they drive back the crowd. A short, downwards chop with the butt levels Ridley's most persistent attacker. Then they form a protective line before the foreigners. They level their matchlocks at the retreating mob, and the withdrawal becomes a rout. At a monosyllabic command, the weapons come down. Johnstone and young Oswald run to Ridley. Eastman stops by Gideon. 'I am fine, Walter, see to Jonathan.'

'You are not "fine", sir.'

Gideon gasps and bites his lip as Walter touches his leg, but the limb twitches. 'You see, you are a liar, sir, as well as a libeller.'

But there is movement in the leg now and the beginnings of returned sensation.

'How is Jonathan?'

'Jonathan lives,' shouts Jonathan.

Laughter, Gideon's a little hysterical.

The Manchus regard them without expression, unless Gideon is altogether fanciful when he imagines they disapprove of the foreigners' levity. They shoulder arms and, quite roughly, pull Ridley to his feet. A pair approach Gideon, but Eastman waves them away. He places Gideon's arm around his neck and straightens up. Gideon supports the rest of his weight on his good, right leg. Surrounded by the Manchus, the party of Americans make their way through the gates to the doubtful sanctuary of the Factories.

From THE LIN TIN BULLETIN AND RIVER BEE

Wednesday, January 30, 1839

Vol. 2 No.3

Which creature is it which unites the strongest sense of self-preservation with the greatest abhorrence of water (Reader, in regard of the last attribute, we exclude the hydrophobic canine or...*dog,* if you'll forgive our bluntness), whose whiskers are sensitive to the minutest adjustment of trim on the vessel which is its reluctant and unconscious carrier, which spreads pestilential disease in its wake and a trail of *dun pellets,* which is resistant to the severest measures which might be instituted by authority to secure its demise, is afflicted by no scruples in its behaviour regarding others of its kind, nay, is a cannibal (and this one has swallowed many a smaller example of the species to make itself all the larger) and, in short, is but one large appetite and a thorough example of vermin? Our readers have it before our sentence has unwound itself (a prolix one, we'll own, and we'll regain our breath). To be short – it is the RAT which is the first to leave the sinking ship.

Not at all relative to the preceding, which we allow was an intemperate paragraph, we feel it our bounden duty to record, as the journal enjoying the largest and best-informed audience in our small community, that five days previous, the gentleman who rejoiced in the sobriquet among the natives of Iron-headed Old Rat was entertained to his banquet of farewell by the Traders who were his rivals and his...friends. To be plain again – Mr J- has decided it is time to leave.

What! My dear sir, you depart so soon? The festivities have only just begun. Two score years and more a Resident upon these Coasts and you choose this moment to make your exit? But how bizarre! Strange coincidence!

At this time the price of drug at Lin Tin *(vide* p.8) has fallen by fully half from what it fetched six years ago (when, mark you, John Company was master). As to the system of draconian measures presently being promulgated and, we'll warrant, most effectively instituted, no trader in Canton can fail to be sensible. However, we do believe such calculations to be foreign to the nature of those modern emulators of Maecenas whose munificent subscription raised the price of the 1000-guinea service of plate presented to Mr J- on this happy occasion of felt sodality and demonstrated gratitude. Could his competitors be pardoned for breathing sighs of thankfulness as they bade God speed to their most powerful rival, or, as they choked into their kerchiefs, perhaps those were tears of gratitude at their deliverance, rather than those of sorrow? Perish such thoughts. In any event, it is matter of general knowledge that the two trusty Mr M-'s shall remain in Canton, while we should be greatly surprised if Mr J- were able to content his adventurous and graspi – *ahem,* his adventurous nature, with perambulations and stock-takings of his extensive Lowlands estates, but should pretty soon be buying – a thousand pardons: proposing himself for some eligible seat of Parliament – and bending Lord Palmerston's ear, not only on account of his old firm, we are sure, but all the Free Traders in Canton.

As regards the price of opium, now well below $400 a chest of finest Malwa or Patna, we believe an interesting and instructive parallel is to be discerned in the history of the yet more odious and objectionable (if 'twere possible) traffic in men. We mean the Slave-Trade. Nine years ago this market was as depressed as may possibly be conceived. In the Slave States the prices of tobacco and cotton were at a nadir never plumbed previously or since, and in consequence of the glut in these commodities, the value of the hands which produced them was lowered as well. The prices of tobacco, cotton, and slaves fell in conjunction. In the marts of the South a fat hog might fetch rather more than a poor specimen of a human being. At this time the Abolitionists, it

382

seemed, might well win their suit by default. In the legislature of Virginia, its members choked by the recent revolt of the slave, Turner, a party gained strength by the day which sought as its chief end the emancipation of these unhappy helots. If they were worth so little, would their owners resist so strenuously the efforts of those who sought to loose them from their fruitless bondage? A scheme of compensation might be instituted which would remunerate the owners on advantageous terms. Alas! The crucial vote was deferred until the winter. In the meantime, the market turned. Daily, the quotations for cotton and tobacco soared. And, as they did, so by equal measure did the price of the slave who cultivated them. In the space of five years the price of slaves, tobacco, and cotton (Unholy Trinity!) had more than doubled. As the wealth of the slave-owners was augmented, so did their determination to protect the source of their profits.

We cannot conceive that the price of opium shall continue to remain depressed in perpetuity. Our readers will not need reminding of the great depression which attended the trade in cotton and especially in cotton piece-goods, two decades previous. Although the trade has been marked by no very great revival in the price of cottons, still it has firmed – and, as matters stand at the present, may furnish no very disadvantageous comparison with the profit to be made on opium, which but a short time ago offered a speedy avenue to riches.

But we greatly fear it does not lie within the comprehension of the Ruler and Administrators of this Empire, otherwise of such subtle and crafty dispositions, to realise they might offer to *buy* out, rather than to *burn* out, those foreigners who have flooded the mart with drug and – in a sense – have contributed to the lowering of their profits through their own unbridled greed.

Nevertheless, in their besotted arrogance, the Chinese are unable to distinguish between honourable and dishonourable foreigners, those who are implicated in this disgraceful trade and those who, to their eternal credit, abstain from it. We much fear that the wheat shall be consumed with the tares in the coming conflagration, that the estimable Mr K- and the virtuous house of O- & Co. shall be implicated in the well-deserved travails of J-, M- & Co. and their ilk.

We attend the consequences of the late events with, we must own, a measure of well-founded trepidation.

Disappearance of servants. Two retainers of the foreign Hongs, Lom and Wong, have vanished under circumstances so suspicious as to arouse the worst misgivings. Two days previous Lom, a man of middle years and a native of Canton, left the Factories with the intention of purchasing fresh vegetables in a market six streets away. By sunset he had failed to make his reappearance. As he was a factotum in whom a peculiar degree of trust was reposed, and, moreover, the wages he was due to be paid the next day considerably exceeded the small sum drawn on account of the comestibles, it is feared he has been kidnapped.

Wong, a youth of some twenty summers, and a strong swimmer, went abroad on the river and was not seen again. His boat was discovered, moored, on the Honam bank. The supposition that he, too, had been kidnapped began to assume the character of a certainty when his elder brother appeared at the Hong the next day with gifts of poultry from his home village in Tung Kwun.

On the literary modes of the Chinese. A celebrated scholar and noted divine has passed judgement to the effect that the Herculean efforts required of the neophyte in gaining a knowledge of the Chinese language are so wholly dispro-portionate to the small rewards which might be hoped to be derived from a course of study in its literature that strong feelings of disappointment must inevitably attend those who win through to a mastery of it. He did not make these comparisons in so many words, but he seemed to place himself in the position of a man scaling a mighty mountain with toilsome efforts in the expectation of discovering a beautiful view yet, on gaining Parnassus's summit, finding the panorama completely obscured by concealing clouds. We own that the musings of the native writers may be sometimes nebulous, yet we ourselves have not found our wanderings among those tracts to be wholly unattended with instruction and even entertainment. Men, perhaps, may more readily agree as to what they *feel* to be amusing than as to what they *consider* to be improving or elevating. The former is the product of an immediate and readily apprehended stimulus acting on the emotions and operating on their organs, notably by forcing the lungs to express the air of laughter. However, men have mentally to debate what they find edifying without the benefit of the corporal evidence of their own bodies' involuntary behaviour. We shall, therefore, discuss as the simpler of the two in our present article the recreational rather than the instructional literature of the Chinese. Thus we shall exclude from our current considera- tion the manuals of the Chinese sages, the treatises of philos- ophy, the poetry, and the eight-legged essay. We shall concen- trate on the prose romance.

This is recognisably the same form of tale in prose as the novel of the West, although with important differences as to its general address and the principles manifested in its organi- sation. That is, *Don Quixote, Clarissa,* and *Tom Jones* belong most distinctly to the same class, if not tradition, as the Chinese prose romances, *Chin Ping May* and *The Dream of the Red Chamber.* We may see why our aforesaid divine failed even to notice for reprobation these works, for, it must be confessed, they are frequently scabrous to the point where they make Chaucer or Rabelais seem fastidious and are imbued with a calculating and worldly lack of scruple of which a Talleyrand need not have felt ashamed. The flagrant flaunting of immorality and, indeed, the revelling in scenes of vice and debauchery distinguishes the Chinese novel from its Western counterpart more, perhaps, in degree than kind when indecent works such as *Moll Flanders* or *Tom Jones* are brought into the consideration. But this is a superficial distinction. The main differences between Chinese, on the one hand, and European or American novels, on the other, appear to reside in their respective notions of what properly constitutes narrative, of how time may be portrayed elapsing, and finally their different surmises as to the expectation of the Ideal Reader. Although no writer (to my knowledge) explicitly addresses himself to these matters, even as *obiter dicta,* they may fairly be said to have become unvoiced and common assumptions which have become conventional to the form.

Examining the first proposition, we shall pursue the argument that the Western novel (American, British, French, German) unfolds itself along a path which to all practical intents and purposes is *linear,* of 180 degrees as the navigator might say, or a reciprocal course. It may ramble, but essentially it proceeds along a course of cause and effects, each contributing to the movement of the whole. The plot is a veritable engine which advances the tale along its rails to a firm destination. The narrative is wound by the wheel of the story into a state of tension and anticipation. The native novel, by way of contrast, moves in a path which is altogether *circular.* It is made up of separate episodes, pretty generally of chapter length, which may refer only unto themselves and be joined by the loosest of threads. It chooses to emphasise incident, character, and language. It usually contains long passages or extracts of poetry, fable, song, and essays, lists of goods, recipes, formulas for patent medicines, and even spells, which may or may not purport to be written by its person-ages and, to a Western eye, may appear altogether dispensable and supernumerary to the author's requirements as failing to advance the tale or deepen the reader's understanding of its characters. This is to misunderstand the nature of the civili-sation of which it is both an adornment and a mirror. They exist *for their own sake!* The one is the form adapted for bearing the fictional wares of a civilisation committed to progress and advance, through the Scientific Explanation of phenomena from an analysis of cause and effect. The other is the cast of a society which looks in upon itself and has no notion of progress but a spiral decline from a golden age to a brazen one, in letters as well as all else. The former is a mighty river pushing to the sea, swollen by tributaries, diverging into deltas, but ultimately meeting its end in the Ocean. The other is a still lake.

As to the second proposition, regarding the different treatments of Time, the novel to which we are accustomed from earliest days may be said to have a clock ticking in its vitals from the moment its first sentence winds it into motion. *Tristram Shandy* is but the extreme example. Not so the Chinese tale, which is bud, flower, and then compost, but as a growth of nature is never subject to the laws and dictates of mechanism. We envisage time flying ever onwards. Some primitive tribes of the Antipodes, if we are to rely on the reports of travellers, see it rather as geographical, with events taking place simultaneously on the same lake, as it were, rather than being borne ever onwards and ineluctably on a river. Such is the conception which informs the native author's purpose. We may think it arrant poppycock. I have a friend of the most distinguished intellect and elevated morals who ventures to disagree. He, of course, is a native.

The attitude of the native author to his subject matter is unwittingly shaped, to boot, by the language he must employ for his descriptions and relations. Chinese is uninflected; that is to say, it lacks tenses. The events which in our own novels are, according to custom, conceived of as having already taken place, however recently, and are as much recorded by the writer as described, where he appears as much chronicler as inventor, working throughout in the historic, are in the native mode conceived of as occurring in an immediate present which (however remote the past in which they are known to have happened) unfolds directly and without mediation before the reader's very eyes. Such, normally, is the condition of plastic or representative art, and perhaps lyric poetry, rather than literature. This through an accident of language. Just as they do not trouble to conform to the laws of perspective in their paintings, so they have no sense of recession or distance from the past, or superiority to it. Of course, it goes almost without saying, there are exceptions to the rules in both languages. Naturally, too, there are advantages and disadvantages in both – but one should have been intrigued to read Sir Walter Scott in native translation. Perhaps even yet…

As to our third proposition, we might expect less divergence between a native and a foreign reader. Both must, after all, be literate; that is to say not only products of a proper education but also members of the leisured class. One needs reading ability of a low order, sufficient inclination, and time abundant to be a regular reader of novels *(as well as indefatigable curiosity and a strong vein of frivolousness – ed.)* As to ourselves, we feel bound to own we do not fall into this category. The chief difference between East and West here resides in the circumstance that fully one half of man, or rather human-kind, are disenfranchised from the readership of the Celestial novel, whereas they are, I dare to say, the staple of the audience of the foreign novelist. I mean…females. Who is as intelligent as man (I dare proclaim it, O, curmudgeon, lay-mentor, and friend!), is eager and curious to sample and know life in all its myriad manifestations, yet is effectively proscribed from acting a part in its varied pageant and making a history of her own? She needs must find this in other lives – and where more convenient but in imaginary lives, in the novel? At least *she* can read, in most cases. Her native sister is, in all but one instance in one thousand, altogether, lamentably, cruelly illiterate.

Howqua's favourite daughter is celebrated, solely owing to the circumstance that she can read and write – yet she is far from a scholar. The exclusion of the sex, by and large, from the prospective audience of the author, and his mind as he composes, may account for the occasional flagitiousness of the native novel, when the ear to which it is addressed belongs rather to a retired or resting scholar and administrator, a man versed and wise in the ways of the world, than to a young and tender head idly turning the leaves in its boudoir *(pace* Sheridan).

Yet, which may be viewed as the final paradox, our

Western novel, with its more perfect and complete audience, addresses itself rather to the individual as hero or heroine, from the delineation and resolution of whose dilemmas, material and moral, most of its energy and interest springs. This tendency is even more pronounced in the literature of the New World where there are in large portions no settled social relationships 'twixt man and man, employer and wage-earner, or skein of connections between the different parts of society — such as fill the tales of the Old World. Leatherstocking treads the soft sod of the trackless forest in an awful silence and solitude in the works of our own Scott.

Quite to the contrary, works in the native tradition, that is of China, are all for relating the adventures of the *group*, that is the family, of four generations or more under the same roof, to whom individual personages are mere parts of the whole, with no intrinsic importance in themselves. Where the Western reader smiles or sheds a tear as he or she participates in the fortunes and vicissitudes of a Pamela, a Joseph Andrews, or an Ivanhoe, the Chinese reader's sentiments will be as fully engaged as he rambles through the labyrinthine record of the prosperity and decline of the great Jar family of the *Red Chamber Dream*. For him the tragedy resides almost in the dismembering of the family rather than the paupering and eventual wretchedness, death, and destitution of its individual members!

In one final respect do the native and Western forms bear a similarity, which is that they both are eminently vulgar forms, mere popular and frivolous entertainment which cannot pretend to the enduring quality of works of scholarship, history, or philosophy. The productions of our own women authors confirm the essential correctness of such an opinion. *(How strange, then, if we may be permitted an interpolation concerning the literary history of our own country, that it should be the soberest, straitest-sided, most God-fearing, industrious-minded religion of the world which should have spawned such a crop. We mean the Puritanism of New England. For the Puritans they were who educated woman and made her literate (to read the Holy and not profane books!), who were single-minded and bore the notion of*

Time as Money, and told the great tale of the elect and the damned. Truly, ye shall know them by their works! – ed.) In one respect, though, is the novel of the Chinese more emancipate than the romance of America. It is truly a mirror of the lives they lead, without dissimulation or pretension, an unclouded reflection of the world as it is, where the material is not falsified to suit or fit some admired model. It is, we say, altogether vernacular. Can this be said of the world of the American authors, empty, shallow, and frivolous as the majority of their works prove? A thousand times no! It will not do, my dear sir, or indeed madam, to present the authentic experience of our countrymen unadorned but you needs must bend it to arrange its conveyance in a foreign vehicle. The derivative *Blackwood's* article, the novel composed after the manner of some supposedly superior author of the Old World, this is the sum and total of our production. Three and sixty years ago our valiant forebears claimed their *political* independence from the British – as to matters artistic it was a different story. We remain still a literary colony of Albion, and if the Hanoverian and his successors could not lay claim to our taxes or prove title to our lands, why they are in possession of our imaginations. This thralldom of the faculties remains to be shaken off – this pigtail of the mind, for at least the queue the Manchu imposed on the Chinese was a mere external token of conquest.

PURSUER

Adoption of extraordinary measures. We do not very readily see those familiar objects of the countryside, milestones, in China. At least, when we do, they are most certainly not to be trusted. To place excessive reliance upon them as indications of the distance remaining to be travelled would be foolish in the extreme and could be attended with serious consequences. One of the most vexatious habits of the Chinese is their disposition to regard distance as a matter of

390

inclination rather than strict measure. Thus, when we interrogate our friend the Hong-ist as to how much of a journey is remaining to accomplish, it will, dependent upon the mood in which we discover him, prove either a matter of miles or of yards. So, in his detestable cant, he will say – 'Oh, too much-ee go, long time walk-ee, walk-ee. Me think-um ten *li*.' This information might be offered if the weather was sultry; then again, on a clear, bright winter's day, the same question might be answered in this way – 'Velly good, no far. You go-um two *li*, walk-um easy.' We have known a distance walked in one direction from a certain spot to another to be described as four *li*. To walk between these same very points but in the opposite direction, or retracing one's steps, the same informant would describe the distance as 15 *li*. How can this be? Why, going the one way is all downhill, returning the other is all uphill!

We should say, from a course of close application to the conundrum of the bizarre reasoning of the Chinese, that the deciding issue in the native mind is the degree of effort or labour requisite in the accomplishing of one's purpose. (Just as the value or worth of any product of Birmingham or Connecticut reflects the quantity of the operative's time requisite for its manufacture.) Thus, to elicit a more nearly correct and nice answer, it might be more appropriate to ascertain the duration of the journey, rather than its extent. The Chinese confuse TIME with MEASURE.

CHAPTER XXVI

The deed is done fast. One wonders whether it has been rehearsed. Too macabre? For the actors that concept does not exist. Nor does it for the victim. He hardly struggles, may have been...drugged, for retributive irony *is* a notion which springs readily to the mandarin mind. Carried on stalwart shoulders in a wicker basket, as an animal to slaughter, trussed hand and foot, an ignominious conveyance to a brutal end, the malefactor is tipped on to the square's greasy stones. Up goes the cross. The executioner crosses his cord around the victim's neck, jerks, and the figure droops like a discarded marionette. Body, participants, and their dreadful, mundane instruments of wood and rope – props in some crude mummery – vanish with a speed and precision which require no curtain to conceal, leaving the square to its quacks and booth-shows. And in the wake of the real-life morality play enacted before them, they too decamp, as swiftly as they may, but with inevitable confusion and clashing.

Too late, the foreigners sally from the nearby Factory, bearing firearms as well as sticks. They are baffled, thwarted. Not only is there no victim to rescue, no assailants to repel, there is no evidence whatsoever of a crime. All have vanished into the thinnest of airs. Can it really have taken place? What they confront is not so much provocation as history, and it has run like water through a sieve.

A blow on a hawker's head consoles. Satisfactorily immediate. Very concrete.

Exactly a fortnight later. Same venue, certainly, same participants, more or less. But this time the river's the stage, the square the auditorium, and the Principal is no wretched, quivering servant but...Commissioner Lin.

He chooses to arrive by water, early in the morning, doubtless impelled by the same reasoning as Jasper Corrigan. This was when Jasper selected breakfast as *his* moment to announce to his employees their entry into the opium trade, two years ago; although, naturally, Corrigan and Lin are entirely at cross-purposes, as the Imperial Commissioner wishes to awe the barbarian into submission and put an end to the drug-trade.

He has been travelling ever southwards for some three months, having received his instructions from the Imperial Hand in Peking on December 31st, which is coincidentally the end of the barbarian year. The journey has been enjoyable, with canal-trips, detours to old friends in new postings (including a convivial verse contest with his own aged examiner and some fellow examinees of the same year), and obsequious hospitality from junior officials on the way. The final arrival in Canton by boat is quite unnecessary and is explicitly designed to intimidate the foreigner.

As such, it signally fails.

Lin, a heavy-set man of fifty, with a long beard and luxuriant black moustachioes, sits in splendour on his barge, surrounded by a staff of mandarins, some of whom are so high-ranking they possess the coveted red button on their own caps, similar to his. In his train glides a flotilla of boats, decorated with tapestries and awnings, their upper framework gilt-ornamented. On these travel the city's highest officers: Viceroy, Treasurer, Provincial Judge, Prefects, Salt Superintendent, Grain Intendants. Some of these scholar-officials look a little bleary-eyed. Soldiers line the walls of the river-forts, while most of the city's population seems to have gathered on the banks. This throng, which is the extraordinary thing, if you have the most superficial acquaintance with the inhabitants of Canton and their ways, is quite silent. As Lin steps ashore – and it is noticeable that he limps and walks with some pain and difficulty – the hush is deafening. Yes, the ears sing.

Where are the foreigners?

They are, sensible fellows, fast asleep. Almost to the man. Only two or three white faces are visible among this press, near the Factories. Of course, they are at this moment quite safe from all molestation or insult. One of them is Gideon Chase? No, he snores. Not until he is a very old man, decades hence, will he recapture those dawn awakenings of a short time ago.

Gideon Chase to Walter Eastman

No, 16 Chow Chow Hong
Canton
March 20th, 1839

My dear Walter,

Matters here present a remarkably bleak appearance, however viewed, and I imagine they should appear no less black when observed from your aspect in Macao. Lin lost no time in issuing his first proclamation in language as plain as its tenor was severe. In its way it was a little masterpiece of the literary art. There can be no room for misunderstanding. He accused the Hong merchants of connivance in the trade in opium (which is perfectly true, of course) and informed those gentlemen that they should be strangled at the stake, did they not secure the surrender by the barbarian traders of *all* the opium held presently in the hulks at Lin Tin. Could anything be plainer? Old Minqua and his fellows were despatched, loaded around their necks with chains, to make their pleas to the Drug-Traders. Johnstone was present and informs me there was not a hint of humbugging about this interview, and Mowqua, who had tears in his eyes, seemed in momentary expectation of death. It goes without saying that Lin is altogether incorruptible. The local officials might have proved amenable to bribes and doubtless resent the loss of their squeezes and perquisites, but they go about in terror of Lin, who is invested with a degree of authority such as is unprecedented in any officer in living memory. He had additionally demanded that the foreign traders should sign bonds, for ever renouncing their participation in the opium-trade under pain of death, and has named sixteen of the most prominent individuals he wishes surrendered as hostages. It is this which is the regrettable part of his policy.

Well, I know you shall rejoice in this news, as do I – or at least my rational self, for I know the difference between right and wrong, and the extirpation of this wicked traffic is also the declared aim of our newspaper. However, as you so rightly declared, I greatly fear that much innocent life and property will be forfeit if Lin persists in his unbending course.

I do not believe I am culpable of an exaggerated foreboding when I caution you that my contributions will very likely become irregular and undependable, so far as concerns the fortnightly erection of your type at Macau. The desire to compose articles has, of course, not left me, but it becomes increasingly difficult to despatch them along the river.

Our contemporary of the *Monitor*, finding himself and his press alike at Canton, labours under no such difficulty. As you may see from the enclosed, he is full of defiance and advises the Free Traders to make a fight of it. This with 400 sailors from the merchantmen at Whampoa and the sloop *Larne* at Captain Elliot's disposal! I estimate there are at least 10,000 Chinese and Manchus under arms in Canton, mostly out of sight in the New City. Were I not here, hostage to the old fool's bellicose whims, I might wish the full consequences of his own folly to be visited upon his head in deserved retribution It is his good fortune neither the Superintendent nor Captain Blake of the *Larne* are madmen, though I wonder if Elliot in Macao is apprised properly of the situation here. Elliot's distaste for the opium trade is, I would surmise, in no way feigned, and I entertain some sympathy for this Englishman and Christian whom duty and conscience pull in opposite directions. His conscience says it is your correspondent's duty to practise those characters he finds difficult to execute but he rather thinks he will take a perambulation to clear his musty head.

Yours always,

Gideon

From THE CANTON MONITOR
Thursday, March 28th, 1839

Arrival in Canton of Captain Elliot. Praise from a quarter which till that moment has been distinguished by the severity of its animadversions must register all the more strongly with the recipient. Such, we trust, will be the spirit in which the gallant Captain Elliot shall accept the thanks and admiration of the Free Traders and ourselves, their declared voice We have discussed unfavourably in our previous issues *passim* his attitude to the Canton authorities when he showed rather too much of the spirit of conciliation to the prejudice of the decided firmness which alone was appropriate. It affords us, therefore, the most unalloyed pleasure to register our boundless admiration for his gallantry in rowing up the river from the Bogue in the gig of the *Larne,* accompanied only by a handful of attendants, *voluntarily to share the fate of the traders imprisoned in the Factories.* We never heard such an instance of cool, cold-blooded pluck in an officer of state – but then Captain Elliot was first a naval officer and we, like Britannia's enemies, with better reason, know the mettle of that service. The gallant Captain presented himself to share the fate of the merchants, offering himself as hostage, in the hopes that his position would protect the heads of his countrymen. He found the Factories an altered place when our servants had taken their leaves, under pain of death, the flagstaff broken, the lanes and terraces around milling with armed men, the river all but blocked by a cordon of boats for six miles from Whampoa. Neither his uniform nor his position protected the Superintendent from the rude jostling and interference of these petty craft, whom one broadside from the little *Larne* would have scattered in terror and dismay. Landing wet, tired, and all but alone, the gallant Elliot ordered his gig's ensign to be lashed to the Factory's splintered pole for, as he remarked, 'there is a sense of support in the sight of that honoured flag, fly where it will, that none can feel but men who look upon it in some such dismal streight as ours'. Write so to Lord Palmerston, my brave Captain!

To speak strictly, the present quarrel involves only the British merchants since the contribution of our American contemporaries with their Turkey opium to the traffic is but a trickle compared with the torrent of Indian opium, and they have always preferred to genuflect to the Chinese and the Almighty dollar rather than imperil a cent of their profits. Supple Jonathan! Profit not principle is his motto – yet his spine was stiff enough when it came to the duties on tea. Still, we much doubt that the other nations can long remain aloof from the struggle – for struggle it is. Britannia shall extend her protection to those of similar complexion to her new subjects when they are threatened by the lawless savages who comprise the population of this empire but, by the same token, when redress of wrongs to her own is the issue, she shall not shrink from inconveniencing others. If, nay *when,* Admiral Maitland shall send naval reinforcement from Trincomalee and measures for a general blockade shall be instituted (which we believe they must), then a very general and protracted interruption to trade must ensue as a natural consequence, as night attends upon day. In the meantime, we most strongly exhort Captain Elliot against accommodation in any form with Lin.

Gideon Chase to Walter Eastman

No. 16 Chow Chow Hong
Canton
April 4th, 1839

My dear Walter,

Only Remedios could have got my mails safely through! What a splendid rascal he is! I have the copies of our latest, but I expect they shan't find much favour except with the Americans, of whom there are only twenty-five of us. (Is that correct enough for Webster? Even if Uncle Noah approves, it is certainly infelicitous.) On Wednesday last, Captain Elliot agreed to surrender all the British opium presently to be found in the store-ships at Lin Tin. The exact quantity this represents is not yet calculated, but it is believed to be about 20,000 chests, worth at prices current on the market some £2 million sterling. Lin rejected beforehand, with some scorn, Elliot's offer of a smaller quantity, denominated in hundreds rather than in thousands of chests. I believe he gave Elliot distinctly to understand that they were not in the position of huckster and customer bargaining for a compromise but the matter was a clean-cut issue of principle. One chest concealed should be sufficient for all at the Factories to be taken prisoner. The Deputy Superintendent, Mr Johnston, was yesterday given permission to quit Canton and proceed to Lin Tin to oversee the surrender. *A Public Notice to British Subjects* was at the same time issued by Elliot to be inserted in the Press, ourselves a recipient as well, wherein he gave notice of the detailed arrangements for the surrender of the opium and the issue of good receipts. It is said these shall be redeemable by HM Government. If so, then the drug-traders can thank Lin for striking a good bargain on their behalf, for they could barely sell the drug at a price which would leave them in profit such was the glut and state of the market these last months. How strange indeed are the workings of Fate!

Elliot's gesture in coming up the river to share the captivity of his countrymen has met with universal praise, as has his comportment throughout the demi-siege, which has been a model of coolness and fortitude in the face of all the insults and nuisances the Chinese could devise to lay upon him and serenity in the very jaws of their trap. His steadfast-ness and evident courage have also done much to take the play away from the hot-heads here, who else would long before have drowned us all in a sea of blood. The state of imprisonment continues, but now that the store-ships' cargoes have been surrendered, I am so sanguine as to believe we need no longer fear for our lives.

It has been a stroke of the most immoderate good fortune for myself, and of *confoundedly* bad luck for the gentleman in question, that Harry should have been up at the Factories drumming up 'a *leetle* commission business' at the time that Lin began his campaign. Although he has been reticent as to this, I understand that he did not expect the Imperial Commissioner to set about his work quite so directly or quite so warmly as has proved the case. Conceive of my surprise, as I now write to you in the full expectation of yours, when he showed me a sketch of Lin's arrival on the river. The question is – did the old reprobate rise at that ungodly hour on purpose, or was he reeling back from some carousal or debauchery which had endured the whole night previous?

I believe we should insert the *Public Notice* on our first page, though the editor's indecision is final.

Yours ever,

Gideon

No. 16 Chow Chow Hong
Canton
April 20th, 1839

My dear Mr Editor and lover of Seegars,

I breathe yet! We are not so very uncomfortable as you seem to imagine. There has not been a servant in any of the Thirteen Factories for more than a month – however, we are well provisioned with foodstuffs, fresh meat and vegetables being daily delivered by the authorities of Canton. There is no attempt to starve us out or to inflict unusual misery upon us, but merely to concentrate our minds – or rather Captain Elliot's – by depriving us of a little liberty and a few services. Certainly, we have all our creature comforts, and it has been rather amusing than disagreeable to have to fend for ourselves. I am the sweeper-wallah, young Oswald is *dhobi,* and Harry fixes a handsome egg. We thought of dyeing Harry's first dozen, which were most conservatively boiled, and employing them on the billiard-table. I, by the by, am the first person in living memory to have got the better of Jonathan on that table. 'A d-d close-run thing.' I believe Lin imagines he plays at billiards – whereas there are so many balls on his table that if he strikes one he will set all the others into undesired motion, He believes his actions may take place in isolation, In reality, they are fraught with consequences.

One unforeseen and happy consequence of the late events is that the threat of violence from outside has drawn our little community close together. Old feuds have been submerged in the larger and common threat, and rivals who have not addressed a word to the other for years are to be seen presenting him with the compliments of the morning and a pinch of snuff or slice of tobacco.

It is now nicely calculated that Elliot has agreed to surrender 20,291 chests, always guaranteeing the merchants compensation from HM Government. It is not, I surmise, difficult to guess from which quarter HM Government will in turn look for compensation.

Is it a fact that the Portuguese have to find 3000 chests from their godowns?

I confess I found your editorial article of the last somewhat of a gloating nature. It is true we oppose the trade – yet there can be no doubt that Lin has also acted unfairly, arbitrarily, and illegally. Living, as I do, with my co-hostages, I own I find it difficult to rejoice in their perplexities, though it should doubtless please my principles. I trust I should always betray a principle for a friend. You, Mr Editor, are, I know full well, of sterner mettle.

We are in hopes our incarceration may soon end.

G.

Frederick J. Remington to Gideon Chase Esq.

No.1 American Hong
Canton
April 22nd, 1839

Sir,

It has been drawn to my attention that on the 19th *inst.* you did visit and attend on the premises of this firm. I am bound to inform you that you are not a welcome guest in these quarters and I should be obliged if you would refrain from repeating the trespass when it would be my most unpleasant duty to have you removed.

I have, sir, the honour to be your most humble, obedient servant,

F. J. Remington

From THE LIN TIN BULLETIN AND RIVER BEE

Wednesday, May 22, 1839

Vol.2 No.11

An edifying mingling. To our loyal and expectant readers we
make no apology for the late appearance of our journal in
the confident anticipation that our desire to insert the latest
news will be considered sufficient justification for the very
small delay and inconvenience occasioned our subscribers.
The increased rapidity which has characterised the unfolding
of the recent events is productive of no little embarrassment
for the compilers of a fortnightly organ, when they may all
too easily discover themselves overtaken by circumstances
and marooned, as it were, on a spot from which the tide has
long receded. Yesterday, May 21st, the stocks of opium held
at Lin Tin were surrendered to the agents of the Chinese
government at the Bogue. We ourselves, together with our
colleague, assisted in the capacity of spectators at this translation of property in company with Mr K- of the house of
Olyphant & Co., when we were present at the express invitation of no less a personage than the Imperial Commissioner
himself in recognition of the good standing of Mr K-'s
house, which has ever remained aloof from the wicked
traffic.

The most perfected and orderly system prevailed by
which stocks as they arrived were meticulously listed, tallied,
counter-tallied, and itemised yet a fourth time in order to
ensure there might be no possibility of theft occurring. We
are pleased to establish it as matter of record and indisputable
fact, which must be beyond the slightest suspicion, that not
one chest was misappropriated and that all which was
rendered up was utterly consumed and destroyed. We would
not have thought it possible in this empire. The situation of
this extraordinary event, the deliberate destruction of over $8
million worth of an eminently portable and easily storable
commodity of high intrinsic value by weight, an action
without parallel in the modern or ancient histories of

401

democracies and despotisms, in the annals of civilisation or barbarism, was Chuenpi at the Bocca's narrows. Lin had caused a most ingenious system of trenches and sluices to be dug on the heights of the precipitous island and filled with ash and lime. Into this destructive liquid was hurled the contents of the opium-chests. Following the elapse of a period of time, sufficient to permit the reagents to perform their work of dissolution, a flood of sea-water was allowed to flow through the system, reducing the consumed opium to the consistency of a sludge or horrid porridge, and washing it into the receiving sea.

Lin observed the proceedings with a degree of complacency and satisfaction understandable in the circumstances in which he found himself a mere ten weeks after his arrival in Canton. He so far forgot his dignity as to run around the trenches, as they filled and discharged, with a nimbleness and agility surprising in a man of his girth. The Commissioner addressed a few words to Mr King, a very great condescension on his part in the minds of the Chinese, and, on his side, Mr King attended with becoming respect, but his demeanour evinced also the plainness and independence of an American. To the Commissioner's question as to whether the British Government regarded the trade in drug as peculiarly wicked, Mr King replied in the affirmative. To the next and inevitable question – why did it not then at once order its subjects to desist? – Mr King was at a loss to reply. Availing ourselves of the very able assistance of our own trusty interpreter, we were able to explain that we, the flowery-flag foreigners, were a nation quite distinct from the British and that we, indeed, had been impelled to take up arms to win our freedom from them. At this, the Commissioner looked mightily pleased and asked if our warships were as large and our cannons as accurate as those of the British. To this, bearing in mind the achievements of Decatur and his frigates, not to mention the numerous privateering captains, we felt free to return a hearty 'Aye!'

Our boat floated among the Chinese war-junks, a fox in the midst of a pack of hounds, but when we repaired to it in some haste that we might make Macao before midnight, we were amazed when we found our half-caste master very coolly gambling at knuckle-bones with the gunner of a Celestial revenue-cruiser.

We moored at the Praia Grande shortly after 1 a.m., having enjoyed an uneventful passage home. We trust that our narrative of these events, which we viewed as eye-witnesses, may be of some interest and even profit to our readers and that they shall excuse any trifling errors occasioned by the haste with which we set up our type.

Curious disappearance of Mr Veale. One of Macao's oldest residents, Mr Thomas Veale, has not been seen for ten days. He failed to return to his house after leaving it in the morning and has not since been sighted by even his closest acquaintances. There are no suspicious circumstances to mark his vanishing. His jacket was found on the beach with no signs to indicate a struggle or violence on the sand around it. It might be supposed that he had drowned while swimming, and the rest of his costume taken by the tide, but it is generally known that Mr Veale did not, indeed, could not, swim.

He had been a resident since arriving *anno* 1779 when he came as a writer in the now defunct house of Magniac & Co. He was ruined in an unwise speculation some forty years ago but kind friends, both native and foreign, combined to restore him to the comfortable circumstances he had enjoyed. He amused himself in the evening of his life by collecting rare birds and plants, his garden and aviary being open to all who cared to view them. In temperament he was sanguine, with a tendency to optimism in most matters, occasionally broken by spells of a deep melancholy (which were not at all to do with his worldly condition). His conver-sation was energetic, animated often to the point of incoher-ence, his looks and gestures frequently wild to a degree, but those with the patience to listen to his anecdotes, usually delivered in a sequence not at all logical or chronological, found in him a valuable fund of the stories of the early trading days of the settlement. He was a representative of the old ways and days of accommodation with the Chinese and moderation in all his dealings. A reward of $100 is offered for information leading to the discovery of his person if he is alive, and his body, if unhappily he is not.

A distinguished patient. A red-button mandarin was discovered in attendance at the morning surgery of the gratuitous hospital maintained for the American Missionary Society in Canton by the Reverend Dr Peter Parker. This former bore with him a description of the symptoms of an ailment which, he said, had long been a source of dolour to his brother, a mandarin of rank equal at least to his own, serving in a contiguous province. Distance and his exigent duties prohibited him from a personal attendance. A few seconds' perusal of the letter, supplemented by a close interrogation of its bearer, sufficed to establish that the absent patient by proxy suffered from a rupture in the muscular wall of the abdomen, or a *hernia*. Dr Parker stated that he would be happy to provide such measure of relief for the sufferer as lay within his powers but that he would need to be furnished with certain physical particulars relative to the anatomical dimensions of the patient. Unfortunately, the mandarin was bound to own that he was a man of far slighter build than his afflicted sibling and could not be used as a model. However, scarcely an hour later, with a swiftness miraculous even within a society endowed with a knowledge of the applications of the awesome power of steam, the mandarin returned provided with the accurate measurements of the waist and loins of his brother. Dr Parker then furnished the emissary with a truss, made up according to the specifications he had been provided. Every doctor, even a man of the cloth in every way so good and so disinterested as Dr Parker, must be gratified to ascertain that his treatment has proved successful.

In a race so generally imbued from childhood with the consciousness of the obligation to requite a debt as the Chinese (so our trusty adviser in such matters informs us), the presents which arrived at the hospital's door – and which in accordance with the good doctor's customary practice were turned away – were less cogent proofs of the efficacy of the remedy than the request for a duplicate and identical garment of support which accompanied them.

It is known that Dr Parker's distinguished patient by proxy was none other than LIN JA HUI, or the Imperial Commissioner himself.

CHAPTER XXVII

Walter whoops. Shingle, spurned by his bare feet, flies in spurts beneath his soles, the brown beads rattling over their fellows. Spray splashes his pumping knees; then, with a resounding crack, he dives into the sea in a flat, flamboyant arc. Surfaces, blows water from his nose, raises hands to sleek back curls which might have adorned his temples even four years ago – redundant gesture, pure vanity – and swims vigorously on his back, while he regards Gideon on the shore.

Harry O'Rourke and Father Ribeiro poke among the bigger stones and boulders beyond the tide-mark. Ribeiro needs some paper-weights for a new dissertation he is composing, having abruptly revised his earlier position on the Rites and Nomenclature Questions and come to agree, God help him, with the schismatics and conniving Lazarists that ancestor-worship bears far too many connotations of genuine religion. Or should one say, *false* religion? Flat, pink stones are what he seeks. (And it was wicked Ow who set about the manipulation of his views.) His cassock bulges with his trophies. Harry cannot help him; he is burdened himself with the paraphernalia of his own obsession. They come to sizable rocks. Harry takes a perch and a swig. Joaquim, he knows, likes to exercise by manhandling huge boulders over the sand. The subtle theologian has been furnished with the body and sinews of a labourer, another little Divine pleasantry. He can be espied from the Ridge, about his exertions, rolling boulders almost bigger than himself, resembling in his black garments a giant dung-beetle pushing its ball before itself. The task is no less Sisyphean, demanding, and pointless than his intellectual labour with his learned dissertation; although the former puts him in better temper for the latter and is certainly healthier than spending hours seated over small print by candlelight. Harry settles himself. Long, long ago (more years than he cares to be precise about) he drew a cartoon of Joaquim at his strange recreation on the beach, which pleased his friend greatly. So now he idly sketches some jagged rocks ahead, with a piece of twisted yellow driftwood before them. The thick, black strokes, these, of one who likes to think of himself as a master of the bold line. (And who is also a little drunk this early mid-June morning.)

Gideon, by the sea, amuses himself by lobbing pebbles at Walter's bobbing head.

'Do you join me, faintheart,' Eastman calls.

'I will not.'

'Has confinement so far broken your spirit?'

'What?'

'Has…Oh, take no notice.' Walter's last words are blown out to sea. He employs a vigorous, efficient breast-stoke; is actually a fine swimmer. Gideon, heavier-boned than his friend and every bit as well set up as the young Joaquim Ribeiro of fifty years ago, is less buoyant than Eastman; so finds it more difficult to propel himself through a medium he regards as threatening. It is no pleasure for him. But Walter powers out to sea, his back dipping and surging with each of his steady strokes until all Gideon can spy is his bobbing head. This, too, vanishes, lost among the flocks of sea-gulls which roost on the khaki waters of the estuary. Gideon would be anxious for anyone else but can stroll along with a free mind in Walter's case. The monsoon breeze, which comes newly from the south-west again, the splendid views of islands, the distance, and the space are delights after his tedious incarceration. He takes deep gulps of the sea-air. He hopes never to have to repeat the experience – which was not exactly a nerve-shattering ordeal but was monotonous in the extreme. Captain Elliot quit the Factories on May 24th, followed on his orders by the entire British community in Canton, who have now swelled the small society of Macao. Some thirty Americans remain in the Factories, unintimidated, uninvolved (so they persist in believing), and under the desire to make up for a great deal of lost business. 'We Yankees,' one lantern-jawed individual remarked to Elliot (perhaps it was Shillingford), 'have no Queen to pay for our opium and must continue to look after our own business.' Gideon, too, plans to return to look after his own and Walter's business, for the irascible editor of the *Monitor*, he and his, are known to be proceeding in a westerly direction from the Bogue at a mean speed of about one knot with the *Monitor's* printing-press, snug in the hold, making their vessel lie very low in the water. Walter has been ungracious enough to express the hope that they might be attacked by pirates – who seem recently to have become more than usually active in the delta. At any rate, he and Gideon plan to steal a march on their rival by carrying the latest, first-hand news from Canton over Pursuer's name. In the meantime, Pursuer, it is agreed, shall avail himself of a little rest and diversion. It does seem to Pursuer, kicking up the sand, that it is more of a printer's vacation than anything else. However, he is still a good-natured, unselfish, and industrious boy, who is incapable of feeling hard done by. He will endure the solitary confinement which is to come; meanwhile, he revels, quietly, in what this day and place have to offer.

'Hut-cha! Hut-cha!'

'What in the name of the...what ails you, Father?'

Ribeiro spreads his legs wider in the sand, the muscles distinctly working under his cassock as he gets his back under the boulder's weight. He says nothing but gives vent to more of his strange grunts, the veins standing out in his face. Gideon is alarmed – the old controversialist is in danger of inducing an apoplexy in himself. He makes to assist him, but the Jesuit shakes his head, really quite frenziedly.

'Hut, hut–cha!'

The enormous, prodigious, gigantic stone rocks an inch forward, an inch back; teeters agonisingly. Finally, it turns on its own centre of gravity and with the greatest ease and willingness in the world describes a turn and a half, Ribeiro exploiting its momentum to the full with a series of light pats. It comes to a halt again. Father Ribeiro dusts off his hands, takes a breath, and strains once more, repeating the performance until he gets to the crucial point where a tiny touch sends the heavy weight rolling again. 'That,' he says, looking back along the foreshore, 'is sufficient to the day. I shall resume the task tomorrow.'

'Is the action symbolical, Father? It seems much like any labour or catalytic action, mightily slow and severe to begin and then accomplished, depend upon it, with a great rush.'

'My son, you spend too long closeted with yourself. Only I am turning a stone – with no other end in view, I do assure you, than to take some exercise.'

'Well, I do calculate it is in the eye of the beholder. I don't think I am overly fanciful.' Gideon frowns; he has a liking for following his ideas right through. This one has interesting-looking implications – revolutions, for instance, political convulsions, scientific discovery, mechanical innovation.

'Come, let us see what Harry has done. Turn your fancy to a fruitful field.'

Gideon thinks he had a fertile conceit, but obeys without demur. Ribeiro, after all, was his first and most important master to whom he is massively, sempiternally in debt.

Harry's rock-formation is going to be one of his successes; quite fortuitously, as he was merely passing an idle hour. He has never been enamoured of marine painting, seascapes, that kind of thing – the very thought makes his pendulous, red lip curl. Even now the water – that unhappy yellow mix of river, silt, and sea – is no more than a frill beyond his stark, blank boulders. Footprints in some cunningly suggested sand end before the shark's teeth of the rocks which Harry has seen as a collection of triangles. These footprints don't exist – Gideon checks. No doubt a little joke of Harry's. The blond driftwood, though, with its crooked, supplicating arms, has had its very essence captured;

it has a quality of yearning, of straining.

'But my dear Harry, this is charged…how to say? *Suffused.* Yes, indeed. It is suffused (thank you, my son) with the instincts of the most sublime and Christian feeling.'

'Pish!' Harry's contempt is vitriolic, but Father Ribeiro, old friend that he is, remains not only unoffended but undaunted. After all, his Society have provided the stuff of martyrs, while Celestial scepticism has been infinitely more rudely expressed than Harry's.

'No, Harry, you are the instrument of a most Divine Plan, see how it resembles a …'

'Crucifixion, you old fool. They should nail you up as an example of having your mind turned.'

'Gideon, my son, bear me out in my view,' Father Ribeiro appeals to his young friend.

'Ha, well…'

'Don't venture to implicate a most intelligent young fellow in your folly, Joaquim.' Harry snorts savagely. 'This is not religion, it is the veriest superstition worthy of some ignorant peasant-woman. I am astounded at you.'

'The humblest it is,' says Father Ribeiro smoothly, 'whom God delights to choose as the vehicles to perform his Works.'

'Damn it twice over, you old fool.'

'Neither I nor you shall be damned on this occasion, unwilling and ungracious instrument though you are. You shall present this to St Paul's as a gift. When the time comes, they shall recite Mass for your stained but immortal soul.'

'I shall tear it up thus, thus,' howls O'Rourke, 'rather than let the damned monks have it, damme.'

At which point the south-west monsoon plucks the sheet from his fingers and drops it to the beach a few yards away. Father Ribeiro pounces on it. He carefully blows off the grains of sand and disposes of it in some hideaway in his priestly vestments. Notably, he refrains from making obvious remarks about divine intervention, but he grins like the cat which got the milk. Harry has another nip from his flask, muttering inaudible maledictions.

'A dram for me,' requests Eastman, who has stolen up on

them, stark naked and shivering. 'Water's darned cold for the season.' Goose-pimples stand out on his alabaster arms and chest. The muscles slide as he works them for warmth, the lean abdomen sharply defined as it goes into his loins and hips, his scrotum, taut, blue, and wrinkled, while his circumcised penis is contracted into an acorn of flesh. Hairs lie streamlined on his fine leg. Gideon smiles. He puts his own linen jacket around the dripping swimmer. The rim of O'Rourke's flask rattles against Walter's chattering teeth.

'Not a healthy exercise,' says Father Ribeiro disapprovingly, 'you should take care not to contract a chill.'

'B-b-b-b-aptism, Father?' says Walter, loping off for his clothes on the rocks. He hurdles the driftwood, his buttocks parting and revealing curls of hair and the ridged cord of his pouch as it narrows into the perianum.

'A ridiculous thing, the human body,' says Gideon. O'Rourke looks up in surprise, but says nothing. He appears to have lost his pen, for he picks up a stray piece of charcoal off the sand and makes some careless strokes on his pad. Walter returns in jacket and trousers only, having dried himself on his shirt.

'Good God, Harry,' he says, 'don't shame me – my member was horribly diminished.'

'My dear boy, your apprehension is groundless, depend upon it. You show yourself a victim of the illusion of regarding it in the vertical plane. It is quite a normal size to us as we regard it.' He shows his drawing to Walter and crumples it.

'Tiffin, and I'd daresay ye'd not object.'

'Curried fowl? The hotter the better.'

'D'ye mortify the flesh today, Joaquim, or will you partake with us?'

'No day is for mortifying,' says Father Ribeiro cheerfully, 'although abstemiousness is to be praised. Today is beautiful, and we have Gideon with us, though not for long. I shall have a most splendid Madeira brought up with the dessert.'

'Then keep the drawing ye've thieved.'

Arm in arm, Walter and Gideon stroll up the beach, laughing, Walter gesticulating to make some point more forcefully, while Ribeiro and O'Rourke – who were that young once, it was in another century – follow with spirits that can never be as light again. But they smile at the boys' backs.

More sand drifts over the twisted corpse of Thomas Veale.

CHAPTER XXVIII

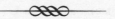

From THE LIN TIN BULLETIN AND RIVER BEE

Wednesday, June 5, 1839
Vol. 2 No. 12

The disinterested spectator who has an eye to historical precedent, having observed the late proceedings and manoeuvrings against each other of Her Majesty's Superintendent of Trade and the Imperial Commissioner, may be pardoned the smile of irony which plays around his lips. On the 24th *ult.* Captain Elliot quit the scenes of his confinement in Canton. On the 30th the little *Larne* (16), Captain Blake, stood out to sea from the roadstead bound for Trincomalee, having delayed her departure well beyond the point of her convenience. As the monsoon is now against her, we regard it as probable to the degree of a certainty that she shall not make Ceylon in under four months. It was known Captain Blake had chafed under the restraints which bound him to this coast and had been eager to weigh in April while the monsoon had not yet changed, but had repeatedly postponed his departure in deference to the wishes of Captain Elliot. We understand that he has left against the expressed desires of the Superintendent in the confidence that Admiral Maitland, the commander-in-chief of the East Indies station, shall support him against the civilian authority.

Now who shall preserve the devoted Britons from the 'cruel, bloody, and lawless savages who populate this empire' (to borrow a phrase from our contemporary) in the absence of the man-of-war brig? But lo! from what unexpected quarter (we do not say undesired) shall protection be afforded? Who is this paradoxical preserver? As the successor of Broke and Nelson dropped below the horizon, whose masts should appear but those of the successors of Decatur – aye, the defenceless Britons have been rescued by their former enemies and fratricides, the Americans! The presence by chance in Macao Roads of the US frigate *Columbia* (60) and *John Adams* sloop (24) as they made their cruise around the world constitutes a guarantee of the safety of person and integrity of property of *all foreigners*. As is her wont (again to borrow from the lexicon of the *Monitor),* America shall extend sanctuary to all victims of tyranny, and not peculiarly to her own citizens and free men.

We do not think it likely that Captain Elliot shall go unsupported for so very long. Once India is furnished with the details of his reports of his late confinement, and the confiscations and indignities attendant upon it, we do not doubt that an expedition shall soon be despatched. His immurement within the Factories shall have provided the good Captain with both opportunity and inclination to wield his pen in the most effective manner. We have it on the best authority that he has recommended the Home Government to request a sum of £5 millions sterling in compensation for the seized opium, to demand the recall and disgrace of Lin, and the opening of new ports along the coast. We much fear that, though such is not at all the Superintendent's intention, these new ports shall be used less as openings for a legitimate and honourable trade than as vantage points for spreading the traffic in poison and the creation of a new class of addicts in regions where demand had never previously existed. Such at least was the object of Gutzlaff and Lindsay on their infamous cruise in the *Sylph* in 1832, with their cargo of Bibles and opium, along the coasts of Fukien and Chekiang.

Lin, we believe, has no suspicion of the hornets' nest he has stirred to get at the tainted honey.

From THE CANTON MONITOR

Thursday, June 20th, 1839

There exists in nature a well-marked phenomenon whereby the hour before the storm is marked by an unnatural quiet. Such an ominous stillness now prevails over the entire delta. As such convulsions of the ether are part of the order of nature; so, too, are they in the little world of man. The price of progress can never be cheap. Civilisation and Christianity may not always find an unobstructed path and, if such proves the case, the forces of darkness and prejudice must be cut down to make a way for the agents of improvement. It is, we would remind our readers, some of whom, following their experience of shifting for themselves, may find the analogy unusually pertinent, impossible to make an omelette without first breaking eggs.

We, it must frankly be owned, cannot wait to see the great Chinese Humpty Dumpty given a forceful shove off his wall of secrecy and deceit and broke all to pieces. Not all the Emperor's men shall put him together again.

It cannot be supposed that the Chinese, in their arrogance and false conviction of superiority, should for a moment imagine that the detested foreigner shall provide the occasion and means of their own betterment. Yet such shall be the case. Once Trade has forced open the doors of the empire, there shall follow on its coat-tails the incontrovertible truths of Christianity and Christ crucified. Nor do we speak solely in a spiritual point of view, for there shall be exposed to the benighted and necessitous masses of this empire cornucopia of cheap and practical manufactures of which they may never even have dreamed. The vast wealth, the burgeoning capital, the useful wares and mighty productive forces of Britain, Europe, and the civilised world, shall be directed to the advantage and benefit of those who have only been accustomed to hurl opprobrious epithets, and worse, at the heads of those who shall transform the mean and burdensome lives they lead in point of comfort and convenience. Lancashire shall yet clothe the heathen Chinaman more cheaply than he may himself. After the storm is the sweet and clear summer's day. We do not doubt it.

FROM A CORRESPONDENT

Sir,

As one of the Britons fortunate enough to have escaped by chance the recent incarceration and cruel treatment in Canton, when I was seeing to affairs in Lin Tin, may I express through your columns the sentiments of my warmest indignation and sympathy for my friends and fellow-countrymen.

Their composure and courage under cruel duress and ill-usage, under hourly threat of death, must evoke outrage and admiration in equal measure.

Should reason for action and redress by the Home Government ever have been wanting, surely it is now not too much to expect Lord Palmerston to bring his attention to bear on the insult offered to flag and representative − not to mention the theft of £2 millions of property.

I have, sir, the honour to be etc.

IRATUS

From THE LIN TIN BULLETIN AND RIVER BEE
Wednesday, July 3, 1839 Vol.2 No.14

(From *Bateman's Northern Intellectual Digest*)

As one of the Poor Commissioners recently appointed to make a study of the laborious classes in this area of England, I, together with the other gentlemen comprising our Board, made up a party to tour the stews of Manchester in which the operatives made their abodes. We proceeded from the centre of the town along straight, broad, and decent thoroughfares until, almost insensibly, the roads and streets became narrowed, winding, and crooked in proportion to the extent of the rubbish and nuisances which infested them and presented such unpleasant, if not insuperable, obstacles to our passage. The new-built offices, mansions, and pleasing houses of the salubrious portion of the town were succeeded by small, mean, and grimy dwellings from the windows of which grey linen was exposed to a sooty air which threatened to render nugatory the patient labours of the launderer. Yet these, it became apparent, were the houses of that upper portion of the artisans who might justly be termed the aristocrats of their class. On turning a corner, we found ourselves in an alley where it was inconvenient for two to walk abreast (as we had been doing), the opposing dwellings and, especially, their upper storeys, being found so close together that the occupants might without undue difficulty have shaken hands across the intervening space and even stepped into their neighbour's bedroom. So near were the roofs that they all but shut out the natural light. A foul odour hung in the air, emanating as well from the interior of the tenements as the heaped rubbish which choked the lane. We arrived now in that quarter where the lowest Irish were accustomed to make their dwelling, directly following their arrival from their native villages. It would be moot whether it would be preferable for them to starve to death by their own empty hearths but in a green and otherwise healthy situation, or to cross the sea and expire of disease in the circumstances in which we discovered them.

A pestilential air overhung those miserable hovels, aggravated as well by the ignorance and insanitary habits of their population as by the unwholesome, and indeed dangerous, situation of the houses. These were built besides the banks of a small river which, difficult as it may be to credit, actually flowed above the level of the buildings, the bed of the stream being of a greater elevation by a few feet than the chimneys of the houses. The damp airs and miasmas of the spot, as may be imagined, would be fully productive of fevers, rheumatism, ague, and pneumonias, a conclusion confirmed by the sound of a hacking cough from the doorway of one of the dwellings, where a woman, who must have been young, cradled an infant in her withered arm. The stream is accustomed to overflow its uncertain banks both in the summer after rains and in the winter when the ice thaws, flooding the street to a depth of a foot.

On instituting enquiries, we ascertained that upwards of three, and often four or five, families might occupy a single cottage, with ten persons residing in a small room, and half that number sleeping in a single bed with no discrimination as to age or sex. The frightful disorders and irregularities which must arise consequent upon the co-mingling of the sexes can only too easily be imagined. Two taps supplied the wants of five hundred souls. There were no sanitary arrangements, waste being thrown into the street. Our informant had been raised in County Mayo and had seen five of her ten children perish in infancy. Her husband was a labourer and navigator, while she had hoped to find employment in a mill.

The fruit of our researches may be discovered in tabulated form in the body of the report.

The city itself may thus be seen as a great drain, sucking down into its maw the very dregs of the urban population and impelling toward it, by an attraction too powerful to resist, the unemployed and wageless of the countryside. Hard as labour might be in the potato- or cabbage-field, it corresponds to a natural cycle of night and day, light and darkness. The agricultural labourer, it is true, sells his time and his body to the landowner yet the town-worker may be said to have sold his soul also. Lit by gas, belching flame and sparks by night or by day, the restless machinery of the factory is never stilled. The provision of an artificial illumination within the shed enables the waged slaves to work by night as well as day and has the tendency of destroying the natural round of toil and rest, the succession of light and dark. The operative in the mill or foundry can have no conception of the state of the world outside, whether brother Sun or sister Moon is in the heaven. To rob men (aye, and women and children, too) of these sensations is surely the worst theft of all – to divest them of their possession of their humanity and to turn them into mere machines, objects. The opium-addict in his daze endures a fate no more pitiable. – ed.

FROM OUR READERS

Mr Editor,

Although I am a loyal and eager *peruser* of your columns and you may find my real name among the list of your subscribers (and contributors), I am made uneasy by the tone of your recent fulminations. Sir, I reprehend them and should be happy to see you repudiate them. The immorality of the opium-trade admits of no debate in my mind, yet I do not concur in the opinion that two wrongs may make a right. Commissioner Lin's recent deeds are culpable on four counts.

Instance the first – the opium confiscated and initially demanded of the importers was not the property of the merchants to surrender but was merely held by them for sale on a consignment basis as *agents*. They had no legal right to surrender it; that resided in their constituents.

Instance the second – the Emperor of China has a most perfect right to formulate such laws as he believes to be in his subjects' interest, but the onus of enforcing them weighs on him, and him alone. He was wrong to attempt to make Captain Elliot their enforcer.

Instance the third – the Imperial Commissioner acted arbitrarily and unjustly in arresting and confining the merchants to the Factories. He had no right to deprive them of their liberty.

Instance the fourth – in refusing to entertain the credentials of Lords Macartney, Amherst, Napier, and now those of Captain Elliot, the Chinese Government closed to itself the possibility of enlisting the British Government's support in forbidding the trade to British subjects. If Captain Elliot were to suppress the trade, he would find himself sued in a British court of law by the importers whose interests he had jeopardised.

I do entreat you, my dear sir, to remember that there are always two sides to a controversy.

PERUSER

These are the specious arguments of the attorney. Lin, to borrow from our contemporary, cannot make his omelette without cracking a few eggs (and there is a fearful aroma of sulphur from not a few of them).

Here is a digest which speaks for itself

OPIUM IMPORTS

Season	Quantity
1800	5,000 chests
1820	6,000 chests
1830	17,000 chests
1838	40,000 chests

This could not be tolerated. How may a ruler leave his subjects in thrall to a thing, a lump of brown sap. Better to be a man's slave than an object's.

From THE CANTON MONITOR

Thursday, August 1st, 1839

Further excesses culminate in bloodshed. At the harbour of Hong Kong an attack by villagers on a British watering-party resulted in one of the sailors slaying a Chinese in self-defence. The attack was altogether unprovoked. The seamen had landed with their casks near a small stream when a group of villagers armed with swords, flails, knives, and picks sallied forth. Some of the watering-party carried sticks with them, but no swords or firearms, and the man Lin was despatched by a chance knock over the head. It is believed Captain Elliot will very properly resent the insult and a punitive expedition, it is to be hoped, shall be sent against the offending hamlet in due course. Watering rights had never been denied in the past either at Kowloon or the waterfall opposite Lamma on Hong Kong island.

Sir,

I have never heard of Bateman's Northern Intellectual Digest. I should be interested to learn if the publication has ever come to your notice.

PERPLEXED

We must confess our own ignorance. We found the Yankee-isms of some of the Poor Commissioners' report passing strange.

From THE LIN TIN BULLETIN AND RIVER BEE
Wednesday, July 31,1839
Vol.2 No. 16

Drunken affray at Hong Kong. Those who hold moderate councils will be dismayed by the latest intelligence of conflict between the Chinese and the English, on this occasion at Kowloon, on the opposite side of the estuary from Macao. A band of sailors, having gone ashore to carouse at the grog-stalls on Chim Sha Shui, became quarrelsome. Owing to the circumstance of the sailors' drunkenness, blows were exchanged with braves from a nearby village, during which encounter an innocent bystander, by name Lin Wei Hei, was bludgeoned to death by repeated blows from an assailant or assailants unknown, but presumed to be one or more English sailors.

Commissioner Lin has demanded that the murderer or murderers be apprehended and surrendered to him for punishment, but it is doubted if Captain Elliot may do so. The enquiries which the Superintendent has instituted point to three or four men as the suspects but he cannot be certain. On the strictly mathematical principles of Chinese justice, a death for a death would satisfy Lin. Any sailor surrendered would expiate the crime in his canon. However, according to the dictates of our justice, Captain Elliot may not surrender an innocent man to die for a guilty.

Lin had been greatly surprised and displeased by Captain Elliot's withdrawal of the British community from Canton and the end of trading. The Imperial Commissioner had fully expected this to resume on the Superintendent's release. The spilling of Chinese blood, innocent blood at that, may try his patience to the limit.

From THE LIN TIN BULLETIN AND RIVER BEE

Wednesday, August 14, 1839
Vol 2 No 17

Captain Elliot's measures unsatisfactory to Lin. Despite every personal effort made by the Superintendent of Trade to apprehend the malefactors at Hong Kong responsible for the murder of Lin Wei Hei, his proposals have failed to meet with the Imperial Commissioner's approval. Three seamen have been arrested and shall be sent home in chains at the change of the monsoon, there to be arraigned and stand trial. It is not known for certain which of the three struck the fatal blow, fatal alike to the villager, Lin, and the hopes of peace, and perhaps it shall never be ascertained. In the meantime Captain Elliot has arranged for the not inconsiderable sum of $2000 to be paid to the relatives of the deceased, a compensation which they have acknowledged as handsome. Lin, however, is reported to be exceeding wroth at the Superintendent's failure to comply with his demand to surrender a prisoner of some kind, his notions of justice being retributive and formal, rather than equitable. In this matter we would support the gallant captain. We know full well the fate of the hapless gunner of the *Lady Hughes* and of our countryman, Terranova, when surrendered to the Chinese for trials whose issues were already decided in the minds of the bigoted tribunal.

We do believe that a descent on Macao by the Chinese, pouring over the Barrier in numbers irresistible by the tiny garrison of Portuguese and Kaffir slaves, is not to be dismissed as a groundless fear. In this case, it would go ill with the Britons who have sought sanctuary there with their oldest ally and, indeed, with the smaller number of Americans, who should by the colour of their skin, let alone their common language, be confused with their cousins.

A tragic relation. The following sad story was confided to me by a native friend who is also a distinguished scholar in his own tradition. A highly placed licentiate of the literary examinations; of the purest morals; upright; sagacious, in an everyday sense as well as regards the working-out of abstruse matters; capable; of a strong will and independent character (as I well knew), yet unusually open and adaptable, his status and position in life had always remained enigmatical to my speculations. Why was he not occupied in administering some populous district when he seemed so eminently equipped to fill the complementary roles of scholar and official? Lesser men than he had been elevated to dizzy heights, nor was it impossible for a man of humble origins but surpassing talents to rise high in the service of his country – there are a hundred Celestial Benjamin Franklins. In the absence of any other explanation, I presumed he had incurred the ill-will of some influential person who had blocked the advancement of what would otherwise have been a promising career. I was proved correct in my surmise, but I had not dreamed the tale could be so shocking.

'I was born in the -th year of the Emperor Chien Lung,' began my friend with a sigh, 'in the town of M-, in the county of L-, in the province of K-.' (And, it may be seen, I have made every effort to conceal his true identity.)

'My father was a tax-farmer. He owned two pawn-shops and held in trust many acres of lineage land.'

We found ourselves seated during the term of this interview in the noble, if perhaps rather cluttered, room in which we were accustomed to hold our conversations. At this time I had known him several years, but had never previously heard (nor did I subsequently hear) him allude to his personal history.

'At the age of eleven I was assigned a personal tutor and began seriously to prepare for the triennial examinations. In my seventeenth year I distinguished myself and overjoyed my father by appearing on the list of successful candidates. I was the youngest of these. We feasted and celebrated many days. My years were still too tender to admit of my being proposed for office, but I joined the ranks of expectant magistrates.

'My father had a business in the county town of Y– and he sent me there to supervise his affairs. During my sojourn there, which grew protracted, I became fast friends with a young man of nearly my years. He was a youth of the most amiable manners, kind disposition, and purity of morals and intellect. He was also a youth of exceeding personal beauty. Alas, his father was a man of profligate and vicious habits who was in the train of rapidly dissipating both his health and the substance of which his family disposed. He undermined his constitution by consorting with low women and was a slave to opium. This greatly troubled my young friend.

'One day I received an urgent message, summoning me to my father's side. I discovered him an invalid, pale of face and emaciated in his body, when all his hair had fallen out. He was fast sinking unto death. I ascertained that he had fallen foul in the transactions of his affairs of the most prominent and powerful family of gentry in the district, among whose numbers were included many office-holders serving in far-flung areas. They had arranged for a hired assassin to waylay and stab my father, doubtless with a baited dagger, to judge by the suppuration and stench of the wound. Shortly, my father expired, having first sworn me to avenge his death.

'I exerted all my literary talents, the remaining wealth of our family, and such worldly acumen as I possessed (alas, little enough at my years then) to bring the malefactors before the tribunal of justice. At length I secured, by dint of bribing the *yamen* runners, the ear of the mandarin. I employed my most winning ways and the most approved stylistic and rhetorical devices to enlist the patronage and support of this magistrate. Later, it transpired that this wretch had all along been in the pay of our family's enemies and my father's murderers.

'At length, after my utmost exertions and at a cost which beggared our estate, I believed I had secured justice and revenge. I proceeded to the county town with all haste and diligence to witness the execution of he who had ordered the slaying of my progenitor. Conceive, then, of my surprise and horror when I saw, bound in a basket and carried to the place of death, my dearest friend!

'The wealthy malefactors had purchased a victim to undergo the penalty so richly merited by the worst of their number. This was my young friend – who voluntarily submitted himself to execution in the stead of the real criminal in order to discharge his family's mounting debts and to provide the drug without which his father would die. His family had been paid a pecuniary reward.

'As the knife fell, I swooned.

'From that moment, my career and prospects in the world were blasted. I left home and commenced my wanderings.'

During this affecting recital my mentor smiled, and his voice was light and gay.

PURSUER

From THE LIN TIN BULLETIN AND RIVER BEE

Wednesday, August 28, 1839

Vol.2 No. 18

Flight of the British community to Hong Kong. How seldom is it that our worst forebodings are borne out in the actuality of the events which unfold, yet it may be seen that in our previous we preached no exaggerated Jeremiad. The very day following the appearance of our organ, Lin acted with firmness and resolution in forbidding the provision of all material supplies, foodstuffs included, to the British at Macao and in commanding the withdrawal of all their native servants. This was to exceed the severity of the measures taken during the 'siege' of the Factories in Canton, when at least those confined had been provided their daily nourishment.

Little after, he placed the gallant Dom Silveira Pinto in circumstances of the gravest embarrassment when he ordered him – under the usual insulting language – to expel all Britons from his little territory. We do certainly have our sympathies enlisted in the Portuguese governor's predicament. On the one hand he is between the Scylla of his hospitable obligations when he is bound to protect his guests, obligation refined and reinforced by his real inclination to aid his country's Oldest Ally, and on the other the Charybdis of his weakness in a military regard, as well as the duty to keep his country neutral in a conflict not of her own choosing, which could jeopardise all her interest in this part of the world. Assuredly, he must answer to Goa for his mistakes, just as Captain Elliot is eventually responsible to Calcutta and then to White-hall and Lord Palmerston.

As matters finished, Captain Elliot had little choice but to retire, doubtless in due season to counter-attack with irresistible force, for at present he has lost even the little *Larne*.

We ourselves were at the Praia but two days previous when we witnessed the affecting spectacle of the Britons' departure, embarking in every and any craft which might fly the British flag. Some of these included barks so tiny as to arouse the worst misgivings as to their safety in the breasts of the Britons' foreign friends (flutterings from which we ourselves were not immune for we do possess English, Irish, and even *Scots* friends who are dear to us), although both parties contrived to conceal such trepidation as they felt. Gallant companions! Would that good men might not be embroiled in this wicked trade. Of temperaments less cold than their late Anglo-Saxon guests (and in several instances friends of many years standing), the Portuguese ladies and gentlemen were many of them in tears. The gentlemen blew their noses, the ladies wept openly and waved salty kerchiefs. Their sympathies grew so warm as to become altogether uncontrollable when there appeared at the quayside three or four English ladies who discovered themselves at this juncture in the most delicate situation which their sex may encompass. One of these ladies had the gravest misfortune to find herself with but two weeks remaining of her term, most conservatively calculated, to run. Such creature comforts as lay within the powers of their American and Portuguese friends to provide were afforded them, Mrs S-, as ever, notable in her great kindness.

We have to say that the weather was inclement, and the barometer continues dropping. A Portuguese navigator of our acquaintance, long versed in the vagaries of the weather around the estuary, doubts that the smallest craft shall complete the scarcely 40 miles' passage across the gulf until the beginning of next month – *if at all*. We trust earnestly he should be mistaken. In the meantime, it is our own fixed intention to visit the harbour of Hong Kong to ascertain the condition of our English friends in their floating refuges.

TO OUR CORRESPONDENTS

The communication signed Post-Meridian has for cogent reasons been ruled inadmissible.

The letter from La Longue Carabine seems to us to make its points accurately and tellingly and shall be printed in our next, together with our reply.

Gossip of the bazaar. It is rumoured that Lin has sent out devious agents and spies into the gambling-houses and the establishments of worse fame in order to take the pulse of the people. Although the Commissioner is, we were ourselves personally impressed as to the circumstance in our brief meeting on the heights of Chuenpi, a man of fearless and irreproachable integrity, who will not swerve from the course he has set himself, he is also conscious that he will accomplish more with the support of the people than without it. One of the agents, we have it on good authority, was none other than Provincial Judge Yeh, an adept at the arts of disguise. To his mortification he discovers that the rabble, though despising the foreigner, are rather annoyed by the closing of illicit sources of income than elevated by the discomfiture of the barbarians. In the hamlets and Ninety-Six Villages outside Canton he finds less feeling against the foreigners than he had hoped. This may surprise the sportsmen among our subscribers!

A stitch in time. The following scandalous story has reached us at the Factories by subterranean but reliable channels. It concerns the family of the wealthy Hong merchant -qua. Into the family the old man's fourth grandson had taken a new concubine, a young girl distinguished alike for her beauty, her modesty, and her intelligence, who deserved a better situation than to be a mistress. Such is life. The young man's father, the second son of old -qua, unbeknown to the patriarch, lusted after his son's paramour from the day she entered the household and longed to know her. He let no occasion pass when he might privily importune her and effect his lewd advances. The virtuous girl spurned his every threat and present, yet dared not inform her master or his grandfather. At length, burning with his lust, the lecher came across the girl in a secluded spot where she plied her needle, and flung himself upon her. She, taken by surprise, and by far the weaker in strength, put up such resistance as she could. Yet, at length, as it must, his weight and ardour prevailed when she found herself flung rudely upon the ground and her clothing in final disarray. The ravisher, making such small adjustment to his own costume as was necessary, was on the point of accomplishing his disgraceful design when she, with great resolution and quickness of mind, discovered that the instrument of her lacy labours might answer the purposes of a weapon and quick as a flash *in penem magno cum impetu confodit hominem et in testiculum.* This latter, unable to contain his agony, shrieked in anguish, thereupon alerting a passing maid to his presence and infamy. Blood-poisoning supervened within days, of which the author of this criminal assault perished.

Unfortunately, his decease presented the wronged concubine in the light of a parricide, the most heinous crime in the Chinese code. It was generally owned that she was virtuous and had acted properly and in self-defence. At the same time her guilt was clearly established. The girl earned great admiration and credit when she spared her family shame and the authorities perplexity by hanging herself on her own girdle. A memorial arch, extolling her virtue, is building in the grounds of the mansion.

PURSUER

Chapter XXIX

Eastman crouches in the bow of the *Sonia*. Through a hole in the low clouds the sun suddenly breaks through, making the sullen sea sparkle. Walter puts a hand over his eyes and squints. Islands spread over the waters on both sides. To starboard is an archipelago of small, low islets with minute beaches of white sand and granitic rocks thrusting into the shallow sea. Beyond are bigger islands, with peaks which are enveloped in cloud. To port is a continuous stretch of land, with hills rising sheer behind the beaches which he assumes must be… 'Lantao!' shouts Remedios obligingly from behind the wheel. Walter had thought it the mainland; they are nearer their destination than he had hoped. The waters which had been bright yellow around Macao have by degrees become less silty and are grey now. Flotsam from the recent bad weather is strewn on the surface and still pitches in a rhythm disquieting to Walter's stomach. He selects a cheroot from his case, prepares to strike a lucifer across the deck, but sees Remedios glaring at him and uses his boot-top. At least there are no bodies on the sea; he had not been looking forward to seeing the half-caste's gloomy prognostications borne out in reality. Most of the British craft seem to have made the crossing safely; only now can stragglers be made out ahead. Or are they? Remedios has steered away from suspicious-looking sails, on one occasion tacking into a little bay to shelter behind a rock. The cannon are double, triple-loaded in the case of the nine-pounder. A schooner called the *Black Joke* was pirated a day or two ago as it crossed to Hong Kong and all but one man murdered – and he has a cropped ear for souvenir.

Now a steep, scrub-covered islet – more like a big green rock than a proper island – looms ahead. They appear to be sailing into a wide anchorage of some kind, with land on both sides, about three miles apart, though whether it is locked by islands or continent, Walter is unsure. It takes an interminable time as the rock grows bigger. Finally, they pass it and descry masts ahead. They are sailing into a magnificent harbour, which nature might have designed for the purpose of a shelter. On each side the land has closed in to about the width of a mile and a half in the narrowest place. The ships and boats are concentrated in the very centre of the anchorage, with tenders scurrying between the craft and from ship to shore.

'The *George* is the ship we seek. Do you know her?'

Remedios takes no notice whatsoever, but spreads his bare feet wider at the wheel. A totem-pole, thinks Walter, would be better company. However, the water is flat calm and a pleasant green, his stomach is better, and he cannot stop his spirits rising. This is one of the most beautiful and romantic spots he has ever seen. Only a few score miles from the flat, alluvial plains of the delta counties, the jagged peaks, valleys, and rugged rockfalls make a wonderful refreshment for the eye and imagination. Walter looks for an introductory sentence -Few places in all our peregrinations can have been productive of such an effect of...

He is interrupted by a whistle from Remedios, who points to a vessel Walter is not far out in imagining a brig but is, in fact, a snow some hundred yards ahead. In answer to Walter's unspoken question and obvious puzzlement, the Portuguese half-caste makes the gesture of a man extending a telescope to his eye. Walter shakes his head. Remedios grimaces in disgust. He keeps his course. A figure grows at the taff-rail of the snow, head and body still one black dot. A few minutes later the face lightens and several minutes after that Walter sees the hands in front of the head, holding the telescope. The hands wave. 'Now this fellow can obviously see me,' mutters Walter, 'but God damn it if I can see him.' He wonders – did Remedios mean him to produce his own telescope from the baggage or was he indicating that they were under observation? Surely, no man's unaided eyesight could be that keen? As he stares curiously at Remedios's tough, brown face, Walter feels unsure. But now the taciturn master utters his first word of the entire journey.

'*George,*' he says succinctly, pointing at the snow. Ten minutes later, Walter may make out the faded gilt lettering on the bow, by the figure-head of the late King. 'Extraordinary,' he says in disbelief. The fellow has eyes as sharp as the kites and buzzards which swoop and hover over the harbour – richer gleanings for their prey than at any time in the harbour's history. Walter tries to count the vessels, and can only get to forty-seven before he becomes confused. Over by the triangular peninsula on the mainland six war-junks huddle together, looking, despite their flamboyant pennants and scallop-edged banners, like a flock of frightened sheep. To Walter's surprise, he can see in splendid isolation two men-of-war, distinctive by their black and white sides, holding themselves aloof from the craft they protect. So Elliot is no longer without a stick.

The figure on the *George* waves again. Walter returns the signal. Harry O'Rourke cups his hands, bellowing in a deep bass which echoes around the anchorage and sends the gulls squawking. 'Repel boarders! Boston redskins, damme!'

Walter shakes his head with disfavour. 'Barely eleven in the morning and in his cups already,' he mutters.

'*D'ye bring your scandal sheet – I've nothing to read.*'

'Now darn him for an old fool. *Be quiet, sir!*'

Walter is furious, but he can't help laughing. Any hope of a secret, even a discreet, arrival has disappeared with the startled sea-gulls.

Heads turn on the decks of neighbouring vessels, faces appear at port-holes.

'There are those who'd flog ye round our little fleet, Mr Yankee, keel-haul you.'

'*I am no damn Yank -*' Walter's indignant denial is quickly swallowed. 'Old buffoon,' he mutters, grinning very much despite himself.

Remedios brings his beloved *Sonia* expertly alongside the bigger snow. He lets his deck-boy take the wheel, handing first Walter and then his bag on to the *George's* gangway. The touch of his hard, muscled hand is surprisingly friendly. Walter nods, before taking the steps of the gangway in athletic bounds. Harry stands back as first valise, then Walter, drop on to the deck. He has a flask in his hand and his breath smells of toffee and toast.

'Good God, you are heavily in liquor, sir.'

'My dear boy, there is nothing else to do.'

Ah Cheong appears, grinning, and takes the bag below, first hefting its weight with insolent suggestiveness. He recognises it as one of his master's. 'Thank'ee my lad. Our haste was so precipitate I quite forgot such fresh linen as I possess, and most of the articles of a gentleman's toilet.'

'You will find all you requested, and some other comforts besides.'

'Too kind, my boy. You have an old hack's gratitude.'

Harry appears genuinely touched by the young American's solicitude, which, in the nature of friendships, warms and softens Walter in turn. O'Rourke takes him by the elbow and steers him round to the mainland-facing side (the *George* points east, away from Canton). Walter throws his cigar-stub over the side, to be met a moment later with a howl of rage. He peers over the side. Assorted bum-boats bob around the snow. Some sell fruit and vegetables; others eggs. In this instance, it has been his peculiar misfortune to have landed his smouldering butt in the laundry-woman's washing. An angry Tanka girl jabbers at him in a dialect which Pursuer, for one, has yet to master but the shirt she holds up, with its scorched hole, needs no interpretation.

'Merciful heavens!'

'I trust it is not Captain McBride's, or you will be thrown

overboard.' Harry leads Walter to a companionway and they descend. The door to Harry's cabin is open: narrow leather berth, folding table, chair, chest, and...giggling barefoot Tanka girl, who drops a shirt and flees, horny soles hissing on the polished wood. 'I see,' Walter comments drily, 'that certain consolations have followed you to this lonely spot.'

'My shirts, sir, are always clean, which is a good deal more than can be said for Ribeiro.'

'That is an extraordinary answer. I expect your sins are scarlet – as the lips of that portrait. Good Lord! – it's the same girl.'

'You are an American and so undemocratic? As a subject, the washer-girl is equal to the grandest duchess.'

'Say you?'

Harry sweeps out of the cabin, or intends to, but the magisterial gait turns into a lurch, and he has to grab the door for support. 'I have yet to acquire m' sea legs.'

'Just so,' says Walter grimly. 'Speaking for myself, I allow this is the most sheltered stretch of water for hundreds of miles around.'

'Well, we are confined to life aboard. Elliot will tolerate no recurrence of the incident with the unfortunate villager. Watering-parties only may land and those under strict discipline. There is a limit to the views I may contrive of yonder peak.'

'Imagine yourself transported, magically, to its crest, and looking down on our puny masts and tiny hulls. That would be an altered perspective.'

'Now I wonder if it's you who's in liquor.'

'Well, I allow I am not the first artist in point of eminence on these shores, far from it, but I'll engage to be the first to take that view to canvas.'

'You may have the climb and that willingly.'

They have come to the end of the main deck of the snow, where Ah Cheong has placed two stools and a small table. Walter is somewhat taken aback by Harry's presumption; presumably, though, the master is an old crony. Following a tiffin, in which ship's victuals do not appear, Walter indulges in a cigar (to be stubbed out on a plate). This relaxes his bowels and involves him in a visit to the heads – one of the inconveniences of shipboard life, despite other ingenious shifts to render existence comfortable – after which a nap seems attractive.

When he awakes, the sun is setting magnificently, over the narrows two miles from the *George*. He goes on deck, to find O'Rourke standing in the chains. In silence, they admire the natural splendours.

Slowly, the red orb floats behind the jagged ridge of mountains seven miles distant on the mainland. Harry sighs. The tropical dusk is short-lived, its transitions brutal. In a matter of mere minutes they are in darkness. Lights glow and twinkle on the hulls and spars of the other vessels, so that the fleet appears as a string of floating constellations to match the sparks in the heavens.

Wordlessly, they absorb the spectacle. And on the other ships, hundreds of eyes share the same sight. Yet in the enveloping night, their solitude is complete. Eventually Harry is first to break the spell, clearing his throat.

'D'ye have in mind some grand coup, boy?'

'I expect that is better left to the gallant little Captain and his marines. Besides, as an American I am a citizen of a neutral Republic.'

'No,' says Harry impatiently. 'I refer to your own concerns. Your journal, sir.'

'Yes?'

'Your rival, it will I trust not have escaped your attention, has ceased to publish. Not enjoying the advantage of your nationality, he has no place situated on *terra firma* upon which he may establish the press he has, nevertheless, preserved.'

'True, we are a few dozen copies augmented in our fortnightly sale.'

'Bah! Petty! Do something large, while you may accomplish it. During the *Monitor's* "eclipse", extend the circulation of your own. Here is the fleet – time hangs on the hands of all. Present copies of the *Lin Tin Bulletin and River Bee* to every ship's saloon, *gratis*. As ye sow, as Ribeiro might say, so shall ye reap.'

'The expense!'

'My dear sir, to the devil with the expense. It is not so much a speculation as investment in your own business. I have no doubts your Yankee employers built their fledgling house on just such measures. They did not want for boldness or imagination in their early days, though in nicety they were perhaps deficient.'

Eastman ponders. He has, packaged against salt and damp on the *Sonia,* two gross *Lin Tin Bulletin and River Bee* which he had been looking forward to selling at some small profit, a peculiar satisfaction of the trip across the estuary being that it should yield both dollars and 'copy'. He supposes Harry is right, though, the old fellow a lot shrewder than he would like people to think.

'I allow you have some reason. Say, did you give free sittings in order to attract more commissions?'

O'Rourke scowls. 'In Calcutta the damned...' he begins, then decides to keep trade secrets to himself. 'It is none of your damned business,' he growls. 'How many of the damned scandal-sheet d'ye have?'

Walter tells him.

'Half a dozen apiece for the large vessels, then, and a brace or so for the small. Whet their damned appetites, but don't slake em.'

'Just so. 'Tis the scarcity of the commodity which creates its demand, if you didn't know.'

'Well, this should be a rare Bee. Let its arrival be clothed in suitable mystery.'

'Ha! After you acted the part of town-crier this morning!'

'Not so much mysterious as *dramatic.* Yes, drama is of the essence.' Harry sticks out his bottom lip pugnaciously. He reflects a moment. 'There's a row-boat under the stern. We'll take her to your pirate's boat and take on the load, pursuant to which we'll pay our courtesy calls and leave a few visiting-cards.'

'Harry, you should have been a theatrical manager, that or a general.'

'Certainly I was passed over for the Academy.'

Strolling carelessly past the snow's other passengers, who line the rail in the darkness, they come to the stern. Dubiously, Walter regards the rope. It appears to end somewhere in mid-air. He cannot see the boat, but the cable yields to his tug.

'Down you go, young fellow.'

Shaking his head at his own lunacy, Walter throws his cheroot over the side and puts a long leg over the rail. Harry sees him sliding down. There is a faint bump as the boat hits the stern, followed by a muffled curse. A moment later Harry hears a low whistle. The old artist looks around and proceeds cautiously to the gangway amidships. He is about to slide down the steps when a friendly hand claps him on the shoulder.

'You bear up well, Mr O'Rourke.' It is the captain of the ship.

'Fairly enough, Captain. We are well provided for comforts, and it's a secure anchorage.'

'Aye, and a noble one. As to secure, we are protected from the elements, but from man...'

'I believe we need not fear for our throats being cut while we sleep.'

'Stranger things have happened while at sea.'

Harry grunts, not desiring to prolong the conversation. The captain, though, has a different mind and exchanges remarks with an increasingly perfunctory O'Rourke for another five minutes. At length the old salt stumps off. A taciturn man himself, he is drawn out by O'Rourke's own brusqueness. Many years ago, Harry committed a dead daughter's likeness to canvas. It lives in the captain's cabin.

'You were a darned unconscionable long time keeping a fellow waiting.'

'Never mind that now, pull to the *Sonia*.'

Remedios already has his boat-hook out as they arrive. Again Eastman marvels at the keenness of his vision, which seems able to cope with dazzle and gloom alike. It is a moment's work to rip open the two bales of newspapers with Remedios's wicked hook. The half-caste master, who seems intuitively to have ascertained their plan, uses the sacking (Eastman had been going to discard it) to muffle the rowlocks. But he will not leave the *Sonia,* much as they would like his services. 'I reckon,' says Eastman, 'that our friend is no novice where this kind of work is concerned, though I have a notion it was poison he circulated in the past.'

'Do you pull, my boy, and I will do the throwing.'

'Directly.'

They work from east to west, approaching the ships from under their bows. O'Rourke grips the anchor-chains for support, while Eastman steadies the oars. Only once does O'Rourke fail to find the deck, and that is when he lobs too hard and the packet falls into the sea on the other side of the ship.

'Gad!'

Eastman giggles.

'Trust in God, my boy, and keep your powder dry.'

Lights and heads in the saloon-ports show the passengers are at their dinners. They appear cheerful. Once or twice they see the silhouettes of the watch on deck, but they are not spotted themselves. 'Deuced poor vigilance,' grumbles O'Rourke, who should hardly be complaining. Steadily, they bombard the fleet, not neglecting the stragglers even if it entails a stiff row. They have been too enthusiastic in their early distributions and must be parsimonious now – two copies for each ship.

Doubling the stern of a schooner, O'Rourke hisses, 'Back up, back up.' Creaking and splashing, a boat comes. Eastman lays their boat alongside the schooner. They wait for the picket-boat to pass. The noise and ragged strokes indicate that it is a merchant crew, rather than a man-of-war's boat – the bosun would ply his rope-end mercilessly, tears would come to the lieutenant's eye.

O'Rourke gestures Walter to go forward. With great care Eastman dips an oar below the surface and pulls gently. The bow pokes out under the schooner's stern, Harry lying flat. He signals all clear. Walter rows towards a group of smaller vessels near the island side of the harbour. Harry takes several good swigs from his flask; a cigar is out of the question for Walter. However, he accepts the offer of some brandy from Harry. Which may help account for what follows.

'That's the *Red Rover,* damn it,' says O'Rourke in a normal voice.

'Quiet, you old villain.'

Eastman knows the vessel in question is one of William Jardine's most celebrated opium-clippers. O'Rourke grins malevolently, reminding Walter of his hideous expression above a ladle of burning brandy. At a Hogmanay, was it? It must have been more than four years ago. How time has wings.

'You confounded young fool, it houses the press of the *Monitor* and its conductor.'

'God damn it!'

'Yes!'

'If I had an auger, I'd bore a hole in her bottom. How many papers have we? We should give him extra rations and food for thought.'

Harry ties string around two bundles instead of one, but then Eastman seizes paper and knife from him. He leaps for the *Red Rover's* netting, rocking the row-boat violently and causing Harry to fall back. The old fellow barks his shins excruciatingly on the thwarts, but can only relieve himself by screwing up his face in agony.

Jesus, Mary, Mother of God, he swears mentally.

Walter's leg disappears over the rail.

'The young fool, he'll get us a volley of musket-balls for our trouble.'

Loud voices drift down to the water.

A curtain is raised from a port-hole, releasing a yellow stripe of light.

O'Rourke ducks quickly.

There is laughter on deck. A glowing cigar-butt falls into the water by the boat. Harry hears what sounds like Eastman's voice. More laughter. Footsteps recede on deck. A moment later Eastman is in the boat again.

'God save the Queen!' he says rather breathlessly.

O'Rourke pushes off. 'Ye madcap young divil,' he says, stress bringing the older, native Mayo to the surface. Eastman pulls hard, stirring phosphorescence around the tips of the oars, as if they were giant lucifers. Drink and elation lend his arms strength.

'Ye young dog, what did ye do in actuality?'

Walter sniggers. 'The paper is pinned fast to the mainmast, "with a poignard". Did you hear me pass pleasantries in the authentic accents of Edinburgh?'

Harry has another go at his flask. 'Young fool,' he says with admiration.

'Ahoy! Who goes there?'

In the darkness they have come too near a black shape which turns out to be a man-of-war. *'Answer, friend or foe.'*

'Row, damn you, your back into it.'

There come a flash and bang from the deck of the frigate.

'Jesus preserve us! Faster – or it will be grape from the thirty-two-pounder we'll be after receiving.'

Now Walter sends the little boat flying along the water – he wishes it were a Meridian racing-skiff and Gideon pulling. The man-of-war does not seem to be troubling to launch a boat, and perhaps they believe them to be a bum-boat, rather than Chinese naval incendiaries. At length, they reach the *Sonia,* where Remedios literally and figuratively takes them by the scruff of the neck and shoves them below deck. At dawn he rows O'Rourke back to the *George,* where the old artist surprises his fellow-passengers when they find him already seated at the breakfast table and well into a second plate of eggs.

From THE LIN TIN BULLETIN AND RIVER BEE

Wednesday, September 11, 1839

Vol.2 No.19

Eligibility of the harbour and island of Hong Kong. It may astonish those of our readers who find themselves presently in Macao, but perhaps not the smaller number whose station is still Canton, that it is our considered judgement that our British cousins in their floating hotels enjoy a more eligible position than do we. We were mightily taken with Hong Kong when we paid the *Fragrant Harbour* our first visit the week previous. No scene could be grander, and we declare that we should be surprised to find an anchorage more picturesque existing at any part of the world. At both west and east ends (the visitor from Macao or Canton approaches from the west) there are narrows before the roadstead widens again to a stretch in excess of one mile. The eastern end of the harbour is the true neck of the bottle. On the starboard side of the Canton boat is the island of Hong Kong, with its precipitous mountain. This is entirely bare, of rock, and attaining, it is calculated by triangulation, a height of nearly 2000 feet above the level of the sea. The shore below this is very narrow and confined, with wild ravines and rockfalls extending behind. As one proceeds east, he encounters a long valley, almost entirely under paddy, with some fruit-orchards and a hamlet two miles off at its end. A stream meanders through this glen where it discharges into the sea. Water-buffalo may be observed in the fields. The valley thus resembles an amphitheatre, with hills and mountains rising steeply on its three sides. Beyond, the interior of the island can best be described as a jumble of wild hills and maze of steep ravines, with one succeeding the other in bewildering disarray. Land property shall never comprise the wealth of this island, but its waters represent a liquid capital. The harbour is both deep and clear and, we assure our readers, different altogether from the turgid and shallow bay of Macao.

We counted seven and fifty sail as we came into the harbour, exclusive of the Chinese war-junks. These are anchored near the spit of the mainland known locally as the Bird Beak Peninsula. Here is also to be found the city of Kowloon (rather, a dirty village) with its mandarin and lousy soldiery. We are given to understand there are two or three fisher-settlements on the south side of Hong Kong. We maintain a close correspondence with our friend in Hong Kong, and shall take pride in printing the latest and most accurate intelligence from the island.

FROM OUR READERS

Sir,

I am certainly no friend of yours and, in a particular regard, no lover of your countrymen. It has, therefore, provided great amusement to me to perceive how during these summer months you Americans have aided us, the British, and more especially, us the Opium-Traders, while your own organ has also been of inestimable value and usefulness. We may fairly describe you and Commissioner Lin both as our most sworn and mortal foes, yet it is difficult to say which of you has aided us the most! Lin, by destroying the surplus stocks of opium, a veritable mountain which overhung our little economy, at a stroke restored equilibrium to the market and raised the profits and prices of the importer! True, Canton and the environs of the estuary are too warm for the smuggler now (as the boats of the Royal Navy also prohibit his movements), but the numerous bays and coves further north, even to the province of Fukien, offer pastures new where a ship's cargo may be disposed of in a matter of hours.

As to you and your fellow-countrymen, Mr Editor, I had long purchased your *Bee* (and, sir, you appear to have but one in your bonnet) for the very good reason that you carried the most recent and reliable informations as to prices and stocks in the Outer Waters. In this regard, your eighth and ultimate page outshone all your competitors, including those of organs devoted to the opium interest! Now what a paradox was this!

I believe the British Chamber of Commerce and our president, Mr Scott, owe a motion of our best thanks to our American cousins for their readiness in getting out our teas and silks for us this summer season. At first, as we watched from our refuge in Macao our American friends stealing the business which would otherwise have come to us, we were envious. We gnashed our teeth. Then, as it became apparent we might remit the profits of our opium in the forms of teas and silks in American bottoms, we rejoiced. We shook our rivals by the hand, not the throat. I understand one million and a half sterling of British trade has safely left the estuary under the protection of the American flag. Nor did the most pious Quaker house scruple to ship a British cargo.

In short, Mr Editor, with enemies like you, I do not need friends.

HONGKONGIENSIS

As to the veracity of our correspondent's allegations and the reliance which may be set upon his facts, we regret to state that they are unimpeachable. Yet different minds, from the same evidence, will often proceed to conclusions which are entirely at odds. Not at any time has it been our policy as conductor of this newspaper to cast any impediment in the path of the legal trade. Profit in itself is not dishonourable, rather the reverse, as indicative of the frugality and enterprise of the capitalist. We were glad to see the British trade continue in American bottoms — we would not wish to see even the speculator in drug ruined. It is true we printed the best Prices Current on this coast — has Hongkongiensis forgotten that his 50 cents still enabled us to print his copy? We find his gloating tone as offensive as it is despicable, but would not wish to deprive him of his fortnightly reading. May Free Trade and Free Press go together, with the latter tending to curb the propensity to excess of the former.

BIRTHS

At Hong Kong, aboard the *Governor Findlay,* Horace Bates master under God, to Mr and Mrs Wilkinson a son, Daniel. Three days previous on the 30th *ult.* to Mrs Grimshaw, twin girls, aboard the *Cowasjee Family.*

COMPENDIA. From time to time we shall, as the whim takes us, compile a glossary of Eastern terms and other curiosities. The subjoined two entries are especially for the benefit of our friends and readers in the harbour of Hong Kong.

Flying fish. These extraordinary creatures, actually scaly denizens of the deep and subjects of Neptune, are possessed, like the members of the feathered tribe, of wings, or, more accurately, large pectoral fins which, when the fish agitates his muscular body and tail in flight, or simple joy of his watery existence, are spread and act as support with the

440

consequence that a simple leap of a few feet into the foreign element of air may be extended into a *flight* of up to 50 yards and beyond even. So nervously and rapidly do they soar that they may easily arrive on the highest deck of the biggest ship, where they land with a *flap* and a *rustle,* their fins spread like the pages of any book. When dissected some species are found to have eight of these. They make a tasty and interesting accompaniment to breakfast when found by surprise on the deck. We have it on the best authority that a shoal were present in the harbour of Hong Kong but ten days ago. We trust they enlivened not a few morning refreshments. Scarcely admitting of belief, one had impaled itself, such was the force of its flight, in the mainmast of the *Red Rover.*

Stinkpots. These count among the most effective weapons in the scanty naval arsenal of which the Chinese dispose. Properly speaking, they are not grenades as we know them, for they are unfurnished with fusees and do not explode. Rather, they smoulder and give off clouds of noxious smoke which blind the enemy and confuse him, and, in a confined space, may even asphyxiate. When tossed in sufficient quantities down, or indeed *up,* on to an adversary's decks they contribute greatly to his dismay and consternation. The ladrones or pirates who infest this estuary place heavy reliance upon them in close-quarter fighting and, our colleague informs us, there is quite a little manufactory of them at a piratical village in the large and as yet unnamed bay to the north-east of Hong Kong island. Also in a road of Our Lady in Macao. Perhaps the skirmishers who stole among the British fleet in Hong Kong roadstead ten days ago and were fired on for their pains by the watch of the *Volage* were furnished with such projectiles or similar. We warrant the smoke can sting, as well as stink.

Chapter XXX

Christmas is coming. How soon a year makes its revolution as you come to maturer years. For Harry O'Rourke, of Mayo, Calcutta, Macao, and now of a floating address which can only be fixed by latitude and longitude, it will be his thirty-eighth in the estuary; for Joaquim Ribeiro, native of the Alentejo in central Portugal, his forty-first. It does not need a Jesuit mathematician to see that the artist and the priest have resided in China longer than their two young friends have lived *in toto*. Harry's Christmases, his New Years, his birthdays pass in a blur not only of alcohol but speed. He cannot remark them. Father Ribeiro, for whom probably, but not certainly, the anniversaries are suffused with Christian significance, the cycle adds up to a litany for a deepening vocation. The dates come as reminders from the real world, ghostly echoes which penetrate, just, the particular chamber wherein he grapples with those elusive, insubstantial issues of correspondence and meaning which, even as he seizes them, recede into a redundant cul-de-sac of history. The world goes on. Issues fail to be resolved, questions answered. They simply cease to matter or are posed in a subtly different manner, which shifts the terms of the entire problem. The river curves round the obstacle, cutting it off and turning it into an island. For Ribeiro, though, the dates of the religious festivals still constitute a life-line – to familiarity, to childhood, to sanity. Gideon is less balanced; Gideon does not work to fulfil God's destiny but for the intrinsic interest of what he studies. The years go slowly for him, at present.

Christmas 1839, though, even for the older men, extends itself. It is a lull. The British still float in Hong Kong harbour, Lin still believes he has got the better once and for all of the hated smuggler, and Captain Elliot and the foreign communities wait for the reinforcement and retribution they correctly foresee as inevitable. If the workings of history can be likened to one of the 'sing-songs', the mechanical toys so popular with bribed mandarins, and its developments to the pendulum which controls the artefact's movements, then the lever has described its arc and our actors are caught in that moment of pause, of illusory stasis, in which momentum in one direction has ended and another beat has yet to begin.

Still, there are larger moments, not apprehended at the time but perceived only in retrospect. A big wheel, in all senses, is associated with the pendulum's steady swing, but this in turn is meshed with tiny cogs, and the smaller the cog, the more frantic its motions.

For Walter Eastman, particularly, the span of his life is measured in fourteen-day increments. Tick-tick-tick. One of the ineluctable nuisances of producing a periodical newspaper of a certain size is that it may not be tailored to fit events, so much as events must be dovetailed to fit its stereotyped column space which, depending on what has to be inserted, appears alternatively as a voracious acreage or a ridiculously finite allotment. These eight pages for Walter exact the same obedience his body has to pay the laws of gravity. Each week, no matter what happens, whether the world falls to pieces or all is stagnant, is celebrated in precisely the same quantity of print. No 'extra' for him, without losing control of the journal's precarious finances; certainly the subscribers would not tolerate less; and the type could not very well be smaller. Vol.2 No.21, for instance, of November 9, 1839, barely did justice to the excitements of the 3rd when Captain Elliot, aboard *Volage,* in company with *Hyacinth,* sailed for the Bogue forts to demand the withdrawal of the Chinese war-junks there anchored.

Elliot did not fear the ancient cannon of the junks so much as the fire-hulks which might be turned on the merchant fleet in Hong Kong during the hours of darkness. Even Walter admitted the justice of the Traders' fears – confusing for the editor of the *Lin Tin Bulletin and River Bee,* but then Harry O'Rourke was one of those who risked being fried.

Two pages of the newspaper were hardly enough for the dramatic, but third-hand, account of the naval action which followed.

Summary: starboard broadside from the light frigates,

followed by turn-about and port broadside.

Score: one junk detonated spectacularly, three sunk, two beached.

British casualties: nil.

An unfortunate (for Walter) outcome of the engagement is that the harbour's floating refugee population is able to put pressure on Elliot (temporarily popular again) to allow them on shore. They deposit stores, cache arms, improvise a defensive battery, build a palisade or two. During this flurry, the editor of the *Canton Monitor* lands his press, intact, on the most level part of Hong Kong's irregular shoreline, erects his machinery, and constructs a wall-less mat-shed structure to shelter it. Obviously, he doesn't lack copy or the inclination to overcome any little difficulties like rain, moth, vermin, pilferers, mud, or insects; in fact, the only difficulty is in restraining some of the pent-up vitriol. Within hours, counter-battery fire is being organised to descend on the head of the conductor of the hated *Bee*.

As the *Monitor* (the name presently lacks quite the effect of the iron-clad connotations it will acquire in thirty years' time) makes a new beginning, roles are reversed. Advantages Walter enjoyed are now passed to the rival. Thus, the *Monitor* from now on will get its blow in first: they decide to print on Monday and appear on Tuesday, as neatly pre-empting Walter as he did them. Walter is now wedded to Wednesday. Given that the ensuing months will very likely throw up more news to report than was formerly the case, this is a formidable advantage. In the times of peace the *Bee* was never in the position to exploit it fully.

The first copy of the *Canton Monitor*, which the editor has regretfully decided not to retitle the *Hong Kong Phoenix,* comes to Walter's notice on a Thursday, January 9th, 1840, to be precise.

'Well,' he says, 'I'm a Dutchman.'

Ridley, who in earlier days would quite possibly have been decapitated as the harbinger of ill tidings, smirks. 'Some are selling even in Canton and it was circulating extensively on the Praia when I landed but an hour previous. I calculate it has quite undone you in the harbour of Hong Kong.'

'Thank you, Jonathan,' says Eastman drily. 'I am indebted for your diagnosis. I expect the ailing patient will die, unless I perform some feat not far removed from the plane of the miraculous.'

'Oh, don't get so darned hot. Yours is the better rag, no doubt of it, but the other villain gives them what they want to read. Not that I didn't see the tale of the needle being extensively circulated.'

'A story with a point. It was the devil's own work to get it out of Master Chase.'

'You will need to mix spice of that kind with your fare. The circumstance that there is no opium-trading during the blockade by the Royal Navy does you no service. Formerly, we all bought the *Bee* for its eighth page, but there is no need now.'

'So you are saying that the prosperity, no, the very existence of my newspaper is most intricately bound up with the fortunes of the drug-traffic? That my success, if I have it, in extirpating the trade will be the very means of my undoing?'

'Say, that's smart!'

'Bah!'

'Bah away, if it does your spleen good. Here's a packet from your pard'ner. What he does and the parts he gets to are a mystery to all. I trust he's no shirker.'

'I'll allow he is no such thing. Take a chair, while I finish imposing upon our readers.'

From THE LIN TIN BULLETIN AND RIVER BEE
Wednesday, February 12, 1840
Vol. 3 No. 4

Latest from Ceylon per Artemis. We have it on the best authority that an armament is preparing at the Cape to chastise the Chinese for their recent misdemeanours in exercising their rights to suppress a contraband trade. St Helena is being stocked with the requisitions of the Quartermaster-General, while the naval magazine at Trincomalee is being emptied of rope, canvas, round-shot, biscuit, rum, salt junk, and powder. Arrack will have to be provided from India to supplement the West Indies rum, which is in short supply.

Home regiments shall not be despatched in the entirety of the force; rather a sepoy army shall be formed, leavened with a few British regiments. Mentioned are the 18th Royal Irish, and the 92nd Regiment of Foot, and, among Indian forces, Robinson's Horse and Thorpe's Artillery. Three transports shall be sent from England, probably in the spring to catch the weathering of the monsoon. We would send those lumbering boxes earlier, even now. As to the wisdom of sending even three ships of home troops, we reserve our judgement. It shall surely be better to despatch seasoned troops, inured to the hardships of weather and the pestilences of the east, than the rosy-faced bumpkins of Oxfordshire or Somerset, who shall drop as plentifully as the sere leaves of autumn.

The naval forces, without doubt, will be the most important part of the expedition. The *Wellesley,* it is said, shall be the flagship of the commander, though the smaller sloops of war and brigs of the East Indies station should be more useful in a practical point of view in an assault on Canton. Perfectly adapted to the task would be the Company's armed steamers, but these may not be able to be spared from the Indian Presidencies and their projected campaign in Burma. We believe the *rendez-vous* of the forces shall be Singapore.

That the campaign in China shall assume the character of a punitive expedition rather than *la guerre à outrance,* we cannot allow ourselves to doubt for a moment. The very timing of the expedition confirms this supposition. How convenient that hostilities should commence at the very end of the trading season in Canton! The fear of Lord Palmerston must be that in humiliating the mandarins he should destroy the very fabric of government in China and lose all the profits Britain stood to make from an opened trade and a market for the manufactures of Manchester and Birmingham. A mere retributive and deterrent exercise would suffice, together with the exaction of a reparation for the expenses of the expedition.

Good may come from evil, if the *casus belli* of the war,

opium, shall be responsible for opening the door to this vast country. We shall see.

From a correspondent resident in New York. Great interest has been aroused consequential upon the invention of a new system or code of communications and signals made by a gentleman who is an inhabitant of this city. The system appears altogether more adaptable in a mechanical point of view, speedier, and less cumbersome than the arrangements of flags devised by Chappe and Marryat which are presently used by land and sea. Although at first sight the alphabet of our inventor, which is arranged upon a system of dots and dashes repeated in various and ingenious combinations of ways, might appear excessively difficult and complicated, a short period of application results in the operator acquiring an easy familiarity with, and even a fluency in, the conventions of the system. As well as possessing a written notation, which may be written thus —• or —•—, the code may be employed as an optical system, not as separate flags, but where a dot becomes a short signal and a dash a long. In this application, it may be used in conjunction with a lamp or a mirror. The advantage of the former, which gives the entire system a great superiority over others, is that messages may be despatched by night or in conditions of poor visibility. The speed of this system when two skilled operators may engage each other in what may be described as a conversation is said to be far in advance of others. Of course, the whole system still relies upon the human eye, aided or unaided by a glass, but its inventor is said to be desirous of conducting experiments by which messages may be sent in this code in the form of electrical charges, or small galvanic shocks, of greater or lesser duration as the case may be, along a cable. It is hoped that such a system would continue to operate in all conditions and, we have it on the best authority, messages sent in this way might be received instantaneous with their despatch at a distance of tens of miles.

447

Samuel B. Morse was formerly a portrait-painter of this city, educated at Yale College, and also a professor of art in New York. He studied as a young man at the feet of the great painters in London, but is an American by birth.

HERMES HERMETICUS

———❦❦❦———

We reproduce below the subjoined article (in translation) which appeared in the *Free Press of Timor* in the November previous. We are indebted to our Portuguese translator and, if he finds his rendering altered in a small way for felicity's rather than accuracy's sake, we know he will not take it amiss as a slight to either his cloth or his scholarship.

THE ARTICLE

We pay a salute and a homage to the awakened morn of conscience! There has come to our notice the noble cries of a younger brother we did not know we possessed! In Macao there prints a journal of knowledge and, more, of edification and moral instruction entitled the *River Bee*. This most esteemed and invaluable production, whose modest guise and habit belies the worth of its contents, appears by the week *(sic – ed.)* Single-handedly, the young editor, and whatever assistants he may call upon, inveigh against the injustice and iniquities of the opium trade which has stained his fellow-countrymen's *(sic)* hands with such deep disgrace. We call him young, for the exuberance and energies of his organ are those of no graybeard. To be veracious, he may impart many unique instances of the habits of the Chinese (of whom we may number a portion of emigrants and indentured labourers here) which casts no very favourable light on the morality of those he champions. It is interesting to note that the very anti-clerical tone of his earlier effusions has been succeeded by a less hostile feeling towards the missionaries, particularly those of the True Church.

We write this under the conviction that our valiant

contemporary neither anticipates nor desires a public recognition and thanks of his good works, nevertheless we feel it incumbent as a duty upon us to bestow some encouragement and mark of esteem of his worth upon him from across the ocean and islands which separate our colonies. We do find the terms of his newspaper rather costly than excessively modest. However, we shall send him, gratis, numbers of our own as they appear. We do not, of course, design by this to solicit copies of his own in return.

To all which we may only reply, 'Obrigado.' The next ship bound for the East Indies shall carry copies of our own organ destined for our generous contemporary.

Contradictory nature of the Chinese. The subjoined two anecdotes reveal the paradoxical character of the Chinese, who, in their slavish thrall to superstition and their extreme worldliness, are at one and the same time both credulous and cynical to the extreme degree.

The first story. A stranger visited an oracle celebrated for the percipience and accuracy of his forecasts and showed him a thread. When the stranger asked how long he would live, the oracle sighed and returned the answer – not long. At this moment the oracle's servant entered and, to his surprise and consternation, saw two oracles. The stranger then left. The servant related this event to the oracle. That night the oracle died. The visitor had been the oracle's own spirit.

The second story. A boy was found sleeping in a tomb. He told his discoverers that, while slumbering, he had dreamed that only those buried in mulberry coffins would be impressed into the army of the shades. The price of mulberry-wood coffins then fell in the town and that of cypress-wood coffins rose. However, when it was put about that the boy had been in the pay of the sellers of cypress-wood, the price fell.

PURSUER

The precise identity, even the name, of the editor of the *Canton Monitor* has not so far been divulged. This is not merely capricious.

We do not need to know his name or his personal appearance. Gideon, Walter, Harry know it, of course. From his writing, from his newspaper, we may glean all we need to know. We deduce, for instance, that he is pugnacious, uninterested in the arts, direct, not a mincer of words, nor a savourer of them, either; is certain about the world, conscious of being in the right, and can be surprisingly fair-minded. He believes he is an honourable man. Ah, and we know he's Irish. Is he black-haired, red-haired, or perhaps a sandy Celt? Greying?

This is not germane to the present narrative.

Probably, had his press been lost in the withdrawal from Canton, smashed by native rioters, dropped off the quay by clumsy hands, thrown overboard in rage by frustrated pirates, then he would have relinquished the struggle without a sense of overpowering bitterness. Circumstances, rather than Walter, would have conspired to defeat him. However, sitting under his mat-shed roof on the edge of Hong Kong harbour, with the means and opportunity of gratifying his ire at hand, recently provoked and charged with all the pent-up fury of a man gagged under monstrous torment, he goes further than, in cooler moments, he himself would think either wise or decorous. Perhaps it is Eastman's reaction which would seem exaggerated from our perspective.

Walter Eastman to Gideon Chase

Rua da Nossa Senhora da Nazare 12
Macao
February 28th, 1840

My dear Gideon,

I make no apologies for the enclosures which accompany this note. Disgraceful and revolting though they are, fit to turn the stomach as well might a dead rat arriving in a box, since your honour no less than my own is compromised in this affair, I am constrained to reveal to you what I might otherwise conceal in order to spare your feelings. I am somewhat encouraged in my purpose by the reflection that you would undoubtedly be made acquainted with the contents in the ordinary course of events by friends (or otherwise) who would feel it incumbent upon them to bring the vile calumnies to your attention. In this case my unpleasant task assumes the character of a duty, when my motives may appear altogether altruistic because wholly selfish and if my action causes you distress, why, I flay my own outraged feelings, too.

Lest you should imagine that I write to implicate you in the defence of my own reputation, I should add directly that I have already set measures in train to seek satisfaction jointly on both our behalves, but where I alone shall act as principal.

Your good friend,
Walter Eastman

From THE CANTON MONITOR
Tuesday, February 25th, 1840

...so we take our leave of weightier matters, recommending Captain Elliot to secure the Home Government's attention in this matter. Passing to smaller, much smaller, nuisances nearer at hand, it will not have escaped our readers' attentions that the journal known as the *Lin Tin Bulletin and River Bee* (which they may have been compelled to notice during our own absence) has, in the unmistakable fashion of a family where the stock was diseased to begin with, degenerated in its procession from issue to issue. Freed of the need to compare its own effusions with those of a sober and responsible organ which consulted the good of the community it served as well as diverted, its animadversions on each and every topic finally became so wild and eccentric they resembled nothing so much as the ravings of a madman. Any topic was grist to its mill, however depraved or licentious, and its columns at length became nothing more nor less than a recital of native lewdness so gross that one blushed to see it read publicly or lying on the table of one's hostess. In this regard, we should say the offending anecdotes were less by Pursuer than *per* sewer, as one gentleman observed to us.

It is an observation unoriginal but true that the contents of a journal must be the reflection of its conductor's mind, and if they be diseased and perverse, then so must his own tastes be called into question. But we are not our Cousin's keeper and if we have not the benefit of a close friend's aid and *services* at the very least our right hand is cognisant of what our left is doing. We recommend our contemporary to a study of 2 Samuel i 26.

The editor of the Lin Tin Bulletin and River Bee
to the editor of the Canton Monitor

Rua da Nossa Senhora da Nazare 12
Macao
1 o'clock a.m.
February 27th, 1840

Sir,

Your most recent, abandoned, scurrilous, and infamous libel upon me was drawn to my attention this morning by gentlemen of my acquaintance. I will not dwell upon the vile and disgraceful nature of these allegations longer than to say that no gentleman could allow them to pass unresented, nor any gentleman deny another satisfaction in such an affair. I should be most deeply indebted if you would communicate to Mr Ridley the name of your representative, so that final measures may be undertaken with such despatch as shall prove, I do not doubt, as agreeable to yourself as to me. Pray be informed, sir, that I consult your convenience entirely.
I have, sir, the honour to be your humble, obedient servant,
Walter Eastman

The editor of the Canton Monitor
to the editor of the Lin Tin Bulletin and River Bee

Hong Kong
March 2nd, 1840

Sir,

While I have the honour to acknowledge your communication of the 27th *ult.*, I am at a loss to account for the very unusual measures you have seen fit to propose. Do you, my dear sir, mean to call me out? I should inform you that this is the nineteenth century, not the eighteenth, and although the combat to the death may be the customary mode of settling differences among the backwoodmen of your own country, I may assure you it is not the appropriate method by which modern English gentlemen regulate the misunderstandings which may from time to time arise between them. I may also add that the duel, latterly, was a form of correspondence between equals. If I have offended you, I regret having done so, but I should remind you that the provocation was gross. In case the tenor of my meaning should have eluded you thus far, I make myself utterly plain – I give you distinctly to understand that I have no intention of standing your fire.

I am, sir, etc.

The editor of the *Canton Monitor*
(Signed)

The editor of the Lin Tin Bulletin and River Bee
to the editor of the Canton Monitor

Rua da Nossa Senhora da Nazare 12
Macao
March 3rd, 1840

Sir,

I have the honour to reply to your communication of the 2nd *inst.* and must inform you that the tone of levity you have assumed in your letter can only compound your original transgression in my eyes. I account your assumption of superiority over me as excessively impudent and unwarranted. I should also inform you that I stand in no need of a lesson in contemporary etiquette from you. The Duke of Wellington called out an opponent in 1829, if my memory serves me correctly, and, I am surprised I need to remind you, Mr Innes issued a challenge to Mr Daniells of the Honourable Company less than ten years ago, which that gentleman was too timorous to accept.

As to 'standing my fire', I take this opportunity of reminding you that the selection of weapons is entirely your prerogative. There is no peculiar obligation to choose pistols. Nor, sir, are you an 'English gentleman'. You are an Irishman. Should you see fit to deny me satisfaction, then the following signed and duly notarised declaration which shall be inserted in your newspaper and mine, with the amendments appropriate to each, would be acceptable to me. The apology should occupy a position of equal prominence with the original libel and be set in type uniform with the rest of your journal.

−Deponent now witnesseth as follows:

Readers of the *Canton Monitor* will have been surprised by the blasphemous and disgraceful allegations of unnatural vice made against two members of the American community which sullied the columns of its most recent issue. I, the editor of the *Canton Monitor,* wholly retract these wicked and monstrous libels which I accept to be altogether without foundation in fact and have now only to regret that I so far forgot myself as to impose upon an innocent and unsuspecting public. These calumnies were both ungentlemanly and despicable in a professional point of view and I undertake never again to repeat them either in a public or private capacity.

A true statement.
John Doe (Witness)

Gideon Chase to Walter Eastman

No. 16 Chow Chow Hong
Canton
March 1st, 1840

My dear Walter,

I cannot sufficiently impress upon you the horror and consternation which afflicted me on reading your letter. Not on account of the malicious falsehood perpetrated in the *Monitor* but your violent and murderous determination to seek what is not redress but revenge. Do we expect anything but lies to emanate from our rival's organ? What weight may we attach to trivial falsehoods about ourselves besides the greater evil that newspaper espouses? In any case the allegations, serious I own, were cloaked and circuitous. I doubt one in ten would catch the author's drift. The biblical reference, to be nice, is, I am distressed for thee, my brother Jonathan, very pleasant hast thou been unto me: '*thy love to me was wonderful, passing the love of women.*' Except by low and depraved minds what is there that may be construed as objectionable in this beautiful passage, as sonorous in its language as noble in its sentiment? I most earnestly beseech you not to endanger your own life or to shed needlessly the blood of a fellow-creature. I am heavily pressed with the conduct of our affairs here and, as well, have more than once had to act the part of translator (and, occasionally, interpreter) as the native linguists now feel it too dangerous to represent the foreigners. At the first opportunity which presents itself, I shall take passage to Macao. Again, I exhort you – do nothing which may cause your friends sorrow. You are most decidedly not your own free agent – but connected by reciprocal duties and rights with the loving expectations of your friends. I believe, if you will permit me a moment's levity, that for you, as for David, the best way to deal with Saul is not to throw his javelin back at him but to catch him asleep in the grotto of Camoes and cut a length, if not from his biblical cloak, at least his top-coat. How say you? I reckon this a good stratagem.

Ever truly yours,

Gideon

PS Or am I the sling-wielding giant-slayer and you the King's son?

The editor of the Canton Monitor
to the editor of the Lin Tin Bulletin and River Bee

Red Rover
Hong Kong harbour
March 6th, 1840

Sir,

Your most outrageous behaviour yesterday evening has left me with little choice but to meet you. I shall be happy to oblige you at the place and time which is convenient to you. Kindly arrange for your representative to meet with Mr Innes, who bears this letter.

I am etc.

Jonathan Ridley, Esq., to James Innes, Esq.

George
Hong Kong harbour
March 6th, 1840

Sir,

Neither party being prepared to withdraw, I believe it our most unpleasant duty to agree arrangements and I shall be obliged if you will allow me to call upon you aboard the *Governor Findlay.* My principal desires you to understand that his motive in *lightly* drawing his stick across the face of your principal before the assembled officers and gentlemen was not to injure but to insult. Failing your instructions to the contrary, I shall have myself rowed across at 6 p.m. this evening. I assure you, sir, of my utmost consideration at all times.

J. P. Ridley

★ ★ ★

GIDEON BITES a tremulous lower lip. His large, strong hands, when he takes them an inch off his thighs, shake. Ridley's knees bump his across the thwarts; Jonathan exerts reassuring pressure. Remedios, who rows, wears his customary expression of brutal impassivity, while the principal, consuming his second cigar, has been behaving with a massively exaggerated composure.

All night, Walter has been gay. His wit has flowed as generously as the champagne, although to those who know him as well as Gid, it might lack some sparkle. Nevertheless, it had been a convivial little gathering, with the undertone of hysteria only serving to stimulate them to wilder flights of conversational repartee. Mirth became quite uncontrollable when Ridley produced two black spheres of lead and hefted them solemnly in each hand. Walter then swept the crackers out of a saucer, handing the balls around as if at an anatomy lecture in one of the medical theatres of Philadelphia: 'There they are, gentlemen, the seat of courage. Seat of courage, gentlemen.'

But, 'Take care,' warned Ridley, with real seriousness. 'I cast them perfectly for you,' and a pall descended in the saloon of the *Sonia*. Which Eastman, drink having made his face pale rather than red like honest Jonathan's, quickly lifted. Going to his cabin, he emerged with some types, which he rattled like rotten teeth. 'These are my weapons.'

'A little late, Walter. The war of words is over.'

'No.' And Walter cast the letters on the table. 'I have not chosen them randomly. There's an N, a P — all from the upper case, you'll note, capital letters to you, Jonathan. Now look — O-P-I-N-I-O-N. There's the giant-slayer, Gid. Remedios, bring the crucible.' And there and then, the glow illuminating the saloon like some devil's punch-bowl, Walter had the half-caste make him two spherical slugs.

'Depend on mine,' Ridley warned, but Walter laughed lightly.

And now, as they pass the eastern shore of Hong Kong island, the two pairs of pistol-balls repose respectively in Ridley's right and left coat-pockets.

It is a beautiful, sunny morning, so cold cannot be Gideon's excuse for shivering. He associates this sort of dismal outing with coaches, mist, marsh. They might be on a picnic, but for the

457

earliness of the hour, for it is true they set out, like duellists anywhere, before dawn.

Although the precise limits of Captain Elliot's powers over Her Majesty's subjects are untested, and he is certainly not empowered to clap an American citizen like Walter in irons, discretion, so far as public insult on a ship's quarterdeck may be called discreet, it has been mutually agreed, shall be observed. Innes, the editor of the *Canton Monitor,* and their other second, a mate from the *Governor Findlay,* lead in the first boat. The other party bring up the rear, while in the middle boat (with Dr MacGillivray, whose presence requires no explanation), rowed by Ah Cheong, is Harry O'Rourke. ('My boy, it would break my heart if...' – 'Fiddlesticks, Harry. I shall not fall, I'll assure you. Do you see fair play done. You are acceptable to my opponent and you will do nothing to injure me. How could I trust anyone else?') So Harry's the umpire and will drop the handkerchief, but the old fellow is woefully unhappy and had a miserable night aboard the *George.* He has a fearful hangover and, instead of his usual straw hat, has donned a funereal black stove-pipe, somewhat reminiscent, as Gideon regards him from the boat behind, of a steamer's chimney.

Forty-five minutes' smart rowing sees them past the familiar open valley under paddy, a tiny island in the harbour to starboard, three native huts of uncertain purpose and worse construction, and then the outskirts of a straggling fisher-village where the junks have yet to return from the night's work. All this while, a rough track has been evident along the foreshore.

'Shaukiwan,' says Remedios, with a jerk of the head backwards, obviously familiar enough with the landmarks not to need to turn. Maybe he catches the stink of drying fish earlier than the others.

'A darned piratical-looking set of rascals,' says Ridley. 'You can safely reckon they have concluded to cut throats as well as net fish.'

Walter smiles with less conviction than half an hour ago. His throat is too dry to allow him to smoke in comfort, but he drums his long fingers on the gunwales. Remedios follows the front boat in to a small cove. They ground on shingle. This,

Gideon notices with surprise, is clear water, the first he has seen in the estuary. The eastern side of the island must lie outside the river's influence. Clouds of tiny fish dart in the few inches of water. Remedios leaps out in his bare feet, not troubling to roll up his canvas trousers, but he makes Walter get on his back. The others have to wade in, the best they can. Ridley curses as he jumps, falls short, and splashes his leather top-boots. Climbing up a stony track, they see steep cliffs before them.

'Don't walk so fast, I implore you,' Gideon calls to Walter. He doesn't speak on his own behalf; he does not want Walter to get out of breath. It would spoil his aim, only mediocre at best, as Gideon knows all too well. What is his adversary's like?

They overtake Harry O'Rourke, whose poor face is crimson, but may not, such is the protocol of the duel, address a single word to him. They do not attack the cliff at its steepest, but turn to the side, where, coming from behind a boulder, they find themselves on the lip of a large, sheer-sided crater. There is surely no history of volcanic activity in this area? But Remedios grins and indicates a labourer wielding a pick. Stone-cutters.

'It's a quarry, darn my mother,' exclaims Ridley. 'Now that's a deuced handsome choice by whoever fixed upon it.'

James Innes, notorious opium-smuggler and quondam prolific issuer of challenges himself, is visible below, striding towards the centre of the quarry. Ridley leaves Walter, gesturing significantly to Gideon to keep their friend occupied in conversation so that nerves do not overcome him, while he himself runs down into the amphitheatre, at imminent peril to his boot-heels and neck, to ensure that Innes steals no advantage. Following a chilly interview on the *Governor Findlay*, Ridley does not trust Innes at all. There is something incongruously effeminate, Gideon reflects, in the way the sturdy Ridley has to mince down the slope to keep his balance. Ridley finishes at a run, then trots across the quarry after Innes. The others see Innes point with his cane. Jonathan shakes his head vigorously. The pair are locked in argument as the rest of the party join them. Avoiding each other's gaze, Walter and his opponent stay well away.

'God damn it,' drifts over from an exasperated Ridley, 'you'll put the sun in his eyes in five minutes' time. Yes, sir, I know that but...'

The argument continues, becoming very heated. Will the seconds issue challenges to each other? Gideon titters nervously.

MacGillivray consults his watch. 'Laddie, they'd better stir a leg. There'll be the marines coming after, unless tha's wha' they're after.' He rattles his bag ghoulishly. 'In the which case, I'll ha' lost ma beauty sleep for nothing.'

Gideon gives a weak smile.

Innes and Ridley have lost all patience with each other. The young American's fists are clenched by his sides. Innes raps his stick angrily on a stone.

'Umpire,' calls MacGillivray, 'd'ye come and arbitrate here. They must abide by your decision.' He gently removes the flask from Harry's hand. The old painter lurches over to the squabbling seconds.

'Sir,' says Innes, 'I cannot allow my principal to be blinded by the rays of the sun.'

'Nor I mine,' snaps Ridley, 'and it rises higher with every second.'

This is true. It is already bakingly hot in the depression. The sun is now a few degrees above the lip of the quarry.

'Darn it,' says Walter, 'I'll give him the shade.'

Ridley opens his mouth to expostulate, but before he can utter a word, Harry says, 'Then the arrangement is also unfair to the other party.'

'How can it be? God damn it, the sun will deprive Walter of any aim.'

'Perhaps, but whoever stands the other's fire against the background of the quarry wall is also *silhouetted* against it. It would act as the sight-screen behind the archer's target or the bowler at cricket.'

'Well, darn me,' says Walter, with some admiration, despite the circumstances.

'Well, what then, sir?' says Innes testily.

Harry thinks a moment. He then takes Innes's cane, looks up, and draws a line at an angle to the quarry wall. He consults his watch, flips the lid down, and says, 'They have, I estimate, seven minutes.'

'Then, in God's name, gentlemen, let us commence.'

460

Innes produces the case which has been in O'Rourke's custody overnight, inviting Ridley to choose from the pair of handsome weapons reposing in the velvet. This Jonathan does with care. They are squarer in the butt than an ordinary pistol, as well as ornately chased. Ridley removes the rammer and is about to load, but Remedios takes the gun from him. Ridley nods. The half-caste is more used to this work, and to coping with it as balls whizz around his ears. Ridley puts a slug in Remedios's palm but Walter, watching closely, says, 'No. Opinion.' Ridley is puzzled, then recollects, not without misgivings, and gives Remedios the ball cast on the *Sonia*. He is sure it is uneven and imperfectly weighted.

Now Innes paces off the distance. At thirty, it is rather long. No one objects.

The duellists are brought together. They stand back to back, pistol-barrels pointing to the sky. The others withdraw. The disadvantage of Harry's calculation of the sun's movements, admirable though it is in other respects, is that it has not left the noncombatants with a great deal of natural cover. All the loose boulders in the quarry are actually in the line of fire.

O'Rourke's deep voice carries across the quarry as he counts.

At thirty, the duellists turn.

Walter fires first, body still moving in his eagerness. The crack echoes off the quarry walls, Harry's stove-pipe hat flies off, the re-echo comes back, and there is the *cree-whang!* of Walter's defective ball ricocheting off rocks.

'Gad!' O'Rourke ejaculates.

The editor of the *Canton Monitor* looks at the editor of the *Lin Tin Bulletin and River Bee* down the line of his pistol-barrel, pauses, and then points the weapon skywards to discharge it harmlessly into the air.

Sighs go up from the spectators.

'Oh, thank God,' says Gideon, tears in his eyes.

As the others advance on him, O'Rourke retrieves his hat and sticks a stubby finger through the hole six inches above his forehead. Wordlessly, MacGillivray returns him his flask.

Eastman arrives. His face is taut and chalk-white with rage. 'Again,' he stutters. 'Again. I have been denied satisfaction.'

Gideon looks at him with horror. 'Walter, you are utterly vindicated. This farce is over. *Over.*' Ridley, too, looks aghast.

Innes smiles grimly. 'He is within his rights. No blood has been shed. What d'ye say, Doctor?'

'I say he's a stupid and vairy impetuous young booby, but one who has a right to stand fire again.'

The editor of the *Canton Monitor* has sweat all over his freckled face. His eyes are green. .

'Very well. Load the weapons,' says O'Rourke in a fury. He turns away and hurls his empty flask into a clump of boulders.

'Darn him for a fool who wants to get killed,' mutters Ridley. 'What can we do except await the issue?'

Remedios turns his back to reload Walter's pistol. The rammer rattles as he forces home the wadding. Either he is devoting more attention to the reload (although none of the others would dream of intimating he might have misloaded on the first occasion), or the phlegmatic half-caste is as put out as the others.

'Ready, Remedios?'

He hands the weapon to his employer.

This time Dr MacGillivray assumes the role of arbiter. 'Wun an twainty, tu an' twainty.'

Gideon mops the stinging sweat from his eyebrows. Can Walter see?

The sun is getting higher all the time but the angle is in his friend's favour. Time is on his side.

'Thairty.'

The combatants turn, more deliberately this time. Walter stands sideways on, thus presenting a smaller target but running the risk, if hit, of having the bullet pierce a greater number of organs than if he were facing straight on.

Ridley sucks in his breath.

Walter levels and fires, first again. There are the flash and the report.

His enemy staggers, drops his pistol, and falls in a spin sideways to his knees. He holds his face.

'Merciful God.'

Gideon and Ridley run towards him. Innes walks behind.

Walter stands stock-still. He lowers his smoking weapon. MacGillivray is already by the stricken man's side. He turns him over and pulls away his crimson hands. The chin is gone and the lower teeth smashed. MacGillvray removes the mangled slug with a pair of forceps. 'Stopped by the molars, thanks to the Lord,' he says, 'it canna have been a strong propellant charge.'

The wounded man groans in a dreadful, bubbling sort of way. Gideon's knees give way and he sinks to the ground but does not pass out. Ridley is very pale.

Walter hands his pistol to Innes, who accepts it without comment.

Nothing can be read into Innes's customary sardonic expression.

'Strange,' says Ridley, 'I thought I saw the ball strike the ladder behind, yet you say it did not pass through.'

'Had it done so, young man, he wouldna be here, but before the dread Tribunal of his Maker, I can assure you.'

'I guess my eyes deceived me. There is much glare off this dust.'

'Aye, well, do you help me carry him. Och, ignore his cries. He can have been cleaning his pistol and had a wee accident. He'll live, but he'll nae be a pretty sight.'

They set off, leaving a trail of blood on the quarry floor. Chinese heads duck behind the rim.

Eastman walks pensively behind the rest of the party. No one speaks to him. Running to catch the others up, which he will do soon, arriving first at the beach to launch the boat...is Remedios. Who has retrieved from the boulders the flattened hemispherical pancake of lead, frayed at the edges, which was once the topmost bullet he had double-loaded in Walter's gun.

He'll use it on his fishing-line.

CHAPTER XXXI

From THE LIN TIN BULLETIN AND RIVER BEE

Wednesday, May 20, 1840

Vol.3 No.10

Armament preparing. The fleet which is destined to wring from the Chinese compensation for the destroyed stores of opium is now, we have it on the best authority, gathering at Singapore, having left Trincomalee at the beginning of the month. Our earlier speculations as to the composition of the forces in the expedition proving but partially correct, we now make amends by listing the land forces as follows – 1. 90th (Perthshire Volunteers) Regiment. 2. 18th (Royal Irish) Regiment. 3. 26th (Cameronians) Regiment. 4. 49th Regiment. 5. Madras Native Infantry (37th Company, with sappers and miners). 6. Royal Artillery, with 9-pounder field-pieces and 9-pounder howitzers.

Of the ships, we know for certain that our old friend the *Wellesley* ploughs up the South China Sea with the monsoon, in company with, most likely, the *Blenheim* (74), another third-rate ship of the line, from the Cape station, with the *Blonde* (44) heavy frigate. *Druid,* another 44-gun vessel, was already arrived from New South Wales last month. We calculate there will be some fifteen other ships, not including the Honourable Company's armed steamers, a class of vessel of which it may be said there cannot exist too many for the purposes of the expedition.

Matters wear an even graver aspect than previously was the case. We would most earnestly impress upon the foreign gentlemen still resident at Canton, and most especially on our own countrymen, the wisdom of a course of discretion. They should forsake Mammon when their own lives may prove forfeit. It may not be necessary for them to go to the extent of the expedient of finding floating refuges away from the immediate environs of the estuary, as our Cousins have done at Hong Kong, but it should surely be prudent to fall back on Macao. True, the gallant Dom Silveira da Pinto's mainly kaffir garrison would not be able to repel a Chinese attack in numbers, but at least our Cousins could take off on to their men-of-war any Americans whose lives were threatened.

Our own particular, esteemed, and deaf correspondent of Canton (deaf, that is, to our repeated urgings to fly his post) will remain in the City of Rams and, with reluctance, for we do not wish to encourage his temerity, we shall continue to publish his reports, as follows:

The Factories deserted. We have become a kind of Crusoe here and, like Robinson, are almost reconciled to our fate. As we take our mid-morning or mid-afternoon constitutional, our heels clatter on the stone flags of those arcades which, even until recently, echoed to the conversation and gay laughter of our friends and contemporaries, and the clinking of dollars and clicking of abacuses under the cunning fingers of the shroffs. Not a soul moves now and we pass unchallenged in those precincts where we once enjoyed a hospitable and warm welcome *(and latterly rebuff and disdain – ed.)*. Why, we even passed our time in a game of billiards against ourself and, if we do not dress in skins, we certainly have our umbrella, a coracle of our very own, and a rack of arms. (Of which latter we would never avail ourself, preferring to perish ourself rather than turn the means of destruction against the wronged and misguided population of this vast city.) Man Friday we have yet to rescue from the clutches of the anthropophages.

Lin rests confident he shall tame the barbarians yet another time. Still, he peruses numerous atlases and charts of the world, which his agents have privily procured for him of the same barbarians, and he has a staff who engage themselves in translating those journals and newspapers of the foreigner which they may purchase or purloin. Ours – we have taken it upon ourselves – they receive *gratis. (I knew nothing of this, sir.-ed.)*

To him therefore, we write an open letter and the sub-pended woodcut *(which has too readily, alas, impregnated our paper – ed.)* is the Chinese translation.

AN HUMBLE PETITION

I, a lowly well-wisher, make communication to Lin, decorated thrice with the Peacock's Tail, a Privy Councillor, elevated ten times, advanced ten times, a Guardian of the Imperial Princes, a Special Commissioner, and an Academician of the Forest of Pencils.

Your Excellency,

No one would dispute, even among those whom you have all too good reason for regarding as your mortal foes, the character you possess of a stern, just, and unyielding judge. You are a devoted and incorruptible servant of your Imperial Master and of your Country and Empire. Rightly, your ire is aroused by the river of poison which flows into the vitals of your nation and daily debilitates and corrupts. Yet I would beg you to subjoin to your virtues of firmness, decision and perseverance, those characteristics of subtlety, compassion, and magnanimity without which an excessive endowment of the former qualities of strength can speedily prove a source of weakness as well as power. Not all the wrong, Excellency, is on the one side. I am bold enough to say this.

The legitimate trade in woollens, tins, lead, ginseng, furs, bird's nests, rattans, tuttenague, and a myriad other wholesome and useful commodities is oppressed to the point of extinction by the vexatious and illegal demands of your subordinates. The dues, impositions, and taxes they levy are arbitrary and excessive and it is matter of common scandal among the inhabitants of all orders and classes in this teeming city that not the tiniest fraction of this huge and illicit revenue shall ever find its way to the coffers of your Master in Peking. Foreigners who would throw up the

466

disgraceful trade are unable to do so, for they would court their own ruin and that of those they represent. Not all foreigners are of the stamp of the hardened and wicked smugglers of opium. Captain Elliot, and I doubt I relate something new or surprising to Your Excellency, is not a bad man. He is far from that. Unlike Your Excellency, his heart is not in his work; yet nevertheless he must do his duty, and pursues it with a zeal and courage which do him, perhaps, even more credit than Your Excellency. Would it surprise Your Excellency to hear that Captain Elliot loathes the trade which your servant has heard him openly refer to as 'a blot on the national character'? That he despises the merchants, whom he regards as lawbreakers, and that he is not on speaking terms with the ringleaders is notorious among the foreigners. He is a man of peace who will strive his utmost to avoid bloodshed. He has a most perfect horror of bringing fire and the sword to the inhabitants of this empire and, I believe, would do almost anything to spare unnecessary loss of life and destruction of property. Even now, it is not too late for Your Excellency to avoid becoming embroiled in the schemes of the men of blood. Yet such, I greatly fear, will be the outcome of these few months.

PURSUER

From THE LIN TIN BULLETIN AND RIVER BEE
Wednesday, June 3, 1840
Vol.3 No.11

DIED

At Macao on June 2nd, *aet.* 38, Lord John Churchill, captain of the *Druid* and fourth son of the Duke of Marlborough, carried away by a violent dysentery and greatly regretted by his brother officers. By his courteous ways, his gentlemanly demeanour, and his large and remarkable condescension he had greatly attached to himself all who knew him.

The above is inserted at the request of Captain Elliot. We are most happy to comply with the Superintendent's personally expressed desire.

From London per Matilda. The radical agitation, we have it on the best authority, which had in no way abated (and perhaps had even been fomented further) by the Reform Act of 1832, reached its climax – as it must – November previous, when in Newport, Monmouthshire, the new Jacobins took up arms. This violent, desperate, and fated insurrection culminated in the deaths of no less than twenty-four of the rebels. In Birmingham, too, there occurred violent affrays and riot. The participants in both uprisings were Chart-ists, that is adherents to the People's Charter of 1838. Atwood, a radical leader and Member of Parliament, had presented a Monster (or monstrous) Petition to the House the July previous, and we doubt not but that this had an ill effect in the Provinces. The demands of the Charter were – 1. Remuneration for the Members of the Parliament. 2. Equal electoral districts. 3. A vote for all men. 4. Annual Parliaments. 5. Vote by secret ballot. 6. Abolition of the qualification in property for prospective members.

It is not so much the aims as the means (if we may be forgiven an unintended pun) of the Chart-ists which we greatly deplore. With the single exception of the stipulation for an election to be held every year (which we would regard as undesirable purely in an administrative point of view, not to mention the maintenance of the public order), we would not take issue with the other demands. The Institutions of the New World, republican in origin and spirit, may be said to be far more radical in the letter than the demands of the Charter. How strange it is then that in practice the operation of those very institutions should prove both moderate and, indeed, conservative, whereas the political and constitutional arrangements of the Mother Country should throw up demagogues like Paine and Atwood who are renegados to their estate. We believe that the difference lies in the temperaments of the citizenry, where the Americans are naturally phlegmatic and independent in spirit. In a democracy, the individual is the unit – he cannot, need not, see beyond himself. He belongs to no caste or corporation, wears nobody's livery, and he perceives the state not as an enemy but as the embodiment and protection of his own desires and interests. He is uninterested in abstractions but is materially minded. In such a nation the power of public opinion (that is the General Will) shall always be greater than that of a standing army (which is unnecessary in any case, for who presses on the frontiers of America?). The newspaper is substituted for the pillory or stocks and the public contempt for the yeomanry. Yet may this produce an isolation to which would be preferable, almost, as a punishment the longest imprisonment, for the felon would have the society of his fellow prisoners, where the solitude of the offender in the community would be perfect.

Establishment of a National Gallery of the Arts. There has now opened in London at Strand a handsome building constructed expressly for the purpose of housing the remark-able paintings, both portrait and landscape, of the day. We would hope to see exhibited there examples of the works of the celebrated Mr O'R–, as his paintings find their way back to the Home Country in course of time. These works are properly the heritage of his nation, rather than the entailable property of whoever happens to hold them at the time by accident or chance – whether he happen to be the original of the work or no.

From THE LIN TIN BULLETIN AND RIVER BEE

Wednesday, July 15, 1840

Vol.3 No.14

Precipitate departure of the British fleet to the north. So! No sooner have our avenging Cousins' keels kissed the river's muddy bottom than they have in two shakes, to be nautical about these matters, weighed and stood to sea. The countenances of our British friends, the Free Traders, were better seen than described. We never saw such long faces. One old gentleman of our acquaintance (a pernickety fellow, for which we always knew him) was quite out of sorts. We encountered him on the Praia. His gait was palsied more than usual, dress funereal and looks gloomy to a degree. 'Well, sir,' we interrogated him, 'how d'you do?' Without a word he cast on us the most ghastly glare and rapped his cane upon the ground, more for support, we are inclined to believe, than any feelings of ire against us on his own part. At the best of times he was a man of few words, and those short and pretty much addressed to the point. 'Hugh,' says he, by which we were a little surprised, since everybody is cognisant of the circumstance that our name begins with what is before XYZ. Turning away from us he resumed his anxious pacing and piercing scrutiny of the sea, empty still. At length we concluded that he had meant 'Heugh!' and left him to his mournful study. He bore all the marks of a drowning man who, thrown a rope, finds it pulled from his grasp and cast to quite the other side of the boat.

We know it for a fact that Captain Elliot himself rues the decision of the Navy. In the few days that the fleet stayed, he did not scruple to show his amazement in private circles that Commodore Bremer's instructions (which must have proceeded from Lord Palmerston himself) confined him to a blockade of the Canton river-mouth, rather than the forcible taking of the Bogue forts, which must more quickly impress upon the mandarins the knowledge of the irresistible power of the Royal Navy. In this we agree with the Superintendent. The river has more mouths than the Hydra, and is supplied by thousands of little branches, only navigable by small craft, and it would prove quite impossible for the entire Royal Navy to cut off the communication of Canton with the sea, let alone the small squadron at Commodore Bremer's disposal.

While we are not yet in receipt of detailed intelligences

regarding the fortunes of the expedition, we understand that it was destined for the island of Chusan, with first landfall expected to be the Buffalo's Nose, a quaintly shaped rock of the Chusan archipelago. The *Conway* frigate (28), Captain C. Drinkwater Bethune, was first to weigh, leading the fleet and transports in three lines. We watched them from the Monte, while our good friend and artistic mentor took them to the life. Our feelings were very mixed and we did not know whether to be pleased or sorry.

Literary notices. There passed into our hands a few weeks since a most extraordinary tome which quite removed us from our everyday plane and time and transported us to a realm which, but for the circumstance that the volume in question purports to be (and indeed *is)* an account, or rather record, of true travels, we might easily have mistaken for that which properly belongs to the province of the romance. Nor do we believe that these papers are of the school of traveller's tales of the ilk of the German baron.

The narrative assumes the form of the author's journal, edited and refined, he most openly admits, with the opportunity afforded by and, indeed, even incumbent upon a general publication. *The Narrative of Arthur Gordon Pym of Nantucket* appeared in serial form in the *Southern Literary Messenger* of Richmond *(Virginia – ed.)* before being printed and bound, which it deserved, in the handsome edition which fell into our hands. We understand it appeared in the United States in August last. Mr Pym and his young companion and friend stowed away on board the brig *Grampus* and, through circumstances not of their own choosing, became bound up in the bloody mutiny of a part of the crew, which was led by a half-caste, Dirk, who yet lives in the trackless fastnesses of the West. The brig, owing to the circumstance of the drunkenness of its captors, foundered in a storm. Following the escape of the few survivors, they endured long sufferings and privations in an open boat, including (O, horrors!) resort to that terrible nourishment which some would rather perish for lack of sustenance than contemplate tasting. Yet, tenacious of life, young Pym addressed himself to that terrific meal.

At length the author and a handful of mutineers were cast ashore upon an island which met them in all providence from the wastes of the sea. Providential, alas, only in appearances, for the cunning savages who were its inhabitants, careful to dissemble their cruel and bloody natures, only made the overtures of welcome the more easily to surprise and murder all but Mr Pym and the half-caste Dirk, who, strange to relate, had become deeply attached to the young Pym. *(Not so strange – does the savage mastiff not lick the hand of its master? – ed.)* At length Pym and his brutal companion effected their escape in a canoe and after further most extraordinary adventures fell in with an American schooner which returned them to the United States.

Alas, Mr Pym survived his hardships only to meet with a fatal accident when in apparent safety once more among the familiar scenes of his childhood.

It is moot whether a work of the imagination, such as the romances of Scott or Fenimore Cooper, or a record of fact, such as the work in question, is the more meritorious, assuming the responses which it inspires in the reader to be equally droll and vivid in either case. We prefer the work of fact *(as do we – ed.)*. However, it is no more than the barest justice to state that the late Mr Pym, an adventurous but *(comparatively – ed.)* uninstructed youth, owed a profound debt of gratitude to his editor, Mr Edgar Allan Poe, the conductor of the *Southern Literary Messenger.*

In conclusion, we should beg to recommend the work to our friends and make so bold as to state that, with all who love a plain and unadorned tale of manly courage and adventure, this will be a favourite volume on their shelves.

The circumstance of our absence from the helm of the *Monitor* will doubtless not have escaped the notice of our subscribers. This was, we regret, unavoidable, but we are returned now and shall endeavour to acquit ourselves at least as well, or as ill, as previously was the case. To the solicitous friends and well-wishers who sent in their notes and cards and gifts of fruit and cordials, we may only add in print the expression of those sincere and grateful thanks we have in many instances been able to reciprocate in person. Those kind friends whom we have as yet been unable to visit or have not as yet encountered in the course of our ordinary avocations will, we trust, pardon the oversight in the spirit which prompted their original offices. While we were yet under the restoring influence of the good Dr M-'s soothing draught, we were unable to recognise the faces around our bed, so we are in hopes that allowances shall be made in our favour.

Good news of the Expedition to Chusan. The latest from Admiral Elliot's fleet is calculated to cheer all loyal British hearts. On the afternoon of the 5th *inst.,* punctually at one o'clock p.m., following due notice and warning, a shot was fired from the *Wellesley* in Chusan harbour at the batteries on shore, which cut down in a cloud of dust the flagstaff of the large red emblem above the Chinese guns when the Chinese admiral returned the fire from his junk and the engagement became general. After five minutes the *Wellesley* hoisted the signal 'Cease firing'. The Chinese on shore could be observed fleeing as fast as their legs could take them, but the old Chinese admiral was made of sterner stuff, for *bang, bang* went his puny broadside and the British ships recommenced piercing the ancient junks, while a shell from the *Queen* steamer hissed away to burst in the city. For the second time the cannonade ceased, on this occasion not to resume. In the city was not a living soul to be seen, while the junks slowly filled and settled in the mud.

The ship's boats were quickly got away and landed under the hilltop joss-house or temple, returning with trophies of spears, gingals, bows and arrows, as well as some wounded Chinamen, some by all accounts fearfully mangled, who were taken aboard the *Wellesley* to have their wounds attended to.

As night fell, it was thought too dangerous to continue operations, but on the morning of the 7th some of our sappers, approaching to blow in the gates, found the place to be deserted.

In the warehouses and cellars of the city were found quantities of *samshoo* or potent rice-liquor, and it is matter of regret to learn that many of the men broke ranks so as to broach the jars and casks, not a few of them becoming quite insensible under the influence of the brew. Many native plunderers had commenced their work of despoiling under cover of darkness, the bolder continuing their depredations during the day, despite being shot on sight by our sentries, and it came as no surprise when at 3 a.m. a fire broke out in the city. This the engineers put out by blowing down the surrounding houses.

Admiral Elliot arrived only after the capture of the city, being brought into the harbour by the *Queen* steamer, Indian Navy, as the *Melville* (74) on which he voyaged from the Cape struck on a shelf outside Chusan and is leaking a great deal in consequence. She may need to be hove down, in which case the *Blenheim* shall also be laid up as, apart from the flagship, she is the only vessel of the *Melville's* size and large enough to carry her. The Admiral has in the meantime transferred his flag to our old friend the *Wellesley*.

We understand that the steamers, of which besides the *Queen* there are the Honourable Company's armed vessels, *Atalanta, Madagascar,* and *Enterprise,* performed sterling service, towing the large sailing-vessels through the narrows and tidal races around the archipelago where else they could not have safely ventured.

Our own losses of men during the battle for Chusan were slight, with none killed and but a few scratched.

As there appears to exist some confusion in Macao, it is perhaps advisable for us to inform our readers that Admiral Elliot and Captain Elliot are not one and the same person. Admiral George Elliot, appointed joint Plenipotentiary with Captain Charles Elliot, is a cousin of the Superintendent of Trade, which will doubtless help them to agreement on the form operations shall assume.

We would remark here that we most unreservedly agree with the instructions from London to transfer the scene of warfare from the Canton River to the north of China. It is true that the source of grievance lies in the south, but the key to redress lies in the north, near the Emperor. His lying and venal servants in Canton, even Lin who must save his head, will never let him know the full measure of the barbarian victory, whereas nearer at hand, even by Peking, the proofs shall be inescapable.

DIED

At sea on the voyage to Chusan, Colonel J. Oglander of the 26th (Cameronians) Regiment after a short illness. Colonel Oglander was second-in-command of the land forces to Colonel Burrell of the 18th. He had the reputation of a good officer and popular among his men. The body was consigned to the deep.

An imposition upon an unsuspecting public. A most impudent forgery has been brought to our attention. There has been circulating in the subscription libraries of Macao a volume of the most extraordinary prevarications of which the legendary Baron Munchhausen would not have been ashamed. This most bare-faced attempt to impose upon the public has its source in America, purporting to be the true adventures of one Arthur Gordon Pym of Nantucket. We have no hesitation in declaring it a farrago of the most outrageous lies and tissue of utter fabrications, which would not deceive a clever boy of twelve. What with attacks by rabid dogs, cannibalism on the high seas, half-caste dwarves, and Polar seas which steam and boil with heat, when the South Pole is discovered to be covered with a lush and tropical verdure, we scarcely know whether to laugh or be outraged by this arrant humbug. The Mr Poe who claims to have found and edited this manuscript by the hand of the deceased Pym cannot pretend in the eyes of the discerning to be any more than a charlatan and impostor. The late Pym cannot be dead, because he never lived.

CHAPTER XXXII

All of Macao is a-buzz with the news. This does not concern mighty victories in the north or deeds of derring-do by the crews of the jolly-boats and cutters, but is perfectly trivial. No one will lose their life as a result of it. The course of the 'war' will not be remotely affected. But because everyone knows the name involved, the affair takes on a personal importance which the latest news from Europe or America, a revolution, say, could never hope to rival.

The Reverend Vincent Stanton, BA (Oxon.), Chaplain to Captain Elliot, has been kidnapped by the Chinese. In the most delicate circumstances. When he could not possibly resist. Even if his cloth permitted. This is the point, you see. He was not protected by his cloth. The Chinese, being nothing if not wily (the weak must necessarily be underhand and tend to prefer tactics like hostage-taking), have seized the Reverend Stanton while he was bathing at Macao. They waited in concealment until the young cleric entered the water at Casilha Bay, stole his black garments first, and then his pink, dripping, expostulating, wholly nude person. Which they carried, trussed, over the

476

Barrier and out of Portuguese territory, and thence by devious waterways to Canton. Where even now he languishes, as Johnstone's favourite, Scott, would say, in a gloomy, most unhygienic and insufferably malodorous dungeon, but is well fed and not otherwise physically mistreated. As Eastman quips with small sympathy, it was his cloth which undid him. What was he doing bathing on a Sunday anyway?

In due course, a ransom note arrives. Naturally, this is rejected. One does not bargain with kidnappers, least of all native kidnappers, and certainly not in time of war. Besides, Stanton has no friends or influence.

Still, a provocation must be resented and the Chinese are massing threateningly behind the Barrier, edicts being issued and batteries set up in threatening positions.

A fortnight later, Captain Henry Smith of the 44-gun heavy frigate *Druid* sails as close to the Macao promontory as his substantial draught will allow. In his train follow the *Hyacinth* and then the *Louisa,* with her six pop-guns. The steamer *Enterprise,* her decks crammed with blue-jackets and Bengal Volunteers, towing more troops and marines in four long-boats astern, heads up to the Inner Harbour.

As bad luck would have it, the day is a Wednesday. That is the *Lin Tin Bulletin and River Bee* has already been distributed and sold. Why couldn't Smith have attacked yesterday, when the *Monitor* was already out and Walter could have reset a half-page? How very vexing.

Still, at least the staff of the paper are free to witness the spectacle which is to follow.

When the deep boom of guns carries over the settlement for the second time in a year, Walter and Gideon are at their good friend Father Ribeiro's house. '*Deus!*' ejaculates the burly Jesuit. 'Now shall we be about to have our throats cut?'

'Well, 'tis a better world ye'd go to, Joaquim,' says Harry O'Rourke equably.

'For the faith, yes. To be sacrificed on the altar of a chest of opium, no.'

'To the roof, Gid,' says Walter, who recognises this as no moment to indulge his natural bent for pleasantry, and with a

'You'll not mind, I expect, Father,' he snatches up an antique brass telescope from Father Ribeiro's collection of instruments.

The staff of the *Lin Tin Bulletin and River Bee* clatter up the staircase to the roof.

'Mind,' says Ribeiro, with assumed indignation, 'the young ruffian only purloins the telescope of Afonso D'Alberquerque the Great.'

'If that belonged to Alfonso, I'm Leonardo, you old cheat.'

'Ah, Harry.'

From the roof the action on both sides of the bay clearly unfolds itself without any intervening obstacles to the two young observers; in fact, they could not be better stationed. As they watch, the *Druid* engages the Chinese battery which protects the Barrier gate. The first cannon they heard, Walter suspects, was a notice to quit, rather than a ranging shot – this from a commander under the direction of the ever humane Captain Elliot.

The frigate now turns to present her broadside to the Chinese positions. Her lines, the swelling, cloudy sails, the striped sides, the sparkling water at her bows, make what is a destructive engine of war into a spectacle of aesthetic perfection. She runs for an immeasurable moment, which could be seconds or fractions of a single one. And then, one by one, not in a flaming unison as Gideon had always thought, her 32-pounders bang and jump in line as the gun-captains take individual aim. Even so, as the guns shoot out huge mushrooms of white smoke with a small filament of flame, she is soon concealed from their view.

'Damn it, let a wind come.'

'If those on shore cannot observe the ship, are those on shore in turn invisible to the ship?'

'I've a notion you ask a frivolous and unanswerable question.'

'I merely pondered whether they could observe their fall of shot. I fancy they might otherwise send a ball through the cathedral façade.'

'Here they go again.'

The smoke clears for an instant as the frigate goes about to fire another broadside, but she is soon enveloped again. Eastman turns his telescope on the battery. It mounts...seventeen guns, and now a few ragged discharges are got off in retaliation, the balls whizzing harmlessly through the air and out to sea.

The one-sided cannonade continues, while the church-bells of Macao ring in counterpoint. Broadside after broadside goes off.

'Observe, Walter!'

Eastman reluctantly lowers his ancient telescope, which one would like to think was once the property of Afonso the Great. 'Well, darn it, they're going in!'

Puffing hoarsely and belching a filthy cloud of smoke and smuts from her stack, the *Enterprise* has got across the Inner Harbour with her pennant of long-boats. Above the panting of the steam-engine, they hear a faint 'Huzza!' from the boats. In a skilful and original manoeuvre, quite novel to either observer and not only because they are military neophytes, the stubby steamer turns sharply starboard on one paddle-wheel, with the rudder hard down, and swings the boats across on their tow-rope, cutting the line at exactly the right moment to catapult them shorewards. A few pulls on the oars suffice, and then the red and blue dots swarm on shore with muskets and cartridge-pouches held high. The pop of the small-arms, the yells of the Chinese, and the regular, deep cheering of the British are added to the score. The combat does not last long. The flanking movement proves the last straw for the Chinese, who are soon fleeing pell-mell across the Barrier, unimpeded and unpursued by the British, whose officers prevent the men from taking pot-shots.

A shriller, more ragged cheer sounds from another quarter: the rooftops of Macao, where Portuguese and other foreign spectators have been witness to the unequal tournament. Gideon is appalled to find his sympathies during the encounter did not lie with the vanquished Chinese.

Walter snaps the brass tube shut. 'There is no time to be lost. Come directly.'

They meet Harry and Father Ribeiro on the stairs who seem to share Walter's desire to get to the scene of the action as rapidly as possible. Hurrying through the streets (Ribeiro close on

Eastman's heels, hitching up his cassock as he trots), they are woefully slow compared to the sensation-seekers and souvenir-hunters who mill already on the beach. Men, women, children, foreigners, Portuguese, Chinese on foot, in sedans, on horseback, upon open carriages, they mingle with and obstruct the grinning sailors and cursing officers.

The Governor, Dom Adrias da Silveira Pinto, trots up and down the sand on his stallion, with a great grin on his face, befitting a neutral who has just had an obnoxious battery wiped out by the side he favours. His aide-de-camp escorts the beautiful Senhora da Silveira Pinto, protecting her with a drawn sword from jostling or insult. Now who could be so ungallant as to insult her?

'Damme,' says Harry, 'if this don't put me in mind of Vauxhall Gardens,' but the reference is lost on present company.

Over by the battery, not one gun of which has been dismounted by the frigate or cutter's round-shot, a lieutenant of marines is carefully spiking the cannon, tamping needles of iron into the touch-holes and snapping them off flush with the breech with a special tool. Pigtailed sailors tread Chinese gunpowder into the sand and ransack the magazines. The sepoys, wild, dark fellows with dangerous eyes, prowl the beach with bayonets fixed. No one comes near them. Seven dead Chinese lie by the guns they served, and there are a few more corpses strewn at intervals on the beach. No wounded can be seen. The bodies by the guns are in most cases badly mutilated, decapi-tated, legless, heads smashed in by round-shot. The sand around them is dark. The ladies are prohibited from approaching these. Further down the beach, the corpses bear wounds, of bayonets or sword-thrusts, in the back. Three sepoys are prodding the sand thirty yards away but no! to Gideon's horror they bayonet a wounded Chinese. He sees the dying man try to grip the bayonet in his breast, but the Indian wrenches it away. No one else appears to have noticed, but a gruff, kindly old voice says in his ear: 'Putting the poor fellow out of his misery.' He turns to see Harry's shrewd brown eyes looking into his own. The older man puts an arm round his shoulders and takes him away. They pass a Portuguese chandler who supplies the *Sonia*. He carries a

Tartar bow and wicker shield.

Eastman has out pencil and pad but is not drawing. He takes notes for his newspaper report while the details are still fresh in mind. Walter's sensibilities, thinks Gideon, are changing.

'Damn my eyes!' Harry roars, the Vauxhall Gardens veneer stripped away in a moment of genuine anguish to reveal the cruder, honest grain of Mayo. 'The divil my foot!' He hops in agony, clutching his gouty old toe. Gideon says in concern, 'I've a notion you've trodden on a sword, perhaps, Mr O'Rourke.'

But: 'Damme, no, a stone.'

'Well, I reckon, too, sir, that Father Joaquim should have amassed all of those by now.'

'Ye poker-faced spalpeen, you. Eastman's a bad influence on ye.'

But Gideon bends over to investigate the loose sand. Feeling something hard, he must put both hands under its smooth, perfect roundness – the buttock of a marble statue surrendered by Arabian dunes, for certainly it is no natural formation. But of course: once he puts his back into the task, the object proves to be one of the 32-pound shot fired by the *Druid* that morning, some 600 of which lie where they struck on the beach. They are too heavy to be carried away easily by the civilian souvenir-hunters. Impact in the soft sand has meant they have come to no harm; in fact, they are not at all distorted and quite fit to be used again, a happy circumstance which, imbued as he is with the values of a neat and frugal service, has not eluded the vigilance of the first lieutenant of the *Druid*, who has detailed men to locate and stack the balls in pyramids. A sailor stands on one, reminding Gideon of tea-manufactory in the old Canton days, when the man slips and his weapon falls and discharges. Fortunately, no one is hit, but the horseplay seems to be attended with more danger than the fighting. Only four sailors have been slightly wounded; one stabbed in the calf in error by an over-eager sepoy. Gideon now retrieves from the sand a long bone. He holds it gingerly at arm's length.

O'Rourke regards it gloomily. 'It is a human femur, to be sure. I need no life-class for that.'

Gideon drops it hurriedly. 'Poor wretch. He perished in the

service of his country. Should Father…'

'Don't be a jackass. I would calculate that bone was months old. Regard how it has been bleached through the agency of the sun and the salt waters.' This is Eastman, pocketing his note-book.

'Our editor is correct, for once,' says Harry, whose letter castigating the *Lin Tin Bulletin and River Bee's* reviewer of Arthur Gordon Pym, or Mr Poe if you prefer it that way (and Harry does), has been suppressed by Walter. Eastman burrows in the sand, coming up with not only the femur but a piece of jawbone and teeth.

'Alas, poor Yorick.'

Gideon turns away in disgust. Further down, Father Ribeiro, shoeless, garments rolled up to reveal calves as fine as those of any of Afonso d'Alberquerque's captains, is engaged in his favourite exercise of rolling heavy weights – not boulders this time but half a dozen heavy cannon-balls. Behind him, he leaves his usual trail of a giant mole. 'If a heretic cleric started these troubles, my son,' he calls cheerfully, 'then let a missionary of the True Church clear his nuisances away.'

'Nicely so, Father.' Gideon leaves the Jesuit to his hobby and wanders back up the beach and into the old town, wondering why it all had to come to this. Walter and Harry swing their legs on a monster piece of captured ordnance and draw the holiday scene.

Green coconut from a huckster proves peculiarly refreshing.

Chapter XXXIII

From THE LIN TIN BULLETIN AND RIVER BEE

Wednesday, August 26, 1840

Vol.3 No.17

A momentous victory has been won in the north, such as will cause to pale into insignificance the petty game of bowls played out on our Macao promontory the week previous. No fierce gongs and wavings of tiger-banners on the one side, nor showers of grape and Huzzas on the other attended this silent contest, which was broken only by the panting of the victor and the sullen murmur of the vanquished. We can almost hear our readers crying – 'To what can you refer, sir, what can have eluded the net of the *Monitor* and its wide-flung allies and informants?' We refer, gentle subscribers, to the penetration of the *Madagascar* steamer up the Peiho or Peking river, hundreds of miles inland, even within thirty miles of Tientsin or the inland port of the capital. This is a most deadly stab in the vitals of the Celestial empire. No other craft could have succeeded in this complex passage, fraught as it is with perplexities and deceptions at every turn. Our own country can claim to have been in the van of this most extraordinary invention, for if Stephenson was its author, it was the Americans who applied the mighty force of steam to its fullest capacity in respect of fluvial navigation.

Yet even ten years ago their Lordships of the Admiralty had set their faces against steam-ships. It was milord Melville, if we are not much mistaken (whose 74-gun namesake owed her keel at Chusan to the help of those very despised steamers), who remarked a decade ago with as much sagacity as prescience that their Lordships greatly deprecated the introduction of steam and felt it their bounden duty to oppose the employment of steam-vessels, for they feared it would greatly tend to the dissolution of the Empire! We may safely presume that had the matter been left to the discretion of their asinine Lordships, the Emperor of China might even today sit securely on the throne in his Palace, safe from the rude molestation of the barbarians in their devil-ships. Merciful Heavens! The Empire owes its existence and preservation to Steam and Manchester!

The Admiralty, we make so bold as to remark, as an institution, betrays in its resistance to beneficial and useful innovation as large a degree of inflexibility and pedantry – indeed superstition and blind bigotry – as the examined and advanced bachelors of the mandarinate in their opposition to truth and the revealed proofs of scientific knowledge. (We talk not of Truth).

Mr Thom and the Blonde *at Amoy.* As he is personally known to us (although there is no marked propinquity in our intercourse) and, more especially, is like ourselves one of the tiny band of interpreters on this coast, we rejoiced as much as his closest friends when we were acquainted with Mr Thom's late deliverance from a wasteful and untimely death while attempting to deliver the British Proclamation at Amoy. The *Blonde* (44), Captain Bourchier, had been with the main fleet which sailed from Macao to Chusan when their Excellencies the Joint Plenipotentiaries, believing it a matter of courtesy to open a communication with the Government of China before bringing the sword to them (that the need for it might be averted), despatched the frigate to Amoy on the voyage northwards of the main fleet.

Mr Thom was put into a boat under a flag of truce and found, when he arrived, a hostile crowd already assembled at the beach. The lieutenant in charge of the boat, who did not require the gestures and expressions of the assembled Chinese translated, judged it best to proceed with extreme caution, a policy to be vindicated by the issue of the next few minutes, for when Mr Thom called to the Chinese in their own language, whether they would receive Captain Elliot's letter or no, they all roared as one man, 'No, we fear you not,' and uttered further threats, making the gesture significant of decapitation (which is so familiar to all of us that it has all the effect of a cheery Tap o' th' marnin' to yeez, sor, and a touched forelock). Mr Thom, taking his station standing on a thwart, still gallantly persisted. However, perceiving some of the Chinese to enter the water, preparatory to seizing the gunwales of the boat, the lieutenant ordered the men to back up on their oars, when the sudden motion caused Mr Thom *(whom for all his other accomplishments we know to be no boatman – ed.)* to topple backwards. An instant after, an arrow flew over the space his body had lately occupied and, striking the thwart, its brittle head shivered into fragments. The emissaries could now see the Chinese preparing to discharge some small field-pieces or gingals at them, which would surely have proved fatal to them in the small boat and at such close range, when the frigate, perceiving the condition to which affairs had degenerated on shore, of a sudden caused its cannon to speak in a language immediately comprehensible to the Chinese. Before the reports had carried, two 32-pound shot had whistled over the heads of the boat's crew and cut a lane through the mob when they at once dispersed in all directions, save the lifeless bodies of a dozen who paid dearly for their temerity.

Our own belief is that it was not a Chinese, properly speaking, who discharged the arrow at Mr Thom, but a Manchu, who would not have understood the language he was speaking, but to prevent the interpreter from making communication would have employed the traditional and favoured weapon of his tribe.

We regard it as a circumstance for particular regret that the object of these murderous attentions should have been one of the few men capable of effecting in their own persons a link and intercourse between the two empires which now oppose each other. To burn boats, to destroy bridges is the counsel of despair. We do not think it mere sodality which causes us to speak so. Certainly, though Mr Thom, like ourselves, was formerly engaged in business with a house of agency here (unlike the other interpreters who are divines in the majority), we do not share many of his beliefs in regard to the Chinese and the merits of the British *casus belli*. Nevertheless, we rejoice at his deliverance and heartily congratulate him.

ADVERTISEMENT

The proprietors of *Sturtevant's Hotel* beg to advise that the hotel is now open after the late events and that all those measures which are calculated to consult the comfort and convenience of their guests shall be undertaken by Mr and Mrs Sturtevant. The airy, healthy, and commodious accommodation which many have found to the benefit of impaired constitutions has been altogether refurbished, while the cellar was secured during the enforced absence of the proprietors. The proprietors extend a particular warm welcome to the heroes of the *Druid*. A capital curry is served at Sunday tiffin.

On the natives' tolerance of lying. With no little justification, the Chinese, are, alas, regarded by many foreigners as habitual deceivers and dissemblers. They will lie unblushingly and perpetrate the most bare-faced falsehoods, yet often enough for no very obvious reason and frequently not even to gain an advantage. It is often an occurrence that a well-born Chinese will dissimulate out of the merest courtesy. He will pretend to understand what you are saying and you may pass a pleasant hour in his company, your host full of smiles and nods, until at length it begins to dawn upon you that your friend does not comprehend a word of what passes from your lips. If you ask a question regarding a matter which is near your heart, the native will always supply you, should he be aware of your inclinations, with the answer he supposes you desire to hear, irrespective of the true standing of affairs.

When you confront him later with the proof and specimen of his own hardihood, he will smile and agree he is a liar. They do not impose upon the foreigner alone, but as a matter of course tell falsehoods to each other. Caught in the perpetration of the most outrageous fictions the high-born native will feel no embarrassment. No particular stigma attaches to the practice, nor is there especial condemnation of its consequences. Now, you may call an American uncouth, foolish, or even dishonest, without having the consequences of your impudence visited upon your own head, but call the same man a LIAR, or presume to doubt the truth of his tallest story, and you may hear gun-fire. To say to a Chinese, 'Sir, I disbelieve everything you say and regard you in the light of a confirmed and habitual liar,' is to say to an American or an Englishman, 'Sir, I understand you are a skilled and faithful mimic and I should greatly desire to be given a sample of your repertoire.'

If they cannot distinguish truths from falsehoods, how may they be expected to receive Greater Truths?

From THE CANTON MONITOR
Tuesday, September 22nd, 1840

ADVERTISEMENT

Lumqua, famous portrait-painter, formerly of Whampoa and Canton, now most respectfully advises all ladies and gentlemen that his studio can be found at Rua da Nossa Senhora da Nazare 11, Macao, where he solicits the favour of their commissions, at rates the most reasonable, not to be compared with foreign portrait-painters, of whom he confidently recommends himself as at least the equal. Also to be discovered at the same premises, Ah Sam, cabinet-maker and fashioner of rattan furniture, formerly of Carpenter's Square at the Factories of Canton, now having completed the translation of his business to Macao.

From THE LIN TIN BULLETIN AND RIVER BEE

Wednesday, October 7, 1840

Vol.3 No.20

Recall and disgrace of Lin. It is with no sensation of pleasure that we hear news of the dismissal of Lin and his summons in disgrace to Peking. Although we ourselves suffered in consequence of his imperious and sometimes high-handed, as well as high-minded, actions, nevertheless we always viewed him in the light of a true patriot and honourable man, for though if the measures he adopted were in the end proven to be as impolitic as they were unjust, his aim was both noble and right – the extirpation of the wicked trade in opium. It was to be regretted that his views on the extension of the legal trade were peculiarly unenlightened, though a longer intercourse with the more moderate foreigners might well have influenced him for the better.

Lin was the last to know of his summary recall. The fall of the Imperial Commissioner from his exalted place on high had been bruited as a matter of common gossip in the bazaars of Canton for some days beforehand, doubtless passing from the venal lictors of the *yamuns* ever southwards, with such of those corrupt functionaries who were also members of secret societies doubtless not neglecting to relate the news to their criminal associates, so that well before the official messengers arrived, the provincial metropolis buzzed with the scandal. The mandarins in the Hoppo's department, for so long deprived of their bribes from the foreigners, a vital and probably in all conscience the major part of their incomes, did not trouble to disguise their glee at the downfall of a just and righteous magistrate.

They know that Captain Elliot entertained a great deal of respect for Lin and that the English Plenipotentiary hoped that Lin and the court might be prevailed upon to make legal the outlawed trade in drug, that a limit might be put upon it and the worst abuses and excesses curbed. This would have dammed at the source the origins of their riches.

Yet Lin was resolved to eradicate the trade entirely.

The Commissioner received the imperial will before his official residence, reverencing in the prescribed manner the communication, which had been brought on horseback by relays of messengers. He retired to acquaint himself with its vermilion contents but, our informants say, maintained a serene and dignified composure when he emerged shortly afterwards. His personal staff were desolated. Within a matter of hours, lampoons had been fixed on the wall of Canton.

We do not believe Lin's life is endangered as the inevitable consequence of his failure, nor do we attach any credence to the wild and absurd rumours that he travels back to Peking in chains. Yet this sad relation does serve to show how vain and transient are the highest honours and powers when they are bestowed at the whim of an autocrat. The populace at the hustings is not more fickle.

PURSUER

From THE LIN TIN BULLETIN AND RIVER BEE

Wednesday, November 18, 1840

Vol.3 No.23

Resignation of Admiral Elliot. Sir George Elliot, lately returned from the islands of Chusan in the company of his cousin and joint Plenipotentiary, Captain Charles Elliot, has, we have it on the best authority, announced his resignation from the responsibilities of the expedition. He is in hopes of leaving shortly for Trincomalee and thence England. During the term of his command as Senior Naval Officer, Sir George has not enjoyed good health, his constitution having been impaired during the service of his country, man and boy. It is not the remittent fevers and dysenteries (which have proved so deadly to so many poor fellows during the short space they have sojourned here) which have forced him to relinquish his post, but the poor health occasioned by an infirmity of the heart. We know, too, that *Captain* Elliot's heart is not in his work of protecting the opium-traders among his fellow-countrymen. How paradoxical is his task! At the one time he is charged with discouraging the illegal trade, yet is given no effective powers to prevent it. Rather his masters expect him to turn the blind eye of Lord Nelson to it.

We are sorry to hear that when the Elliots arrived at Chusan at the end of September, on their journey southwards, they found an epidemic raging among the garrison, which had taken away a good many poor fellows. The troops had been stationed in the rice-paddies and marshes in close proximity to the noxious exhalations emitted at night which must have affected their healths adversely and, which tends to prove the truth of this supposition, those troops who had pitched their tents on the summits by the joss-house lost not a single man while the angel of death tarried here and there among their less fortunate brethren, who found themselves encamped in the valleys and declivities.

Through a glass, darkly. As there appears to be a supposition, very generally though incorrectly held, and more pronounced among those who are *not* our readers than among those who are, that we are prejudiced against the missionary gentlemen, both as linguists and as divines, we are pleased to take the opportunity of dispelling the former at least of these most unjustified charges. It is true that many of the missionaries are but indifferent scholars of the Chinese language (including the Chentleman from Chermany who loves to distribute the Good Word with the chests of drug); yet they may also count among their number such accomplished specimens of scholars as Morrison the senior, Rémusat, See, and let us not omit the great Jesuit missionaries of the past. We find it most significant that when Marshman came to the mighty task of translating the Bible into Chinese, he should have chosen to begin (and end his own labours) with the *New* Testament. This circumstance is accountable not by reason of any intrinsic difficulty in translating the language of the Old Testament word for word. The most beautiful, terse, and sonorous language of the Bible of King James is at one in its limpidity and exactness in both Testaments. The evenness of tone is, to be sure, quite deceiving, for though the various books of both Testaments are by quite different hands and composed at widely varying periods of time, and in different languages (viz. Hebrew, Greek, Latin, and even others) the very success of the translation of the scholars of King James confers upon it a most deceiving and spurious uniformity. Holy Scripture may partake of the nature of the Truth of Divine Revelation, but its expression is most variable.

Now for us, educated men and women of the nineteenth century, the language in which we read it is quite archaic. Familiarity from youth with the more notable passages gives them, from excessive hearing, all the meaning of a bell monotonously tolling. To hear of the brazen idols of the Old Testament, the temples, the city walls, the gongs, trumpets, and cymbals, is further to have our sympathies removed. The entire effect is to operate upon our imaginations (the eye of the mind) as if we were looking at events, already sufficiently distant, through the wrong or diminishing end of a telescope. The struggling figures become so tiny as to appear like insects rather than real, struggling, suffering men. But not so when the Scriptures are translated into Chinese! A thousand times no! The words for *idol, temple, gong* (yea, even the *cross* in the slow and lingering death of a thousand cuts) are as live and real to them as the artefacts they represent. On every hand they see idols and temples, hear gongs, and walk on city walls very much like those of Jericho. To talk to, say, Mr I-, of forsaking idols (save that of Mammon) is meaningless. To tell a Chinese to run out, like Moses, and break up the idols of the city gods as the prophet did that of Baal, is to incite him to a most desperate act of civil insurrection. Nor are these exhortations couched in the learned expressions of a dead language or the antique form of a still living tongue, but in the most contemporary and pungent idiom of the

Chinese, as is the nature of translation. By changing the form of Holy Writ the translator also most drastically alters, if not its matter, its effect. Much like the unhappy savant of the novel, the reverend scholar rendering the Scriptures into the native tongue breathes life into a body long moribund. Is it a wonder, then, that he creates monsters (but not in the manner in which the ignorant among the natives believe he purloins the organs and eyes of dead children), or that the Chinese are loth to receive the Word of Life?

PURSUER

CHAPTER XXXIV

Captain Charles Elliot, RN, to Gideon Chase, Esq.

> *Louisa* cutter
> Macao Roads
> November 23rd, 1840

My dear Mr Chase,

As an American citizen, under the protection of the Republic which has remained a neutral power during the term of the conflict which the Royal Navy has carried along the coast and rivers of this empire, your astonishment at the presumption of the chief of one of the belligerent parties in writing thus to you may only be exceeded by your embarrassment. However, I am emboldened to address you both by reason of your reputation in the foreign community as a gentleman of Public Spirit and, if I may further presume, from my own knowledge of your Character and Attainments as has been made evident in your writing and scholarly pursuits. Without further burdening you with compliments which would be as tedious for you to receive as they would be supererogatory for me to bestow, I would venture to ask you, my dear sir, whether I, on behalf of Her Majesty, and Her Government, and also on behalf of what, despite temporary disagreements may have obscured, is the Mother Country out of which issued the seed from which sprang the sovereign republic of which you have the honour to be a citizen – on behalf of all these, I say, and whatever sentiment they may inspire in you, I have the audacity to speculate if I might prevail upon you to lend your services to my personal staff as a translator and an interpreter. I should need to call upon your accomplishments in that order of priority. I may say that this is in no way intended as a slight upon your grasp of the vernacular dialects of the Coast and Interior, nor is it to say that I am blessed in the execution of my duties with an abundance of linguists, for we sorely lack men with a command of the different Chinese languages, but that as the prosecution of the war advances, and as the Chinese are brought to a knowledge of their own manifest inadequacies in a material point of view for the conduct of a struggle which must be cruelly uneven, we shall require men of attainments and ability in the literary language of the Chinese as the time approaches for communication, negotiation, and in the fullness of the time, *deo volente,* a treaty of peace.

Furthermore, and in no way must you imagine this as reflecting upon your personal courage, it would not be appropriate for the citizen of a neutral country to be exposed to the hazards necessarily incidental to pursuing duties where of their very nature he should confront the Chinese in close proximity and very likely without the benefit of arms. I believe you are already acquainted with Mr Thom's narrow escape at Amoy.

Lest you should hesitate for fear of aiding and abetting the enemies of China, and through a most understandable unwillingness to participate in the persecution of a weaker party, I should assure you that by helping to make the passage of arms as brief as possible and precluding the logical extension of hostilities to the areas of great population in the north, you should in fact be consulting the welfare and safety of the innocuous and unoffending people of this empire, who are not at all to be blamed for the policies of their masters. I believe it to be sufficiently well known among all who know me, as well as notorious among those who do not, so I do not court disbelief or derision when I profess it – to gain the most from the Government of China that is consonant with honour and propriety at the least cost of human life among its subjects has ever been my aim.

It is perhaps inappropriate to mention to a gentleman and scholar of your attainments the question of remuneration and I certainly do not do so now in order to influence your decision, which must be made for very different motives. However, I should merely confine myself to the very bald statement that the salary of Company Rupees 35,000 is attached to the post, remittable through the financial instruments of the East India Company at Canton or Calcutta.

I have, my dear sir, etc.

Ch. Elliot (Signed)

H M Joint Plenipotentiary and Chief Superintendent of Trade in China

Gideon Chase, Esq., to *Captain Charles Elliot, RN*

Rua da Nossa Senhora da Nazare 12
Macao
November 24th, 1840

My dear Captain Elliot,

I have the honour to reply to your letter of the 23rd *inst.* and I most willingly acquiesce in your proposal in kind and flattering terms to attach me to your personal staff in the first instance as an interpreter and in the second a translator, on terms which I want the delicacy to refrain from describing as exceedingly handsome, and if I take issue with any of the terms of my appointment, it is implicit in the order of words of acceptance. Such, sir, is the cunning which a course of study in the Chinese language induces in its followers. I shall stand the same risks of service as Mr Thom, Mr Morrison, and Mr Gutzlaff, *and* face Kishen's loaded antitheses and word-orderings.

I have, believe me, my dear Captain Elliot, the honour to be your very trusty, obedient servant,
Gideon Chase

Ah Sam scratches his bald head, then scrutinises the diagram before him. He picks his nose, by way of relief and variety inspecting the grey mucus on his finger, which he rolls into a ball. He is baffled by what Young Inky Devil wants. This is like no curio-cabinet he has fashioned before, and there *have* been some strange commissions: the mahogany thunder-box with the wicker seat, the lepidopterist's specimen-case, the false-bottom security-chest (which was the item nearest Ah Sam's heart). But what in the name of fornicating progenitors can this be? It basically takes the form of a baseboard with two boxes which must be capable of sliding into each other on grooved insertions. Young Inky Devil made gestures of a huge, unintended lewdness as he demonstrated how one box penetrated the other. Ah Sam made him do it several times before he allowed himself to catch on. Then enthusiastically mimicked Young Inky Devil.

'That's right, that's right,' said Young Inky Devil in his own barbarian tongue.

'Me hab got — old fellow now but still can do,' said Ah Sam, not daring to look at his convulsing workmen.

Otherwise, there was a hole to be cut in the front of the box, a removable panel inserted inside the back of the larger box, three-quarters down, and a flap on the hinge. Also a mirror and two integral doors which could be opened by a rod from outside. Fornicating fathers.

Then Young Inky Devil wanted the joints sealed with pitch, a gross affront to a real craftsman. 'I don't produce cheap rubbish like your barbarian sing-songs,' Ah Sam said coldly in his own tongue, which went straight over Young Inky Devil's head. Fortunately Stripling Who Knew Talk wasn't there. A very dangerous fellow, he was. Hadn't he listened to the workmen wondering who sodomised whom, and then the fellow had asked for a cup of tea in a perfect Tung Kwun accent.

Fear of *him* was the only reason Ah Sam accepted the inky one's commission.

Now he pushes the boxes in and out of each other. Probably a set of bellows. They did melt lead next door. But why teak for the boxes then? A waste of fine wood. He smears his own mucus along a join, sniffs, and takes up a pot of varnish.

'The principle,' Walter pontificates to Father Ribeiro, 'is one of the most extraordinary simplicity.'

'So,' says the Jesuit gloomily, 'are the cardinal principles of theology.'

'Well, Father, I've a notion that this instrument may be a tool of the devil, who has a preference for simpler things. There is nothing new about the casting of the image, which is altogether as if it were a *camera obscura* – take a grasp upon yourself, Harry, or you shall have an apoplexy – and the picture is thrown upside down and, of course, reversed from right to left, as with that device, on to the back of the inner box. A convex lens of a meniscus design fixed over the aperture at the front of the outer box would produce a brighter and … sharper image of the scene, or, indeed, person, viewed. If it collapsed and extended, like a telescope, rather than being fixed into the body of the cabinet, then the focus and distance of objects represented might be varied without recourse to sliding the boxes.

'Now, where Daguerre has most brilliantly succeeded is in retaining and permanently fixing, as it were, the image cast. By treating a polished plate of copper, plated with silver, which is fixed at the rear of the second box, with a solution of reagents – to be precise, iodine, in the greater part – he has rendered that surface so sensitive, so voracious of light that it absorbs in the most astonishing detail any scene or personage which should play against it. If treated with bromine, as well as iodine, the plate is further sensitised, shortening the time required for its exposure to light most considerably. When the plate is held over heated mercury the effect of the vapour of this reagent is to further clarify the image, when it is finally fixed by a powerful solution of common salt.'

496

Walter halts triumphantly, and is a trifle disappointed by the reaction of his audience. 'I had the gunsmiths fashion me a brass tube and pivoting disc of the same material to act as cover and lens-holder respectively.'

'Ah, like a telescope,' says Gideon.

'Quite the reverse, my dear Chase,' says Walter sternly.

'And, my son, of what use is this invention? I believe nothing good proceeded out of France in the last fifty years.'

'*Use!*' cries Walter. 'Why, my dear Father, there are one and a thousand applications. At a stroke, it shall...' Walter catches sight of O'Rourke's crimson face and bites back his words, which would have been '...make the painter extinct'. (Of both landscape and portrait to an equal degree, he thinks.) Instead, he says, 'Every man shall be a Hilliard, a Poussin, a....Lawrence.'

'Pshaw!' says Harry rudely.

'But how very democratic,' says Ribeiro. 'I did not believe you were a radical, my son.'

'Well, Father, I don't believe in debasing principles, or lowering standards to accommodate those of the mass. However, I do say that to talk of raising the universal standard to that of the genius is another issue entirely.'

'Poppycock.'

Walter elects to ignore this.

'How simple! Merely impregnate your plate and insert it within the box. Slide that receptacle an inch or two forwards or backwards to clarify the image. Remove the brass cap or disc to expose the plate to the light of the sun. Wait for it to take the image – smoke your cigar the while. And, like magic, the perfect representation – *sans* effort, *sans* skill.'

'You mean,' says Gideon with some excitement, 'that it lies within the power of the common man, of myself, who wants all aptitude to represent, to take a perfect likeness of the world I see, as well as does Mr O'Rourke? And all by the power of the sun?'

'Indeed so. And now,' says Walter, who only needs a little encouragement, 'the machine.'

Father Ribeiro looks doubtful and Harry O'Rourke ferocious, as Walter places a handsome chest of camphor-wood on the table, the Jesuit put in mind of Zoroaster, not to mention some private worshippers of the golden orb, while O'Rourke thinks balefully of the Venetian charlatan.

'Pandora's box,' says Walter gaily.

'Is that it?' asks Gideon, disappointed. 'It has every appearance of being an ordinary aromatic cabinet, such as I might purchase anywhere in Carpenter's Square.'

'That, you foolish boy, is its travelling guise,' and from the chest Walter produces an object the like of which they have never seen before.

'It is, gracious me, like...a weapon, with the protuberant barrel of brass.'

'No, not a weapon, a boon to mankind. And how few originators may claim that. Even the power of steam is harnessed for war, but this is wholly innocuous.'

'Do not underestimate the old Adam, my son.'

'Have you the reagents?' Gideon asks eagerly. 'For we could contemplate an experiment with the device.'

'It is too late in the day. To gain the most perfected results we should require brilliant sunshine.'

'Hah, so you don't work miracles. I need an umbrella merely.'

'And to be impregnated with the fruit of the grape-press, rather than bromine.'

'Damme, you go too far, sir. Thank'ee, Joaquim, not to the brim.'

'Now these, though, may serve to amuse,' says Walter, removing some plates from a large leather wallet.

'Good God! The fort and bay! To the life! No, I cannot credit. It is...It is altogether unlike any painting I have ever seen – a piece of the world, yes, and yet the world bleached of its essence – I do not mean its colours. God in heaven, you have stolen this image from the world's store!'

Walter smiles complacently at Gideon's excitement. More wonders are to be displayed, he knows.

'Remedios! The villain. It is *him,* the scar on his cheek, the scowl. And the old barber and eye-scraper! But, Walter, Remedios's hand has failed to become solid... it seems to vibrate or be in a fog.'

'Ah, yes, it was the devil's own work to get him to sit. He

would whittle with that damned dagger of his. A Chinaman's your best subject.'

'Indeed,' says Harry drily, 'better still, an opium-addict in his reverie, or a corpse – even better. Ideal objects for your…what d'ye call it?'

'Heliogravure or Daguerreotype.'

'Then how long does it take, Walter, for the plate to become imprinted?'

'Up to the half of an hour in adverse conditions.'

'Oh.' Gideon looks disappointed. 'Then you may not take a man running?'

'N-o-o-o,' says Walter reluctantly, 'that still requires the painstaking observation and imagination, not to say genius, of a painter of the front rank.' He warms to his sentence as he speaks it, seeking a chance to mollify O'Rourke. 'It is dependent upon your distance from the object, the further the better. One could successfully portray a 74 under sail at two miles, or a steamer at a greater remove, but you could hardly see…'

'Portray! Object!' Harry spits. 'You do not portray it – you take it, sir.'

'I am not sure, Mr O'Rourke, sir, what you can mean.'

'Bah!'

'My dear Harry, you are too hasty with our young friend, our young friends. After all, I can see directly what the consequences may be for the artist. The device of Daguerre may not be, to speak fancifully, the designing murderer who would make pretensions to succeed you as the monarch of all you surveyed, so much as the handmaiden of the artist. Why sit outside in all manner of inclement weathers when for – ten minutes, my son? – you might take home a faithful copy of the original to look upon at your leisure? Why, Harry, to think you might have been spared hours of sitting with Mr Jardine or Mrs Marjoribanks.'

'Damme, the Scottish skinflint would rather have the…'

'Daguerreotype.'

'Thank'ee, than the artist's interpretation of plane and mood. What d'ye sell 'em for, boy?'

'Well, sir, I could hardly contemplate…'

'You are a humbug, sir. Young, but a humbug. A humbug but

young. A young humbug, sir. Yes. Are you ashamed, sir?'

'No, sir.'

'No, sir? Well, I shall have to take you down a peg, sirrah.'

'Is this a challenge, Harry?'

'It is, but in my own good time, and on my own ground and terms.'

From THE LIN TIN BULLETIN AND RIVER BEE

Wednesday, December 2, 1840
Vol.3 No. 23

Keshen. He is the Viceroy of the metropolitan province or Pechihli, whom we now know to have been designated as the successor of the disgraced Lin Ja Hui. The governorship of Chihli is the most coveted post in the empire. As his name might suggest, he is a Manchu, and one closely related to the clan of the Emperor. He it was who received Captain Elliot with snuff and presents of beef, eggs, vegetables, and other fresh comestibles at Taku on the Peking River and persuaded him to return to the south. He made no objections about receiving Captain Elliot's communication, unmarked by the letter *pin* or 'an humble petition', where formerly Captain Elliot had been most rudely assaulted for his temerity on a similar occasion before the gates of Canton in 1836. A man of about fifty years of age or upwards, stalwart, remarkable for a queue of extravagant length, and a mandarin of the red button and peacock's tail. He appears less inflexible than Lin.
PURSUER

Fate of Captain Anstruther and Mrs Noble. We are now apprised that the gallant Captain is still alive and as well as may be expected, having been seized while out sketching in the countryside of Chusan two months ago. He was slung by the ankles and wrist on a pole and carried off like a porker rather than an officer of the Madras Artillery, when he was stealthily conveyed to the mainland by his kidnappers. We understand that he is held in Ningpo. Excited and emboldened by their success, the mandarins have put out rewards for Barbarian Heads.

Mrs Noble, taken under slightly different circumstances, is also said to be alive in Ningpo. She was shipwrecked in the *Kite* surveying vessel, of which her husband was Master, under command of Lieutenant Douglas of the *Melville,* which was lost with her crew and a party of marines. She was the only survivor of the wreck and lost both her husband and infant child. She was treated with great cruelty, being carried in a cage so small that she could only sit doubled up, with her chin resting upon her knees. As she passed from village to village on her way to Ningpo she was exhibited in every place. She is a Scotswoman, red-haired and tall of stature.

From THE LIN TIN BULLETIN AND RIVER BEE

Wednesday, December 16, 1840
Vol.3 No.24

...and altogether the discovery and its applications are of far too momentous consequence and potential benefit to mankind for it to be kept a close secret. In the spirit in which M. Daguerre unveiled his discovery to the generality of the public on August 19th the year previous, in return for a small pension from the government of France, we shall also not delay in revealing the particulars to those among our readers and ever cherished subscribers who should wish to imitate the process and mount experiments of their own. They should find them of endless fascination and amusement. We speak from personal experience. Having furnished instructions above for the manufacture of the boxes and a diagram, drawn by our own hand, for we find those of the original (dare we say it) less than perfectly clear and prolix as a consequence of a native Gallic love of over-embellishment, besides being unsuitable in some particulars for service between the Tropics, we shall now directly proceed to a discussion of the apparatus and solutions of reagents requisite for the sensitising of the silvered surface of the copper plate. In all essential particulars, the information is drawn from the *Historique et Description des Procédés du Daguerreotype et du Diorama,* composed by M. Daguerre and published by his relation and associate, M. Giroux.

The following comprise the barest apparatus necessary, though experience will advise the employment of additional items in respect of convenience and speed:

1. Copperplate.
2. Frame (to hold plate at corners)
3. Buffing-board and chamois leather.
4. Jeweller's rouge.
5. Sensitising box and porcelain or glass dish. (The Chinaware hand-warmers for containing charcoal, which are used by the native ladies and are exposed for sale on the third stall at the Native Bazaar in Macau, answer admirably for the purpose.)
6. Crystals of iodine.
7. Small trays with glass covers.

For the enhancement or *development* of the image transferred to the plate in the chamber of the *camera obscura* the following are requisite:

1. Cubic enhancing-box, with metal or porcelain dish.
2. Spirit lamp
3. Mercury.
4. Thermometer.
5. Common salt.
6. Sand-or hour-glass.

We have ourselves in our own essays in the new art (for such it is) found that a developing-box fitted with legs serves the best, for then the lamp may be placed beneath it with the greater ease in order to heat the mercury and elicit its vapours. Folding or retractable legs are not so strong as those permanently fixed into the body but are certainly of greater convenience when going a voyage or if stowage-space should be limited. The food-boxes and lamps such as are used by the natives to keep their food warm may, with slight modifications, be well adapted to the purposes of the Heliogravist.

Thus we flatter ourselves that the machine we have described resembles in all essential particulars its French prototype, and that we may even have improved upon it in point of serviceability and sturdiness.

SOLORIENS

An instructive cruise. Through the kind instrumentality of a friend, colleague, and, at one time, subordinate, though junior now only in years and senior infinitely to ourselves in accumulated knowledge and wisdom accrued, we were enabled lately to take our first passage on a steamer. We are aware that such an admission may serve to inspire feelings of scorn and contumely calculated to excite derision and pity in the bosoms of our friends, rather than the envy and astonishment we should have been inclined to expect. 'What! Not boarded a steamer! My dear sir, have a care what you say, and you an American! The Canton River is not to be mentioned in the same breath as the mighty Mississippi – keep your shortcomings and manifest inadequacies to yourself.'

We are aware that the river-boats of our own country are inclined to make a bigger roar when they 'go up' than either the *Madagascar* or *Enterprise* in the discharge of their 32-pounders, but should wish to be spared that interesting and elevating fate. We did once cross the Hudson on the steam-bridge, but we should hardly call that lubberly device a vessel proper. No, we should merely add in extenuation that we have taken a China residence for far too long and that our more recently arrived contemporaries and compatriots have the advantage of us in this respect.

There was no need to be rowed out to the *Nemesis*. Her shallow draught (she draws but six feet fully laden, more commonly five) enables her to come into the Inner Harbour and, indeed, we might have lobbed an orange through the windows of the Governor's Palace from the larboard (we apologise for our backwardness, *port,* as the mariners now say) paddle-box. This interesting vessel is made in the entirety of iron as to her hull (the *Jardine* and the Honourable Company's armed steamers are wooden, viz, *Queen, Madagascar, Enterprise,* and *Atalanta)* and Captain Hall assures us she is the first iron vessel to double the Cape, though not, we understand, without incident when a gigantic wave struck her off the coast of Africa and started a split in her side halfway down her length. This cracked to a depth of seven feet and though planks and bolts were applied to her hull, it was feared she should split in twain. Happily, the storm abated.

She is armed with two 32-pounders, on pivots fore and aft, which may throw shot or shell, brass 6-pounders and iron swivels on the sides, and, on the bridge, between the paddle-boxes, a tube for Congreve rockets, as well as bearing the usual complement of boat-guns and small-arms.

The impression she gives with her small masts and tall chimney-stack is of length and lowness, an appearance borne out by the recitation of her physical dimensions, which are of a beam of 29 feet compared to a length of 184 feet. She displaces 630 tons and her engines are of the order of 120 horse-power. She has two sliding keels, which may be raised into the hull, and is divided into seven water-tight compartments to resist wreck and shot-holes.

Of the man who commands this vessel, suffice it to say that Captain Hall is as distinguished for his courtesy, kindness, and hospitableness and good breeding as he is noted for his seamanship and courage. He is not a stranger to these shores, having been midshipman on the *Lyra* under Captain Basil Hall during Lord Amherst's embassy to China in 1816 when he passed some weeks in Macao. What were our surprise and pleasure when we discovered that Captain

Hall had gained his experience of steam-boating in a different capacity on the Delaware and Hudson rivers! He entertained pleasant memories of those scenes and personages of his youth and of our country in general. He had been invalided from the Royal Navy on the ground of infirmity, although to regard him now, the picture of stalwart, rude health, nothing could be more difficult to imagine. At present he holds the rank of Master-Commanding, RN, though actually in the pay of the Government of India, that is, the Honourable Company. Strange to say, he holds no official commission or rank from the Home Government and, that being so, like the rest of the steamer-commanders, could not read the Articles of War to his crew, who, in fact, are not under martial law! Now what a strange anomaly!

We do suspect that the steamers and their crews are in some measure looked down upon by the officers and men not only of the stately line of battle ships and dashing frigates, but also even the bouncy, impertinent little brigs and sloops of war, as a set of grubby, foul, greasy, sooty, sweating operatives of landlubbers rather than the fine seamen they are by training and experience. We grant the black clouds, sparks, and flames which belch out of the stack of the *Nemesis* are more suggestive of the mill and iron-works than the white horses of the sea, that we have ourselves seen her stain the snowy, billowing clouds of the *Melville* and draw the wrath of the master on that towering quarter-deck, freely also do we own that the task of coaling in port is a labour the filth of which it is difficult adequately to represent in words (though a painting or Heliogravure could), while the settling fine dust makes the eyes water, the nose to run, and the throat rasp. Yet, for all that, there is something not altogether ignoble, majestic even, in the sight of three such vessels in line abreast, steaming for the setting sun, with their wheels churning the sea to a maddened froth, for beauty is in the eye of the beholder.

Although the *Nemesis* has yet to see action (Captain Hall was sorely tempted during his voyage across the Indian Ocean to aid the young Sultan of the Comoros islands against his designing uncles and to render material assistance to the Governor of Mozambique, Brigadier Joaquim Pereira Morindo, in the attempts to suppress the slavers), the other steamers have already proved their worth many times over. The only fear of Captain Hall is the circumstance of a shot splintering a paddle-box which is altogether vulnerable, and the only argument against the wholesale employment of the steamer as a perfected arm of marine warfare. (But are not the masts of a sailing-ship equally vulnerable, even to chain-shot?)

Such accidents of chance were far from our minds when we took our cruise around the Kap-sing-moon with the band of the 18th playing such patriotic airs as 'The Roast Beef of Old England', 'The British Grenadier', not to mention 'Rule Britannia', and, as a special mark of Captain Hall's regard and politeness, a most spirited rendering of 'Yankee Doodle'. It was quaint to see the fishermen, working at their nets, jump up and gesticulate when they were alerted to the approach of the strange, fiery craft by the sounds of the tunes floating over the waters. The splash of the wheels, the throb and beat of the engines, the hiss of the steam, added their contribution to the orchestra's medley, as the band attempted some appropriate music of Handel, not forgetting the boom of the 32-pounder's salute as we heard the strains of the 'Grenadier' a second time. All the while, we dashed along, cheered and invigorated, the spray flew, the gulls circled, the wind sang through the rigging. We undertake we shall not forget this day for a long while.

'Now, gentlemen, pray remain still as statues for the duration of the plate's exposure to the light. Not so much as a muscle may twitch.'

'Good God, sir, I trust we may blink, or d'ye have eye-patches for us?'

'Blink by all means, Captain Hall. Harry, endeavour to look more pleased with the world.'

'I am not pleased with it. I think I'm grown too old for it and had better get along.'

'Then leave an exhibit for posterity. Do you put your hand over the chair. Jonathan, hold MacQuitty by the ears – you must answer for his behaviour.'

'Sir, you talk of a gun-dog. He'll be stiller than any of us, our friends and the gallant officers included.'

Walter moves along the verandah, disposing of his friends' limbs, hands, heads, swords, telescopes, as he will. The naval officers seem to enjoy the rigamarole much more than the civilians. It seems to flatter their self-esteem, though not so much as being portrayed on a shattered quarter-deck by a proper marine artist. Or bridge, in the case of these steamer-crews.

'Worse than being made an apostle in a painting of the Last Supper,' grumbles Johnstone.

'Not so at all,' ripostes Walter. 'That would go on for weeks, even with the preliminary sketches accomplished. You'll be as free as a bird in ten minutes.'

'Aye,' which is O'Rourke, 'but you're not, damn it. You have to take them as they *are*. I can change what I will. You may be the democratic representer, sir, but you have no liberty.'

'Well, I allow so. But I shall take the liberty of requesting you not to gesture to make your points. Now, stock-still all. Ridley, you are not to make them laugh.'

The gorgeous parakeets in the missing Thomas Veale's aviary squawk and chatter, a peacock, no less conscious of its dignity and ruffled feathers than Harry O'Rourke of his, steps over the ancient lawn. The house has been turned over to naval and marine officers as a club, pending the return (no longer expected) of its owner. The sight is too much for MacQuitty's hunting instincts, and, with a bark, he's out of Ridley's lap and snapping at the wire.

'God damn it, Jonathan.'

'I haven't moved a muscle, I'll assure you.'

'Nor me,' chorus the officers.

Walter grunts. He has a sand-glass in his hand. After a few minutes the top chamber has run dry. He swings the brass disc over the lens of his camera. 'Thank you, gentlemen.'

'That's all?'

'You shall view the results in due course, and I shall be inclined to believe you shall not be disappointed.'

Captain Hall is the only naval officer present to be dressed in mufti, a sober black jacket, which makes him look like a clerk but for the powerful thighs which strain at the confinement of his white trousers.

He offers Walter a cigar from his box (fellow-addicts) and says, 'You'll take some fine prospects, and no doubt engagements, too, if you get on the *Nemesis* again, Mr Eastman.'

'That, I'll have the liberty to observe, is a big "if", Captain.'

'I'll see you aboard, Mr Eastman, my authority runs that far, I believe. Recollect, too, Mr Chase is not without influence in the quarters where it might matter.'

By now O'Rourke looks extremely sour. His stubby fingers flick at the rattan of his chair.

Walter says, 'I guess I'm much obliged, Captain Hall, for your kind offer,' his formality a veneer for some qualms (of trepidation as well as conscience). 'I'll present you gentlemen with the fruits of your indulgence and my own labours right away. I shall withdraw inside for some little time,' and he carries off his paraphernalia, aided by Remedios – this latter an unlikely but very willing assistant who has been behind the contraption all the time, glowering and toying with the hilt of the dagger protruding from his sash, as if daring anyone to move.

Harry scrawls across the back of a Chinese proclamation, which comprises part of Gideon's work for the Plenipotentiary. He prods back his pince-nez. He mutters. Ridley winks at Colin M'Dougal, the irascible mechanical wizard who is chief engineer of the *Nemesis*. For Harry, this little sketch is a conjuror's trick for children, a *jeu d'esprit,* a spirited rally.

'Two minutes and thirty-two seconds,' says Ridley, who has been timing Harry. He flips shut the lid of his hunter. 'Which is, let us recollect, one fifth part of Walter's requirement, and we've been leaping around like hop-frogs.'

'You've captured the line of my leg well,' says Captain Hall, looking at Harry's sketch. 'I shall commission a portrait of my vessel from you, Mr O'Rourke, if you have the kindness.'

'But before we see action,' says Lieutenant Pedder, a red-haired fellow. 'We'll not want the shot-holes in your canvas, nor the splintered boxes.'

'But, my dear sir,' says Ridley, 'I had the impression Keshen was suing for terms at the Peiho.'

'So had Captain Elliot,' says Pedder grimly. 'Gutzlaff says Keshen is making a monkey of the Plenipo. While we were within knocking distance of the Palace door, he was all smiles and accommodation. Depart again for the south – and, lo, all the doors are closed and frowns are the order of the day. During which time, thanks to the Plenipo, the batteries at the Bogue are put into repair. We shall see a few more brave fellows buried before John Chinaman knows reason.'

'You embarrass Mr Chase,' says Captain Hall in a neutral voice, so that Gideon is uncertain whether he is reprimanding his first lieutenant or making a simple statement. He would imagine the bluff and active Captain Hall would have little patience with the Plenipotentiary's hesitations and niceties.

'Captain Hall, sir, do you believe you and your ship's company will still be in these seas today twelvemonth?' Ridley enquires.

'Mr Ridley,' Hall says, 'this Boxing Day you have taken my officers' pay from them with your cue, and I doubt not but that you shall be defeating them at billiards again the next.'

Walter's muffled voice comes from the library of Veale's bungalow, cursing the hapless Remedios. He is possibly the only man ever to have done so without getting his ribs tickled by four inches of steel. Glass tinkles and breaks; there is the whirr of a bottle rolling on an uneven wood floor, ravaged by damp and white ant. 'God damn it, you three-handed idiot, stand back. Cook-boy, bring water.'

'Well,' says Harry O'Rourke with great complacency, 'this is a regular process, is it not? D'ye think he can transmute lead into gold with his iodine philtre?'

'Give the boy his chance,' Captain Hall murmurs. 'Give him time.'

'We could all do with some of that commodity, sir.'

From within, a cry of purest anguish. Walter emerges with the product of his exertions. He is nearly in tears of rage. 'Spoiled! Spoiled! Where is he? The rascal! I'll cut off his darned queue.'

Now Remedios, even if it were wise to make such threats about him, doesn't possess a Chinese pigtail.

'Look at this – it's *ruined!*' Walter screeches. 'Bathos! Ruined.'

The portrayed gather to peer at the image. Walter has not troubled to protect it with glass. Exclamations of astonishment and pleasure follow, which merely add fuel to the fire of Walter's agony.

'Well, by Jove, is that what I look like?'

'Gad, Pedder's swollen his chest fit to be broke.'

'Look'ee here, that's where I cut myself with the razor this morning.'

'Capital. I should like one for my sisters, if 'twere at all possible.'

'Most faithful to life,' Captain Hall observes more moderately.

Walter shakes his head in disgust. He jabs the plate. 'Now, darn it to perdition – look.'

Gideon examines the composition. And there, at the very back, in the doorway of the verandah, where bright sunlight makes the image especially vivid, though smaller than the arranged officers and gentlemen, is the (grinning) Ah Cheong. Pinching his nose, on the way to the roses, he holds aloft a…chamber-pot!

Pedder guffaws coarsely. Walter groans. Harry's eyes behind his pince-nez are bright with spite; he smiles maliciously as Gideon passes the plate to him. 'Well, my dear boy,' and the brogue is almost a lisp, 'your machine is altogether voracious – it will have the whole world in its maw, if it may. Gourmand and gourmet.'

'An unfortunate accident,' says Walter. 'It shall never happen again.'

'The essence of the whole process, sir,' snaps Harry. 'Select your subject, sir, or it will select you.'

This is double Dutch for Pedder and his shipmates who are tired of sitting in the pleasure-garden and are ready to fall in with any madcap idea of a wild boy like Ridley, such as: 'Gentlemen, I guess we have been immobile too long. I

510

conclude for us to engage in a race.' Which is to run to the bottom of the Monte, hire sedans, place the astonished coolies inside and sprint with poles on shoulders, whooping, gasping, the lung-searing half-mile or so to the top.

Crestfallen Walter is left with O'Rourke.

CHAPTER XXXV

Keshen, a mandarin of the Red Button, ten times advanced, ten times promoted, Holder of the Peacock's Tail, a Cabinet Minister, an Imperial Kinsman, a Guardian of the Princes, makes the following communication to E-lut, the Barbarian Eye.

Matters of great moment were decided by us in our meeting in the north. These are not matters which may be lightly or precipitately undertaken. You refer in your petition (lit. pin) to outstanding issues and the delay in carrying out promises. At this moment, it is not convenient to discuss these issues and a favourable opportunity will certainly soon present itself. In the meantime, the barbarian ships may as customary resort to Canton to conduct their trade and carry the cargoes. This is certainly a circumstance highly satisfactory to view and which your nation may regard with satisfaction. The big ships do not need to loiter around the mouth of the river, as this is certainly not advisable for the health of the men.

Saying this (I) trust you enjoy the fruits of prosperity and good fortune.

Taou Kwang, -th year, -th moon, -th day.
Gideon Hall Chase
A true translation

N.B. This letter is unsatisfactory in the extreme. As well as employing the objectionable term Barbarian Eye for the Plenipotentiary and the offensive term *pin* for his ultimatum, neither of which characterised the mode of communication

511

as between equals in the Peking River, the author of this most evasive message clearly means to indicate that he proposes a resumption of the Canton trade on the old terms and within the old system. As the month for the sailing of the ships approaches in three months' time, he knows very well that it is incumbent upon the British shippers to get their consignments out with the smallest possible delay. Were this the case, then he would have succeeded in deferring the entire issue for a twelvemonth. The reference to the line of battle ships and the welfare of their crews represents a desire to indicate a consciousness of the possible weaknesses of the British expedition. Intelligence of the shocking mortality and illnesses among the troops at Chusan will have reached Keshen's ears long ago from his spies and informers on that island, the movements of whom between the maze of islands in the archipelago and the city of Ningpo on the mainland will scarcely have been inconvenienced, let alone impeded, by the patrols of the Royal Navy. The parting good wish with which his communication concludes is a barely disguised insult, which represents an attempt to degrade the Plenipotentiary and Superintendent of Trade to the status of a merchant and speculator.

It will not have escaped Your Excellency's attention that there is no mention of a payment in money in compensation for the opium stocks confiscated by Lin.

G.C.

Gideon has not been successful in getting much breakfast down. There are no dainties in the wardroom of the *Nemesis,* such as might tickle the palates of officers of more elegant sailing-craft like *Calliope,* or even the brigs *Hyacinth* and *Larne* – who are their consorts for the day. Captain Hall insists that he and Pedder eat the same hard tack as the men (though he has twelve dozen crates of claret of his own in a hold somewhere in one of the seven water-tight compartments of the steamer, above the shells and canister-rounds). The steward, as a concession, has brewed coffee for the translator, who softens a fragment of biscuit in it.

This is a man who doesn't demur at a native breakfast of rice-gruel, pickles, and dyed offal. His limbs feel fluffy, head clear and empty.

On the river, mist floats. The sailing-ships have their crews aloft, spreading canvas. Small ripples form at their bows as the sails flap under a light breeze. The *Nemesis* and the *Queen* have been feeding their boilers with indifferent coals and cords of best quality hardwoods since dawn and, at a signal from *Calliope,* Gideon feels planks tremble beneath his feet. Now there is the odour of the estuary, stirred by the paddles. The steamers wait for the sailing-ships to stand out of the anchorage, pouring black billows from their stacks, sneezing and wheezing patiently like a line of elderly invalids. The white sails give Gideon a catch in the throat. How beautiful, he thinks, can be such terrible engines of war.

The steamers shudder as their captains ring for full power and the great beams below begin to deliver their shocks. Soon, they overtake the frigates and brig. They do nine knots to the sailing-ships' five, and will reconnoitre and sound for shoals. They carry a native pilot, a demi-piratical Chinese from Cheung Chau island near Hong Kong, but the river's changes can deceive even him. He has been well-primed with cherry brandy.

Gideon has been taking shelter from the wind on deck, but Captain Hall sends orders for him to come to the bridge, which is an entirely unprotected structure, connecting the two large paddle-boxes on either side, bare except for the ship's officers, the launching tube for the Congreve rockets, and some small brass cannon. By contrast, the sides of the steamer are sand-bagged and protected by anti-boarding nets. If the marines and blue-jackets lie down, they will not be hit. Captain Hall is jealous of his men.

'Request this rascal, Mr Chase, to pay a good deal more attention to his work. The fellow does nothing but spit and smoke, and, pray inform him, he shall not have another bottle – no, not so much as a glass.'

'I do beg to inform you, Captain Hall, such is the customary requisite and comportment of the river-pilots. He is as competent and trustworthy as any of his class.'

'That, sir, is what I give myself concern about.' And with a series of gestures which need no explaining Captain Hall points to a rope, his low yard-arm, and the pilot's neck. This latter's expression does not change.

Pedder has his telescope out and now informs Captain Hall of a signal from *Calliope* that she is grounded. It is fortunately a clear day. Bells ring and the *Nemesis* turns 'on a sixpence', as Pedder says, the rudder assisted by the feathering of one wheel, and within minutes they run alongside *Calliope*. The captains converse through their hailers: no need to lighten the frigate, she's on soft mud.

'Damned glad of our help now,' mutters Pedder, 'filthy blackamoors though we are. The tide's dropping.' The pilot shrugs his shoulders. Mr Crouch, one of the mates of that 74-gun monster the *Wellesley*, seconded to *Nemesis* for these operations as gunnery officer, grins as he overhears Pedder's comments. The *Nemesis* throws a rope to the frigate. The steamer's wheels thrash the water, the rope rears out of the sea, becoming a hemp rod, creaking and squeaking. The *Nemesis* stands still, reminding Gideon of a bull pawing the ground. Then, inch by inch, picking up speed, she makes ground and suddenly she's off at a rush, pulling the bigger *Calliope* at a good five or six knots. A cheer goes up from both ships.

By half past ten, the frigates and brigs having grounded twice each and been towed through some tricky channels by the redoubtable *Nemesis,* they near the Bogue forts and Chuenpi island. Gideon can see four more British ships on the other side of the Bocca Tigris channel and large sails, probably the line of battle ships, coming up the estuary four or five miles behind them. The crew now proceed to a second, heartier breakfast, or possibly early dinner – 'Jack liking to fight on good victuals and a full stomach,' as Pedder says. The smell of frying onions turns Gideon's stomach. After this, the galley-fires are extinguished, a somewhat nonsensical precaution on an iron steamer, though doubtless vital on wooden vessels under sail.

The *Nemesis* comes to a temporary anchor under the forts of Chuenpi, a mile off. When Pedder lends Gideon his telescope he can see the tiger-masks and the banners and mantles over the embrasures. Tiny figures run to and fro. The gun-crews at the 32-pounders fore and aft on the *Nemesis* load their big pieces.

'Shell, I should think, Mr Crouch,' enquires rather than commands Captain Hall of a fellow-professional, 'for the forts, reserving our grape and canister for the troops and entrenchments?'

'Aye aye, sir,' comes Crouch's answer, which little exchange, with the deferences and allowances paid on each side, settles the terms of service for the duration.

Gideon doesn't notice.

Pedder has his glass on *Calliope*. A moment later, a signal breaks from her mast. The first gun of her broadside goes off, followed shortly by the thirteen others in quick succession. The flash comes first, then the report, and the echo off the hilly islands. The 'cannon's roar' is not a roar at all, but at distance quite flat and muted. It is, therefore, a terrible surprise to Gideon when the bow-gun of the *Nemesis* discharges with an ear-piercing crack and boom. A great jet of flame shoots out. Then a cloud of smoke hides the gun-crew and, momentarily, their target. Gideon sees Pedder's lips counting. High up on the hill there is a flash and puff of smoke, just below the fort.

'Good practice,' Gideon hears Captain Hall say, before further words are obliterated by the blast of the after 32-pounder. Its shell bursts squarely within the walls, raising a cloud of dust and masonry. The sailors cheer. Now the gunners have their range and timing, each shell exploding within the fortifications or above the embrasures, as they wish.

'We'll close,' says Captain Hall to Pedder. They steer in to the shore at half speed, presenting only their bow to the fort's main battery. Gideon sees the flashes at the embrasures. Until now he has been too frightened by the *Nemesis'* own guns – surely they must burst with such force – to worry about the fire from the Chinese battery. Now he experiences the thoroughly disagreeable sensation of hearing cannon-balls whirring over head. He has his shoulders instinctively hunched, neck down. The balls seem low enough, indeed he sees a spar struck in a shower of splinters, but Pedder says, 'Too high, sir. Their aim's poor and powder weak.'

Hall nods. 'God be thanked.'

Gideon is surprised to hear the captain's confession of weakness. He wishes he were in the waist with the marines and sailors, instead of on this hideously exposed platform. Now there comes a whirring far lower than any previous, and two fountains of spray spout behind them.

'Capital.' First lieutenant and captain smile.

Gideon is horrified. The wheels turn remorselessly, their steady splashing interrupted by the explosions from the 32-pounders but always reasserting itself in the ringing in Gideon's ears. The steamer turns broadside on, still panting. They are within long pistol-shot of the shore.

This is insanity! The forts will pulverise them, however erratic the aim of their gunners, or feeble their powder. Gideon sees entrenchments on the shore-line, bristling with troops, pikes, and banners. The yells of defiance are clearly audible and, Gideon imagines, so too must be the cool, composed orders of Captain Hall, the rattling of the marines' small-arms on their accoutrements, and the clatter of a loose plate on the smoke-stack (how has that escaped Captain Hall's stern vigilance?)

'Grape-shot, if you will, Mr Crouch.'

Gideon recognises the banners waved in the entrenchments. 'These are Manchu troops,' he informs Captain Hall. 'Tartars,' he adds, as Captain Hall shows no signs of recognition. 'Their bravest troops.'

'Canister on top of the grape, Mr Crouch.'

Crack-crack-crack overhead go a volley of matchlock-balls from the earthworks, the last striking the starboard paddle-box.

'Good shooting, that,' says Pedder, with genuine appreciation.

'They may achieve the same from the back of a moving horse. Kites are a favourite target of their marksmen.'

'Indeed? Pray inform your marines to stay down, Mr Wheeldon.'

Just after the Manchu marksmen discharge another volley, several of the balls this time rapping the wooden rails of the *Nemesis* or clanging against her iron hull, Captain Hall swings his vessel violently round and, double-shotted with heavy grape and the canisters of musket-balls, both 32-pounders rake the trenches with fearsome results. The effect is of a blast from a giant blunderbuss or shot-gun: banners, flagpoles, lances slashed in half under a hail of lead, the earth around the breastworks driven up as if by a huge invisible flail. Where there was display, defiance seconds before, now there is carnage. Screams reach them. A wounded man crawls out of the back of the trenches, another staggers after. At an order from Lieutenant Wheeldon, the marines crouch, rest their muskets on the rail, and fire a volley. The two Manchus fall. A bell rings and the engine slows. Around goes the steamer. This time the guns discharge canister only. Cannon-balls from the forts on the hill rush overhead, harmlessly striking the water beyond the *Nemesis*. Gideon can now see why Captain Hall brought them to an apparently foolhardy range: the fixed guns of the forts cannot be adjusted to a sufficiently low angle to threaten the *Nemesis,* but fire their shot unavailingly overhead. The foreground of the picture they present is a zone of safety.

Pedder passes him the telescope. In the short space of the action, the forts have become unrecognisable, the parapets smashed, walls breached, guns dismounted, earth-bags ruptured, and corner-works beaten into rubble. Such is the power of accurate, concentrated fire from shell-guns. Yet another broadside goes off from the *Calliope* and, in their position, they hear the shells hissing overhead. A few seconds later follows the rumble of the bursts.

But now Captain Hall has spotted a battery eight hundred yards upstream where the river shoals and widens and, the siren lure of inclination for once prompting the call of duty, he takes his novel craft through the shallows to engage.

Pedder gazes anxiously over the bow. 'Shoaling rapidly,' he says in a worried voice. 'I believe this is a sand-bank which must be exposed at low water. Good God! I can see the bottom.'

But Captain Hall is imperturbable. 'We draw but five, Mr Pedder. We may retract the false keels if necessary and, with the powder and shot we have expended, we are lightened.'

Pedder looks doubtful. 'I'll put a leadsman in the bows, sir. I don't trust this rascal,' gesturing at the native river-pilot, who has managed to secure further supplies of drink from some obliging tar and by now is blind drunk, leaning against the rocket-tube with an inane grin on his face.

'Very well, Mr Pedder. We'll slide and bump our way through, if we needs must. I seem to remember doing the same on the mud-flats of the Hudson.' Here Captain Hall smiles in an avuncular way at Gideon.

At this moment, gouts of flame and smoke break from the embrasures of the low battery. The cannon-balls howl over the *Nemesis,* causing Gideon to dive for the deck as the top five feet of the severed smoke-stack topple on to the bridge with a great clang of disintegrating parts. Neither Pedder nor the Captain move a muscle.

'They are better gunners here, Mr Pedder.'

'Capital shooting, and recollect the age and quality of the pieces they serve, sir.'

Captain Hall avails himself of the first lieutenant's telescope. 'Ha! No masonry but earth redoubts, faced with grass.'

'I should think a shell thrown in among the rascals would flush them out, sir.'

'D'you think so? I daresay. But let us see some nicer work from our gunners. Load with round, Mr Crouch.'

All this while, the leadsman in the bows has been calling out the soundings. From three fathoms the water becomes two, then one, then barely five feet. Captain Hall brings his ship about, steams fifty yards further upstream, swings her round on one wheel and full rudder. Still the soundings are ominous. Then, 'Two fathoms,' calls the leadsman, and in quick succession, 'one and a half, one, sir, five feet, sir,' and Captain Hall puts the paddles into reverse smartly. He orders a second leadsman in the bow but not before the battery fires again, one ball hopping over the water like a pebble skimmed over a pond and narrowly missing the port paddle-box, while the others whirr overhead. The soundings show a channel of sorts and Captain Hall takes the *Nemesis* through at two knots, then has to slew her violently round again, which presents her sideways on to the Chinese gunners' third shots. This time a ball goes straight through the iron side, pierces the plate on the other, and continues its progress over the Pearl estuary.

'Deuce!' says Pedder.

He orders a ship's boy below, who reports no damage: the round-shot passed straight through the narrow *Nemesis* without even breaking a water-barrel.

'Interesting,' says the Captain to Crouch. 'Can this be a stronger charge? Or perhaps they've bought some of our own cannon at Singapore, or even from our Cousins.'

'Begging your pardon, sir,' returns the latter. 'They've got a long barrel brass 'un there, and if it's fixed without recoiling on sprung ropes, then the...'

'...force imparted will be prodigious. Well, Mr Crouch, you had better silence it.'

'Five and a half feet, sir, and shoaling fast. Do we pull up the sliding keels?'

'No, we'll lose way and sail off the wind like a seventy-four.'

At this point the *Nemesis* bumps on the bottom, before lurching off again. Pedder looks as agonised as if it were his own bones being scraped. There's a crack from the starboard paddle-box. Pedder rushes over. One of the floats has broken. Captain Hall brings the steamer round again.

'Stop the engines. Let her go through the water.'

The silence is broken only by the hiss of steam.

The *Nemesis* floats gently through on the tide.

'Three, three and a half, sir, five, six, seven, eight fathom, sir,' comes the leadsman's cry. The beam begins to thump again. They are within five hundred yards of the battery. Crouch, in accordance with the captain's orders, has loaded with round-shot. Whether Captain Hall has altered the load for reasons of humanity or simply to give his gun-crews better practice is uncertain to Gideon. At any rate, shot will do the earth-works little harm. The gunners will actually have to score a direct hit on the Chinese cannon to dismount them, where a reasonably thrown shell would kill all the men serving the guns.

Crouch personally lays the bow 32-pounder, pulling the lanyard himself, and the *Nemesis* shudders. Grey smoke hides the view, uniting with the dirty black clouds belching out of the amputated smoke-stack. When it clears, a fierce cheer rises. One of the Chinese guns is lying on its side. The after 32-pounder fires at the same moment as the battery. Although the Chinese gunners enjoy a far bigger mark, neither they nor their ordnance can match the *Nemesis* and, besides, their aim has been spoiled by the hit on the battery's prize early eighteenth-century Portuguese monster; so that their shot fly harmlessly through the rigging of the steamer without so much as knocking off a spar or block. The after 32-pounder, though, also misses, its shot kicking up turf four feet below an embrasure. The gun-captain swears atrociously.

'Line was good, Mr Dawkins,' says Captain Hall calmly, 'and we're closing. Leave it as it is.'

At the bow-gun, Crouch repeats his earlier success and this time Gideon can see the ball smash into the Chinese cannon in a shower of sparks and splinters, knocking it right off its mountings. Three of its crew lie across their wrecked gun. It is now possible to see that the other pieces in the battery have been abandoned by their crews, all but the centre cannon, whose rammer can be observed thrusting his tool into its mouth. Moments later, it fires, the ball passing very close by the starboard side. The officers on the bridge murmur in admiration.

'Upon my word, these are brave men, Mr Chase, very brave men,' says Captain Hall warmly. 'You may depend upon it. When you're ready, Mr Crouch.'

With the bow 32-pounder now firing with its sights on the point-blank, Crouch puts his ball straight through the embrasure, seemingly down the cannon's mouth, for it jumps straight up before turning end over end backwards. Astonishingly, most of the crew seem to have survived, including the doughty rammer, who leaps on to the intact parapet and shakes his instrument defiantly.

'Game,' says Pedder, 'to the last.'

In the waist of the steamer, a musket pops. The Chinese stands stock-still for a moment, so that Gideon believes the marksman has missed. Then the Chinese gunner releases the rammer, which stays upright for a second as he collapses slowly backwards.

Lieutenant Wheeldon lowers his musket and grins. Gideon cannot look at him.

With the battery silenced, the *Nemesis* steams back into mid-channel, where she takes a company of the 18th Royal Irish on her decks and three boatloads of the Madras Native Infantry strung behind in her wake like a kite's tail.

Under sporadic fire from a battery below the main fort of Chuenpi Heights, which still holds out, Captain Hall lands the troops and takes three more shiploads without sustaining any damage beyond the spray of a near-miss, which drenches the cursing, red-tunicked soldiers on deck. After this mundane ferrying, he presses on up to Anson's Bay (favourite sketching spot of O'Rourke's in the balmier days of the early century, though infested with pirates), where it is his reward and singular good fortune to chance across a squadron of fifteen war-junks. Pedder whoops at the sight, while the crew cheer at the chance to pit their remarkable vessel against other ships and superior odds, besides the prospect of *prize money.*

The guns are already loaded with fused shell, but Captain Hall wishes to try out the Congreve rockets, great iron missiles, longer than the sturdy captain himself, and tipped with exploding heads. Crouch watches with professional interest and a degree of pardonable scepticism as one is loaded into the tube. He finds it, despite its fearsome appearance, bristling with fins and somewhat rusty after the rigours of a sea-voyage, even with a protective coating of grease from the manufacturers, rather similar to a child's toy or firework. The steamer chugs on to where the anchored junks lie broadside on.

'Ten guns a side and heavy metal by the looks of it, which is one hundred and fifty guns in all. Say two broadsides from the beggars before we engage, and that's three hundred shot.'

'Indeed, Mr Pedder, but I doubt if one shall find us.' Captain Hall gestures to Gideon to stand away from the rear of the rocket-tube. Somewhat more unceremoniously, he kicks the redundant river-pilot, who topples off the bridge and on to the packs of the men of the 18th, who give him a good cuffing for his pains. They are some four hundred yards from the junks when, after careful adjustment, squinting, and the holding up of a wet finger to the wind, Captain Hall discharges the Congreve rocket. There follows a tremendous hissing in the tube, which drowns the noise of steam. Sparks and hot air rush out of the end, and for a few seconds nothing else happens. Crouch does not trouble to hide the smirk on his honest features. Then *whoosh!* and with a burst of flame the Congreve rocket shoots out of its tube, soaring up into the heavens as a fiery ribbon and describing a majestic, symmetrical parabola, at the summit of which it is already appallingly apparent to Gideon that the missile is going to descend and strike the nearest junk, a circumstance perhaps more obvious to the crew of the junk than the *Nemesis,* for the groan from the Chinese – both sides looking up from their immediate tasks of laying guns and tightening ropes – precedes the gasp from the British. A long time it hangs at the zenith, then drops, spitting flame more fitfully. Gideon is reminded of his hunting accident so long ago when he fired his ramrod by mistake. An eternity later, the rocket plunges into the junk. What happens next exceeds the expectations of all, including even the firer of the missile (who has been aiming at a junk three vessels to the left), for with a great flash and roar, the wind from which smites the faces of all on the bridge of the *Nemesis,* the heavy craft disintegrates into a thousand pieces. Wreckage is thrown high into the air, and a pillar of smoke marks the spot lately occupied by the junk. Debris starts coming down, splashing the still water in front of the steamer. As the *Nemesis* proceeds at full speed, through the calm sea, fragments of junk continue to rain out of the sky, a shattered plank or two clattering on to the bow. And…before Gideon's horrified eyes, a human arm, including the hand and fingers, suddenly lands with a heavy thump, failing to bounce. He cannot believe what his own eyes have seen. He turns to Pedder, but the first lieutenant is concentrating on the next target. Captain Hall surrenders his place at the rocket-tube to the weapon's designated operator. Crouch looks as stunned as if the rocket has hit him, which, in a manner of speaking, it has.

'There, there…do you see…' is all Gideon can manage.

'Interesting effect, Mr Crouch, I'm sure you're in agreement.'

'Prodigious. The destructive power is extraordinary – but the more so the accuracy. I could not believe a rocket might be so precisely delivered.'

'Well, you will perceive the conditions are almost perfectly suited to its employment. By some happy chance I believe it must have penetrated directly to the magazine.'

A second rocket has been fitted into the tube, and this hisses away, but the operator has insufficiently lowered its trajectory with the closing distance and it soars over the mast of the centre vessel of the flotilla. Chinese sailors are visible hauling up their anchors with frantic urgency. Their gunners discharge ragged, inaccurate broadsides. Another Congreve rocket sails away, on a flatter trajectory this time, pierces the side of a junk, and detonates with a flash. Seconds later there follows a series of smaller twinklings and then, with a roar as big as the first explosion, the entire junk blows up, scattering pieces far and wide. In the dirty fountain bodies fall through the air. In quick succession the *Nemesis* launches ten rockets, scoring eight hits. Five junks explode as spectacularly as the first two, while the others catch fire and are beached by their fleeing crews. A brisk cannonade accounts for another, and the gunners pitch shell among the running Chinese on the beach.

Up a winding creek, the look-out descries three more masts and the *Nemesis* ploughs through the narrow entry, this time throwing grappling irons on to the junks, which have been abandoned by their crews just as the steamer appears around the corner. These she tows out as prizes into the main channel. Debouching on to the river and returning to the battle at the fort, they find a strange calm prevails. On the other bank the frigates *Samarang* and *Druid* and the sloops *Modeste* and *Columbine* lie at anchor. They should be engaging the forts at Taicocktow island opposite Chuenpi, but their guns are silent. The forts, too, though battered and, as Pedder can see through his telescope, with the rendering knocked away from the brickwork, are still in Chinese hands, though no longer returning fire.

Thank God! thinks Gideon. They have surrendered!

In mid-channel the *Wellesley* has finally arrived. A small boat is rowing back to a group of Chinese junks near Taicocktow, having apparently visited the British flagship. They *must* have surrendered. But, no, a puff of smoke from the Chinese fort on

North Wantung island gives the lie to this. Moments later the side of the *Wellesley* erupts in smoke and flame, and the struggle recommences, with pretty puffs of smoke in the sky and on the hillside from the exploding shells, fountains in the water from the fall of the Chinese shot, and the red ants of the 49th and 18th Regiments swarming out of their boats and advancing in lines up the slopes of the island. The *Nemesis* receives orders to support the troops, Pedder reading the *Wellesley's* signals through his telescope, and she steams into the shallows in grand style, blazing away with her two big guns, rockets, and smaller brass cannons and swivels. Wheeldon, the lieutenant of marines, goes ashore with his men and a party of blue-jackets to join the assault. Captain Hall seconds Gideon and Pedder to the shore-party.

On the beach it is warm and close. Steaming at nine knots, the *Nemesis* had created her own breeze. Encumbered with knapsacks and full cartridge-pouches, the men sweat. A shell from a frigate hisses over their heads and, quite a long time later, explodes near the fort. Pedder assembles the blue-jackets and, conscientious officer that he is, checks their muskets are primed and loaded. Wheeldon's marines are ready a good deal earlier, and such is the rivalry between the officers and the mutual dislike of the men of the two services that he sets off without the blue-jackets.

Gideon remains with Pedder. At length they are off, the men striding quickly to overtake the red-clad marines. They hear the pop-pop of distant musketry above, feeble after the shattering reports of the naval 32-pounders. Halfway up the hill, Pedder, eager, but also aware of the limitations of sailors ashore, makes his men halt. He has them gather their breath and offers Gideon a drink from his own water-flask.

Above them come the cracks of matchlocks and gingals, firing raggedly and without coordination. Then there follows the single, slamming crash of a volley of disciplined British musketry. A slight pause, and again. The men shuffle impatiently; the boatswain Davenport, a harsh, myopic, knowledgeable man, looks at Pedder, but even under Company pay, as an ex-man-of-war's man, he is too smart a seaman to question an officer's orders.

'Well, my hearties,' says Pedder, pulling out his flask, his prominent Adam's apple working above his stiff-collared tunic, 'let's be in no hurry to haze the Chinese.'

The boatswain's fingers fidget with his cutlass-handle. Pedder offers Gideon another drink. He declines. Although thirsty he is aware of the naval party's impatience and does not wish to antagonise the men. At length, Pedder carefully pushes the top in to his canteen and packs it away. He leads the tars up a goat-track with deliberate slowness, the sailors colliding in their eagerness with the man in front.

The firing is now audible as sharper cracks. No more volleys come but the crackle of free fire. They are in a little dip covered in rough grasses. Gideon can see one of the stunted pines which may be found on the skylines of the estuary, so he knows they must be nearing the summit. From the brow, they see the fort is already taken. One red line still advances in perfect order; the other is pouring through a breach in the fort in the shape of a wedge. Smaller groups climb scaling ladders. Pulsing swarms surround holes in the ground, which must be the Chinese trenches. Pedder orders his blue-jackets down in skirmishing order, sensibly as ship's discipline is not necessarily directly transferable to the exigencies of a land battle and hand-to-hand combat now seems to be the order of the day. The sailors whoop with joy. At increasing pace the party trot down the hill, Gideon cautiously bringing up the rear. Pedder topples headlong, falling on his face. The men check their charge, for that is what it has become, but their first lieutenant bounces up, wiping scuffed hands on his trousers and grinning cheerfully.

A company of sepoys have surrounded the foremost of the Chinese earthworks in advance of the fort and are firing randomly into the trench, running along the mounds and discharging their muskets kneeling down, before standing to reload. Surely this exposes them to the Chinese?

Pedder and the boatswain are on the lip. The blue-jackets arrive, raise, and then lower their muskets. Gideon scrambles to the top, sand spilling into his light boots.

The trench, forty yards long, three wide, and some two deep, is choked with the corpses of Chinese soldiers, sprawled in the awful, careless shapes of violent death. Many more, some scores, Gideon estimates, are still alive and apparently uninjured. These run up and down along the bottom of the trench, treading and tripping on the bodies of their dead comrades. The Indians take pot-shots at them, almost every report telling with effect. A man running down the trench towards Gideon throws up his arms and falls sideways to his knees, face resting against the rough wall of the trench in the attitude of Christian prayer. Blood wells from a hole in the back of his head. Another endeavours to climb up the walls of the hole but a sepoy bayonets him in the eye and, again, in the throat. He falls upon a pile of bodies, still breathing, and the Indians shoot him in the spine.

The Chinese uniforms, of black cloth, are embroidered back and front with representations of animals: phoenix, dragon, but mostly duck.

A soldier, a young lad of nineteen or twenty, manages to scramble up and grab the loose cloth of Pedder's trousers, below the knee. White and sick, Gideon does not need to translate the plea. The boatswain draws his cutlass from his belt and strikes the Chinese on the arm, with the flat of the sword. Pedder restrains him, and is in the act of pulling the boy from the trench when there is the flash and bang of a musket. The Chinese slithers back into the hole. A moustached sepoy grins on the other side of the trench. Pedder stares at him over the pile of bodies. It is possible at this point to step across to the other side of the trench on the corpses which fill it. A wounded Chinese runs down the trench to the blue jackets, followed by three others. The sepoys' muskets crack, and the three Chinese at the rear go sprawling.

Pedder jumps into the trench. Bang! goes a sepoy's musket just in front of his face, dropping the Chinese like a steer and sending Pedder, cursing, into the walls of the trench, temporarily blinded. His side-whiskers have been singed by the flash. A second sepoy fires into the twitching body of the Chinese. One of the shot Chinese at the rear flops on his stomach towards Pedder. Blinking, the first lieutenant of the *Nemesis* drops to his knees and shuffles towards the man with his hand extended. A third sepoy jumps down behind the Chinese, drives his musket-butt into the back of his head where it joins the neck, and then with one foot on the stunned man's shoulder blades stabs him twice on either side of the spine in the small of the back. Pedder tries to knock the musket-barrel away, only cutting himself on the bayonet. More Indians jump in, one treading accidentally on Pedder's injured hand. They drag bodies off the top of the heap to kill those still breathing or hiding below, and as Pedder crawls into the melée of boots and blades, Davenport the boatswain jumps in and pulls him out by the collar with a: 'For God's sake, sir, get out, or they will kill you, too.'

Gideon gives Pedder his hand. There's blood on his palm, which the young American wipes on his white trousers.

'Are you hurt, William?'

'No, thank you, Mr Chase – which is more than can be said for the poor beggars of Chinese below.'

'Your pistol, sir.'

'Thank you, Davenport. *Where is their officer?*'

The naval party press uphill towards the fort. More Madras Native Infantry are killing Chinese in a small slit trench one hundred yards to their left. Pedder looks resolutely to the front. His cheek pulses. Ahead, three red-tunicked officers of the 37th Madras Native Infantry stand on a small knoll, pointing to the fort with their canes and taking turns with a telescope. Spiking-parties in the distant embrasures are rendering the Chinese cannon useless.

'Ah, Pedder, my dear fellow,' says a veritable giant of a man, well over six feet tall, with a chest like a boat's water-breaker, 'you are finally arrived. There's a good fellow, lend me your telescope.'

'My dear Edwards, I suggest you apply the glass towards your rear, rather than to the fore. Do you know of the misdeeds your blackamoors are perpetrating in the trenches?'

Edwards looks down the hill and shrugs those broad, red-clad shoulders, making his brown leather belt creak. 'In their present condition I can do nothing with them. They would as soon stab me through the vitals. When the lust of blood is upon them...' And the giant turns his back.

'Gad! They've thrown a cannon over the parapet. Your glass, James. I must insist categorically on my right...'

Pedder pulls a face. The sailors fidget with their weapons. Armed, in addition to their issued firearms and cutlasses, with home-made implements more suited to the mass brawl euphemistically described as boarding than land combat, they look more like a gang of robbers than the troops they are not. Pedder motions them on.

Although the spiking-parties have hammered and broken off their nails in the touch-holes of the majority of the fort's cannon and, indeed, have dismounted and dislodged several of them, there are still isolated pieces of fighting continuing, fiercer, if anything, than the main battle and bombardment. As they approach one of two small square towers in front of the fort's main gates, a flash and a *boom!* come from a loop-hole on the first floor, followed by a clang as the boatswain's shattered cutlass is sent spinning out of his hand. Before the two pieces of metal have hit the ground, the blue-jackets are firing back, their shots sending chips of masonry showering to the ground around the slot in the wall. Smoke hangs around the oblong loop-hole. Gideon spots the long barrel of a gingal being retracted.

Pedder ties his own handkerchief around the boatswain's injured wrist. 'That was pretty shooting, sir,' says the petty officer. 'A cable's length, which is very fair for their matchlocks, confound them.'

'You are mistaken, Davenport,' says Gideon. 'That was a gingal's ball, which is several times heavier than a matchlock's bullet – and the men who served and discharged the piece are not the official levies of the Emperor, but braves or volunteers from the hamlets around Canton.'

'Well, I recommend you to impart that piece of information to Captain Elliot,' remarks Pedder pointedly, 'he who is at such pains to spare the "unoffending population" the horrors of war.'

The blue-jackets are spread out in a semicircle before the tower, having reloaded their muskets, waiting for a glimpse of shadow at the loop-hole. As the gingal-barrel appears again, they discharge another ragged volley and an able seaman gives a cry of triumph as his shot fails to strike the wall but penetrates the narrow opening.

'A tot for any man who does it again, no, hang it – a guinea.'

But Pedder's jubilation is short-lived as Lieutenant Wheeldon and his marines arrive with a rocket they have stolen from Fanshawe's Bengal Battery. Pedder's jaw clenches as the marines run up to the fort, taking advantage of the time taken to reload the gingal, and at a distance of less than thirty yards fire the great iron arrow straight under the slot. In the ball of flame, smoke, and white dust, it is possible to see pieces of the rocket-tube go flying through the air, a hot piece of iron burning Gideon's fingers when he picks it up. The gingal-barrel hangs drunkenly through a jagged hole four feet across, which has taken the place of the neat slot, and its gunner droops over the barrel. The back of his jacket has caught fire. The marines send, on the command, an orchestrated volley through the breach. Next, the sergeant hangs a powder-bag on the door, lights the fuse, and retires. The explosion splinters the heavy wood and iron door, and then the marines, Wheeldon to the fore, charge in and up the stairs. Soon after, Wheeldon trots out again, sheathing his glittering, unsullied sword.

The sailors mutter among themselves, Pedder standing by himself in a lonely, bitter silence. Gideon now discovers himself, to his own great confusion, leading their little party to the fort. He drops back to walk with Pedder.

All resistance has now been mopped up. By the battered parapets are bits of bodies. An arm lies near one dismounted cannon, a pair of legs by another. A corpse with a head missing and a torso lie like any objects which have had their casual uses superseded.

Pedder says, 'You are quiet, Mr Chase – but this is womanly work when compared to the sights I have seen at sea.' He goes on to explain that shot, good old-fashioned solid iron, will make a worse mess of the human body than shell. 'There are no piles of guts here, Mr Chase, and I have slipped on intestines when I have boarded a ship that struck to heavier guns or superior handling. You'll see the blood has caked the dust as if it were bibulous paper – it collects in pools on a deck. Which is why the gun-deck of the *Wellesley* is painted red. Sit on this cannon, Mr Chase. I recommend you drink this.'

A few minutes later a messenger arrives with a note

requesting Gideon's services for the commander of land forces. Pedder ignores him as he leaves.

What has he done to offend the first lieutenant?

CHAPTER XXXVI

From THE CANTON MONITOR

Tuesday, January 12th, 1841

Reduction of the Bogue forts. If there existed any among our community who was as yet ignorant of the speedy and decisive victories won by British Arms in the north and we doubt that such could exist, even outside the readership of the *Monitor,* though perhaps there might still reside in the *yamuns* and camps of Canton some blinkered mandarin or rude Tartar obstinate in the conviction of his race's superiority, there remains now no excuse for such a lapse of attention. The rumble of the guns, audible alike in Macao and Canton (but not in the anchorage of Hong Kong), would serve to convey sufficient intimation.

The saucy mandarins of Canton, who earlier had cause to congratulate themselves on the happy and to them inexplicable circumstance that the consequences of their own insolence were being visited on the heads of their brethren in Chusan and not on their own, have now seen their strongholds smashed to porridge about their ears. For the last week the river has been as full of wreckage and timber as it has been with the bodies of dead Chinamen, often fearfully mangled and all horribly bloated by the action of the water and the process of decomposition inevitably ensuing after such a prolonged immersion. Would that the law of nature might be suspended and the purulent and stinking corpses be driven up the stream to Canton to bob before the residences of the mandarins! They may yet feel the effect of a bomb tossed among their roofs from one of those extraordinary craft, the steamers.

Keshen is reported all of a confusion and ready to agree any terms E-Lut the Barbarian Eye might care to dictate. We trust that the Plenipotentiary shall not, through misplaced moderation, throw away at the bargaining table the advantages won by force of arms.

The Battle of the Bogue, as it shall doubtless be known, was a glorious affair, with not one British sailor or soldier killed and four wounded, these for the most part with scratches and contusions. On the Chinese side some five or six hundred are estimated to have fallen. It was wonderful to see how prettily and with what precision the steamers threw their shell, venturing all the time with impunity into the narrowest and shoalest of openings. During the almost four hours the unequal struggle endured, there occurred a space of some fifteen minutes during which Kwan, the Chinese Admiral, who had been a particular favourite with the officers of the *Wellesley* in 1838, requested and was granted a truce. He wished to recover his cap and red button of office, which had fallen overboard in the heat of the contest! It was recovered and sent to him when he sent out a row-boat to receive it.

The Chinese and Tartar troops appeared altogether unversed in the conventions of modern warfare and would not surrender, greatly exasperating our men by continuing to fight on when apparently taken prisoner or discovered in impossible situations and by firing from the rear in concealed positions when the ground had been to all intents and purposes taken. In the heat of the moment, many Chinese were shot who might otherwise have been spared, but in the prevailing circumstances no blame may attach to the men.

Convention signed by Keshen at Chuenpi. This event took place on the 20th *inst.* when the treaty was celebrated with a reception in a pavilion by the river's Second Bar some days subsequent, Captain Elliot going up the river on the *Nemesis*. We understand that the Tartar Plenipotentiary has agreed to pay over an indemnity of $6 million Spanish against the stores of opium stolen by Lin, his predecessor. The island of Hong Kong is to be ceded to the British crown. In return Chusan is to be restored to the Emperor and it is agreed that no more territorial demands are to be made upon him.

Most, if not all, of our fears are thus realised at a stroke. We heartily concur with Captain Elliot in the opinion that the island and harbour of Hong Kong are a most valuable and eligible position upon the coast of China, separated, defensible, and ideally suited in all respects for conducting a maritime trade with the city of Canton. The Factories were altogether too vulnerable to Chinese interference or attack, Macao likewise, sited as it is upon a promontory. However, at a remove of some ninety miles from Canton, at the mouth of the river and surrounded by water, Hong Kong is indeed a most valuable possession. Yet why must we surrender Chusan? There is no need to barter island for island. Britannia could have enjoyed possession of both. Sterile, wild, rocky, and infertile, Hong Kong has nothing to recommend it but its position and its deep water. Chusan and its associate islets are fertile, green, wooded, and among the most beautiful and romantic archipelagoes which the world has to offer. Furthermore, it is well situated as regards access to the Emperor and Peking. We shake our heads and verily do wonder.

From THE LIN TIN BULLETIN AND RIVER BEE

Wednesday, January 27, 1841

Vol.4 No.2

FROM OUR CORRESPONDENTS

Mr Editor,

As an habitual reader, and indeed subscriber to your organ, I was not a little surprised to perceive any mention of the recent battles by land and sea joined at the Bocca all but suppressed in your journal. To what may this extraordinary lapse be attributed? The account of the battle at Chuenpi is old news in the bazaar. As one rides along the Praia of Macao, it forms the common topic of conversation, while on the verandahs, it exercises a veritable monopoly. Yet when one peruses the columns of your last, this engagement merits three paragraphs (none too long) or, to put it differently, eleven short lines. Yet, occupying, indeed invading, half of a page is an antique account of the forcing of the Bocca forts some two hundred years ago. Now what do I care for Captain Weddell, his pinnaces, or his 'bloude redde flagge', the play his sakers made on the Chinese forts? This, sir, is not what I buy a newspaper for – I like my viands a little fresher. My monarch is Victoria, not the first Charles.

CONTEMPORARY

During the absence at Hong Kong of the Bee's principal conductor, I venture to reply. The decision to print both accounts was mine and mine alone, for which I feel no need to make apology. The one is complementary to the other, and a disfigured, dismembered, and mutilated half-truth without it. Nevertheless, we trust our account of Captain Elliot's reception by Keshen at the Second Bar was sufficiently vivid. It is penned by one who was a participant in as well as a witness of the Events he described.

PURSUER

Formal occupation of Hong Kong. This event took place on

Tuesday the 26th *inst.* A small detachment was landed from the *Sulphur* surveying vessel, Edmund Belcher captain, and, arriving on the narrow rocky beach of the north-west of the island, proceeded to a small knoll overlooking the harbour where, amid three loud huzzas and under a discharge of musketry, the Union Jack was raised. The British merchantmen and men-of-war lying in the harbour responded with a *feu de joie* of their cannon, which echoed and re-echoed off the massy granite peak which commands the anchorage. The kites and sea-gulls soared and screamed in alarm, no less than the lousy Chinese soldiery on the spit of land opposite the island.

This was a fine day for all foreigners and not merely the British merchants alone. Free and unrestricted entry and departure from the port, where no imposts shall be levied, such is the order of the day and desire of Captain Elliot. He should declare Hong Kong a neutral as well as a free port, where even Britain's enemies shall be free from harassment by British cruisers and all property deposited, whether by friend or foe, equally respected. At last we shall have a sanctuary and, still more important, a *point d'appui* from which all China may in the fullness of time be opened.

We do earnestly trust that not one ball of opium shall be allowed to sully the shores of the island though, alas, ships carrying the deathly cargo have already made the harbour their refuge and resort. The war and the trade in drug have been regrettable – yet may good come of it all: if Hong Kong shall be the place where a legitimate and non-clandestine trade can flourish, then a healthy and honourable livelihood which will benefit their fellow-men shall be open to all who might otherwise embrace a nefarious living. Not by any specious morality or maxim of *'Do unto others as you would be done by yourself'* are most men swayed but by a cool consideration of profit and loss. Let profit for once be the prerogative of the good, then in despite of their own natures the evil shall be compelled to do good.

A cunning trick. An old friend of ours, and an acknowledged master, had for some months felt slighted by us. Our too ready adoption of new ways and ingenious machines had displeased him. A man of manners ordinarily brusque enough and conversation short and much to the point, his indignation was difficult to discern beneath his usual face. (All know it conceals the kindest of hearts.) When we paid a call to his residence last week, we were surprised to see a new brass knocker fixed to his door. It was his habit to leave this door ajar, and visitors would be received or turned away by his native major-domo as his humour took him. Now, as the door was closed, we reached up our hand for the knocker, much fearing he was seriously indisposed, when to our vast consternation *we touched nothing but wood:* the door! Out jumped our friend from a place of concealment behind us with a shout of triumph, terrifying to the neighbours, and clapped our hand to the representation of a knocker he had painted on his door. In his high glee he became impossible to restrain. 'Now, sir,' exclaimed he, 'am I such a useless being? Is my craft to be thrown aside for a chest of reagents and a box of wood? I defy you and your inventions, sir.'

In great confusion, and properly rebuked, we made our retreat. We never meant to offend him – we love him as the father we never had, and give wider circulation to the anecdote in handsome amends.

SOLORIENS

From THE LIN TIN BULLETIN AND RIVER BEE
Wednesday, February 24, 1841
Vol.4 No.4

The subjoined proclamation recently appeared on the walls of Canton, which we reprint not from any feeling of self-interest, but as an indication of the poor faith of the mandarins and unhappy turn of events.

PROCLAMATION

Now the barbarians have become grossly insolent again and their hardihood is really too much to endure. Hourly, they lurk in the Outside Waters, amassing their cargoes, consorting with the lowest ruffians of the black-haired race [i.e. the Chinese), *suborning native traitors, and corrupting women and children. Taking advantage of our kindly and merciful feelings, they wax daily bolder. Now is the time for patriots to emulate heaven. Bravely rushing on them, let us kill them every one.*

Rewards of 550,000 are offered for the heads of the following Barbarians:

One – The Barbarian Ee-lut. Strike off the head and the monster dies.

Two – Ba-Lee-Ma. Commander of the Rebel Navies.

Three – Ma-Lee-Son. He adopts civilised ways and speech only the more completely to deceive.

Four – Chai-A i-See. A Barbarian of the Flowery-Flag Barbarians. His nation and the Red-Head Barbarians fought a war thirty years ago, yet still he aids E-Lut. He is therefore doubly a traitor. He knows writing better than Ma-Lee-Son and is a young man of surpassing personal goodness. This man is very dangerous. Slaughter without the smallest mercy.

It seems that Keshen has no intention of keeping the promises made at Chuenpi last month, and another war appears inevitable. Mr Morrison met Keshen's representatives a fortnight past with the object of securing the ratification and implementation of the agreement at Chuenpi, but in the present circumstances such a meeting would be unwise in the extreme. Needless to say, the river has yet to be opened to trade or cargoes loaded or unloaded at Whampoa. According to a daring Portuguese captain of our acquaintance, new fortifications are building on the river-banks, the demolished forts put into a state of defence, new cannon mounted, and stronger magazines constructing. Especial attention is being paid to the islands of Anunghoy and

Wantung, Chuenpi as an isolated strong point having been
found wanting.

FROM OUR CORRESPONDENTS

Mr Editor,

As it is your repeated assertion that your columns are
open to your readers and the community you serve, I experience less hesitation than I should when I submit to you for
favour of insertion the following proposal, which has long
been of concern to me. The favourable reactions in private
of my friends and their urgings to get up a petition on the
subject have incited me to a boldness and presumption I
should not otherwise feel.

Have you, sir, ever reflected that the most commonly
repeated lie which may enjoy circulation in polite society, as
well as in the appointed sphere of commerce, is that which
traditionally ends not only a correspondence between equals
but also between manifestly superior and obviously inferior
parties? I refer to the expression in which the writer states
that he has the honour to be the addressed's most humble,
obedient servant or some similar species of nonsense. In nine
cases out of ten, this is the purest humbug where the
correspondent may well wish to say, 'D-n you, sir, I do not
give a fig for you or your opinions.'

Now the practice is perfectly acceptable as facilitating a
peaceable intercourse between individuals but when it
comes to an official correspondence, this is to take the whole
matter too far. According to my calculations, the time taken
for a clerk to write the expression, even confining himself to
the shortest and least deprecating of formulae, is at least
twenty seconds. Assuming the volume of official correspondence in the various ministries and departments of state to
be, estimating from the number of *employés* and the mean
rate at which they may transcribe, 80,000 letters per mensem
or almost one million per annum, and considering the

average terms of remuneration to be £75 or $300 per clerk, then the aggregated cost of so many humble, obedient servants is, unless my figures are faulty, in excess of one thousand per annum! This does not take into account the cost of ink, wear of quills, etc., where I estimate that the employment of such otiose addresses and valedictions consumes 600 gallons of ink and 5000 miles of writing in five years – or more than the distance between England and China. In total, I calculate the possible savings as sufficient to purchase a second steamer such as the *Nemesis* – and what return might that not produce?

SCRIBENDUM

Our friend in the bazaar, who is the possessor of an abacus, disputes our correspondent's grasp of the mathematical science. However, we cannot take exception to his views, which appear sound, if somewhat enthusiastically held. In conclusion, we subscribe ourselves his very obliged servants and eagerly await the favour of an elaboration of his most interesting proposals.

From THE CANTON MONITOR
Tuesday, March 2nd, 1841

The difficulties which present themselves before the conductor of a weekly periodical as distinct from a daily journal may best be considered when we state that the appearance of our last, February 23rd, anticipated by three days the recapture of the Bogue forts and postdated the evacuation of Chusan by four and twenty hours. Thus, through, we should say, no laxity on our own part, we were unable to have intelligence of both these events of moment, still less to insert them among our columns.

Kwan is dead. The gallant old Chinese admiral died at his post in defence of the Bogue. His body was recovered, bearing in the breast the marks of a bayonet wound, and treated with every mark of respect. He was a great favourite of Admiral Maitland three years ago. As darkness fell, the

Blenheim saluted his memory with a salvo of minute guns. On our side there were five men slightly wounded. It is believed the Chinese who fell number about one thousand.

The day following the battle, the fleet, with the steamers in the van, pressed up the river and at Second Bar, scene of Keshen's wily promises and prevarications but a month previous, found themselves presented with the strange spectacle of an American man-of-war moored in mid-stream behind an obstructive raft of heavy timbers. This was the *Cambridge,* formerly the *Chesapeake,* which the American house of Russell & Co. had sold to the Chinese but a short time previous. She was gaudily bedecked, had two eyes painted on her bows, and was well armed with heavy cannon. Alas, the Celestial commander had moored her so that only her bow-guns could be trained on our vessels as they approached the raft, doubtless wishing that she might perceive the enemy with her eyes as they approached. She was herself, owing to this circumstance, so conveniently positioned to be raked through her whole length that it could not have been more advantageously contrived if Commodore Bremer had himself had a hand in the stationing of her. She went up very quickly, the powder on her decks exploding and throwing flaming timbers all over the river.

Despite these easy successes, opinion in the fleet and among the troops is very inflamed against Captain Elliot. We ourselves are very puzzled as to his reasons for evacuating Chusan and handing it back to the Chinese *two days before he attacked the Bogue forts!* These forts had also been in his possession barely a month previous. This game of take and give must be as confusing to the Chinese as it is to our own men. How shall Lord Palmerston decide?

Restoration of Captain Anstruther and Mrs Noble. These, as well as several lascars and sepoys, were returned unharmed to their friends on Chusan by the Chinese authorities. The men manned the rigging and cheered as the two junks conveying them from Ningpo arrived in Chusan harbour. Captain Anstruther was kept pretty busy in drawing for his gaolers likenesses of the Queen of England, the Prime Minister, Captain Elliot, the Commodore, and Brigadier Burrell. This kept him in tobacco and other little luxuries of the kind.

From THE LIN TIN BULLETIN AND RIVER BEE
Wednesday, March 10, 1841
Vol.4 No.5

A most daring expedition is projected, which shall be under way even as our subscribers pick up this newest number and break their fasts of the night previous. As you, gentle reader, drink your coffee or small beer, we shall be...but, hist, there are prying eyes and everywhere straining ears. The privy agents of Keshen would reap rich reward for the notice they could give to their master, sufficient to permit him to erect a battery of obstacles to our progress. We shall have been gone – this we may tell you – long before the dawn. And, when we return, you shall read of our exploits at your leisure. In the meantime, we are pleased to enjoy the opportunity of correcting reports of the Second Battle of the Bogue, which appeared a day ago among the columns of our degenerate contemporary. The *Cambridge* was not destroyed by cannon-fire, as the *Monitor* appears to be under the delusion, but was boarded and powder-trains laid to her magazines. The Chinese had already fled, leaping over the starboard side as the British came over the larboard.

Captain Elliot took his station on the *Nemesis* rather than one of the line of battle ships, transferring himself from the *Wellesley* to that gallant little steamer. The courage and coolness of the Plenipotentiary were a great source of encouragement to the men. A shot had gone clean through the steam-chest of the *Nemesis* when Captain Elliot, against the advice of Captain Hall and his officers, was adamant in his refusal to leave the bridge.

As the batteries were stormed, Captain Hall went ashore himself under fire to plant the flag when a gigantic Tartar officer discharged four arrows at him but each time narrowly missed the chosen mark. This officer was shot himself by one of the marines, the *pluck* and coolness of this archer being much admired.

In all, 460 pieces of ordnance were captured at the Bogue, among them four huge Portuguese brass guns at South Anunghoy Fort, stamped with the date 1627.

We have the information from a participant, and are in hopes that this shall make amends for our lapse in inserting so little concerning the First Battle at the Bogue during our absence. – *ed.*

CHAPTER XXXVII

As the *Nemesis* strides along at a steady six knots, her decks have about them the air of a picnic rather than impending battle. It is a good thing no unsympathetic officers from a sailing-ship can see her – there being no way in which the crack frigates and stately ships of the line could ever traverse waterways as narrow or as shallow as this – for their comments would raise Captain Hall's scanty hair, make his thick mutton-chops bristle. In fact, Captain Scott of the *Samarang* and no less a personage than the Plenipotentiary himself are on the bridge of the steamer today. Scott is, theoretically, in command of the vessel. Hall takes this well. It is very likely the fashionable and well-connected frigate-captain would make a fool of himself without Hall's promptings. For even though the crew of the *Nemesis* are not part of the Royal Navy, the air of slovenliness and idleness about them is no more than an appearance. Where the crew of a sailing-vessel – be it sloop or 74 – would be constantly employed in putting on a cloud of sail, taking it down, adjusting ropes, pulling on blocks, tarring rigging, the watch on a steamer have relatively little to do. Below, the engineers, artificers, and firemen, inmates of a hell of flame, smoke, and coal-dust, slaves to the boilers' and furnace's inordinate appetites, toil half-naked in a mist of sweat and grime, their efforts orchestrated by the ring of the telegraph. On deck, the watch line the rail, pointing out the sights (which is, of course, only part of their express duty of keeping 'a sharp look-out, my men'). The gun-crews lounge around their monsters (which are already loaded with double charges of ball and grape), and the troops and marines below the bridge occupy themselves with nothing more arduous than the role of passengers.

Two very special passengers do not have to sit in the waist, but have the freedom of the craft. Gideon is again officially attached to Captain Elliot and has to wait upon him on the bridge (which platform is now screened with an awning, as March in the estuary is baking hot), but Walter and Harry O'Rourke roam where they please. Two huge, newly painted eyes in the native style adorn the bows of the *Nemesis*. Wonderful eyes, ever so slightly slanted, demi-Celestial, delicate corners, outline in white, red pupils, and thin fold of blue eyelid. Now, more than ever, the flame-spitting *Nemesis* resembles a sea-monster. These were quite beyond the capacities of the ship's painters, honest fellows, and represent Harry O'Rourke's *entrée* to the vessel. He spent two hot afternoons, quite drunk, seated on a rig of planks and ropes lowered over the side, with the ship's dinghy in attendance below in case of mishap.

'Did Michaelangelo drop off the Sistine ceiling, impertinent boy?'

Walter owes his passage on the steamer to the assistant editor's influence. They are perhaps the only civilian allies the lonely Plenipo possesses.

Harry is seated at the bow in a cane chair he had brought on board by a grumbling gig's crew; he has a glass of grog in his hand and is pretty pleased with himself. Walter is perched on the after 32-pounder, enjoying a cigar and exchanging blue stories with Lieutenant Wheeldon RM. He gets on rather better with Wheeldon than Pedder. In the steamer's wake hop the usual towed boats from the *Samarang* and the *Atalanta*.

They have been under way nine hours, departure even earlier than announced, at 3 a.m., but forty-eight hours later than Walter's deliberate false alarm, and are travelling up that Inner or Broadway Passage, debouching behind Macao, which offers an alternative route to Canton from the seaward estuary. They are to see no cormorants this time.

At this point the channel is four hundred yards wide. During the progress of the expedition it will become so narrow that in order to extricate herself from false openings the *Nemesis* will occasionally have to turn in a little under her own length, shoving her bow into the rustling grasses of the bank.

The telegraph rings urgently. Captain Hall has spotted stakes in the water. The wheels slow their revolutions as the *Nemesis* swings on full rudder. Hall has acted precipitately, without consulting Scott. However, the commander of the elegant, snowy *Samarang* can understand the other's concern for his vessel, filthy steamer or no (and he's starting to get a glimmer of the different sort of seamanship and skill required). The jolly-boat is lowered over the side. It transpires that the stakes are firmly embedded in the river-bottom. Scott looks serious. It will be hard work on the windlass, perhaps impossible. Hall knows better. He has cables bent to the stakes and lashed around the stanchions of the *Nemesis*. Full astern is rung, the paddles turn, slowly, slowly, but with all the 240-horse-power of the steamer and – hey, presto! – like a tooth yanked out by a string tied to the knob of a slamming door, the stake comes out of its muddy home and back shoots the steamer. The soldiers cheer. Scott raises an eyebrow at the Plenipo, who taps his beaky nose. Again, the crew of the dinghy tie the cable around a stake, back up, and see the success repeated. The stakes come aboard for firewood.

On steams the gun-boat, ever northward, pressing down the sedge and rushes, getting stuck briefly, sliding over a muddy bottom at four and a half feet before finding the deeper channel. Merchant's mansion, villa, fields, hamlets of astonished villagers pass by before they meet their first challenge. At a narrowing of the river, a system of submerged rafts and stakes forces them through a passage which guns have been trained to sweep along fixed lines. Hours of experimentation by the Chinese gunners have ensured that any craft passing will be raked with shot, day or night. It is, in effect, a prepared interrogation, to which the *Nemesis* answers, fittingly, with her freest weapon: the rocket. Off they shoot, swishing through the air, trailing sparks and flames – great witch's broomsticks. They are fired in a flat trajectory, instead of the 45-degree angle of launch used on the hill-forts of Chuenpi, rushing straight out from the bridge over the heads of the passengers. Thanks to the exceptional accuracy of the Congreve rockets on this windless morning and the over-eagerness of most of the Chinese gunners, who have fired too early, betrayed their positions, and warned the *Nemesis* of the ambush, a dangerous situation becomes remediable. The explosive rocket-heads burst on impact with the Chinese batteries, setting one stockade on fire. Scott can hardly believe his eyes. Steam and rockets indeed! Smart work with the telegraph and rudders brings the *Nemesis* out of the lethal zone but not before one small mast has been cut in half and an iron swivel-gun knocked into the water. She is lucky to escape with so little damage. Now her guns and rockets commence punishing the Chinese in earnest. With the batteries silenced, she wrenches out the last of the stakes, and continues upstream.

In quick succession that afternoon, she shells three forts and lands storming-parties (the soldiers and marines not wishing to be wholly outshone). Miraculously, no one is hurt (except Chinese, that is) and not so much as a splinter is knocked off the boats of the *Atalanta* and *Samarang*.

The dismounting of the swivel-gun leaves a convenient gap in the side of the ship. Walter is struck by just how convenient. Splendid opportunity! The entire complement of the *Nemesis* are watching the bank where the last of the three forts has just been hit simultaneously by a Congreve rocket and the deadly burst of a fragmenting shell. He is thus able to unpack from his bag, unobserved, tripod, camera, and presensitised plate, erecting the apparatus where the swivel-gun has been screwed into the rail. To the surviving Chinese, scattering on the bank, the brass lens has all the appearance of the barrel of a new and still deadlier weapon of war (which perhaps it is), the more destructive for its small size and apparently innocuous wooden body.

The wheels of the *Nemesis* turn slowly, the dripping floats individually visible rather than a blur. She just holds her ground, without any forward movement. Walter has on his focusing screen: boats, the men at the oars, with the gunners loading the bow-carronades on the small craft, the blue-jackets and marines running at the battery, and streams of fleeing Chinese. Smoke and flame pour from the buildings and earthworks. Of course, there is no way in which his exposure time can be sufficiently shortened to cope with these fast and violent events. He thumps the rail and curses. What a dramatic scene! To miss it is frustrating, maddening.

Harry O'Rourke sidles up, smiling maliciously. He shows Walter the rapid outline sketches he has just executed and from which he will work in the studio. Walter groans, actually groans. The gig comes under the rail. They require spikes. Blowing up the Chinese cannon will waste powder and they do not wish to take the guns and burden the steamer, thus increasing her draught. With extraordinary dexterity Walter has dismantled his tripod and is going over the side with his paraphernalia before the boatswain, who has charge of the gig, has realised what is happening.

'Blast your eyes! Aha. I do not believe you should be here, sir.'

'Walter, where in damnation's name are you going?' Untypically, this is Gideon, over the rail.

Walter lights a cigar with great complacency. 'Do not let me delay you, Mr Davenport. Pull away, men, and I shall give you something to drink my health on our restoration to Macao. Goodbye, Gideon.'

The boat pushes off. Elliot and Scott have spy-glasses trained on the shore, while Captain Hall is inspecting a broken float in the starboard paddle-box. The boat is quickly ashore. Walter struggles to keep up with the rest of the party on the hill. They disappear into the blazing fort.

A little later, some marines emerge, with five or six Chinese, their hands bound behind their backs. Captain Elliot calls to Gideon: 'Mr Chase, do you kindly go on shore and extract such intelligence from these prisoners as you may – especially with regard to the navigation of the river ahead and the whereabouts of the shoals. As to their dispositions about defence, I am not at all particular.'

'Yes, sir. Er...what shall we do with the prisoners afterwards, sir?'

'Release them, Mr Chase. Release them, of course.'

Gideon is mightily relieved. Thank heaven there are no sepoy detachments in their expedition.

He finds the Chinese, all regular soldiers of the Green Standard, squatting on the muddy bank, guarded by a tiny midshipman with a boarding-gun, a large trumpet-mouthed blunderbuss. The first thing Gideon does is to turn the boy around to face the river. The Chinese soldiers, having ascertained they are not to be tortured or drowned, freely volunteer information. There are, apparently, forts, two more rafts, a field of stakes, and a boom ahead, as well as a squadron of war-junks. They keep looking behind Gideon at the smoke pouring from the stack of the *Nemesis*. As they mutter, Gideon overhears: they believe the Congreve rockets both propel the ship and act as its armament. What they cannot believe is that they will not be shot at if they go. Finally, the middy drives them off.

Gideon continues up to the fort.

The rocket-bursts have not been as devastating as the explosive shells at Chuenpi, although the single fragmentation-bomb thrown by the *Nemesis* has pocked the inner walls. Nor are the dead as appallingly mutilated as those at the Bogue. It is difficult to see marks on some of them. However, in a corner of the bastion, where a rocket has driven in and dislodged the sand-bags around a cannon with the force of its explosion... *'Walter!'*

Eastman and Wheeldon have a dead Chinese artilleryman between them, his bare powder-blackened arms around their necks, feet trailing on the ground – Eastman, who, Gideon notices, has not even the grace to give a guilty start. They drape the corpse over the breech of the cannon. Walter spots the rammer and his eyes brighten. He puts it into the dead man's hand, but it falls out. And again. 'Damnation.'

Wheeldon tries to break the stick across his knee and fails, but, standing it against the cannon, he uses his sword to hack it in half. He strews the pieces at the dead gunner's feet. 'Capital.'

'Yes, that is a fine detail, sir.'

Walter kicks at a ruptured sand-bag to bring more debris down. Pulling at some wicker baskets filled with earth, he completes the scene of destruction. Wheeldon brings a tasselled lance from where it has been flung down by escaping soldiers, another pleasant touch. Walter now addresses himself to the management of the camera, he, Wheeldon, and it, the only standing whole objects in the devastation.

'A little further back, Lieutenant Wheeldon, I'll have the liberty of requesting, and, pray, unsheath your sword again. Yes, arm to the side. Handsomely. Now, if you'll stand still as the dead man. Fine.'

Gideon must stay silent while the exposure is completed.

A wasp hums in the bright sunlight, settling on the Chinese artilleryman's left thumb.

'Thank you, you may move now.'

'Walter, this is...'

'Ah, Gid, I shall press you into service. Would you be so obliging as to carry the box of plates and the tripod? I am for ever in your debt.' Walter is frisky, jaunty, not a trace of embarrassment. He is perhaps a little too natural with Gideon. They leave Wheeldon to the task of making the fort innocuous.

On the *Nemesis* Harry O'Rourke has retained, somehow, a place at the bow, where he sits in his cane chair while Ah Cheong holds a parasol above his master's head. He sketches the gun-crew, who are engaged in cleaning meticulously the 32-pounder and then reloading it with grape and canister. Gideon will not be popular with the gunners, for on receiving his information and learning that the war-junks are very likely the most immediate challenge, Captain Scott will order them to draw the charge and load with round.

A string of rather feeble explosions, watched by Wheeldon and his men halfway down the hill, leaves the fort looking intact: the Chinese powder has been insufficiently strong in the quantities optimistically employed by the lieutenant of marines. He comes aboard sheepishly, but no time is to be lost. Within a minute the *Nemesis* is under way, sneezing and puffing past the sedge and paddy. The marines and soldiers settle down on the decks to clean their equipment.

'Mr O'Rourke, Mr O'Rourke.'

All heads turn to the bridge rather than the addressed. Captain Hall has a speaking-trumpet to his lips. *'Sir, I must request you to come off the bow. You may be picked off by matchlockmen or gingals on the banks.'*

'Damn their aim, let them. Only my plaguey creditors can lose.'

A cheer goes up. Harry doffs his hat...but he has a long swig from his flask. Then he kicks Ah Cheong in the backside, so that he is in front of him. Also he switches from pad to easel, which shields all but his hat from view. Thus immured, he becomes absorbed. Walter has no idea what he paints; cares less. They settle to the monotonous dirge of the leadsman. Captain Elliot interrogates Gideon as to the state of morale of the Chinese captives he ordered released. He is less interested in accounts of their new general. Gideon is in the middle of informing the little man he towers over, Elliot's head birdily cocked to one side in total concentration for that moment, when, looking at their wake for inspiration (how to reduce an expression, a deadness of the eye, a crook of a prisoner's shoulder to a meaningful statistic for the Plenipotentiary?), he sees junk-masts behind them. One, two, three...nine altogether. *Behind* them? Now how has this come about? They have passed absolutely, categorically nothing. But there are the masts, sailing away from them, three-quarters of a mile behind. They might have been hiding down a creek and been waiting to make their escape, but Gideon could swear he has seen no opening into the main channel, however well disguised. He alerts Captain Elliot, who has a word with Scott and Hall. The telegraph rings, the thud of the beam shakes the ship. Full *ahead*? Well, doubtless Captain Elliot's ambition is to navigate the Broadway Passage successfully, rather than destroy ships. Three minutes later, rounding a bend, nine war-junks appear.

We're caught, Gideon thinks, without fear, as he knows the capabilities of the *Nemesis,* but with respect for the clever pincer-strategem of the Chinese. But their strategy seems to be stronger than their tactics or at least their will to fight (demoralised by the death of Kwan?), for before the steamer has a chance to fire a shot, the panic-stricken junk-crews turn their craft around to flee, four running aground in their hurry and another three soon following. The *Nemesis* does not waste time or ammunition on these craft but, lobbing a well-placed shell into a fort, proceeds along the sinuous waterway. From the nearby bank – Captain Hall having run in close with great daring to avoid a sand-bank in mid-stream – comes a flash and *phut!* Harry's hat jumps off his head, then spins into the river. Running to the side of the bridge, Gideon sees it float along the hull, a large hole clearly visible in the brim, to where the paddles splash. Under it goes, trodden down by the wheel, comes up smashed, stuck to the paddle, then disintegrates in the water.

How strange! thinks Gideon. I run to watch the fate of the hat, not to see if Harry is hurt. O'Rourke plainly is unscathed. He paints *ferociously.* Walter comes past with his tripod and his box. 'The old fool! I'll be shot with him!' He erects his apparatus on the bow, neither man looking at the other. Walter's movements, too, are jerky, like those of an angry man. From rushes near the river a line of angry flashes erupts from a gingal-battery. The *Nemesis* replies with her own small swivels and also grape from the brass 6-pounder on the bridge, as well as the pair on the port side. After the twenty seconds of firing, Gideon's ears sing. A blood-covered man lurches out of the rushes, collapsing face-down into the brown shallows.

O'Rourke mixes a colour in his palette moodily.

Eastman is fiddling with the back of the camera. Gideon knows he must be reloading with a freshly sensitised plate. Half a mile ahead is a wooden stockade on the left bank; on the right is a large blockhouse, from which the black muzzles of three cannon protrude. The *Nemesis* trudges up at half ahead, thus allowing the two surviving junks afloat to make good their escape – no point running herself aground in pursuit of such small prizes. Three flashes with little balloons of white smoke come from the side of the blockhouse and, quite quickly, one fountain is raised two hundred yards ahead in poor line. The other balls hop across the water, all missing widely.

'The guns are fixed into masonry,' Crouch the master-gunner remarks to Captain Hall. 'Their powder's weak, too.'

'Still, Mr Crouch,' says Hall. 'Thank God *you* are not serving those pieces.'

Captain Scott has descended to lay one of the 32-pounders, which now replies to the battery. The whole steamer shudders and for a moment the front of the vessel is hidden in smoke, which the wind of their own passage soon dispels. Walter and Harry, Gideon checks anxiously, are still there, though both rubbing their eyes. They must be quite deaf.

'Missed,' shouts Captain Hall jocularly to Captain Scott. 'Do you regard me place a rocket nicely on the roof.' Adjusting the Congreve tube, Hall stands back. Halfway to the fort, travelling in good line, the rocket is deflected from course by a gust of wind and carries over the top of the blockhouse. Captain Hall smiles.

The next 32-pound shot is square on target and they hear the thud of its impact above the beat of the steam-engines. The battery has not fired back at all, which inclines the consensus on the bridge to the opinion that it is deserted and the gunners fled after the first shot they fired. They chug past the stockade – also silent.

The river now bends so sharply as to double back upon itself. The stockade is perfectly situated to take advantage of the difficulties in which a sailing-ship would find herself, though for the *Nemesis* it is a relatively simple matter to cut power to one wheel and turn on full rudder. Her after 32-pounder fires into the wooden posts, bowling over three or four and driving up a great geyser of spray and mud from the marsh behind. The steamer appears to be retracing her steps, for the river is describing such a winding course that they have come back perhaps a mile in three minutes, though they cannot see the part of the river in which they were, hidden as it is by a spit of paddy. Pedder confirms the suspicion, which has already struck Gideon, by referring to a pagoda which was previously on the larboard side and is now to starboard. Gideon had not even noticed it before, though it was he who had spotted the junk-masts...*which were obviously not behind them at all but in this very spot!* Pedder checks the ship's compass. Because she is iron, the steamer plays havoc with this instrument, fitted though it is with counteracting plates along the lines of Airey's system. It does confirm him in the conclusion already drawn from his seaman's instincts.

Gideon goes forward to where the two competitors are apparently absorbed in their separate tasks, Harry over the steamer's right eye, Walter the left. Walter is in a state of high excitement. He chatters to himself: 'Oh, fine, fine. Handsomely. Could not have been bettered had I the rudder myself.'

'What could not have been improved? I thought no achievement was perfect?'

'Ah, Gid, amiable boy, smart lad, delightful fellow. This has truly been a remarkable day for your friend.'

Gideon glances at O'Rourke. Whether the ferocious scowl and pouting lip are caused by nothing more than his usual desire to concentrate and keep his pince-nez on, or additionally by the irritation of a gleeful Eastman close at hand, it is impossible to say.

'Have you, er, successfully transferred the image?'

'Taken the picture, Gid, *taken* it: such is the correct expression. Indeed I have.'

'Beg pardon, sir. You must move a little to the side, thank'ee.'

Gideon steps smartly away to allow the 32-pounder to traverse on its carriage while the crew clean and load it. 'But, Walter, you are unable to pose your subject or arrange your background, and besides we were travelling at a considerable velocity of speed – as fast as a horse and carriage.'

'My dear Gid, you omit to take into account the *angle* of our approach. Recollect, we steamed at the fort, and the junks, head-on for a distance of a mile or more. Where I could not have hoped to take a Daguerreotype of the bank as it passed, I am confident I have a satisfactorily composed, and exposed, picture of Captain Scott engaging the small fort. I should hope Captain Hall will engage all future forts in such a manner.'

'Heaven forbid! My dear friend, think of the risks to which you have exposed your person! You were the first point at which fire was directed! I should say you were the very mark of the Chinese gunners and if we are fated to be struck, you will be the inevitable victim.'

'I do not care.'

'At least Harry is somewhat safer behind his easel – and his requisites do not have all the appearance of a deadly weapon.'

'My dear Gideon, it was Harry who lost his hat.'

Walter is so plainly enjoying the argument that Gideon desists. He leans over Harry's shoulder and sees that his representation of the late scenes is taken from a point, say, one hundred yards behind the *Nemesis* and fractionally to the right. It is at the sharp bend. Harry is quite jolly again; usually, he is very touchy about having half-finished work scrutinised. 'Not a hostage of any position, d'you see. The boy's perspective will be dictated by his situation – can't step off his little spot – besieged, surrounded – it might as well be by sharks. Hmmm. But I, I, sir, have wings.'

'Where is the battery, Mr O'Rourke?'

'My dear boy, I must own I hadn't remarked it, until it fired. I'll paint it in, I'll paint it in.'

'Yes, because you have Captain Scott pulling the lanyard and the great flash from our own cannon-mouth. If you will permit me to be so bold as to make such an observation, the composition suits the colours you always favour.'

'D'ye say?' purrs O'Rourke.

'It is no accident the old rascal has a preference for sulphur, flame, and brimstone,' says Walter. 'S-y-c-o-p-h-a-n-t,' he mouths silently at Gideon, who, ignoring the photographer, says, 'And also, Mr O'Rourke...'

'Harry, dear boy, Harry.'

'...you are in addition not a prisoner of the, ah...*temporal sequence,* of the specific moment. That is, you are at liberty to insert – as you shall the blockhouse – any object, or person, subsequent to the main composition. And, indeed,' says Gideon, becoming rather excited, 'good heavens, you may *anticipate.*'

'I'll settle,' says O'Rourke grimly, 'with great contentment, for my liberty to choose what I put into the frame – at any time.' And he adds in a piercing whisper, 'Recollect, did he not take the chamber-pot as well as the flowers of Veale's garden? I'll covenant for a few objects he'll not care for in his damned heliogravure. The loading number is afflicted with an itch in an indelicate portion of his anatomy well suited to Rubens. I'll say no more.'

Walter says coldly to Gideon, 'We'll pursue this interesting discussion at leisure in Macao. But for the moment, as, in your view, I am immured by the moment, I am too pressed to debate further with you.' The effect of this decisive rejoinder is a little spoiled by the fact that Gideon has ducked under the bulwarks halfway through the sentence as a shot screams overhead, lower and better aimed than any yet. Neither Harry nor Walter flinch, but continue with their tasks. Two junks, survivors of the original squadron of nine, lie half a mile off, near a side-branch of the river. They are under sail and also being poled. Smoke drifts from the stern-chaser of one. Another flash and bang, and a fountain spurts wide and short of them, indicating the first shot was a fluke of wind or unusually strong powder. The telegraph rings again and the *Nemesis* picks up speed. The chase is on.

The junks seem to be steering for a shallow, reed-covered branch off the stream, no doubt in the hopes that even the steamer's exceptionally shallow draught will be unable to cope. The river winds in great lazy loops, the junks popping in and out of sight. Captain Hall is unable to resist a long shot with a rocket, sending a missile streaking from the tube at seven hundred yards range when only masts can be spied three bends of the river away. Over water, land, marsh it flies, dropping in a perfect arc, out of sight. It must be water or soft ground, for there ensues no explosion. He fires another, 'just to spoil the rascals' navigation' – and this time there is the *crump!* of an explosion, followed by a continuous stream of smoke. Splashing round the bend, bustling, huffing, puffing, cannon now loaded with double charges of grape and canister again, the steamer *finds itself in the middle of a large town!*

'Well,' says Pedder in some awe, 'stab my vitals.'

Astonishment spreads down the steamer, starting from the bow-gun and working through the bridge, until even the men in the boats towed behind are leaning out, trying to see beyond the bulging paddle-boxes. Most amazed are the three civilians. How can they have missed this place before? It is possible, barely, to accept that the river may have cut itself new channels in a few years, flooded the land, abandoned its old bed to crack in the sun, forsaken its straight route to imitate a serpent – but this is the work of man they regard, not nature. Warehouses line a decent waterfront of about a hundred and fifty yards, lighters float by jetties, and there are hundreds, if not thousands, of boats: sampans, small junks, a ferry-raft, a galley of some kind...and a skiff and wherry of unmistakably foreign design. Surprise replaces Walter's earlier irritation, and he catches Gideon's eye on the bridge. 'Corrigan's?' he mouths. Gideon grins and shrugs. This will remain one of the river's puzzles.

The town, a trading-town rather than a market-town for country produce, as Gideon quickly sees (then the river *has* passed this way for many years) is compact, densely built, even crowded. You could step from tiled roof to tiled roof, bound over a street; yet all around is nothing but field and marsh. The crowding is willed.

Flame and smoke wave from one of the roofs – a secondary warehouse off the river-front. They can hear the tiles smashing as they slide off the roof. Up the river, the two war-junks are disappearing into a shallow tributary.

'Your rocket, sir, I believe has fallen on that house.' The Plenipotentiary addresses Captain Hall. The latter nods respect-fully. 'Well, Captain Hall, I should wish you to drop anchor here. Have the goodness to command the gig and jolly-boat to be away in five minutes. Mr Chase will accompany me on the shore-party.'

'If I may presume, sir, the risk to which you shall expose yourself...'

'Thank you, Captain Hall, for your concern. Have the sailors and marines prepare themselves. They shall need scaling-ladders and axes as well as their small-arms. Train the cannon on the river, away from the town. There is no need to keep our fires up, but place springs on the cables.'

'Very well, Captain Elliot.'

Crowds have gathered on the water-front. Elliot sits straight-backed in the jolly-boat by himself, Gideon at the tiller with the coxswain. Wheeldon and his marines follow in the gig.

'Don't like the look of this, sir,' the coxswain confides to Gideon. 'Cap'n Cook went the same way, sir.' Despite his own nervousness, Gideon laughs. The boat bumps on the quay in utter silence from the crowd of thousands. Without waiting for the marines, Elliot climbs up the slippery ladder, the crowd giving way before him. Gideon can see the nimble midshipman of more than a quarter of a century ago. Wheeldon swears horribly in the gig. As he hurries up a mossy flight of steps the marine lieutenant's sword catches between his legs and trips him. Gideon helps him up. They hurry after the Plenipo. Moses going through the Red Sea, thinks Gideon of Elliot's progress through the crowd. The lane stays open for them, Elliot's small figure strutting in front. Gideon tells Wheeldon not to look behind at his men.

At length Elliot stands before the burning warehouse. For the first time, he turns. 'Lieutenant Wheeldon, your men may pile their muskets here. Place the ladder adjacent to that wall and have a man mount and knock a hole into the roof, near the joist there. Mr Chase, request of the natives to provide buckets and a supply of water. Lieutenant Wheeldon, any native pillagers are to be dealt with severely.'

'We're going to put the fire *out?'* Wheeldon asks in amazement.

'I believe it lies within the powers of marines,' says Elliot, proceeding to walk the tiny street in company with Gideon, hands behind back as if he were pacing a quarter-deck.

'Shall I mount a guard over the arms, sir?'

'You will need all your men, lieutenant. I anticipate no attack from these unoffending people.'

Wheeldon's eyes roll in his head. However, orders are orders, and this is the supreme commander. With Chinese assistance a bucket-chain is soon formed, and as the marines hack down blazing timbers and clear wreckage, the fire comes under control. Wheeldon's eyes keep flickering to the stand of muskets, only to hear the Plenipo gently say, 'I fancy you would be a good deal safer on the ladder, my dear fellow, if you unbuckled your sword.'

Wheeldon looks very inclined to disobey this recommendation (order?) until Gideon volunteers: 'I shall hold it for you, Lieutenant Wheeldon.' Even so, the marine is most put out.

'Bring out those bales,' the Plenipotentiary calls. 'Stack them by the muskets. Let no one touch them, Mr Chase.' As Gideon is about to translate for the crowd's benefit, Wheeldon brushes by, muttering savagely: 'This is the damnedest, queerest war I ever fought.'

A heavy, oily reek wafts from the burning warehouse, really quite sickly. Despite the heat and fumes, the crowd press in with rather less respect than before, though quite obviously without any aggressive intent. A decrepit old fellow in rags at the front, so frail he may barely stand without assistance, and supported even now by unwilling bodies in the press, sways ecstatically. Gideon's nostrils twitch. He unsheathes Wheeldon's sword. Lurking figures by the salvaged bales run off into the gloom of an alley.

'I say, bravo, Chase!' Wheeldon calls from the ladder. This is really not bad from a Yankee and the next best thing to a sky-pilot (Wheeldon has the functions of divine and linguist inextricably confused, since they seem so frequently merged in the same person on this coast).

'Now, Mr Chase, I perceive you to react excessively,' Captain Elliot admonishes him. Gideon takes the naked sword and plunges it into the bale, feeling it cut through a certain amount of resistance. The sensation is not unlike what he would imagine it would be if he stabbed someone. The shiny blade, when he withdraws it, is discoloured with a substance that looks like dried excrement. Gideon sniffs.

'Captain Elliot, sir, this is Malwa opium.'

'*Opium?*'

'Of that I have no doubt. The balls have been unpacked from the wooden chests, I dare say for purposes of concealment.'

Elliot looks appalled. A marine, red coat scorched brown in patches, emerges from the flames, dragging another bale.

'Belay that,' Elliot commands.

From the crowd a pompous-looking man in scholar's gown advances on the Plenipo and his interpreter, except that advance is perhaps too positive a word to describe the sideways, cringing approach, clasped hands and capped head bobbing and pumping all the while.

'Take these...these parcels of death back into the conflagration,' Elliot commands.

'Back into the *fire*, sir?' The marine can hardly believe his ears.

The obsequious Chinese tugs at Gideon's coat-tails. 'Excellencies,' he fawns in the most barefoot delta dialect, which belies his robes of office, 'to you I owe...'

'Is this villain the proprietor of this house of death, Mr Chase?' Elliot does not even wait for an answer. 'Tell him he's a confounded rascal and will get no help from me. Would you kindly ascertain, Mr Chase, the number of the ordinary population hurt when the rocket fell? I trust there were none? Capital.'

'Back, sir?' the marine enquires again to confirm the general lower-deck opinion as to the insanity of all officers – which, apparently, increases in proportion to rank, reaching a perfect apogee of lunacy in the commander-in-chief.

'Back in, my man.'

The glee on the opium-broker's face turns to utter dismay. Elliot pushes him brusquely aside. 'Instruct this man to retire into the crowd, Mr Chase, unless he wishes to feel the prick of a bayonet.'

The bales of opium feed the dying blaze briefly. The charred timbers of the building glow in the dark, but the fire has been prevented from spreading. The shore-party retire to their boats. One marine has lost his musket but three boys in the crowd help him find it and the smallest urchin is permitted to carry it to the quay beside the marine.

The returning party discover the *Nemesis* surrounded by small boats of all kinds, and a smart trade going on over the side in eggs, fresh vegetables, and firewood. Captain Hall greets them at the gangway with a cheerful, 'Hulloa, the fire-engineers!' and, once Elliot is piped aboard, 'Sir, I have taken the liberty of allowing small parties of natives on board in turns in the belief...'

'I congratulate you on your acumen, Captain Hall. A very good decision.'

'Thank you, sir. I am very much obliged for your kind approval.'

Gideon converses with some of the Chinese on the steamer, who inform him that the town is called Heong Shan, that the mandarins have escaped in the two surviving war-junks, that they could pursue and capture them, for the mandarins have no pilot and will have to anchor in the darkness. A man volunteers to guide them the ten miles to his village the next day and confirms they are on the correct route to the main river at Canton.

That night the *Nemesis* maintains an ordinary watch, keeping the guns loaded but without troubling to put up boarding-nets.

The next day sees the water becoming even shallower, so that it is difficult to say whether the steamer is fording across shallows in the river or slithering over flooded paddy-fields, so blurred are the margins. One of the ship's boats is actually caught overnight in a field as the water recedes, but floats back the next morning ...

...and, having taken a fort before tiffin with the aid of peasants who volunteer help in extracting a field of submerged stakes, late in the afternoon of that day the *Nemesis* breaks through into the main Whampoa channel to join the light squadron near the Pagoda at Second Bar.

As the *Madagascar* blows steam off through her whistle to salute her muddy consort, the Plenipotentiary leaves the *Nemesis* and boards *Calliope,* a jackass frigate of 28 guns, more of a brig with pretensions than a proper frigate like the *Blonde* or *Druid*. The transition from steam to sail comes as a surprising anticlimax to Captain Scott and Lieutenant Crouch, looping back along the path of progress much as the river did. They feel the wind somewhat taken out of them.

Harry? He'd like to pour the concentrated salt solution with which Eastman is fixing his exposures right down that egregious young man's throat. A powerful emetic, indeed.

From THE LIN TIN BULLETIN AND RIVER BEE
Wednesday, March 24, 1841
Vol.4 No.6

An anonymous correspondent has furnished us with the letter which we print below, as we are desirous to impart its contents to a more general audience. Knowing well the officer to whom it is addressed and even better cognisant of what his own wishes would be, we have not thought it fit to identify him by name. We believe the letter was copied and forwarded by one of his subordinates, eager that his superior's abilities should not pass unnoticed by civilians as well as by his brother officers.

Commodore Sir J. Gordon Bremer, KCB to *Captain — of the steamer N—.*

HMS *Wellesley*
Whampoa
Canton River

Sir,

I have the honour to communicate to you, on the express instructions of the Plenipotentiary, His Excellency's high satisfaction with the conduct of your crew and officers during the most recent hostilities. Commander Scott of the *Samarang* had held the command of your vessel, you relinquishing your authority temporarily, but the Plenipotentiary has instructed me to tender you his warm congratulations and his thanks for the invaluable assistance you yourself were able to afford Captain Scott with regard to the handling of the steamer.

It will doubtless prove a source of additional gratification to you that this class of vessel should have proved itself so perfectly adapted to riverine warfare and the intricate navigation necessary for its successful prosecution. It may be said that no other description of vessel could have safely made such a passage. I sincerely congratulate you on your achievements, not least the small toll of only three men wounded during these operations and shall not fail to bring your actions to the notice of the Lords Commissioners of the Admiralty.

I have the honour etc.

J.G. Bremer (Commodore)
Senior Naval Officer

(We ourselves would only add that we believe this is no more, and perhaps less, than the doughty captain deserved. We do know that

his dearest wish is for a commission in the Royal Navy. - ed.)

From THE CANTON MONITOR

Tuesday, March 23rd, 1841

An easy and illusory victory. We entertain no very strong hopes that our aims will be accomplished through the successful outcome of the latest skirmishes in the Canton River. This can make no difference to the Son of Heaven in Peking. What are a few hulled junks, some spiked guns and breached forts? We assume, even, that he shall hear the truth as to his subordinates' manifest failures. It is much more likely that he shall receive reports of a great victory over the barbarian trumpeted by the venal interests of Canton. A decisive blow is wanting in the north, as exemplary as it would be just. We have in mind a blockade of the Yangtse River or the destruction of the dykes along the banks of the Yellow River. Such a deed would speedily bring the Emperor to his senses.

By this, we do not mean to belittle the extraordinary achievements of British arms in the last several days. The post of honour, in the van, belonged to the Navy and, especially, the steamers. By this, also, we do not mean to disparage General Gough, who in the scant weeks since his arrival from Madras has altogether 'shaken up' the land forces on succeeding Brigadier Burrell (who was a good soldier but old and infirm). What a sight it was! British men-of-war floating in the heart of Canton before the dear old Factories! The *Nemesis* steamer made the journey by a route hitherto impassable, save for flat-bottom barges and small junks. The Plenipotentiary himself was numbered among the company during this most daring raid. While never sensible of any other feeling than the most unmitigated respect for his personal courage, we strongly reprobate the manner in which he may be said to have thrown away the fruits of victory. Never was handsome opportunity so prodigally wasted – unless it was by the same commander at the Peiho River! The Chinese richly deserved chastisement – not once but twice did they fire on the flag of truce. On the first occasion, the day after she had found her way into the main river, when the *Nemesis* was passing the Bird's Nest Fort in the heart of Canton, the rascals fired on the white flag (whose meaning they well knew, not having scrupled to employ the signal themselves). Captain Hall exercised too great restraint, merely throwing a rocket on to the fort and then, after contenting himself with such a modest measure, retiring. A sailing-ship might not have been able to effect such a convenient exit, which would have spelled the destruction of the fort about the saucy gunners' ears. Two days later, in the general resumption of hostilities, the *Nemesis,* aided by the *Modeste* and *Madagascar,* wrote *finis* to the excesses of the fort with their shot and shell. Its chief had reported the *Nemesis's* forbearance as a signal victory for himself!

The second instance when the Chinese manifested their poor faith occurred when the circular fort at the Dutch Folly fired on Captain Elliot as he went to the Factories under the protection of the flag which all civilised nations but the lawless savages of this empire know how to respect. By the guns and rockets of the *Nemesis* the insult was resented with all promptitude.

At half past one o'clock p.m. on the afternoon of the 18th, Captain Hall and Mr Morrison raised the flag again at the Factories. Under the terms of the armistice, trade is to be reopened and British men-of-war are to take their station in the river to protect the Factories. Yet the Gates of Canton *still* remain shut in the face of the foreigner. When the Entry Question might have been resolved at a stroke, when a steady bombardment from the guns of the ships in the river might have culminated in an unconditional opening of the gates, an opportunity was lost for want of that firmness and decision in negotiation which had already been so conspicuous in the dash and vigour which had distinguished all the military and naval operations.

Clearly, the Chinese and their 'All-Destroying' General Yang have not been taught the lesson requisite. We see no sign of contrition in the Chinese, rather the reverse. The loss of life on their side has merely served to enrage them and the moderation of the Plenipotentiary, viewed only as pusillanimity, to embolden. For one, we should welcome the chance to give the villains the drubbing they deserve so soundly and to bring them to a proper opinion of themselves.

Vessels participating in the Assault on Canton:

Calliope (28) Captain Wilkinson
Herald (26) Captain J. Nias
Modeste (18) Commander H. Eyres
Algerine (10) Lieutenant Mason
Starling armed schooner, Lieutenant Kellett
Hebe armed schooner
Louisa (6) cutter
Nemesis steamer, master-commanding W. H. Hall
Madagascar steamer, master-commanding J. Dicey
Ship's boats to the number of 40 under the direction of Captain T. Bourchier and Captain C. Drinkwater Bethune.

From THE LIN TIN BULLETIN AND RIVER BEE

Wednesday, April 7, 1841

Vol.4 No.7

Reinforcement to the Expedition sought. It is now known Commodore Bremer steamed for Calcutta in the *Queen* last Wednesday. He is desirous of securing further troops from the Governor-General of Hindoostan, to which plea it is feared Lord Auckland may turn a deaf ear. Commodore Bremer, we ourselves have good grounds for believing, will especially represent the case for more steamers to be despatched to assist in river operations, preferably the iron-hulled class. We believe Lord Auckland may well be more prodigal of vessels than of men, especially in the light of the fashion in which, all are agreed, the steamers have proved themselves so suited to this form of warfare. To the hazards of the river they are almost immune, while defying the guns of the Chinese to the extent that it would be no exaggeration to state that two more vessels of this class would bear the same usefulness as ten regiments of native troops. Owing to the circumstance that the armed steamers already employed here (viz. *Queen, Enterprise, Madagascar, Atalanta* and *Nemesis)* are the property of the East India Company, we believe it will be no very difficult task to obtain consorts. The Honourable Company in its wisdom and discretion is fully cognisant of the difficulties in the way of exerting influence on the Canton authorities unsupported by ships which can traverse the whole length of the river, even past the city if necessary. The reversals which Lord Napier suffered in 1834, with the heavy frigates powerless to pass Whampoa, must be vivid still in the minds of the Indian and Home authorities. We know that the iron steamer *Phlegethon* of the Bengal Marine, sister ship in all respects to the *Nemesis,* lies at Lord Auckland's disposal and her attachment to the Expedition would be fervently desired by Commodore Bremer. We have it on the best authority, from the men of steam themselves, that the iron-hulled vessels, being lighter than the wooden *Queen* and her consorts, draw half their depth in water. The Commodore went to India with the north-east monsoon and, by the time he has assisted at the deliberations in Council, will find the gentle south-westerly winds assisting him back to China. Commodore Bremer has made openly known his desire to return within a matter of six to eight weeks, as he is by no means alone in the opinion that the present truce shall be short-lived. He wishes to direct the siege of Canton and to be first to march through its gates. In his absence Sir Humphrey Le Fleming Senhouse of the *Blenheim* (74) assumes the post of Senior Naval Officer. Sir Humphrey will be able to count on the presence and assistance of the *Calliope* still as Commodore Bremer has *absolutely* refused to countenance her return to Valparaiso and the South American station.

Murder of officers from HMS Blenheim. The bodies of Mr Toole and Mr Bligh of this ship were found washed up on the shore six days previous, together with that of Mr Field, mate of the schooner *Snipe,* who had accompanied them in their row-boat. It had been supposed they were kidnapped when they failed to return to their ships eleven days beforehand. Their bodies bore the marks of spear-wounds and Mr Field had had his ears cut off. It is presumed they were taken by surprise, murdered, and their mutilated bodies thrown into the river.

CHAPTER XXXVIII

From THE LIN TIN BULLETIN AND RIVER BEE
Wednesday, May 5, 1841
Vol.4 No.9

Recall of Keshen. This high officer has been summoned to Peking in disgrace, loaded with chains. His fall is thus attended with even greater ignominy than his predecessor Lin's. Moreover, as a Manchu and an Imperial Kinsman he shall feel the degradation even more keenly. The truce and treaty he negotiated with Captain Elliot in January is, we have it on best authority, the source of the Emperor's wrath. The continued reports of Chinese victories, when all here know they have suffered an unbroken series of reverses, costly alike in men and resources, had led the Emperor to expect much. The untruths thus rebounded on Keshen's own head.

Gazetted appointment. To be Magistrate at Hong Kong and Superintendent of the Gaol, Captain W. Caine of the 26th Regiment.

The Magistrate shall try all persons, other than natives, in accordance with the precepts and practices of English law. His jurisdiction over Chinese shall be in accordance, however, with Chinese custom and usage, all descriptions of torture excepted. His power of punishment over Chinese resorting to Hong Kong to be limited to fines of not more than $400, three months' imprisonment, and floggings of not more than 100 lashes.

Perpetrators of more serious crimes are to be handed over for the Plenipotentiary's decision.

Gideon Chase to Walter Eastman

> No. 16 Chow Chow Hong
> Canton
> May 11th, 1841

My dear Walter,

Although the Factories present the most desolate and abandoned appearance, with scarcely a soul to be seen, other than a handful of our own countrymen and the most hardened and brazen of the British smugglers, strange to relate little deliberate or wanton destruction is evident, and our office is quite as it was, with the lock unbroken. The rumours you hear from our friends regarding your obedient are rumours. I may assure you I am in good spirits, tolerably cheerful and the bowels regular. So far from nurturing murderous designs against myself, I cogitate schemes of revenge against my friend's enemies, wanting any of my own. I am, I expect, something of a hired assassin, a free-lance. Master Ow, my old Chinese teacher, who has provided in his character and personal history matter for our organ already, takes an especial delight in the use to which I have turned his instruction. Wheresoever and howsoever I can *dish* the mandarins he encourages me to do so. If I may find an infelicity of style or an incorrect or misapplied quotation from the canon of classics, I am to be sure to show it up pitilessly in order to humiliate the perpetrator. In fact, the implacable old pedant has of his own initiative sent several such to me. I do believe he is more delighted to notice an error in syntax or inappropriateness of expression in the communications of the mandarins than any ambiguity or contradiction in the substance. In this he is at one with his enemies, the mandarins themselves, who are a good deal more put out of countenance when the foreign stripling remarks their flaws as stylists than when he detects them in a conspiracy to make some cunning alteration or addition to the wording and sense of a treaty or proclamation. On occasion, it might be one and the same thing, as when they failed to elevate the character for Queen Victoria one line above the other characters in the same sentence, as they would for 'Emperor'. Really, I expect they would rather be shot from the cannon's mouth than accord it such treatment. Passing strange that the form and the representation should provoke almost more passion than the reality. I had returned from a walk with our friends of Meridian (who must have been the spies who informed you I was assailed by the blue devils) when, once again, I was assailed by confusions. Did I act altogether wrongly in assisting Captain Elliot? And had I overlooked the strong element of personal advancement and ambition in all his actions (for we know he *did* conspire discreditably to secure the post)? Harry then entered, somewhat warm with wine, I fear, and, on being apprised of my doubts, said, or words to the effect:

'My boy, selfishness and honour are one and the same. Men will not act by grand plans or formulations of a scheme of ideas, or even by the impulsion of a vested interest, but in the very first instance by the notion they entertain of themselves – and this picture they draw of their private characters is one to which they will address themselves with assiduity of purpose over many years: no portrait is more intensely drawn, Gideon, than the self-portrait.'

At least I trust I have captured the old fellow's drift.

But how strange the mandarins are! Captain Elliot had requested me to furnish him with one of Morrison's translations – I believe it may have been the Sermon on the Mount – for him to show yesterday to one of the senior mandarins, the Prefect of one of the Metropolitan Districts of Canton. This latter *winced*, truly he grimaced in pain. Captain Elliot, under the impression that the nobility of the doctrines therein expressed had worked some sensation upon the feelings of the mandarin, enquired eagerly if the Prefect had been favourably affected by the precepts. This mandarin made a slight movement of the expression in his face, as if troubled and perplexed deeply in his emotions. Of course, the meaning of the Scriptures had been productive of no such effect upon him. He was merely shocked by some solecism of Morrison's style (which, I feel bound to own, is not patrician). I quavered as I interpreted his words for the Plenipotentiary. The Prefect's answers to other of Captain Elliot's questions proving as evasive as they were unsatisfactory, we retired. The Plenipo had come up from Hong Kong with Mrs Elliot, as you know, but following this thoroughly suspicious interview, he quit the Factory that evening, preferring to sleep on board the *Nemesis*. He shall return to Hong Kong tomorrow, having spent only two days here as against the twelve at the beginning of April directly pursuivant to the ending of the hostilities. I fear his words to Sir Humphrey Le Fleming Senhouse on the occasion of that earlier departure (can it have been less than three weeks past?) to the effect that he entertained no uneasiness for life and property at Canton have appeared less than prescient in the light of subsequent events. He must surely regret them, reported as they were with such scorn by our contemporary. Having commanded Sir Humphrey to withdraw the ships from the Factories to Whampoa, on the 8th what does he find but boat after boat of Chinese soldiers passing down the river in full view of the Hongs. The spectacle can surely have had no other purpose than a design to intimidate us, the foreigners. We hear fire-rafts are being prepared and divers trained who shall use augers to bore holes in the devils' ships. I expect they would have a hard time with the iron *Nemesis,* but, in all seriousness, I do fear that the fire-ships, let loose with a favourable tide, might wreak sad havoc with the ships moored in the river.

I scarcely know whether to rejoice in Chinese success, for they have much right on their side, even though I do not feel so strongly on the issue of the opium as do you, or to fear for the safety of our friends, who have shown us such kindnesses. Nor do I much doubt that a rent forcefully torn in the veil of the government's obduracy, cruelty, and ignorance will not but benefit the population at large.

I am certainly at one with Captain Elliot in believing that the people may be successfully detached from their rulers for patriotism, so far from being a force to reckon with, barely exists among them. Did we not see with our own eyes the country folk voluntarily assisting us to clear the river and coming forward with correct and useful informations? Have they not supplied from the first all the provisions for the ships in the harbour of Hong Kong?

I expect the present peace should be measured in weeks rather than months, if not days and hours. Uncertain as I am to the nice timing of fresh fighting, I have no doubts as to the outcome of the issue again. This is no war but a pleasant hunt for the victors and massacre for the vanquished.

I take my station in the Factories at the request of Captain Elliot (a good man whom I am more than happy to assist) and by personal inclination, but I doubt if even the Americans may prolong their business here much longer. If, peradventure, I am in circumstances which permit of me forwarding news of an interesting or dramatic nature, I shall, of course, take every opportunity and all pains so to do.

Ever yours,

Gideon

PS. There has just arrived a letter from the Prefect. Evidently Captain Elliot's seed has born strange fruit. The Prefect has submitted a list of questions. It is my own belief that they are not calculated to be impertinent, although

Morrison thinks otherwise, but are posed in all seriousness.

INTERROGATORIES

1. How tall is Jesus?
2. How long are his mustachioes?
3. Ditto his fingernails?
4. How rapidly can Jesus indite verse?
5. Of what rank are his brothers?
6. How was it filial to leave his family and repudiate his father by saying he was the Son of the Emperor?
7. Are 30 silver pence the equivalent of less or more Carolus dollars?

Morrison is ransacking the Holy Book for apt quotations. I can think of a few, but as to the mustachioes I think Holy Writ is silent.

PPS. And yet is it not conventional to portray Jesus as bearded, and are not all the beards of a median length? Why so? Do ask of Harry if he left by yesterday's passage-boat. As Papist and artist, he should be furnished with an ingenious answer.

G.

Walter Eastman to Gideon Chase

Rua da Nossa Senhora da Nazare 12
Macao
May 17th 1841

My dear Gideon,

The briefest of notes. Now, when Elliot arrived in Hong Kong on the 12th, he directly ordered all the men–of–war and transports to weigh and proceed up the river. He will be coming up himself at any moment, catching up the rest of the fleet in the winged (or wheeled) *Nemesis*. It looks all up with Canton at last and the Chinese. Either firmly attach yourself to Elliot and his staff in your capacity as linguist and seek safety there or fly with the British merchants. Do not count on the circumstance that you are an American proving a defence against the rabble of Canton or the Tartar troops. Do not tarry to glean matter for our columns. Rather, depart.

Your concerned friend,

W.

CHAPTER XXXIX

E lliot's small figure casts a huge shadow in the dying sun. The Plenipo is dwarfed by Gideon and the guard of burly marines as they lower the flag outside the English Factory, but this serves to emphasise rather than detract from his authority. The Plenipo's moderation is by now notorious among all ranks of the military, yet over and above his universally admired physical courage, he seems to delight in exposing not only his own person but those of others to delicately gauged risks. These have mostly to do with fine calculations of time. Since wind and tide were unfavourable for the clumsier sailing-ships, particularly the troop transports, up till four hours ago the only vessel on hand in Canton was the *Nemesis*. This while thousands of Manchu troops poured into the suburbs, new batteries were erected in plain view of the river, and citizens left the gates bearing their worldly possessions on their backs. Only on the morning of this day now ending, May 21st, did Elliot issue his proclamation recommending all foreigners to leave Canton. Most Britons are already at Whampoa. The stragglers, and many stubborn Americans, only get away in boats on the afternoon of the 21st. However, several Americans remain, their attachment to the dollar proving stronger than that to their skins. One, Coolidge, is a subscriber to the *Lin Tin Bulletin and River Bee* – and, thinks Gideon, they can ill afford to lose one of that body.

On the pull back to the *Nemesis*, which is anchored some way above the Factories, Chase requests an oar for himself. The sailors laugh good-humouredly, one of their number surrendering his place to the young American (who will surprise by matching them stroke for stroke against the current) and sitting in the stern-sheets as a passenger next to the Plenipotentiary. Even Captain Elliot smiles, but a mournful Gideon is not skylarking. This was the route he rowed with Walter in their Meridian days, in their snowy shirts, on those glorious mornings in anticipation of the mighty breakfasts of old. Those dawns are gone, and the river is empty now of all craft except for theirs.

Evening falls on the *Nemesis*. No lights show from the shore and with the usual throngs of native craft and their colourful lanterns absent, the steamer might as well be anchored in a ribbon of ink. In the brightly lit wardroom, the officers are merry. If they are slightly taut, as well they might be, this makes their conversation all the sprightlier.

Elliot is sombre.

So, too, is his American linguist.

J. R. Morrison, the senior interpreter after the German Gutzlaff, merely translates official documents. He has no sympathy with the Plenipo's style and methods and is as cheerful as the servicemen about the prospect of action. He splits a walnut with a ferocious grip on the silver crackers (gift to the mess from Lieutenant Pedder's sister), showering shell and kernel on all and sundry. He offers a piece to Gideon. The nut is quite blackened and rotten. Gideon declines with a wan smile. Elliot has scarcely spoken. Shortly after, he leaves to go on deck, requesting his subordinates to be convivial as long as they wish.

It is ten o'clock.

After a few moments Gideon also goes up. Respectful of the Plenipotentiary's mood, he does not proceed to the bridge but goes to the bow. The crew of the 32-pounder are checking the lanyard of the gun, which is already loaded with grape-shot. The atmosphere on deck is quite different from that prevailing in the ward-room. Seamen and marines are tense and nervous. They spoil for a fight, and expect it imminently. Gideon sees lights down the river. The boatswain Davenport tells him they are the small frigate *Pylades,* brig *Algerine,* and the *Modeste,* which have arrived in the last hour. The bigger 28-gun *Alligator* is a little farther downriver, off Howqua's fort. Off the Factories, between themselves and three small men of war lie two still tinier vessels, which prove to be the graceful little *Louisa,* Elliot's favourite cutter, and the *Aurora,* no man-of-war but a schooner belonging to the house of Dent. Gideon knows her well. And so they are no longer alone; his spirits lift.

At eleven o'clock, when Gideon has just finished explaining nautical 'bells' to Wheeldon, who has the sublime effrontery to pretend he doesn't know about them, there is a shout from a sentry on the *Modeste.* He hails again. Now Gideon, who has been on deck longer than the officers who have just spilled out of the ward-room, full of wine and bonhomie, and whose eyes have already adjusted to the gloom, can make out dim, moving shapes upstream. Too low to be ships, too massive and clumsy for boats. What on earth can they be? An instant later, a plume of flame rises from the river, casting twisting shadows over the moving water. At that moment the sentry discharges his musket from the *Modeste,* shortly followed by five swivels on the port side of the *Nemesis.* On the heels of the sharp barks from these small pieces come shouts and cries from upstream. Further tails of flame appear.

'Fire-rafts!' says Wheeldon. 'Good God!'

Captain Hall is on the bridge before the words are out of the marine officer's mouth. At the bow there is a flurry of activity around the anchor. The *Modeste* can be heard getting her boats away, but it is too dark to see. The Plenipo makes his, appearance on the bridge, talking in a low, calm voice to Captain Hall, who replies in the same tone. Wheeldon rushes off to gather his marines. Bells ring in the engine-room. Gideon hears thumps, crashes, curses from the passageways below – presumably the firemen and other engineers rushing to their stations. Armed with ropes and boat-hooks, seamen pile over the side into the gig and long-boat. The boatswain bangs into Gideon, swears, and lashes out with his rope's end. He runs off without seeing it is the interpreter. Gideon goes on the bridge to avoid interfering with the crew as much as to offer redundant services to the Plenipo.

Elliot greets him with a concerned, 'You are not wounded, I trust, Mr Chase?'

Gideon stops rubbing his arm.

Elliot says, 'We are fortunate our attackers were thrown into a panic and ignited their combustibles in too great a haste. Another few minutes unobserved and we should have found ourselves in a pretty pass.'

Gideon reflects that they seem to be in one anyway.

The flames are discernibly nearer, brought to them on a favourable tide: this must have dictated the timing of the attack, as four or five o'clock in the morning might have caught them more unawares. The boats have vanished into the darkness between themselves and the fire-rafts. Gideon regrets he did not take an oar this time; he could have been of practical assistance without imperilling human life (except his own, which doesn't count, of course). He hears splashes on either side – not boarders, but the paddle-wheels starting to turn.

'All ready, sir.'

Elliot consults his watch. 'Nine minutes, Captain Hall. Capital work. My compliments to Mr M'Dougal.'

'I should not be greatly surprised if their batteries open very shortly.'

'Nor I. I leave our dispositions as to defence in your very capable hands, of course, Captain Hall.'

Hall bows, a courtly gesture from that strong and silent man. The steamer passes her own boats safely and, steered with great skill, tows a line of blazing rafts in to the bank. Just as she lets go, the darkness is split by a great flash and a bang. Hall's teeth show white.

'We were too close in for them to hit, unless they lowered their sights,' Gideon thinks. He is now, he flatters himself, almost a veteran of these manoeuvres. A string of flashes and reports from further downstream indicate that the batteries are firing on the other ships.

Now the *Nemesis* shudders as her two big guns go off. There is no moon, and Gideon guesses the discharges are meant to unsettle the Chinese gunners as much as damage the emplacements.

'Attend on them,' Captain Hall calls through his speaking-trumpet, 'stand their fire and aim at the muzzle-flashes.' Elliot nods approval. Next time the two 32-pounders fire a split second after the Chinese, and in the momentary glow it is possible to see the shadowy figures of men on the parapets of the batteries. 'Damned brave,' says Hall, 'rallying the men to fight the guns and exposing their own persons.'

'They don't want courage,' Pedder says, 'but science, that and discipline.'

Near the Factories there is a bellow and huge flash from a gun of considerable size.

'Dear God,' Pedder exclaims. 'The *Louisa*.'

They wait in silence. Again the big gun roars.

'Our smallest craft,' Elliot says, 'and their largest piece. It'll make matchwood of them at this range.'

'Three hundred yards to mid-stream,' Hall remarks gloomily, 'if it is as much as that, and batteries on both banks.'

The *Louisa* and the *Aurora* reply with their small guns, perhaps disconcerting the Chinese but also betraying their positions.

'*They can't move off!*' Hall says with sudden realisation. 'The tide is against them!' A moment's consternation, if the naval officers can be said to be capable of it, before Hall reflects out loud: 'We cannot reply to the gun, we'd risk hitting the schooners. It needs must be a rocket, thrown high.'

'Well,' thinks Gid, 'that's smart of him.'

The operator brings the rockets to the tube.

'An elevation of...hmm...seventy-five degrees or twelve turns of the screw,' Hall muses. 'Now, sir, there's not a gun made, not even at Carron, that wouldn't burst if abused so.'

'True, Captain Hall, but a mortar?'

'Then, sir, with respect, you talk of something utterly distinct.'

'Granted. I have no desire, my dear Captain Hall, to disparage this extraordinary craft, its crew, or appurtenances.'

The large gun goes off again with a flash that lights the whole river. It is quite definitely concentrating its fire on the two small sailing-vessels. Captain Hall adjusts the direction of the tube, having fixed on the elevation already. The rocket rushes off, even more spectacular at night than by day, a rain of sparks showering the river. Up, up, it soars, impossibly high, just a red dot now. All faces turn upwards. It wavers, begins to drop.

'I should estimate that was at least ten times the height of the *Melville's* mainmast,' remarks Captain Elliot to Pedder, very democratically.

'I should not disagree, sir.'

The missile starts to pick up speed, turning into a long comet as it approaches its terminal velocity and leaving a wavering, ghostly trail imprinted on the spectators' retinas. Harry could explain the phenomenon, thinks Gideon in the instant before impact.

The rocket bursts well beyond the sand-bagged gun and, in fact, it must be…'Upon my soul!' exclaims Elliot. 'It must have landed in the Factory Square.' So far from showing any compunction or embarrassment, he begins to laugh. Gideon can see that the Plenipo finds a relief in the simplicity of action which is probably more to his personal taste than the policies of moderation and conciliation which he has enforced on himself and wears like a hair-shirt.

A battery on the southern bank, near the Honam temple, opens on them. Hall commands the two big guns to reply with shell. He has another Congreve rocket loaded into the tube. Elliot removes his cocked hat (he is in uniform tonight and must have suspected the likelihood of fighting) to scratch his balding head. 'This is strange,' he comments, 'to the best of my discernment, they appear not to have hit the *Louisa* or *Aurora* – and yet the range must be almost on the point-blank. This is damned queer. Would you not say, Captain Hall?'

The commander of the steamer, however, is too busy supervising the fitting of the Congreve rocket. He twirls the elevating screw on the launcher. Pedder rings on the telegraph for half-astern. The steamer backs up. 'A higher trajectory still and greater range should stop it passing over the target,' Hall says. He nods to the operator, who sets the rocket off. As usual, those on the bridge stand at a respectful distance from the exhaust-gases. Flames and sparks pour out. The orange shower becomes a storm. The tube shudders, the rocket clattering inside.

Pedder shouts frantically, 'It's stuck!' Gideon freezes in horror. The Plenipotentiary looks death in the face. He wears a smile of mild amusement. At this juncture, Captain Hall steps through the torrent of sparks, the orange particles dancing around his knees, thrusts his arm in, past the elbow, and shoves the rocket forcefully out of the tube. This assistance is all that is required to send the rocket rushing off. It spins erratically, though, and falls short of the battery into the river.

'My dear Captain Hall,' says Elliot warmly, 'we all owe our lives to you. But, my dear fellow, you are hurt.'

Hall is pale as he receives the congratulations of all on the bridge for the prompt and gallant action which indeed has, in all likelihood, saved their lives, for the rocket would have devastated the bridge had it burst in its tube. He tries not to hold his right hand, but in the end flesh and blood have their way. He winces.

'Better to see the surgeon, sir,' Pedder advises. Hall ignores his first lieutenant.

'I command you to leave the bridge, Captain Hall, on pain of disobedience.'

With obvious unwillingness, but not a word of argument, Hall goes down to have his badly burned hand cleaned and dressed.

Concentrated shell-fire from the 32-pounder pivot-guns and the well-placed shot and grape from the brass 6-pounders have silenced many of the shore-guns. In the case of the major battery by the Shameen sand-bank, near the Factories, the valiant Chinese gunners have had to be silenced twice, on the second occasion when they were rallied by their Tartar officers.

Suddenly, a strange sail appears ahead of the *Nemesis*. 'Junk ahoy!' shouts the look-out.

'Now where in God's name did that tub pop out from?' This is Pedder, theoretically in command of the vessel. Any doubts that it may be a trader, strayed or drifted inadvertently into the battle (in which case the Plenipotentiary would have spared her), are dispelled when she blazes away at the steamer with two large gingals on her poop.

Pedder rings full-ahead and pursues. The bow-gun bellows,

striking the junk's stern with a round-shot and sending up a shower of splinters in the flickering glare of the beached fire-rafts, but the gunner's target, the junk's rudder, is unscathed. The junk moves surprisingly swiftly. It has sweeps out. As it disappears into the northern bank, Pedder becomes quite profane. They drop to half-ahead and turn violently on the starboard wheel, sending their wake surging into the riverside. The bank opens before them: the mouth of a large creek. They seem to have lost sight of their quarry. The look-out calls to port. The character-istic ridged junk-sail is there. Then the starboard gunners shout that they have a mast, too.

'By God!' Pedder ejaculates. 'Look ahead, it's a fleet of the beggars!' The junks are moored in lines, head to head and stern to stern. 'Fire-rafts by the bank, hundreds of them!' The Chinese, it is clear to Gideon, have concentrated their entire junk-flotilla for protection here, while the fire-rafts are reserved for further night-attacks. 'I wonder,' ponders Pedder, 'if we shouldn't save our shot and powder and cut 'em out. They could lay trains to the magazines.'

'Capital notion,' drawls Captain Hall, stepping on to the platform, 'in fact, why not have the two birds with the one stone and use the combustible rafts?'

Pedder looks relieved. A chance to distinguish himself in temporary command is every first officer's dream, but present circumstances are really too trying a baptism. Within minutes the boat-crews are getting away again. Gideon's request to go aboard some junks to scour for official correspondence or plans before they're blown up is flatly refused by Captain Elliot.

In the next three hours the boats will destroy no less than forty-three heavy war-junks and thirty-two fire-rafts: Pedder's first estimate proving wildly exaggerated. 'Go to it with a will, men,' he encourages them, as they keep returning for fuses and kegs to lay powder-trains.

With all boats out of the way of falling timbers, the *Nemesis* backs up on her wheels to await the first series of explosions. The bridge will not be disappointed in the work of the boatswain and gunnery officer. In a chain of devastating eruptions, the powder-stores going up not simply one after the other but in a pattern of every other junk for six vessels, then each remaining second junk going backwards again, a whole row of vessels are blown to pieces. Hall observes grimly, Pedder with a boyish jubilation. 'I say! That's devilish fancy work. Have you seen better in the Vauxhall Gardens?'

'I guess I wouldn't know, Lieutenant Pedder. I have never been to London.'

'Haw! My dear fellow.'

'But the pyrotechnical displays of the Chinese are really quite something to behold. In days gone past we have enjoyed such in Macao.'

'Well, hoist with their own petard now, I fancy, sir. Good God! Those are men in the water, bodies rather.'

Gideon follows Pedder's pointing finger. As he does so, a complex sequence of detonations ravages a second row of junks. Is it his imagination, or does he see human figures going up among the planks and timbers?

'The poor devils must have hidden themselves, or not been able to flee ashore like the others. I wonder they didn't surrender to us.'

'Can you wonder, Lieutenant Pedder, after the quarter meted them by the Madras Native Infantry? I believe that is the title of that corps of murderers.'

'This is the Royal Navy,' Pedder says coldly, turning his back on Gideon. Who forbears remarking it is no such thing but the Honourable Company's Bengal Marine.

To the boatswain's great chagrin, four junks which have failed to explode have to be hulled at the water-line with round shot at less than fifty yards' range. Leaving them filling slowly, as the first watery light of day starts to thin the blackness, the steamer chugs up the creek on the sort of reconnoitring and surveying mission to which she is ideally suited. This waterway, of whose existence Gideon has been quite unaware in all his years at the Factories (can the river, he ponders, hold any further surprises?) describes a circuitous route which more or less follows the line of the city walls two miles away, though having a tendency to go northward. The boats sweep along the banks, flushing out refugees and taking several prisoners. Three miles up the creek, with the Plenipotentiary glued to the eye-piece of his telescope,

Hall coughs discreetly. 'Sir, if you will very kindly indulge me, if you will follow the line of my finger: to the west of the water-wheel, there is a small track which curves past those pools...'

'...*fish-ponds*,' volunteers the interpreter.

'...which then becomes a kind of causeway raised above the level of the paddy-field.'

'Flagged, I believe, Captain Hall,' says the Plenipotentiary, handing the steamer commander his telescope.

'Indeed, thank'ee, sir. It then joins a bullock-track which snakes up to the Heights two miles distant, unless my eyes are greatly weakened.'

'It does and they are not. A capital route by which the land forces may proceed to investing the city, I should think. There is a respectable beach here and the causeway would carry light field-pieces. As to siege artillery, I am less certain. Obliged, Captain Hall, I shall remember this, in addition to all your other services.'

'You are very kind, sir,' Hall mumbles. He seems unsteady. Elliot looks at him sharply. 'Support him before he falls,' snaps the Plenipo, moving not a muscle himself as Pedder jumps forward to catch Hall.

'Now take him below to the surgeon – he's not to rise. You can tell the sawbones a tincture of laudanum would do no harm at all.'

'Aye, aye, sir. What shall we do with the prisoners, sir?'

'Let Mr Chase question them, and then release the rascals.'

'I'll cut off their blasted pigtails, too, and send 'em squeaking home, in a manner of speaking, sir.'

'You'll do no such...'

'Thank you, Mr Chase, that will be quite enough. Leave the commander of the steamer to his own business and kindly serve me by eliciting what you may from our captives.'

'But, sir...'

'That is all, Mr Chase.'

Gideon leaves the bridge. By the time he has finished, at eleven o'clock, the sun is high in the sky and his jacket transparent with sweat.

And Captain Hall will be tossing in the initial throes of a four-day fever.

Rua da Nossa Senhora da Nazare 12
Macao
May 23rd, 1841

My dear Gideon,

How I envy you! Truly, I long to be conveyed on that magic vessel, to journey on which is more akin to flying on the Djinn's carpet than voyaging over water in any ordinary way. To watch the panorama unfold before one's steady gaze, to spread one's legs upon its platform and seize the remarkable views and sights with the charmed eye and necromantic plate – could any prospect afford me greater gratification? Here I sit, immured in bales of tomorrow's (God knows where we will find our subscribers, let alone how convey their copies to them, with every species of boat taken up) and generally in a lather. The subscribers shall have to wend their way to us, much like the mountain to Mahomet.

Our friends arrived this morning, so exhausted as to be well-nigh dead (at any rate to all sense of appearances). I was able to offer a biscuit and a glass of claret to fortify the inner man. Ridley was in great distress. That sturdy youth laboured under the oppression of a most abject despair. How had the fates conspired to deal him such a heavy blow? Was he wounded? Had he left behind all his substance, the not inconsiderable amounts he had won with his deadly cue? Was anyone killed, hurt, or missing, with, under the circumstances, strong presumption for concern? This was it. MacQuitty was the cry. Where was MacQuitty? He'd been on the quay – remembered him barking, said MacLean. Didn't Johnstone carry him aboard, Ridley having the tiller? Now Jonathan was darn-ing everyone's mother and worse. I swear he was near to laying about him with his mighty fist – he was on the point of blubbering. (In fact, Gideon, there *were* great tears rolling down that brown, unshaved, and manly countenance.) For a dog, Gid, a *dog*. Don't be altogether amazed if you see him at the wall of Canton, brandishing his stick and whistling, 'Here, boy, here.'

Corrigan, who puts his dollars above his own miserable life, has, I hear, elected to remain, detaining young Oswald. Let the Chinese have his head if they must. I am given to understand that Canton is to be assaulted. Is this so? Send all the news you may to,

Your good friend,
Walter

PS. I had the extraordinary gratification of being able to exhibit all my plates (all, that is, that successfully took, which is a dismal and merest fraction of all that I endeavoured to submit to the light, especially with regards to my earlier experiments) at the studio of Samqua, the portraitist who has his premises next door. You recollect the 'provocation' of his notice in the *Monitor?* But he is a most obliging and estimable native. I believe I can use him to add to our revenues – we have, by the by, exchequer problems. The burning forts on the Broadway are an extraordinary composition, if I say so myself, with the criss-cross lines of the rocket-trails still evident in the sky, and *'Lieutenant Wheeldon RM astride a shattered battery'* evoked remarks and comparisons I should blush to repeat. Harry, of course, is full of spleen, and hardly speaks.

Gideon Chase to Walter Eastman

> *Nemesis*
> The Factories
> Canton
> May 23rd, 1841

My dear Walter,

By now you will have heard of the attempt made on the ships in the river by the fire-rafts and of the great duel with the shore-batteries. Feeling in the fleet is greatly excited against the Chinese for the underhand way in which they broke the armistice and tried to surprise the ships. I do not concur in such nice notions – it seems to me that the weaker party must perforce always rely on the advantage of a sudden blow. The rules of war are a luxury for the strong and an imposition on the weak. Kidnapping (as we saw at Chusan and Macao) and the seizing of hostages are the only truly efficacious measures which the Chinese may consult.

I expect you have welcomed Jonathan and our other friends at Macao (and, I hope, provided them with comforts and conveniences) for their departure was hasty and ill-prepared and I should think they pushed off the quay unprovided with razors or fresh linen. I regret to say that not all our countrymen were got away in time. Mr Coolidge and a number of others are believed captured by the Chinese. It is my considered belief that we need not entertain strong fears for their personal safety.

No British sailors were killed and but few wounded. One man was injured by the blast of his own cannon. Captain Hall recovers as well as might be hoped from the burns to his hand and arm, sustained in a piece of great heroism on the bridge of the *Nemesis*. I attach an account. The *Aurora* and the *Louisa* were caught in an awkward position near the bank and unable to sail away. However, they escaped with but trifling damage thanks to the ingenious expedient hit upon by their commanders when they by turns veered out cable and shortened it in again – thus altering the range and deceiving the Chinese gunners by playing merry games with their range and timing on the river. We have chosen a small place called Tsingpoo to make the landings. This will not be for a day or two, during which time the transports will be got up, boats commandeered, troops supplied, and all the rest of it.

I fear the latest events may well sound a death-knell to Captain Elliot's hopes of detaching the populace of this province and the metropolis from their rulers. To carry sword and fire to the town and its contiguous hamlets is not well calculated to recruit the hearts of its inhabitants. Already, tactless measures – which perhaps seem rather lenient than excessive to the perpetrators, but constitute a mortal insult to the victims – will have sullied the reputation of the foreign forces. I was a disgusted witness of such acts on board the *Nemesis*.

We have steam up and springs attached to our cables, to boot, and the greasy smuts from the stack soil this paper as I recline against a brass 6-pounder. Still, you are not the man for appearances.

Your affec. friend,
Gideon

PS.Anchor weighed. We are further to explore the creeks and tributaries for suitable landing-places.

Gideon Chase, Esq., to Major-General Sir Hugh Gough, KCB

Nemesis steamer
May 24th, 1841
Three o'clock a.m.

My dear General Gough,

I have the honour to forward to you by this emissary, under separate cover, a specimen of the translation which you were so good as to request of me to provide yesterday evening. While sensible of your several pressing duties both in a military regard and as a loyal subject of Her Majesty, and of the most humane desire not to cause unnecessary alarm or perturbation among the population, I should wish to point out that a proclamation of this nature requires a large amount alike of thought as to its content and of careful expression as to its wording that the language should not demean its subject and thus be productive of an effect opposite to that which is intended. The Chinese are most sensitive to such blunders. The difficulty is increased by the circumstance that while it is requisite the notice should be intelligible to the populace at large, it should at the same time prove acceptable in its forms to the mandarins. I should have liked more time. However, I trust that the translation conveys something of the spirit of the original, and I attach it whilst assuring the General that he may always rely on the services of his humble, obedient servant,

Gideon Chase

(Letter marginally annotated in the hand of Major-General Sir Hugh Gough, 'too damned wordy by half')

PROCLAMATION
of their
HIGH EXCELLENCIES
THE COMMANDER-IN-CHIEF
of British Land Forces
and THE PLENIPOTENTIARY
and CHIEF SUPERINTENDENT OF TRADE
to the
worthy
CITIZENS OF CANTON

It is not the intention of General Gough or the officers and men under his command to cause needless destruction to life and property at Canton. So far from wishing to harm the population of the CELESTIAL FLOWERY EMPIRE, they wish even to spare them all unnecessary fright and inconvenience. Therefore, they communicate freely to them the following information.

Today is the anniversary of the birth of the QUEEN OF ENGLAND. This is an occasion which HER MAJESTY'S loyal subjects prefer to mark with demonstrations and tokens of the honour and esteem in which they hold HER. More especially, it is customary to discharge salutes from the great guns, one for each year of her age. This is twenty-two, she being a young woman. HIS EXCELLENCY the Commander-in-chief of British Land Forces is at pains to make it known to the CITIZENS OF CANTON that during this celebration, which will take place punctually at noon, they should not surrender to panic since the cannon-fire is *without shot* as the guns are loaded only with powder.

Taou Kwang, -th year, -th moon, -th day

A true translation
G.H. Chase (Signed)

Delivered by the long boat of the Hyacinth *at 6 o'clock a.m., May 24th,* 1841
Gideon Chase, Esq., to Major-General Sir Hugh Gough, KCB

> *Rattlesnake* transport
> Canton River
> May 24th, 1841
> Three o'clock p.m.

Sir,

I wish to register my strong protest at the use to which my services have been put. I regard it as hypocritical and provocative in the extreme, as well as being an action in the long term to be attended with consequences which shall prove highly deleterious to the known policies of the Plenipotentiary, to send to the citizens of Canton a proclamation assuring them of their immunity from the guns of the British fleet as a preliminary, a bare two hours after the discharge of an innocuous salute, to a general, indiscriminate, and destructive bombardment of the town. In what sense may the civilian population of the city understand any similar future declarations from the leader of the British Expedition other than as cynical and heartless pleasantries?

I have the honour etc.

G. Chase (Signed)

May 24th, 1841 4 p.m.

'Thank God, Mr Corrigan, and you, Mr Coolidge, sir. We never expected you rendered so soon.'

'We…ah, every hour of our captivity has been of the interminable duration of a month to us. But at any rate, we are not harmed. Our Chinese captors very kindly returned us to the Factories after releasing us.'

Behind the ten Americans, flames rise from the suburb to the rear of the devastated Factories. A pall of thick, black smoke hovers over the city. The boom of ship's guns carries down the river. Gideon gestures to the file of marines behind him to assist the released prisoners as they stagger over the rubble.

'Our boats wait to take you off, gentlemen. Your travails are over. Mr Corrigan, sir, I'm heartily relieved to see you safe and sound. I guess old misunderstandings may be submerged in…'

'Pah!' Corrigan spits venomously, staining the flagstones brown. 'You be damned.'

Gideon recoils.

Coolidge says, 'A boatload of our countrymen were taken, which you presently see before you, Mr Chase. I regret to say, the small dinghy in which young Oswald of your former house and another were effecting their escapes was stopped by village braves and…well, sir, we have good reason for fearing the worst.'

'I am desolated. He was a fine lad.'

'I calculate they mistook him for a Briton. We had difficulty convincing the Tartar general as to our nationality. He believed, if I recount rightly, correct me, Mr Corrigan, sir, that if we were not English then we should speak a different language and wear different clothes.'

'This way, gentlemen. You are safe now.' The sergeant of marines gestures to the longboat of the *Rattlesnake* transport.

Gideon proceeds to reconnoitre the buildings to ensure there are no other foreigners taking refuge there. The enraged citizens of Canton have sacked the New English Factory. As Gideon steps through the splintered doorway, he crunches on chandeliers. The staircase has been destroyed and even the fine polished stone floorings torn up, while the large marble statue in the Great Hall has been toppled. It lies in three pieces. The portrait of George III hangs in ribbons. There is no one in the building. Other of the Factories have been sacked, none vandalised quite so ruthlessly as the British. The American, Chow Chow, and Swedish Factories have managed to escape quite unravaged.

In Hog Lane he encounters old Minqua, the security-merchant. He advances on Gideon, shaking his head and pumping his hands. 'Too much-ee make trouble,' he wails, 'all building make-ee fall down.' Then he sees it is Gideon. 'The Co-hong is ruined. Ruined,' the security merchant says in his own language. 'The Prefect has given the buildings into our charge-but of what avail when the mob has ransacked it?' He walks off, shaking his head.

Gideon re-emerges into the square. This is now full of red

uniforms and a group of sepoy artillerymen with a small field-piece and short, wide-mouthed mortar. Where in the name of the Merciful have they come from? A large, mutton-chopped officer strides up to Gideon. 'What the devil do you mean by this? Who in hell's name are you, sir?'

'I might request the same of you, sir,' responds Gideon, admiring his own coolness.

'Pratt of the twenty-sixth. Now oblige me with your identity, sir.'

'I am Gideon Chase, an interpreter of the Plenipo's staff. I am come on my own initiative to take off Americans, my fellow-countrymen, whom native friends had informed me were to be set at liberty here.'

'You are in the middle of a battle, Mr Chase. I recommend you quit this scene with all celerity. I may not be responsible for your safety. I believe you have certainly exceeded your authority.'

'Very well.'

Gideon gets into the gig of the *Rattlesnake,* seething with fury. He has never been so angry, not in all his life.

The Aide-de-camp of the Commander of British Land Forces to Gideon Chase, Esq.

Canton
May 24th, 1841
8 o'clock p.m.

Sir,

I have the honour to be instructed by General Gough to return to you your letter of today's date. General Gough regrets that the very unusual tone you have chosen to adopt in your communication makes it impossible for him to receive it.

I have, sir, etc.

W. Browne (Capt.)

May 24th, 1841 11 p.m.

From his position of isolation on the mast-head of the *Rattlesnake* Gideon can see there are two more fires in the city. Explosions twinkle as shells from the ships in the river fall upon the suburbs in the dusk. The surgeon of the transport is in the other mast. He appears to be sketching. The man nods in a friendly way to Gideon, but the young American ignores him – an uncharacteristic piece of rudeness. Further up the river are the bright, starry flashes of shell-bursts and the warmer flame from the cannon-muzzles themselves. Rockets rush away into the city to immolate themselves at the end of their flights in balls of fire.

That I have contributed to this, thinks Gideon bitterly. He could fling himself sixty feet down into the water with shame and vexation. He feels lost and confused in the immediate sense, as well. The land actions seem far less clear-cut than the river-fighting, where an operation can actually be seen unfolding for most of the time, the river facilitating movement, bearing the men and the ships, and yet also closely framing and delimiting the scene of the action. The sprawling, ill-defined, and messy exchanges on *terra firma* are far less transparent in their meaning to the uneducated eye than the combat on the water, where the units are material, bigger, and more discernible: ships, not individuals. Of course, this has been unusually emphasised by the static nature of much of the naval action, the big 74's and frigates used more in the role of floating batteries, towed into action and then anchored, than as sailing-vessels, while the steamers have served mostly as tugs. Now Gideon tries to puzzle out Gough's strategy, for he has been kept in the dark for some time now, whereas the cheerful Pedder of a few weeks ago was always willing to explain. The sporadic gun-fire in the river comes from the steamers and fifth-rate jackass frigates and the sloops engaging the sand-batteries on the banks and the island forts in mid-stream. But what were soldiers doing at the Factories, when the main force embarked upriver so gaily in the early afternoon?

Gough, Elliot, Sir Humphrey Le Fleming Senhouse, Morrison are on the *Nemesis*. Which has failed to return. Are they holding their landing-point, or have they become lost?

Perhaps they have already broken into the city, where the fires beckon. Gideon sighs, lets go his hand-hold for a second, and relaxes. At that moment there is the whipcrack of a shot through the rigging, followed immediately by the dull thud of the lead burying itself in the wood.

Some sharp-shooter has taken a pot-shot at him!

What's more, the fellow has obviously attained a high degree of proficiency with his clumsy weapon. Had he not moved the slug would have drilled him straight through the head. He is, in fact, he recalls, at about the same height and distance from the bank as the target-kites he and Walter saw the Manchu matchlockmen flying. Down he shins, putting the trunk of the mast between himself and the shore. He can just hear Harry O'Rourke: 'Silhouetted against the flames, dear boy. It's a mee-racle you're not dead.' Halfway down he remembers the surgeon. 'Mr Cree!' He climbs back up to his post. 'Mr Cree, we are being fired upon!'

'The deuce we are!'

In a moment the surgeon is swarming down his mast.

Gideon feels a slight roughness in the wood. Unevenness and splinters just there. He probes, and digs out the matchlock-ball. How heavy it is. He bends his arm, is about to throw the bullet into the river, but checks himself and instead drops it into his pocket. It can be a charm, perhaps worn on a watch-chain.

When he ever gets a chain, that is.

May 25th, 1841, 7 a.m.
The longboat glides over the water in an eerie silence. On the right bank buildings smoulder. A charred timber crashes to the ground, sending a flight of sparrows arcing over the river. The wood glows orange briefly and then becomes grey again. Stillness returns. They can hear the water dripping off the oars of the gig twenty yards behind as the sailors pause in their stroke. Gideon is forgivably uneasy: his longboat is nothing more than a munitions-barge. They carry boxes of ball-cartridge, stacks of Congreve rockets, 12-pounder shell for the howitzers, some enormous mortar-bombs, and bags of powder. The gig bears…water-casks. As they round the bend by the Fati flower-

gardens, scene of many a legitimate excursion in the days of peace and, Gideon is glad to see, still smothered in spring blooms and quite unravaged, they spot a man-of-war sailing-ship moored in centre stream where the river widens to well over a mile. Its side explodes in jets of flame, smoke blossoming, the roar of the broadside following the *ee-ee-ee-ee* of the shells over the longboat. Gideon's head goes into his shoulders, but he turns to spot the salvo burst long seconds later on the northern bank, well inside the Old City. The target seems to be a mansion a little below the mosque. Gideon can just make out the two trees growing insanely out of the top storey of the minaret. That would be, let me see, he thinks...the Tartar general's yamen. A general bombardment now commences, the ships further down the river joining in, until the rumble of the distant guns is a continuous muted thunder. The flash of shell twinkles intermittently in the city, concentrated around the targets of Government Arsenal, Manchu parade-ground, and Governor-General's residence. Gideon can see the shells bursting through the green roofs of the larger buildings. Smoke starts to rise again. There is already a dark bank of it, high in a sullen sky. Just as Gideon turns to the bow again two remarkably heavy explosions close after each other shake the Old City. Looking back, he sees a pillar of debris and smoke, shot through with fire, rising above the Arsenal. The oarsmen cheer, and are answered by the seamen on the men-of-war. Her guns are run out through the ports again, and moments later another broadside sails towards the city.

The ship slips behind them and then disappears around the Fati bend, but every five minutes they hear the thumps of her discharges, fainter each time. It is a sultry day. Birds sing sweetly and cicadas buzz. An hour into the row, the men are clammy with sweat. However, they complete the passage without incident: the river has been swept of hostile junks, and no one is so bold as to take a long shot at them from cover.

About three miles above the city, half an hour down the newly-named *Nemesis* Creek, they pull in to the right bank. Two steamers, one easily recognisable as the celebrated iron-hulled vessel, are anchored near a most workmanlike wooden landing-stage erected by native sappers under the direction of their engineer officer. Moored by the jetty, a little armada of almost a hundred ship's boats and commandeered junks lie under the protective guns of the steamers like a flock guarded by two black sheep-dogs.

Only a picket of four marines remains on the jetty. Leaving the boat, Gideon tells the seamen not to wait for him after they have unloaded the munitions. Strolling on, he finds a quarter of a mile distant a company of some seventy or eighty men of the Madras Native Infantry holding a large temple set in handsome grounds. These form the rearguard Gough has left to secure a retreat which it is inconceivable he will ever have to make. Impeccably turned out, white cross-belts stunningly blanco-ed, the sepoys on guard present arms crisply to Gideon. He returns the compliment with a semi-military gesture, half salute, half deprecating wave, appropriate to the anomalous status of interpreter.

Within the temple buildings, the other sepoys make their morning meal over fires casually lit on the floor. Clad only in loin-cloths they squat on their long, thin shanks, combing out oily black locks. Their wild eyes roll, and Gideon shudders to see them sharpening their bayonets on the flagstones. The gilt and gold leaf on the temple idols have all been torn off, while in the search for precious stones and specie a hole has been hacked into the giant Buddha's belly. Other sepoys are defecating in the gardens, bright yellow ropes of excrement. No doubt, thinks Gideon in a state of general mild shock, the product of their diet of pulses. He cannot see their English officers.

Anywhere is better than this place, Gideon decides, and heads briskly up a bullock-track.

The sun rises high. It really must be the hottest day of the year so far, and heavy and humid as well. Gideon removes his jacket. The track becomes a causeway over rice-fields. Figures shimmer in the distance. Is it his imagination? Trees or the black shakoes of the 18th Royal Irish? He steps out smartly.

Crack goes a bullet over his head, followed by the thump of the report behind him. Without even looking for the signalling puff of smoke, Gideon breaks into a run. Another bullet whipcracks overhead, while a third kicks up the mud at his heels. He has, unfortunately, to run in a straight line. To step off into the flooded field would slow him terribly. It is about half a minute before he is shot at again.

Thank God, then! Only three men, who must reload each time. The next shot comes nowhere near him. The third man, obviously the best shot of the trio, having already splashed the foreigner's trouser-leg, waits a long moment before letting fly again, and then Gideon feels a plucking at the coat in his arms before the report reaches him. Why is he bearing such an encumbrance anyway? Is he going to tea at Alice Barclay Remington's? Into the field he flings it, pumping his arms furiously with renewed momentum. He is young and fit, and his wind and legs do not fail him. No more shots come. Nevertheless, he hardly slows but keeps running at an easy pace. He has gobbled up a surprising distance. The far-off black dots clarify into the shakoes of the 18th, as he first thought, and not a vestigial tree-line. He slows to a trot, then a fast walk, and, as the breeze of his momentum dies, finds he is bathed in sweat, his shirt a second skin. Wiping the stinging sweat from his eyes, he sees a group a few hundred yards ahead. Catching them up, what is his surprise to see they are not troops at all, but dusky, bare-legged women, young boys, and stick-shanked old men, carrying all sorts of pots and baggage. These are the camp-followers of the 18th, who had their station at Trincomalee, in Ceylon, before taking ship to China. These carriers, cooks, cleaners, and perhaps mistresses are distinguishable as a more delicate-boned people than the Madrasis who follow the Sapper and 37th Company of the Native Infantry. Gideon hurries past, noting a boy who carries a Chinese vase in one hand and a trussed, live chicken in the other. Those lumpy cloth bags tied with string probably contain further spoils. Soldiers are spread out over the entire plain, plodding through the rice-fields, the stragglers half a mile ahead. The sepoy artillerymen have broken up the small causeway with their pieces, and are having to manhandle the light guns in the paddy. Small clumps of disorganisation everywhere. Frantic red-faced officers cursing their men for confounded blackamoors or a set of idle clodhoppers from the bog. Then Paddy should have no difficulty on this ground, thinks Gideon wryly. But why the hurry? The Heights, the small hills opposite the walls of Canton, are some two miles distant. Surely it would be best and safest to arrive in orderly fashion; after all, a few minutes or an hour saved are as nothing in a campaign.

'Bang!' goes a gun on the left, too heavy for a matchlock or musket, but not a cannon's boom. It can only be a gingal. Smoke rises one hundred yards distant. More reports follow, the dirty fumes of Chinese powder concealing the view. The sepoy artillerymen make to unlimber their pieces, throw a shell into the Chinese skirmishers, but their European officers countermand it. A quick volley is got off, then the 18th rush in.

'On, boys, on with the point – these pagans won't stand bayonets!' This is their ensign, a fresh-faced boy of about sixteen, barely young Oswald's age. The red tunics vanish into the screen of gun-smoke. Cheering, shrieks, and yells come out of the fog – whether Irish banshee or transfixed Chinese, it is difficult to tell. As it clears, Chinese can be seen splashing across the rice-rows. An Irish infantryman kneels in the wet, fires, and drops the rear of two gingal-bearers, who flops forwards, wriggles, and then lies still. Some of the Chinese skirmishers abandon their heavy pieces to make good their escape. As Gideon, on the causeway, comes level with the spot, he sees blood staining the water. The corpses float, in fact. The stagnant water and heat will aid the process of decomposition, he thinks. These could also cause a problem with disease. Or will it be fertilising for the crop?

On the right flank, the advancing forces have run into another pocket of Chinese resistance. Their defence seems remarkably feeble and ill-coordinated. Puffs of smoke betray the ineffective ambuscades. How hot it is. No relief.

A burly sergeant of the Royal Irish, wading below Gideon, parallel to the causeway, puts his hands to his throat, half-turns, and, as his knees give way, slips into the paddy-water.

In a moment, Gideon is running down the side of the raised path to get him out. He has heard no bang. Is it true that you do not hear the shot which hits you? He *was* very near the man. Nor, when he turns the soldier over, is there blood or any sign of a wound whatsoever. He recalls how obtuse he was in the case of the coolie bitten by the cobra during the flood at the Factories. Perhaps…but the sergeant's thick boots and tight gaiters are proof against his fumbling fingers, even if a snake could have stung him through them.

The world dissolves into a bright orange flash. It darkens into a purple ball. Somehow, his face is in the mud. A voice a long way above him says, 'Ye thievin', mutherin' hound, would ye take the boots from a dead man? Ye'll think twice afore ye boot from a Christian agin.'

Boot?

Do you mean steal the boot, my good man? thinks the stricken Gideon with a mad, inconsequential pedantry which is almost sublime. What an interesting word. Noun used as verb, which would indicate, would it not, familiar usage, phenomenon of common occurrence among the rude soldiery. Connotations also of *freebooting*. He giggles. And groans as a shafting pain like a hot needle sears through his skull. He must not open his mouth again. Or, as he gasps, move his head unless very gently and slowly. He makes it to all fours, overcoming a desire to retch. There's salt sweat in his mouth and streaming down his face – and as he wipes it away, he sees it's blood. He can feel the lump on the back of his head where he was struck. Oh, God, his skull throbs. He gets onto his feet unsteadily. The sun is blinding. He lurches into the water by mistake, but decides to splash some on his face anyway. It is not much comfort but alleviates some of the stinging of the cut. He wades on. Four soldiers are stretched out on the bank of the next field. Their haversacks have been removed and placed beside them. Regaining the causeway, Gideon sees a knot of men around a prone figure. The ensign undoes the victim's stiff leather stock and gently lifts his head to a flask. The casualty is a middle-aged man with red side-whiskers, deadly pale and babbling in delirium. Should he tell them not to give water to a man shot through the body? They really ought to know better. Still, he doesn't want to court another blow.

On he stumbles, his passage a little Calvary.

'At least I do not have to bear arms or provisions.'

His own voice comes from a distance. The sun is pitiless. Each throb in his skull seems like a nail from the sky. The sepoy gunners curse in their liquid tongue, forcing their 6-pounders through the slush, slipping and falling over themselves. Juggernaut, thinks Gideon inexactly. Bliss awaits the self-immolated. The stink from the fields is atrocious – nothing but night-soil goes on them, that and stone jugs of urine. The hills seem just as far away as they were five minutes ago. For the first time, the crackle of distant musketry goads the troops into further efforts. The fire spatters irregularly, followed by the crash and roll of a disciplined volley. Once more a feeble popping precedes the sweeping echo of the volley. Wild cheering rings down from the Heights. Shimmering before Gideon, a line of red dots, ants, crawls slowly up the slopes. Clouds of white smoke, seemingly very clean at this distance, swirl in the air, occasionally hiding parts of the ant-swarm.

Jets of white spurt from the line; seconds later the slam of the third volley reaches the fields. The smoke must be rising on the hot air, rationalises Gideon, trying not to think about the pain in his head and to surmount the plane of the corporeal on the approved lines of the stoicism of the sages, for there is no wind at all. Would that there were – he tears off his shirt, is going to dip it into the paddy-water, thinks better, and wraps it around his temples and neck as some protection against the sun's rays. Shading his eyes, he sees stone structures near the tops of the hills. The ragged shooting comes from these buildings – forts, presumably, which were not there seven years ago when he walked the city walls with Walter and their friends of Meridian. The first field-pieces have come through the paddy and a battery of three guns commences firing at the forts, the shells exploding above the parapets in the familiar stars of smoke and sparks. Troops of the 18th come past Gideon at the run, knocking him sideways, followed by the Indians of the 37th Madras Native Infantry. Gideon presses on stubbornly. The battle is getting nearer. He cannot see too well, but the shooting is discernibly nearer – louder, with less time elapsing between the flashes and the thumps. He decides not to look at anything ahead but to keep his eyes steadfastly on a spot on the ground ten feet in front, no matter what. Indeed, for a while he shuts his eyes completely, having checked there is nothing for him to bump into on that featureless plain. This becomes boring, so he opens them again, but still walks without reference or perspective. He is as a somnambulist. The boom of cannon and the rattle of musketry hardly impinge on his reverie of pain and fatigue.

He will get above his body, float while it walks on, observe himself. 'Or at least my mortal integument.' It is requiring more effort to walk. He finds he is trudging up a slope. The forts are very near. What else?

The firing has stopped.

Red-tunicked bodies lie on the hill, a good many. Higher up, Chinese and Manchu soldiers in black and blue lie in piles or alone, in those disjointed postures to which familiarity can never reconcile the eye.

An officer of the Royal Irish looks strangely at Gideon. Gideon stares back. The officer is an apparition, with a powder-blackened face into which trickles of sweat have carved stripes like the decorative cicatrix of the West African, not to mention a moustache singed off on the right side. His sword is broken three inches below the hilt and, as the man slowly sinks to his knees before collapsing on to his side, Gideon recognises the appalled expression on the officer's face as the mirror of his own regard of horror and pity for the other.

A moment later, he jumps and flinches as a bullet flies past with the high, ugly twang of a ricochet off rock. He never heard the shot itself. But the shock snaps him out of his trance. As time begins again, so his head starts to ache, and he scrambles up the hill to the shelter of the fort. Pop, pop, pop, from the parapets, followed by the big bang of a wall-mounted gingal. Mercy! The Chinese still hold that fort. Tumbling down the slope with a shower of bullets and gingal-balls ploughing up the dirt around him, Gideon skids behind the shelter of a clump of boulders at the bottom. He hears groans. Peeping from cover, he sees the officer of the Royal Irish lying on the ground, shot through the thigh. His cries are too awful to endure. He runs out, picks the fellow up, and carries him in. He is so smart about it that he is only shot at twice.

For the moment there appear to be no reassuring blobs of red in their immediate area. Somewhere, over on the other side of the hill, in the three hundred yard gap between the Heights and the city wall comes a fierce exchange of gun-fire, the British no longer discharging in volleys. What can they be doing? Indian stragglers come over the last of the rice-fields, half a mile away on the left flank. Between these troops and themselves, to his unmitigated horror, Gideon sees black-tunicked forms in straw hats flitting through the broken ground. They have: a gingal, swords, rattan bucklers, spears, and a matchlock or two. These look like Cantonese irregulars, village braves. He shudders to think of his fate if he falls into their hands. To their right is a line of trees, an irrigation ditch, and an overgrown garden with the large, semicircular horseshoe-shaped blocks of masonry which Gideon recognises as tombs for the wealthy citizens of Canton.

Any port in a storm.

'Please,' he entreats the wounded and moaning officer, 'to be quiet as you may.'

Lifting the man across his shoulder, he stumbles down the hill at an increasing pace. Had it been uphill, he might have had to leave the wounded soldier to his fate. Once in the grove which shelters the cemetery, he feels more secure. They will need to go to the end, and then round to where the firing is. This has intensified, with the boom of artillery swelling the musket-fire, but the shots are muffled by the intervening hill.

At one point, hearing voices, Gideon has to place his companion on the grass. He crawls on his belly to peer over a tomb. An old man and a young boy shelter within the curve of the grave. They stare at him without expression. Probably, Gideon imagines, paralysed with fright. 'Don't worry, Uncle and Little Brother,' he whispers in the local patois, his command of the words of reassurance almost certainly terrifying them even more. He picks the Royal Irish officer up again and, stooping beneath the burden, hurries across the cemetery. From the top of a small knoll he can see the city wall of Canton and the chain of forts opposite on the Heights. British and sepoy troops with artillery are under enfilading fire from forts and walls, but the deadly play of their own cannon is gradually silencing their enemies.

The ground, though, is littered with British dead and wounded. It seems the Chinese have exacted their highest price yet. Under a barrage from their supporting artillery, the red lines advance in formation up the hill. Their bayonets glitter in the sun. Chinese fire from the forts becomes frantic, increasing in intensity and rapidity at first, but then becoming feeble and dying away. Soldiers fall in the scarlet ranks, but the advance is steady, the fire they are taking is galling rather than withering. Some of the ants bear scaling-ladders. As these are placed against the fort walls, the first two flung down by the defenders, four ants dash for the gate and race away. Ten seconds later, a great flash from the powder-bags, smoke, and splinters whirling in the air and, mingled with the roll of the explosion, deep-voiced cheering. The ants pour in through the breach. Sporadic shooting follows, soon silenced, then the odd shot at strange irregular intervals, eerie silences, cheers – all to no discernible rhythm. From the sounds it is quite impossible to deduce what form of action corresponds to that jagged syncopation.

A few moments later, the Union Jack breaks from the ramparts and is draped over the wall.

This is the moment…there is a time and tide…taking a deep breath, clenching his jaw, Gideon moves out of cover with an unconscious man on his back. He scuttles over the grass. He would never have thought he could move so fast. As yet he seems to have gone unremarked. Coming over a hillock and out of a line of bushes, he arrives at the road which runs between the city wall and the Heights. Having waited to recover his breath, he sets off at a dash. No shot immediately follows. Four hundred yards to go. The sun, moving away from the river and city, starting to descend into the west behind the Heights, casts an orange glow on the forts, but where Gideon runs, in the gauntlet between city and fort, below walls and hill, it is darker, full of pools and oblongs of shade. Bang! goes a sniper's gun from the ramparts of Canton. *Yea, though I walk through the Valley of Death.* As if in answer, a discharge of protective musketry comes from the forts, and under cover of this fire, Gideon stumbles safely up the hill. By the time he lurches through the splintered gate, his legs have turned to curd. Strangely, he is not much out of breath.

May 26th, 1841, 5 a.m.
Chase twitches. A huge Manchu soldier with a broad-bladed sword is trying to chop his foot off. He has a pistol. It won't fire. This significant, and by no means unusual, dream of a young man dissolves into the grey but infinitely less disturbing reality of an orderly of the 18th pulling at his boot.

'Tay, sorr.'

'Ah, thank you kindly. You don't have some coffee?'

'Sorry, sorr, on'y tay, sorr. Anither American gentleman requested same as yeez, sorr, if Oi remembers right.'

'Thank you, er, private.'

'Eggs for breakfast, sorr. Foraged hen's eggs, with compliments o' th' officers mess o' th' 18th, sorr. Paddy's a dreadful scavenger now, sorr. Token o' regard for yeez, sorr, from the brother officers. Shall Oi say ten minutes, sorr?'

Gideon arches his back. He is horribly stiff, but his head no longer hurts. And he has a clean shirt. He has passed the night in the square keep in the centre of the fort, preferring the stone flags to verminous straw.

The eggs slide down welcomely – greasy, frazzled, black at the edges, and more than a hint of grit in the saucepan. O'Rourke's favourite meal of the day. Yet he has never enjoyed the huge spread of dainties at Harry's hospitable table as much as these crude offerings.

The heat and sultriness of the preceding day have abated – yet is the weather still heavy. It is dull and overcast, carries a threat of impending violence in itself. The hot tea in these circumstances is actually very refreshing. Suitable for British weather maybe? He ducks into the squalor of the keep again. He would like a handkerchief. Unfortunately, his own and all his personal requisites, were in the pocket of the coat he threw away so thoughtlessly the previous morning. Life over property, though, unless you're a Chinese-Yankee with a Scottish upbringing.

'Gin'ral's compliments, sorr, and would yeez attend him at

599

earliest convenience on the Heights, sorr? T'ank yeez, sorr. A mirror and a razor, sorr. Oi'll bring yeez hot wather and soap directly, sorr.'

I don't think this fellow could 'sir' his own officer as many times as he has done to me, Gideon thinks as he contemplates his sunburned face in the borrowed field-mirror. Scraping the razor over the tender skin is exquisitely painful. As he dabs on more lather – this snowy beard and those rheumy eyes a vision of a distant future – he hears a rumble qualitatively different from the crack of the light field-pieces. They are going to work early, he thinks. Last night, fatigued as he was, his sleep was made uneasy by the distant grumble of naval bombardment from the river. This is heavier even than the ships' great guns. Gough must have his siege-pieces up. Refreshed, cheeks stinging him into liveliness, he departs for an interview with the brusque general, which he imagines shall be at least as astringent.

The staff cluster around the Great Man, some blue naval uniforms also present. Gough uses a powerful ship's telescope to sweep the city. The view is tremendous, an extraordinary panorama. Gideon takes in his breath. This is Canton viewed from a perspective he has never before enjoyed. Spread below him is an ancient, forbidden city, its labyrinthine, weaving lanes, crooked streets, maze of creeks and canals no longer an insoluble puzzle but open as a relief map; green roofs of substantial houses, flimsy grass mat-sheds, square fortified towers, pencil-slim pagodas, bulbous spires of Muslim mausoleums, all jostling the other for light and precedence in a haphazard, planless geometry. Here and there shell-holes in the roofs or the black space cleared by conflagrations actually seem willed, an extinction of clutter. A huge fleece of smoke still hangs in the west, three miles away, over the naval arsenal. Shimmering at the end of it all is the grey ribbon of the river and, beyond, the alluvial plain, rich and well watered, sheltered by the violet smudge of mountains in the distance.

'Prodigious prospect, you'll agree, Mr Chase.'

'I guess so, General Gough, sir.'

'Now, m'boy, we have use for you, if you'll not spurn us.'

'I am yours to command, General Gough, in most things.'

'We generals are accustomed to command in all things. However. Sir Humphrey, pray present your spy-glass to our young friend. Now, Mr Chase, we seek targets for the guns. We do not wish to rain an undiscriminating fire upon the heads of the population of this city, even did you or the Plenipotentiary allow us.'

Laughter.

'I perceive six or seven square strong points in a particular quarter of the north-western metropolis of some seven or eight storeys...you are amused, sir?'

'I crave your pardon, General Gough. Those are pawn-shops. They are built thus so as to be secure from bands of robbers – they have no stairs but access from ladders, which they haul up at night.'

'Throw a bomb on top of 'em anyway,' suggests a young staff officer.

'Hurt the rascals in the pocket – they'll still have their miserable skins.'

'To the extreme east, Mr Chase, the remarkable long, walled rectangular ground near the French Folly fort, near enough half a mile from the river, d'you follow my pointing finger, sir? If you'll apply the glass, you'll remark a large building and an extraordinary number of small huts in rows. Captain Browne inclines to barracks, our naval friends to magazines of powder.'

'That, sir, is the Examination Halls.'

'Mr Chase?'

'Those are the cells in which candidates ambitious for office will sit the various literary examinations which will assess their capabilities as scholar-administrators. Thousands may sit at a time, as you may judge from the extent of the buildings, which occupy an area fully as great as the military parade-ground, which lies directly after the five-storeyed red pagoda which confronts us behind the wall. Now these examinations are conducted in circumstances of the greatest secrecy and security. Why, should a candidate die during the three days' ordeal (which is not at all unknown), he may not be brought out save through a hole especially knocked into...'

'Mr Chase, you are informing me that those buildings are the

601

hatching-ground, the spawning-place of the mandarins who have been confounding us with their knavish tricks and damnable deceptions?'

'Of the mandarins of this province, who must nevertheless serve away from home under the regulations of...'

'They're all the same to me. Mark the range for that, Pratt. Mr Chase, do I offend your tender susceptibilities?'

'Why no, General, I expect I can already hear the chuckles and glee of my preceptor.'

'Can't understand you, Mr Chase. Talk in riddles, but I hear you're straight enough in an extremity, what?'

'Two and a half miles, sir,' says Major Pratt, 'while the guns shall be sited on an elevation, of course. I say, what a capital notion. Never liked school myself. Urchins wouldn't have minded a few shells pitched into Rugby school.'

'Haw!' laughs the General. 'This shall sting worse than rods, I'll wager. The artillery-park must be situate behind the rearmost fort when the siege-train is brought up.'

'Very good, sir.'

Gideon is surprised. They still await the arrival of the heavy guns, then. As if on cue, there is another mutter on the horizon, as of a bombardment far distant. The ADC grins. 'Celestial artillery, hey?'

'They have reinforcement from the north?'

The ADC points. A white veil drifts across the plain towards them from the mountains on the far side of the river, twisting and winding as it comes. Within seconds it is over the water, then rushing over the city spread below. As the first puff of wind cools their faces, soon to grow into a mighty buffeting, forked lightning laces the sky over the city with veins of gold.

Torrential rain starts to fall.

Gideon Chase to Walter Eastman

Heights of Canton
May 26th, 1841
7 o'clock p.m.

My dear Walter,

I am come to this spot a little later than the main body of the troops, but in time to witness much of the action. The gentlemen commanding in the Naval Brigade, of some four hundred men, are returning to their ships in half an hour's time. They will convey this to you. So this must be the briefest of notes. I have got myself under canvas, but it is raining hard, and has done so all the day, with the consequence that the mud in the courts of the forts comes over the top of our boots. The troops only wait for the command to take the city. They could do this without the big siege-guns, but General Gough is a fine commander who wishes to spare his men as much bloodshed as is possible. I do fear for the citizens of Canton, especially when the Indian troops get in among them. I hear they sent out under a flag of truce yesterday, but doubt if General Gough entertained their overtures favourably. Would you send up clothes to me? Gideon.

May 27th, 1841, 6 a.m.

Chase sneezes. Water trickles down the back of his neck. He finds he is shivering. The weather is as changeable as the Chinese. He reflects that discomfort is relative. It only seems so cold because the heat of twenty-four hours ago was so oppressive. This would be pleasantly temperate for New England. However, the bedraggled group of army and naval officers around General Gough, though soaked, are in high good spirits. Water pours from the brim of Captain Sir Humphrey Le Fleming Senhouse's cocked hat, no doubt as it is designed to do in still more inclement conditions on the quarter-deck of a 74.

Behind them, a messenger toils up the slippery slope, which is awash with rivulets. He slips more than once. The senior officers have their eyes on rain-shrouded Canton, not the assassin of their hopes from the rear. He speaks to the ADC, who gains the general's attention. Gough turns impatiently to the runner. He breaks open the seal, the ADC sheltering him beneath an umbrella. Can this be the order for an immediate attack under protection of the weather, without prelude of a bombardment?

Gideon's pulse beats quicker.

The officers close around the land commander. Gough reads the short message without expression. His hand drops to his side. He stares at Canton spread before him. He looks at the anxious faces. Le Fleming Senhouse raises his bushy grey eyebrows. Wordlessly, Gough hands the naval commander the sodden note. It takes a moment to read the blurred and smudged lines. Senhouse crumples the paper. His face turns puce. Taking his cocked hat off, he flings it on the ground. His trailing sword follows.

'I protest.'

This is all Senhouse says.

Gideon watches the furious naval commander walk down the hill by himself. It is a little while before the general's entourage breaks up and he leads them down the slope.

The ADC retrieves the hat and accoutrements of the officer of the senior service. It may be seen he is an obliging young man. One day, though, he will be a field marshal himself.

Gideon Chase to Walter Eastman

No.16 Chow Chow Hong
Canton
May 27th, 1841

My dear Walter,

Yours found me on board the *Rattlesnake*. It is good of Captain Elliot to allow us the conveyance of our correspondence in the steamers with the official despatches. I cannot begin to express my sorrow on hearing of Remedios's misfortune. To have been run down in such a manner partakes of the worst bad luck – yet why was the *Sonia* not carrying navigation-lights? At least if he has lost his ship, still he escapes with his life. I do not know how we shall manage to distribute our papers after this. No doubt it is not beyond you to contrive some arrangement.

The terms of the truce here are that the Chinese shall pay an indemnity of $6 million within one week and one million directly, but their troops, of whom some 45,000 (to Gough's 2260 or 2261, if we count your servant) shall retire to a distance of sixty miles from the city, and that the Chinese shall bear all the costs of repairing and rebuilding the Factories. The British forces shall not remove from the Bogue until all is paid. The Plenipo has made the arrangements with all three Imperial Commissioners, the Tartar General, the Viceroy, and the Governor, in hopes that they may not be able to disown the treaty by degrading the officer who made it.

The Hong merchants acted as intermediaries, which I think was mistaken on the part of Captain Elliot.

The British troops are not best pleased by all this – they should have liked to have the Chinese smart, and at least have marched into the city with their bands playing. All ranks, high and low, are implicated in this mutinous sentiment. Senhouse and Gough can hardly speak, such is their choler. Gough, I believe, is truly concerned for his troops in their exposed, unhealthy, and precarious positions, and for that reason alone would have liked to have seen them snugly quartered in the city.

On both sides, the situation remains hazardous.

You will be glad to hear that I am quite the old campaigner, and both safe and well. (A slight summer cold excepted.)

Yours ever,

Gid

Nemesis steamer
Canton River
May 27th, 1841

Sir,

I believe I had the satisfaction of personally conveying to you on the Heights of Canton the sentiments of my warm admiration for the zeal and gallantry displayed by you during the fighting of the 26th *inst.* in the advance on Canton. However, I feel that it is further incumbent upon me to communicate formally to you my sense of indebtedness. You were observed to walk up to the Heights under the most galling fire and in the coolest fashion and then further to distinguish yourself by rescuing Lieutenant Frobisher of the 18th Regiment, who has since, unfortunately, expired of the mortal wound he received.

You maintained a post of honour throughout the conflict, displaying a great carelessness of life and limb. It is not, unfortunately, within my power to confer upon you recognition of your services. Nevertheless, I may congratulate you upon your deliverance from a most dangerous position, much of which you owed to your own steadiness.

I have, sir, etc.

H. Gough (Maj.-Gen.)

May 28th, 1841, 2.30 p.m.

Gideon's comfortably digesting tiffin gets the most ferocious wrench as the pounding on the door startles him out of his chair. He has been sleeping like a log.

'In God's name, Chase, open the door.' That sounds very much like Johnstone's voice.

Gideon picks up his ink-stone, however; ridiculous though it seems even to him, it is actually a rather formidable weapon, well capable of cracking the thickest skull. Who says the pen is not mightier than the sword?

It does turn out to be Frederick Johnstone. Gideon resists the temptation to brain him. The poor fellow is in a pitiable state. 'Quickly,' he gasps, 'before he gets himself into a worse fix.'

Without troubling to enquire who or what, Gideon merely picks up his coat (that clearly vital piece of apparel which also contains his sodden pocket-handkerchiefs) and clatters down the stairs after his old colleague. (Contact with the military has obviously influenced a naturally cautious and reflective nature.)

In Hog Lane lie the bodies of two Chinamen. Gideon knows they are corpses by now – the posture cannot be imitated. A third native crawls by the wall of the Hong, blood leaking from his thigh. As a shot rings out from the roof, he collapses on to his face.

'Ridley,' whispers Johnstone, 'grief has driven him out of his mind.'

A hat passes along the parapets.

'Jonathan,' calls Johnstone, trying to communicate loudly enough to be heard, without sounding aggressive, but succeeding only in producing a crafty quaver. 'Do quit this foolishness, there's a good fellow.' This elicits no immediate response from the roof – other than the unmistakable quiet click of a gun being cocked. Johnstone hurriedly retreats behind the corner of the Factory. He mops his brow and sighs. 'Oh, goodness mercy.' He looks around for Gideon and then peeps around the corner. The idiot Chase is standing in the middle of the lane. 'For God's sake, Gideon,' he hisses, 'get under cover.'

'Why? I calculate he is not going to conclude to go the whole hog and shoot *us*. And, as I recollect, he is a very straight shot.'

The hat moves away from them in the direction of the terraces behind the Hongs. A long barrel protrudes through the parapet. Two shots crash out in rapid succession. Gideon jumps behind the corner. Really, they were amazingly loud in the alley.

'He must have a veritable arsenal with him.'

'No,' says Johnstone gloomily, 'only a brace of Colt's repeating revolvers.'

'I was of the mind that we could dash on to the roof while he was reloading.'

'They carry five shots each in a revolving chamber.'

'Heaven save us! The barrel seemed as long as a musket's!'

'It is a most infernal nuisance, God damn it,' says Johnstone with passion. 'They're Corrigan's, by the way,' he adds, 'the revolvers, I mean.'

'Jonathan,' Gideon calls up, cautiously, 'now, you really must stop. Captain Elliot has declared a truce and, whatever your personal feelings, and your honest exasperation cannot exceed that of the British troops or their officers, you must abide by its terms. The war is over, for the moment.'

Ridley stands up, revealing himself on the roof, holding two huge, smoking revolvers. The barrels are about a foot long. He is wearing a stove-pipe hat, also of inordinate length, and it is the hat, rather than the guns, which makes Gideon think he is dealing with a madman.

'Not for me it isn't,' says Ridley with appalling lucidity. He drops down again. A further two shots crash out. They hear the ricochets whining over the tile roofs of the native city.

'I can hardly blame him, I guess,' says Gideon. 'Young Oswald was a fine, smart young lad.'

'Oswald?' laughs Johnstone with bitter incredulity. 'Oswald? We should be so fortunate. It's that darned cur of his, God damn it. Ridley was searching the terraces while we were putting the office to rights. Then this damned rascal Chinaman, see, spots Jon, and gestures. Nothing unusual, d'you see. Chop your head off, white devil. No one could take offence. But this rascal gets on all fours, Gid, and starts barking. Then he stands up, puts his hand under his mouth for basin and plies his chopsticks with the other hand. Then he has the darned gall to pat his stomach, belch, and grin.'

'My God! They *ate* MacQuitty.'

'Well, you know Jonathan's impulsive nature as well as I. It was but a moment's work for him to enter the Hong, knock us aside, pull up a floorboard, and bring up the Colts. As we stood there, he ran out and shot the villain dead, without ceremony or compunction. Just like that, sir. Then he got on the roof and he has been blazing away ever since.'

'Done like an American,' says a quiet voice behind them. 'Does he think he is in one of the wild territories of the West?'

It is Lieutenant Pedder, with a file of blue-jackets behind.

Gideon ignores the anti-American sentiment by taking the question literally. 'He is from New York,' he says primly. 'If you will not take offence, Lieutenant Pedder, I guess you won't be needing firearms to deal with our friend.'

The boatswain of the *Nemesis,* that grim and sardonic man of few words and those pungent, thumps a belaying-pin into his hand with meaning. 'Pressed a few Yankees in my time, beggin' yer pardon, sir, so it makes no difference to me.'

'Well, Davenport, I guess this one would hardly object to serving on the *Nemesis* if it meant he could slaughter more Chinese. He means *us* no harm, I do assure you.'

'They killed his dog,' explains Johnstone, giving it the doleful pronounciation of *dawg.*

'The fiends!' exclaims Pedder. 'The murdering, black-hearted devils! Jove, no wonder he's taking pot-shots at them. I'd do the same myself.' A murmur of sympathy passes among the blue-jackets, Britons all. 'Well, we must use him gently, the poor fellow.'

No more shots have come. Gideon tries to count back, from memory, the number of bullets fired. Johnstone has had the same idea, for he announces, 'I calculate he has only two chambers remaining before his ammunition is exhausted.'

'Capital!' says Pedder cheerfully. 'Davenport, do you impress some natives into our employ. Drive them out before the rear of the Factory – they'll have a sporting chance. I believe I saw one or two piratical-looking rascals loafing around the terraces.'

'Aye aye, sir.'

The boatswain is off before Gideon can remonstrate.

'Get a ladder from the boat-shed, my men. We'll board him fore and aft.'

While three men hold the ladder out of sight around the corner, ready to dash in and place it against the wall of the lane when the signal is given, the remaining blue-jackets wait on the stairs to the roof of the Hong. From above, two carefully spaced shots blast out over the roofs. Screams come from the terraces.

'Now's the time, my jolly boys,' sings out Pedder, and with a concerted rush the blue-jackets dash on to the roof from two directions, Gideon scrambling last up the ladder. He is in time to see Ridley, stout Jonathan, iron-fisted Jonathan, stove-pipe hat knocked flying, borne to the ground in a welter of bodies, but not before he has punched the boatswain squarely on the nose.

'Don't hurt the gentleman, there's good men,' Gideon enjoins them. There seems to be blood everywhere. Ridley's shirt has more red than white area. Fortunately, it turns out only to be the boatswain's leaking nose.

Pedder collars Gideon. 'I say, what in hell's name am I meant to do with him? Clap him in irons? He'd have got a blasted medal two days ago. And he's a citizen of a neutral Republic.'

'Entrust him to his friends, Mr Pedder. We shall go guarantors for his good behaviour. They shall keep him in a room, locked fast, until he is restored to his senses.'

Pedder hesitates. 'Very well, then – against my better judgement. I'm confiscating these brutes, mark you.' He waves the enormous revolvers. 'I'll find better use for them than him, I don't doubt. I believe they are manufactured for Uncle Sam's navy in any case.'

'But they are not Mr Ridley's to relinquish,' Johnstone says.

'Well, it's him or them,' Pedder says firmly, 'when combined they seem to be a somewhat deadly combination.'

'Oh, very well,' Johnstone sighs. 'Are you going to behave yourself, sir? You have caused a deal of trouble to your friends.'

Ridley looks very sulky.

'You shan't be let up until you have given your parole.'

'I refuse.'

'Well, then, sir, you shall be sat upon all night by these sturdy gentlemen.'

Ridley considers his position for a long minute. At last: 'Oh, God damn it, all very well. You have my word.'

Johnstone nods to Gideon. Better leave the Meridians to sort their own mess out, in all senses.

He retires down the ladder where he finds the three dead Chinese have disappeared.

HBM's Plenipotentiary and Chief Superintendent of Trade in China to Gideon Chase, Esq.

Nemesis steamer
Canton River
May 28th, 1841

My dear Mr Chase,

I sincerely congratulate you on your safe deliverance from the events of the past week. It would have been a sad blow indeed, were I to have lost the services of one of my little band of interpreters.

The City and Suburbs now being in a state of General Pacification, I should wish you to investigate the condition of affairs prevailing in the Countryside. For this purpose, you will be provided with an escort of sepoy soldiers who would accompany and protect you.

I wish it distinctly understood that it is my express desire and command that you shall not expose yourself to any unnecessary hazards during the course of this mission.

I have etc.

Ch. Elliot

Gideon Chase Esq. to the Plenipotentiary and Chief Superintendent of Trade

The Factories
May 28th, 1841

Sir,

I have the honour to acknowledge receipt and to reply to your communication of today's date.

I should prefer a party of seamen from one of the ships in the river. If this meets with your approval, I should land at dawn tomorrow behind the city.

I am, believe me, my dear Captain Elliot, your very trusty, obedient servant

G. Chase

May 29th, 1841, 5 am.

Wild duck fly overhead, while the blue-jackets wade through the glutinous mud below. Gideon remembers his shooting-trip in the Whampoa marshes. Would he aim any straighter now? The birds strain on. Does their formation not resemble the mathematical notation for infinity, or is it 'less than'? Walter would know. The pressure of the Colt Paterson in his groin reminds him to ask Pedder when he gets back. The first lieutenant of the *Nemesis* is strong on navigational and kindred calculations. Kind of Pedder to loan him the weapon. He strongly suspects they are trudging through not paddy but an irrigation canal which has lost its identity during the heavy rains. Ahead is the puff-ball of trees which betrays a hamlet. The *fung shui* grove is in the rear, in the most auspicious site.

Strange: no dogs bark. The settlement is very small, probably merely an outpost of the larger, walled village two miles off. The houses appear quite deserted. A loose shutter bangs. Going into one of the largest dwellings, Gideon's nose is assailed by a sweet, *green* smell (which is how he categorises it), though also ripe. Buzzing in the corner and...bodies in the gloom. He thought so. Out he jumps. However duty asserts itself: it is his brief to find out how death arrived. He holds his breath. What seemed one body was, in fact, three, all young children, all with cut throats. He bumps against something soft behind, then falls over an upturned stool. Above him swings...the mother. It must be. The face is horribly contorted, tongue swollen and protruding. Gideon has to breathe now. Oh, God. The part of him which is cold, questing, rational, which never appears in everyday affairs, which is not cynical but is unshockable, which will imprison him in isolation after the year 1872, takes his mind over. The woman's hands are not bound. They dangle at her sides. She chose to die, then. She was not murdered, therefore. She committed suicide. She jumped from the chair which tripped him.

She cut her children's throats.

Outside, he is sick.

He continues the search. Two blue-jackets have strayed from the party while he was in the house. He finds them in the loft of the largest house. They have found an earthenware wine-jar the size of a man's torso. One is seated, drinking from a pannikin. The other is trying to get his hand and a tin cup down into the neck of the jar.

'Blast it, Bill, give us the ladle, will you?'

Gideon bounds up the last rungs of the ladder, kicks the pannikin flying out of the man's hand as he has it raised to his lips, seizes the other by his sailor-collar and flings him to the ground one-handed. Both are well set-up fellows of his own age and height. He pulls the Colt from his belt, cocks it with both hands...

'Now, look'ee here, sir.'

...and lets drive at the wine-jar point-blank. In the confined space the roar seems as loud as a 32-pounder, having a concussive effect as well as deafening them. Coarse powder-fumes sting and blind. Gideon finds his nose is bleeding and he seems to have sprained his wrist. A torrent runs over his boots. The jar has disintegrated into shards. A sickly smell of liquor fills the stale air. Like cat's piss, Gideon thinks. He waves the men out with the revolver-barrel; he is finding it difficult to hold the heavy weapon. Descending, he falls down the last six rungs of the ladder, banging his coccyx and dropping the revolver. The men prove remarkably solicitous, handing him to his feet and dusting him down. 'Here's yer pistol, sir, reg'ler pocket-cannon, that is.'

'Hurt yer wrist, have ye, sir? Let me strap it up, sir. Give Bill back 'is red 'andkerchief on board, sez I. It's 'is blasted signalling-flag.'

In fact, they seem to like him the more for his recent rough treatment of them.

Outside, the rest of the party have the house surrounded, their weapons levelled. The boatswain eyes the two strayed seamen suspiciously. His fingers itch for a rope's end. Alas, he can only stroke the butt of his musket. Leaving the hamlet, they pass through the same rich countryside, dotted here and there with handsome mansions, the villas of wealthy city-folk. Ow has mentioned them to him, Gideon recollects, though the tales of golden lads capping each other's verses in wine-drinking forfeits, while regarding the reflection of the silver moon, hardly correspond with the present desolate appearances. Looking into a villa, they see a body floating face down in a non-refulgent lily pond. Again, the corpse bears no sign of external violence or duress.

'It's damned rum, sir,' says the boatswain, 'we ain't seen no sign of nobody, unless they're dead, and nobody's taken one little pot-shot at us yet. I call that damned queer, sir.'

'I share your unease, Davenport. I guess the owners of these substantial houses have fled, or are in the city – but what of the villagers? I much fear an ambush is preparing.'

'Well, sir, this ain't no band of redskins, if you'll pardon the liberty, sir. We'll take 'em as they come, sir.'

'Thank you, boatswain, I repose implicit confidence in you.'

A much larger settlement with a moat and wall, slotted for small-arms, is coming up ahead. They must approach on a causeway, in file, and Gideon, the nape of his neck crawling, feels bound to take the position of danger. The iron portcullis leading to the interior has been blasted with powder-charges. Four dead bodies in a square before a temple bear stab-wounds in the chest. The sailors confidently identify these as from the bayonet. The temple has been devastated and plundered. It is also infested with 'nuisances'. Continuing to the rear of the settlement, they find rice-straw fires burning in the grates of houses.

Most startling discovery: the *fung shui* graves have been opened.

Not in the way of mere grave-robbing, pyramid-pilfering, or some such mischievous vandalism – those deeds partake of the nature of a little unofficial ventilation, scratching of the topsoil compared to this. No, this is a thorough, professional job, no doubt of it, with the tomb laid open like a gutted steer, pit-props, a horizontal shaft driven in the side. Gideon's mouth drops.

'It's them nigger sappers,' the boatswain deliberates, clearly impressed despite the use of pejorative language.

Screams come from the grove of banyans behind the tomb.

'Good God, what are those villains doing?' Pulling the Colt from his belt, Gideon runs into the trees without looking to see if the men are following.

Four Indians have a Chinese woman on the ground, one holding each foot and hand. Her trousers are on a banyan branch. A fifth lies on her, his muscular brown buttocks bare as he pumps and lunges. Another two have a young girl by the hair and are in the act of thrusting her to her knees before one of their number. He is unbuttoning himself.

Still running, Gideon fires into the air. The sepoys turn. The rapist resumes his pleasure, but the standing sepoy takes the precaution of fastening his breeches again. The Indians look at their muskets, which stand against the banyan's trunk at a critical distance of about fifteen feet.

Time slows.

Gideon, still moving in, has opportunity to observe the smallest change of expression in the Indian faces. What fierce, savage countenances they are! He can see the bloodshot veins in their eyes, the bright, red gums of one, stained with betel, the hairs coming out of the nostrils of another, the hand stealing behind the back of a third...*to a knife!* As the seconds begin to speed again, Gideon presents the heavy Colt on the run. Then he has to lower the revolver to cock it in both hands. The sepoy's hand is behind his ear. The index finger of his free hand points at Gideon. Too late, almost, Gideon lets fly with the .34-calibre ball, the gun bucking in his hands. The slug goes well over the sepoy's head, but the flash and smoke fortunately spoil his aim and concentration and the thrown dagger, likewise, misses Gideon. An instant later, a well-placed belaying-pin, hurled by the sinewy, unerring arm of the boatswain, takes the sepoy square between the eyes. Those orbs roll, and he drops soundlessly on the spot. Gideon pulls back the hammer of the Colt – to apply to what purposes, he's not quite sure – when the boatswain interposes his thumb between firing-pin and cap, pushing the long barrel down to point at the grass. 'That's enough, sir. We have the rascals,' he says in quite a kindly way.

The sepoys glare at the blue-jackets. Can they, Gideon wonders, be maddened with *bhang?*

One of the blue-jackets, Bill, earlier miscreant with the rice-spirit, retrieves the woman's clothing from the bough. The other female, Gideon now sees, is a girl of no more than nine or ten years. The older woman takes her hand, still holding her own trousers, and runs off with the girl out of the grave into the fields. Her plump white buttocks wobble. The sailors guffaw and cheer.

'Silence!' snarls Gideon.

The sepoys look sullenly at him.

'Make 'em sit, sir?' the boatswain suggests. Gideon nods. What is he to do with them? He can hardly shoot them out of hand, assuming himself ruthless enough to do so. Theoretically, they are on his – or at least Captain Elliot's – side. They may well all be attacked at any moment, despite the formal truce, in which case they should all have to combine to defend themselves. His mission is to explore and gather information, not to act as the provost-marshal. Besides, it would not be practicable to take them prisoner under the circumstances.

'I'd like to flog every blasted mother's son of them,' the boatswain growls.

'Boatswain, do you gather their muskets. Er…'

'Hoskins, sir,' Bill identifies himself.

'Thank you, Hoskins. I guess I'd be obliged if you would relieve these fellows of their ammunition-pouches…'

'They'll have sixty rounds of ball-cartridge, sir, less what they've fired away, o' course,' says the cheerful Hoskins.

'…and then remove the flints and priming from the pans of their muskets.'

'Aye aye, sir.'

That, thinks Gideon, is the first time I have elicited that particular affirmative response, which augurs well for the intrinsic merits of my stratagem. 'Leave them their bayonets, for the moment. Keep them under your guns during the period of our withdrawal. We shall deposit their powder in the field yonder which they may discover when we shall be out of range.'

This is all accomplished without mishap. As his party crosses a dyke into a field of cane, Gideon sees the sepoys running to get their weapons. By the time the Indians have seen to their muskets, though, the sailors will be out of sight in the tall cane, so there will be no chance of the odd revenge-shot coming their way. Gideon, nevertheless, takes his party crashing through the cane at a smart pace. Emerging, they find themselves on a slight rise, the only high ground in the flat landscape, apart from the Heights of Canton, which appear disproportionately large some six miles to the south-west. Between themselves and a big village three miles to the north is a tributary of the main river, which is full of boats. Smoke of cooking-fires rises from the settlement, which looks heavily populated, with people on the walls and milling outside. Gideon can spot flashes of colour, mostly red, which appear to be waving pennants, while every now and then there is the glint of...

What?

'Spy-glass, sir,' offers the trusty boatswain.

Gideon pushes the segments backwards and forwards until the scene leaps into focus. (This is only the fourth time he has ever used the instrument.) How extraordinary it is, annihilator of distance, insufficiently celebrated instrument of clarification and acquisition. Is this how Walter focuses his camera obscura? He must ask why it would be impossible to place a telescope over the lens to capture the images of distant objects or persons. It must be impracticable, else Walter would have done it already.

Suddenly, Gideon's heart leaps into his throat, all whimsy banished.

Armed men parade in front of him. They seem within pistol-shot, if not close enough to touch. Appalled, he lowers the tube to confirm he is the victim of the illusion his intellect, if not his senses, apprehend. Now he sweeps the distant village again. It is a riot of brandished banners, flags and placards; a jumble of weapons, implements of all kinds. The arms include, on a quick and (it must be admitted) somewhat shaky inspection, two ancient cannon, ornamented along the barrels in relief; matchlocks, spears, gingals; even humble hoes and rice-flails are brandished. Not one man is clothed in uniform, either of the Manchu banners or the Chinese Green Standard, but wear plain blue or black. Gideon snaps the tube shut. The men look to him for orders, but this time he disappoints them by sitting abstract-edly on a rock. He shakes his head, muttering to himself things like... *the utter destruction of all his policies ...virulence of the town which has spread to the environs...*

'Sir?'

Gideon blinks at the boatswain. Rain is falling.

How long has it been doing that? 'Sir, the men await orders, beggin' yer pardon.'

'We shall, ah, fall back upon the boat.'

'Yes, sir. Very good, sir. By the way what we come, sir?'

'I expect that we shall not lose ourselves. This countryside may be deceiving in its uniformity. I guess we should have blazed a trail. Is there anything wrong, boatswain?'

'Beg pardon, sir, wouldn't the Chinese be ready and waiting for us the way we come, sir? And them murderin' Hindoostanees, sir.'

'Good gracious, I hadn't considered!'

Gideon scans the horizon. All very well to see the river glint from even this modest eminence: a different matter entirely on the ground. 'We cannot approach nearer the braves and the militias. We are already dangerously near and…'

'Don't you worry yourself, sir. Jack'll eat rabble like that afore his breakfast.'

'Without meaning to disparage your gallant Tarpaulins, these…never mind.' Gideon is silent while he plans a path which will take them over the dykes and back to the river without approaching too near centres of population. 'I have it.'

'Very good, sir,' says the boatswain, with misplaced suspicion, who has had enough of this holiday from naval officers. Flighty as a shuttlecock, this Yankee. And he wishes he'd stop calling him a boatswain, instead of a bosun.

May 30th, 1841, 11.30 am.

'Dear God,' says the ADC, shocked out of his urbanity, 'there are thousands of the buggers.'

Gough looks grimly at the mass on the hillside. He, for one, will enjoy dispersing this presumptuous mob. Cheated of the chance to march into Canton, he will vent his irritation on these insolent ruffians.

On one hill: silent, orderly red lines, glinting with brass and blanco, neat field-batteries of howitzers and rockets unlimbering and forming, discipline and science, hierarchy and professionalism.

On the other: a shapeless crowd, waving motley weapons, spilling down the slope and into the valley. Ardour and vehemence. Enthusiasm, spontaneity.

On the former: just under 2000 men of all ranks.

On the latter: maybe 8000 or 9000 incensed peasants.

The shouts of defiance and abuse drift across the valley. The undisciplined mass is not quite the formless rabble Gough imagines it to be. It does possess a cohesive logic of some kind, common instincts of advance and self-preservation, a mutual understanding. It begins to pullulate and tremble, not unlike a jellyfish. Bolder elements advance down the slope, impelled perhaps by pressure from behind, a little further than they would feel wholly comfortable. These stinging tentacles coil, retract, shrivel, then roll forwards again. At length, with a shout of defiance, a group of several hundred dash down the hill and, at extreme range, loose a fusillade from their gingals before scampering up the hill again with shrill shouts. As this provokes no retaliation from the silent red lines nor have the gingal-balls told – the gunners are encouraged to make another foray.

'We shall,' drawls General Gough, 'throw a few rockets into them, by way of a small chastisement for this impertinence.'

No sooner said than done.

But how interesting.

What has proved so efficacious against capital units of the enemy, against hard, inanimate, expensive, and relatively immobile lumps – of masonry, so be it, of forts, or wood, in the case of junks – turns out to be far less devastating when fired at soft, self-dispersing, thinking flesh and blood. Alas for Gough, these are not objects at which his batteries now aim. True, within minutes the lowering sky is crisscrossed with a net of vapour-trails, but they do not trap this aggravating, fluid enemy. As the iron broomsticks fall, blazing out of the grey, the insurgent peasants simply judge their likely fall and scatter, individually, shamelessly, according to their separate notions of self-preservation rather than a uniform command. Large holes form in the milling crowds, where the rockets will drop – in most cases harmlessly, the missiles frequently burying themselves up to their tail-fins in soft ground which the rains have converted into a quagmire. As well might Gough flog a jelly-fish, or the water which is both its element and main constituent.

'Damn it to hell,' says the ADC, while the great man remains impassive.

'Have the howitzers drop a shell on them, Major Orville.'

These work better, their smoke-stars flashing their bursts over the opposite hill. Figures fall. Some do not rise again. Most do. As they are not soldiers, they do not feel obliged to receive the enemy's fire in a vertical and exposed position. Skirmishing-parties, if they can be called anything so formal, race down the hill to fire as quickly as they can. For the first time, red-tunicked figures drop. But the lines immediately close up the gap, shoulder to shoulder again.

'They're standing the fire deuced well, those rascals,' says the ADC, who is quick to acknowledge an opponent's coolness and pluck, whether it be the trial of war or a cricket-match.

'General Gough, sir, the gunners have fired away all their shells. There was only a small store.'

Gough shows no emotion.

'Some hours may elapse before they can be brought up, sir.'

The general blows his nose (it has had a tendency to run all day). 'Ah, Colonel, oblige me by taking the Company's troops over the valley. I much doubt if these bumpkins will stand the bayonet.'

'It shall afford me the most unalloyed pleasure.' The officer glows. But Gough, who was very nastily wounded at Talavera in the Peninsular War, remembers how the Spanish and Portuguese irregulars and *guerrillas* galled Marshal Toult's crack regiments. He, therefore, adds: 'You should separate the infantry into small sections. They may engage and chase the enemy at their discretion.'

The colonel's face falls a little. However, orders are orders, even if it means engaging rabble on their own terms. He salutes, a little frostily.

For the first time a cheer goes up as the sepoys and Irish start to cross the valley under a heavy barrage of rocket-fire, the white smoke-wakes interlacing to form a canopy. The popping of musketry intensifies on the other side. With the red ants halfway across, sheets of rain commence falling without warning from the black sky. Thunder trundles in the mid-distance, as if some metal object were being broken up by irresistible forces. So overcast does it become, so torrential the rain, that visibility is cut within minutes to a matter of yards. The general might as well be a hemisphere distant in a pea-soup fog on Ludgate Hill for all that he can see of his troops. The ghostly swishing sound overhead causes puzzlement until identified as the sound of the rockets in the rain. Only the orange melons of their jets can be seen, except when, briefly, lightning flickers to illuminate the terrain, figures and groups frozen as if in a Daguerreotype.

Gough ponders. He ought to recall his detachments. The dangers are obvious in broken country, separated, no communications, outnumbered, even if it is only by a mob, and no integrated command.

Squelching behind. 'The compliments of the Plenipotentiary, sir.'

'Mr Chase! You will find a welcome where I am.'

'Sir, your kindness may turn to displeasure when I inform you that the Prefect of the City has disclaimed to Captain Elliot, through Mr Morrison, all knowledge and responsibility for this violation of the truce. The country folk have risen without reference to the governors in the city, and the Prefect is presently exerting himself to secure their dispersal and withdrawal to their homes. Unlikely though his assurance may sound...'

'Mr Chase, I do not doubt it for one minute.'

'Why, General Gough, sir, you greatly surprise me.'

'In that event, Mr Chase, I possess an important advantage over you in a military regard – surprise being one of the essential prerequisites of the successful attack.' Gough's voice has no difficulty carrying, though Gideon has to raise his over the downpour.

The lightning bathes the plain white again. For some time there have been no shots.

'Captain Waring, pray have a general withdrawal sounded. I should wish a substantial body of men, two or three companies at the least, to scour the countryside for our stragglers. They are not to exceed a radius of two miles from here in their search. Mr

Chase, you have not been shot at today, though I marvel you have not been struck by lightning.'

'In order to protect myself from the electric fluid, General Gough, I fly kites in the manner of my countryman – tho' most of them are insubstantial vehicles, extravagant conceits of the imagination.'

'Mr Chase, I don't pretend to understand you. However, take a glass in my tent with my aide and myself before you return to the river. I cannot say I like the present state of affairs.'

From THE CANTON MONITOR
Tuesday, June 1st, 1841

Fruits of the campaign thrown away with profligate folly. Such is the belief which unites all ranks of both services before the Gate of Canton. A universal disgust is felt with the Plenipotentiary, not only in a military regard but also in mercantile circles. The City was ours! Only imagine – ours we say! Sweet would have been the cup of victory, but it was wrenched from the lips of the eager conquerors. We are quite at a loss to explain Captain Elliot's conduct, save that he has done the same on previous occasions when the Chinese were on the point of being taught a final lesson.

Above, we have recapitulated the story of the operations on the river in which the Navy and especially the steamers were concerned, and now feel it mere justice to adumbrate the exploits of our land forces under the valiant Gough. The plan of attack, as implemented at noon on the glorious 24th, was to separate the force into columns, the smaller body to take and secure the Factories, the main force, divided into four brigades, to assault the Heights of Canton to the north, the veritable key of the ancient city. The expedition bound for the Factories comprised some score of men of the Madras Artillery with a 6-pounder and a 5-inch mortar, the same number of sappers directed by an officer of the Royal Engineers, and not more than 250 men of the 26th Cameronians. This small number, under Major Pratt, performed sterling service, assaulting one of the buildings to rescue a group of American gentlemen who had been held hostage.

The remainder of the little army, numbering less than 2000 men of all ranks, were towed up the river by the *Nemesis,* the long lines of white boats, bunting, flags, and uniforms presenting a brave spectacle, though the burden of 80 boats confined the doughty steamer to but a tardy progress. The greater part of the 49th crowded the decks of the *Nemesis,* standing packed like herrings in a barrel. The naval brigade of 400 men were placed under the command of Captain Bourchier. As the current of the river presented also some impediment, it was not until the evening of the 24th that the force arrived at the spot fixed upon for a general disembarkation when only the 49th were landed, taking possession of a large temple which they then handed to the Company's troops. The Chinese were perceived to send up signal-rockets.

In the morning the remainder of the expedition were landed without event. The weather continued sultry, the mercury rising throughout the morning until by mid-day the thermometer stood at 90 degrees. The nature of the ground presented severe difficulties for the detachment bringing the guns up, but, nothing daunted, the men in their columns raced each other for the sport of arriving at the forts first. Alas, a good many fine fellows collapsed of sunstroke, the cases not infrequently terminating fatally.

Dash and manly British vigour prevailed in the march over the cunning and spite of the Chinese, who vainly attempted to make up in guile and want of scruple that which they lacked in science and courage.

Early on the 27th, as Gough tarried to unleash his eager battalions, the news of the truce came through. Some 15 fell and 112 were wounded, who suffered vainly for their country, while the Chinese losses must be more than twenty times that number. Of the British casualties the high proportion of 15 were officers. The wounded were brought down to the *Nemesis* for attention.

Some three days following the ransom of the City, a rabble appeared on high ground to the north when they were dispersed by British patrols. One of these became lost in the darkness but fought their way through to the lines again.

The men in general behaved very well. There was little opportunity for plunder or inebriation, the troops rather protecting the houses and abandoned property against Chinese robbers and marauders. It had been among General Gough's express instructions to the troops to show forbearance and mercy to the Chinese, in despite of their cowardly ambuscades, and as well as the lively satisfaction which it must afford him to contemplate the achievement of his arms, the general must feel sensations of complacency with regard to the good discipline which prevailed in all ranks during a most confusing and trying campaign.

From THE LIN TIN BULLETIN AND RIVER BEE

Wednesday, June 2, 1841

Vol. 4 No. 11

...and as we have many times remarked in the past, can take neither pride nor enjoyment from the recitation of a catalogue of inevitable reverses and humiliations inflicted upon a proud and frequently courageous people, who in many instances – and not only among the number of the strong, the grown, or the male – preferred death by their own hands to the dishonour of defeat and defilement.

This latter of our heads of discussion brings us to the mention of scenes of distress to which we are only emboldened to allude by reason of their inevitable effect on the policies of Britain and more especially the line of conduct which is associated with the name of Captain Elliot, and as such as we would be failing in our duty if we ruled such news inadmissible in our columns, we briefly adumbrate them. Rape, robbery, arson, and murder were the order of the day among the Indian troops. When their brutish appetites were slaked, they did not scruple to mutilate the outraged flesh of their victims. Their behaviour around the village of San Yuan Li became so offensive to the inhabitants that they rose as a man in defence of their hearths, their temples, and their daughters. What commenced as a spontaneous demonstration by the village-folk, armed only with such rude agricultural implements as came readily to hand, became something altogether more serious when the drums were beaten to summon the village militias and arms broken out to them. Those trained bands were originally formed for the defence of the hamlets against rival clans, the Hack Cars, pirates, and also, let us say it, the agents and publicans of the Emperor.

By the morning of the 30th about 10,000 men had massed opposite Canton. They stood the fire of the regular British troops and, had rain not commenced falling, would have made the issue altogether less predictable than in the preceding battles the British fought against the official levies of the Emperor.

During the hours of wetness and darkness which followed the exchange, one of the British patrols of the 37th Madras Native Infantry became lost in the paddy-fields. Their plight being soon perceived by the keen-eyed inhabitants who, naturally, were accustomed to the ground since childhood, they were in a short time surrounded by a vastly greater number of armed enemies. The sepoys, when commanded by firm and resolute officers who possess their confidence, constitute a most formidable body and it might be supposed they would make light of their disadvantage in a numerical sense when opposed by men, however brave, whose sole occupation was not that of waging war. Yet what was the horror and dismay of their officers when the roaring volley that should have scattered their assailants was attended merely by the snapping and clicking of gun-hammers. The rain had soaked the powder in the flintlocks and rendered them useless! Nor in the unceasing downpour of rain was it possible to reprime them with dry powder, even had they not become directly flooded in the short space necessary to present the piece to the shoulder and fire. Perceiving the strait to which the soldiers were reduced, the villagers became greatly daring, stabbing at the men with spears and attempting to dart in among them with knives and swords. Matters looked even graver when some braves returned with poles to which were fixed large hooks. These were employed to snare soldiers and drag them from the ranks. Lieutenant Hadfield commanded his men to fix bayonets and formed them into a square. Thus situated they were able for a while to beat off the attacks of their tormentors. Yet, as a man slipped, the villagers were able to cast a hook around Ensign Berkeley, wounding him in the body as they did so, and to drag him by main force from the ranks. A most desperate struggle then ensued, in which young Berkeley was recovered and put in the middle of the square. A stalwart fellow who appeared to be the leader of the villagers was able in the confusion to wrest a musket from a sepoy when he rapidly primed it with dry powder beneath an umbrella and contrived to discharge it by thrusting a slow-match into the pan. Owing to the fortunate circumstance of the haste with which he was forced to proceed, the shot failed to take effect in the breast of Lieutenant Hadfield, whom he had selected as his chosen mark, but the ball merely plucked at his sleeve, inflicting a slight graze upon the flesh beneath. As the soldiers, harassed and vexed at every pass, were unable to preserve a firm footing on the treacherous ground which, soaked already, was rapidly being churned into the consistency of a morass by the feet of the combatants, their square was rapidly losing its shape. Although discipline never wavered, some of the sepoys only removing their boots the better to preserve their footing, matters had begun to wear a very grave aspect. At this moment a company of the Royal Marines, despatched expressly for the purpose of searching for the missing detachment, came upon this grim and silent contest. As they were armed with the new percussion-muskets, the mechanism of which is impervious to the weather, they were able to scatter the attackers and relieve the native infantry with a single, well-directed volley. They escorted the sepoys to safety and shelter and, amazing to recount, not one man of the company was lost or killed, though several were wounded.

In this incident we find the seeds of a transformation of the relations between the Chinese and the British and, by contagion of example, with all other foreigners resident here, exhibiting features characteristic of the worst and best of both sides. Regard for the coolness and steadiness of the sepoys must be tempered with revulsion from their propensity to theft and murder, admiration of the firmness and science of the officers with condemnation of their high-handed desecration of tombs and temples to construct batteries or merely to satisfy a vulgar and macabre curiosity to look upon the disinterred corpses. (In the deluded belief that the bodies were preserved in a fashion similar to the embalmed mummies of Egypt.)

Until this moment the conciliatory policies of Captain Elliot had stood some small chance of success. The truce he made in March, which was so roundly denounced in the merchant press, enabled cargoes of tea worth at least £3 million sterling to be loaded and taken out of the river to the open sea. Does he not deserve the plaudits of his government for this astute act? His wise and subtle object of detaching the sympathies of the native peoples from their rulers was evincing every sign of realisation. The Manchus, not the British, it was who massacred without mercy a million of the citizens of Canton under two hundred years ago. The very country folk assisted our steamers in their passages up the byways of the river! As the Indians began their forays to the north of Canton, so they destroyed all chance of a popular accommodation with the British. The foreigners are presently hated more than they have ever been. Worse, Elliot's forbearance on the Heights, shortly followed by the inconclusive engagement between the village militias and the British troops, has given rise to a myth of heroic proportions, circulating now with the swiftness of wings, concerning the valour of the people and their triumph against the foreigners. As the British ships dropped down the river, the jubilation of the country folk redoubled. Simple folk! *They believed only the evidence of their own eyes!* The foreigners departed, so they had been forced so to do. Who inflicted this signal reverse upon the barbarians? Why, they had! And this in despite of the traitorous wiles and supine cowardice of the city merchants and mandarins. The City Prefect it was who, accompanied by Captain Moore, bore the odium of instructing the country folk to disperse. This wholly adventitious circumstance sets a mine under the entire foundation of the Plenipotentiary's policy. The success of his actions had depended upon the preservation of the finest of balances between firmness and conciliation – he wished to gain the fear, and therefore respect, of the mandarins, without alienating the sympathies of the populace. So far from attaining this, he has merely antago-nised the people without succeeding in cowing them and thus has the worst of all worlds. Shocking though it is to say so, to have sacked the city and put to the sword all its inhabi-tants would likely have been attended with consequences less deleterious, at least in the short term. It is very difficult to win a war when the stronger party imposes its own limita-tions upon itself.

CHAPTER XL

Gideon gapes. He had expected the beautiful anchorage of Hong Kong again, of course. But the extent of development on shore is extraordinary. He was prepared for nothing more than the 'jumble of wild ravines' and a desert shore, with perhaps a handful of tents and a few sailors and Chinese. Yet this is like strolling through a large fair in some populous town. Where he and Walter walk, on a foreshore extended by wholesale flattening of the hillocks and rocks above the beach, they mix in a crowd of sailors in best white ducks, Irish soldiers in red, coolies, hucksters, fishermen, lascars, mountebanks, laundry-girls, fruit-sellers, boothmen, and barbers. The square of Canton was nothing to this. Like white pepper-pots to the East are the tents of the military lines, but these are outnumbered now by the ugly mat-shed constructions: wooden huts some one hundred feet long, with the chinks in the walls crudely plastered in mud, or often not at all, and rude grass-weave roofs. They can glimpse through the crowds the men lying on their palliasses inside, or smoking while they clean their accoutrements.

'I should think it a most dangerous practice to smoke in there.'

'My dear fellow, there is no way on earth in which you could prohibit a confirmed devotee from the indulgence of his pleasure. Discipline would suffer by being brought into contempt.' Walter bumps into a huckster. Both apologise to the other.

'Mercy! What is this? I have seen riots at the Factories for less.'

'These, Gid, are *our* natives, or, should I say, the British natives – here by choice and inclination.'

'I have yet to see a more unsavoury or villainous crew.'

'I allow so, and we see them by daylight.'

They come over the top of a rock and down the other side at a run to find a gang of Chinese in chains breaking stones and beating down earth.

'I retract that. *These* are certainly the most rapscallion crew I have ever seen.'

'Caine's crew – and you are right: proven rascals all. They are the culprits detected in flagrant misdemeanours and expiating their misdeeds in a term of hard and productive labour. Fine notion.'

'Hmm.'

Continuing along the bridle-path, which is really very well constructed and surely follows the line of the old native foot-track, they come to the western side of the large valley which is the most characteristic feature of this side of the island. Beyond, shining in the distance, are handsome-looking whitewashed buildings, the most permanent edifices yet constructed, it would seem. 'Those,' says Walter, following Gideon's gaze, 'I hardly like to tell you what or whose they are. But I give you one clue: our enemy is more substantially housed than we.'

'Is that a fact?'

'Unfortunate, but true.'

'The other brick building directly behind us?'

'Where our contemporary should be – the gaol.'

'Ha! Well, an inauspicious inception for the poor Plenipo's prize acquisition, but better things have come from worse starts.'

'I think I see what you mean.'

'Hulloa!'

They look back to the military lines. An odd procession creeps towards them, much like a disjointed caterpillar. It sorts itself out as three palanquins, with a train of baggage-coolies behind. The bearers of the middle palanquin appear to be having particular difficulties, not surprising since the occupant is corpulent Harry O'Rourke. 'I allow,' says Walter, 'the felon's lot in the road-gang would be preferable to that of these poor fellows. What are you about, you old elephant?'

'I have the Plenipo's commission,' says Harry with great sweetness, 'to get me to the top of yonder peak and draw what I see.'

'Darnation bells,' says Eastman between his discoloured teeth.

'Well, Harry, I allow that's a mighty condescension on your side. I was ignorant as to the circumstance that you were a surveyor in addition to your other parts.'

'I don't disdain anything,' says O'Rourke cheerfully. 'Make our numbers up.'

'Well, I had a mind to look at the fisher-…'

'We're agreeable, Mr O'Rourke,' Gideon says, 'it should be a most diverting expedition.'

Two hours later – when Walter has not spoken to him for at least half that time – Gideon, knee showing through torn trousers, and sweating like a pig, still does not regret his decision. The procession picks its way along the bed of a dry stream, clambering up what must be in wet weather innumerable little waterfalls. It is dreadfully steep in places, so sheer that Gideon fears for Harry as his bearers stagger and slip, almost dropping the little box but never quite doing so. The old fellow is beaming all over his big red face.

The passengers in the other palanquins, it turns out, are Captain (now Major) Caine, the seconded magistrate from the 26th Cameronians, and a young English boy, Harry Parkes ('Thirteen and three-quarters, sir') who is some in-law of Gutzlaff, the Plenipo's Chief Interpreter. Gideon detests Gutzlaff, but resolves not to be unfair to the boy. He would not be at all surprised if he were an orphan like himself, sent out by aunts or uncles. As they come to a sheer rock face, young Harry Parkes and Caine descend from their palanquins, the major instructing the bearers to await their return there, but old Harry (O'Rourke) is immovable, merely shouting some jovial remark out of his conveyance.

Caine shakes his head. 'He'll break the beggars' backs, then we'll have to carry them down again.'

They all move across to where niches have been cut into boulders and take a zigzag path across the mountainside, Walter cursing as he stumbles. He looks remarkably sullen.

Gideon decides to cheer him up:

> 'On a huge hill
> Cragged and steep, Truth stands, and hee that will
> Reach her, about must, and about must goe.'

he recites down cheerfully.

'Hold your God-damned tongue, or I'll cut it out.'

'Temper, temper. *No man is...*'

Walter's dreadful Anglo-Saxon oath rings out over the hillside, sending Gideon hastily after the others. The remainder of his expletives are fortunately unintelligible. Harry Parkes looks interested and repeats the strange expressions to himself. Caine grins. The boy seems to have a liking for words. They follow O'Rourke's palanquin, which bounces and rocks like a boat on a rough sea, tilting backwards at slopes as a yacht might climb a wave. Gideon has decided not to look down until they reach the summit, a characteristic deferral of present gratification for future rewards which it might not be too far-fetched to apply to his entire approach to scholarship and life, in so far as the two are separate for him: steady toil towards an immolating moment of verity.

The slopes of the island are quite bare, unrelieved granite and sandstone, flaking away at spots of weakness, with many major landslips and subsidences of the past evident. Gideon imagines the rains must be hugely destructive without any roots to bind the soil. However, for them the landslides are a convenience and an aid, making it possible to ascend in a straight line without having to move sideways to conquer the incline. An hour later, Walter still silent, still bringing up the rear, they have a rest. O'Rourke stretches his legs. Young Harry, still full of boyish energy, lobs stones down a water-course. He claims to have seen a snake. Certainly there are no other animals. 'Oh, what a lovely view! Do look, Mr Chase, the ships are so tiny.'

'I shall reserve a greater surprise for myself at the top, young Harry. By the by, did you know the natives regard snake as in the light of a great delicacy?'

'Eugh!'

'Your reaction is entirely understandable, for it was also mine. In fact, the meat is not unpleasant, resembling fowl, with the consistency of a firm fish. Should you like to sample some with my native friend one day?'

'Oh, rather! Mr Morrison says I am to learn the native tongue as I am at an impressive age and should not lose the opportunity.'

'Impressionable age, Harry. Yes, that is a fine notion. You must do your best to make your mother and father proud of you.'

'Mama is with the angels, and Papa has joined her.'

'*I thought so!* I mean, I, too, had lost my parents at your years. Come, we shall walk together.'

There remain a few hundred feet to the top. The two youngest members of the party scramble on ahead of the others. Gideon holds Harry's hand as he jumps across a pool of stagnant water. Some moss does now cushion their steps. Gideon will not look down until he is seated on a boulder which he establishes as the highest spot. 'Well, let me regard from this bad eminence. You rascal, take your hands away.' Harry's childish laughter rings across the peak as the others appear, the top of O'Rourke's palanquin first.

'Heavens! What a prospect!' Gideon is amazed, delighted. There is neither haze nor cloud, perfect weather after last month's savage rains. The air is so transparent one might see for ever. The harbour is like a glass of green liqueur, its masts as big as match-sticks, the chequered hulls of the men of war the size of dominoes.

'An elevation of some two thousand feet,' says Caine, joining him. 'The RE took it by triangulation.'

Gideon grunts, wishing to preserve the illusion of his solitary enjoyment. From this height, all is made clear, obvious, simple, as at Canton. To the left, which is to say the west, extends the straggling bazaar or native quarter, of flimsy, higgledy-piggledy huts. Even from here, the squalor is evident. The township has just sprung up, without rules or plan. In the centre, the neat and orderly rows of the military cantonment, the mat-shed construc-tions looking tiny at this distance. On the bluff immediately behind – the Battery. Beside that, two or three tiny cubes, which must be the dwellings of Johnston, the Deputy Superintendent and temporary chief administrator of the island, the Harbour Master (whoever he is), and, indeed, of the chief magistrate himself, who is such an intrusive presence at Gideon's side. Immediately to the right are the mat-shed church and the large parade-ground. A mile and a half further on to the east lie Jardine's godowns in a cluster opposite a small islet in the harbour. Behind them, the large valley of rice-fields with the Chinese hamlet at the back. Just visible is the quarry where Walter stood the fire of the *Monitor*. On the opposite side of the harbour, on the mainland, is the dirty walled 'city' of Kowloon, invested by paddy, about a mile and a half distant from the shore. The triangular white sand peninsula of Seem-sa-joy, thrusting into the harbour, can from this elevation be seen to resemble the bird's beak of its Chinese name; though at sea-level the title has always been inexplicable to Gideon. Does this mean the geomancers have in some remote past visited the summit on which he now stands? The bearers were certainly very familiar with the path. To the rear of Kowloon City extends the curtain of mountains, running perhaps thirty or forty miles east to west, which insulates Hong Kong and Kowloon from the rest of China.

'Mr Chase! Mr Chase!'Young Harry Parkes draws him to the side of the little plateau. Here they face across the open sea and estuary in a south-westerly direction. The monsoon is invigorating in their faces. Islands stud the sea for miles. Below is the fisher-village of Little Hong Kong, with its own anchorage shut in by a nearby island. Diminutive junks and sampans, smaller even than the tiny ships in the harbour, wait to leave for the evening's fishing.

'Oh, how jolly it is!'

'Beautiful indeed, Harry.'

'A fair prospect.' This is Walter. Though grudging, at least he is speaking again. Gideon nurses him back to good humour with conversation on topics of interest to Walter.

Harry O'Rourke has set up his paraphernalia and is getting down to work. Easel does not adequately describe his rattan stand, which is narrow relatively, but very wide, almost semicircular, designed – as it turns out – to receive his unusual canvas. Packaged in the form of a scroll, this unrolls to eight feet. Caine, joking about his name, puts in a cane at each end. O'Rourke settles down to his panorama. He is cheery, suspiciously so, but does not appear to have been imbibing, a steady hand and eye, rather than inspirational agencies, being appropriate to this particular commission. For instance, he doesn't object to the little group behind him spying on his work. However, as the preliminary marks with the charcoal mean nothing to anyone, with the possible exception of Walter, they soon drift away. Caine has caused a hamper to be brought up, somewhat idiosyncratically provisioned with hard-boiled eggs, cold custard, devilled fowl's legs, sausages, ginger beer, salt fish, sugared almonds, pickled onions, game pie, a pot of jam, cheese, quince tart, raisins and curry.

'Oh, *lovely* grub,' exclaims young Harry, beside himself with glee. The arduous climb has done nothing except whet his young appetite.

'Tell me, my boy,' asks Walter sternly, 'are you the concoctor of this most extraordinary bill of fare?'

Caine nods resignedly. 'He is. Gad, my dyspepsia.'

'Ha! Ha! All the more for me. For *me!*' Harry dances round with a drumstick in his hand.

'Well, that's good, I guess. Do you make amends by carrying over to Mr O'Rourke this plate of curry and eggs with the compliments of Mr Eastman, for which he will thank you. Smart lad.'

'They'll hang him, that or admiral of the fleet,' says Caine, his eyes softening a little below his bushy eyebrows.

'I guess so. Say, it's very pleasant here on the mountain.'

'I should venture to express the opinion that we have experienced a fall of some three degrees of mercury. Small as it may sound, that is a greater drop than one could contrive in removing one's person anywhere under six hundred miles to the north.'

'Is that a fact, Major Caine?'

'Are you calling me a liar, sir?'

'Ah, no, Major Caine. You don't understand. This is our Federal way of speaking. Mr Eastman meant merely to make a statement indicative of his mild surprise and appreciation of the ingenious comparison and esoteric information. Is that not so, Walter?'

'Why, sure, I meant no offence.'

'Nor was any taken. Thank'ee, I will have a cigar.'

'Mr O'Rourke sends his compliments, sir, and he'd like you to send some raisins and custard to follow.'

'He shall have them. But sit you down. Smoke?'

'Oh no, thank you, sir.' Young Harry flushes with pleasure. Would Eastman really have given him a cigar, Gideon wonders? 'MacGillivray believes this summit would make a capital site for a sanatorium,' Caine reflects through a blue haze. 'I expect he's right, you know. Many of the poor fellows down there would doubtless recover when exposed to the beneficial airs on this peak. It resembles an oven of hell in the town.'

'Yes, indeed,' says Gideon, 'the mountain itself is responsible for blocking out the monsoon breeze altogether. I believe the inhabitants have a superstition to some such effect.'

'Have they?' says Caine carelessly. He finishes his cigar. A little later he lies on his back and goes to sleep.

O'Rourke is making good progress with his sketch. A sketch in oils, this is, fashion of the great man's youth. The panorama is strikingly faithful to the original of the view before Gideon. He moves quietly away to Walter. 'I calculate,' he says, 'not that I grudge Harry his commission, that such a task would prove more perfectly adapted to the Daguerreotypic process. Could you not have exposed a plate in a fraction of the time Harry shall take, while you would still be able to leave it to be imprinted for as long as you chose, as the picture was not moving?'

Walter shakes his head. 'It would be damnable difficult. You see, Gid, there are all manner of…Well, in a word, it cannot be done with the niceness you'd expect. I should not be able to capture the whole scene round through my lens in the way in which you or I may with our human eye (not to mention H's superhuman eye). It will only cast a limited, a circumscribed view of the scene onto the plate: say from the headland there to the beginnings of the bazaar in the far west.'

'You should have to expose many plates, then, and perhaps join them together for the whole picture.'

'In a nutshell. But, you see, to estimate where one ended and the contiguous began would be a task, as I say, demanding great niceness of judgement for it to be attended with even the smallest success. It is hard enough when attempting a smaller subject. You have seen my headless men. Were I able even to cut the plates to size, then there should be the unwanted effect of shade and light. Regard the cloud slowly appearing from the west, yonder the sun blazing. Each plate would be a record of a different moment. And today is a remarkably clear and even day. No, 'tis far better left to old Harry.'

They find *young* Harry tickling the snoring Caine's nose with a stem of grass. The magistrate swipes with his hand at the annoying insect before opening his eyes with a 'Drat!' He smiles, though he was enjoying his siesta. 'Now, Harry, play by those rocks there and mount us a guard against rascal Chinamen. Good boy.' Caine waits for him to get out of earshot. 'Orphan, don't you know. And with devilish pretty sisters, I hear. One's married to Gutzlaff. She won't last long, if the fate of the previous Mrs Gutzlaffs was anything to go by.'

'Poisoned all of them, so they say,' says the malicious Eastman.

'Heard that, too. Don't believe it myself. It's a wicked climate. Did the little beggar pack any Hodgson's? No, ah, well. Let's hope he survives this infernal heat. Splendid lad.'

When Caine comes to again, the sun, which rose over Jardine's settlement is going down over the native bazaar. O'Rourke's bearers reverently bear his canvas. The great man deigns to go down the hill by his own means.

The sketch he will complete in the town.

From THE CANTON MONITOR
Tuesday, June 15th, 1841

The recent campaign has caused many gaps and vacancies to appear in the services, notably among the officers, the high mortality among which corps we had occasion to remark and regret in our last. Some of these vacancies, happily, shall only be temporary during the convalescence of their incumbents, while others partake of a sadly permanent nature. For in addition to the casualties directly attributable to the action of the enemy, many more poor fellows have fallen victims to sickness after the trying Canton campaign. Over half the strength of some Companies are on the list of sick in Hong Kong. However, it is an ill wind indeed which blows no good at all, and it is a source of a somewhat melancholy satisfaction to us to print the appended list of promotions. These, as is usual, are not, of course, gazetted but merely acting ranks, which would require the seal of approval in London. Our contemporary appears not to understand the meaning of the expression gazetted.

To be acting COMMANDERS
John Ashegarde Codrington-Browne
Hon. Julian Beauregard Witherby
Peregrine Semple

To be acting LIEUTENANTS
Raymond Hanlon Wilson
Sir Henry Wilson

To be SAILING MASTERS
John Brown
Joseph Smith

Mr H. Sprent, sailing master of the *Wellesley*, is promoted into the *Rattlesnake* following the death of Mr Brodie, her captain.

The sad news of the death of Captain Sir Humphrey Le Fleming Senhouse at Hong Kong on Sunday merits separate mention. Sir Humphrey had distinguished himself during a long and eventful career, being wounded in the service of his country, man and boy, on more than one occasion. At the age of sixty, he might have expected to enjoy a few more years of active service. His responsibility as Senior Naval Officer in the absence of Commodore Bremer was a heavy one. Alas, his earthly hopes were dashed – a sad and salutary reminder of the awful and ineluctable Orders of the Greater Commander of all Men.

By the doctors Sir Humphrey is diagnosed as dying of a remittent fever. We do not believe it, or if we do, his illness was severely exacerbated by a bitter chagrin he experienced on the Heights of Canton when betrayed by the Plenipotentiary.

He died of a broken heart. Of what else?

This gallant Christian warrior shall be buried in the Protestant Cemetery at Macao. Mistrustful of Captain Elliot, his brother officers do not care to inter their leader in the soil of Hong Kong which they fear the whimsical Elliot may well hand back to the mandarins. As to ourselves, we do not find it in our hearts to blame them – their choice partakes of as great a rebuff and insubordination as their discipline permits them to indulge. Nevertheless, we feel bound to own that we ourselves have every confidence in the security and prosperity of the infant and newest possession of Britannia.

In token whereof, we shall from our next re-Christen our journal:

THE HONGKONG GUARDIAN AND GAZETTE.

Land sales. Auctions were held in the large No. 5 mat-shed yesterday. Some gentlemen had attended from Macao two days previous on the deluded assumption that the sales of land were to take place on the 12th. These were postponed two days when further preparations proved necessary. In this regard we have to observe that the auction even when deferred two days occurred under confused and frequently mysterious circumstances. Division of the land was the responsibility of the commanding officer of Engineers. Distinction was made between marine lots, facing the sea, and suburban lots on the other side of the new road. The marine lots, which we would broadly regard as the more desirable, each enjoyed 100 feet of frontage, but their depth varied according to the shape of the coast-line. Calculations to ascertain the total area of each lot, and to ensure that all were uniform, were, as might be expected when the shapes answered to none of the usual forms known to geometry, of a complexity difficult to imagine. Only 50 of the anticipated 100 lots were ready for sale and the purchaser's own calculations, rueful in the one case, jubilant in his neighbour's, confirmed the judgment of common sense and plain eyesight that the dimensions of some lots were patently unequal to those of others. So much for the arcane mysteries of the mathematical science. In this regard, the aid of Mr O'R-, the painter, was invaluable to many of his old patrons.

Bidding for the land related to its annual rent and not its outright enjoyment in freehold, although the

Plenipotentiary has assured the merchant gentlemen that he shall press the Home Government to part with the title in return for a lump commutation of two or three years' rent. As much as £265 was paid for some lots, as little as £20 for others, in keen bidding which would not have disgraced the sale-rooms of London. Purchasers had to engage to construct buildings of a minimum value of $500 upon the plots within one year, and a surety of $500 was required, the rate fixed at 4s. 4d. to the dollar.

All native claimants to these lands were required to prove their claims.

From THE LIN TIN BULLETIN AND RIVER BEE
Wednesday, June 16, 1841
Vol.4 No. 12

The language of man is at one and the same time an expression and instrument of his needs and, for those who follow him, relic and evidence of that experience. Words may be fashioned, invented, changed to an end. And the worthiness or otherwise of that end, is to be discerned in ...the lexicon of that manifestation. Now, we are witnesses to the rise and spreading abroad of an interesting new expression and addition to the grand and main stream of the English language. From dark and subterranean sources comes this new upwelling. As is almost invariably the case with such new words or phrases, no man can with conviction point to its author, the first originator, though many, perhaps, would try to appropriate to themselves that distinction. In this case, though, we take the liberty of doubting it. LUT or LOOT is the queer word, which rings so strangely and uncouthly in our ears. We doubt if one of our gentle subscribers has yet heard that sound – we should be heartily sorry if they had. We ourselves heard it first when we were reduced to a very sorry state and, in fact, mistook it for a more familiar word, appertaining to the clothing of the pedal extremities. Presently in common usage among all the troops, the expression originated among the Company's sepoy soldiers and is a corrupted version of an expression of the chief dialect of Hindoostan. Its very sound helps evoke its meaning, for though it is not a case of onomatopoeia, the effort of its utterance and the play of expression imparted to the muscles of the face, the lips pursed and pushed forwards, the eyes wide and eager, enact the signification of the word. What does it mean? Why, so far as we have been able to ascertain from diligent enquiry, it means *plunder* (itself a Teutonic word, having its origins in the Thirty Years' War) though mayhap wanting that word's heavier Teutonic legitimacy. For plunder was the soldier's recognised perquisite in those times, whereas our modern officers, who should be restraining the pilfering habits of their men, but too often not merely connive in them but also indulge their own bent, are officially charged with repressing the practice.

It seems that when Commissioner Lin (who, we hear, by the by, finds in his verse a solace for exile) seized the 20,000 chests of opium, he violated the rights in property of the owners – but when it came to Chinese goods – why, it's only *looting*.

PURSUER

Not many months since *(vide Lin Tin Bulletin and River Bee* Vol.3 No.24) we shared our knowledge of the new invention of HELIOGRAVURE with such of our readers as might have felt a curiosity. During the elapse of this short time, our diligent *practice* of the novel methods has as inevitably suggested numerous reflexions on its *theory*. These we propose to impart to such of our subscribers as might have constructed their own cabinets from the plans we printed.

Now:

1 – It seems to us, though it did not at the inception, that it is as much art as science. No two individual operators will ever take the same scene or portrait in quite the same fashion. We do acknowledge this. The minutest deviation in

angle (viewpoint and perspective), framing (that is, where to place the border between that which shall be represented and that which shall not), and moment selected to make the exposure (of which more below) – all or severally each contribute to the final result. It is quite surprising how tiny and apparently insignificant differences will be productive of hugely distinctive results, just as two gun-shots on slightly divergent aims will be close together at twenty yards and perhaps a quarter of a mile distant when they eventually fall, or rivers having their sources within a hundred miles of each other may discharge into different oceans.

2 – The heliographic method is at once *Democratic* and *Imperial*. Democratic because after a little simple trial and error, not to be compared with the labour of learning the painterly craft, excellent results may be secured by all. Imperial because it is a most voracious medium, which is capable of annexing the entire solid world and recreating it in two dimensions, instead of three. It is possible, in theory, to expose sufficient plates so as to capture the entire little world one daily inhabits, not to mention his friends, acquaintances, and (more difficult, we grant) mortal foes.

3 – And as corollary of the foregoing, it is a method which finds *multum in parvo*. It might be the artistic embodiment of the principles of the philosopher of Ancient Greece (the name of whom momentarily escapes us) whose especial recommendation to the notice of his contemporaries was his notion of the world as composed of infinitely tiny particles, invisible to the sight, all independent and separate from the other but aggregated in the visible objects of the universe. This limitation – the Republican tyranny – imposed upon the operative by his lens and limited frame, means he needs must take only *segments* of the world. Alas, to paraphrase Mr Turner, we do not have pictures made up of bits but pictures of bits. The heliogravist's views and his borders are arbitrary, partial, peculiar. He must be content with parts, not wholes; shards, not the mirror; abruptness, not continuity. His must be an unfinished story, not a rounded tale.

4 – Time is his deadly foe. Oh! How has this not

perplexed and mortified us! Those few minutes, seemingly so short in any other avocation of life, prolong and extend themselves into an eternity of anxiety and frustration, while we pace up and down, our palms damp and an extinguished cheroot between our livid lips, for all the world like some tormented and expectant father in the last moments of his wife's confinement. Ah, but did ever father see so many deformed or still-born births as we? So many ruined plates, with the faint image of too much light, the Stygian black of insufficient exposure, or the dreadful blur and fog which is the consequence of the slightest movement?

Just as the Congreve rocket (we have it on the best authority), that witty weapon, is better adapted to play upon the stationary fort or ship, rather than a scattering mass of men, so our instrument is more suited to take the likeness of inanimate things. Here, however, we do believe that the remedy lies rather in the scientific or mechanical aspect of the process than in the *artistic*. Already the period of exposure has been contracted by the treatment of the plate with bromine and other 'quickstuffs' and we have no doubt that further discoveries and advances may be made, involving the glass of the lens or perhaps the provision of an artificial illumination, man-made lightning. We are sure that we shall see, captured on the Daguerreotype, not only the running man or the race-horse in motion, but the wings of the bee in flight, even the cannon-ball cutting through the air. All things shall be seen, even as in a peal of thunder across a darkling plain. Even now, when our attempts prove successful, our plate is nothing so much as a piece of the congealed substance of time, sliced out of the body of the changeling world. It is an instant frozen, purloined. It is the river of time arrested in its flow, before it melts and rolls its waters on, for what is ten minutes but as a blink in eternity?
SOLORIENS

'Oh, capital stroke, sir. Oh, well played that man.'

Applause spatters from the crowd. A marine officer retrieves the ball, lobbing it into the centre of the pitch with aplomb and accuracy such as a grenadier might envy. Pitch is the white sand of Kowloon and ball, ridged sphere of crimson leather, gives only a single, sullen bounce before coming to rest near three sticks of driftwood. This is wicket – hieroglyphic and acrostic significance of which has formed topic of conversation more amusing to Walter Eastman than his hearers. As the cricket-match is between the officers of the Navy and Army, the marine officer can act as a neutral. The two umpires, certainly, are members of his corps. They wear red-coats, as opposed to the shirt-sleeved players, which even from the boundary can be observed to be heavily stained with sweat. Due to the intractable nature of the pitch, the bowlers are obliged to deliver their balls as full tosses, which confer an immediate advantage upon the batting side. The adjutant of the 26th facing the senior middy of the *Algerine* scores another success as he strikes the lob with the full meat of his bat, sending it soaring to land in a mass of scattering parasols and frothing petticoats. The young ladies giggle frantically. They are not very clear about the rules of the game, although several gentlemen have taken the trouble to explain them in detail. Some of the young ladies, for instance, appear to think that the object of the game is to strike a spectator with the horrid little blood-coloured ball which *surely* cannot be as hard as it looks, just like a little cannon-ball. The ungallant gentlemen cheer ironically as one of the young ladies, wrinkling her pretty nose with effort, flings the ball back underhand a distance of some twelve feet. More tittering.

Walter raises his eyebrows. 'Why do they not send the charming creature in to wield the cudgel in this baffling game? I allow it would make it a power more interesting.'

'Oh, no, Mr Eastman,' says Harry Parkes in dismay, 'that wouldn't do at all. Why, girls are always blubbing. There ain't one I haven't seen do it, when it came to it. They couldn't even *field* for you.'

'Is that a fact now, young Harry?' says Gideon Chase, smiling but secretly agreeing, though he does not dare do so openly in front of Walter.

Miracle! With a new over and bowler, none other than the

ingenious Colin M'Dougal, chief engineer of the *Nemesis*, the ensign of the 26th facing the ball is clean-bowled middle stump, M'Dougal's extraordinary three-revolution, whirling underarm delivery whizzing just below the bottom of the bat. Huzza! go the tars.

The Chinese watching begin to have an inkling, as Ensign De Quincey trudges towards the boundary, handing his bat on to a lieutenant of the 18th Royal Irish: the object must be to strike the other stick-man's shrine, the thrower helping you by bouncing the ball off your stick and, of course, if he hits your shrine, he releases you from the running against your rival. Thus the compradore of Dent & Co. explains it. The villagers watch grimly. They remember another game of cudgels when Lin Wei Hei had his head stove in.

'How puzzled the Chinamen look! It must seem a rum affair to them.'

'You must study to gain an understanding of their tongue, Harry, as did Mr Morrison and myself; then they would no longer seem so strange.'

'Mr Morrison says the more he learns of them, the queerer they seem.'

'Well, he may have justice.'

'Who are those ladies? Are they married to anyone? Or are they the officers' sisters?'

'Ah, ahem….um, Mr Eastman, Walter, who precisely are…in the nice sense…do you think….er….those ladies might be?'

Walter comes to the rescue. 'Oh, those girls are *everyone's* sister, Harry, in a manner of speaking. They shall be jolly with the officers and, indeed, perhaps, with the men, too.'

'They are very pretty, but some of them don't speak English.'

'They speak French, some of 'em, but, Harry, there's enough now. Don't stare at them so, but go and render some assistance to Major Caine while he selects his staff.'

'Bat.'

'Very well. Off you go now.'

'Thank you, Walter.'

'My dear sir, that was not the first unhandsome fix I have got you out of, nor the last. Damnation pretty, aren't they? I'll allow

I feel the sensations of a rising interest myself.'

'Well, I do not. Well *caught,* sir. Good luck, Major Caine.'

Caine acknowledges with a jaunty twirl of his bat, which he manages, generally, like a sabre.

'D'you know, old friend, this game is played so slowly, I allow I could contrive to capture it on the Daguerreotype.'

'You may be right.'

'Yet, I like the principles. I have a notion it could be adapted into a game more suited to the spirit of the New World.'

'Indeed?'

'Why, certainly. We'll get rid of the wickets. I don't care overly for the wickets. They give you but the single chance. The game's too darned unforgiving. Knock 'em down, and you're out of the great game of life. What do emigrants come for except for the second chance in life? *So,* sir, no wicket to defend and we'll give them *three* misses. I like the number three, as you know. This will encourage them to be more emphatic and attack and amass more points, rather than merely defend what they already have. Is that not a pioneer for you? On the same tack, why have the two hitters...'

'Batsmen, sir.'

'Whatever they are called, there is one too many for me. The spirit of the backwoodman is simplicity. We'll have just the one. The running up and down is monotonous, and shall be redundant with the just one. There is more drama in running a circle or triangle, still better.'

'You are running away with yourself now.'

'Ah, well. Jonathan would know. I may ask him when he lands. Hulloa, the major has sent the ball straight into the midshipman's hands.'

'Oh, well caught, sir, well caught,' shrieks Harry Parkes, unable to restrain sportsman's instincts, though he hero-worships Caine.

'Now they're all walking off,' Walter complains. 'What is happening, Lieutenant Wheeldon?'

'Caine was eleventh man, for obvious reasons, as you perceived. Now they're all out and will take tea and sandwiches before the Navy have their innings.'

'I see, sir. An armistice pending resumption. That seems to fall in with the Plenipo's notion of captaincy.'

'Not,' says Wheeldon mysteriously, 'if there's a new captain. You are invited most cordially to refreshments, gentlemen.'

From 𝕿𝖍𝖊 𝕳𝖔𝖓𝖌 𝕶𝖔𝖓𝖌 𝕲𝖚𝖆𝖗𝖉𝖎𝖆𝖓 𝖆𝖓𝖉 𝕲𝖆𝖟𝖊𝖙𝖙𝖊

Tuesday, June 29th, 1841.

Vol. 1 No. 1

It is a trite but true observation and, indeed, one which comes to us on scriptural authority, that new wine will burst old bottles. Under the circumstance and verified result of that ancient experiment, then, we make no apology for the appearance of a new organ of opinion and news, younger even than the colony it shall serve and whose name it is proud to take. For we do anticipate and presume, we must freely own. Lord Palmerston has yet to ratify and approve the taking Hong Kong by Captain Elliot (one of the few wise actions of the misguided Plenipo), yet we cannot believe that he should countenance the handing it back to the Chinese government. The island in every respect answers the need of our traders for a secure position in the vicinity of Canton from which they may conduct their affairs in security and freedom. Trade without imposts, open to all nations, is a principle already written into the charter of the island by Captain Elliot's proclamation. When sales of land and specified lots have already been made, it is difficult to see how our Home Government can do otherwise than formalise those arrangements already existing at the present time. We repeat, we do not doubt it will bless these.

There will always be difficulties. We do not presume to make light of these. The place has not been won at a small cost. Yet the sacrifice makes the island all the more valuable to the Hong Kong-ites. Deaths among our men caused by the resistance of the Chinese have been few, yet the losses which the Chinese failed to inflict, the unhealthy climate has augmented. We learn to our deep regret and sorrow that

Lord Edward Clinton, lieutenant in the *Modeste,* died at Smith's Hotel in Macao from the consequences of a gingal-ball in the knee before the wall of Canton. This had been extracted from the place where it had lodged in the bone but, the young man refusing to undergo the performance of amputation, inflammation and mortification supervened, followed by fever, from which he perished in the greatest distress. Fever has cut a wide swathe in the ranks of the Services, sparing neither rank nor distinction. Half the companies of many a ship, as well as the land forces, are laid up with agues and intermittent fevers. Commander Brodie of the *Rattlesnake* perished in delirium on the day the last issue of our old *Monitor* appeared, while Captain Wilson, Adjutant of the 18th Regiment, expired shortly after, also of a remittent fever. He had only shortly disembarked from the *Futty Salaam* transport. Both have been buried in the new cemetery at the top of Happy Valley.

On a more auspicious note, Commodore Bremer is returned from Calcutta in the *Queen* steamer. He comes back as Joint Plenipotentiary, which will greatly please all with the interests of Hong Kong and Free Trade at heart. We believe we are not deluded when we say we are in hopes of seeing a new and more vigorous policy promulgated.

APPOINTMENTS

To be CLERK OF PUBLIC WORKS – Mr Bird.

To be HARBOUR MASTER AND MARINE MAGISTRATE at Hong Kong – Lieutenant W. Pedder, late of the *Nemesis.*

To be ASSISTANT HARBOUR MASTER – Mr Lena.

(Mr Lena, we would inform our readers, is an Italian gentleman who performed sterling work with the Expedition in the North.)

Atrocious crime. This outrage occurred at an isolated warehouse east of Jardine's outpost, near the large Quarry, in the early hours of the 15th *inst.* Lieutenant Philips had retired for the night to his quarters above the godown when he was alerted by a small sound. He was on the point of returning to sleep again when, after a small interval, he heard the noise repeated. Persuading himself it was the splash of the waters in the harbour or the scurryings of a rat, he turned over, only for the unmistakable rattle of metal upon metal to impress itself upon his auditory sense. Springing from the bed, but in his precipitate haste omitting to furnish himself with a weapon, he descended the stairs when he found himself surrounded by a band of piratical Chinese, armed with spears and swords. Putting up a desperate resistance, although receiving a severe wound to the hand in doing so, which almost severed his thumb from his palm, he was so successful as to contrive to wrest a spear from one of his assailants and, thus provided, fight his way to the water-gate. Beset by superior odds, severely wounded by a sword-thrust in the body and a blow to the head, he was hard put to prevent the rascals poking at his ribs and, finally, in desperation, flung himself into the water. The ruffians endeavoured to follow in their boat but by dint of diving under and swimming below the surface, he was able to elude their best efforts at pursuit. Perceiving the reflections of their torches to grow fainter upon the waters, he struck out for the small rock in the harbour known as Kellett's island, where he arrived wet, exhausted, and more dead than alive. We never heard a more striking instance of cool pluck and fortitude.

ADVERTISEMENT

most respectfully directed. Mr Smethwick, who shall be charged with the management of the house at Hong Kong, looks forward to welcoming gentlemen and ladies from both Macao and Hong Kong, as well as extending a special welcome to the officers of the Navy whose requirements he is especially equipped to fulfil.

From THE LIN TIN BULLETIN AND RIVER BEE

Wednesday, June 30, 1841

Vol. 4. No.13

The growth of Hong Kong continues apace. We find not so much the buildings remarkable, many of them being insubstantial and mean in the extreme, as the influx of population. Prior to the British occupation, we do not believe there can have been upwards of one or two thousand souls on the whole island, scattered in three or four fisher-villages, at Little Hong Kong and Chek Chu on the south and Shaukiwan on the north coast. Since then this aboriginal population has been swelled in the most dramatic fashion by an invasion of emigrants from China. We believe there may be six or seven thousand of these. Without injustice, these may be described as the very scum of Canton. Who else would resort to such a place, ninety miles from the capital and all the haunts, acquaintances, and conveniences which make life comfortable and familiar, but men of the most unsettled and lawless habits, who are in many cases refugees from the justice and retribution they so richly merit. We say men, for these are mostly single individuals, wanting families, though naturally there already exist our women of the town. Already booths, houses, and all manner of debaucheries exist within the nest of iniquities which is the native bazaar. No viciousness is unknown.

The boldest robberies and piracies take place daily (and nightly) on the island and in the waters surrounding it. These ruffians have become greatly daring since the war. The naval mandarins have even less ability to suppress these incursions than they commanded in the past, while the Royal Navy must look to the conduct of greater things than the apprehending of a few pirate-boats. Even as the Plenipotentiary was making a tour round the entire circumference of the island by steamer, a passage-boat was pirated a stone's throw from Hong Kong harbour, the Portuguese master stabbed to death, his mate's ear cut off, and two gentlemen passengers wounded.

We should add that we do not believe these are insurmountable problems, so much as the teething pains of the infant dominion. Such is inevitably the nature of new settlements that they attract the rude, and rough, and the licentious. It behoves us, though, to add (as if we needed) that the first settlers of the New England 'plantations' – for the world *colony* did not exist then, or at least had not yet been resuscitated from the body of a dead language – were religious men of the purest principles and most ardent zeal. Perhaps too zealous and too principled. The same cannot be said of Hong Kong. The first substantial brick buildings, it seems, are dedicated not to Jehovah but to Morpheus and Venus. While the bare-headed soldiers worship under a roof of thatch in the mat-shed church, the chests of drug repose snugly in the godown, while in the br – but we desist.

Climate and Disease are rather the true enemies of Hong Kong. Sanitation and a Hospital are its immediate *desiderata,* rather than a new Battery in the harbour.

FROM OUR CORRESPONDENTS

Mr Editor,

It is my feeling that this question was best addressed while he was alive to the late and lamented Mr Veale, he owning the splendid aviary and gardens in Macao. However, as you and your assistant appear to dispose of a ready fund of knowledge concerning the local waters and the habits of the natives, I beg to request elucidation on the natural as well as political history of China and to seek out the best information of the flora and fauna of this coast as well as its human, or inhumane, inhabitants.

Sir, is it true that the poisonous snakes and reptiles here may shuck their skins, discard their mortal coil, and emerge as a new creature altogether? I was a short time since presented with such a spectacle in Hong Kong.

ADAM

This is a most pertinent and interesting enquiry. There is such a serpent in the colony. At the termination of the sixth month, or June as it is vulgarly known, it tends to divest itself of its paper-thin coat and go abroad in another. While in title and appearance it in no wise resembles its old self it still speaks with the forked tongue of untruth and is every whit as venomous. By the unwary it should be avoided at all costs.

Caught napping. Subscribers to our contemporary, that obstinate and dwindling band, who should be well advised that when Dick Turpin changes his *nom de plume* his occupation is still that of *gentleman of the road,* or highwayman as we ruder fellows should like to term it without circumlocution, these unhappy readers, we say, may have found among yesterday's smudged and dreary columns, among the dismal tracts of countryside through which Dick likes to lead them, a spot of some more than usually appealing interest. Our friend actually had an interesting anecdote to impart. Good Lord! Wonders will never cease. In the account of the adventures, travails, and lucky escape of Lieutenant P— lurked some glimmer of excitement and romance. Alas, our self-appointed Guardian was rather too tenacious of the whole truth, for he kept and guarded most of it to himself (if, indeed, he knew it).

In the breasts of the alert there may have arisen perplexity and the sensations of unease, as quickly stifled as felt. For one does not have to have remained in Hong Kong longer than a day to have ascertained that the Jardine godowns are veritable fortresses, secured with gates, railings, and locks, with communication to the blank upper storeys possible only through the agency of a long ladder which is habitually raised after dusk. The quarters above, which for obvious reasons Mr Matheson prefers to rent out to young and athletic officers of the services, partake of the nature of an arsenal, with racks of guns, even rifles, swords, and pistols.

So how came it that our hero admitted the robbers ('Ah, but he went down to them, sir,' the demurrer would say – to which we should reply: 'That, sir, is pretty much the same thing, only the latter is *much* more foolish than the former') and that, having done so, he compounded the error by going down unarmed when, by dint of leaving the ladder unlowered, he might have smoked a cigar and amused himself by taking pot-shots at the rapscallions all evening?

The simple answer is – *he was not alone.* Our friend, rather the butt of his brother officers at the present than the object of their sympathies, had taken a native companion to his quarters and she, in league with the assailants, who *did* come by boat, privily admitted them when our cavalier had to make his exit already in a suitable condition for a long swim, as he wore no clothes. Disciplinary proceedings are being instituted against him.

ADVERTISEMENT

Mr Richard Robinson, mason, of Calcutta, begs to present his compliments to the gentlemen and ladies of Hong Kong, where he is lately arrived. He is expert in the dressing, mortaring, and laying of stone and brick and has supervised the construction of many of the most handsome and substantial houses in the 'City of Palaces'.

He begs to draw the attention of the public-spirited to his willingness to accept commissions, of which he regards none as alike too large or too small. He is residing at No.5 Queen's Road, where all interested parties are urged to direct their enquiries.

CHAPTER XLI

'I have no wish to go, Walter, even to accompany you. My refusal is both categorical and vehement. I have no interest in debauchery of this nature.'

'O'Rourke is coming.'

'Harry is old enough to sin, and repent at leisure, if he wishes.'

'They are pretty little girls, I'll warrant you, Gid. "Delightful fillies", Wheeldon said.'

'Lieutenant Wheeldon is a soldier. One should expect that kind of behaviour of his caste.'

'Well, by God, I am the editor of a rag and I expect it of myself. Still, if you cannot be tempted…'

'I cannot, and I regard it as a very ill wind that blew them off course from Batavia.'

Silence follows for a while. Walter sends a succession of smoke-rings through the boughs of the banyan tree. They are under canvas at the top end of the Happy Valley, along with a good many other civilians, including the Meridian boys, who have come to open an agency for Corrigan, and a few companies of troops who have been moved from the western areas while their mat-shed barracks are pulled down and permanent accommodation constructed.

Pools of stagnant water still lie around the valley. Walter puffs away philosophically, enjoying the dusk. Really, he is quite incorrigible. 'Strange, you appear to have no interest in the fair sex,' Walter muses.

'I don't,' Gideon snaps.

'Well, I allow you will some time.'

Gideon abruptly gets off his stool to go into the tent. He is going to lie down on his cot and read some more Kant, when he sees Walter's tin trunk open under his camp-bed.

The tripod, camera obscura, assorted bottles, dishes, and rods occupy an intolerable amount of space in what ought to have been study-room at the rear of the tent. Developed plates spill out of the trunk. Gideon frowns at one through its reflective glass cover. The Daguerreotype is of a familiar but decidedly odd object. Odd, at any rate, in isolation. He picks it up and tilts it so that the glass no longer reflects.

A foot.

Human foot, that is.

Nothing else.

Bit of ankle in it also, of course.

The next one.

Same study.

The third plate – another foot.

Ditto fourth.

In an increasing frenzy of irritation and mystification, Gideon pulls more out, throwing them on to the trestle-bed, the floor, where they clatter together. Madly, he wonders – are they the same foot? Which is left, which right? Which another's?

'Ah, I thought a stand of muskets had collapsed to judge by the clangour. Do mind not to break the glass covers, or they will scratch.'

'What are these?'

'Feet.'

'Yes, I can see that.'

'Beautiful, are they not?'

'Why, in God's name, have you taken representations of hundreds of feet?'

'No – hundreds of representations of feet. Oh, I'll allow that is the prettiest, tenderest, shapeliest, loveliest portion of the girlish anatomy! Ah!' And suiting gesture to word, Walter brushes his lips against the instep of a foot.

Gideon can only stare.

'They are all female, I can assure you, Gid. Look how small, how delicate the bones, the translucence of the skin, that delicate tracery of its blue veins.'

'Good God, you *are* insane.'

'Now, Gideon, look at this. The roundness, yet squareness of that dainty heel, the angle as it meets the ankle. The perfect symmetry of the cables of dainty tendon as she flexed her toes. The alabaster flesh of the outside edge, the rose-blush of the sole. And the toes! See here, such pretty toes, a perfect shape to the foot, the second toe longer than the great toe (the greatest sign of beauty to the ancients, Gid), the charming small toe there. Now this is the same foot, Gid (same owner, my lad) but at a different angle. Side elevation, that is, from inward. The inside ankle, how strongly it is set into the foot, glorious! Wonderful! Worshipful! The line from the instep to large toe, the sweet scoop of flesh in the arch under. Oh, this is the best. No, this is. *Two* feet – look, peeping out like shy mice from beneath the petticoat. I took them from above. She has rather longer bones than the others, do you see?'

'Desist, Walter. This is a spectacle tedious in the extreme – as well as offensive and gross to the last degree.'

'But my dear Gid, the girls were quite content. You should have heard the giggling. It was a ceremony a good deal more innocent than many they have known.'

'Are these of the…trollops whom we saw at the cricket-match?'

'If you must employ such language…yes.'

'Appalling, perfectly disgusting.'

'Not at all,' says Walter imperturbably, packing his plates away with care.

'I wonder at you, Walter.'

'Why? I worship beauty in all its forms. This shall be only the beginning of my collection. I love to peruse and study them in an idle hour of leisure – my own, my darling beauties.'

'Go away, and leave me to Kant.'

'By all means.'

After Walter has left, Gideon starts to shake with laughter.

Kant, then, goes spine down over his face as he convulses with hilarity on his cot. 'God damn it,' he says. 'God damn it.'

'God damn what?' enquires Jonathan Ridley, peeping in. 'God damn the moskiters, I say. Look, my darned arm is an ugly mass of bites. Torment — I cannot sleep. They feast on me — varmints.'

'That is bad,' says Gideon. 'But I know a native poulticer who could fix you a lotion and plaster to alleviate the irritation.'

'Ach, too darned late. You haven't suffered.'

'No, Ridley,' says Walter from the tent-door. 'You see, my cigars keep them away. They cannot abide the smoke, if you've noticed. Not a bite.'

'Say! That's right! Not a mark on either of you pair. Fred wore his clothes all night, but I chose to be eaten alive, rather than be roasted.'

'Keep your tent-flap tied,' Walter advises, 'and, whatever else, refrain from lighting your lamp until it is all secured. You may then catch a few winks of sleep tonight.'

'Sleep's not what I'm after, if you take my meaning.'

'Indeed, perhaps the stings will rather have stimulated than depressed your appetite.'

'It is not a sting,' Gideon says coldly, 'such as a bee's or a hornet's, but the insect pierces your skin to draw and consume the blood.'

'Let it suck away. Do you expect O'Rourke is immune on account of the pox which very likely riddles his frame?'

'Most likely. Jon, catch up my tripod and the plate and buffing-press there. We shall depart now, or we shall be late, and that would never do.'

'*Adios,* Gid.'

'Harry, how d'ye do, my smart lad!'

'Very well, sir. Oh, sir, Mr Morrison has instructed me not to speak with you gentlemen.'

'Lordy, Harry! But why?'

'I don't know, sir. At least, I don't really understand why, sir. Oh, I am heartily sorry.'

'Well, it is most disagreeable of Mr Morrison and the

Reverend Mr Gutzlaff, who I am sure is the principal behind this affair, most presumptuous, but as they are your guardians, you needs must obey their commands, which they see as consulting your best interest and for your own good. But it's odd, deuced odd. Walter?'

'Darned queer, disobliging fellows, but there you are. No two ways about it. I'll allow it's certainly through no wish of your own, Harry. But you feel free to cut us when you see us here on the Praia the next time you pass with Mr Morrison or Mr Gutzlaff to enjoy the sea-air. No, I'll say we won't call you out.'

'Oh, thank you, Mr Eastman, and you, Mr Chase, oh, you have been so kind to.....'

'Now, don't blubber. Recollect, only girls behave so. You just keep your bat straight, like the fine lad you are. Have a handkerchief.'

How kind Walter can be, thinks Gideon.

'What's a brothel, Mr Chase?'

'Hey? Er...um....Walter?'

'Oh, very good question, Harry. Smart lad. A broth-el is a small gratuitous soup-kitchen where gruel and beef-tea are dispensed to the sick, needy, and deserving, in order to keep body and soul together.'

'Oh, people are silly.'

'You have made a very adult observation, Harry. Now run away with you, like a good fellow, and we'll pretend we are the most perfect strangers when next we meet.'

'Huzza!'

'Yippee!'

'My God, Walter, you are as cool as a cucumber, and no two ways.'

'I accept your compliment.'

From **The Hong Kong Guardian and Gazette**

Tuesday, July 6th, 1841.

Vol.1 No.3

The morality at Hong Kong continues to give rise to concern. As champions of the island, we do not believe that it is necessarily more unhealthy than Chusan (a more green and beautiful place) where, our readers will scarcely need reminding, the troops still dropped like flies. We are certain that with the erection of the new barracks, construction of a military sanatorium on the sea-front or at the top of the mountain, and the institution of sanitary reforms both in the bazaar and outside, the most distressing and long lists we are obliged to print shall become matters of the past. The sickness among the troops and Navy has been fearful, nor have civilians been altogether spared, though the incidence of serious cases among them has been more rare. Strange to relate, the sepoy troops have suffered more in this regard than the European regiments, dysentery, fever, and cholera having taken off many a man. The sorry state of the native Companies, with as many as three-quarters of their strength now on the sick-lists, is attributed to the poorness of their present accommodations, many of them lying in their own filth in circumstances of the utmost squalor, and to their dietary practices, with sustenance confined to pulses and weevily rice.

Most malignant has been the Hong Kong Fever – a species of remittent fever. The symptoms exhibited in the progress of this disease are quite different from those of the cholera or of dysentery, with which it is not to be confused. The sufferer becomes, hot, restless, and delirious by turns, calling out and prey to hallucinations to the most touching and affecting degree, shortening sail in a storm if he be a sailor, or under the impression that he is preaching to a congregation if he be a man of the cloth. (And these, in His Mercy, He does not spare.) Finally, after enduring the most awful and agonising torments of thirst and a parching burning of the whole body, interspersed with, strange to relate, violent shivering and sensations of the utmost chill, an apparent recovery is made by the victim.

Oh, cruellest irony! the respite is but short-lived, short as the life of the afflicted, for within a matter of hours, rather than days, relapse occurs with a repetition of the previous symptoms, only aggravated, until the victim becomes comatose, expiring shortly afterwards.

It is not unknown for a victim to recover from the second onset of this terrible disease, yet it is true to say that he is never the same man again, and he shall never be wholly free from minor visitations and repetitions of the sickness.

The cause of the Hong Kong Fever is still matter of dispute, even among the medical profession. Dr MacG-, long a resident on this coast, believes it is the same, or a similar form of a, sickness he noticed and attempted to treat among seamen encamped at Dane's island and the marshes of Whampoa in 1828, while Dr Scott at Macao has never seen it before. Surgeon-Commander Raison of the *Futty Salaam* transport recollects seeing a similar fever at Valparaiso, while officers who have cruised the West African station have seen a similar ailment prevalent there. The Hong Kong Fever is not altogether unknown among the natives, but a smaller proportion of them are afflicted, and those with more trivial symptoms, when compared to the foreigner. Happy Valley is particularly notorious on account of its prevalence in that locality. Troops encamped upon high ground, though not altogether spared, appear less susceptible to attack by the disease, but those on low and, especially, damp sites feel its ravages most keenly. One opinion has it that the foul miasmas of the air may collect in the hollows on low, broken ground, while yet another school of medical thought opines that the decomposing granites of which the hillside in Hong Kong is chiefly formed give off noxious vapours as they deteriorate. The natives say that the foreigners have been punished for disturbing the dragon which lives in the valley by their digging of irrigation ditches and draining-channels. Whatever the reason, and we ourselves incline towards the first adumbrated, it should only be a matter of the most common prudence to construct new barracks for the men on the more open, southerly part of the island where their constitutions might be the better protected.

The cortège winds through the valley. It is rather different in its details from the military funerals which have become a familiar sight to the Chinese inhabitants of Wong Nei Chong hamlet over the last two months, as they snake their ways along the insidious paths to the new cemetery. This one, for instance, has no four-man files of red-coats, or straw-hatted blue-jackets, in its train, marching in slow step, with their musket-barrels pointed at the ground, butts held in the elbow's crook. No band plays melancholy airs. There will be no volley discharged over the rough grave, and the flag draped over the coffin is not the cross of the Union Jack (though to these villagers this is a subtlety un-apprehended at merely another barbarian burial) but the jewels and jaunty lines of the Stars and Stripes. Among the mourners who follow the dead man, there are a few scattered uniforms of red and blue but since, like himself, most of his friends were civilians, they are habited in sombre black with hats to match. Despite the awful heat, they wear gloves. All things considered, it is a large train. The dead man was popular. Nor are the mourners exclusively his countrymen but — saddest sight of all, at any funeral — those come to mark his departure are mostly young.

As was he.

Gideon draws his breath in gasps. They would be long gasps, if he didn't shudder so. The heat in these clothes is like nothing he has ever known. Does it pour like molten lead off the hills to accumulate in the plain? His chest heaves again. His face is wet, whether with sweat or tears it is difficult to tell since both are salt. He rubs his stinging eyes. Harry O'Rourke is definitely weeping. Weeping and sober. He stumbles in the ruts that gun-carriages, laden down with caskets, have cut into the pathways. Gideon takes Harry's elbow, and the old fellow presses Gideon's hand against the ancient black broadcloth of his coat. Even out in this inferno, Gideon can smell the odour of must and camphor-balls from it. The baked earth is quite hard underfoot. It would be all too easy to sprain an ankle. Water has evaporated from all but the deepest pools and puddles. What is left is coated with scum and algae.

The procession halts at the foot of the western slopes. Earlier parties have cut crude steps into the soil; they crumble already. By now the graveyard has a startlingly large population. Some six or seven rows extend across a quarter of a mile of hillside. The leading mourners slide the coffin off the borrowed gun-carriage. Gideon, fittingly, has been chosen as a pall-bearer and must now leave O'Rourke mopping his face with the handkerchief hidden under his tall hat. There are six of them, all strong, brawny lads (as was their friend). They manage the box quite easily, even as it tilts back sharply to take the steps. Someone's coat rips. 'Oh, darn,' they hear him whisper softly. A giggle quickly turns into a half-sob. The grave waits, narrow and a little over six feet in depth. Surprisingly, there is some water at the bottom. Springs must well all over these slopes, Gideon thinks, for the valley's two brooks flow fiercely in rainy weather. Not the best choice for a graveyard. The slit stares blankly. In the mound of spoil earthworms and cockroaches crawl. The pall-bearers place the coffin by the graveside, on top of three ropes. Gideon stands back.

That awful, dire hole, obscene in its simplicity.

Is that what his friend has come to? Is it what he will come to? It cannot be true.

It is.

'This is my only sure knowledge of the future.'

'Hush.'

Gideon looks round; he did not think he had spoken at all, but he had. How dreamlike it all is. Now he no longer feels sorrow. His misery has fled. He floats above emotion, rising superior to his own body, to the others, to grief. A sob rises in his throat; his shoulders shake; and his face is wet, trickling with tears. Yet his mind is serene. It is a stranger's body which shudders, with shaking shoulders. He puts his hands over his face. What a strange split this is, between himself and his body.

Mourners pile flowers on the other side of the grave. Corrigan's sombre face shows no emotion. The Reverend Elijah Bridgman, the deceased's and Gideon's countryman, begins the simple service, assisted by the Reverend Vincent Stanton, once kidnapped by the Chinese while bathing at Macao. The address concentrates on the virtues of the deceased, his blameless life – the impermanence, instability of human life, exemplified by his sudden end. *For everywhere in life there is death.*' Bridgman stops droning.

They begin to sing, the Americans more certainly than the British.

We'll all gather at the river...

Alice Barclay Remington, singing like an angel, smiles tremulously at Gideon through the tears her black veil cannot hide. The hymn comes to its end. Stanton takes over. Though an Englishman, he knew their late friend rather better than Bridgman, being a young man of the deceased's own age. His words dissolve the calm induced by Bridgman's generalities, and we must imagine the next hymn broken by sobs and much manly blowing of noses.

Throats are then cleared. Coughs relieve dryness. The British seem comforted by the slower, melancholy music of the last hymn, which was more to their taste.

The party uncover their heads, exposing them to the sun and uncaring sky. They pray. A moment's silence follows. Then the pallbearers prepare to lower the coffin. Gideon feels quite calm.

'Quick! Catch Chase! Catch him, I say!'

The sun glows orange, then purple. Of earth the sky smells. His cheek is cool, pleasantly so. He closes his eyes.

From 𝕿𝖍𝖊 𝕳𝖔𝖓𝖌 𝕶𝖔𝖓𝖌 𝕲𝖚𝖆𝖗𝖉𝖎𝖆𝖓 𝖆𝖓𝖉 𝕲𝖆𝖟𝖊𝖙𝖙𝖊

Tuesday, July 13th, 1841

Vol. 1 No. 4

OBITUARY

On no account are we to be represented as belonging to that shade of opinion (alas, not unknown here) which commonly holds the value of life among the men of the Services to be somehow cheaper than that prevailing among the civilians. Yet, although we have only noticed the losses among the military and navy as names in our columns, we feel it behoves us to remark in somewhat greater detail the passing of a young man widely known among us when we took our residence at Canton, popular to a degree, and remaining there almost half the years of his short life. We refer with the deepest sadness to the late Mr Jonathan Ridley who passed away but a few days ago in Hong Kong.

Mr Ridley was an American gentleman, from the state of New York, of English and, on his mother's side, we are given to understand, of Dutch ancestry. He did greatly resemble Admiral Tromp in the face. He had been in the house of Meridian at Canton and Macao for more than ten years, interrupting his sojourn in China only to voyage to the Sandwich Islands as supercargo and then for but a nine months' cruise. He had been staying under canvas in the Happy Valley when he succumbed to the Fever, greatly surprising all his companions and friends, among whom he was a byword for strength, resolution, activity, and his manly accomplishment and dexterity in all the virile pursuits young men love to follow. He had almost won the last regatta at Canton, but for his partner's too great sense of fairness. In all its hateful manifestations, the fever ran its course. His temperature rose. It dropped. He tossed, he called out in all the agony of his delirium, reliving the country scenes of his childhood which had been passed among farmyard things, when while conscious and while his faculties were in the thrall of his strong will, he had scorned to utter one word of complaint or reproach. By his friends his life was despaired of. He seemed to rally, called for refreshment, slept a little. Soon he was again exhibiting all the symptoms of the serious derangement of his system, passed into unconsciousness, and, little after, this amiable and valiant young man breathed his last. His demise is sensibly apprehended as a sad loss not only by all the close and boon companions of his days but also by those who felt the impress of his qualities in even the fleeting association they enjoyed with him.

We condole with *all* his friends.

He was buried in the cemetery at the Happy Valley by a large party of both English and American ladies and gentlemen.

FROM A CORRESPONDENT

Sir,

In consequence of the shocking mortality among the men, I feel emboldened to venture an expression of opinion in your columns, trusting that any roughness or infelicity in expression will be redeemed by its intrinsic worth. As a serving officer in the junior service, I only give utterance to sentiments which are commonly felt by many brother officers of my own age and rank, that is to say among those whose wits are still fresh and uncrusted by years of prejudice and unreasoning repetition of drills and paradings. So many, men and officers, have fallen victims not to the enemy's shot (he has no shell) but to the climate, that we needs must ponder the necessity for certain reforms, all within the jurisdiction and proper province of the quartermaster-general. (By this I do not intend to cast mean aspersions upon the present distinguished officer in our Expedition.)

I have often thought the Queen's uniform could not have been designed upon worse principles than if a synod of wise men had been got together to invent the most impracticable and useless garb which could possibly be tailored for men serving in the field. In this climate, the heavy shakoes and stiff leather stocks are not only cumbersome but positively dangerous. To keep a line of men out at midday, clad in these articles, is to ensure decimation by sunstroke. The tunics and trowsers are loose in the wrong places and tight in the worst, so that the final and ridiculous consequence is that the best part of the physical energies of the men who wear them is spent not in harassing the enemy but in uselessly distending and compressing three yards of cloth. Nor, if we were huntsmen, could we desire a brighter plumage or a better mark than that provided by a red tunic, with the white cross-belts indicating the bull's eye.

Sir, I believe reform is long overdue and without apologising for my enthusiasm, I have the honour to subscribe myself,

ACHILLES

There is much of truth in what our correspondent says. We do doubt whether the War Office will institute the reforms our ensign or lieutenant desires until he is at least a general. There are no minds slower to change than the military.

Erratum. A trifling error crept into our last, p. 1, col. 1, line 3. For 'morality' read 'mortality'.

'You do not rise until MacGillivray assures me it is safe for you to do so,' Walter admonishes his patient. 'Lie back and don't argue, for remonstrance is useless.'

'Oh, very well,' says Gideon pettishly. 'I'm perfectly able to get about, though.'

'You are not the best judge. Now, it is time for your cold compress.' Gideon submits unwillingly to Walter's amateurish ministrations, but enjoys the touch of his fingers. 'Say, look what you just did – all run down the back of my neck!'

'Just what the doctor commanded.'

'How long was I oblivious?'

'About six hours. You came to your wits at seven in the evening, when you took a draught of bottled soda-water, and then fell fast asleep – a far healthier slumber than the first – until the morning when you woke unconscionably early and promptly fell asleep again after giving me your salutations.'

'Do you know, I calculate I remember nothing at all. It is as if that afternoon had been stolen from my life. I remember bending to go to lift...Jon's coffin...and then no more.'

'Well, poor Jonathan is gone for ever, and you scared us all by stepping out of time for the short period you did. MacGillivray says, "a wee touch too much heat and dehydration," but I incline towards a full sunstroke.'

'Where am I?'

'In Macao. No, no – don't excite yourself. I only jest. This is Pedder's. At least we are out of the Valley of Death. I *had* considered removing you to Macao but the weather is lowering.'

'It seems cooler indeed.'

'Now look at these.'

'Walter!'

'Yes, I am delighted with them.'

'Ah, no, Walter. Ah, no. This is to exceed…you are lost to all sense of decorum.'

'My dear Gideon, I intended no disrespect to Ridley's memory. He was as good a friend to me as he was to you. I allow he would not have objected. I cannot for the life of me (I did not meditate that pun) think of a better subject: the waxy complexion, perfectly suited to the silver and black of the Daguerreotype, far better than the high colour and ruddiness of life; he does not move and thus affect the exposure. All lies peaceful in the slumber and solemn dignity of death. I do not capture a transient moment, with all the artificiality of a pose and a feigned expression and emotion, so much as his entire condition: true and unaffected. Yet is he impermanent flesh, on the road to dissolution and decay. I have secured a memorial to him which is proof against the ravages of mortality.'

'Well, I guess I really don't know what to think. But it is my surmise that Jonathan would have boxed your ears for this.'

'Do you know, old friend, I was in momentary expectation, all the while, of him leaping up from the bed to do just that. Here — now these, too, were successful to a degree: the sun blazing, light brilliant, air clear to the point of perfect transparency. With the consequence that the times requisite for the submission of the plates to the action of the light were very sensibly shortened. In fact, Gid, this is the ideal moment to take a Daguerreotype — the thought occurred to me simultaneous with the opportunity presenting itself. When are people stiller, living people I mean, than when at prayer or in painful contemplation? The black clothes afforded me splendid contrasts…here, see for yourself. And the composition! More luck than design, I'll own: the different planes to lead in the eye, the heads all bowed, with only one looking up (which only emphasised the otherwise uniform pattern), the yawning hole, that dreadful box, the flowers on the pile of spoil.'

'Well, I own, Walter, I see some redeeming value in this. Your act is still cold, inhuman and macabre, but it is a memento, in some sense, of our dear friend and our last respects paid to him.'

'Then it is yours.'
'Oh, no…'
'I should very much like you to take it, my dear friend.'
'Thank you, Walter.'

From THE LIN TIN BULLETIN AND RIVER BEE

Wednesday, July 14, 1841
Vol.4 No. 14

OBITUARY

The American community experienced a sad loss the week previous when Mr Jonathan Ridley, a merchant at Canton, contracted a fever and died during a sojourn in the island of Hong Kong. He was a person of the most amiable disposition, unaffected manners, loyalty of heart, courageous to a degree, and yet possessed withal a kind and affectionate nature. By all his grieving friends his demise is sensibly apprehended as a great affliction. A full heart prevents us from saying more.

FROM A CORRESPONDENT

Mr Editor,

This shall be my last on the subject, I contract. I congratulate you on your essay on the science of Daguerreotypism and its correspondence with our notions of TONALITY, TOTALITY, AND TIME (June 16, 1841, Vol.4, No.12). At least, such, I surmise, were the topics it most ably discussed by implication. These seemed notable and valuable opinions to me. I am pleased also to note – I trust that I do not stand the deluded victim of my own hopes – some moderation and modification of your views on the relation of the new science to the painterly craft. I heartily concur with your judgement that the man behind the machine is as important to the final consequence as the machine itself, which would seem to elevate its operations to the status of art, rather than mere mechanical reproduction, as is the case of an engraving of a painting. Where singularity, a uniqueness of vision may manifest itself, then we may be sure we are squarely on the plane of art. I am an old man now – these were also the opinions of my youth. To have held them then – in the prime of Gainsborough, Reynolds (that tyranny!) – was the rankest heresy and those in whom it might be detected exiled to the furthest and loneliest reaches of their profession. A most pure and exact transcription of the topographical, if so I may term it, was then deemed the acme of perfection. Such was the conventional wisdom of the day. Today, it is all different. We may be sure that the received opinions of fifty years hence shall equally be quite contradictory. But if the orthodoxy of my youth were to be given credence as the finality of perfection, then the Daguerreotype is truly the assassin of art. I, sir, should be redundant. Painting could go the way of…I do not know…the bow and arrow. Perhaps there are painters even now in Paris or Amsterdam, Rome or London, Madrid or (I do not say New York) Florence, who see their nemesis approaching, a black cloth over its head. I, sir, do not share this gloomy view and am inclined to believe that Painting has secured the services of a New Ally, rather than been confronted in the lists by a Deadly Adversary. (Are the English not the friends of the Americans?) Heliogravure an art? Why, certainly. But then painting is equally a science, an investigation of natural philosophy and a celebration of geometry where progress is founded upon experiment and discovery. In this regard, I should thank you for the loan of the plates of the funeral we but lately and sadly attended. In regard to the deadly enemy of Daguerreotypism, you are, I should say, in no wise mistaken when you identify him as Father Time. (Would that the causes of the late sickness were as easily discovered.) However, I venture to suggest that you are deluded when you assert that mechanical improvement shall vanquish him. I do not doubt that progress shall be made, and that soon, in the operation of your toy, but to shorten the period of exposure of the plates to the sun (say, even to a second or two) is not to strike down your enemy but to render yourself into his very clutches. You, sir, are then in far worse straits than ever you were before. I trust you shall have the indulgence to give me yet further space among your columns to elucidate this proposition, which may seem somewhat bizarre at first airing. *(You have and it does. – ed.)*

Painting, I should say, may as an activity be compared to a still pool. Meditated, mulled, and representing the world through the eyes and imaginative faculties of the artist, it cannot be said to have occurred at any definable moment – that is, it may *represent* a particular time or occasion, but it *is* not that occasion or moment and it also stands outside that time and is not confined by it. The Daguerreotype not only represents that moment, it *is* also that juncture or concatenation of time and circumstance and is subordinate to the laws of aging. It is not a pool, but a stream –its artefacts whirled helplessly along in the current. Even as you complete your heliogravure, *now* becomes *then*. When the process is 'improved' to the point of the operation occupying only the space of a few seconds – then is the vice of time merely tightened. A scene of Rembrandt, of Titian, vanquishes Time. In each of their paintings is nothing but grandeur or sublimity, however trivial or minor the subject. It is a timeless meditation. But in the Daguerreotype of today, as viewed in a hundred years' time, there shall be pathos only. A painting is immortal, the Daguerreotype is a reminder of death.

In private conversation, sir, you have remarked to me that the painter is limited, whereas the possibilities of the Daguerreotype are infinite. I venture to turn your proposition on its head: it is the heliogravist who is limited. You have no colours. (Do not talk to me of 'tint' for the plate.) Now, I do not speak of mere prettiness, but it is the gradation of tones, the merging of colours, the invention, use and siting of light in a painting which enable the cunning artist to employ Time as his servant, whereas the Daguerreotypist is the slave of process. By artful use of shade, a play with perspective, of oppositions in tone and line, of merging or of contrasting colours, the skilful painter may impart to his works the *illusion* of distance – as in a landscape – of motion and change, and because he may bestow on his work a direction in space he may also suggest a shift in the values and scale of Time as well, if I may give currency to an expression. I talk of the painter in oils or water-colour, who may achieve his effect aided or unaided by instruments and glasses, with his foregrounds of brown and his horizons of silver and blue. You, sir, know my passion is to draw but my pen and my ink – I own to a lesser extent – may also have the advantage of the Daguerreotypic image in this respect. (Have you, sir, no handier word for what you contrive to do?)

Finally, I would state the sibling relation as between Painting and Daguerreotype is as the relation between your Newspaper and a Drama, say, of Shakespeare. You would, I am sure of it, accurately report the true facts of the death of Hamlet's father, the detailed ramifications of the troublesome division and bequest of the estate of Lear (I can almost imagine your account), yet could you give us the whole Soul of Man? I do not think you could.

I have the honour to be, sir, your very humble obedient servant – but not the Sandglass's.

PIG MENS

Our plate of our own face even now is in the passage-boat to Macao. As to the arguments of our loved and respected correspondent, some tax our understanding greatly, and we shall seek him out for further explanation and enlightenment in private. Fiat lux *may be both our mottoes.* – SOLORIENS

CHAPTER XLII

Roaring fills his ears. Even if it were possible to open his eyes against the cloud of stinging spray, Gideon would see nothing in the darkness. His senses are dead. Even the skin of his face, continuously lashed for hours on end by the particles of spray, has lost feeling in a general numbness. There is just the regular up and down lurch of the ship – and Gideon is long past seasickness. Two feet of water cascade down the length of the tiny *Louisa,* knocking men off their feet and escaping only slowly through the scuppers. Not a sail has been left intact on the masts, the mainsail was torn to tatters hours ago, and the others followed in quick succession. The jury efforts rigged on Captain Elliot's expert orders gave way a little later, but not before they had got the cutter out of desperate trouble on the lee shore of some nameless island. Now the wind howls through the rigging as they scud along under bare poles. Gideon has never heard such a sound. Is it the ropes vibrating or simple force of the wind? He clings to the hand-rail as another torrent of water roars through the ship; he is barely able to keep his feet. He is, of course, soaked through. Dim figures rush about in the spray-laden gloom, but with purpose and resolution in their movements. Gideon trusts they would tell him if they were abandoning ship. Timing the next movement of the *Louisa* as she climbs seemingly endlessly up what must be a mountain of a wave, he stumbles and falls downhill on the slippery deck to the wheel. The helmsman has just been unlashed from his post and is endeavouring to restore the circulation to his limbs, while no less a personage than Commodore Bremer has taken the wheel. Elliot stands by the former subordinate who is now his equal as Joint Plenipotentiary. If there was ever any lurking sense of jealousy or rivalry, it has vanished now, blown away in the tempest and need to cooperate for common survival. The ship shudders as a wave strikes her beam, but then, between them, the two Plenipotentiaries fight to bring her round. Bremer looks grim, though the fear in the helmsman's face is not mirrored in his own. Elliot, though! The Plenipo is transfigured. Gideon has never seen him like this. Joy suffuses those careworn features, which the interpreter has rarely seen without some shadow of anxiety or inner conflict hidden behind the creased brow. Now all is simple – perilous, but simple. The wind and seas pose a far greater threat to the Plenipo's life than Commissioner Lin's men ever did, but he seems to find an exhilaration in the directness of the combat against the elements which he never knew when winning his victories at the Bogue and Canton.

'Mr Chase!' he bellows jovially in his interpreter's ear, 'I am quite sorry to have been instrumental in bringing you to this pass. How d'you do?'

'Very well, sir,' Gideon tries to shout back but salt has made his throat hoarse.

'Mr Chase came from his sickbed, Commodore.'

Bremer nods briefly.

'We'll keep running with the wind, Gordon. I have no idea as to our whereabouts, but I trust we are past the Ladrone islands.'

'God knows,' says Bremer gloomily, knowing his words will be carried away on the gale, but Gideon can read his lips in the glow of the storm-lantern. 'I trust so, at all events, Charles,' the commodore shouts back.

'A clear sea, Mr Chase,' Elliot yells into Gideon's ears with what he imagines is reassurance, 'and no matter if the waves are like mountains, we shall not founder. I have seamanship enough for that, I'll warrant. Hey, Gordon?' And Elliot's eyes dance with joy. Down slithers the ship again, on, on, on, down and down, until Gideon thinks she cannot possibly plunge deeper, but still deeper down in the trough of that monstrous sea she goes, blown down and sideways across the face of that mighty wall of water until at last, when Gideon thinks she must strike her bow into the very bed of the sea, she lifts her nose. Clouds of spray pass across the moon, and as a hole appears in the canopy, Gideon may see the huge mass of the wave towering over them, dark, smooth, and opaque, with a crest of foam at its summit, as high, he thinks, as the peak of Hong Kong.

'Oh, God preserve us.'

Now up she comes, born up irresistibly by the mass of waters, the deck tilting, men falling back in the stern, cannoning into the mast, the wheel, the Plenipotentiaries, each other, but Elliot has the wheel steady, she does not waver, right up that liquid slope, like a greyhound after a rabbit, on she climbs, ever upwards, till at last she seems she must be flying, shooting over the moon and spray which alternately blind and reveal, black or silver at the will of the wind. And there they are. They hang suspended, looking down in a sudden break on the valleys and mountains around. Then the spray blinds them again. A long moment they stay. Poise sustained. Elliot whoops like the thirteen-year-old middy he once was. Gideon feels sick for the first time in hours. He looks at Elliot again. 'I'll always remember him like this,' he says aloud, in absolute confidence that the hurricane wind will shred his words, which it does. But is there a wink of complicity in the Plenipo's eye? Down they start to drop, like a lead, and the gigantic helter-skelter begins once more.

In the recesses of the enormous waves there is a kind of peace, for they are sheltered, briefly, from the spray and foam, which flog them so mercilessly on the summits. At these moments the vessel seems a ghost-ship peopled by spirits, and isolation is complete. Is it his fancy, or does the brave little ship seem to be climbing the waves more slowly, lifting her bow to return from the abyss with a fraction more reluctance? She seems sluggish, lower in the water, tardier to respond to the Plenipo's guidance. Perhaps Elliot is tired. But Bremer frowns and for the first time Elliot looks serious.

A seaman, his bare feet purple, pads towards the wheel, not omitting even at this juncture of conflict with the elemental to touch his curl to the senior officers. Bremer takes the wheel, while Elliot follows the seaman down the vessel. He returns, shaking his head, for a shouted conference with Bremer. To Gideon he says, 'We have started, Mr Chase. A matter of a few planks, but she's filling. You may be of most use at the pumps. No seamanship is required, merely a strong back, and you'll free one of the sailors.'

'Willingly, Captain Elliot. I mean aye aye, sir.'

As he runs up the deck, which resembles nothing so much as a wooden slide, he notices for the first time that he is shivering in his wet clothes. Shuddering, more precisely. The work on the pumps will make the blood race round his system again. He hopes. And trusts.

As he arrives at the chain-pumps, he coincides with the lurch upwards in the wave's cycle. His ears are greeted with the awful sound of groaning planks. Can the vessel be breaking in half? Peering down, he sees water rushing in the hold, cascading backwards in a little ocean of its own as the *Louisa* at last lifts, while still more swills through the scuppers and down into her interior. Spray in the air is so fine that it is difficult to breathe, let alone see. When it clears, the men are still pumping furiously. Steady streams of sea-water spurt out, to be torn into spray in the wind. Gideon relieves a man from his post.

'Six feet of water in the hold,' the fellow shouts at him. 'Pump for your life, sir.'

But Gideon needs no urging. Stripping off his soaked shirt, which affords worse than no protection, he throws himself into the work. A little later he kicks off his shoes, and can no longer be distinguished from the seamen, for he is as sinewy as they, if a little paler-skinned. The rhythm of the strokes exerts a calming effect on him; much worse to be unemployed. He no longer tortures his eyes by looking at the sea through the spray, but regards instead the brimming hold. No doubt about it – despite their most valiant efforts – and Gideon works as hard as anyone, the water is slowly, almost imperceptibly gaining. Clank, clank, clank, go the pumps, but they only delay the inevitable. Now there's an object lesson in life, muses Gideon, still being keen on object lessons in life, and pausing to sneeze and wipe his nose with the back of his hand: it doesn't matter how small an advantage or disadvantage, credit or debit, may be – for only give it time and the accumulation will tell. Tip the balance fraction-ally to one side, with the weight of a feather, and the result is inevitable. Now, can this be true of human vice and human virtue, good and evil? Weak, deluded, not wholly bad men, men with substantial goodness in their natures, producing when

675

aggregated and afforded sufficient space and opportunity a colossal wickedness? Then, he consoles himself, imperfect humanity, flawed natures, men not irresistibly impelled to what is good, may if there exists the tiniest inclination to a tendency to good, combine to form a cause whose sublimity is beyond their attainment as individuals. Yet, as individuals, there may be little obvious difference between the respective adherents to good and bad, or their toleration of injustices. Straws and camel's backs. But what is good and what bad? Can it just be a matter of perspective, with one seeing it quite differently from another? Never mind camels, *his* back aches.

'Land ho!'

That mariner's cry, which usually rings so joyfully on a sailor's ear, strikes dread into every heart. The men at the pumps miss a stroke, all looking instinctively to their commander at the wheel. The wind works itself into a paroxysm, sheets of spray blind them all, and they must grip mast, bulwarks, or ropes to avoid being blown bodily away, such is its extraordinary force. For half a minute it is impossible to see your own hand before your face. When the ordeal is over, the wheel is blank, no guiding hand behind it. As horror fills them all, a hand grips the lowest spoke and little Elliot pulls himself up, followed by Bremer. Elliot laughs. The Commodore now comes forward, holding on tightly. 'The Plenipo is going to beach her,' he tells the crew. 'Find some sand, if we can. It is a gamble, men, but we cannot go on. She's working herself to pieces.'

The crew murmur their agreement – the only liberty (and in their canon of unswerving obedience to orders it does constitute gratuitous presumption) which they have taken so far.

Bremer takes Gideon aft with the cabin-boy. A petty officer volunteers to stand in the bow to guide them in, while a skeleton shift remain at the pumps. Gideon can hear a new sound, waves breaking on a shore. His teeth chatter, whether from fright or chill, he's not sure. The wind does seem to be dropping a little, though. A messenger comes from the look-out: dead ahead, cliffs to port, a small headland to starboard.

'We must get past this island, Mr Chase,' Elliot says, 'or I fear we are lost. The men have to get some canvas up or we shall be

676

blown on to that lee shore.'

Elliot, calm as if he was at a regatta in Portsmouth, directs the tacking. They beat and beat about. The jutting headland looms ever nearer.

'Gracious!' exclaims Gideon. 'I can see figures on the shore.'

'There is,' says Bremer drily, putting his hand on the young man's shoulder, 'no more engrossing a spectacle than to watch a ship fight for her life, while you are safe. I have seen a vessel tack all morning and afternoon in the Dead Man's Bay and finish a wreck on Chesil in the evening. It is but to delay the inevitable.'

Gideon gulps. The headland is within pistol-shot now, waves smashing against it, white and hissing. Elliot shouts to the men, spins the wheel, and they are past with some ten feet to spare. Gideon takes a deep breath.

'A miss,' calls Elliot cheerfully, 'is as good as a mile.'

'Splendid, Charles, old chap. Capital work,' shouts Bremer. The men cheer.

'Sandy beach, Mr Davenport thinks, to larboard, sir,' gabbles the cabin-boy, 'but a very narrow entrance.'

'We'll take it.'

Elliot brings them sharply about, and they drive in like an arrow. Dark cliffs flit past. The breakers are a roar: Elliot's face ecstatic. The boatswain Davenport, who must wish he was on his steamer, runs back, and with a shock which flings them all to the deck – all bar Elliot, whose chest is driven against the wheel – at last they strike. Even as he is slung to the deck, Gideon is amazed by the noise and force of their impact. He can clearly hear the stout planks splintering. He picks himself off the deck and, as he does so, the retiring wave pulls the *Louisa* back, the sand and shingle grating under her keel. Someone is groaning on the deck. Not Elliot, though he has to suppress a quick wince from the pain in his ribs.

'Quickly, now there's smart men,' he commands, 'over the bowsprit. Davenport, Stancliffe, do you take the injured man. Mr Chase, fasten this rope around your waist. I shall come last with Commodore Bremer.'

And, suiting his actions to his words, he kicks off his buckled shoes and makes a start with the buttons on his coat. The first men already struggle through the shallows. Gideon prepares to jump. He waits for the wave to retreat; it hisses and rattles like a snake, before launching himself into space. He lands on all fours and is swept painfully up the pebbles by the next wave, water going up his nostrils. Coughing and gasping, he scrambles on hands and knees through the seething, receding foam, and is pulled to safety by a strong hand. They watch the two shadows on the bow. Elliot, recognisable as the smaller one, waves Bremer to go; then, taking a last look back at the yacht, jumps himself.

Moments later, the entire complement are on dry land, wet but alive.

From The Hong Kong Guardian and Gazette

Tuesday July 27th, 1841

Vol. 1 No.6

The saints of old were in the salutary habit of regarding the trials sent them by the Lord as in the nature of tests designed to try the faith and as exercises for the soul, rather than as simple tribulations of the flesh. In just such spirit has our fledgling community here accepted the late visitations of the elements. To have inflicted upon our heads the one typhoon of the 21st was sufficient chastisement. To have sent us but five days later the second tempest of the 26th was the act of a stern Father. Yet is his Awful Justice tempered by Mercy, and his ways are Mysterious. We do believe there may be a deeper Good at the bottom of it all.

The first typhoon of the 21st July was of a force and duration unparalleled in our time on the coast and said to be the worst in living memory. We spent much of our days with the old *Monitor* in Canton, where these hurricanes, in God's Mercy, who has set a bourne on their roamings, may not extend. However, our friends in Macao never saw its like and the opinion is corroborated by the natives where the bazaar in Hong Kong has been altogether destroyed. The devastation wrought by the typhoon in the harbour of Hong Kong was frightful. The anchorage was crowded with shipping and junks which felt the full force of the elements, native and foreigner alike. Many of the ships were utterly destroyed, being smashed to driftwood on the rocks and shore, or capsized by the giant waves, while the force of the wind and seas left one vessel marooned some hundreds of yards up the hillside where it had been blown by main force! Even the large men of war and transports in many cases broke loose of their moorings and the crews had to fight for their lives. Some of these, alas, were forfeit.

The *Nemesis,* iron-hearted as well as plated, chose to ride the hurricane in Kowloon Bay with her engines running at half speed into the storm, which sufficed to keep her stationary and out of harm's way. As is highly characteristic of the course these hurricanes follow, the period of fierce winds and torrential rain was followed by a short interval of light airs and clear skies, when it was possible with impunity to venture out of shelter, before, in less than the elapse of an hour, the full fury of the elements was known again; so that it may be seen the violence of the heavens was not as an unrelieved or unbroken infliction and it would not be altogether exaggerated to state that the island knew not two but *four* separate storms. Of course, the seas were still heavy in the harbour, the waters having been agitated both inside the roadstead and outside in the open sea where they swept through both ends of the anchorage, so that it was impossible to land from the vessels. In the morning the shore-line and anchorage presented the sorriest scene we ever saw – and hope never to witness its likes again. Bodies and wreckage littered the beach, while dismasted ships lay helpless and crippled in the middle of the harbour. The steamers were better able to cruise for survivors of the shipwrecks than the other vessels and, once again, proved their worth over all other descriptions of small craft. The *Nemesis* ranged outside the harbour and cruised in the vicinity of the small neighbouring islands, scouring the seas and beaches for any who might have escaped the wrath of the elements. They discovered the captain of the *Prince George* transport on a small islet, which he refused to leave under any circumstances, even threatening violence against his would-be rescuers, until he had found the body of his drowned wife.

On the land, the town presented one picture of unrelieved chaos and destruction. All the mat-shed structures were without exception blown down and, in many instances, had vanished entirely by the morning. The more substantial buildings, however, of brick, tile, and masonry, withstood the winds with, in most cases, but trifling damage of slates and tiles blown off or windows broken. Jardine's Town at East Point escaped largely unscathed and has subsequently served as the headquarters for arranging the efforts directed towards the reconstruction of the town and the relief of the pressing wants of its population.

The coming of the second, lesser typhoon five days later could not have been better timed for frustrating the efforts of civilians and military to set matters right again if the enemies of the colony had planned it. Less potent in itself, this disturbance had its consequences aggravated by the circumstance that most of the population had to withstand its ravages and the rigours of the ensuing rain deprived of any shelter whatever by the first visitation of the elements. Such measures of reconstruction as had already been set in train subsequent to the 21st were in addition made utterly vain and redundant when the second typhoon damaged them beyond repair. The town and harbour are still much knocked about, but we are in anticipation of works being speedily set in train which may even hasten the development of the public works in the colony beyond their previous and quite rapid pace.

Recall of Captain Elliot. For the last five days Macao and Hong Kong have been alive with rumours which bade fair to rival even the effects of the typhoons for the speculation and interest which they aroused. These concerned the fate of Captain Elliot and, some believed, even his impending dismissal and the repudiation in no uncertain terms of his actions by Lord Palmerston. Such have now proved all too well founded. We believe we do not flatter ourselves unduly when we say that the first premonitions of such event initially appeared in our last of seven days ago. It was owing to our close friendship and connection with certain merchant gentlemen that we were thus able to anticipate when, not for the first time, commercial intelligence proved superior to the system of the servants of government. Captain Elliot would thus have learned of his relief from his responsibilities at his breakfast-table, while he perused the *Hong Kong Guardian and Gazette,* perhaps even with a smile of scorn and contumely.

The growing displeasure of milord would have been manifest in the opinions conveyed in the succession of official despatches to the contents of which the Plenipotentiary alone would have been privy. Even now, Sir Henry Pottinger is on his way with the despatches and the letters of authority which shall finally remove this most eccentric and dilatory agent of government from the scene of his misdeeds. His errors were those of omission rather than commission. By failing to exploit to the full the opportunities won for the Crown by British Arms – the men and officers of the Services whose successes and achievements owed nothing or little to his direction – he substantially betrayed the trust and authority reposed in him. The failure to press the Expeditions up the Peiho in 1840, the handing back Chusan, the inexplicable retirement from Canton earlier this year, were all so many instances of incompetence and vacillation, which doubtless amazed Lord Palmerston as much as they frustrated the Plenipotentiary's commanders at the time and place of their occurrence. The effect, manner, and practical consequences of Captain Elliot's withdrawal amount, we do not doubt, to a recall in disgrace. To secure the Chinese as much as possible, while systematically neglecting the interest of his Country, seemed with him to be as much the proof as it was the end of a rational policy. The possible circumstance of his inexperience or unfamiliarity with the wiles and deceits of the mandarins cannot reasonably be advanced as excuses or extenuations in Captain Elliot's defence, since he had resided on this coast in one capacity or the other (and his first post was the humble one of Master Attendant on Lord Napier, from which in light of his subsequent actions it appears he was quite unfitted to rise) for nearly seven years to the day of this issue. It is notorious that he intrigued most scandalously to secure the dismissal of his chief, Sir George Robinson, in 1836, having been the author and instigator of a most irregular correspondence with the Foreign Office behind his superior's back, and that he made every effort shamelessly to ingratiate himself with Lord Auckland and Lord Palmerston (short, it goes without saying, of actually obeying the latter's express instructions) – and, all in all, we do not find it in ourselves to pity him meted out with his just deserts.

From THE LIN TIN BULLETIN AND RIVER BEE

Tuesday, July 28, 1841
Vol.4 No.15

It has ever been the peculiar fate of the prophet that he shall be without honour in his own country. As with those grim and unyielding greybeards of old, so it has proved in the modern instance of Captain Elliot, who bears an altogether more percipient and merciful character than the Ahabs or Daniels of the Good Book, still less the cantankerous Biblical old gentleman who devised the fearful fate of setting the bears on the children. No one could deny, nevertheless, that Canton has not been as the fiery furnace or lion's den for many of us, besides the gallant Plenipo. (Who have walked, too, through the Valley of Death at Hong Kong.) It is our own strong and well-considered belief that the vested interests of Manchester, that pernicious and hard-aspected lobby of traders as piratical under their beaver-hats and top-coats as the unknown gentleman who has lately been in the habit of making so many depredations on our local shipping – that cut-throat crew, we say, have been responsible for the accomplishment of this fell and woefully ill-considered purpose. Instrumental, we do not doubt it for a moment, in pouring poison into the ear of Lord Palmerston has been Mr J-, formerly of the house of J- & M-, who has very likely proved a deadlier enemy to the Chinese in White-hall than ever he could have been, even proscribed, on these coasts.

Our ever scrupulous contemporary's account of the demise of Captain Elliot was characterised by all his customary adherence to fidelity. All the while the Plenipotentiary is supposed to be gnashing his teeth and rending his uniform of blue and gold over the *Monitor's* (Excuse us – the *Guardian's)* report of his recall, he was in reality conducting an heroic battle – against the elements. So far from his enjoying the smallest opportunity to read a newspaper, any journal would have been ripped to shreds the moment he produced it from his pocket (always assuming that post-captains, Plenipotentiaries and such like are in the habit of carrying newspapers in their pockets). Why, the very stout canvas of the sails was torn asunder by the wind as if it had been the flimsiest paper. As all the world knows, Captain Elliot and Commodore Bremer were caught in the first and most violent typhoon, of the 21st *ult.,* while at sea, and despite all the extraordinary coolness and smartness exhibited by Captain Elliot in his efforts, seamanship which won him the hearts of every man jack of the little *Louisa's* complement, he was forced to beach the ship on an unknown island, probably far to the south-west of Hong Kong. Struggling through the breakers, the officers and men ascended from the exposed beach, lashed by the full fury of the typhoon, and – chilled and half-drowned – found such shelter as they could in the lee of a formation of large rocks halfway up the hillside where they passed the night in conditions, as may be imagined, of the most acute cold and discomfort, but heartily glad to be alive. When morning broke, they gazed from their elevation upon the most awful and desolate scene it is possible to conceive, with ships and junks wrecked or foundering, spars and planks upon the beaches, and the naked bodies of the wretches who perished in the convulsion carried on the face of the dirty, white-capped sea. Strange to relate, and we have it on the best and most immediate authority, it was the pangs of *thirst* and not hunger which now began to torment the little company, shivering though they were, with not more than a pair of trowsers apiece to cover their nakedness. We can only assume that salt had exacerbated the dryness of their throats. Officers and men alike presented a picture of dishevelment which would have been ludicrous had it not occurred under circumstances so dangerous and tragic. The high officers, especially, appeared in the most unlikely guise, stripped of gilt, of braid, stocks, and cravats, fine shoes and silk stockings as well as magnificent hats, and barefooted and naked to the waist, they appeared in no wise different from common seamen or street arabs (especially in the case of Captain Elliot, who is of slight build), save for the air of authority which still clung to them and of which no ordeal could strip them, and the deference naturally paid them by the men. Within an hour, they had spotted some Chinese fishermen on the strand and signalled to them (the officers judging it better to take the risk of discovery by the Chinese, which in course of time was inevitable, rather than trusting to the mercy of the elements or remaining marooned). At this point it perhaps is incumbent upon us to add that the party had escaped *altogether* without resources, being unprovided with arms of any description – other than the offensive or defensive uses to which Jack may turn nature's endowment of the four limbs – even to the extent of a clasp-knife, as well as being wholly unprovided with food or raiment. They were soon surrounded on the beach by the natives. Now on the head of this man, Captain Elliot, was a bounty of $100,000 promised by the mandarins these many months, while in lesser sums according to their various degrees there was blood-money on the heads of his lieutenants and subordinates. To confound the *Guardian* according to the system of its own estimation and, better and most irrefutably so, according to the nicest scale of values, the worth the Chinese themselves set upon the heads of their foes, Elliot's was considered the most valuable while that of Commodore Bremer, friend of the Free Traders, whose declared aim has always been to reduce Canton and its forts to rubble, was by now worth sensibly less dollars than that of the Flowery Flag interpreter. Fortunately, all clouds tending to possess silver linings, their appearance was not such as to excite suspicion that they were Great Barbarian Eyes, and for the sum of $3000 the fishermen were prevailed upon to take the Plenipotentiaries and a few others to Macao. Three thousand! When Elliot alone was worth thirty times that without incurring any risk of detection and punishment by the mandarins!

At this point a circumstance occurred causing matters to look the reverse of happy when the bodies of Chinese were discovered lashed to spars, which greatly excited and disturbed the fishermen, who at first were inclined to suppose they had been bound thus by the British and murdered in the water in cold blood. However, the rapid interposition of the interpreter soon allayed their suspicions when he was able to point out to these simple men that the drowned Chinese had in all probability themselves tied their bodies to the wood for purposes of flotation and buoyancy before entrusting themselves to the waves from their foundering junks. During the course of the tedious journey to Macao, which took the best part of a day, the bizarre passengers (bizarre in that craft) were obliged to spend much of their time out of sight, which sorely tried their patience as the posture forced them to rub their noses among the fish-scales and bloody innards with the doubtful benefit of some stinking oil-cloths to cover them. At one point during the passage, their junk was intercepted by a Chinese vessel of war in the vicinity of St John island. Preferring to confront their captors boldly in the knowledge of certain detection, rather than to be taken in the ignominious positions of conceal-ment, what was the surprise of Captain Elliot and Commodore Bremer together with their staffs when the captain of the war-junk coolly regarded them with his arms folded on his chest from his quarter-deck, with fifty yards of space intervening between their vessels, before sheering away to leave them unmolested but perplexed in the extreme. No very obvious explanation came to mind at the time to the foreign castaways, nor subsequently has a plausible reason for the action of the Chinese commander suggested itself to them. *(Other perhaps than a very laudable desire not to delay the restoration to comfort and safety of some very battered mariners – the well-known readiness of foreign ships and their crews to preserve life at sea and rescue Chinese beleaguered by the watery element inspiring a reciprocal kindness in the breast of the nameless Chinese captain, who might himself have once owed his life in some mortal peril to the interposition of foreigners.* – PURSUER). Certainly fear could not account for his strange hesitation as it was perfectly apparent that little or no resistance was to be apprehended. A few hours later Captain Elliot was stepping on to the safety of the Praia at Macao, followed by his ragged band. The compradore at the godown was able to furnish them with some oddments of clothing cast off by Portuguese sailors which answered the purposes of decency if not ornament, and in but a short space the Plenipotentiaries were proceeding up the hill to the fort, most strangely habited, Captain Elliot in a pair of the large canvas trowsers of a common seaman, the constricting vest of a cabin-boy, and two left shoes, while Commodore Bremer's striped trousers, which we have it on the best authority had a large rent in the seat, flapped about his knees in the steady breeze. Recognising the faces of the high officers with remarkable astuteness under all the circumstances, the Portuguese officer on duty was all for turning out the guard, who had to be restrained from presenting arms and saluting by Captain Elliot and Commodore Bremer as they presented such a truly ludicrous appearance.

In due course a ship was sent for the remaining men.

Arrivals. In Hong Kong harbour, the *Phlegethon*. This interesting craft, sister ship and in all respects twin of the

Nemesis, entered the harbour under her own steam a few days past. She was constructed at Birkenhead in the yard of Messrs Forester and under the supervision of the designer of the *Nemesis,* Mr Laird, of the Birkenhead Iron Works Co. She must have found the harbour pretty knocked up, but the surprise was mainly confined to those who beheld her, for the *Nemesis* had passed through the eastern mouth or Lye Mun an hour or so before and to all intents and purposes was now steaming through the western straits of the anchorage, having circumnavigated the island at the extraordinary speed, we should calculate, of 40 knots. Her appearance occasioned much rubbing of eyes, even the *Nemesis* being thought incapable of showing such a clean pair of heels. As is the case with her older, but no uglier, sister, she is classed as a vessel of the Company's Bengal Marine. Her attachment to the force is worth ten regiments, the light-draught iron-steamers having proved themselves of even greater utility than the heavier wooden steam-ships. The *Nemesis* had recently arrived from Macao, where she had ridden out the second typhoon in the anchorage.

The *Phlegethon,* alas, was no harbinger of good news, for either Captain Elliot or, indeed, his enemies. In the official mails she bore notification that Lord Palmerston had to disapprove of the Convention made at Chuenpi in January between Keshen and Captain Elliot. Now, our contemporary and his patrons (for the organ is merely an old thing by a new name) may wish to secure the replacement of Captain Elliot by a chief whose simpler measures would consult their interests more efficaciously but, whether they like it or not, do it with a good or ill grace, they must own that Hong Kong is the child of the Plenipo. He alone created it, and from out of nothing. The choice of situation, the decision to press for its cession, the bold measures of public works, the land sales, the appointment of the Government Officers, the present burgeoning of efforts – all are due to him. Without the Plenipo's personal intervention, there would now be no little town at Jardine's settlement, no profits to be made through speculation with the land, no warehouses, no trade.

Yet their Great Ally and Protector, Palmerston, now wishes to remove all this from them! (Yet if Palmerston is the enemy of Captain Elliot, we warrant that he has a powerful protector in the Duke of Wellington, who has always counselled moderation and a course of conciliation in dealing with the Chinese – the Statesman and National Hero who gave his protection to the Catholics will assuredly shelter a former and zealous subordinate from the wolves of Manchester).

Will the Free Traders render Hong Kong without a squeak? Nay, we think they will show rather more fight than did the Chinese!

Beware, ye who would replace the Captain – he alone brought his craft safely to the beach. You are all in the same boat as he!

A Jerem-iad. We confess ourselves heartily tired of hearing the adherents to the party of the Free Traders descanting on the topic of their own liberality and large-mindedness. Their behaviour is more than a little like that of the tiger in his indulgence, who will permit the jackal to take his pickings after he has satiated his own mighty hunger. If it did not suit the Free Traders to have markets open, they would not scruple to close them to interlopers. It is merely *cheaper* and more *profitable* to act the part of the Universal Benefactor. Such are the discoveries of the Economists.

In the old times, before the emancipation of the Americas, the Home Fleet (those wooden walls so frequently appearing among our contemporary's columns) constituted the most formidable expense for the Government of England. The first, second and third rates each required to bring them into being at the Dockyards a forest of oak – yet in order to deny her colonies and their markets and produce to the rival Powers, to France, to Holland, to Spain, Britannia must possess those line of battle ships, each costing almost as much as a palace, for their cannon it was which decided the issue in those grand battles of Nelson's day.

Now what do we have? Why, the Navy is cheap! Cheaper by far than the army! The 74-or 120-gun monsters of fifty years past are outnumbered by the sloops, the brigs, the corvettes, the light frigates, and now the steamers – that is, the vessels of the *foreign* stations. These are the real guarantors of Britannia's wealth, who shall protect our Mr J-s or our Mr M-s, not to say their valuable trade, from pirates and potentates such as Lin. It is not *utilitarian* in a material point of view to spend millions when, by opening a few markets, the entire Home Fleet of Nelson's time could have been halved at a stroke! Thus, appositely for the doctrine of numbers, of the sum of the greatest good, it is the many small ships (Oh, democracy!) and not the few aristocrats of the battle-line which protect Britannia's Empire.

New naval academy. This has been founded at Portsmouth harbour. HMS *Excellent* shall be the Royal Navy's new gunnery school. She is an old first-rate with the masts taken out of her, but we warrant she shall be a reforming and revitalising influence on the ways of the fighting sea-farers. Until now, the guns of a ship and the evolutions of the gun-crews in the handling of the ship's ordnance had been matters left to the discretion of their individual captains and gunnery officers. The use of sights (or their absence), the timing of the discharges as the ship rolled, the aiming-points on the enemy, whether mast or hull, the making-up of the cartridges and the combinations of shot, had all been peculiar to each vessel and captain. In many cases, we have it on the best authority, the gunners operated according to principles handed down from the days of Blake, if not Drake himself. But no more – the lore and craft of the veterans shall be reduced to a scientific and uniform system, with what results we have yet to discover. The steamer captains of our acquaintance are as a man enthusiastic as to the founding of the *Excellent,* the officers of the sailing-vessels less so. The school, so they say, is not within the tradition of their service.

Yet how strange is this Tradition. When we first took our dinner in the ward-room we were astonished to see the officers remain seated when Mr Vice proposed the Loyal Toast and more so to see them Bless the Queen and drain the glass without rising from their chairs. 'Oh, sir, this is our tradition, I am surprised you did not know,' one of the young gentlemen of the gun-room informed us with a distinctly superior air. This ancient tradition was not, as one might suppose, founded by Alfred, but a dispensation of the late William IV, who struck his royal head on a ship's beam some ten years ago!

If our esteemed correspondent and colleague seems to have water on the brain we trust that our subscribers and friends shall understand the reason. – ed.

CHAPTER XLIII

'You are sure, quite certain, that it must be he? Oh, how can it be? It is too terrible.'

'For your years and your prodigious attainments, you are a darned noodle.' Walter neatly folds, rather than rips in half, the *Hong Kong Guardian and Gazette* of August 3rd, 1841, which we know, of course, to be volume 1 number 7, and passes it to Gideon, who is every bit as distracted as his words would suggest.

'Oh, the terrible, terrible news. I may hardly credit it.'

'Will you hold your tongue?'

'How can you exhibit such callousness? I, of all people, know it is assumed merely, but...'

'It is not. And you do not know me well enough to say so. I could not say it of myself with any degree of certainty. As to callousness, it is that of our friend in question which passes belief.'

690

'Surely, there must be some mistake?'

'Read for yourself.'

The apprehension of the leader of the band chiefly responsible for the daring piracies around the waters of Hong Kong, which, we may reveal, occurred this forenoon a matter of a few hours before we had concluded our operations at the press, will rejoice alike those whose habit or necessity it is to travel between that settlement and Macao as much as those permanently fixed in either place, who have the interests of the new Crown Possession at heart. This bold malefactor was caught in flagrante delicto, *his sword still reeking with the innocent blood of his victims, on the decks of the craft he had all but seized. The capture of the pirate-leader was entirely owing to the vigilance and alertness of the officers and crew of the* Phlegethon, *the more commendable in that the vessels and customs of the waters in which she presently finds herself were alike novel to them, although the captain was first alerted by Lieutenant Oliveira of His Portuguese Majesty's Navy, whose suspicions were excited by the strange arrangement of the sails of the lorcha in a secluded situation by Cheung Chau island, long notorious as little more than a nest of pirates. Lieutenant Oliveira, the aide-de-camp of the Governor of Macao, was – unhappily for himself as matters transpired (which we shall shortly see), but happily for the public – afforded passage on the steamer to Macao, whence he was returning after an inspection of Hong Kong. We should not like to call him a 'spy' for* de mortuis nil nisi bonum.

As the Phlegethon *approached, great activity was discerned on the deck of the lorcha and, when the glass was applied, a general brandishing of weapons observed. Full steam on both wheels imparted an extraordinary velocity to the* Phlegethon, *which veritably seemed to fly through the water, while the rascals ahead endeavoured to pile on all canvas. Too late! She was upon them. Choosing not to put out boats but to come alongside, the captain turned the steamer when it seemed she was on the verge of squarely ramming the lorcha. There then occurred a circumstance tragic to a degree which a little patience and prudence on the part of the young officer in question might have averted, the pirates being taken and unprovided with any means of eluding capture. However, not for the first time, discretion was shown not always to be the companion of valour among the military caste, or at least its younger members. Heedless of the remonstrances of the men and cries of warning from the officers,*

*Lieutenant Oliveira jumped from the bridge of the steamer on to the
starboard paddle-box and with a single spring was on the deck of the
lorcha. Drawing his sword, one more suited to the ceremonial duties of
the aide, for which we doubt his temperament fitted him, than the needs
of a boarding-party, he advanced upon the pirate-leader. This latter
evaded his blow and, as Lieutenant Oliveira's blade shivered against the
mainmast of the lorcha, stepped coolly in, burying a dagger to its hilt in
the breast of this unfortunate Portuguese officer, who directly fell dead
upon the deck. Perceiving the fate of Lieutenant Oliveira, the captain of
the steamer ordered a marine furnished with one of the new rifles to pick
off the pirate-leader for him, which he did, the man falling severely,
though not mortally, wounded as the ball took effect in his chest. The fate
of their leader impressed itself so disagreeably upon the pirates that they
offered no further resistance to the marines and blue-jackets. They were
all clapped in irons and taken to the gaol of Hong Kong where they lie
presently, awaiting trial and, no doubt, execution.*

*A circumstance which at first greatly puzzled their captors and which
no doubt principally contributed to the band's success in eluding capture
thus long in these crowded waters was the absence of a second vessel by
the pirated ship. The efforts of the private vessels hired by the merchants
of Hong Kong had been directed towards scouring the neighbouring
waters and islands for a trim pirate-vessel when the actual method
employed by the villains was to embark on their chosen prey as deck-
passengers at Hong Kong before rising upon a signal from their leader.*

*This chieftain, a villainous-looking fellow with a pronounced cicatrix
on the left cheek, sturdily refused to volunteer his name but his identity
has subsequent to his capture been disclosed as a half-caste of Macao,
named Remedios.*

'Gracious heavens!'

Walter has remained silent during Gideon's faltering reading,
although he has had a puff or two at his cigar. Outside can be
heard hammering of masons and scrape of shovels, sounds
already so familiar on the ear of the residents of this island that
they register only as a background lullaby, the infant colony's
own version of the liquid bird–call and musical waters of less
mercantile frontiers.

'D'you know, Gid, strange to own, but I allow I can't grudge
paying the old villain his fifty cents. That's the most striking

piece of intelligence I have yet read. It is a prodigious irony, is it not?'

'I am sure I don't know what you are talking about.'

'My dear Gid, to read about ourselves, almost, among our rival's columns. I had no conception it might be Remedios.'

'Poor Remedios. What will they do with him?'

'Hang him and good riddance. The fellow is an unmitigated rascal.'

'He has served us well.'

'And doubtless feathered his own nest while he was at it. The scandal! Can you conceive of the disgrace if his connection with us is discovered?'

'It is my calculation that he would have laid down his life in service of us.'

'I cannot conceive of the circumstances in which he could have aided me – other than if his own skin had been threatened, when he would be acting to preserve his own life in the first instance. Damn him, I say, I owe him nothing.'

'Well, I shall not stand by and do nothing. You greatly disappoint me, Walter.'

Gideon Chase, Esq. to the Marine Magistrate at Hong Kong

Sturtevant's Hotel
Hong Kong
August 6th, 1841

My dear Lieutenant Pedder,

I have the honour to write to you concerning the case of Pedro Remedios, who is presently incarcerated in the gaol of Hong Kong. This man is known to me as a first-rate seaman, rough and daring, it is true, and perhaps not over-nice in his choice of company or evincing due judiciousness in all his actions, but possessing, behind an exterior which may well strike those who do not know him as sullen and intransigent, a good and loyal heart. Under different circumstances and with a happier dispensation of the fates, I do not find it difficult to conceive of him performing sterling service on

693

the deck, maybe even the quarter-deck, of a British man-of-war.

Without entertaining the slightest desire to inform you of the nature of your duties – I entirely lack the presumption – I feel it incumbent upon me to point out that, contrary to accounts which have appeared in the local press and which now seem to have been accepted as the indisputable truth of the affair, no blood had been shed upon the lorcha prior to the arrival of the *Phlegethon,* while the act of Lieutenant Oliveira in jumping down on the vessel with a drawn sword, while that of a very gallant officer, was neither prudent nor considered, and there exist strong grounds for maintaining that Remedios acted in simple self-defence.

The crew and passengers of the lorcha are, of course, witnesses that an act of piracy by Remedios and his followers did in this instance take place, but there are no further proofs forthcoming that they were involved as principals or accessories in the series of earlier piracies in the vicinity of this island, if indeed these were all the responsibility of one band. While it is incontestable that Remedios has committed a serious misdemeanour, I trust that he shall not suffer the full rigour of the law on merely circumstantial or unreliable evidence, such as the testimony of such of his erstwhile followers as are willing to incriminate him under duress or in order to save their own necks. With regard to this, when I visited the gaol today to be turned away by the havildar on duty there, I heard the sounds of corporal punishment proceeding from the yard, the sound of the rattan and the cries of men being quite unmistakable.

In conclusion, sir, I appeal to your sense of fair play, of Britishness, and ask you not to succumb to any prejudice on this issue.

I have etc.

G. Chase

Office of the Marine Magistrate
Hong Kong
August 7th, 1841

Sir,

I have the honour to be instructed by the Marine Magistrate to reply to your letter of yesterday's date. While the Marine Magistrate considers your communication to open a most irregular channel of correspondence, he understands your feelings on the subject and assures you of his best attention at all times. He cannot comment on the merits of the case before him, other than to say that he has formed no opinion and will form none, except on the facts of the case. He believes those facts with which he has been acquainted to be correct in all essential particulars.

With regard to the action of the guard, he was correctly performing his duty in denying you entry to the gaol. The employment of the rattan in particular and corporal punishment in general are part of the criminal code of this settlement, but Lieutenant Pedder believes your ears must have deceived you on this occasion, as there was no such punishment recorded to have been inflicted in the register of the gaol that day. The use of all descriptions of torture was, of course, expressly prohibited by Captain Elliot in his enactment regulating the mode of government appropriate to the Chinese emigrants to this island, which stated that they were in all other respects to be governed according to their own customs and usages.

I have, sir, etc.

G. Lena
Assistant Harbour Master

Enclosures

Marine Magistracy
Hong Kong
August 6th, 1841

Sir,

I have the honour to bring to your attention the case of the alleged pirate, Pedro Remedios, who claims to be a citizen of Macao. I understand this man shall be brought from the gaol on the 8th *inst.* for trial before you. I must dispute your claim to jurisdiction over him, as he is a Portuguese citizen, who was taking passage to his place of residence at the time of his arrest. As the schooner was 18 miles (nautical) from Macao at the time of the incident and his ensuing capture, the jurisdiction must reside in the Governor of Macao. However, I need hardly remind you, the officer slain during the boarding was in the Portuguese service and not, therefore, under the protection of the Crown.

Pray consider me, sir, as one at all times ready to consult your interests entirely.

Wm Pedder (Signed)
Protector of Chinese (Fisherfolk)
Harbour Master and Marine Magistrate at Hong Kong

Marine Magistracy
Hong Kong
August 7th, 1841

Sir,

I have the honour to acknowledge receipt of your communication of the 6th *inst.* I have to reply to your points under the following heads, in the order in which they were raised:

1 – Those apprehended in Acts of Piracy on the high seas are by the common consent and custom of nations to be tried and, if proven guilty, punished by those who have succeeded in detecting and apprehending them. This holds as well in the South China Sea as the Spanish Main.

2 – By their infamous acts, those engaged in piracy, without Letters of Marque, forfeit any claim to the Protection of the Law of Nations. They retain their rights under Natural Law.

3 – That the lorcha was nearer in distance to Portuguese soil than British at the time of the boarding is of inconsiderable significance, as the interception took place on the high seas. The captain of the *Phlegethon* confirms his position at the time, which has been erroneously reported as Cheung Chau island. I try this case in virtue of my office as Marine Magistrate and not as Harbour Master at Hong Kong.

4 – Lieutenant Oliveira embarked on the *Phlegethon* in a private capacity and not in an official or public role and therefore, as a guest, enjoyed the privilege of protection from his hosts. Remedios is tried not for resisting arrest by an agent or servant of the Crown but for the murder of a civilian.

5 – Admiral da Silveira Pinto has personally expressed his keen interest in this case and requested for it to be tried in a British court. The sentence of death, if passed, shall be passed by HBM's Plenipotentiary in China.

I need hardly assure you, my dear sir, that all the proper forms and precedents shall be adhered to most scrupulously that the accused may receive a fair trial. In conclusion, I take the opportunity of reciprocating your sentiments and assure you of my continuing pains to regard your interests.

I am, sir, your most obedient servant,

Wm Pedder (Signed)
Harbour Master and Marine Magistrate at Hong Kong
Protector of Chinese (Fisherfolk)

From # The Hong Kong Guardian and Gazette

August 10th, 1841

Vol. 1 No.8

Regina v Remedios

The above case was heard in the court of the Marine Magistrate and consequential upon the public interest aroused by the particular circumstances of this affair, there was a large press of numbers in the Public Gallery with the consequence that the vast majority of those who attended had to stand in the open air. As an unlooked for and happy contingency of the late typhoons, the great devastation wrought by those disturbances, which had afflicted the entire colony, had not spared the courthouse of the Marine Magistrate, which had suffered the extreme indignity of having its roof blown quite away. The proceedings were therefore transferred to a temporary mat-shed built without walls, which enabled an infinitely greater number of gentlemen, and interested Chinese, to view and hear the case than would otherwise have been so within the original and more straitened precincts of the court.

We ourselves discovered our situation to be within the 'walls', so-called, of the court, that is, at least sheltered from the sun's oppressive rays by the building's thatch, and within the bounds of an imaginary line which might be extended between the corner-posts, yet our predicament was unenviable and prejudicial in the extreme to our taking notes of the proceedings, such was the jostling and press of the throng around and behind us. This was neither conducive to order nor decency and if our account should appear to have any shortcomings with respect to accuracy or completeness, we beg our readers to remember the circumstances in which we were obliged to labour. We most respectfully recommend to the authority charged with the ordering of these matters that a separate and unimpeded position be made available to the chroniclers of its doings.

Nevertheless, we present the following in good conscience.

Marine Magistrate – Have the prisoner brought up.

Sergeant of Marines – Bring the prisoner up.

Marine Magistrate – How do you plead to the charges brought against you?

Marine Magistrate – You must answer me.

Marine Magistrate – Mr Teixeira, direct the prisoner to answer me. He must answer me.

Interpreter – *commands the prisoner in Portuguese.* Prisoner declines to respond. Interprcter addresses him in the Chinese dialect. Prisoner remains silent.

Marine Magistrate – I direct that a plea of Not Guilty be entered in the Court. Clerk of the Court, record that.

Mr Lena – Yes, sir.

Marine Magistrate – Major Caine, you may read the charges preferred against the accused.

Major Caine – Pedro Remedios, you are duly charged that on the -th of the month previous you, together with parties known and unknown, conspired to seize the schooner *Albertine,* that you did effect the accomplishment of this illegal and violent act, that during the commission of it you were surprised by the *Phlegethon* steamer cruising for pirates, that when a boarding-party led by Lieutenant Oliveira boarded the schooner you stabbed Lieutenant Oliveira in the side, so as to cause his death, and further resisted arrest. You are also charged with the piracies of the *Hebe, Water Witch,* and *Caroline,* and numerous murders and arsons both ashore and at sea in which your accomplices have incriminated you.

Marine Magistrate – What does he say?

Interpreter – Sir, I do not wish to say this word.

Major Caine – Take the prisoner down.

Marine Magistrate – Take the prisoner down. Now call the first witness. *(Oath administered by Mr Lena.)*

Major Caine – You are John Jones, captain of the *Wellesley's* top mast?

Jones – Formerly was, sir, thank'ee, sir. Seconded boatswain of the *Phlegethon,* sir, to replace Mr Cartwright, sir, on Mr Pedder's recommendation, sir. Thank'ee, Mr Pedder.

Marine Magistrate – Silence in the court. Answer Major

Caine's questions with a 'yes' or 'no'. You were a good seaman, Jones.

Jones – Aye aye, sir. *(Laughter.)*

Marine Magistrate – Silence in the court.

Major Caine – Jones, you stood on the wheel of the steamer as Lieutenant Oliveira went across.

Jones – Yes, sir.

Major Caine – What did you see?

Marine Magistrate – You may answer, Jones.

Jones – Aye aye, sir. *(Laughter.)* I saw him stab the Portyougoose lieutenant, sir.

Major Caine – Who stabbed Lieutenant Oliveira?

Jones – The man what stood there in irons, sir. The cove with the squint and scar, sir.

Major Caine – Thank you, Jones, you may step down. You have done your duty.

Marine Magistrate – Call the next witness.

Mr Lena – Call the next witness.

Sergeant at Arms – Call the next witness.

Major Caine – You are Hop Ah Fa, native of Singapore, now resident in Jardine's Bazaar, a ship chandler in the native junk-trade?

Interpreter – *translates.*

Hop – Yes.

Major Caine – Where were you on the – th *ult.?*

Hop – I was on the schooner.

Major Caine – What was your business there?

Hop – I was recruited to rise on a signal and overpower the captain and mates.

Major Caine – *(addressing Marine Magistrate)* – Sir, do you note that. This man did not design murder.

Marine Magistrate – Very well.

Major Caine – Who recruited you?

Hop – The accused.

Major Caine – You may step down.

Hop – Am I free?

Interpreter – No.

Marine Magistrate – Bring up the prisoner.

Mr Lena – Bring up the prisoner.

Sergeant at Arms – Bring up the prisoner.

Marine Magistrate – Pedro Remedios, I find you guilty of murder and piracy on the high seas, for which the penalty is death. The Plenipotentiary shall confirm and pass sentence. May God have Mercy on your Soul.

The accused received intelligence of his doom from Mr Teixeira with every sign of apathy and, indeed, the most perfect indifference. We have to regard him from his manner and appearance as the most perfect specimen of a thorough-going piratical rascal we ever saw, which in our experience of these matters, which fortunately has been inextensive, is not always the case when beardless striplings of appearances positively cherubic have stood accused of the most revolting and sanguinary crimes. The villain cast a most perfect glower on us as he left (we had just completed a line in our pocket-book) such that we will heartily congratulate ourselves on our good fortune in never having discovered ourselves in such unfortunate circumstances that he might have encompassed a mischief towards us.

A disturbance was made in the body of the court during the course of proceedings when the Chinese Hop Ah Fa was testifying. Consternation, which had spread through the ranks of the spectators at the thought that the remnants of Remedios's band might even then be meditating some desperate design to rescue their leader, was soon succeeded by a very general sensation of disgust when the author of the interruption was perceived to be a foreigner. This misguided young gentleman had to be forcibly removed by the marine guard under their lieutenant, who handled him with a gentleness and consideration which his outburst little deserved. We do know him, and we are happy to state it, as an estimable, if deluded, young man, and the circumstance that he succumbed a few hours later to an ague which had lain dormant some weeks subsequent to his being shipwrecked may explain, if it does not extenuate, his eccentric behaviour.

Arrival of the new Plenipotentiary. This happy and auspicious event occurred, as all at Macao know, but a day and a half ago. Sir Henry Pottinger and Admiral Sir William Parker, together with their respective staffs, arrived in Macao on the *Sesostris* steam-frigate, having come from London in a remarkable swift passage of sixty-seven days, no less than ten of which were spent at Bombay! We believe this must be the fastest passage ever made, surpassing any achieved by even the swiftest tea-ship.

Yesterday, Sir Henry and Vice-Admiral Parker stepped ashore in Macao, having been ferried from the *Sesostris* by our old friend the *Nemesis*. We do not speak for ourselves merely when we say that we should have regarded it as more fitting if these high officers of the Crown had resorted directly to Hong Kong as the Crown's newest Possession. Still, the lapse (if such we may properly term it) is understandable when the settlement has developed from its origins in so short a space of time. Doubtless, the Indian Government had no exact notion of the state of affairs here.

The *Queen,* which is the vessel which brought Sir Gordon Bremer to India and back but a matter of weeks previous, was greeted under a salute of guns of the appropriate number from the batteries and ships in the harbour. It is perhaps a suitable juncture here to note that Sir Henry is *sole* Plenipotentiary, while Admiral Parker – though senior in rank to Commodore Bremer, who was recently appointed Joint Plenipotentiary with Captain Elliot – is merely the Senior Naval Officer.

Sir Henry has distinguished himself in a long and adventurous service of his country in some of her wildest and most far-flung territories. Presently two and fifty years of age, he served in India as a boy-soldier in the early years of the century, in the Third Mahratta War with distinction as a young officer, and during the last four years has been Political Agent in Sind. He has a reputation, justly earned and deserved, as one of the most energetic and enterprising servants in any of the Company's Indian Possessions. It is said that he speaks five languages fluently and often passed as a native while engaged in secret tasks for the Honourable Company. He was created Baronet for his services in Sind.

In all his actions we do not doubt that he will prove an able, resolute, persevering, and steadfast leader who, to judge from his character as revealed in all his previous deeds, will not allow himself to be deluded and confused by the Chinese, or shrink from appropriate measures. We cannot imagine a character more distinct from that borne by the late Plenipotentiary.

Addendum.

Too late for inclusion in the body of the above, we have heard – to our great and unfeigned delight – that today Sir Henry (whom we shall henceforwards unambiguously refer to as the Plenipotentiary) has issued a notification to the effect that all arrangements which Captain Elliot and his deputy, Mr Johnston, have made to date with regard to Hong Kong shall remain in force until Her Majesty's pleasure is known. The effect of this resolution is that the land sales, contracts, prices, *etcetera* made during the previous busy year shall remain legally binding and enforceable on the parties concerned. Oh, decision worthy of Solomon! We also have it on the best authority that Sir Henry regards the successful prosecution of the war in the north to constitute his chief task for the moment. In this we concur, having always recommended it as the most sagacious policy – that is, the one most likely to be attended with a success in the south and least likely to result in unforeseen consequences for the property of the foreigners at Canton.

Sir Henry is an Irishman, which information we divulge with pride: we heard him speak ourselves in accents which bore great resemblance to our own. In stature he is tall, stalwart but not corpulent, florid in complexion, vigorous in his language and military in bearing, but also alert and sensible of the views of others.

Formula for an improved quickstuff

Many gentlemen who have resorted to our office and studio, having complained of the inordinate delay in the taking of their portraits owing to the long period during which the plate must necessarily be submitted to the action of the light in the camera (though the same have expressed their full satisfaction with the ultimate result), we are happy to announce our perfection of a new and improved process. This consists in the application to the plate of a novel and more sensitive mixture which we have taken the liberty of dubbing Eastman's Novel Patent Accelerator. By a process of experimentation and trial and error, we have arrived at a formulation which contrives to be both manageable, easily storable, and to a great degree imperishable, as well as rapid in its action. We were able to manufacture lotions of great sensitivity early in our experiments but to greater or lesser degrees these proved either excessively inflammable, too readily vapourised from even a stoppered flask, or else so noxious that they must have constituted a great hazard to the mixer and proved potentially injurious of the operator's health. The following mixture, for which we give the recipe, is admirably suited on all counts and will reduce the period of exposure from five minutes under the most perfect conditions to the fraction of one minute.

EASTMAN'S PATENT ACCELERATOR

To prepare, introduce a small amount of chlorine gas into a glass vessel containing iodine. Care should be taken at this stage of the manufactory, as it is the only operation attended with some slight risk to the concoctor. The gas will liquify the iodine. The compound is then diluted, most conveniently at the time of use, in two parts of distilled water to one of the Accelerator. Four grains of gelatine should now be added to the compound. The plate must be steeped in a shallow tray and submitted to the action of the Accelerator until it is first of a rose colour and then a deep purple. Finally, coat the plate over dry iodine crystals from three to five seconds until dark gold. The resulting coating will drastically reduce the time requisite.

We were spurred to the invention not by the grumblings of our friends so much as by the exigencies peculiarly inherent in a new order of commission, which was to take the Daguerreotype of Mrs G–'s two children.

SOLORIENS

Chapter XLIV

'Well, sir, at least you have stopped these strange fits of weeping.'

Chase shivers in the bright sunshine. He hugs his knees to stop them trembling. Far below, the junks huddle in Chek Chu harbour. Ant-figures work on the new barracks being constructed on the long headland beyond the old village and its picturesque temple.

'I guess I have the command of my intellectual faculties, even if my body, or parts of it, are not amenable to direction.'

'Now, that's more like the old Gid.'

Chase smiles through teeth that chatter. But he wishes he could talk to serene old Ow or Father Ribeiro.

'Now, Gid, your eyes mist suspiciously to me. Here, you had better have my coat around your shoulders.'

The sun blazes down on the rocks and waters below, but goose-pimples tighten the skin of Chase's bare forearms. It is nearly 100 degrees out on the exposed hillside, but the south-west monsoon is not blocked here by the huge peak which overhangs the harbour and town on the island's opposite coast and creates such an unhealthy stillness.

'I feel better here, Walter. The climate on this side is more like that prevailing in Macao.'

'Well, I allow so – and not only that: this anchorage greatly resembles in its curious shape that of Macao.'

'Gracious, Walter! That was what was preying on my mind, without my realising it at all. Your eye is remarkable, truly so, and you are right – it is a double anchorage.'

They stare at the peninsula with renewed interest. 'What would you describe it as – an ox-bow, maybe?'

'My dear Gideon, we are newspapermen and compositors, not peasants or Mongol horsemen. No, 'tis a letter "x" from the lower case, with ships in the concave hollow on each side.'

'I defer to you, Mr Editor.'

They enjoy the prospect a while. So clear is the water that from their elevation they can see submarine rocks and moving shoals of fish. Chase tries not to shiver.

'Do have a cigar – it shall help you.'

'I doubt it.' But he accepts.

'Puff away like a steam-engine, you'll feel the better for it.'

Chase leans back against a boulder, feeling very light-headed. The deep depression which has afflicted him for the last three weeks does not disappear, but he feels a little more tranquil. 'We have failed,' he says calmly, 'in everything we had set out to achieve, with such glad hearts.'

Walter laughs, shocking Chase. 'Now, don't be so down in the mouth.'

'Alas, it is true. We and Captain Elliot alike are the losers in this contest.'

'I have never seen it in the light of a contest.'

Silence. But they are old friends, who have been together through too much to feel uncomfortable.

'What a beautiful summer's day after the storms. I should like greatly to paint the blue of this sea.'

'Not to take a heliogravure?'

'As a matter of the purest fact – no.'

'Then you do astound me.'

'I astound myself, old friend. I was in need of astounding.'

706

'Then, Walter …'

'Yes, old friend?'

'I have to tell you…with sadness which passes beyond utterance… I cannot…that is to say, my days, I feel, on this coast are *numbered*.'

'All our days are numbered – tho' I take your point, old friend. I sense it, and your feelings, as much as you do yourself.'

'Of course, Walter, I should not wish to fail you. You may depend upon me to stay with you until you find suitable assistance in the production of the paper.'

'One of your most signal failings, Gid, and I fear it will endure into your old age, as it is fixed in your character, is – perhaps it is all part and parcel of your several mighty accomplishments – is a deep (don't stop puffing for a moment) obtuseness. Yes, you never listen to me, sir.'

Chase looks puzzled.

'I, too, lack the inclination to continue – no, it is not the consequence of any decision or behaviour of yours, but rather springs from the same sources. I will not produce another *Lin Tin Bulletin and River Bee* after the next or perhaps its fellow.'

'Walter!'

Eastman smokes complacently. His pale face is no more sarcastic than usual, eyebrow raised no higher than the customary half an inch.

'How can you leave it in, in…'

'Very easily, my dear Gideon. I shall walk out of the office and never step into it again. I shall not even bestow the backwardest of glances upon it. Let Sodom and Gomorrah be razed – but I shall not be turned into a pillar of salt.'

'Is it Macao and Hong Kong you mean, when you talk of Sodom and Gomorrah? Or perhaps Canton? I trust *I* am not to be cast in the role of Lot's wife.'

'Hong Kong, I allow, is a very Sodom, but choose for the other, for I'm darned if I can care any more.'

Gideon reflects, unconsciously sucking on the cigar now and blowing smoke into the flat, scorching air. After a while he says, with forced cheerfulness, 'I guess we shall not read first of our demise among our friend's columns, that at least we are spared.

I shall compose a special obsequy to our journal, to Pursuer at the very least – I may do so without braggadocio, for he is but my assumed character and only as much I as he is me.'

Eastman's butt goes spinning down the hillside. 'Then the editor, I can inform you, shall not print it. I require no such thing, sir. There will be no funeral oration over the body of my creation.'

'But there must. How can there not be? I own I am in sympathy with your feelings as to the matter – but there must be a small notification. We could place it near the subscription list. And if we bear such a gloomy notice, then some lighter animadversion in the body of our page.'

'There are no "musts" about the matter. I have phrased my answer in the negative.'

'Do you, Walter, mean seriously to say that, without rhyme or obvious reason, explanation, apology, or warning, you shall cease to publish the *Lin Tin Bulletin and River Bee?*'

'Yes.'

'That it will simply cease to be, vanish, be remarkable only for its absence?'

'Yes.'

'Then you amaze me.'

'I see you belong to the category, old friend, which will have things in the round, which does love an end, causes, the balance sheet drawn and equalled. But, my dear Gid, the world is not like that – it *is* untidy, there are no reasons, the final sum never balances. There is no blank end, only…the succession of moments leading on to something else. The line is drawn through the ledger quite rudely.'

'You often rebuke me, Walter, for flying with my head in the cloud while my boots sink in the mire. What is your intention towards our subscribers – who have paid for a full year and shall be cheated for a good six months of it?'

'The sale of the press will secure them the refunding of such of their monies as has not been accounted for.'

'And Harry's little capital?'

'He will forgive me.'

'That he will. I trust you will not forgive yourself. That is if you are the man I calculate you are.'

'Hmm.'

Further silence. The insects continue working on the roof of the barracks.

'How will it end, though, Walter? This unequal contest, dragged out though it has been, cannot endure for ever; surely nor can a vile and wicked trade which even its conductors own is to a degree odious and immoral.'

'Oh, it shan't go on for ever, don't you know, old friend. Pottinger's the man. Some Convention, or Congress, or Pact, or Treaty of Nonesuch or Somewhere will cap it all – end it for those of you who like their wars ended smart and clean. But it won't end anything in a true sense, old friend. Can't.'

'I guess Captain Elliot would dispute that.'

'You great booby, that is precisely what sets Elliot apart – he does know. But his own career is not ended – far from it, I have a notion. He will find supporters at home – Gladstone, the Iron Duke himself. The only end, Gid, is death. The soldiers and sailors, our friends, who laid their souls to rest here – Jonathan, also, who was a fine fellow and loyal friend, as you – did they go to their final account with all settled? No – they were unready, Gid. As will you and I both be. They were snatched away – by flying ball or winged pestilence – it hardly matters which, I allow the consequence is the same. They'll never see your conclusion, Gid. The story ended for them at a moment of merest insignificance – save that it was the hour of their death.'

'Well, I guess Father Joaquim would contest that, too.'

'God bless the good Father – but as to me, I'm an Unbeliever.'

'Ah, but Walter, when it must end, and it must, is with the exit, by death, of *all* the actors, ourselves among the number. That is as inevitable as the victory of the British. And what shall become of us then?'

'At this moment, Gid, I know I am immortal, I know the hot sun on my knee, the smell of smoke in my nostrils, the refulgent sparkle of the sea below. Be content with a knowledge of that.'

APPENDIX I

Entries from *A Gazetteer of Place Names and Biographies Relative to the Early China Coast* by An Old Hand (William Brown), Kelly and Walsh, Shanghai, 1935

BELCHER, Sir Edward. (1799-1877) Great-grandson of Jonathan Belcher, Governor of Massachusetts. Entered Navy as midshipman 1812. Post-captain 1841. Admiral 1872. Circumnavigated the world in the surveying vessel *Sulphur* 1836-42. Seconded to Chusan Expedition 1840. Directed landings in Canton River, May 1841. Took formal possession of Hong Kong island January 26th, 1841, and planted flag at Possession Point (q.v.). Knighted 1843. Led Expedition to Arctic 1852. A difficult man but a brilliant navigator.

Publicns. *Narrative of a Voyage around the World, performed in Her Majesty's ship* Sulphur *during the years 1836-42, including details of the Naval Operations in China from December 1840 to November 1841 (2 vols)*, London, 1843. *Narrative of a Voyage around the World in the* Samarang, *London, 1848.*

BOYLAN, A. J. (1792-1880) b. Dublin and brought up on uncle's estate in Co. Mayo. In employ of East India Company at Calcutta 1817-24. In Country Trade, Singapore, 1824-26. Clerk at Innes & Co., Canton, 1827-30, and later Jardine Matheson & Co. Editor of *Canton Monitor* 1830-40. Founded and edited *Hong Kong Guardian* 1840-62. Friend of William Caine *(q.v.)* whom he supported in the Caldwell scandal of official involvement in brothels and piracies and during the ensuing Hong Kong Civil Service Abuses Enquiry (1860). Mounted press campaign of vilification against the unpopular second Governor of Hong Kong, Sir John Francis Davis (1844-48) on behalf of the merchant community ('...supercilious, pompous, and a pedant and humbug to the last. We possess no knowledge as to the identity and abilities of Sir John's successor, but this we do know: he cannot be a worse Governor. There was none since Pilate.') Horsewhipped publicly in Queen's Road 1846 by Australian barrister for report '...scum of the Penal Settlements presently imposing upon the public as attorneys in the court'. Earlier in Canton days fought duel with Professor Gideon H. Chase *(q.v.)* in culmination of campaign over mutual libels. Later supported Chase when the latter was American Consul in a dispute regarding extra-territoriality and the jurisdiction of the Crown Courts in Hong Kong over American citizens on the China coast.

Chairman of the Hong Kong Club in its Wyndham Street premises. Said to be a relation on his mother's side of the painter A. H. O'Rourke (q.v.). m. Josephine (*née* LeClerc), Hong Kong, 1845. No children. A well-liked but peppery character of old Hong Kong, known popularly as Mr Ancient Boiler. Suffered from a congenital speech impediment and facial disfigurement which necessitated the services of an interpreter in conversations with strangers. Retained the colour of his bright red hair until well into his fifties. (See Conyngehame's reference to the lost O'Rourke portrait.) d. Bournemouth of a brain haemorrhage.

BREMER, Sir (James John) Gordon. (1786-1850) Son and grandson of naval officers. Distinguished himself as midshipman and lieutenant in Napoleonic wars. First Burma War 1824-26. Knighted 1836. Established Port Essington N.T., Australia, 1837. Commodore and Joint Plenipotentiary (for two months) in China 1841. Rear Admiral 1841. Two sons, four daughters.

CAINE, Colonel William. (1798-1871) Of undistinguished origins. Boy-soldier in India. Commissioned Ensign in Company's service 1814. Arrived Hong Kong from India via Singapore as Adjutant of 26th (Cameronians) Regiment 1840. Regimental Judge-Advocate. Appointed Chief Magistrate in Hong Kong by Captain Charles Elliot *(q.v.)* 1841. Denied leave to campaign in north China with his old regiment 1842. Legislative Council, Hong Kong, 1843. Colonial Secretary, Hong Kong, 1846-54. Lieutenant Governor 1854-59. Retired 1859. m. Lucy, 1846, a notable and popular hostess whose charm and gaiety assisted Caine greatly and helped secure his position in the civilian community. Treated Assistant Magistrate Charles Batten Hillier 'like a son'. Implicated in land speculation in early years of Colony from which he amassed a large private fortune, and also involved on periphery of Caldwell brothel and piracy scandal. Failed to secure Governorship of Straits Settlements 1858.

Sought honours and decoration in vain in the last 12 years of his life in Ramsgate. Petitioned the Queen, complaining of 'disgrace and neglect', 1864.

Caine Road, Hong Kong, is named after him. No children.

CHASE, Professor Gideon Hall. (1816–1908) Early Sinologue and writer, honorary Consul. Friend and correspondent of James Legge, Sir Thomas Wade, Sir Edmund Backhouse, Leopold von Ranke, Jakob Burckhardt, Max Weber, and J. W. Dunne. b. Boston. Parents not known. At Canton in the house of Meridian & Co. 1833–38. Editor *Lin Tin Bulletin and River Bee* 1838–41. Left China for the United States, November 24th, 1841. Contributed to *The Dial*. Joined Transcendentalist group at Brook Farm and left August 1842. Texas 1842–43. Interpreter to US Consul, Shanghai, 1843–52. Acting US Consul, Canton, 1852–55. Shanghai 1855–56. Assistant Principal Morrison Education Society, Hong Kong, 1856–60. Hankow 1860–61. Official Adviser to Chinese Government 1863–72. Professor of Chinese, Heidelberg University, 1872–77. Visiting Professor, Edinburgh, 1877–78. Hong Kong 1879–80. Peking 1880–81. Boston 1881–83. Hartford, Conn., 1883–85. Rome 1885–86. Visiting Professor Oxford 1886–88. Rome 1888–1908. m. 1852 Constance Bewdley (1825–1909), widow of the Rev. John Bewdley. Two sons, Walter (1854–1944) and Nathaniel Joaquim (1856–72).

Chase's significance, like James Legge's, is as a bridge between the first generation of the 'pioneer' scholars of the Chinese language, such as the Rev. Robert Morrison *(q.v.)* and Abel Rémusat, and the second generation, Clementi, etc. His considerable prestige with the Chinese Government and personal friendship with Viceroy Li Hung Chang and Prince Kung assisted in reform and modernisation in the last quarter of the 19th century. The increasing wildness of his non-academic views caused the decline in his reputation which immediately preceded and followed his death in Rome in 1908, but should not be allowed to obscure his contribution to China studies in the middle and late years of the last century.

Hon. Doctorate University of Gröningen, DCL (Oxon), FRS, FRGS, *Légion d'Honneur,* etc. Publicns. *Desultory Footnotes on China,* Philadelphia, 1845. *Dictionary of the Chinese Language,* Gröningen, 1874. *Dishonourable Company,* Edinburgh, 1879. *The Red Chamber Dream,* transl., London, 1881. *Dubieties of the Colloquial,* Boston, 1883. *The Impermanent Delta, or an Account of a Journey Overland from Kowloon to Canton,* Hong Kong, 1881. *Byways better than Highways,* Hong Kong, 1882. *The Victory of the Vernacular: or an appreciation of the works of S. L. Clemens,* private printing, Hartford, 1886. *Giambattista Vico,* Naples, 1902.

CHEK CHU. Ancient fishing village on SW coast of Hong Kong island. Later named Stanley, after Lord Stanley. Contains old temple, reputedly headquarters of the notorious pirate Chang Li Po in the early 19th century. Clear waters a popular haunt of turtles and sharks. Its headland the site of Stanley Prison.

EAST, Dr John. (1800-49) Surgeon, educ. Edinburgh University. Surgeon on East India Company's ships. d. typhus Shanghai.

EASTWOOD, Christopher. (1816-76) b. Farnham. Merchant. Arrived Hong Kong 1844. Shanghai 1844-72. Deputy Vice-President British Chamber of Commerce.

ELLIOT, Captain Charles. (1801-75) b. Dresden where his father, a Minto, was a diplomat to the Court of the King of Saxony. As a midshipman served against the Barbary Corsairs and was present at the Bombardment of Algiers on the *Minden* 1816. Lieutenant on *Hussar,* Jamaica station, 1822. Commander of the Hospital Ship, Port Royal, 1826. Post-Captain 1828.

Retired from active list 1828. Protector of Slaves, Guiana, 1830-33. In London during the passing of the Parliamentary Act freeing all slaves in British Possessions with £20 million compensation. Master Attendant in Napier mission 1834. Chief Superintendent of Trade and later Plenipotentiary in China 1836-41. Replaced by Sir Henry Pottinger *(q.v.)*. Left Hong Kong August 24th, 1841. Protected by Duke of Wellington after recall from China by Palmerston: 'You have regarded my instructions as so much waste-paper.' *Chargé d'affaires* in Republic of Texas 1842-46. Governor of Bermuda 1846-54, Governor of Trinidad 1854-56, Governor of St Helena 1863-69. Admiral on retired list 1865, d. Exeter.

Described by *The Times* as 'unfit to manage a respectable apple-stall' and twenty years later as 'that gallant, wrong-headed little man'. Of steadfast personal courage and infirm conscience.

His name is uncommemorated in the Colony he founded.

ENRIQUES, José. (1775-1848) b. Lisbon, editor *Timor Free Press* (1825-47). Coffee-planter Brazil 1801-12. Wine-shipper, Oporto, 1816-20. Goa 1823-24. Timor 1824-47. d. at sea en route Manila.

GOUGH, Field Marshal Sir Hugh. (1779-1869) Adjutant of Colonel Rochford's Foot at age 16. 78th Highlanders 1795. Severely wounded at Talavera 1809 with 87th (Prince of Wales's Irish) Regiment and again wounded at Nivelle 1813. Major-General 1830. China 1840-42. Threatened to shoot Indian camp-followers out of hand at siege of Amoy, August 26th, 1841, en route to north China with the newly arrived Pottinger *(q.v.)*: 'That which in England obtains the name of theft deserves no other title in China.' Commander at defeat of Mahrattas 1843 and in Sikh wars 1845 and 1848. Field Marshal 1862. A doughty warrior.

GUTZLAFF, Reverend Karl Friedrich August. (1803-51) Born Pomerania of humble family, son of a shoemaker. Largely self-educated. Attended Missionary College and sent to Far East. First wife died in Bangkok 1831. Gutzlaff voyaged by junk to

Macao and narrowly escaped murder at the hands of the crew. Employed by the Free Traders at Canton to reconnoitre openings for the opium trade in north China on the *Sylph,* 1832, in company with H. H. Lindsay. At Macao 1834-39, during which period he married Mary Parkes, cousin of Sir Harry Parkes *(q.v.).* Chief Interpreter to Captain Elliot and Sir Henry Pottinger 1840-42. Magistrate at Chusan and Ningpo during the temporary British Occupation. Pottinger wanted to make him consul at Foochow, following the opening of the five consular ports by the Treaty of Nanking in August 1842, but only a British National was acceptable to the Home Government in that role. Assistant Chinese Secretary at Hong Kong and on the death of J. R. Morrison *(q.v.)* in August 1843 appointed Chief Secretary. Founded Chinese Christian Union 1844. Returned briefly to Pomerania and then back to Hong Kong in January 1851. Died August 1851 and is buried in the Colonial Cemetery at Hong Kong.

A controversial figure – 'that sinister eye' – and regarded by many as a hypocrite, if not a murderer. Retained his strong German accent all his life.

HALL, Rear Admiral Sir William Hutcheon. (1798-1878) Entered Royal Navy 1811. On 1816 Amherst mission to China. Lack of preferment and patronage led him into the navigational branch of the service. Sailing-master 1823 and visited the United States 1820-23, during which period he learned steam-navigation. Left Navy, ostensibly on grounds of ill-health. By 1839 Commander of the newly built *Nemesis.* Distinguished himself in China. Commissioned Lieutenant 1841, with accelerated promotion to Commander 1843 and Post-Captain 1844. Distinguished service in Crimean War in the Baltic, present at bombardment of Sveaborg. Rear Admiral 1863. KCB 1867. Inventor of iron bilge-tanks and Hall's Patent Anchor. Married the daughter of his old Admiral.

FRS 1847. Publicns. Co-author with W. Bernard M.A. (Oxon) of *The* Nemesis *in China,* London, 1846. A first-rate seaman who only enjoyed the fruits of success comparatively late in life.

HAPPY VALLEY. Expansive plain and the most noticeable geographical feature of eastern Hong Kong island. Originally part of clan lands of old Chinese village of Wong Nei Chong (Yellow Earth Brooks). Largely under paddy at the time of the British Occupation. Originally mooted as the European residential area by the Colonial Engineer, to be linked to the harbour by a canal constructed by Jardine Matheson & Co., but the area proved unhealthy. Paddy was reclaimed, native cultivators bought out, a nullah built, and a circular carriage road and riding-track constructed. Entire area turfed to provide a race-track. Colonial Cemetery occupied the western side of the valley from earliest days. Morrison Education Society for illegitimate Eurasian (politely 'Chinese') foundlings occupied the hill on the eastern side until 1849.

JOHNSTON, Alexander Robert. (1808–c.1860) Born into a legal family. Father was Chief Justice of Ceylon. Writer in the Government of Mauritius 1828. Appointed Private Secretary to Lord Napier 1833. Third Superintendent of Trade 1835. Second or Deputy Superintendent 1836. Accompanied Captain Charles Elliot *(q.v.)* to voluntary incarceration in the Factories November 1839. Supervised the handover of the confiscated opium to Lin. Negotiated the release of the Rev. Vincent Stanton *(q.v.)* August 1840. Unofficial Governor of Hong Kong June–December 1841 and in the same season in 1842 while first Elliot and then Pottinger campaigned in the north. Censured by Pottinger December 1841 for conducting land sales in his absence. 'You have entirely exceeded the authority vested in you.' Sick leave granted 1843. Returned to Hong Kong 1845. Retired 1853, with pension. Request to Secretary of State for Colonies, 1856, for honours refused.

JOHNSTONE, Frederick. (1810–78) b. Salem, Mass. Clerk in Meridian & Co., Canton, 1831–39. Macao 1839–42. Hong Kong 1842–43. Traded on own account in Hong Kong 1843–45. Founded his own firm in Shanghai 1845–57. Bought out partners of Meridian & Co. under acrimonious circumstances

1857. President American Chamber of Commerce Hankow 1862-65. d. Batavia 1878.

MORRISON, John Robert. (1814-43) Son of the Rev. Robert Morrison, the translator of the New Testament into Chinese. Himself a competent, though not a great, linguist, and forced to undertake a heavy burden on the death of the older Morrison in 1834. Befriended Gutzlaff's young nephew Harry Parkes *(q.v.)* and acted as his first Chinese teacher. Continued work of Morrison Education Society as a memorial to his father, but on transfer of the Anglo-Chinese College, Malacca, to Morrison Hill, Hong Kong, in 1843, under James Legge, the Society became increasingly dominated by Americans. d. fever Macao August 1843 and his death described by Pottinger as 'a positive national calamity'.

NAPIER, William John. (1786-1834) Eighth baron. Midshipman RN 1802. Trafalgar 1805. Retired as Post-Captain to family estates in Selkirkshire. Sheep-farmer. Succeeded to title 1823 and returned to active list. Chief Superintendent of British Trade in China 1833. d. Macao 1834.

O'ROURKE, Augustine Henry. (1772-1853) Minor painter. Resident of Calcutta, Madras, and China coast. b. Co. Mayo, Ireland, son of Michael and Patricia O'Rourke. Father an architect. Worked in draughtsman's office in Dublin 1790-91. Student at Royal Academy, London, 1791-93. Studied in Florence 1793-94. Portrait-painter Calcutta 1795-98, Madras 1798-1801. Macao c. 1802-39. Hong Kong 1839-40, Macao 1840-53. O'Rourke's reputation was somewhat more obscured than it might have been when a conflagration in the home of a wealthy merchant patron and collector in Shanghai in 1857 destroyed most of his works. A similar fate had overtaken the painter's drawings and sketch-books during his lifetime when his own house in Macao was burned down. His servant was arrested for arson and confessed to the crime, saying he had not been paid for five years, but was released on O'Rourke's personal intervention. A charming sketch for a theatre programme of Sheridan's *The Rivals,* staged in Macao in 1837, survives, including a self-portrait of the artist as Mrs Malaprop. Two early Daguerreotype photographs by an unknown hand of his paintings 'Driftwood on the beach of Macao' and 'At Mrs Shillingford's Soirée' do not inspire the conventional veneration which contemporaries appear to have felt.

PARKES, Sir Harry Smith. (1828-85) British Minister to Japan, Gazetted Minister to China. Friend of Sir Thomas Wade, Professor Gideon Chase *(q.v.)* and Colonel 'Chinese' Gordon RE (Gordon of Khartoum). b. Walsall, Staffs. Grandson of Rev. O. Parkes, father an ironmaster. Mother d. 1832 and father d. a year later in a carriage accident. Joined his cousin (Mrs Gutzlaff) and his two sisters in Macao. Befriended by J. R. Morrison and on the latter's death in August 1843 by (John) later Sir Rutherford Alcock of the British consular service. Student Interpreter Amoy consulate 1844, Foochow 1845, Acting Interpreter Shanghai 1846, Chief Interpreter Amoy 1849, and then given home leave of 18 months. 'Arriving at Folkestone, I hurried to the best chop-house I could see, and ordered an English beef-steak with potatoes and ale as concomitants...' Appointed Acting Consul at Canton in 1853 by the Foreign Office over the head of the Governor of Hong Kong who did not wish to see a linguist appointed in what was known as the 'Battle of the Interpreters'. Helped sign first treaty with Siam. One of the three Allied Commissioners in charge of Canton in Second Opium War (1856-60). Suggested taking lease on the Kowloon peninsula to the new Governor, Sir Hercules Robinson, 1860. Captured by the Chinese in violation of a truce arrangement and imprisoned in Peking for 11 days as a hostage in 1860. Of 26 Indians and British captured only nine survived; Bowlby of *The Times* tortured to death. Knighted 1863. Consul at Shanghai 1864. Revived the North China branch of the Royal Asiatic Society. With the collaboration of Professor Gideon Chase *(q.v.)* aided Colonel Gordon in his role of special adviser to the Chinese Government against Tai Ping rebels in 1864. Gordon: 'Dear Sir Harry Parkes, The rebels all know me, and the most of the chiefs have my photograph. I believe they would toast me if they ever caught me, but at the same time think they trust me to some extent.'

d.1885, 'worn out with work', of fever at Peking.

Five sons, two daughters. Eldest son Douglas Gordon Parkes d. of fever, Penang, 1894. Eldest surviving daughter m. J. J. Keswick of Jardine Matheson & Co. 1884.

PEDDER, William. (?-1854) Lieutenant RN. First Lieutenant of the *Nemesis*. Harbour Master and Marine Magistrate at Hong Kong, 1841. Retained post through successive administrations. d. at Ryde, Isle of Wight, at his sister's house while on home leave in March 1854. Pedder Street, Hong Kong, named after him. Succeeded by Captain Watkins and in 1858 by his old clerk, the former gold prospector, A. L. Inglis.

POSSESSION POINT. Small hillock on north-western coast of Hong Kong island on which Sir Edward Belcher *(q.v.)* raised the flag to claim Hong Kong for the Crown in January 1841. Subsequently notorious as a site of taverns and brothels in the late 19th century. Celebrated in the vulgar shanty, 'Possession's Point'. Presently occupied by a tree and an iron water-pump, long disused.

POTTINGER, Sir Henry. (1789-1856) Fifth son of Eldred Curwen Pottinger. b. Mount Pottinger, Co. Down. First Governor of Hong Kong and Plenipotentiary and Superintendent of Trade. Educ. Belfast Academy. Sent to sea at the age of 12. Joined the East India Company's naval service 1803. Transferred to army service in employ of the Company after his family petitioned Castlereagh in 1804. Commissioned Ensign 1806. Became a proficient native linguist. At the age of 19 volunteered for a secret mission with fellow-officer Captain John Christie and with two servants and a native horse-dealer scouted an area between Persia and India for 1500 miles, disguised as Afghan merchants. Christie killed in a Russian attack while in Persia. Pottinger promoted to Lieutenant 1809, Captain 1821, Major 1825, and Colonel before being transferred to the Political Staff of the Bombay Presidency. Appointed

Political Agent in Sind 1836. In charge of the logistical arrangements for Keane's expedition in the Afghan War 1839. Returned home in 1840 after 27 years on the subcontinent without leave. Appointed Hon. Major-General in the Company Service and made Baronet. Appointed HM Plenipotentiary and Superintendent of Trade in China. Travelled overland via Suez and then down the Red Sea to Bombay and Macao. Spent 24 hours in Hong Kong, August 19th, 1841, before hurrying north to prosecute the war in the limited six months of the campaigning season. Captured Amoy, August 25th, and in quick succession recaptured the Chusan archipelago, took Chinhai and Ningpo, and was narrowly restrained from sacking Ningpo by his own interpreters. Returned to Hong Kong, December 1841. Moved the headquarters of the Superintendency of Trade from Macao to Hong Kong, February 1842. Rejoined the armed forces at Chusan, August 1842, and ascended the Yangtse with the Fleet, captured Shanghai and Nanking. In 1842 negotiated the Treaty of Nanking and formally gained the cession of Hong Kong. The treaty made no mention of opium, but opened China to western penetration with five new consular ports. Terms very unfavourable to China, but the Treaty formally ended hostilities. In September 1842 Pottinger informed by the new Tory Government that Hong Kong and Chusan were not to be regarded as permanent conquests. At the ratification of the Treaty at Government House, Hong Kong, Pottinger sang Irish and Manchu songs with Imperial Commissioner Keying.

Pottinger's initial popularity with the merchant interest waned and turned to mutual hostility when he banned freehold-land sales at Hong Kong in 1844 and only permitted leasehold. Quarrelled with the military over their retention (to this day) of prime sites in the centre of Hong Kong and their responsibility for the disastrous fever epidemics of 1842 and 1843. Left Hong Kong on HMS *Driver* in 1844 and, against his will, was forced to share the ship with a Spanish naval officer. Governor of the Cape, 1846, Madras Presidency 1846. d. at Malta 1856 on the way home from India. A headstrong and quarrelsome man who was personally incorruptible but distributed patronage to the numerous Irish relations in his train, including the incompetent

Colonial Engineer A. T. Gordon. Saw his task in simpler terms than Elliot and was correspondingly successful.

Commemorated in Pottinger Street, today a rather mean alley. m.1820 Susanna Maria, daughter of Captain Richard Cooke of Dublin. Three sons.

REMINGTON, Alice Barclay. (1814-48) b. Boston, Mass. Youngest daughter of Alexander Remington, third partner in house of Meridian & Co., and Harriet (*née* Hollis). Resided in Macao with her uncle and aunt 1835-42. Returned to America via Alexandria, Rome, Paris, London, and Liverpool. m. Richard Brown, banker, of Boston 1843. Two sons, Frederick William (1844-1923) and Edward Joseph (1846-1919). Her letters and journal of the years 1836-41 are cached with the Bodleian Library and constitute a valuable source of material for study, particularly the detailed accounts of the war March 1839-November 1841. d. of purpureal fever, Boston, 1848.

STANTON, Reverend Vincent. (1815-?) educ. Exeter College, Oxford. British Chaplain at Macao. Kidnapped August 1840 and held in chains at Canton. Colonial Chaplain at Hong Kong, September 1842. Founded St Paul's College for the training of Chinese ordinands to the Anglican Ministry 1843.

VEALE, Thomas. (1759-c. 1840) Oldest resident of Macao in the 1830's, a distinction he shared with the historian Sir Andrew Ljungstadt. Came to Canton to work for Hollingsworth & Co. in 1779 and later Magniac & Co. (to become Jardine Matheson & Co. in due course). Fiercely anti-American, but mother b. Nantucket. Mother's family Loyalists in War of Independence and emigrated Caicos Islands, British West Indies. Veale ruined in an unwise speculation in 1801 but his debts paid off for him by a subscription among the Chinese Hong merchants and foreigners. Kept a remarkable aviary and tropical gardens in his retirement. Disappeared under mysterious circumstances and his body never recovered.

APPENDIX II

Edited passages from *The Morning of my Days,* the unfinished and unpublished autobiography of Professor G. H. Chase.

And so the image, always abiding, of a childhood all too short, remains that of the frozen pond, with the flat and gelid wastes around hidden beneath their integument of white, the surface of the waters half-transparent, brittle, yet in the end opaque to our discernment, while beneath that glassy roof the fish flutter, tantalisingly, half-glimpsed as an idea or memory struggling to the surface of our thought. Boston and New England are, while I conjure my recollections in exile, the land of winter, of wintry thought and a chill, uncompromising and unforgiving cast of mind, not ignoble in their way, but anathema to the warmer doctrines of the Old World and that South in which I presently discover myself and shall likely end my time. I do not see the rustic colours of our New England Fall, those blazing leaves, but the white of snow and the black of a gloomy sky, when I cast my mind back into the scenes of youth. When young I, too, drank at the fountainhead of that puritanism which left the individual refreshed in the astringency of its doctrines but alone, isolated, and justified only by his simple faith. I was something of a prig, too, I fancy.

...stark, then, as were the morals and intellectual habits of that place and time, they were of the essence of the life of the mind as it unfolded in the middle and early years of the last century. (The last century! How strange it sounds!) For what were the twinned modes which dominated our thought, as well the vulgar as the scholar's or the scientific mind, so much as a passion for the actual – for the *real* – and a sensibility which was informed by the emotions and devices of the melodrama. Now I may have already anticipated the disbelief of the reader. The first proposition might perhaps be received as plausible, if not self-evident, but does the second, if true perhaps of the uneducated, not constitute the grossest insult to all our *savants* of the last fifty years? On the contrary, I should always be inclined to assert the existence of a bridge between the high culture and the popular mood, the mould of the colloquial and the specific forms assumed by higher discourses. The grand stream is fed by innumerable petty tributaries. Often enough, as in the misuse of the proper signification of a word which when sufficiently widely misunderstood becomes the accepted usage of the academy, the vulgar anticipates the proper and may be said to be the chrysalid of the later orthodoxy. Thus, the crude mechanism of the drama of wrong-doing and retribution, of murder and apprehension, corresponds most closely to the *modus operandi* of the elevated intellects which have done so much to make the preceding century one when mankind accomplished the greatest progress and improvements in recorded history. The entire schema of the popular entertainment reflected faithfully – or at least was part of the same way of looking at the world as were – the discoveries of Darwin or the deluded propositions of Engels. Do the man of science or the social scientist, both searching for the laws which govern the behaviour of the physical world or the world of man in aggregate, not investigate, deduce, and proceed generally from a mass of accumulated evidence in the way of the police detective? Even the painter experiments to gain his effects by trial and error. And the process of inquiry instituted by the scientist in the field of medical discovery follows precisely the same course of an 'interrogation' and elimination of suspects from his work of investigation as that of the 'sleuth' and a final revelation of a murderer, not the less deadly for being invisible, or hateful for his insidious and agonising effects upon the human constitution, than a dagger in the breast. The discoverers of the efficacy of quinine bark against malaria shall always be viewed by me in the same light as the relatives of the murdered man regard the successful officer of the law.

Furthermore, the entire development of the melodrama is linked with our modern revolutionaries' understanding of process (to use their own term upon themselves). To them, history is a melodrama; that is, it is a succession of acts and actors, of *dénouements* and, above all, of climaxes. The one stage of history leads inexorably to the other, with no slow shift of the *mise en scène* but a most ruthless, violent, and wholesale doing away with 'props' and actors. Slave, feudal, bourgeois, and proletarian orders end and begin in violent cataclysms more reminiscent of the primordial world of the volcano than of man, for the laws of pseudo-science operate with the same melodramatic force as those of science. And what could be more melodramatic than the struggle for evolution or the iron law of Malthus? Malthus, the parson who became the professor at the East India College at Haileybury? And it is a view of the human nature which is ultimately falsified, for it deals in blacks and whites, just as the hero, heroine, and villain of melodrama, in absolute good and absolute evil – in the confrontation between them and the ultimate victory of good and the discovery and routing of evil. Here is where the Puritan and the authors of the Communist Manifesto are at one in their conception of man. There can be no other common source for these streams than in the primitive doctrines of the millennium and the apocalypse, and their schematic views of time and elapse, as well as relapse. The Book of Revelations and *Capital* are equally of the Judaic tradition.

Theirs is not a view of human nature which I ever shared, or at the very least I lost it early in China. It is not the spectre of absolute evil which is so shocking as the intimate commingling of good and bad in human beings, the occurrence of the wicked in a familiar and quotidian aspect. The purveyors of opium, in the days before the Treaty, William Jardine, Lancelot Dent, James Innes, and their ilk – with many of whom I was on familiar terms – could not be described as malevolent in their everyday social intercourse. To the contrary, they were many of them large-minded, hospitable, and kindly men who might have risked their lives to save mine. It is more truly shocking to see good men in a bad cause than bad men in a bad, and nothing more truly disillusioning than to see bad men enlisted under the banner of good. How I could wish for some *catalyst,* some alchemical ingredient that, tossed into the crucible of men's actions, would free the dross from the gold of a man's nature and send the impurity to the top as scum, where it might be skimmed and removed! Or that there existed a key which in all respects fitted the bizarre twists and turns of a man's contradictory character which, inserted, should turn the tumblers of his soul and unlock that which was noble in him from the base. Vain wish! As soon find the philtre of eternal life!

To return to my first assertion: that I have lived through and am still enduring in, and doubtless shall conclude my life in, a span of time wherein men have experienced a passion for the recording of the actual, to accumulate *fact* – this may perhaps be a contention easier to justify. *Wie es eigentlich gewesen war,* as von Ranke stated to be his aim, may be taken as the motto of the purest and most elevated intellects of the time. Mill writes of 'that series of great writers and thinkers, from Herder to Michelet, by whom history, which was till then "a tale told by an idiot, full of sound and fury, signifying nothing", has been made a science of causes and effects; who, by making the facts and events of the past have a meaning and intelligible place in the gradual evolution of humanity, have at once given history, even to the imagination, an interest like romance, and afforded the only means of predicting and guiding the future, by unfolding the agencies which have produced and still maintained the present'.

It does appear to me that without the scrupulousness of a von Ranke, the hopes of a Mill are in vain, but I take both as instances of the perfected development of scholarship in the preceding century – and I do not mention the great de Tocqueville, whose most casual observations, *obiter dicta,* including those passed on my own country, should be engraved on the very stones of Liberalism and Democracy. But, until that time, there was little sense of the past as a subject worthy of faithful representation in its own right, so much as a mine from which the writer might extract anything that should suit his polemical purpose or personal notions and, not infrequently, mica or fool's gold were quarried in the stead of the genuine article. Again, I do not believe I am unduly fanciful in citing a change of attitude among *hoi polloi* as well as among the *literati,* for the spread in the early and middle years of the last century of the organs of dissemination of facts and opinion – by which I mean newspapers, those vehicles of information and prejudice – was so prolific as to represent a Babel of tongues (and my own small and piping voice among that pan-demonium).

...nor could the world of art long remain immune where the spheres of science and scholarship had already been affected, for the discovery of photography (which I have the temerity to observe was no accidental invention, just as the discovery of the Americas was inevitable, but a reflection itself of a changing view of the world) came as a pebble hurled into its still depths. Photography, I believe, to borrow its own terms, was the point of focus at which those irreconcilables, art and science, the high culture and the low, could be brought together, where elsewhere a coexistence was impossible. And both photography and journalism, offspring on the sinister branch of art and literature, were the most powerful agents of this novel passion for the actual and the real, alliance made yet more potent where the photograph might be reproduced as an article of news in itself. Yet how deluded was this search for truth, literal truth, and how fallacious its instruments, for there is small verity in the newspaper or the photograph, though both purport to be fact in its purest form. At best, how often is their apparent fidelity contingent on the prejudices, expressed or unconscious, of the producer, not to mention the consumer. At worst, how easily may their evidence and proofs, seemingly so incontrovertible, be falsified and twisted in unscrupulous but skilled hands into a travesty of the actual! Perhaps the essential truths may only be possessed in utter contrivance, where the artifice is openly acknowledged, as in a painting or a work of fiction where no facts may be found at all. The effect produced by photography upon painting, it now seems to me, in the latest work of France, has been to isolate the artist from his public, to make our modern painter insular, private, abstracted, to free him from the tiresome representation of the surface of things, but also to exile him to a realm where taste and knowledge are the private possession of the craft. Their work, treating still in its way of the world we all inhabit and in which we have our being, resembles nothing so much as a cryptic code to the outsider, a message and description of the mundane world, but couched in a cypher to which only an *élite* hold the key.

But I wander, and I am no *littérateur* or a connoisseur of the fine arts, but a philologist. (I had been looking, all my life to know what I was – and when my student informed me that such I was and always had been, why I experienced a feeling of the most lively gratitude towards her.) Prior to this, I had conceived of myself as a fisher (of words, not men), or as a Daguerreotypist on the banks of some mighty stream. For what is a dictionary but a photograph of the river of language at a given moment? And its definitions but as temporary dams, or low-lying islands, whose meanings will not hold for all of time and, indeed, may be wholly obliterated as they fall into desuetude and are no longer heard on the lips of men. Just as a river will take the simplest and easiest course as the most efficient, so at last the tendency of language is to eschew circumlocution, to become briefer and simpler, but not straighter necessarily, for the most efficient path, the line of least resistance, may not always be the shortest distance point to point in a geometrical sense, but consist in a meandering. And, as its course swerves, so the words alter, and may bear a wholly distinctive meaning from where their usage lay a century past. And as the geographical river plays its practical jokes, leaving the trading town three miles from its new banks as it changes its course, so, too, is the change in meaning of words, as our language flows on, productive of bathos and humour to the modern reader. And as the main branch flows on, so, too, does it become swollen and enriched by the contribution of tributaries, as the usages (for instance) of our Federal English, as Webster, our first Noah, dubbed it so primly, became added to the grand branch of Old England – the fountainhead whence all the literature of the language flows. (Though through what different scenes it has passed in the last eighty years!) From time to time the stream runs underground, passes through dark and subterranean caverns of our society, among thieves, prostitutes, and outcasts, and then comes bubbling and gushing up in the spring where sunlight plays on those words, once barred from polite usage, but now enriched in the fertile mud of the colloquial. Thus is fed the stream of language. Yet the tendency of language is to *diverge* as well as divulge, at its most primitive levels. It is perhaps our most subtle and detailed mode of communication – yet it may also isolate. Where dialect reigns then we talk of a delta. I have known villages ten miles apart in China, whose tongues were mutually incomprehensible. And in my own time has the language of my own country not steadily proceeded away from its common source in Old England, so that the usages which a hundred years ago were common to both have become fewer and the distinctions greater?

...both those dear friends and instructors I was not destined to keep beyond my young manhood. The one nearer my own years, following my first departure and, as I thought then, my last, from the coast of China some sixty and more long years past as I write, I never saw again but once, fleetingly, eighteen years after: and how we talked the steamy night through, I plying him with the little comforts I knew he loved so well, he in a wicker chair on my verandah, limbs stuck out in the careless way he always had, head thrown back as he gestured vigorously to make his points in his old manner. How those scant hours flew, as we discussed till the dawn old friends long scattered, many of them dead, and the events of that distant past. (At that very moment history appeared to be repeating itself in China with the Allies knocking at the gates of Peking, while in our homeland the thunderclouds gathered. In our own country, we should perhaps have been mortal foes.) He worked, latterly, as the manager of a tobacco plantation in Luzon, and in the time intervening between our meetings had travelled once to Europe but never returned to America. He was a Virginian. Every year thereafter, we corresponded, his gay and amusing letters an endless source of delight to myself and my family. 'We have been hard pressed to cope,' he wrote once, 'with the visitations of Messrs Typhoon, Drought, & Co.' He died not young but, alas, when he still might have hoped for more years, of an affection of the lungs. He never married.

The greatest genius I was privileged to encounter when I was young was that of a painter, Mr O'Rourke. I only heard of the death of my old friend E- some two years after the event, in Germany, when sadness was tempered by the circumstance that I only heard the reverberations of the event of his passing. In the case of my older friend, I was not spared the most pitiful and affecting sights of the deathbed, for I chanced to be visiting Macao at the time. For some years he had not been well, his spirits additionally oppressed by a terrible misfortune as concerned his works and, indeed, he had not worked at all for the last three years past, infirmity having so far sapped that mighty spirit as to rob him of the old quickness of response between eye and hand. 'I will do it quickly, or not at all,' he would say, for to pretend never to take pains was his little pleasantry upon the world and the least discerning among his many friends, for all the world knows that genius consists in the willingness to take a thousand tiny troubles. At length, having been much weakened, to the point where he was but a shadow of his old hale and hearty self, his clothes (all of which, he used to declare, were of the previous century) hanging loosely upon his shrunken frame, he withdrew to the chamber and retired to that bed whence he was destined never to rise again. His oldest friend on that coast was also he to whom I owed my profoundest debt as my first initiator and guide into the mysteries of the Chinese language. This great teacher was also a cleric, priest of the great order or, properly, Society, of Jesus, and in every respect an equal of his mighty forebears in China, Verbiest and Ricci, and a coreligionist of Mr O'Rourke. It was, of course, not only his solemn duty but also his deepest wish to shrive the soul of his dying friend, who, I regret to say, had conducted his life altogether without reference to the 'small print' of the sermons and precepts of religion narrowly defined by narrow men, but always in such a way, as regards the cardinal principles of the Sermon on the Mount, that his great and generous soul could never have been in jeopardy. To the inexpressible joy and relief of his old friend and final confessor, he died in the bosom of his own Faith, having made a sufficient contrition – when I withdrew from the room – and embraced his Saviour. His end was one long and excruciating torment and his friends could only welcome his relief and removal from that dreadful trial from which he never shrank, though his ability to do that which made life worth the living had vanished long before. In my own old age, as I look upon a hand which shakes and speckles the page as I write, a feeble, waxy, and veiny claw, which once could with a single convulsive grasp reduce a whole orange to pith or send a boat dashing along the waves, as I look on the outward sign and emblem of my mortality, I ponder whether the pain of our ends (for lucky is he who passes away all unknowing in his sleep) is that which defines the meaning for our entire lives? For, commonly, an end is that which governs the sense of all that has gone before, which confers a significance. Men do love a conclusion. Yet death comes abruptly – who is ready, but would rather not say: 'Stay, I have found no meaning to my days'? In those dying throes which rack our frames, are we to assume that the path we have trod, the progress and steady accumulation of the days of our entire lives, the purpose of our whole existence, has been to lead to that awful suffering? Alas, the sensations of the present moment, which is to say our corporal side, are the strongest and to inhabit that present only, without the power which may recall the dear scenes of old, is to die as a prisoner in a cell of the securest prison of the loneliest island. No, as a beast.

To me, though, the days of my youth, of the bright morning of my life in China, are the most vivid. What does the Jesuit say? Give me the child until he is seven, and I will give you the man. As I write now, those vanished companions, all in their graves now, every one, but young and quick again in my mind, sit around that glowing table in the Factories, their faces flushed, eyes bright, full of anticipation and the expectation of the realisation of all their lives' dreams. Ours was a convivial community, full of good fellowship and good humour, and – such may be the surmise of an old age unduly mellow – even the petty feuds, rivalries, and enmities from which our little community was, alas, not free served in the end to sustain the unity of all and to impart some slight piquancy to a mix which might otherwise have wanted some interest. Do the opposing forces of an arched stone bridge, such as span the canals at Soochow or Canton, pressing together at the top, not resolve themselves in the greater strength and stability of the entire structure? To turn in upon ourselves, to become preoccupied with our own bickerings and jealousies, to be obsessed with our own insularity, was a relief from the threat outside. The antagonisms which existed among the foreigners were but as wires which served to bind them to themselves yet tighter against the Chinese, for we inhabited a little refuge washed by an alien sea. By a way of contrast, when men wish to turn the minds of their fellows against another group, say a confederation of men which threatens their interest, they 'focus' their hatred on an individual; they make that which is properly a conflict of classes 'personal'. Thus Robespierre and Lin are the focus of the obloquy. Yet the conflict of interests of which they are part began without them, shall end without them, and is largely beyond their control. How well do the powerful and influential know how to poison minds in this way, to turn men away from the consciousness of their own interest! In this sense the newspaper has superseded the pulpit.

...but the rest of my life does not seem so colourful when compared with those short years, so soon gone, to lack some vibrancy as I remember, though there have also been adventures and excitements of both an outward and an inward kind. I do believe that, in the history of the individual and also in the wider chronicle of the evolution of our human societies, there are some years where the essence of all that is new is a concentrate, where development is – to coin a queer phrase – 'telescoped', where the perspective of the years is foreshortened. (Do we not also look at the years and personages gone by as if through the wrong or diminishing end of a spy-glass?) And in these watersheds of change, that which is new and that which is old, the revolutionary and the ancient, invention in its infancy and that which is to become extinct, all come together in a medley of the shocking and the incongruous. Speaking for myself, it is speed, the attainment of velocities undreamed of a hundred years ago, which has modified most my view of the world and time.

Does this not reflect an inner sense of accelerating time? As we grow older, the years go faster, till they speed by all of a blur.

To mark and to make sense of such a passage, men look to measure in Anno Domini, to fix by what they believe are endings, signatures on a piece of paper. How deluded is this formality! Treaties, Congresses, Conventions mean nothing, except to the participants – the stuff of history is less tangible, but lies in a popular mood whose ebbs and flows are not measurable by the month or year.

Yet there is also a seamless aspect to the affairs of man in society, the image of generations handing down their torch – a torch which, in defiance of the laws of the natural world, glows more brightly, stronger, fiercer, with every new possessor. This, then, is the moral continuum, characterised in its highest form by the sacred relationship between pupil and teacher, bestower and receiver. And just as I have received, so now do I give in my turn: yet only now do I understand that truly it is more an honour to receive than to give. I am old now and I was young. This is the common history of mankind, which each individual must trace in himself as if it were a unique truth and not a universal truism. It was true of our predecessors and shall be true of those countless more who shall come when we are gone, wandering down like white sheep after us to the dark shore of eternity. To you, reader, I reach out my hand. I was a man!

Canton, February 1980 – London, July 1985

ABOUT THE AUTHOR

Timothy Mo was born in Hong Kong in 1950 and educated there and at St John's College, Oxford. His novels have won the Geoffrey Faber Memorial Prize, the Hawthornden Prize, the E.M. Forster Award from the American Academy of Arts and Letters, and the James Tait Black Memorial Prize.

He is now based in South East Asia after more than twenty years in London.